OAKVILLE OBSESSIONS OMNIBUS

Kick Start, Kick Back, and Kick Home

KALLYN JONES

Oakville Obsessions Omnibus

Kick Home, Kick Back, and Kick Home

Copyright 2025 by Kallyn Jones

My Creative Jones Press

Editor: D.A. Sarac/the Editing Pen

Copy Edit: Taming the Ink

Cover Art: Modified Deposit Photos Illustration

Cover Design: the Jones Design Studio

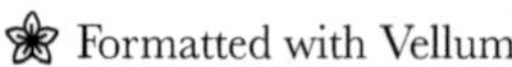 Formatted with Vellum

Kick Start: Book One

A LATER IN LIFE ROMANTIC MYSTERY

A Note About Autoimmunity

Kick McKenna, our heroine, is an autoimmune patient like me. Her experience neither represents the entirety of mine nor is it meant to represent anyone else's journey. As the saying goes, when you've met one autoimmune person, you've met one autoimmune person. As so often happens, one person's healing balm can cause another to flare, even when they share the same diagnosis. Our human bodies are fascinating, for sure. The regimen that Kick uses to help her back to health is unique to her experience. The truth is, for the sake of the story, I went easy on her. If you are someone who shares similar health issues to her and manages them by different means, the story doesn't seek to judge or criticize your methods. Whatever gets you through the day is a blessing. I hope you're able to make the most of each victory. XO

For the autoimmune warrior.
You who work your buns off, even though it may not look like it. You who sometimes find yourselves flat on your back for days or weeks on end, through no fault of your own. You are seen. May your setbacks stay minor and every victory —no matter how small—be huge.

Hard Out Here

Kick

"You've got to be fecking kidding," I muttered, staring at my doctor's sharp jawline on the video screen as she quietly spoke to her assistant.

Morning sun streaming through the window warmed my left shoulder, promising a perfect September day. With the oppressive humidity finally gone, my customers were more likely to sit outside on the patio than inside. It made the '80s girl in me want to belt out "Walking on Sunshine." I made a mental note to play an eighties mix later.

I wished I could be outside, enjoying an iced Americano and a quick break. Instead, I was stuck in my office, dealing with my body's shortcomings. Despite major victories in my decades-long battle with autoimmunity, this new flare was a doozie.

I absorbed the news from my test results as I waited for the doctor and eagerly let myself be distracted by a photo of me with my kids. We stood together, all smiles, at my coffeehouse's ribbon-cutting. I hadn't seen those proud smiles in months, and I missed them. These three were the reason I'd worked my butt off to get better. Bad news or not, I wouldn't give up on them now.

"Sorry for the interruption, Kick," Dr. Chaddha said, her face returning to the video chat window on my laptop.

"No worries," I answered, hoping a soft smile could hide my anxiety. We were running five minutes behind with about fifteen minutes of appointment left.

"So," she continued, "did you receive the new dietary guidelines we sent through the portal?"

I flipped through the pages I'd printed off. "Yup. You really think restricting stuff like artichokes is necessary? I thought prebiotics were important for my microbiome."

Dr. Chaddha lifted her copy of one of my many recent tests. "Given this lab panel, yes. A low-FODMAP plan will let your gut heal. Trust me." She dropped the papers. "After six weeks, we can address it again, depending on how closely you follow the regimen."

"What do you mean, how closely?" I sighed, tucking a wayward curl behind my ear.

"Well, did you see caffeine and chocolate on the list?" She pressed.

"Yes," I muttered. Or whined. A little.

"I meant to have my assistant put decaf on there too."

My brow creased. Was she kidding? "What? Why?" I'd prepared myself to stay engaged and positive through our tele-appointment. Truth be told, I expected some heavy-handed advice. Bringing an autoimmune condition into submission was ridiculously hard. I'd done it already. But the good doctor stepped on my pride with this directive.

"I sell only fair-trade, organic beans. And they're third-party tested for mold." I felt my face dropping into a stubborn frown. "The water is reverse-osmosis filtered. I don't see the problem here, other than the ones inherent in caffeine. Also, I've already been limiting it."

"Nice to hear." Dr. Chaddha scribbled on her tablet. "I want to make sure you're not reacting to the product itself."

"You understand my business is called the Perked Cup, right?" I said, hearing the sharp edge in my tone. How the hell does a barista abstain from her own product? How was I supposed to recommend a new flavor I couldn't test? I didn't think the good doctor would approve of the swish-and-spit routine either.

"This leads to my next point." A nervous smile crept across her face as if she were bracing herself.

Holy hell, now what? I couldn't imagine the news getting any worse. I gripped the edge of my chair, not sure I wanted to hear it.

"You've had a hard year with your dad passing. Plus your business responsibilities. And family."

As if I needed reminding. "Everyone has their issues, Dr. C. Everyone has bad years too."

"Not everyone has autoimmune diseases," Dr. Chaddha continued firmly. "If you want to avoid undoing all your past progress, I suggest you take three months off while you work my program."

If I had been drinking that Americano, I'd have done a spit take. As it was, the normal kaleidoscope of test-result butterflies in my stomach beat their wings into a frenzy. I was sure they were working up a tornado in there. I didn't lead a take-three-months-for-yourself kind of life.

I'd heard about other patients doing this, but the ones I knew of were either kidless or retired. Maybe I could do it in a year once my youngest graduated high school. But the kids weren't the only people who needed me. My employees did too. With the summer over and most part-timers off to college, we were already under-staffed. Then there was Dad's cigar shop.

Dr. Chaddha's dark eyes narrowed. "Perspective is the key, Kick. Remember, you're lucky to be alive. You've been blessed to come this far. Don't stop now."

My belly laugh after her comment sounded a tad hysterical to my own ears. Staying alive had already cost me a fecking fortune. Dr. C's current set of recommendations had me staring down another path ending in a mountain of bills. Yet I should stop working for three months? Hire others to fill the gap? I bit my cheek to keep from snapping.

"Sorry to interrupt, Kick, but I need you in bathroom number one." My morning manager's strained voice over the intercom made me jump in my chair.

"What happened now?" I pressed the button and asked, ignoring my doctor's frown. Didn't she realize the interruption kept me from crossing full steam into Rudelandia and chewing her out? Was I solving world peace? No. I sold coffee to my neighbors. At best, it encouraged them and gave them a boost in their daily grind.

The tension in the discombobulated voice amped up. "Something big that it requires us both."

Right. Deana wouldn't bother me with a minor issue. Ever the eternal optimist, her anxious tone turned my internal tornado into an F4. "Be right out," I told her.

I turned back to my webcam. "Listen, Dr. Chaddha, I need to fix whatever is happening here. I'll take your advice into consideration though."

"Mrs. McKenna, you haven't set up your IV schedule. Plus Audra needs to do your life coaching session. Give you her recipes."

JaysusMaryandJoseph. My arms phantom-ached at the thought of new bruises and collapsed veins. Time off was one thing, but I swear I had PTSD from the last round of intravenous therapy. "I'll think on the IVs, and Audra can upload the files to my portal."

"Will you at least consider cutting back your hours? It's critical to relieve stress somewhere. And if you can't make our meditation sessions here, at least do it at home." Exasperation hovered in Dr. Chaddha's normally steady inflection.

A tightness settled in my chest while the tornado switched to full-blown nausea. I nodded at the monitor. "Thank you for your time, Doctor. I'll be in touch soon. Promise."

We cut the tele-session, and my shoulders slumped. How the hell had I ended up feeling back at square one? And there lay my doctor's point. Autoimmune patients sought management, not cures.

Even before this appointment, I monitored everything I ate, drank, how I worked out, slept, et cetera. It was all-consuming, though the real challenge lay in keeping it from being soul-consuming. Then there were years like this one when as soon as I thought my ducks were finally in a nice, neat row, life whacked me head-on and the little feckers waddled off again.

The rhythm of my footfalls in the hallway out to the dining room gave me some headspace to reflect. This flare was more evidence of my failure "to do health." Moreover, I feared my body would continue to betray me, no matter how many hoops I jumped through to keep it in line.

Kill the pity party and find Deana.

I took the last few feet of tile to mourn the progress I'd lost in my recovery. Inhaled deep and shook it off. I might struggle, but hell if I'd let my thyroid run me over. Taking a cleansing breath, I turned the corner toward the serving counter and remembered Dee had told me to meet her in the bathroom.

Deana Douglas, the source of the earlier voice, paced the restroom hallway. An OUT OF SERVICE sign stuck to the first door.

I groaned. "Did someone flood the toilet again? You could've just called the plu—"

Dee grabbed my arm and tugged. "Get in here."

I jumped, expecting to get wet feet, but the floor looked dry.

She pointed at the sink. "In there."

A large ziplock with smaller bags lay in the porcelain bowl. "Is that—"

Deana nodded vigorously. "We used to call them dime bags."

"I remember," I breathed, wondering if today's kids still called them that. "Did you look inside? Were they in the sink?"

"Yes. And no—they were taped to the side of the vanity. If I hadn't changed the garbage, I might've missed them." Deana fanned her face. "I think we need to call the police."

I bent over, sniffing, making sure they contained cannabis, but the little bags didn't give themselves up without opening them. Since I didn't have on gloves like Deana, I let it go. "Did you notice who used the bathroom this morning? Also, shouldn't we just throw this away?"

"Kick"—Deana heaved a motherly sigh—"someone tried to use our café... *your* café as a drug drop. We can't ignore it."

"Shit."

Dee was right. She was also late.

"Don't you have to get out of here too?" I asked.

Dee scrunched her button nose, reminding me of her doppelgänger, Gladys Knight, bracing to hit a big note. When she had walked into my café, responding to my ad for a barista, I immediately thought of the megastar from our hometown, Detroit. Dee possessed the same class, sparkling smile, and hint of an edge. It's what initially bonded us—that and shared memories of growing up in Motown.

Deana untied her apron and folded it, tucking it under her arm. "You sounded off when I buzzed. I texted Genesis, and she's saving me a seat." Her granddaughter Geneva was about to play the *Hungry Caterpillar* in the first-grade fall play, and Dee was stepping out for an hour.

I waved her on. "Go ahead. Take pics of little Geneva for me please. I'll call this in."

"But—"

"Go before you get stuck answering questions and miss the whole play." To distract her, I added, "Maybe we can hang some of your recent work in the dining room again."

Dee chuckled. "I see what you're doing. Yeah, we can do that, especially with the senior portrait season underway." She turned for the door. "You're telling me about your appointment when I get back."

"Not going anywhere," I murmured. *Yet.*

As a Bob Marley song later reminded me that everything would be all right, I swiped at a curl stuck to my sweaty cheek and pulled my elbows together to stretch my middle back. Then I donned a pair of gloves and looked around my café. Keeping it in order brought peace, especially during a crazy day like this one.

A senior officer from the Oakville PD had come and gone after questioning the staff and me forward and backward. There were only two other part-timers currently on the schedule. Officer Miller had shown me his sincere disapproval of my lack of security. Upgrading the system had been at the top of my list at the beginning of the year. He also complained about my letting Deana go to the play. I promised to have her give a statement at the station.

A quiet hum finally settled over the café as I swayed to "Three Little Birds." I opened the display case and moved the leftover breakfast pastries to make room for lunch items. Next was the bar top—a raw-edged hickory counter that looked more like a piece of art—the centerpiece of the space. It made me smile when it shone and was something I could quickly set to rights.

I let my hand rhythmically glide over its smooth surface while I lengthened shallow breaths, letting my thoughts go. Since giving my statement, I'd racked my brain to remember every customer we'd served.

Inhale for four. Hold for four. Exhale for five… Again.

As the streaks of cleaner evaporated, I caught the dark hint of my reflection in the glossy finish. The silhouette of my big curls shadowed the warm browns in the wood. They were extra exuberant on washdays like this one and reminded me of the Irish dancing competitions I'd been dragged to as a kid. For years I'd fought to tame the curls with dryers, irons, and goo. We'd called a truce when I embraced their wild nature and found better products. Presently I didn't have the heart to corral them in a scrunchie. Maybe later.

The distraction eased my mind and caused me to miss the woman sliding onto a stool at the end of the counter until she spoke, startling me.

"I heard you talked to your so-called doctor," my mother commented, setting my heart pounding.

She'd been in a good mood when she arrived with her neighbor. Perhaps she sincerely wanted to know about my appointment. I'd almost rather talk about that than who had tried to use my bathroom as a drug drop. The logic there escaped me, but maybe expecting a drug dealer to use logic was my first mistake. It ended up not being a large amount of cannabis anyway, thank goodness.

I stopped wiping and gave it a shot. "Dr. Chaddha confirmed

the flare. She gave me a plan though." I scanned the dining room, hoping the subject would drop. I didn't see her friend. "Did Shirley leave?"

"Yes." My mother, Bobby Allen, lifted her cup to her lips, wearing a judgmental expression. One of her favorite forms of torture, it kept me always guessing, although it didn't necessarily equal an impending temper. "Did you lock your office door? My suitcases are in there, remember?"

"I don't lock it during business hours. But the back door is secure, and your cases are tucked under my desk. They'll be safe until Rachel's ready to drive you to the airport."

Bobby clucked her tongue. "We're already cutting it close."

"You'll be fine to go as soon as Deana gets back." My daughter, Rachel, currently manned the drive-through.

I reached for Bobby's cup. "Let me refresh this. It's probably cold." Still uncertain of her mood, I hoped a little kindness would allay her.

I handed her a new latte along with a nervous smile. She took a loud slurp and set the cup down.

"When will you see a real doctor and fix your nonsense once and for all?" She moved her forefinger up and down in my direction, further indicating I was the nonsense.

Annnd we're off.

"Dr. Chaddha *is* an actual doctor. She trained here at Lord University. Her methods are cutting-edge. Besides, regular doctors spent twenty years telling me nothing was wrong." I didn't dare say what they actually said since Bobby also thought my disease was in my head.

She shook her head, pushing button number one. "If you'd handled yourself like a bloody grown-up all those years ago, you'd still live your fancy NFL life, retired husband or no. You certainly wouldn't be working yourself to death in this backward town."

I rolled my head to stretch my neck. This was our game, our mother-daughter dance. In my head, I still waited for my dad to butt in with *"Now Bobby, let our Katie Girl be..."*

"You're the one who hates Oakville, Mother, not me. Moving to

North Carolina and shortening the winters was the first step to feeling better." I sighed, shaking my head because an explanation was an exercise in futility. "Plus you know I hated the spotlight. What little still pops up on occasion drives me batty."

She tsked my first comment and ignored the second while rubbing her knee. "We all feel pain, Kick. Feeling pain means you're alive."

Tension traveled south back to my stomach, reminding me of what my doctor had said about stress. I spelled stress B-O-B-B-Y. "Definitely alive, Mother."

I spun on my heel to get away, looking out the window. It would be a welcomed relief to have her gone. Six blissful weeks of a seniors' cruise.

"Take care of her, Katie," my dad's weak voice sounded in my head. *"Maybe she'll finally find happiness."*

I begged the universe to let this trip do the trick. The universe had been stubbornly silent though.

Another deep breath kept my pulse in control. The café emitted the best aromas—blends of coffee beans, obviously. Once I completed the tapering-off period, I'd have to settle for only the smell for a while. I knew I'd survive. I had already learned to live with the smell of fresh pastries I couldn't eat anymore. For the first time that week, I reminded myself this was temporary pain for long-term gain.

I took a moment to gaze up at the mural of cats I'd painted near the ceiling, their colors done in the same warm latte-and-coffee-bean hues. Their playful curiosity represented the way I wanted to live life even when it seemed difficult. I waited for the peace of the dining room to fill me. Since opening the Perked Cup seven years earlier, I'd found my center within its walls. Relief came from the door chime, announcing a new customer.

A man strolled through the door. With the light streaming from behind him, the details were blurry from where I stood. Or Deana was probably right about needing stronger glasses. He was tall and lean with a familiar, immature swagger.

"Hey, beautiful."

As I stepped to the register to meet the new arrival, the blur became a recognizable face. A local kid the same age as my oldest, Dylan, named Garrett. I cringed at his words, hoping it wouldn't show, reminding myself to put the customer first.

The thing was, flirting would always be a part of my business. I knew this going in. I preferred friendly banter, but some men didn't understand the difference. I accepted it. Usually. However, when an attractive young man came in, my internal thoughts generally gravitated toward *who's your daddy?* never *want a sugar mama?* A twenty-nothing boy would always stay a boy for my intents and purposes.

With my body throwing its age in my face, it wasn't even slightly humorous. Perhaps he'd get the hint if I ignored it. "What can I get you?"

He flashed a cocky grin. "A large iced latte."

With an indifferent nod, I spun on my heel and filled his order. Remembering to upsell, I called over my shoulder, "Interested in a snack?"

"Other than you?"

I swear, the boy tried to make his pecs dance. It looked more like they spasmed. "Garrett—"

Rachel rescued me from making a serious mistake and rebuking him when she bounced around the corner from the drive-through. Without a word, she dipped her chin to me and stepped up to the glass case, her sapphire eyes showing the friendly patience I lacked. I gladly let my daughter take over for a moment.

Garrett pointed at a small case on top of the large food display. "Why are these separate from what's down here?"

"That's our gluten-free Blarney Scone," Rachel informed him, pointing to the sign on the upper corner. "It's lavender-almond flavored, which is great. You don't have to be gluten-free to choose it." She pointed to the larger case. "This one is our traditional blueberry recipe. We keep them separate to avoid cross-contamination." Rachel fitted her hands with a pair of disposable gloves.

"Guess I'll do the blueberry one. Thanks."

I handed Garrett his cup and scone, and he winked. "And thank *you*, gorgeous."

"It's Mrs. Mack, or Kick, please. You can skip the sham flirting too."

His shoulders stiffened. "Can't I cheer you up? You were frowning when I walked in. You just… you know, should smile more. Especially considering…"

Garrett piqued my curiosity. Bobby had needled under my skin, but I was sure he'd caught me squinting to figure out the mystery of his blurry form. "Considering what, exactly? And why can't women have all the facial expressions?"

He lifted a shoulder as if he'd never considered my question before. "You know, for your age. You should be proud you look good."

Boy, did I want to backhand the backhanded compliment right off his pretentious mug. I shook my head, wondering if he would ever get it, while dismissing it all the same. "Have a good day, Garrett." *Don't let the door hit you in the ass.*

He strutted out without another word.

I put my arm around Rachel and rested my head on her shoulder. "I thought your generation was supposed to be woke."

Having three inches on me, Rachel kissed the top of my head and rubbed my free arm. "Silly Mama. Even if some of us are woke, that one's still dreaming of the fifties."

"No kidding." I shook my head and grinned at Rachel, then grimaced when Bobby chimed in.

"You're such a chip off the old block. If you didn't flirt so hard, they wouldn't bother with you." She cackled from her perch at the counter. "You asked for it."

Annnd there went another button, possibly the biggest one. Did I ask for it? Sometimes my mother could twist her arguments, making me think up was down and I was a complete lunatic. Hell, she was the one who had drilled into me to smile no matter what.

I turned to Rachel, looking to grab a minute alone. "Can you cover for a few? My fat jeans were in the washer, and this pair squeezes so hard it's making me nauseated. I'm going to change into the backup pair in my office."

"Really, Kick? Fat pants?" Bobby scoffed.

"Yes." I bit back, saying no more because screw her. If I told her my current weight, she'd never let it go. Besides, every woman I knew had three sets of clothes. There were the ones you wore as a reward for working your ass off, the ones that fit on normal days, and the fat ones. Actual numbers didn't matter. After achieving the impossible and losing a hundred pounds several years prior, watching thirty reappear practically overnight was as off-putting as the return of the bone-deep fatigue.

"Sure, Mama." Rachel pity-laughed. "I'll be fine. Gran can help if we get a mini-rush."

I chuckled at my mother's sputtering and hustled to the back. Bobby had been one of my first employees, along with my father, and my son, Dylan. But Bobby and Dad made better customers. He'd pushed me to open an authentic Irish pub, but I didn't want my kids doing homework in the back of a bar. My body couldn't handle the late hours either. So, I'd designed the Perked Cup with the rich woods of a pub combined with bright windows, coffee, pastries, and a patio.

As soon as I could afford it, Deana came on board, saving my butt and my spirit. And I had to find more people immediately.

Five minutes later, after digging through my bottom desk drawer and only finding a spare pair of shorts, I sheepishly returned to the front, wearing them. I'd worn low-cut cowboy boots with my jeans. They were comfy and helped my feet last a long day. I caught my reflection in the mirror hanging over the office door. I looked like an extra in a country video, not a respectable forty-six-year-old entrepreneur. At least my bloated belly found peace. Unfortunately, my daughter had lost hers.

Rachel stood at the register, leaning back as far as her waist and neck would allow, while another neighborhood boy leaned over the counter, leering.

"Jonn, please, you know Cody and I are together." Rachel defended as I approached. She kept a polite smile on her face, though her fingers twitching at her thigh gave away nerves.

"Isn't it time you try out a real man? Dump him, babe," Jonn drawled. "Everyone around here knows Cody's a loser. I'll treat you right."

Whoa. "Thanks, but…"

My daughter the peacemaker was terrible at standing up for herself unless her brothers were the ones annoying her. Jonn stretched out his fingers and stroked Rachel's forearm. He tried to hold her hand, but she snapped it up to her chest, clasping her hands tightly together. The boy bled arrogance. The kind coming from money and too much spoiling, like he owned the town and everyone in it.

Perhaps the loss of his mother a few years prior contributed to his lack of manners. I decided it was a good day for me to educate the neighborhood boys after all.

It didn't matter that my favorite Prince song filled the dining room. It muted in my ears as my daughter's frantic gaze slashed to mine. All the stress, arguments, and annoyances of the morning scurried up my spine like steam ready to boil.

Screw with me, push my buttons, make me spend all my money on medicine and fancy grocery stores. *Fine.* Ask the impossible of me and poke me with needles. *Whatever.*

But don't. Mess. With. My. Kid. I tucked a stubborn curl behind my ear, ready for battle.

Okay, Jonn boy, class is in session.

Wicked Game

Thomas

RESISTANCE COMING FROM THE LOCKED DOOR DIDN'T REGISTER WITH Thomas Harrison's brain. He simply pulled the handle again, with vigor. He was on a mission, and a closed cigar shop didn't jibe with his schedule.

Then he saw the sign: PLEASE INQUIRE AT THE PERKED CUP FOR ASSISTANCE. SO SORRY FOR THE INCONVENIENCE. ~ THE STAFF AT MICK & HUGH'S.

Inconvenience?

That had to be a joke. Thomas tried the door a third time. Not a joke. He didn't have another thirty minutes to drive to a different shop and make it to the Durham Forest neighborhood on time.

He pivoted and found the Perked Cup's signage, taking off at a brisk pace. He fully expected to deal with a pimply teenager ignorant of cigars. No matter. When he found out his new boss liked an occasional smoke, he knew exactly what to bring to the Welcome Back social in the dean's garden.

Starting off on the right foot was paramount to making sure the man was an ally and as hands-off as the former dean had been.

Thomas hoped a few thoughtful trinkets would help him build this rapport. Christ, the hoops he'd been jumping through to honor his contract with Lord University and keep his obligations to the other team in France wore on him. He could use a close friend at the university, and his initial conversation with the new boss suggested they shared some interests.

He reminded himself to nod and smile if someone brought up hurricanes at the party. It was September in North Carolina, what did they expect? They were lucky a quick shower was the only thing forecasted for the afternoon. He feared humanity might devolve, what with its reliance on small talk and the latest viral video. Then again, meaningless topics like the weather always irritated him.

Time spent locked away in his lab and at his property had an adverse effect on him. It affected his ability to "people," as his lab assistant called it. He feared it might be killing his soul too. Plus the mantle of professor still didn't feel comfortable on his shoulders. He wondered if it would ever fit.

As he opened the door to the coffeehouse, the blower nearly sent his fedora airborne. He grabbed at the hat to keep it in place. Thomas's gaze lifted, and he was dumbstruck.

A barista with shoulder-length curls was giving what-for to a customer. She told the boy what he would order and how he should behave in her establishment if he wanted to continue being served. Her head bobbed in a pointed rhythm to the Prince song playing in the background, turning her brunette curls into physical exclamation points to her arguments.

She stepped back, her curvy hip leaning into the back counter, her brow furled and focused.

She let a girl hand the boy his order. Keeping her tone low and rational, like a professor schooling a disrespectful student, she said, "Now, Jonn, thank Rachel for graciously making your iced mochaccino."

"Th-thank you, Rachel." The young man touched his credit card to the reader while stammering, his brow pulled into an angry V.

The barista folded her arms and nodded to the girl. "Thanks,

Rachel. You can take the drive-through again." Her gaze shifted back to Jonn. "I'm going to tell you to have a nice day, and it's not BS. I really do wish you a better day, Mr. Graham. Then you'll return the kindness and go."

Was it wrong how her *don't fuck with me* air turned him on? Thomas considered doing something to piss her off—just to hear what she'd say to him—and ducked his head.

The boy took the cup and turned.

"Jonn—" she warned.

The kid grunted and murmured, "Have a nice day, Mrs. Mack."

"Thank you, son. I don't mean offense. But I won't tolerate any more of this behavior with my daughter, my employees, or another customer. We clear?"

Jonn nodded again and left, silently stepping around Thomas.

A smile woke inside him, and it might have reached his eyes. Thomas didn't smile much lately. The work didn't allow it. He sure appreciated the woman's lesson though. He liked the authority she held as she spoke, as much as her words.

She was fire.

Or was the spark igniting in him? Like glimpsing himself in a mirror, Thomas recognized his frustrations in her tight brow. A hint of sadness.

His attraction to her was instant, but he only had time for the occasional quick hookup. Something about this woman said she would consume him.

Like attracts like. Right. He saw his work in all areas of his life. *Guess the Law of the Instrument applies to scientists as much as it does to carpenters,* he thought.

"Look at Nathan Detroit," a voice snapped beside him. A brief look around, along with a fast flip through his mental memory bank to the *Guys and Dolls* reference, suggested the senior citizen at the bar spoke about him. Did she have a problem with a man wearing a suit? If he had to be in academics, he'd be damned if he went the patched-elbow blazer route.

The barista wore a friendly smile, reaching her eyes, as she turned from the back counter and greeted him. "Well, hey there, handsome. Is Maggie feeling better? Oh—" Her eyes flashed wide as she took Thomas in. "I'm sorry. You're not Hugh."

Another smirk caught him off guard. "Not according to my license."

The woman blushed, the light pink complementing her porcelain skin. "I'm sorry. My Uncle…" The lady at the counter hissed, and the woman adjusted her words. "My father's *friend*, Hugh, often wears a similar fedora. It's dumb… Not the hat. Your hat is very handsome." She gestured to her eyes. "I think I might need distance lenses. Anyway, what can I get you?" She raised her hands in a "stop" motion. "Wait, let me guess… A large Americano?"

"Good guess." He nodded. "But I'm here for cigars, actually." He pointed over his shoulder. "The sign said—"

"Oh right. One second." She held up a finger and leaned around the corner. "Rachel, I have a smoke-shop customer. Tina's due in five. You can cover for me again, eh?"

"Sure, Mama. Have Gran sit at the register. I'll get the rest."

The barista tucked a burnished curl behind her ear and took a long breath before addressing the scowling older woman. "Five minutes. I swear, I'll be right back."

Mother, daughter, and grandmother. Thomas took note. Neither looked too much like the other. The youngest wore her hair in long, raven curls, looser than her mother's coils, while the eldest woman kept hers in a straight, blond bob. He supposed both younger women favored their fathers. *Yeah, he spent way too much time contemplating genes and epigenetics.*

The barista approached with her hand extended. "Kick McKenna. Is this your first time visiting us?"

Thomas shook the offered hand, noting her confident grip and kind eyes, the hint of sadness still there. They were hazel—deep and earthy with splashes of bright gold. They reminded him of walking in the woods on his property. A subtle, pleasant warmth bloomed from his fingers to his elbow.

"Thomas Harrison. Nice to meet you… Kick? I've been loyal to the Durham lounge near campus, but it closed last month."

"Yup." She sighed. "Frank mentored my dad with his shop. The man earned his retirement." A somberness chased the smile away for a few beats. Kick shook herself and headed toward the door.

Thomas followed her across the parking lot, mesmerized by the sway in her purposeful stride. Out in the sun, Kick's chestnut hair came to life as a light breeze danced through it. A few strands of mahogany and gold wrapped around the deep brown. The colors reminded him of the cabinet he'd built for his office over summer break.

An edginess crept through him. *No time for this*, Thomas scolded himself again. The side of his right hand still tingled from her touch. He flexed his fingers and grazed it on his suit jacket, his other hand carrying his briefcase.

Kick opened the door and swept her arm inside. "Welcome to Mick & Hugh's. Again, I apologize for the staffing problem. It should be resolved soon. Are you interested in a particular brand?"

She looked up and frowned as if she were mad at the song that started when she tapped a row of switches. Tula's "Wicked Game" filled the store, but it was near the end, so whatever bothered her about it wouldn't last for long. "Fecking girl," Kick muttered under her breath.

"Pardon?"

Kick turned and lifted the corner of her mouth. "Nothing, I'm sorry. What kind were you looking for?"

"Padrons. I assume they're in the humidor?"

She nodded and pointed to the glassed-in space. "The line sits on the middle shelf. Help yourself."

Thomas took a joyful inhale when he stepped into the enclosure. The aroma from the leaves set him at ease while brightening his thoughts. If he didn't have to hustle to the luncheon, he'd consider chatting Kick up, welcoming a distraction from his stalled research.

He approached the register with an open box. "Mind if I take the whole thing?"

Her laugh bubbled, too husky for a giggle and... sexy. "Of Family Reserve? Anytime. A new shipment is due Wednesday anyway." She lifted the lid. "We've already sold two. Are you okay with that?"

"Fine."

"Is it safe to assume you have a humidor at home for these?"

Thomas patted his briefcase. "Most of them will be given away this afternoon, and there's a travel one in here for the rest."

"Perfect. Are you celebrating something then?" She glanced at him and added, "If you don't mind my asking."

Thomas liked her scrunched nose. He took it as a "hope I'm not offending" demeanor and liked it as much as her "take no bullshit" one from earlier, only this was cute. "I don't mind. I run a genetics research lab at the university and am taking over a biology class for someone on sick leave. There's a faculty social at the new dean's house this afternoon."

"Ooh, cigars are great for schmoozing. Nicely done. Are you at Raleigh State? My son—"

"No, no." Thomas interrupted. "I meant Lord University in Durham."

"I see." They completed the transaction, and Kick said, "Please come back again. I'm still sorry about the inconvenience. One of the owners died this summer, and the other partner's wife is dealing with a bad bout of pneumonia. I think Maggie's almost back to normal though."

Thomas furrowed his brow. Maybe he had a minute to spare. He tossed his thumb over his shoulder, toward Kick's café. "Is that the Maggie you referenced earlier?"

"Yup," she answered, blushing. "Sorry about that too."

Thomas snapped his fingers. "You called me Hugh, and this is—"

"Mick and Hugh's. Right." Kick turned toward a tablet sitting on the counter and scoffed.

"Everything alright?" Thomas asked.

Kick shook her head, then nodded as if she hadn't decided. "It's fine." She inhaled deep and lifted a corner of her mouth. "Thank you."

"No problem," Thomas answered, shoving his hands in his pockets. "I didn't mean to pry. It's none of my business."

Kick's straightened and laughed. "No worries. It's been a day already, but it'll turn around. It's early yet, right?"

"Sure." A flier caught Thomas's eye. It advertised an open-mic night at the Perked Cup. He lifted one. "This is tonight?"

"It is," she said, shifting her back before straightening again.

"I see." Thomas often relaxed by playing guitar, but it had been ages since he'd heard someone else live. He doubted he could make it back in time though. He turned back toward Kick. "Hey, do y'all ever—"

"Oh, *hell* no," she muttered. Her hand fisted at her hip. "Maybe Bobby was right about me."

Thomas tipped his head to the side, a crease in his brow. "Pardon?"

"Or there's something in the water." Her face contorted, looking a lot like anger. At what, he had no clue.

"Why do men think they're the answer to my problems?" Kick's eyes slowly surveyed every inch of him, leaving Thomas feeling like the scolded boy from earlier. He stood straighter, waiting for clarification.

"Let's get one thing clear." She tapped her finger on the counter for emphasis. "I. Am. Not. A. Cougar. I don't need to get my groove back. I don't *want* to be completed." She leaned in slightly, dropping her voice to a growl. "Sure, I roar. Sometimes I purr. But prowl? *Boy*. I. Do. Not. I've never auditioned for the role of MILF, and man-cubs like you need to quit assuming I have."

"MILF?" Thomas blinked.

"A mom I'd like to… Never mind."

He raised his hands in surrender. "I didn't mean to—"

Kick cut him off again, her voice growing louder. "Yeah, I know. You only wanted to compliment me. I'm not in the AARP yet, but I don't do young men in any fashion. No one's interested in your charity either."

He suddenly couldn't get away from the delusional woman fast enough.

With a quick shiver, her demeanor chilled. She strolled to the door, gestured for him to leave, then said, "Thank you for stopping by."

Thomas's tight grip on the steering wheel eased as his '69 Camaro made its way west. Driving was another form of meditation to him, and it lightened his indignation at Kick McKenna's rant. The engine's roar, the machine bending to his will, relaxed Thomas's clenched jaw, let him know he still had control. By the time he navigated the neighborhood on the edge of Durham Forest, he'd forgotten about the fiery woman and her wrong, knee-jerk assumptions.

Thomas's mind was back in the game, focused on his job and making a new friend. Hopefully, this boss wouldn't micromanage. He already had people doing that from France.

Roar, she'd said? Hot damn. His engine had revved at the sight of her flame. Well, too bad for Kick.

He found a perfect parking spot near the dean's sprawling colonial and stepped out of the car. An ominous cloud formation appeared right on time. He reached for his beloved briefcase, and his shoulders dropped with renewed frustration.

Of course.

In his haste to leave the cigar store, he'd left it behind. *Damn it all.*

3

Settle Down

Kick

"G REAT, YOU'RE BACK." I MET D EANA AT THE END OF THE DISPLAY case, her warm smile the perfect prescription to help me jump into the lunch rush. After locking up Mick & Hugh's, I'd stormed back to my café and chilled a minute in my office, finding calm after another unwanted come-on. I was three for three in a weird day that was only half-done. This Thomas guy should've been old enough to know better. I mean, he was handsome, with soulful gray-blue eyes, a chiseled jaw, and a sexy chin cleft. But he probably still lived with his mom. Or roommates.

No. Just no.

I spent the time examining my interactions with Garrett and Thomas. Then came Jonn Graham. He'd had a crush on Rachel for years, but he'd never been so brazen before. I didn't know what had gotten into him. I hoped Jonn would take my scolding to heart and change his attitude.

If not for the stressful morning, I would've answered Thomas with a polite "no, thank you." Most days, that was all it took. No harm, no foul. Unfortunately, Professor Harrison had stumbled upon my last nerve and set me off. I saw my mistake and let the embarrassment wash over me. At least it beat guilt.

Deana laughed at my greeting as I retied my apron. She held the bus bucket of dirty dishes. "I've *been* back, Kick. Long enough to see you charge past me like Satan's hound had chomped on your heel." She took a long glance out the window. "Still, you beat the rain. It's about to open up."

Well, hell. There went my last hope for a perfect September day. And lunch on the patio. I bent to look out the window. I hadn't noticed anything looming earlier, but I'd been preoccupied. The dark cloud didn't look too big. Maybe my day would brighten once it passed.

Deana tapped me on the shoulder. "Want to tell me what's going on?"

I shook my hair and pulled it back, using the scrunchie I kept in my apron pocket. "Just men. All morning. Men."

"Another diehard fan find you?"

There was a frightening thought. Dee had found my silver lining. "Thankfully, no."

She chuckled harder, then lowered her voice, leaning in closer, getting serious. "Are you sure your mama had nothing to do with it?"

"Probably."

"I wasn't here, but I know you'd have been fine if Miss Bobby weren't hanging around. That woman has the passcode for pushing your grouch buttons."

I looked up to see my mother bringing her cup to the bussing box; then she sat back down at the bar.

"What are you up to?" I asked her, trying to sound cheery and not suspicious.

"I sat in the sunny corner after serving those two women gossiping about their grandchildren." She pointed to two locals who met here weekly. "It's cold here by the door." Her comment came out as an accusation, but I was tired of being baited.

"What I mean is, shouldn't you and Rachel have left for the airport by now?"

"My flight is delayed. Some storm in the Midwest made the plane late. You'd think they'd have a better system by now, considering there's always weather."

The little girl in me strangely welcomed Bobby's temporary animosity toward the airline. At nearly forty-seven, I still thought it was nice when someone else made it on her shit list. Except for when the attention turned to my youngest, her ultimate scapegoat.

Deana and I established ourselves at our stations, my part-time staff filling in where needed. I changed the topic and asked Dee, "How was your *Hungry Caterpillar*?"

Her face filled with pride and love. "Geneva's a natural. I told Genesis to put her in an after-school theater class."

I was about to recommend the camps Rachel attended when she continued, "But I want to hear about this doctor's appointment. Is it as bad as we thought?"

We leaned against the counter, monitoring the house, but forgetting the conveniently silent lady sitting at the bar. The chill in the stainless steel of the work area moved through my braced arms. It cooled the last of my hot temper, helping me gather my thoughts. I raised my hands, my thumb and forefinger a smidge apart. "There are things to figure out, but I'll get through it."

"Don't play coy, Kick," Deana scolded, crossing her arms. "Some weeks I see more of you than my husband."

I leaned into her for privacy. "You were right about stress. Dr. Chaddha said the loss of Dad, coupled with a hot summer and Liam's last year in school, et cetera. It put me over the edge." I shrugged. "It's a decent-sized road bump."

"I hadn't thought about your impending empty nest," Deana added. "I remember that year. It was terrifying and exciting. Gordon and I spent Maceo's senior year planning the trip to London we took in September. But I was afraid of the quiet house when we returned."

"Hey," I said, tapping her arm, "don't remind me."

"Sorry. What's the doctor want you to do about it?"

"Added therapies and food changes to stop inflammation. I can't have any caffeine until the New Year. I'm still processing it up here and here." I touched my head and my heart, knowing from experience these change-ups required their own version of the stages of grief. I had to let past progress go and accept this new starting point. It would be the Zen thing to do. I wanted to scream and punch a wall, which might have helped for a minute. I wouldn't recommend making coffee with a broken hand though.

"We have great decaf."

"Oh, that's out too, for at least six weeks. And I have to meld something called a low-FODMAP food plan with my autoimmune Paleo one. I think it leaves chicken, green beans, and blueberries."

A chuckle burst from Deana before she caught herself. "Tell me you're joking."

I grabbed a rag and wiped the counter. "I am. Mostly."

"Cute." She bumped my hip. "You've got this though."

My nails tapped a rhythm on the stainless steel. "The doctor wants me to take three months off. Can you believe it? I can't possibly, not when Hugh needs help too. But maybe I should cut back hours here?"

"Am I *not* here for you?" Deana spread her arms. "Let me hire some folks. *Use* me, boss lady."

"You have enough going on yourself," I countered. "I don't want to dump my issues on you. Not when you watch the grands in the afternoon and your photography business is gaining traction."

Dee's hands moved over each other in a circular motion. "Spread it around. Give me some. Give Dylan some. You know."

I shook my head. My oldest, Dylan, worked the counter at the cigar store. He'd done it primarily to spend time with his granddad. Now he worked to fill in the gap. But he was finishing up grad school and getting ready for big things in the tech world. "Dylan's thesis project is ramping up. He should cut back at the smoke shop, not add more hours." I tapped my chin. "What would you think about Jake taking over for me as night manager?"

Jake Quick was a young veteran who worked evening hours at the café while he finished his business degree. He'd already bumped up to full-time hours and did many of the things I'd require of a manager.

"There you go." Dee nodded her head.

"You wouldn't mind sharing the second office?"

"Not at all. I'm mornings; he'd be nights. Delegating would do you some good."

"Thanks." I wanted to hug and kiss Dee. I crossed my fingers Jake would be up for the promotion. I wasn't certain what his post-graduation plans were.

Deana's eyes warmed, the mother in her coming out full force. "This isn't the end of your healing. You've come too far already. The staff and I'll do what we can to help."

A loud scoff broke our private bubble. "Isn't your drama queen act exhausting? It sure tires me," Bobby butt in. My shoulders fell. We should've waited until she left. Then again, she was already supposed to be gone. "No wonder you keep complaining about low energy."

"Now, Miss Bobby," Deana said, "Kick's worked hard to get this—"

"The help's defending you now?"

Deana walked off toward the drive-through, muttering, "One Mississippi, two Mississippi..."

I bit my cheek and let her go. She'd be back in a heartbeat anyway.

I whipped around and glared. "You will never speak to her like that again."

Bobby waved me off with a flick of her wrist and a smirk. "Just admit defeat and convince Hugh to sell Mickey's bloody smoke lounge. You know you're looking for an excuse to get rid of all this. Quitting is what you do. Ever since you quit dancing, you've flitted from one thing to another like a drunken butterfly." She cackled at her own joke, the master gaslighter on a roll. "Maybe then you'll feel better and have time for a man again. You know if you hadn't been so focused on yourself, you wouldn't be in this shit now, right?"

"Hang on." I threw my rag down. "Are you saying—?"

"If you had stopped whining about not feeling good, you wouldn't be alone," Bobby snapped. "It's past time someone pointed out the obvious. Your father used to shut me up on this, but he's not here anymore, is he?"

Ah, the mother of all buttons, right there. The source of my nightmares for eight years. Life's biggest guilty verdict. I'd collected a lifetime of them. "There would've been an accident either way, Mother," I protested.

"I wasn't there, Miss Bobby, but even I know one thing isn't the other. Nobody gets out of life without struggles. I don't think you have." Deana's bravery knew no end.

I hustled over to the drive-through, my cheeks so hot I was certain they looked sunburned. "Tina, you have Rach's spot now." I pulled Rachel toward the back. "Take my AmEx card from my wallet and get your grandmother out of here. If her plane is still delayed, go to the airport and buy her lunch. Hell, shop for all I care, just *git her awa*. Please, sweetheart." Though raised in the Midwest, my father's Irish lilt found me when agitated. A memory flashed of him asking teenaged-me to take Bobby anywhere and give him peace.

Rachel gave me a quick hug. "Sorry, Mama. I heard some of that, but the drive-through was too lit to leave."

FORTUNATELY, THE LUNCH RUSH KEPT US BUSIER THAN A TWO-BIT hooker on BOGO night. Putting smiles on customers' faces soothed Bobby's cruelty. Deana switched the music to my alt-rock playlist to kill my temper and keep me bouncing, even though it wasn't her taste. By midafternoon, we had a break and took our lunch together. We shared a table in the sunny corner. Dee ate a Santa Fé chicken wrap and chips. I had a Cobb salad and apples with a dip from home. I noted how the lunch didn't fit the new low-FODMAP plan. *Well, hell.*

I wore my reading glasses as I tinkered with the upcoming schedule, figuring out where I could take time off for appointments. I decided to give acupuncture a try, hoping it could work in lieu of IV therapy.

"Feeling better?" Deana asked between bites of her wrap.

"The *momster's* gone, so… yeah."

"Kick, your mama has more issues than *People Magazine.* I mean, where are you with all this?" Deana asked, waving her free hand toward my laptop screen.

"Still absorbing."

"But you've done it before."

"There's the thing." I sighed. "When my stomach went haywire and the pain amped up, I thought going back to the original regimen would fix it. It's also why I joined the HIIT group. When I asked Dr. Chaddha why it didn't work, she said it was courtesy of the dreaded P-word."

"Which P we discussing?" Deana asked.

"Perimenopause," I moaned. "Apparently the rules are different now. Doesn't matter that it's only been five years since the last big protocol and the weight loss. Something about estrogen and my metabolism being more stubborn now than before. Here I thought it was almost impossible *then.*"

"Oh, shug." She patted my hand. "That'll settle down."

"I don't know, Dee," I said, a hitch catching my voice.

"What are you really afraid of?"

I set my pen down, along with the reading glasses. "Worst case?"

Dee's eyes managed to show sympathy and say "duh?" at the same time.

"I've worked hard so my best years can be ahead of me. But what if this is as good as it gets? What if I spent my best years being sick and there's nothing left? You know how the Psalm I like reminds me of the good stuff?"

She nodded. "Psalm Sixteen?"

"Yup. Right now I'm trying to believe 'the boundary lines have fallen in pleasant places,' but I can't. The boundaries are choking me. I want more."

Dee squeezed my hand. "There's your stress talking. Have you tried meditating?"

I felt my own eyes flash with annoyance. "I've looked at some apps, but none seem right. I don't know. It's adding more stress when I think about it, like I can't cut it there either."

"I'd be happy to show you the app I use." I didn't know Deana had tried mindfulness. She piqued my curiosity. "Either way, everyone meets their fears now and then. Did you know my Maceo and his wife are having issues? It's not his health, but he's terrified his vision of the future is about to go bust."

I shook my head. Poor guy. Dee had great kids.

"I'll tell you what I told him: don't cross bridges before you get to them. Let me help. Leave the hiring to me. Have Jake do scheduling. Shoot, he can help with staffing too. He's a smart boy. He's a wonderful choice, Kick." She stretched her arms to their sides and began shaking her hands and flapping her arms. "Now, do like me and shake this off."

I complied while laughing. "You do this with your grandkids?"

"Better believe it." We took a deep breath and giggled some more. The action had a remarkable effect, and I honestly felt better.

"You got this. Plus we'll be here to keep you in line and on track. Before you know it, this will be a memory and something else will bother you."

If we'd lived in Ancient Greece, the woman would've been an oracle.

4

Simple Man

Kick

"A peace offering, Kicky," my best friend's smoky voice said to my back. A plastic container squeaked across the counter as I turned around. It had to be yummy. She was a fantastic baker. I had watched Cyndi Sendaydiego walk in from the parking lot, and she'd accurately assessed my level of peeve. She had promised to help me set up for the open-mic night, and fatigue was setting in thanks to the crazy morning. I took a moment before greeting her.

I lifted the corner of the container and sniffed. "Lumpia," I whispered in awe. Okay, this was a good apology. She'd been experimenting with gluten-free flours, claiming they made her tummy feel better too.

"Papa's recipe, modified of course," Cyndi confirmed. "These are the best so far."

I didn't have the heart to tell her the rolls were probably off the menu for the foreseeable future. Besides, how much worse could a few goodies make me feel? I'd pop some activated charcoal and cross my fingers afterward.

I lifted my eyes and caught true repentance in hers. "Thank you, chica." I grabbed two forks and two knives, handing her a set. We had time to catch up before the show.

Since she'd arrived late, I expected her to come in ragged or at least frazzled. Instead, Cyndi looked like a million bucks, from her silky black, chin-length wedged bob to her wedged flip-flops. Being tiny, she was into wedges.

Her tan skin glowed, and her beautiful gray eyes (one of the traits courtesy of her mother's European ancestry) glowed.

A low-cut, V-neck tee couldn't hide a tiny hickey. I instantly knew why she'd stood me up.

She lowered her sunglasses to the tip of her nose and flashed a smile. "Anytime. Sorry I missed helping. It looks great in here though." She twisted uncomfortably in her seat as I studied her. "I accepted an offer I couldn't refuse."

"You got some." I crossed my arms. "What's his name?" Cyn didn't cancel often, and between us, it was usually me asking for a hand. She'd been through a lot and fought her way back too. She worked hard and played harder, as they say. And possessed a metabolism I'd sell a kid for. If I were in her shoes, I'd also take a detour when given the opportunity.

A grin started at the right side of her mouth and slowly spread to the left. "Manu."

"Seriously? You skipped out on me for tanned and exotic?"

Cyndi had the nerve to close her eyes, lick her top lip, tilt her head back, and squeal. The students studying on the far side of the dining room looked up from their books. "Make sure you add tall to the visual." She smirked, picking off the lumpia wrapper.

I laughed at her antics while my stomach growled, and I dug into my plate. We had each other's backs when it counted. We became close while rooming together at Michigan State University. Like any successful lengthy relationship, we'd learned which battles to pick and which to let go.

"You're forgiven if you tell me about him," I offered with a smile, cutting my rolls into pieces. "You know I live vicariously through you." I swallowed my bite. "Oh, Cyn, these are heaven. Thanks, sweets."

"You're most welcome, Kicky." Cyndi went full finger food with hers, speaking between bites. "Manu runs a food truck. I'm helping him with his books so he can get a permanent space next year. Anyway, I took him to lunch, as I do with all new clients. We started talking, and…"

"You liked his menu."

She nodded her head and licked her upper lip again.

"Think this one will be serious?" I asked lightly, ever hopeful she'd take the plunge again.

"*Pfft.* Did I say relationship? It's sex. We're too busy for more."

"Hey, fam." My youngest, Liam, flew through the front door, eyed our food, and reached for one of my rolls.

Cyndi tapped his hand away. "Get your own food. These are Mama's." *Yeah, we had each other's back.* Liam kissed his godmother on the cheek. "Fam?" she asked. "This is new. Do I count as a fam?"

"You're Aunt Cyn," Liam countered. "Of course you're fam."

"It's not new," I added. "Between your business and his after-school activities, you haven't seen each other in a while."

"Yeah, thanks for coming out tonight," Liam said, rounding the counter to fix a drink and a snack. He lifted a cup toward Cyndi, asking if she wanted one. I'd been so caught up in myself I'd forgotten the first rule of running a coffeehouse—the blasted coffee.

"Yes, please, dimples. Are you nervous?" Cyndi used her pet name for him, but my kids were used to multiple nicknames. It was how my family showed both approval and disappointment.

"Naw," he said with a sassy grin you find in a high school senior. Liam ruled his world. "This is my practice crowd." He leaned down and kissed my head since he'd already grown nine inches taller than me. I liked how he'd never fully entered the "moms are idiots" stage. Then he flashed us his killer dimples, the reason for Cyn's nickname. It was a habit the girls in his orbit encouraged. My baby was growing into a beautiful man regardless of my readiness for it.

Liam turned his attention to me. "Can I take this stuff to your office? Gonna bust on some homework before the show."

"Definitely, Weeman." I nodded and shooed him away. "Want

me to send the band members back as they arrive or keep them out here?"

"Send them back, please." With the backpack still over his shoulder, a plate and cup in his hands, he shuffled to the office. I swore I heard a table of girls sigh.

It was our first open-mic night of the fall. My newly promoted night manager, Jake Quick, helped me set up the sizable pieces, then I gave him the night off to celebrate. The minute I'd offered, I regretted it. I still waded in denial regarding how much my health had backtracked.

A few minutes before the start time, my father's business partner, Hugh Reynolds, entered and slid onto the stool next to Cyndi.

"Hugh!" She threw her arms wide and leaned into a hug.

"I should come in here more often if this is the greeting I get," he answered with a smile in his eyes.

"You could come in more often, period," I said, leaning across the bar, receiving and returning a kiss to the cheek. "Great to see you. Is Maggie well?" He nodded, eyes bright. We'd both been so distracted since Dad's funeral, it felt like I'd lost both men over the summer.

"She gone?" he asked.

"Honestly, have you been staying away because of Bobby?"

Hugh raised his hands. "She's been a bear since the funeral, plus taking care of Maggie… I'm sorry, Katie, but I didn't want the missus around Queen Bobby's temper."

"Tell me about it," I answered. "You'd think she might've liked Dad or something." Hugh had been my father's best friend since moving to North Carolina. Unfortunately, their wives didn't feel the same. "It's great to see you. Can I get you anything before I start this shindig?"

"Did I see a piece of the quiche I like?"

"We still have a couple, yes."

"Add a decaf the way I like it, please."

"Got it." I set about making Hugh's belly happy and fixed a cup of decaf for myself, following the dietary sheet's recommendation to ease into the coffee abstinence.

As the after-school crowd headed home, the dining room buzzed with warmth and excitement. Customers settled in for a few hours of the unexpected. The sign-up sheet always held its share of singers and bands, but the number of poetry performances and even stand-up acts had been growing. I hoped the teens who performed saw the Perked Cup as a safe place to develop their talent.

Waning light from the sunset brought my focus to the amber illumination in the space. The coffeehouse was ready for the day's third act.

I filled a small glass of water and popped an anti-inflammatory supplement, coaxing my body to hang in there, letting the smell of the roasted beans and hiss of the machines sustain me. This might have been my plan B, but the Perked Cup was intended to serve the community along with a fine cup of java. Whether people stopped by for a quick cup of "get you going" and a smile in the early hours, a story hour and social time for moms and their littles midmorning, a quick boost and to-go lunch, a safe place to study after school, or an evening gathering spot, I enjoyed putting smiles on people's faces. I was still living the dream and hoped I could hang on to it.

While walking off the stage, having introduced Liam's band, Metaphorical Chemistry, I noticed Professor Harrison lingering near the door. I knew he'd come for the attaché. A cardigan had replaced his suit jacket, and the fedora had disappeared.

I planned to approach him directly but ended up tossing him a shy wave from the safety of the service area. I didn't know what to make of him now that I'd calmed down. Perhaps I'd read more into the formality of his suit and arrogant demeanor. Now he stared at my son's band as if taken by them. He seemed more casual and yet —I don't know—isolated. It was like he was unfamiliar with being in public. It seemed strange for a professor, even a young one.

My waving caught his eye, and Thomas moved to the counter. He leaned in to hear me as I asked, "You're here for your briefcase, aren't you?"

Relief flooded his face as his shoulders visibly relaxed. "Is it here?"

"In my office. I'll go get it." I gestured to an open spot next to Cyndi. "Have a seat."

"Mind if I get a coffee too?"

I laughed at the question, tempted to shoot him my typical sarcastic response, but I didn't know how he'd take it, given the way I'd yelled earlier. "Not at all." I tapped the shoulder of one of the part-timers. "Madison can take your order, and I'll be right back."

Walking out with the heavy briefcase in hand, Liam's words stopped me from the stage.

"Most of y'all know my mom runs the café. She's worked her ass off"—I shot him a glare, which got me a dimpled smirk in return—"to make the coffeehouse something we could be proud of." He looked over his shoulder and back to the small audience. "The band and I thank you, Mom, for letting us play."

As far as I knew, no one had told him about my day, the diagnosis… any of it. His words were a reminder that while some people knew which buttons to push to bring you to your knees, others knew which ones could make you soar, make the bad days worth it.

My nose tingled as he settled his guitar and quickly added, "This is for you." They proceeded to play Lynyrd Skynyrd's "Simple Man." He'd tinkered with the song on his own for years, but I didn't know his band had earnestly practiced it. When Liam was little, he took to the idea of a song about a mother and son. He'd belt it out from his car seat while we ran errands.

He changed the opening lyrics from "only son" to "youngest son." I bit my lip to keep my emotions tight. The gleam in Liam's eye said he knew he'd gotten to me. My memory flashed to the day he pranced into preschool without a second look back. That's a funny thing about parenting teenagers; their toddler selves tended to hide in their growing bodies. They wait within shadowed memories, quickly jumping out when you didn't expect it. The reminder he was the last of my children occasionally sucker-punched me too. It was easy to go about my daily routine, forgetting how the raising part of my job as a mother was ending. I was crazy about this kid with a heart bigger than the planet, and I didn't know what I'd do after he left.

I returned to the service area and almost teared up again when I caught the emotion on Cyndi's face. Family by choice could be better than blood. Then I saw the spread in front of the professor and laughed. It didn't occur to me he'd settle in, though my reaction probably came more from a release of emotion.

I raised the briefcase. "Here you go. If you're staying, I could keep it back here. It's kind of heavy for the undermount hooks." I gestured to an open space on a shelf at the end of the bar. "I promise it's dry and safe down there."

"If you wouldn't mind, thank you." He smiled and finished eating his… sandwich wrap, the last slice of quiche, and a piece of shortbread.

I gathered Thomas's plates and wiped the counter when he finished. It was an excuse to take a big breath and humble myself. The band had finished, and the overall volume of the room had lowered for a poetry reading, so I didn't have to yell. "I want to apologize for earlier. I'm sure you didn't mean any offense in asking me out. I mean, of course you didn't. And I don't usually take offense when it happens."

Nice going, Kick. How far down your throat will this foot go? "Anyway, you were kind of my last straw in a morning with tough diagnoses and rude customers, not to mention some eejit left weed in our bathroom. I think my pushed buttons were looking for a target and I overreacted… So yeah."

His eyebrow popped up in question. "I didn't… I meant to ask if there were other open-mic nights. Specifically on the weekends. I'm often busy at night."

Cyndi and Uncle Hugh had watched our entire exchange, and they burst out laughing at my expense.

"Oh shi-it," I stuttered. I didn't have a stutter, but my brain had shorted out.

Please God, let me become invisible. Grant me this one little thing. Pleeaase. I looked down at my arm. Super pale. *Still visible.*

"Can we start over?" I extended my hand in greeting as I felt the blush rush up my chest to my hairline. "Kick McKenna. Chief coffee brewer. Also self-absorbed foot eater. Sorry, open-mic nights are always on Mondays. Weekends are for themed nights or single-act bookings."

A sweet smile reached the corners of his eyes, making them crinkle without pulling at his lips. He took my offered hand and shook it once with purpose. "Thomas Harrison. I'm familiar with the foot-eating habit. Bad for digestion."

"Great sweater, my dude," Liam told Thomas before he asked me if the band could hang out in my office again. They wanted to review their set without groupie interference. Plus Liam's best friend since first grade, Jacklyn Moore, was new to the band. That they had stayed friends through awkward years and ridicule from classmates made me proud.

"He's not a dude, Lee. Dr. Harrison is a professor," Cyndi said.

Thomas tipped his chin. "Thanks, pal. Thomas is fine though, unless you're my student. I liked your music. Has the band played together long?"

Uncle Hugh added his compliments, and the three males put their heads together, talking about music and future school plans.

Cyndi pulled me in to whisper in my ear. "Is this the guy with the zoot suit you told me about?"

"Shh," I scolded. "I never said zoot suit. Those are from the roaring twenties. See his pants? They're more…"

"*Mad Men.*"

"Precisely."

She nudged my shoulder. "What do you think though? He has potential."

I laughed, caught the men looking, and bit my lip. I turned back to her. "The whole Mr. Rogers thing is a bit weird, don't you think?"

Cyndi's eyes shifted toward the fellas without turning her head.

She studied Thomas for a moment, and I hoped she wouldn't crack a joke at his expense. For some reason, I felt protective of him.

"Remember the semester you made me watch the classic movies with you for a class?"

I wrinkled my nose, wondering where Cyndi's thoughts had turned. "Sure."

"I had a mad crush on young Cary Grant. He was *fiine*." She drew out the word and sighed. Her eyes flashed to the side again. "Professor-man has the same vibe. And face."

I ducked my head to look at Thomas without him noticing. Raven hair, cleft chin. The eyes were lighter, but she had a point. I nodded slightly.

Cyndi added, "I bet his female students swoon when he walks into a lecture hall."

"Bringing back memories?" I teased her, then bit my lip, regretting the comment. "Sorry."

"No worries." She smiled as if remembering something. "Even if it was wrong, some of those memories are awesome." Cyndi tucked some hair behind her ear, and her eyes dimmed. "It ended up being only half as bad of a bad habit as Joel was."

I tried not to flinch at the mention of her ex-husband. I'd introduced them and felt the sting of his infidelities personally, but this day had been hard enough. I didn't want to add more spilled milk to my guilty feelings. I stepped away from the counter. "Gotta introduce the next act."

After a few minutes of clapping and talking, I was back across from my bestie while the men still conversed. The current topic involved the merits of Stevie Ray Vaughn. Liam excused himself, and Hugh and Thomas switched to cigar talk. There was only one more singer scheduled, and the crowd had thinned. I couldn't wait for the performances to end so I could leave too. My pillow called to me.

I quickly tipped my head toward them to silently ask Cyndi if she'd noticed Hugh and Thomas still chatting away.

She scooted a stool away and leaned over so no one could hear. "Get in there and flirt with him." She even swatted my hand.

"What? No." I croaked, still embarrassed about my earlier behavior. The men glanced at us, then turned back to their tête-à-tête. I stage-whispered, "I meant… isn't it weird how they're getting along?"

"It's cute," Cyndi answered. Then she added, "So he's a little odd with the clothes, and maybe there's an air of a superiority complex. Come on, Kick, maybe the universe is sending you a message."

"Funny," I started, "I thought the universe gave me the silent treatment."

"That's because you keep declining its calls." She squeezed my hand. "Life doesn't wait around for you to feel like it."

Fatigue influenced my snapped response. "So I should, what? Wrap my hand in his collar, drag him to the back, kick the kids out of my office, and bang his brains out?"

She sighed with her own pent-up frustration with me. "It would be a start. Come on, Kicky, there's nothing wrong with a little fun." She leaned in and kissed my cheek. "Whatever. Night, chica." She pulled her purse strap over her shoulder and mouthed, "Think about it."

I bobbed my head to agree while Hugh swallowed Cyndi in a goodbye hug. Then she shook Thomas's hand and gave him a wink. They both watched her strut out the door, then turned to me.

"Well, Katie, time for me to get back to Maggie," Hugh declared.

After giving him two carrot cakes in to-go boxes and receiving the same bear hug Cyndi had, I introduced the last performance. I'd left my reading glasses at the counter and had to do the trombone-arm stretch to read the scratch on the clipboard. Then the boy didn't show. I gleefully wrapped up the evening while the dining room cleared out as if someone had yelled "fire!" I couldn't wait to leave the clean-up to Madison and Liam. He was finally responsible enough to lock up for me.

They approached at the same time.

"There's an aura in my vision, fam," Liam said, his eyebrows knitted tightly together with the sign of an early migraine.

"Did you take your spray?" I asked, reaching up to brush his curls off his face. Of my three kids, Liam's hair was most like mine.

"I forgot to put it in my backpack."

"Lee," I scolded, shaking my head. Jax offered to take him home, and I waved them on.

I turned to Madison, who looked a little peaked.

"You know how I'm supposed to close, Mrs. Mack?" she asked.

"There's a rumor going around to that effect," I responded.

"I have a sore throat." Her eyes popped when she swallowed.

Annnd my pillow would have to wait a bit longer. I sent her home, rang up two more to-go cups, then noticed Thomas rising to leave. I walked to the end of the bar and held up his briefcase.

"Don't want to forget this twice," I said with what I hoped was a friendly smile and not a tired grimace on my face. It was an idiot move to let Jake have the night off and not arrange for another part-timer to close.

"Today was the first time I'd ever forgotten it," Thomas said, looking down at the attaché. He gave me a shy smile. "You have a nice place."

"I apologize again for earlier. And please come back."

"I'll try." The smile grew as he dipped his chin good night. Cyndi's voice in my head urged me to do more, be playful, be… hell, *not me.* But my body didn't care. It took everything I had to follow out the last of the customers and lock the door. It was ten minutes before closing, and the day demanded it end.

I flipped over the chairs and swept the floor. Stevie Wonder encouraged me not to "worry 'bout a thing" while I danced a slow cha-cha with the broom, hoping it would give me enough of an energy burst to leave the café clean. The day's earlier tension settled in my hip, making me limp. I had a cane in the office, though using it while straightening the dining room was impossible.

My mind distracted itself from the pain with can-do thoughts of recipes to experiment with when a vigorous knock at the door startled me.

Thomas Harrison stood on the other side.

5

Crossroads

Thomas

HE WANTED TO LAUGH AT THE MISUNDERSTANDING BETWEEN HIMSELF
and Kick, but her assumption offended him. She received the
benefit of the doubt because of the way she'd comported herself in
the evening. Thanks to the people around her, including her
customers, he figured their first encounter was a one-off.

Didn't mean he held an interest in a friendship, though he did
like talking to Hugh. The man had convinced him to visit Mick &
Hugh's over the weekend. He'd mentioned watching college football, and Lord University was playing an away game. As far as the
Perked Cup went, Thomas could stop in now and then. Kick made
a damn fine espresso, and the food beat the hell out of the small
plates from the faculty party. He could push down any attraction
and keep it to an eye-candy-only situation. He was friends with
plenty of attractive people, and it never bothered him.

Thomas's first mistake occurred when he looked up after placing
his briefcase in the Camaro. If he'd kept his head down, he would've
driven home perfectly ignorant and fine. On autopilot, he checked
his surroundings, glimpsing the graffiti on the brick wall next to the

47

Perked Cup. He did a double-take, hoping the foul words on the brick wall were an aberration due to being lost in his thoughts. But no.

Something told him to remove his gun from underneath the front seat, tuck it into his waistband, and walk the perimeter of the café, especially the back alley. If the so-called graffiti artist lingered, he'd hold the idiot until the police arrived. One lonely camera guarded the back alley, and who knew if it worked. No indicator light showed. Someone had damaged the back door lock. It held but would need replacing immediately. Kick had to get a security upgrade. Wasn't it handy Thomas knew a guy?

Thomas froze when he turned toward the café's door. Silhouetted by low lights, Kick danced with a broom. His heartbeat picked up as he observed her swaying with her pretend partner. She knew what she was doing. Despite favoring her right side, she moved with fluid and grace. Kick threw her head back and smiled at a private joke, loose curls falling into her face when they tipped forward. He wished he knew what was so funny.

She was stunning like this. Even in the shadow of her hair, her porcelain skin glowed. The delicate tone suited her. Thomas shook himself from his stupor and resumed walking. *Give her the information and go home. No distractions.*

Her startled smile upon unlocking the door surprised him. Their interactions had been awkward at best all evening.

"I know I handed you the briefcase this time," she said.

He shook his head. "The case is fine, thanks. It's…" He turned and pointed. "You should see this."

"Oh hell. What now?" she asked around a yawn.

Thomas waited for her to lock the door, then stepped aside. A cane had leaned against the table with her purse. She used it as she traveled the sidewalk. He wondered where the limp came from. They both shined their phone lights on the wall in the unusually dark space. A streetlamp, which should've lit the area, sported a rock-sized hole he bet was new. The two sentences were still visible, thanks to neon yellow paint.

Your a drug sellin hoe

and

Jesus is cuming.

"JaysusMaryandJoseph." Kick sighed, her disappointment and defeat settled into her features, pulling at his heart. Her fingers hovered over the letters in the second line.

"Don't touch it. You could leave fingerprints if it's still wet," Thomas warned. "Not sure if it matters, but just in case."

The hurt on her face broke his resolve, and a wave of anger washed over him. A few minutes earlier, and he might've been able to beat the little asshole for this. He couldn't leave her to deal with the vandalism by herself. What if said asshole was watching and waiting? Something about the act seemed more violent than the words suggested. It had Thomas's hackles raised.

On that thought, he scanned the parking lot one more time.

Kick kept staring at the paint and said, "I'm too tired to laugh about the grammar, but seriously? Is this a _U_?"

He gestured toward the wall as the humor in the words hit him too. "Maybe the overspray suggests closing the _O_?"

"Nope," Kick answered and pointed again. "There's a downstroke with a terminal, here. It's almost a serif. I think the overspray is chalked up to lack of paint skills. This genius thinks 'coming' is spelled with a _U_. That's like a second-grade spelling word."

She took a breath and yelled, her body shaking with each word, "I hope Jesus enjoys it!" Then she muttered, "I am too _through_ with today."

A chuckle sputtered from Thomas. He bit his lip to hold it in. "I didn't realize y'all had a garden tool display either." He cringed at the dumb pun. Why did this woman have him on edge?

As she turned the key in the door, her hands shook and she grumbled, "I know, right? I should've guessed this shitty day would end weird—vandalized by the Chick-fil-A cow."

Another snicker escaped from Thomas as he nearly lost his composure. Fortunately, Kick didn't notice his puff, like that of a kid hitting their first note on a trumpet.

. . .

THOMAS COULD'VE KICKED HIMSELF FOR STICKING AROUND WHILE she gave a statement to the police and arranged to have the paint cleaned. It didn't take long for him to do his part, but he felt bad about leaving her alone. Her features were a mix of anger and exhaustion—utterly spent. Thomas hoped Kick didn't play poker. From what he'd read of her pretty visage, she'd lose big.

He did not understand what was wrong with him unless the late hour affected him too. It wasn't like his current situation was new. He'd been laser-focused for a while. Women stayed low on his priority list since he'd moved to North Carolina. When one occasionally landed in a slot on the list, she learned the deal up front: no attachments, no commitments, and an expiration date was imminent.

He sat in a chair in the corner where the stage had been and found his thoughts mulling over the song her son, Liam, played earlier. The lyrics of "Simple Man" running on a loop in his head became an indictment of the way he lived.

When had it happened? The problem was, he remembered each time his life had taken a turn toward more complication. Hell, he couldn't remember the last time he'd followed his heart for the sheer joy of it. He'd locked it up tight in a box, keeping emotions at bay and helping him stay the course. But the song reminded him of other things. Things that used to be important. Life shouldn't be so complicated for one man; then again, maybe it should. From another angle, he carried enough baggage to fill a cargo plane.

The song looped through his head another time, and he found a speck of encouragement in the words. Maybe it would help to have more people in his life. Yeah, he could stop back here once in a while, remember what it was like to be normal.

"You don't have to wait with me for the… the guy… Steve? Seth? You know, with the key thing."

"You mean the locksmith?" Thomas asked.

Kick offered him a bottled water, which he gladly took.

"Yes," she gasped, falling into the chair next to him. Her cane dropped to the floor. "Brain fog is the most annoying part." She rubbed her eyes and continued, "What's with the broken lock though? The officer thinks whoever did it used the music as cover."

"I'm not leaving you here with a bum lock. What if they come back?"

They sat in a shy silence, sipping their water. Kick hummed to Don McLean's "Crossroads" playing over the speakers. It gripped him in the chest more than anything she'd done so far. To say this woman differed from most of the women in his life would've been a gross understatement.

"Did you know your logo makes a double helix?" Thomas blurted, uncomfortable with his thoughts.

Kick smiled. Despite the exhaustion showing all over her face, the smile lit her up. "I do know, yes. Few people notice because I meant it to be subtle. Good eye."

Thomas shrugged his shoulders. "I'm a geneticist. What's it mean?"

She took a pull from the water bottle. "I go out of my way to provide a different cup of coffee. Sure, we have syrups and such, but most of our customers appreciate our effort to make the base product as healthy as possible." Kick clicked her tongue. "Not that it's helping me now."

"Can I ask you something?" The double helix reminded Thomas of an earlier conversation. He suppressed the voice in his head, telling him to mind his own damn business.

"Stephon," she answered, leaning back into the perfectly worn leather chair, her eyes closed. Between the dark circles there and the slight tremor in her hands, he assessed Kick to be at her breaking point physically, if not emotionally.

"Pardon?"

"Stephon's my locksmith. Sorry. Go ahead and ask."

"No need to apologize." Thomas sat in silence while he gathered his words. "I'm having trouble reconciling who you've been this evening and—"

"The card-carrying member of the bitchy cliterotti who chewed your ass up this morning? Yeah, me too."

Thomas burst out laughing. It started as a quiet snort and grew into a hardcore belly laugh. His hands and core warmed and hummed with an old sensation. He concentrated on it, certain it had nothing to do with attraction. Then he spotted the confusion on Kick's face and quickly pulled himself together.

"It wasn't a joke," she deadpanned.

And the laughing fit resumed. Lord, he couldn't remember the last time he'd laughed, let alone split a gut. Her words tricked his self-control into dissolving, but it had been looking for a release. His day was stressful too. Maybe not equally, but close.

He sat up and found Kick staring, nonplussed, her arms crossed at her chest. The pink Perked Cup T-shirt she wore complemented her ivory skin. The neckline scooped without being too tight or too low. Now, what her arms were doing to her cleavage? He looked away to keep from ogling. It was rude. Plus he'd be damned if he'd let a great rack bend his focus. Or his will.

Thomas pulled himself together. "Bitchy what?" He raised his hands. "Never mind. Anyway, I wouldn't say that… Alright, maybe you were… a bit." One last deep sigh and he was back to his proper self. "Earlier, you mentioned a diagnosis and weed?"

"You don't want to chalk my behavior up to an irrational, female, Irish-American temper?"

"Should I?" Thomas looked around the open area. Large, rustic tables anchored one corner. This comfortable leather lounge area offered a different experience, as did the industrial bistro sets scattered throughout. Kick had thought hard about appealing to each type of customer. You didn't get this kind of insight by being a selfish hothead. No, it wasn't a foul temperament he'd run into earlier. Something had her off her game.

Kick sighed, sat upright, toed off her boots, and pulled a heel onto the seat, resting her elbow on her knee. "It's nothing that won't work itself out. I've seen some dumb shit in my café, but I've never had a customer tape a bag of weed to the bathroom vanity before."

"Is that what the graffiti was about?"

She lifted a shoulder. "Maybe? Except how would a vandal with bad grammar know about it?"

"Unless both criminals are the same person. Maybe he's mad you took it from him," Thomas added, rubbing his chin.

Kick yawned, making her jaw pop. "Ooh, good idea. When I check in with the OPD tomorrow, I'll see if they've thought of it."

"And the diagnosis?" Thomas asked.

Flicking her wrist, Kick answered, "Just a setback."

Thomas raised a hand. "I didn't mean to pry. Really. It's my research. My brain's always thinking about genetics. The way it contributes to illnesses fascinates me."

"Okay." She studied him intensely, then muttered, "You asked for it." Kick straightened her back and began. "I have two autoimmune issues: Hashimoto's thyroiditis and celiac disease. I was close to remission, but it's been a rough summer." Thomas's bouncing foot filled the silence until she continued. "My dad was Hugh's business partner. He's the one who died in June."

"My deepest condolences. How awful."

Thomas wondered why Kick did a double take. Then her spine appeared to collapse over her knee. "Thank you. My son and I are trying to help Hugh keep things going until he's back full time, but he never liked working the front of the store. He needs time to figure out what to do next." Kick sat up, lifting her hair off her neck. "Anyway, big surprise, I hadn't been feeling well. This morning my doctor confirmed the flare and a possible third autoimmune attack, blaming all the stress."

"I see."

"Can't begin to explain the mountain of garbage between my mother and me. With Dad gone…"

"It's worse?"

"I'm getting buried by it."

Thomas thought back to the morning. "The lady sitting at the counter this morning."

"Yup." Kick removed her hairband and redid her ponytail while Thomas's gaze rested on the pointed tip of her ears. Something about them made him soften to her plight even more. They held a correlation to an old spirit—and suffering.

"My mother says I'm a hypochondriac, seeking attention by pretending to be sick. At least she's out of my hair for now."

Thomas lifted an eyebrow and smirked. "Tell me you didn't hire out an assassin."

The question brought a sly, delightful smile to her face. "You did get the correct first impression. No, she's on an extended cruise. I hope doing something for herself will soften her somehow." Kick put her foot back down and sat straight. "Now you know. And again, I apologize for earlier."

Thomas didn't want to be moved. He couldn't care less about the plight of sick working mothers who didn't understand the concept of balance. Yet he found himself probing. "Is there a plan? For your flare."

Kick collapsed back into the chair, and Thomas watched the weight of her world grow heavier. "Yup. There are temporary dietary changes. It's like a detox thing." She let out a low sarcastic laugh. "And I have to change the way I work out." Her hands flew to her head in a brief, upset burst. "Shoot, I forgot to tell Cyn I can't do boot camp anymore. She's going to kill me since I talked her into joining the class."

Thomas rubbed the bridge of his nose, feeling the effects of his long day. She didn't make any sense, and his own tiredness tested his patience. "I thought exercise is paramount to improving your health. What are you supposed to do?"

"This part I remember without notes. Since my workouts have been wearing me out more than they should, for the foreseeable future, an hour-long moderate walk is better than squeezing in a hard workout for a short amount of time. It's been stressing my adrenals, causing cortisol levels to rise." Kick turned her head and gave him a small smile. "My dog will like the slower pace anyway. Still, the group was fun and supportive."

"Will Cyndi be your walking partner then?"

Kick shook her head. "She prefers machines to nature and must have bodies to ogle. My dog is my little nature buddy."

Thomas's brows pulled together. "How little are we talking?"

"Research, huh?" She shrugged and lowered her hand to knee

height. "Koosh is tougher than she looks if that's what you're asking. Anyway, I'll be fine once I process everything." Kick tucked a stray curl behind her ear. "Lately it seems like every few months everything I know to be true flips on its head… *annnd* now I'm whining." She turned her gaze to Thomas. "Sorry. Life truly is good. 'The boundary lines have fallen for me in pleasant places.'" She bobbed her head as she recited the words.

He turned to her, surprised by their familiarity. "Psalms?"

"Yes. You know it?" Kick's face perked up.

"Certain things in life imprint themselves so deep they never leave."

She nodded.

Thomas settled uneasily into the club chair. He didn't like to think of Kick walking alone, even though he knew women managed fine on their own every day. Still, he'd bet money the dog wouldn't matter if trouble came their way. He quietly sipped his water, keeping his thoughts to himself. He didn't want to risk stumbling into another argument with her. Besides, since she meant nothing to him, it didn't matter.

Wasn't there an uptick in attacks on women on local greenways though? The news reports made it sound like the victims were at fault for running alone. Hell, one of the reasons he ran at all was for the peace to get away and sort through his thoughts. It would suck to have to stay constantly on guard.

THE LOCKSMITH CAME AND WENT, LEAVING THE PERKED CUP SECURE again. Not to Thomas's standards, but it would do for now. Thomas couldn't get over how much their security lacked. He turned to Kick as she relocked the front door, pulling a business card out of his pocket. "First thing tomorrow morning, call this guy. Please."

She dropped the key in her purse and took the card. "Excuse me?"

He tipped his head toward her hand. "This man is like a brother to me. He's also a security expert. Promise me you'll call him and bring your business into the twenty-first century. I promise he'll take care of y'all and won't overcharge."

She looked up toward the streetlight, the broken one. "Jaysus, more money. Some days I'd swear if you cut me, I'd bleed Benjamins."

Thomas placed his hand on her foreman. The contact buzzed, and she quickly withdrew. He mirrored her action, though more from the shock of the feeling than the sensation itself. If he'd slowed his thoughts, he'd admit he liked it.

"Promise me you'll listen to his advice. There's too much invested in here to risk a successful break-in."

Kick admitted, "It's been on my list for a while."

Thomas fought a relieved grin. "Now you know who to call. Banger's the best."

"Banger?" Kick shook her head. "Never mind. It's too late to consider where he got the name." She hooked the cane over her arm before placing the card in the same pocket as the keys. "Thanks for this. For keeping me company too." A huge yawn shook her body. "I probably would've slept through the knocking when Stephon finally arrived."

"You did," Thomas said, keeping his smile shaded. He took a step backward and nodded his head. "Have a good night then."

"You too. Thanks again."

Kick leaned against the wall and began scrolling through her phone.

Why wasn't she walking toward a car?

He planned to wait and make sure she pulled away safely. Isolation didn't trump being a gentleman after all. He unlocked his door, opened it, and froze. *She's capable, asshole. Just slide in.*

Thomas turned around. "Why aren't you moving?"

Kick looked up from her phone. "I'm too tired and in too much pain to bike home."

He tipped his head. "Bike?"

Her eyes had returned to the screen. "Yeah, car's in the shop." She gave her phone a waggle. "I ordered a ride."

"I should go."

"Yes, you should."

It was a challenge more than agreement. Yet he couldn't leave her there. She'd given him an out, letting loose her problems earlier. And she'd set them straight. Eventually.

She'll be fine. Slide in and go. Damnit. He set his chin and called out, "Get in."

She waved him off. "Seriously, Thomas, you've done enough. I owe you a month's worth of free coffee at least. Go."

Thomas shook his head with purpose. "I'm taking you home. You're not riding with a stranger."

She approached the car, her eyes narrowed and lips pressed into a similar thin line. "Like I know much about you?"

"Have I hurt you? I'm here. It's no problem. Get in." He nearly growled, his last ounce of patience slipping away. He reached across the front seat and unlocked the passenger door. Thomas watched her notice the classic Camaro.

Despite her weary gait, her eyes brightened, and she gasped the way most women fawned over babies. "It's mint," she stated, not questioned.

Thomas nodded his head, and her smile placed another crack in his dried-up soul. *Simply a fellow muscle-car lover.* But this felt different from the occasional gear-head chatter. It *meant* something to have Kick notice the car, like appreciating the vehicle meant she appreciated him.

As she passed the hood, her hand slid over it, first the tops of her fingers, then her hand flipped, and she glided her whole hand over the surface—a genuine caress. Thomas lost his breath. His eyes tracked each finger's exploration, nearly at eye level from his vantage in the driver's seat, swearing he felt them on his body, on his — He cleared his throat and swallowed.

"Beautiful," she whispered.

Agreed, he thought.

Kick opened the door. "Well done, professor. I have a newer Camaro. I love it to bits." She slid in, shut the door, and buckled the belt. The corner of her mouth ticked up. "I bet the rideshare driver wouldn't be so grumpy." Had their shared taste in rides energized her some?

Through his foggy head, he wanted to bite back that he should be in bed. But it would've been cruel, considering how thoroughly exhaustion showed in the way she carried herself despite her car enthusiasm.

To confirm, she collapsed into the leather seat and declared, "Jayz, even my hair feels tired." She was right. It didn't have the same wild bounce it showed off in the morning.

Thomas stole glances at Kick as he drove. Her eyes closed, so he relaxed the leash he kept on his desires, watching her almost continuously thanks to empty streets. She looked perfect in his car. The leather seemed to embrace her like it didn't want her to leave, like the seat was made specifically for her.

"One thing I don't understand."

"Shoot," Kick answered without opening her eyes.

"You thought I was asking you out, but you wear a wedding ring."

From the corner of his eye, Thomas observed Kick's thumb turning said ring on her third finger. "It's a mother's ring. My daughter's birthstone is a diamond, so a jeweler friend repurposed my grandmother's wedding ring and added the boys' stones to either side."

"So you're not married."

"What?" Her brows furrowed into a deep V.

He cringed. Of course she was single. She would've called her husband instead of letting Thomas wait around and help her otherwise. "I'm sorry. Dumb question."

Kick chuckled, her eyes still closed, her voice gravelly when she answered. "No worries. I'm too spent to judge. And no. I *was* married." She raised her left hand. "My hand felt bare after, so…"

"I see." Thomas shut his mouth to keep from further embarrassment. He couldn't shake how much he hated the idea of this woman being alone. He didn't know why he cared.

GPS did its job, and he pulled into Kick's driveway. Thomas touched her hand to wake her and caught the peaked flush on her face. Hoping he wasn't overstepping, he lightly placed the backs of his fingers on her forehead and damned if she wasn't warm.

"Shit, Kick, I think you're sick."

She started, patting around her face. "Oh. It's nothing." She gave him a shy smile. "Par for the course for pushing so hard today. No worries."

He stared at her for a beat before saying, "Want me to see you to the door?"

Kick silently waved off the question. Well, fine. She was a grown woman.

She opened the door, stepped her right leg out, then turned back with a sweet smile. "Thank you for going way above and beyond. I hope you stop in again sometime. I'm serious about the free coffee too."

Thomas's eyes tracked Kick limping around the car, and the pull grew. In the headlights, the sheen on her face was more pronounced. He saw the graying of her pale skin, the slowness of her steps. Seeing this side of her really did anger him. Not at her, but for her. She shouldn't have to put up with it.

Christ, one minute you're fighting lust, the next you want to protect her from the world. But he couldn't protect her from her own body, could he? There wasn't anything Thomas could do for that. *Put it in reverse and drive. Let it go, man.*

He rolled his window down. "Hey, Kick?" She turned back to him without approaching the window. "When are y'all planning to go walking?"

She tapped her temple and whispered. "Argh. Stop making me use my brain." Her eyes tipped up to the sky, tongue rolling in her cheek like she was scanning a mental calendar. "Wednesday, Friday, and at least once over the weekend. Why?"

"What time on Wednesday?"

"Seven thirty. After Liam leaves for school."

He had a faculty meeting not long after. "I'll come with you."

"It's fine, Thomas. I don't need a—"

"I'll be there," he declared, using the tone he used with an obstinate student.

She narrowed her eyes and parked her hand on her hip. He suddenly felt like the student waiting for a correction. Thomas popped his head back into the car to add some distance. She wasn't a young girl to be handled. Kick was an experienced mother—a fascinating woman—but he wouldn't admit it.

"Fine. Do what you'd like, *professor*. Meet me here, but I'll only wait ten minutes. I have a lot to take care of before I settle into the new schedule." Kick turned toward the house and wobbled, then stopped and looked back. "I promise I won't be mad if something comes up."

He thought he heard Kick say, "I'm used to it," but she'd already resumed her stagger to the house.

Thomas put the car in gear and cranked up his Blues station.

No big deal, he thought. He liked to exercise anyway.

What harm could it do?

6

It's Easy to Fall in Love (with a Guy Like You)

Kick

Friday morning, around eight o'clock, I kept wondering what the hell I was doing walking with Thomas Harrison on my local greenway, my dog's leash firmly in hand. As expected, he'd canceled Wednesday morning, but I didn't mind. Unloading my problems in one blurp to a relative stranger had the unexpected result of clearing my head. In the past, honest sharing had made close friends run for hills, so I had expected Thomas would do the same.

That first slow walk on Wednesday nearly drove me bananas though. I kept catching myself trying to power through. Then Liam gave me an idea to try. So far, so good. Except every time I paused, Thomas would walk ahead of my dog and me.

When he did it initially, I had my head in my phone or had let the dog sniff out an interesting find. And when I looked up? Whoa, the view made my eyes pop.

It was a warm, cloudless morning, so I wore a pair of hiking shorts and a tunic-length tank over my sports bra in case tummy bloat showed up. Thomas, however? Who knew a b-o-d-y was under the suit? The archaic rule of walking five steps behind a man didn't seem so bad if it meant following an ass like his. Add in muscled shoulders and biceps, I worried about getting the vapors if he overheated and took off his tank.

"Mind if I ask where your nickname came from? Is it short for Catherine?" he asked.

My dog, a hound-mix rescue named Macushla, found a communal pee spot right as an Eevee appeared in the app. I was already close to evolving my first one, and the silly excitement of it made me hum. "What'd you say?"

He turned and came back to us. "I asked about the origin of your nickname." He looked at my phone screen. "What're y'all doing? You're going to trip over something with your face in the phone."

"Sorry, Professor Grumpypants." I showed him the Android. "Liam suggested *Pokémon Go* might help me slow down without getting frustrated. I tried it out for a short loop yesterday. Koosh liked it too. You should play." I batted my lashes with vigor. When his scowl didn't dissipate, it occurred to me my sunglasses obscured the joke. "Sorry, we're slowing you down." I shrugged. Embarrassed and disheartened, I confessed, "I didn't know what else to do. It goes against my nature to dawdle."

Thomas took his phone out of a pocket and downloaded the app, his appeasement lifting my spirit. It wasn't long before we were catching critters and easing our way down the path, my dog enjoying her fill of smells thanks to our meandering pace.

"The nickname, huh?" I said after catching a Squirtle with high combat points.

"Just conversation. And curiosity. You don't have to—"

"It's fine." I chuckled. "After Monday, you had to notice I'm an open book. Anyway, it's short for Kathleen. I didn't like it for a long time. It was my introduction to a lifetime of tug-of-war between my parents."

"How so?" Thomas's dour expression morphed into one of interest and empathy. I couldn't help but notice how he gave his attention fully, once he decided to. It didn't take long for the floodgate, known as my mouth, to open.

"Dad always called me Katie, my mother took to Kick. She got the name from her obsession with the Kennedys, who had a sister with it. Typical to Bobby's side of the family, it was more of an insult. The more I objected, the more they used it. I begged teachers to call me Katie, or even Kathleen, at school, but only one ever overrode Bobby. Since it was the seventies, the adults stuck together."

"Sure."

"It's water under the bridge. At the time, classmates used it to tease. You know, *Kick me, Kickball.* It took a while to realize they only did it to those who let them. My dad's mom helped me own the name and turn it back on the playground bullies, as well as the ones in the family."

Figuring I'd said enough, I walked on in silence, working with Macushla to walk on my right.

"Aren't you going to tell me what happened?"

"Seriously?" I didn't think even Deana knew the full story of my name, beyond the Kennedy sister connection. No one ever really cared.

Thomas shrugged. "I have a feeling it'll be a good story."

What the hell. I continued, "While waiting on the bell one morning, this monster of a girl targeted me. She started in on the typical teasing, so I said, 'How about I *kick* your arse?' Then we threw down."

Thomas stopped walking and leaned in, a mischievous grin on his face. "Kathleen McKenna, were you a fighter?"

"Only in defense. Or if someone picked on my friends or my little brother." A light breeze diffused the blush threatening to overheat my already warm face. "She threw the first punch. The principal called home anyway."

"As they do."

"Yeah. Granny Allen was staying with us, and she came to the office since both my parents worked." I laughed at the memory. "The principal told Granny I'd been suspended for three days for swearing and fighting."

"Yikes."

I nodded. "When I insisted the other girl threw the first punch and I'd said 'arse' and not 'ass,' Granny did her five-foot-one best to get in the man's face. She was adamant European swear words didn't count in America and defending oneself wasn't fighting, so he had no case against me. She negotiated it down to taking the afternoon off. Then we stopped in a Sander's ice cream shop and ate hot fudge sundaes. It ended up being worth the cuts to my knuckles."

"Cuts?" Thomas's eyebrows knotted in confusion.

"The girl had braces." I laughed. "I miss Granny. She scared my mom." I held up a finger. "Wait. Not true. Bobby was afraid of *her* mother, but Grandma Sullivan was mean. Bobby respected Granny Allen. I could breathe when she visited." As if it was a suggestion instead of a statement, I took a long inhale and slowly released it. "I took her stance on European swear words as far as I could as a kid. Still use some of them when I'm upset."

My gaze had fixed on Macushla inhaling some scent in a stand of weeds as I shared my story. Opening up to Thomas felt both uncomfortable and natural. I didn't consciously want to but kept finding myself compelled. After stopping, I looked up at him, waiting for the next question, and felt his gaze piercing not only through my sunglasses but through me. I took a deep breath to fight the tightness in my chest, wondering what the outcome of his assessment would be.

The gentle roll of the nearby creek soothed the fluster. Two other women with dogs and a couple ran by us, getting in exercise while the temperature was still enjoyable and—I assumed—before taking off for work. But we weren't a couple, and I didn't want to be a part of a couple. What I *wanted* was the confidence boost of a successful run, not the head-muck that came from a body forced to putter.

He quietly said, "You seem comfortable with the name now."

I laughed at the memory he evoked. *Three generations from my mother's family had gathered around a kitchen table—the first holiday meal after my playground fight. My aunt had used my nickname with her particular bite. "This one thinks she's a kick, doesn't she?"*

"If you mean I kick arse and take names, then yes," I'd answered. It was the first time I didn't let their use of the sneer shut me down.

The spanking had been worth it. And Daddy had given me an extra dessert to apologize for the women's behavior.

"Yeah. Embracing it had the opposite effect on Bobby," I told him. "She's the one who hates it now. But it reminds me to fight for myself. Sometimes literally."

My phone vibrated in my hand. "Ooh, a Jiggly Puff popped up." *A Jiggly Puff should look like a middle-aged mother.* We slid our fingers across our screens to catch the Pokémon. "You're going to get ahead of me in no time. My kids say campuses are loaded with Pokéstops and gyms."

"I'm not playing this on campus," Thomas countered with a sardonic chuckle. His brow knitted back together like it was the default position.

"Suit yourself. It's getting fun." We spun a Pokéstop, and I received a gift package to give to a friend . I heard his phone notification ping. "There. I sent your first gift."

"This is ridiculous," he groaned.

"Come on, Gramps." I chuckled, giving Macushla a wiggle of her leash. "We're almost to our halfway point."

Thomas surprised me with more thoughtful questions, showing me he was honestly interested in my life. He shared what he could about his research but clarified it was considered top secret. Then he received a call, reknitting his brow and returning his face to a state of grumpiness.

"Excuse me. I have to take this privately." He stepped off the path, disappearing into the woods. "*Oui, Grand-père.* What can I do for you?"

"No worries," I called after him. "I'll take Koosh down to the creek." I wasn't sure if Thomas heard, but I made sure he could find us when he finished. Was he French on his mother's side? I liked that he still had at least one grandparent after sharing about mine. They had all died. I wondered if the man lived in France or here in the States.

I waited while the dog splashed in the creek, delighted to see water Pokémon show up on my screen. Between catching them and mulling over our talk, I didn't notice Macushla cut from my right side to my left after spotting a squirrel. Moreover, I paid no attention to the leash. She charged after the thing, taking me out with the efficiency of an NFL safety tackling a running back. One second my feet were firmly planted on a leaf-covered, shady foot path, the next they'd swapped positions with my head. In the process, my ankle twisted, and I might or might not have heard a *pop*.

I lay on the ground, wondering why the stars were out at the same time as the diffused sun rays that dotted my face. An intense pain shot up my leg from my shoe to my thigh. Macushla apologized with whimpers and kisses.

"Shit. What happened?" Thomas crouched down and helped me sit up. As he fixed my Michigan State ball cap, his worried expression threw me. I didn't know what to do with his concern, even though any friend would have done the same. It had to be this new-old idea of friendship with a *boy*. After becoming a single mom, Cyndi took on the role of my plus one on the rare occasion I needed it. Or my dad did. Befriending a man had become a foreign concept after years spent in the divided world of husbands and wives.

He brushed debris from my calf, revealing a shallow gash from a piece of broken glass. My screaming ankle had me reaching for the laces to loosen them.

I remembered the Pokémon game and called out, "My phone—"

"Here," Thomas answered, placing it in my hands. "Nice job picking a case. There's not a scratch on it. Unlike you." He stood and grabbed my hands, pulling me up onto my good leg. "Is there a clinic nearby?"

I pushed away his advancing hands, embarrassed enough. "Sorry, pal. None within walking distance. It's only a sprain anyway. An ice pack and Ace bandage will be fine."

He lifted my wrist and draped it across his shoulder, his other hand at my waist. "Lean on me at least." He took Koosh's leash in his free hand.

We step-hopped for a couple hundred feet at a snail's pace

before the ache in my leg became a roar. I was determined to make it back home with whatever pride I had left. Besides, what was the alternative? Sit on the ground and cry? It had been stupid to take my attention from Macushla. She could never resist a good chase.

We came to the steps leading up to my neighborhood, and I almost did cry. Only four blocks to home and an ice pack, but the cement flight might as well have been a hike up Mount Mitchell.

"Shit," I said. "I forgot about the stairs." I tried to hold on to the railing and one-foot hop. My good ankle rolled, making me land on my butt again. The zing to my sacrum manifested in a guttural groan.

"Enough." Thomas scooped me up in his capable hands. He managed the steps and kept the dog out of his stride like he practiced the maneuver regularly. I opened my mouth when we reached the top step, but he warned, "Not a word about putting you down. We're going to your house and then to a doctor."

"No, Thomas. It's okay. Really. I'm too heavy for this. I'll—"

"I said enough, Kick. Your ankle looks rough. We should make sure you don't have a hairline fracture."

"This is embarrassing," I growled with frustration. But hey, now I really knew Thomas would scram, right?

"You have a hard time taking help, don't you?" he bit back. We had to make a ridiculous sight—he and I arguing as he carried me. Only Macushla acted happy to be in our little trio.

After a couple of beats of silence, I answered, "It's not what you think. It was a hard lesson learned many times over."

Thomas's gaze snapped to mine as I interrupted his thoughts. "Pardon?"

"I used to ask for help. Despite what people offer, I've learned the quickest way to lose a friend is to share about a struggle. As soon as the words were out of my mouth"—I snapped my fingers on my free hand—"Poof. They disappeared."

He inhaled deeply and adjusted his hold on me. "What about your current friends? Cyndi or Hugh or others?"

"They have their own issues," I answered with a sigh. "When I first got sick, my mother's response to the devastating news was

'Nobody wants to hear your sob story.' It was a cruel and cold thing to say. But she turned out to be right. So, I muddle through tough times. They eventually pass."

"On your own." The way he said it told me Thomas understood.

"If I can afford to hire help, I do. Otherwise, yes. Obstacles usually resolve given enough time." My foot began a throb so strong it had its own heartbeat. "*Jaysus*, it hurts."

I tucked my head into Thomas's neck to focus on my breathing, hoping to slow the pounding. Something about being in his arms, inhaling his scent, relaxed me, if only a little. He had a point. It was nice to let him carry me. A girl could have gotten used to it. One day.

Yet my scarred past cautioned me against getting too comfortable. It was my God's-honest truth—a shoe always perched at the ready, waiting to drop. But boy, it would be so nice if the shoe stayed put for once.

Thomas smelled amazing, even with a little sweat, more from the growing heat than our pathetic exercise. I inhaled deeply, recognizing sandalwood and lavender, two of my favorite oils to diffuse in the house. An underlying essence that was uniquely Thomas and equally relaxing. My body gave in to his hold.

"Did you just smell me?" he asked with a rattled edge.

Hell yeah. "No." I deflected. "I'm trying to adjust my breathing and slow my heart rate to see if it'll slow the rate of swelling. Sorry." His heartbeat pounded against my side, almost as fast as mine.

"Don't apologize." We came to an intersection. "Which way?"

I pointed straight ahead. "Are you sure you don't want to put me down? I won't mind."

"Kick, stop. I'm fine." He adjusted me as we made our way across the street.

"At least you're finally getting a decent workout."

The corner of Thomas's mouth lifted, and his eyes formed the kindest crinkles. "I lift more than you in the gym."

Okaaay then. "Really?"

The crinkles deepened as his smile transitioned to a chuckle. "Why do you sound excited?"

If a person could slump while being carried, I did. "I've gained weight with this setback. I'm not supposed to care, but it's the easiest thing to measure when it comes to health." I took a long sigh. "It's embarrassing."

Thomas assessed me from head to toe. "You're embarrassed? About your appearance?" He shook his head. "I understand not feeling well, but you look—"

I set my fingers over his lips, not sure I could handle a joke. Thomas didn't know how raw the topic was thanks to Bobby. And I'd had enough of oversharing for the day.

"Fine," he said through my fingers. "You look perfect…ly fine."

"Really?" I asked again, like a desperate teen.

"Yes. I was going to say more, but I was afraid you'd wallop me with your free hand."

"I'd never."

Thomas's sarcastic laugh had me thinking of the morning we met, when I'd yelled at him. A step around a tricycle in the sidewalk sent a zing up my leg and shut me up. I welcomed the distraction since I already regretted telling him too much.

I focused on my up-close view of his shoulders and arms, which testified to his workouts. The emotions he stirred in me were ancient. I'd forgotten how to recognize them, let alone know what to do with them if I did. So, I chalked them up to gratitude and settled into the ride.

Besides, there was no way I'd allow a spark of interest for a man so young. I'd made a vow that ran deep and long, straight to my core beliefs. He might not be as young as my son, but he was off-limits in my book. And I offered him nothing.

I tried to lighten the mood with a joke. "I think I understand the retro clothes now."

"What're you talking about?" Thomas passed me a look of incredulity. I feared I'd insulted him.

"If your female students knew this"—I patted his hard-working chest and almost died—"was under your suits, they'd be all up in your business."

A shy smile returned to the corner of his mouth. Hell, it was sexy too. Then guilt tried to stir, as it always did if I considered moving on.

"Are you… complimenting my body?"

"Stating facts, Professor. Isn't that what scientists do?"

"Nothing's wrong with my clothes. It's rude when people show up to class like they've just rolled out of bed. Professional dress shows I care about my classes. Besides, my students think I'm a fine teacher, thank you. Seems to work."

"We haven't hung out much, but you kind of seem a bit hermit-ish. Frankly, it surprised me you picked teaching for a profession." Thomas's Adam's apple bobbed as he stared straight ahead, his eyes forming irritated slits under his brow.

Argh. I'd gone bitch-clit again.

I immediately regretted my words. Why did I seem to turn into the Wicked Witch of the Southeast around this poor guy? Since our times together had been on bad days for me, what did I really know about him? Once again, open mouth and insert purple-swollen foot.

"Can I take my words back? They're unfair since I still hardly know you. I'm sorry."

Macushla tried to stop and smell who-knows-what, and Thomas efficiently kept her on track with a slight correction. "Apology accepted." We continued for a few steps in silence before he gracefully explained, "I spend most of my days in the lab. But lecturing has been a surprise. I took the class as a favor, but it's reminding me there's more to life than research. The lab tends to follow me wherever I go if I'm not careful."

We stepped off a curb, and I hissed at the jolt of impact. "Hanging in there?" he asked.

I nodded, unable to speak for once, and turned my head back into Thomas's shoulder, blowing quick breaths to get above the throb.

"Stop smelling me, please," he clipped. "It's creeping me out."

"I'm trying to meditate," I snapped back. "My doctor wants me to learn it to help with stress, but I haven't had a chance yet. I figured Lamaze breathing might help with the pain.

"Keep it up and you'll hyperventilate. You're breathing into your chest."

He did his best to inhale into his belly and had me follow him. It surprised me how much it helped. I mumbled into his neck, "Left at the next corner. You'll recognize the stone facade from there. Maybe you're right about the doctor. I should call Dylan and have him take me to the Urgent Care. Where did you put my phone? I could call him now."

His adjustment was more of a jostle, like a physical reprimand. "For Christ's sake, let me take you. I can have my TA cover today's lecture. Then I'm not due at the lab for hours."

I returned to my breathing, trying to close out the neighborhood noises and escape the pain. The sound of landscapers mowing lawns aggravated the throbs in my foot.

Thomas lightly tapped my arm. "Don't fall asleep on me. I didn't see you go down, but it looked like you might have blacked out when I found you. You should be checked for a concussion too."

"Leave it to me to get a TBI from tripping. I wasn't sleeping though. I was trying to meditate again."

"It's a good idea. It may be more important than your workouts."

"Not you too," I groaned.

I knew the moment Thomas recognized the stone porch of my house. His strong shoulders relaxed, and I worried again about how much work I'd put him through. At least I wasn't bloated since bloating could lead to gas. And just… *nope*. If that had happened, I'd have run home, sprained ankle or not.

Then he said, "I use a meditation app. I can show you how it works if you'd like."

I rolled my eyes like a teenager. "The blasted universe won't leave me alone, will it?"

Thomas's chuckle rumbled through his chest, making me want to purr. *What the hell?* The pain had to be fritzing my brain. I'd even forgotten to ask him about the phone call from his grandfather.

. . .

Sunlight spilled through the bathroom window, a warm and golden dawn. A shadowed man crouched in front of me as I sat on the edge of my tub. He pushed a curl behind my ear. I didn't recognize him, but somehow I knew I loved him. His hair was shoulder-length and queued, with a gorgeous peppering of silver at the sides. I couldn't see much of his face, aside from a chiseled jaw.

This man's love was so deep it brought tears to my eyes. Despite the yellow light coming in the window, there was a cool essence around him. It's what diffused my view of his face, his body, and his clothes.

Then he spoke. "You own my heart and soul. Open your eyes and find me."

I sprang up, sitting in a cold sweat. Though dizzy, it wasn't from the pain meds in my system. The dream was so vivid every second of it clung to my thoughts like a sticky irritant. It swirled in and out of my head to keep me from falling back to sleep.

Replaying the vision created a deep lament. I'd had the dream so many times in the past five years my longing for an unknown man built to this unbearable level. I was desperate for clues about him, but the dream rarely changed.

I hated the foolishness even if no one else knew about it. Who fell in love with a fantasy? But my heart hurt for him. I scanned my memory again for evidence the man was *him*—the other love who haunted my dreams—but *he* was bigger, broader. His hair receded with waves. Then there were the dimples no one could ever forget. No, this was a different man, and the guilt I felt was almost too much.

The first time I had the dream, I thought I'd met an angel and glimpsed an afterlife. As time wore on, I became more attracted to his presence, silly as it sounded. His voice softened the hardest nights. The days following a dream drove me insane as I'd ruminate on who he could be, if he were real, if I'd ever find out. Granny Allen had told me plenty of stories of the Fae as a child, but none of them involved handsome dream-men like this. Since they'd become their own version of torture, I either wanted an answer or to be left alone forever.

I wondered if dating in the real world would make him go away. But my health, the kids, the business, and then my dad's passing had left no room for it. I thought about Cyndi's comment again, about the universe sending me messages. But the universe could also wait until my ducks aligned again.

I grabbed the crutches nearby and maneuvered into standing with a wince. I refused opioids, and standard pain meds were wearing off. I prepped a mug of ginger tea and a snack to go with the next round of drugs once I'd made my way into the kitchen. I turned on music to clear my mind and help me sleep some more, hoping the mystery man stayed the hell away this time.

Maybe I'd try the meditation app Thomas installed on my phone. Professor Thomas Harrison—he was an enigma shrouded in mystery. Why didn't he want to speak to his French grandfather? Every time I visited the memory of our walk, Thomas's face grimaced after his phone rang. And the mad dash for privacy, like he couldn't get away from Koosh and me fast enough. I didn't know whether to sympathize or fear what it could have been about.

Why were the answers I craved all so elusive?

7

Cold Little Heart

Thomas

THOMAS SAT AT HIS DESK, STUDYING THE MARKS IN THE QUARTER-sawn oak—anything to delay checking in with *Grand-père*. He shifted his shoulders to remove his blazer, only to catch sight of it already resting on the coatrack in the corner. He triple-checked the lock on his office door. Ran a hand through his hair. His laptop booted up, glaring at him with its bright light, mocking him. *Coward.*

Images of new acquaintances shuffled through his mind, including the students who'd taken the time to stop by during office hours, revealing an interest in biology beyond a checked box for graduation. Two showed promise as future undergrad assistants in the lab. Agreeing to teach a section of biology had its pluses. So did doing a favor for the dean.

Thoughts drifted to Kick McKenna making quick work of the rude kid when Thomas had stepped into her coffeehouse. Too many students had the same air as that boy, as if Thomas received them not quite ready to adult. He secretly wanted to turn a few lectures into what he termed "applied biology" and teach basic life concepts, like Kick had done.

Kick's face continued flashing through his mind. Thomas hadn't responded to a woman in such a primal way in a long time. Her vanilla-and-tropical scent surrounding him while he carried her, or the few times his fingers brushed the side of her breast. He'd awakened, forced himself to not stiffen like a preteen boy. She would've jumped out of his arms and hobbled home for sure. He chuckled at the proverbial picture, then felt remorse. He hated her pain.

Thomas couldn't shake the notion Kick could help keep him from losing himself. Favor or not, he'd taken on the extra work of teaching out of fear. He hoped exposure to more students, and people like those at the Perked Cup, would keep him sane. His isolated life wasn't only making him "grumpy," as Kick called it. Thomas feared he'd become a sentient statue, outwardly representing the man he used to be, but inside was nothing but cold stone.

Reliving these new moments beat the hell out of his usual ruminations. Had it really been ten years since the last ascension ceremony? It was when he'd developed his plan to go into research. Paul's ascension had been as beautiful as the others Thomas had witnessed in his time with the secretive *Felidae*. He wondered where the kindhearted man was presently. Could Paul help their cause from the other side as much as he'd hoped? Lately, Thomas recognized the same weary gaze the man had carried when looking in the mirror at his own visage. But he planned to make his contribution here, on this side, and then he'd ascend. Some days the idea thrilled him so much he swore he'd do a dance during the ceremony. The days Thomas dreaded most were the numb ones, where he no longer cared either way. Those days, he was certain he'd become that statue.

With the laptop ready, he took a cleansing breath and entered the login information. Unlike his teaching computer, this was a tiny machine with one job. Using an encrypted network, his friend and colleague, Banger, had set up, Thomas logged onto the website for the Felidae Society. The eyes of a graceful black jaguar stared out from the landing page. Obsessed with security and deflection, the Felidae presented itself as a conservatory for protecting endangered cats. They'd raised millions for the effort since the front end of the site went live.

This backdoor kept up the ruse in case the wrong person found it. It protected the closed world in which Thomas lived. The group purposely chose the mysterious big cat as the fake face of the Felidae who also lived in the shadows, walking and sleeping near people without anyone knowing.

Anxiety flowed through his fingers as he typed in his information. Too much hung on his latest round of experiments, and they had failed. He entered the update as if it were any other report, hoping no one would notice. His fingers moved as quickly as possible so he could get in and get out while those in Bordeaux, France, slept soundly at the Felidae headquarters.

Thoughts drifted to Kick again and her stubborn attempt to limp home with a sprain. Her nose scrunched when she insisted CBD cream and ice would suffice. But he had to be sure there wasn't a hairline fracture. He kept returning to the memory of her wrinkled-up nose and the way she fidgeted in his arms until she'd surrendered, relaxing, giving him her trust. The victory in their moment together outshone any progress in the lab. It was the kind of emotional success he looked for in his work. It was the kind of victory that made him feel something again.

Or he needed to get laid.

His phone rang fifteen minutes after Thomas began correcting quizzes. "*Grand-père*. How are you, sir?" The cheerful greeting sounded forced to his ears.

"Good to catch you, young man," Alaric Kraus, *Grand-père* to those in the Felidae, responded. The predicted urgency transmitted over the phone, a crisp contrast with his usual tone of warmth and encouragement. "I will cut to the chase," he continued. Thomas smiled into the phone. Modern idioms didn't come naturally to the unique leader of the Felidae, but *Grand-père* practiced them. Thomas was also pleased to hear Alaric's more ancient, Northern European accent stayed firm. It was the first thing to draw him in all those years ago. "What happened?"

Thomas sighed, owning the disappointment. "What can I say? I hit a wall. You saw the evidence of Toni's transition? I'm confident about her. It's the why and the how that still hide from me."

"Perhaps it means she's not worthy to be Felidae. Have you thought of that?" The old man's voice boomed before Thomas could answer. The remark stunned him; of course Toni was worthy. "She should move in with you. I keep telling you this. Fresh samples would help your work, and a change would be good for her. A new start."

A shadow passed by the frosted glass window in the door. Thomas willed the person to knock so he could end the call. Unfortunately, the shadow made a sharp turn and moved in the opposite direction. The lab associates usually texted if they had an emergency anyway. He reluctantly returned to the call, determined to end it as soon as possible. He had an unending loyalty to the Alaric and the Felidae, but family came first. The superior attitude of the Felidae leadership grew tiresome.

"Toni's overwhelmed and not only by the Felidae," Thomas countered. "She's staying with Joe in Virginia for her health. He's taking the lead in her transition, per my direction. I'll visit them before I see you." He paused, then added quickly, "That is, if there's still a reason for me to present in October."

"What do you mean, if there's still a reason?" Alaric snapped. "I want you here. You'll come. You have a month to fix this, no?" *Grand-père*'s confidence was a breath of fresh air in the beginning. Lately it had morphed into obstinance.

"Fine." Thomas considered defying the order to attend the fall meeting. Others did, but he'd given his word. "Anyway, the first goodbyes are the worst, and as long as Toni's husband is living in the memory care center, she's staying near him. If we push too hard, she'll leave us. Then where would we be?"

"True, true," Alaric conceded. "The husband. You Harrisons are a strong stock."

"Technically, Toni's a Paci."

"Are you saying she hasn't changed her name yet?"

"No." Thomas backpedaled. "Her identity is squared away, but we're still new to her. She relates more to the Italian side of her family. Hell, the memories she holds of Joe are from photos and stories from when she was a girl. It's a lot to navigate, *Grand-père*."

"Yes. I see."

Finally. It could be nearly impossible to make the old ones understand the difficulties of life in the Felidae, not that Toni was a member yet. Locating a relative midtransition was the lightning strike Thomas had almost given up hope of finding. Alaric, and the few his age, gladly separated themselves from the modern world. They had created the Felidae to be a refuge from it.

"You're not discouraged, are you? You sound different," Alaric said.

"An idea is floating around in my head regarding the research. Should we also study regular people? One of my other relatives or even a friend, perhaps?"

"Friend? Surely you're not wasting your time on laymen."

The idea was so reprehensible to *Grand-père* he said it as a statement. To him, Felidae Society members who worked in the outside world were equal to zookeepers. Thomas grew most frustrated with the prejudice, though he understood the motivation for it. The Felidae lived in fear of being found out.

"How's *Grand-mère*'s team doing?" Thomas changed the subject to avoid answering.

He envisioned the old man's hands animating his *pfft* as it came through the phone. "Ellie's people are holing up in Oxford. They're keeping everything close until October."

This was new. Thomas and the Oxford crew had a great working relationship, but he had needed no cross-team input lately. "How odd," he said, "my new first assistant came from them. She's been a great help and hadn't mentioned anything off. I've been planning to call Nigel and thank him for the recommendation."

"If you must. Don't expect a long chat."

"I can look into it though."

Again, Alaric made a decidedly French sound of doubt. It reminded Thomas why the man felt like family when they first met. He'd missed having elders in his life.

He finished the call with promises to press on while fielding more feeble attempts at encouragement from *Grand-père*. He'd bought himself some time by telling the old man it would take at least the month to get fresh results.

Thomas's eyes blurred as he finished the quizzes. He didn't know why he'd taken them from his TA, other than a desire to get something accomplished. He removed his guitar from its stand, settled onto the love seat tucked in a corner, and played to clear his head.

Thoughts shuffled again, from concern for Toni and how hard it was to transition, to how long he'd have to be absent in the middle of the semester. He resented the insistence on in-person meetings now, with videoconferencing so easy. He hoped his students excused his absence.

Through it all, he kept wondering how Kick was healing. Carrying her home had been like handling a firework shell and hoping the fuse wasn't lit. He cringed at memories of adjusting her and causing more pain. Thomas relived the shame of letting her think his struggle was because of her weight and not the situation in his shorts. Kick had no reason to be ashamed. He hated accidentally putting that on her but still believed the truth would've been worse. She made no qualms about his attractiveness, which he appreciated. She had also made it clear she'd do nothing about it, thank goodness. Kick wanting more—hell, anything—from him was unacceptable. He'd get himself sorted and work their new relationship into an easy friendship, something suitable for both their schedules.

He unconsciously played the Prince song he'd heard when he entered the Perked Cup. It wasn't his usual genre, but the connection between the song and her warm, forest eyes created an earworm he couldn't shake.

NOXIOUS GAS FILLED THE CRAMPED SPACE WHERE THOMAS crouched. He ached everywhere, especially in his heart, as the shock from Uncle Theo's death set in. Joe hadn't returned either, leaving Thomas utterly alone. Again.

This terror gripped him like no other. His helmet had been

knocked away with the blast, and he tore off his mask, desperate for the gas to take him. He begged for the peaceful finality of death. He was on the edge of consciousness when light rays broke through the fog. A female figure reached for him and stroked his face, pushing back his hair. The yellow light surrounding her shadowed frame quieted him, giving him hope.

Her full lips smiled brightly, but he couldn't see much else. The smell of air after a spring rain at home replaced the repulsive stench of the surrounding gas.

"Believe in us." She spoke in a low purr.

Shaking his head, he cried out in anguish, "It's been so long. I don't know if I can anymore. Are you even real?"

The woman he loved without reason squeezed his hand and answered, "Find me." He crawled after her as she faded away. A loud crash woke him as his head hit the hard floor. Thomas had rolled off the love seat in his office.

A pounding knock at his office door threw off the effects of the dream. They had tortured him for too damn long. Thomas used to fight waking up so he could linger with his dream angel. Now he resented her and his unending need for her. He despised himself for craving an illusion.

What were dreams anyway but the brain stem processing energy while the prefrontal cortex rested? The keyword there being *energy*. They occurred mostly during times of stress, and the failure in the lab had him on edge. After the stressful phone call to *Grand-père*, that had to be the answer.

"Professor Harrison? Is everything okay in there? I thought I heard your voice," his associate, Presley, asked through the door. She knocked twice again.

Thomas swung his door open midpound. "What?" Her startled jump clued him to the rough nature of his greeting, and he paused, remembering Kick's comments about surliness.

"Sorry to disturb you, Professor. I texted and called, but you didn't answer." Her eyes scanned him, and Thomas wondered how bad he looked. "I-it couldn't wait," she stammered.

He forced a smile. "Don't worry about it, Presley. Come in,

please." He gestured toward a visitor's chair. "I could use the distraction." Lowering himself into his oak chair, Thomas asked, "Please tell me it's good news?" Light from the streetlamp outside his window made a delicate shadow pattern on the wall over his shoulder. Thomas checked his phone and noted the time. He'd slept for over an hour.

"Look at this." Presley slid a folder across his desk.

Thomas sifted through the report. "We determined it was junk a while ago."

His assistant stood. "If I may?" She separated the papers into three piles. "I don't think it's *all* junk. Look." Presley leaned across the desk, pointing. "The variants here and here are the same, but the control samples show no sign of them." She gave Thomas a bright smile, stirring his pride. Breakthroughs in the lab were fulfilling, but the discoveries of a promising protégé were golden.

"Do you think we're looking in the wrong place?"

"No, Professor." She sat back down, staying at the edge of her chair. "What if what we're looking for isn't in the same place for every person? I think we should expand the reach."

Thomas thought about who had provided his study material and the number of possibilities even this tiny genetic pool offered. "Like a recipe? You think there may be multiple ways to, say, make a cookie?"

If it were possible, Presley brightened more. "Oh, there are endless numbers of cookie recipes, Professor. One of my housemates eats Paleo, and she came home with a package of them last weekend. They looked normal, but their ingredients were totally different." Presley's energy flowed from her as Thomas considered her point.

"Do we have enough samples to expand upon?"

Presley rubbed her knees as she stared at the wall behind him. Thomas could practically see her mind running through the catalog of tubes back in the lab. "I think so."

"Then do it. Write up a plan we can go over before our staff meeting in the morning. Will tonight be enough time for it? You can fill in the details later." Thomas could already think of ways to implement Presley's idea, but it was her baby. A good mentor should allow the student room to bloom.

"I'll make sure it's enough time. I'll go over a few more things in the lab if it's okay." She collected the papers and set them back in the folder.

"Works for me. Remind me to send Nigel a care package of North Carolina goodies. I owe him for recommending you to my team." He meant it as a sincere compliment, but a deep blush rushed up Presley's face and neck. He waited for her to say anything, but the young woman stared at the floor. Thomas stood and turned his back to give her a second. "I have to get to the lab myself. I'll escort you back."

As he slipped into his jacket, Presley gravitated to a table by the small sofa. She bent to study a photo on it. "Wow," she gasped with awe. "This picture is amazing."

Thomas knew it well. Nearly a hundred years old, he kept it nearby as a reminder of why he worked so hard.

Presley pointed at it. "This guy in the middle looks exactly like you." She stood and smiled again. "I see why you're into genetics. There's some strong DNA running in your family."

His promising assistant was one of his brightest so far, and she did not understand how right she was.

8

No Scrubs

Kick

DEANA HAD AN APPOINTMENT MONDAY MORNING, SO I OPENED THE Perked Cup, welcoming the morning flow while keeping my crutches nearby. A weekend of rest, ice, massage, plus all the allopathic and naturopathic anti-inflammatories I'd thrown at my ankle had it on the way to healing. The hardest part of serving customers so early had been convincing myself that smelling the coffee while drinking a glass of lemon water would wake me up. The caffeine moratorium was underway.

Another of my favorite scents floated to my nose after the door chime rang. For a split second I thought my father had come in before opening the cigar store, like he used to do. A tsunami of emotions washed over me when reality caught up with my primal brain. The amount of life that could fit itself into a single moment overwhelmed my senses. I grabbed the back counter, my knuckles blanching with the effort to stay upright. No wonder my energy constantly dragged. Seeing Hugh's face chased away the minute of sadness. I'd forgotten my father and his close buddy often wore the same cologne. He hadn't used it when he visited last week.

He situated his wife, Maggie, on a stool, took her jacket and purse, and hung them on the undermount hooks. Then he settled on his own stool. Watching how Hugh still courted Mrs. Reynolds, after nearly fifty years married, gave me hope *even if my shot had failed*. Maybe my kids could break the cycle with their own happy endings. I wondered if my parents ever even tried.

"Look at you two honoring me with your presence this morning." I leaned across the counter and hugged them. "What can I get you?"

Maggie coughed, the remnants of the pneumonia hanging on. Hugh spoke for them. "Our usuals, please. We've missed breakfasts here."

"Let's cross our fingers the cruise will snap Bobby out of her funk."

"Unless they're doing lobotomies aboard the ship, I wouldn't hold my breath, honey," Maggie said. Hugh corrected his wife's criticism with a touch to her arm, but with a smile, I let him know it was fine. I didn't believe my words either. I carefully moved through the service area, filling their orders while Rachel worked the drive-through. She'd bailed me out when a virus traveled through our skeleton crew.

Hugh took a sip of his latte before stretching his neck to look over the counter. "You're limping, Katie. What happened?"

"And here I thought I'd perfected the air cast waddle." I leaned on the counter for a beat, giving my foot a rest. "It's sprained." I relayed the crazy story of tripping over Macushla's leash on the greenway and my mortification over Thomas having to carry me home. Thankfully, they stayed quiet about the Thomas part. No one else had. Hell, Deana had us practically married off already. Thomas had stopped in one other morning last week, wearing a similar suit and fedora as he wore when we met. Dee had remembered the description and immediately hit it off with him. She'd given her approval, *as if there were anything to approve.*

My real problem consisted of how often I'd thought about him carrying me. It felt nice to be in his arms for our long walk home, despite the humiliation. His smell and the squeeze of his arms came back to me at random times, shaking me.

"Shouldn't you be off of it?" Maggie tsked.

"I've been resting it, but duty called. We're short-staffed at the moment."

Hugh's eyes filled with a pang of unnecessary guilt. "I'm leaning too heavily on you too. I'm sorry."

I patted his hand. It wasn't all that bad. Most of my duties included covering deliveries, letting Hugh know what products to restock, and counter sales when I wasn't at the café. Okay, maybe I was working too much. "It's temporary. Everything will be fine." Eventually.

Maggie leaned in. "I'll work the floor today. Liz is scheduled for the afternoon, so you can rest."

I gave Maggie a kiss to the cheek. To be honest, guilt ate me up too. The business and camaraderie my father and Hugh had built up had virtually disappeared over the summer. "It's good to see you're feeling better."

Right then, Jake Quick entered the café and greeted us. He'd been with me since leaving the military three years prior, so he knew the extended family. Becoming my night manager strengthened his position as an honorary McKenna. "There's one of my brilliant fixes now."

The Reynoldses pivoted between Jake and me, confused.

"You're looking at the Perked Cup's new night manager."

Hugh shook Jake's hand. "Congratulations, young man. Guess you finally have that degree?"

"Thanks, sir. Two classes this semester and one next, then I'll be in the clear." We chatted a bit more before Jake headed into the back to do paperwork.

Hugh looked at his watch. "You said night manager. It's still morning, Katie."

"Yeah, well, thanks to my ankle situation and Deana being out today, he's here early. Jake and Dee are in charge of our hiring search."

They both finished their breakfasts while I helped another customer.

"I do have a specific to ask," Hugh said as I worked near them. "I don't mean to pile on—"

"Not at all." I cut in. We both needed to stop tripping over our guilt. "Ask away. You know the smoke shop is important to me too."

He blushed and said, "Well, I'd like to run the gift-card poker games again. Dylan is pulling together a group one Saturday a month. But what would you think about a seniors' game again? If I organized it, would you mind hosting? It could bring the regulars back in, you know?"

I couldn't keep a huge grin from spreading across my face. Hugh's idea suggested he was back and crawling out of his funk. Maybe I could do it too. "I'd love to. It's a wonderful plan."

Hugh added, "A couple of people have shown an interest in working the counter too." He winked at me. "You should be off the hook with the other duties soon."

Music to my ears. Checking another box off my to-do list almost made my ankle stop throbbing. Most of the ducks still wandered in the wild, but a few were lining back up.

I said goodbye to the Reynoldses right before Big John Graham surprised me with his appearance. We knew each other from the local Chamber of Commerce meetings, but our worlds didn't overlap anywhere else. Aside from the aggressive, workaholic personality he showed everyone, I'd often wondered if I'd offended him somehow. I couldn't figure out where the offensive mistake happened though. The café provided coffee for the meetings, even when I couldn't attend. But he'd always kept a national competitor's to-go cup glued to his hand. I wondered if Young Jonn had told his father about our encounter.

"Well, hello, Mr. Graham. This is a surprise."

"Call me Big Jonn, Katie." He perused every inch of the dining room as he glided to the ordering area.

"Katie?" My father's friends were the only people to still use the name, and it didn't settle right in my ears. Perhaps the name itself didn't fit anymore.

"Don't the men in your life call you Katie?"

The men in my life? Thomas's face flashed before me, throwing me off. Big Jonn threw me a cocky flash of teeth that might have been a grin. It reminded me of the playful yet immature way Liam tended to use his smile to get his way, common for a teenaged boy. But for a middle-aged man?

I was still unpacking the odd comment when Big Jonn waved his hand. "No matter, Mrs. McKenna." This time he drew my surname out like it was heavy in his mouth, as if I were claimed property. But he'd always come across as an old-school "man's man." In Chamber meetings, he reminded me of some sports agents I'd met in my former life. I chalked up the bravado to a misguided sense of the importance of appearances.

"Gimme one of y'all's coffees with cream. I thought I should take a few minutes out of my day and check on you."

"Really? Oh, okay." My neck suddenly heated. I took a scrunchie out of my apron pocket and pulled my curls back. Then I washed my hands and made Big Jonn's order. I passed the mug over.

"I haven't seen you at the Chamber meetings since earlier this year. Then I heard about the attempted break-in and vandalism. Is everything okay, Mrs. McKenna?" His tone gentled with a concern I had never experienced from Big Jonn. Then again, we'd only ever spoken professionally.

"It's Kick, please. Yes, there were some setbacks this summer, but I plan to be back soon. As for the other, the town has nothing to worry about. The store's security is being upgraded."

"Kick… cute." He smiled in a teeth-flashing way. Women in the area tended to throw themselves at Big Jonn's muscles. And money. Active in the way he led his family's third-generation construction firm, he had plenty of both. *He went through women the way a pub patron went through free peanuts.* It made any appeal disappear from where I stood.

He pressed his hands together. "Let me get to the point. I heard about the bag of goodies found in your bathroom. From one entrepreneur and single parent to another: Do y'all need help?" He lowered his voice to a whisper. "If y'all're selling drugs to make ends meet—"

I raised my hands in defense. "Hang on, the police know the stash wasn't mine. Why would I call them if the cannabis belonged to me? And why would I leave it in a bathroom?"

He turned to look around, then met my gaze again. "This place is adorable. Even if I didn't do y'all's interior, you made the best of it."

"Um—" Is this the root of my transgression in his eyes?

"Anyway, would a loan work for you? I'd like to help quell the rumors." He tapped the counter. "Your little café has become important around here."

Rumors? My brows rose. This was quite the jump. "I'm fine financially, thank you. We think it was a nitwit kid who thought they could hide the bag and pick it up later. Probably after school. On the other hand, what rumors have you heard?"

He set his cup down. "People are concerned about you being a single mother and all."

"I'm not the only one in Oakville, let alone the Triangle. Or the world."

"It doesn't look good, Mrs. McKenna. They think you're selling drugs to kids out the back door and said your manager actually found them in your office to cover for you. They're calling you…" He whispered again, "Immoral. Like the graffiti said."

"Immoral?" I squeaked. Was he serious? Cyndi loved to call me a nun. "The café's a safe place for kids after school. I'd bounce anyone caught selling drugs here."

Big Jonn touched my hand. Let it rest on top of mine as if it had been invited. The gesture reminded me of his son with my daughter, only not as aggressive. "Good to hear. *I'm* not doing any accusing, mind. These are just things people say. Terrible things… You're sure no one on staff's selling it?"

I laughed. "You're kidding, right? The police interviewed each employee. No one fussed over it. They know I'd fire them in a hot minute too."

He took a pull from his coffee and shrugged. "Of course they do."

"Who are these 'talking people,' Big Jonn?" I wanted to confront them head-on.

"No one to worry about, Mrs. McKenna. Just some posts on the city's Facebook page. I thought y'all should know." He stretched his hands toward me, then back. "Like I said, your little business is important." Big Jonn sheepishly tilted his head and gave a light chuckle. "I was prepared to buy you out and keep you on as manager, if it would help. Figured you could help me in return."

JaysusMaryandJoseph, I couldn't believe my ears. "Thank you for this enlightening information, Mr. Graham. I assure you, the café's fine. I also spoke with Detective Ross over the weekend. The OPD isn't worried about the incident, and neither am I."

There was something small he could do for me though. Just because we didn't click, it didn't mean we couldn't be friendly. I made a point to never turn away a potential business ally. I added, "If you want to pass that information back to where it came from, I'd happily give you free coffee."

"Big Jonn," he insisted. He took another pull from the mug, set it down, and walked away, leaving half the drink. "I'll see what I can do. If anything else comes up, give me a jingle." He chuckled from his belly this time. "My number's on the billboard on the corner."

"Got a minute, Mama?" Rachel asked. She cleared her throat several times as she made her way into my office. Instead of casually dropping into the club chair as I expected, she remained standing, her gaze settling on the clerestory window above my printer stand. Storm clouds were usually the only things visible from her angle, and it was a clear day.

I removed the reading glasses I wore to see Rachel better and discovered she stayed blurry. Scheduling an eye appointment went to the top of my to-do list. I gestured to the chair. "There's always time for you, sweetie. Whatever it is, spill."

"It's probably nothing." A nervous giggle escaped her lips, giving my heart a small stab. Why the hell was my girl nervous around me?

I inhaled the essential oils diffusing in the corner closest to me—lavender and sandalwood with a drop of rose. I'd chosen it to relax so I could focus on paperwork instead of my ankle. I flipped the ice pack on my propped-up ankle, put a smile on my face, and caught her expression in the light. Something was off. "Are you sleeping okay, Snow? You look pale. Are you eating?"

Rachel sank into the chair with dramatic flair. "My stomach's been bothering me, but it's just school. Everywhere I turn, there's a fork in the road, and I don't want to screw it up by taking the wrong one."

I thought about Six Forks Road—a major road in Raleigh, the city we edged—and its initial origin as a six-way crossroads. The intersection, and the original community, were long absorbed by the capital city. Problems had a way of doing the same.

"Is this really about school or your personal life?"

"Yes?" Rachel said, biting her lip, her lower lids shiny. "I think I should drop my education major. Or maybe come back to it later."

Crud. I wondered if her double theater-education major would pull her in two directions. I wasn't thrilled when Rachel showed signs of bite marks from the acting bug. In her years at Pierce University, she'd been molding herself into the proverbial triple threat while I'd secretly hoped she'd work with me. But I'd never press the issue. Truth be told, the girl began singing, dancing, and acting before she formed proper sentences.

"Why?"

"The senior production is intense. The more time I put into it, the more I want it to be spectacular. It's become overwhelming." She shifted in her seat. "You think the teaching thing can wait?" Rachel's eyes brightened as she moved to the edge of the chair, explaining the details of the original musical, the agents and producers who planned to attend the performance.

She slumped back down. "What if I regret going for it?"

I leaned on my desk, resting my chin on my folded fingers. "Regrets come more from doing nothing. If you're pulled in this direction, there's no reason you shouldn't test the waters. Besides, teaching shouldn't be a consolation."

I remembered the years she used to line up her dolls and stuffed critters to play teacher. It reminded us of the Disney princess she favored, with her dark hair, sapphire eyes, and ruby lips, surrounded by pretend animals and Little People. She didn't simply look like *Snow White*; she acted like her too. It became her identity.

"You know, Snow, forks aren't necessarily about right and wrong. They can be a choice between two amazing things."

Her lips twisted with confusion. "I don't understand."

"You're loaded with so much talent you can *choose* what you want to do. Relax and see where it goes. When the road turns, follow it with open curiosity. You don't have to have all the answers right now. Hell, look at how I've had to reinvent myself."

"What if I'm afraid?" She dipped her chin, and a tear fell. My drama princess.

"Life is scary, sweet girl. Living is facing your fears, and the easy path often has a way of ending up the most painful."

A dark cloud seemed to park over her head as her shoulders pulled farther down. My girl might've loved her drama, but I didn't take to this shift at all. "You mentioned multiple forks. Is something else going on?"

Rachel chewed on her lip as her eyes traveled to the window again. Had all this been the warmup to the actual issue? She hemmed and hawed, then spilled. "This is really, *really* hard. But I don't know who else will give me an honest answer. You know? It's not like I can ask the boys or anything."

"What would you ask your brothers?" Where was she going with—

"*IsAnOrgasmTheSameWithSomeoneElseAsItIsWithYourself? OrIsItSupposedToBeDifferent?*" She blurted out the words in her rush to get them said.

JaysusMaryandJoseph. I jumped in my seat and banged my ankle on the side of my desk. "Fecking hell!" The pain made my eyes roll.

"I'm so sorry. I'm so sorry," Rachel chanted as I tried my best to wave her off. Talk about forks in the road. We'd driven off into a ditch. We had to get back on track, or I feared she'd never ask me anything of consequence again.

Buck the hell up and give your best grown-up advice.

Deep down, I floated, knowing she'd trusted me enough to ask me something so sensitive and not rely on her equally inexperienced besties for answers. Or, *God forbid,* her older brother.

"It's fine, sweetheart. I should've kept the brace on." To gain a moment, I searched my desk for topical pain cream and rubbed it in before setting the ice pack back on my black-and-purple cankle.

With the time it took to resettle, I time-traveled to Rachel and me in our minivan, listening to TLC. "Waz a sckwub, Mama?" Her squeaky voice imprinted in my memory as I'd simplified the story of "No Scrubs," for her preschool mind. Had I known then what I knew presently, I would have told her a scrub was a boy named Cody Dalton, and she should abide by the wisdom in the lyrics.

"Tell me this: has Cody ever learned to drive your Accord?"

Rachel swung her foot as she answered. "No. But mostly we Netflix and chill when we get time together."

I shook my head. "The boy refuses to learn a manual transmission, and it's a *surprise* he can't find his way around what makes you hum?"

"*Mom,*" she scolded.

I raised my hands. "Seriously, the boy's about as useful as a football bat." Cody wasn't a trust fund baby per se, but he lived like one. From where I sat, their relationship had run its course a while ago.

"Then being with him should be better than with my b-o-b?"

Are you kidding me? "Absolutely. And it doesn't do him any favors to fake it."

"Please stop." Rachel mumbled, "Maybe this was a mistake." She stared at the floor a beat, then rolled her wrist. "So you're saying I need to teach him how to…?"

"First ask him if he wants to learn." The boy was *terminally* lazy.

"True." Her defeated tone broke my heart. I wanted better for her but didn't like how the journey to better would have to begin with the pain of a breakup.

I wanted to give her hope, but I also knew Rachel asked more than a mechanical question. This wasn't about navigating parts. It was a talk about navigating the heart—a heart at a crossroads.

I shifted my foot off its perch under my desk and strapped on the air cast. "I hear kids talk about their sex lives in the café. Don't look so shocked. They're loud little buggers." I leaned toward her, wiggling my fingers to get Rachel to grab them. "Anyway, it's like they're trying to understand it by wandering around a dark forest with a flashlight. They find a piece—say an orgasm—and declare 'I found sex.' But it's not the *whole*. Then they shine it somewhere else and see hookups and say 'Oh, here it is.' But it's only horizontal exercise. So they still aren't putting it all together."

I squeezed her hand. "Ask yourself if you've found pieces of it or all of it. The bits satisfy some people, but I think you're saying you want more. Understand?"

"I'm not sure. How will I know I've found what I want?" Her brilliant blue eyes met mine with hope.

"You'll know in the connection. When the pieces are in place, it feels like the best worship service and Christmas morning rolled into one. Not because of the how, the what, or the why, but because of the *who*."

Rachel's nod told me she'd heard. I hoped it helped, not only with her lazy boyfriend but with the choices she faced. Like any mother, I wanted her to be fearless.

I tapped her hand. "One more thing, though I'll probably regret this more than anyone else. Please, Snow, break your give-a-shit meter. Smash it to pieces right now."

"My what?" She giggled, looking at me like a marble had sprung loose.

"Most women take until they're thirty to trust themselves; until they're forty to stop giving a shit about what other people think; and until they're fifty to realize no one was thinking about them in the first place. I believe it's why so many ladies in their sixties and on are carefree. They live by the meme 'Dance as if no one's watching,' because they figured out everyone's so busy navel-gazing that no one ever was watching. Save yourself the self-induced pain and criticism."

Rachel bit her lip, glanced up, and smiled, contemplating what I said. "What if I end up pissing you off?"

I wrinkled my nose and grinned. "If it comes to it, I'll do my best to eat my words. Promise." My heart lightened at her trust and the new turn our relationship had taken. The continuous background aching of my ankle lessened. I chalked it up to endorphins coming from helping my daughter. I treasured the revelation that my girl was becoming something I'd never had growing up. Rachel was my friend.

"And here I thought you'd tell me to get a better rabbit or dump Cody's ass." She laughed.

"Oops. Too much?" I cringed, then chuckled. "You could do those too."

The warmth returned to her eyes. "No, Mama. But it's time to get back out front. As soon as my shift finishes, I'll schedule time with my adviser. *And* I'll talk to Cody."

"There's my brave girl."

Rachel's gentle waves bounced in her ponytail as she turned the corner to the hallway and stopped short. "Oh hi, Professor," I heard her say. Knowing there was only one professor who visited the café lately, I dropped my head into my hands.

9

It's My Life

Kick

THOMAS CLEARED HIS THROAT. HE STEPPED INTO MY DOORWAY WITH his head down and hands in the pockets of his black, pleated slacks. A black dress shirt and silver tie topped them off. The missing suit coat allowed for rolled-up shirtsleeves. Why did my eyes linger on his forearms?

He lifted a hand, pivoted, and pointed his thumb over his shoulder. From this angle, his ass nearly melted my eyes. The material fell over said backside like a waterfall flowing gently down a mountain, as if the field of flax that grew this linen had been planted especially for him.

Perhaps I was looking for distraction from my embarrassment.

"I could head back out if you're busy," he said.

"How much did you hear?" I scrunched up my nose. Thomas came across as old-fashioned to me. Maybe it was the suits, but this might be the moment he'd had enough of me.

A slow grin spread across his face as he crossed his arms, then his ankles, and leaned against the doorjamb. "I should schedule you as a guest lecturer for my class while I'm gone next month. It is Biology after all." He took a step toward my desk. "May I?"

Flustered, I straightened my spine, ready to defend myself, unsure how to read him. "Be my guest."

He took the club chair Rachel had used. He lifted his gaze to meet mine with eyes as bright as his tie and smirked. "A football bat?"

My hands flew to my hair and ended up tucking back stray pieces. "Oh Jaysus. The thing is… see, their relationship should've ended already, but I don't want to interfere." I stared at him for a beat. "Why didn't you say something?"

"Y'all caught me off guard, and I froze. It was… an unusual conversation for me."

I'll bet. "My kids and I are unconventional on purpose. I knew a long time ago I didn't want my daughter relying on a boy to teach her what her body liked. So when she started menstruating, I…" My hand flew to my mouth. In my embarrassment, I almost over-shared about Rachel. I felt my skin heat and almost cried.

"What's wrong?" Thomas asked, suddenly rising out of his chair.

I shook my head and waved for him to sit back down. "I almost told you something private between my daughter and me." I kept shaking my head, willing it to go away.

Thomas leaned in. "Hey, you didn't though."

"It's something Bobby would do, has done many times. I can't believe I defaulted to it."

"But you checked yourself. It says a lot in my book. I'm not judging. Not this or your advice… shit… I stopped in for coffee and wondered how your ankle is healing."

I leaned my head on my hands, the tension flowing out my fingertips. "It's what you'd expect."

"Do you need pain meds?"

I woke my phone, checking the time. "In an hour." I reached under my desk and set the bag of melted ice on my desk. "This didn't last long."

"How about a refill?"

"No, I'll…" I didn't know why Thomas kept wanting to do things for me. He'd even checked in with texts over the weekend. Somewhere in the back of my brain, a voice reminded me that friends helped each other. If Cyndi had asked, I wouldn't second-guess her. I handed him the bag. "Thanks, and thank you for thinking of me."

"Does it feel weird?" He smiled and stood.

He did *not* throw our talk about asking for help in my face. "Why did you?"

Thomas shrugged. "I honestly don't know. Most people don't get my attention. But you… Your smile is a treasure. I hated to see pain take it away."

"Are you telling me to smile more?" I asked, tiny bristles shivering down my neck. "Because I'll have you know, I might prefer my men friends to be pretty and silent."

He shook his head and laughed, turning for the door. "Wouldn't dream of it, Kick." His hand tapped the jam twice before he added, "A man who demands a smile from a woman doesn't know what makes a woman smile in the first place."

"And you do?"

"No, Kick. *You* do. It's just fun to be around to see the light shine when it happens."

I wiped the perspiration off the back of my neck when he left me alone. Did the man have any idea how he kept blowing me away with the simplest words or gestures? And I'd nearly bitched him out again. I hated the boxes my family threw me into and never let me escape. For all intents and purposes, I'd almost done the same thing to Thomas.

"Called Banger yet?" Thomas asked, sitting across from me in the dining room. When my stomach grumbled, I walked out front with him and grabbed lunch.

I swallowed my bite of salad and answered, "Your security guy? It's on the to-do list."

"Do y'all want me to arrange it? This upgrade should happen now; don't let your ankle put it off."

"Oh my God!" Rachel cried out from across the room.

We turned toward her, along with everyone else. Several sets of customers filled the dining area, including Mr. MILF, Garrett. He sat with a group of friends and acknowledged me with an ambivalent chin tip. I chalked it up as a victory for me and growth for him.

I waved Rachel over since I shouldn't go to her. She showed us her phone, her forehead quivering with hurt and fury. A picture of a naked woman in a shower, her leg up on the tub edge, stared at us. The caption said it was Rachel and called her Oakville's favorite slut.

I brushed a small tear off her cheek. "This isn't you."

"I know. But everyone thinks it is. Look at the comments. It's going viral."

My stomach flipped as I read the misogynistic filth written about my daughter. As a general rule, in dance classes since she could walk, Rachel defaulted to proper spine and shoulder alignment. It broke my heart to see her curl into herself next to me.

At a loss, I turned to Thomas. "Is there anything I can do about this? Should I call the police again?"

"I could call Banger," he offered.

"Can he handle something like this?"

He leaned in, eyes narrowed. "Definitely."

My phone pinged with a text from Dylan. When I swiped it, my stomach turned again. "What the hell is going on?" I showed the phone to Rachel and Thomas. "Someone threw a brick through the window at Mick & Hugh's." I clicked on the photo Dylan took of the attached message: WE WON'T STAND FOR IMMORALITY IN OAKVILLE.

The shopping center maintenance company had the minimum requirement for surveillance. I doubted there would be decent footage of the person who threw the brick. I guessed this was related to the earlier vandalism and the horrible gossip Big Jonn had mentioned, but why did it turn on Hugh too? Did it have to do with my helping out somehow?

"Okay, Thomas. I'll call him after I speak to the police. Again." I hugged Rachel. "Don't worry about the photo, Snow." I pulled back to wipe her tears and catch her gaze. "Go about your semester on campus. You don't have to take any more shifts here. Deana, Jake, and I will handle the café, okay? Focus on classes, and I'll get this sorted."

"But what about the…" Her voice hitched, and mine followed suit. My hands itched to choke the monsters who so stirred the vitriol in the comments. Vandalizing my store was one thing. Someone had attacked one of my babies—"the things people said?"

"It's wrong and cruel, and those vile people pile on to make themselves feel superior, sweetheart. I'll find a way to fix it." I took her chin between my thumb and fingers. "Hold it up. You hear me?"

She gave me a tearful nod.

THOMAS CHECKED THE TIME ON HIS PHONE. "I HATE TO DITCH Y'ALL like this, but I have to get to the lab."

A police cruiser parked by the smoke shop as I was hobbling out the door. I waved a casual hand in front of my face. "It's all good, Thomas. Thanks for coming by." I pivoted toward Mick & Hugh's. "I'm sorry I can't walk again this week, but maybe next week?" Thomas's hand wrapped around my bicep, making me turn back.

"Kick?" He bent his knees slightly as an aggravated navy gaze met mine. It struck me how Thomas's eyes could change with the light from silver to navy. Or maybe it was his mood. "I didn't stop by to schedule a walk. I like your shop and the crew. Why don't you want my help?"

"Want your help? Can't you see what's going on here? I've got enough to balance without trying to meet the needs of your hero complex." I'd snapped, not only my words but my emotions. A shock ran down my arm from where he touched me.

"Hero complex? Come on…" Thomas drew in a long breath, his face shifting. Like a magic trick, the irritation I'd kindled died, and his eyes softened to tiny crinkles. "Talk to me."

I released the breath I'd been holding, but my chest hitched. My tears had long dried up, being replaced with this annoying, reflex. I chalked it up to having cried myself into a deficit eight years before.

"It's…" I tipped my head up to the sky, collecting the stampede of thoughts. "Someone told me about rumors going around that I'm selling drugs to kids. This cigar shop incident feels connected. I want to know who's doing it and make it stop. And now they're messing with Rachel?" I sighed, returning my gaze to Thomas. "I wish my dad were here, but I'm glad he's missing it too."

His grip on my arm loosened and became a friendly caress. I'd have paid for a hug at the moment, but we weren't those people. Yet his expression and the tenderness in those strokes, reaching around my shoulder and to my back, communicated we might be able to be better friends. Then again, upset women had a way of wringing out the emotions in the most locked up of men.

With a grave tone, he responded, "I'll call Banger from the road and see if he can come by in the next twenty-four hours. Text me after you're done with the police, alright?"

I nodded my head in agreement and appreciation. We said our goodbyes, Thomas moving to his car and me to the police cruiser across the parking lot.

Hours later, my ducks were back in order——the police report filed, the broken window boarded up, and Rachel tucked safely away in her apartment. Her roommate, Isabella, had called their posse over for pizza and a cheer-up session. Liam was at band practice and planned to stay late to do homework. A fresh dose of pain meds worked its way through my system as I sat in the quiet of my living room. Too keyed up to watch the latest bingeable cable show, I sat in a corner of my leather sectional sofa and gave the meditation thing a try.

I was beat from the day and the pain, and Thomas, if I was honest. My thoughts short-circuited whenever they turned to him. An unwanted attraction mixed with guilt I didn't want to admit, let alone visit. I couldn't remember a man having flummoxed me before. Thomas's quiet persistence drew me in, and it had to stop. I could deal with friendship at arm's length, but no more.

I stretched my legs out, placed my hands in my lap, closed my eyes, and focused on breathing.

Inhale, two, three, four. Hold two, three, four, five. Exhale, two, three, four.

I should order dandelion tea. Local honey too. Liam wanted frozen dinners, and I refused to buy those hot pockets…

After ten minutes, I'd mentally planned out the next three days, had a list of groceries, and remembered it was time for Macushla's check-up.

Typical for me, whenever I quieted my mind, it took off like the latest SpaceX rocket.

Shit.

Perhaps I needed to give the app thing a try. If Deana swore by it, it had to be something. The app loaded, and I shifted my body into the directed seated position. So the problem was with my posture? Huh.

I followed the instructions for the twenty-minute session. It was calming while also invigorating. I felt fantastic. My ankle no longer throbbed, my chest opened with deep breaths, and the tightness in my spine eased.

The session ended with me thinking this could be a good thing. Dr. Chaddha, Deana, and Thomas were right. Meditation could be the key to turning my flare around, and I wouldn't have to do the IV treatments.

Having veins both small and deep, my body protested the treatments as much as it benefited from them. My last foray into my doctor's treatment room ended up with repeated blown veins and subsequent track marks scarring my hand. *Om*-ing my way back to health held a definite appeal. It was a hell of a lot cheaper too.

I became aware of a change in light while my eyes were closed and relaxed. I opened them to find a soft, barely blue glow surrounding my skin and stealing my breath. I leaped off the sofa, hoping to escape it, remembering to land on my good foot at the last minute.

"What the hell?" I shook my head, hoping my eyesight was playing a new trick on me. But the light, the glow—whatever—stayed with me. I limped around the living area, attempting to shake it off, yelling every swear word I knew.

It undulated an inch or two above my skin, the movement growing around my wrists, ankles, knees, chest, and lady bits, like it was swaying to a rhythm. The color in those areas shifted to a darker hue. I swore I heard a low hum and spun toward the shelves surrounding my fireplace, my eyes catching on the sound system, making sure everything was off.

Should I call an ambulance? Nope.

I'd probably end up having a psych evaluation. I crossed the space to the kitchen sink, letting a hard stream of cold water splash over my hands.

The icy chill shocked some sense into me, letting me know: (1) I was awake. A thought I might be lucid dreaming initially flitted through my mind; (2) If I calmed enough, the light died down; and (3) I needed to recheck the labels on *everything* I'd recently put in my body.

I'd had some oddball symptoms over the years, but this one rivaled the weirdest. Hell, it beat out my recurrent mystery-man dreams. I spent some time researching the side effects of my pain medicine and the CBD tincture I'd taken in the morning, though I was sure if a hallucination were a possibility, it would've happened right away, not twelve hours later.

At the end of it all, I logged onto my doctor's patient portal and scheduled the IV treatment. Meditation definitely was not my thing. Dr. Chaddha, Deana, and Thomas could all go jump in a lake. I only hoped my veins would hang in there this time. And that this glowing incident was a one-off.

These Dreams

Kick

I awoke the next morning with a wet face and pressed my palms to my cheeks. The Dream Man had visited me again.

Some nights the visions were like nightmares, because I wanted him to leave me alone. Other times they left me hopeful, and I tried to sleep as long as I could, enjoying our time. This dream crushed my spirit. I couldn't shake how real he seemed, though I didn't know how to find him. It wasn't like someone could Google "hot, middle-aged, silver fox." Okay, you could, but it didn't help. Thankfully, the filters on my modem kept the creepy stuff away. Besides, I'd bet money the object of my dream time wasn't a porn star. My brain never worked that way.

Unsure how to solve this mystery, I rose and put one healing purple foot in front of a well pink one. Liam left early for school, allowing me time for a light workout. Focusing solely on bicep curls and floor work gave me enough mindfulness, thank you very much.

Thomas's friend, Banger, had scheduled a meeting for ten at the Perked Cup. Anticipating the expert's input, I pondered my daughter's safety. Her building had security cameras, but college kids often propped open exterior doors. While it would bring comfort to have a solid system at the café, the mother in me sweated most over the viral photo.

Banger McHenry pulled up to the café on a Harley at precisely ten o'clock. I heard the bike before I saw the man. He was shorter than Thomas yet as wide as my son, Dylan, a former linebacker.

His bright blond hair, cut military close, gave off a special-ops vibe. Warranted, I suppose, for the head of a security firm. Banger's nose carried the telltale jag of a previous break. The center of his blue irises were so pale they almost appeared white, but with a wide navy outline. I started when my gaze met his, grateful for the counter separating us, though I doubted it would deter a guy like him.

His eyes scanned the dining room, a grimace telling me he didn't approve. My first impression second-guessed Thomas's judgment.

"Kathleen McKenna?" He scowled.

I slowly slid my hand out to him in greeting. "Kick, please. You must be Banger?"

"Gotcha."

"Thanks for meeting me so quickly."

We moved to a table in the office where Banger produced a check sheet covering every detail of a business's security requirements. In as few words as possible, he grilled me on the current alarm system and walked through his ideas for an upgrade. With all the blood, sweat, and tears I'd put into the café, it was difficult to view my surroundings with the same skeptical eye. I became equal parts grateful, panicked, and resentful of the need to upgrade.

I tucked a curl behind my ear. "This looks like an overkill response to some pranks."

Banger didn't coddle or patronize me. He pulled the morning paper from his satchel, opened it to the Opinion Page, and laid it on the table. The headline stared at me, mocking: DRUG DEALER MASQUERADES AS INSPIRING ENTREPRENEUR.

I sank into my chair. "I know. I read it earlier." The rumors Jonn Graham warned me about had surfaced, the article mostly half-truths and innuendo.

"This isn't a prank, Kick." He jerked his thumb over his shoulder toward the front of the store. "Sales are down. Correct?"

I nodded my affirmation. Customer traffic had come to a stop. I hoped the pull of a caffeine addiction would override the smear campaign quickly.

"My company will help."

I took a deep breath and capitulated. "I guess you're right. Can you show me the camera placement again?" My hatred for being treated like a victim equal to how much I hated being treated like a perpetual patient, I decided to appreciate his straight talk.

After another twenty minutes of schematics, it was a relief to let him examine the café by himself. I gave up any ideas of inroads to a future friendship with the man. I finally empathized with those who gave me a hard time about resting bitch face. Banger possessed a resting asshole face. Or maybe it was a resting psycho face?

Though Thomas and I had moved past our initial prickliness with each other, I could see where the two men found common ground. They both walked with airs of otherness, like they might not completely fit in with us regular folk.

An hour later, I jumped again when Banger cleared his throat. I'd been composing an ad for baristas. I cursed an annoyed, *shit* under my breath.

Banger strode over and placed his adjusted schematic on my desk. His suggestions made sense, even as he explained them via drawings and grunts. A sense of renewed security had already taken hold in my gut, though the changes were only on paper.

We sat for a quiet minute as I reviewed his plan once more, envisioning how the monitoring would work. Banger cleared his throat, interrupting my thoughts. "Your logo has a double-helix in it."

"Yes," I answered. "Not many people pay attention to it, but it was intentional."

"It's weird," he grunted.

"Thomas liked it." I wasn't sure why I was defensive. I found it interesting they both picked up on the design. I thought the lines representing the hydrogen bonds—as I remembered it—were subtle and doubled fine for steam.

Banger shrugged. "He *would* like it. No offense."

I considered explaining the concept but decided a quick "none taken" sufficed.

He shook his head as if shivering and said, "I still can't believe you've gone this long without decent security."

You'd think I'd done it as a personal affront. "We don't have anything worth stealing here. Most of the transactions are electronic. Hell the students even have credit cards these days. I don't want it to feel like a fishbowl, especially since the café is a refuge for more than me."

"Someone already tried to break in. You'll appreciate thorough coverage. If you'd had these cameras"—Banger pointed to spots on the schematic—"you'd know who left your surprise package in the bathroom."

True. "I-I just…" I'd been so tired the night of the graffiti, and honestly, the weed and mangled lock both felt like pranks. Why did anyone care?

Banger tapped on his tablet and laid it down, showing me a satellite picture of the shopping center. The image was clear enough to see Liam taking out the trash.

"Welcome to the fishbowl, Kick." His voice was eerily gentle, like he was teaching me a new law of the universe. In hindsight, he was. The dose of reality scared me more than a slanderous newspaper article. Banger continued, "My crew will make sure you're safe." His eyes narrowed and he added, "I Googled you. You used to live much… bigger."

Ah yes. Here we go. Too many people—men in particular—assumed I spent my money on designer labels and hair appointments because of how life *used* to be. "Which is why things purposefully changed when we came here." I took a breath to keep myself in check. "I've built my life *my way*, Banger. For good or bad."

I left my desk and stood by the clerestory window, watching clouds pass. I hated people making assumptions about me and money. "Between my medical bills, our family foundation, and other responsibilities, the discretionary account isn't what most might assume it to be. Given the complexities I can't control, I like to keep life as simple as possible."

"Family Foundation? *You're* the McKenna Family Foundation?"

"Yes. I… We are." A manager ran my nonprofit assisting autoimmune patients who couldn't afford the out-of-pocket costs of their treatment. I preferred to stay behind the scenes. Website photography even focused on staff and patients. In place of my time and energy, a sizable percentage of an inheritance and settlement I'd received went to keeping the foundation running, especially when fundraising efforts ran light.

He made a gruff "Umph" noise, then asked, "You set for the install tomorrow, same time?"

"Yup. I'll be here. I have a medical appointment in the afternoon though. My manager, Jake Quick, will be available then."

11

Anything Goes

Thomas

Stepping into the Perked Cup, Thomas knew Kick was at the helm before he saw her. A Prince song filled his ears. She used music to create atmosphere. If the eighties and nineties classics played, Kick and her crew buzzed behind the counter in a happy mood. Classical music meant calm, for the after-school study crowd.

He heard an edge in Kick's voice as she conversed with a customer. An annoyed sigh preceded her answer. The polite yet adamant "go away" vibe was clear to everyone in the shop, except the bozo pestering her.

"Looking like the yards gained record might break this year," Bozo said.

She handed him a to-go cup. Good, he'd leave soon. Hairs on the back of Thomas's neck prickled. Kick gave him a blank smile. "Records get broken, as they should. New players need something to shoot for."

"Won't you be sad?"

"Not at all."

Thomas swore Kick hadn't inhaled since he first glimpsed her.

"When are you finally gonna take me up on watching a game together? I'll buy the beer. Maybe we could catch the one tonight at Finnegan's Wake?"

As much as he acted like it, Bozo didn't know her. She couldn't drink beer. It wasn't gluten-free.

Kick sighed and shook her head. "No, sorry. I'm… swamped right now." She squeaked a fake laugh. "I even forgot about tonight's game. I'll read up on it tomorrow."

"Maybe the next one. Or we could—"

Thomas's hackles rose fully. The guy wouldn't take the hint. Thomas made his way around the line and behind the counter. He wouldn't have made it that far unnoticed under normal circumstances. This man had Kick off her game in more ways than one. Thomas slid an arm around her waist and dropped a kiss on her jaw, just below her ear. A buzzing sensation spread across his lips, a physical manifestation of a hum. Like being able to touch your favorite song.

Kick froze as her eyes shot wide open, but he couldn't tell if it affected her the same way.

"Good afternoon, darlin'." Ringlets fell into her face as Thomas grinned at her. The lavender-and-vanilla scent from when he'd carried her filled his nose again. He inhaled deeply. A third exotic fragrance mixed with the two today, making his heart race.

Given how he acted on impulse, Thomas expected Kick to either go along with the ruse or fly off the handle and wallop him. She shocked him when she stayed still as if someone had shocked her with ice water.

Bozo turned to Thomas. "Y'all are together?"

"Ah—" she began.

Thomas offered his right hand. "Thomas Harrison. Kick's significant other." Christ, he'd gone off the deep end, his desire to protect Kick growing. He simply offered an easy solution to make her problem go away. No harm, no foul. *He hoped.*

"Jim Porter." He turned back to Kick. "Why didn't you *say* you were taken?"

Kick did a double take between the men—at least she moved again. "It's not—"

"We're new." Thomas interrupted her, perhaps a little foul.

Her brows rose as her jaw gaped, but she didn't set anyone straight.

Jim dipped his chin and grinned like he was in on a secret. "Gotcha." He raised his cup and stepped away from the counter. "Thanks for the pick-me-up, honey. Let's hope the pass reception record stands, yeah?" Sketching a wave, he sauntered out the door.

Kick answered with a slow nod as a red flush spread up from her chest.

Thomas smiled wide. "You're welcome. Can I have a large Americano please? For here."

"*I'm* welcome?" Kick's cool demeanor finally melted as she leaned in and grumbled, "You *kissed* me, and"—she pointed to her chest—"I had it handled."

"It was an innocent greeting to the cheek." He heard a low growl from her throat. "Oh, come on. Everyone here knew that idiot was bothering you. Except for him. What was with the football talk anyway?"

She turned to the espresso machine, muttering, "Jim talks smack to get attention. A harmless hazard of the job. So what if he pressed a little harder this time?" Thomas darted out from behind the serving area and sat on a barstool in time for Kick to hand him the finished mug. "You don't think you overreacted?"

He took a quick sip and vocalized his approval. "Do *you* think he'd have left if I hadn't stepped in? If nothing else, I expedited his exit."

"Argh." She spun on her heel, stopped, and turned back, defeat in her voice. "Anything else I can get you?"

Thomas leaned back and glanced at the display. "The chicken wrap."

"Chips?"

He pointed at plates in a rotating display. "What are those?"

"Gluten-free brownies. Everything in this case is gluten-free."

"Are they any good?"

"Better than regular."

"Can I have one instead of chips?"

She shared an exasperated laugh and shook her head. "Of course."

It sounded like bells ringing.

The music had switched to the Staple Singers, which he preferred to pop. She let a new employee finish the last customer and leaned onto her elbows in front of Thomas, her eyes narrowed.

"The thing is, why can't *my* no be sufficient? I understand it's bad business to piss off customers, but you walk in, snap your fingers, and Jim's in line." Kick rolled her eyes. "It bothered me as a young woman, but it's *beyond* frustrating now. I see now why some of my friends embrace the invisibility of menopause."

Thomas winced at her comment. An invisible Kick McKenna was an oxymoron. He imagined her well on in years, still commanding a room. "Men are taught to press on and keep their eye on the prize. That kind of shit. It's a poor answer, but it's the game, Kick. You have to know it too."

"Games change, people change. Hell, laws change. Women aren't property anymore. Why can't the other half of the population accept it?"

"Give it time."

"I'm afraid Starfleet uniforms will be the fashion when *the time* finally comes." Kick sighed, dipping below the counter to retrieve a sleeve of napkins. She filled three nearby dispensers.

Thomas took a few bites, enjoying the food almost as much as the company. For some odd reason, a fired-up Kick kept lighting something in him. He also heard what she had to say. Without looking up, he muttered, "I'm sorry, Kick. I shouldn't have butted in. My hackles went up when I sensed your discomfort."

Kick stayed near, wiping down the counters and checking the monitor every few seconds. "It's okay." She sighed. "Unfortunately, it's not illegal to be an asshole. I mean Jim... not you."

Thomas couldn't help his smirk.

They stayed silent for a beat as they went about their business until Thomas couldn't take it. Despite his tiredness, he wanted to talk to nonacademics, forget about the research for a bit.

"New glasses?" he asked.

Kick paused her wiping, blew at a curl. "Yeah. These are progressive lenses. Another reminder I'm getting old. Cyndi said I look like Lisa Loeb. If I can't live in the nineties anymore, at least I can look like I do."

"They're ho—"

She folded her arms and glared. "Don't you say it."

"Why?" The glasses gave Kick a sexy librarian vibe. She had to know she was hot.

"What's with the antics? Why aren't you surly?" Kick pressed.

"Is it a requirement?"

"I might prefer it." She twisted her lips, studying him. "I'm not sure what to do with cheerful, encouraging Thomas."

Ah yes, there was a reason he'd stopped in for a meal despite working all night and testing through lunch. A dose of Kick's spirit was like a shot of B12— Hell, it became the whole alphabet of vitamins. He wanted it more than the caffeine boost. The esprit de corps in the café had been lifting his moods whether or not she worked a shift. But it, too, was Kick's doing. She possessed a superpower for bringing people together.

He usually only found this lifting energy with his family or Banger. Lately his family had become a source of worry, while Banger had a darkness growing behind his eyes.

The man occasionally disappeared on secret, freelance missions, making use of his security skills. Thomas suspected his friend had become involved in something especially grim.

"Sorry to disappoint," he smirked and took a bite of the brownie. "What's wrong with being nice?"

"Too much like flirting." Kick took an awkward step back and scanned the new security monitors. "We don't do that, Thomas."

The morsel stuck in his throat. Was he flirting? Definitely. Would it be so bad though? Being here made his blood feel like it flowed right again. A deeper part of him, the quiet place holding his locked box, didn't want to admit that flirting with this woman meant more than it usually did.

Thomas gladly focused on Kick's obsession with the monitor Banger's team had installed. He figured her eyes were traveling to it for the same reason a tongue fusses with a sore tooth. They both could use another subject change too. "What's going on with the monitor?"

Kick's exhale of relief almost insulted Thomas's ego, but he ignored it.

"Jake's in the back, finishing up with a new hire he's taken on by himself."

"Oh?"

"It's a big deal for me… the delegation." She blew out a breath. "It feels like I'm giving my kids the keys to the car."

Thomas paused in midraise of his coffee cup and set it back down. "I bet y'all had a hard time there."

"I threw up the first time Dylan drove off by himself." Kick nodded ruefully.

Thomas barked a laugh, getting a few head turns from it. He didn't like the image in his mind, but it didn't surprise him either. "Jake's a smart guy. He won't hire a chump. I can tell he thinks the world of this place. Of you."

Kick laughed. Though Thomas hadn't meant to make a joke, he'd take it. "Thanks." Her brow furrowed as she watched someone walk by the corner windows. "And thanks for shaking off Jim earlier. Right or wrong, he'll give me a few months' peace now."

Thomas didn't like to think of that bozo loitering and picking up where he left off. He didn't like Kick being under surveillance either. He also buzzed with annoyance that *he* might not be enough to send the guy away for good. Where did that come from?

The significant-other comment was a joke, not wishful thinking. One friend helping another. Right? His normally noisy brain, constantly running new formulas in the background, went silent.

The person Kick had been watching entered the shop. Her creased brow slid into a neutral mask after a determined sigh. He recognized it from his own dealings with overprivileged students.

"Afternoon, Jonn, what can I get you today? A mochaccino?"

"Word around here is you're short-staffed."

"Oh. Nope. We're okay. Thank you."

Thomas's hackles awakened again. He was near certain that was a lie even if Jake hired whomever he had in the back.

The kid tapped the counter like an old-time salesman going for the close. "Dad said you could use someone from an influential family. I can be that person. Part-time's fine with me too."

"He said what?" Kick's eyes flashed in surprise. "I'm sorry, he's wrong. We're fine. Doesn't your dad have anything you can do?"

"I don't like his business."

"I understand. My kids aren't interested in mine either. They're their own persons."

Jonn brightened. "Yes. That's why I'm going to work with *you*. You get me, Mrs. Mack."

Kick laughed. "You might be right but not in the way you think. I'm sorry, son." She leaned into the counter. Right then Thomas recognized the kid as the one she had set to rights the first time he'd walked in. She continued, "Go to school. Find your calling, like my kids have. You won't do it here though. I'm sorry."

Jonn balled his fists as he pivoted on his foot and stalked toward the door.

"Anything I can get you to-go?" she called after him. "On the house."

"No!" His bellow caused some customers to look up from their laptops and a few to take out their earbuds.

Kick blew out a slow breath and rolled her shoulders as she moved back toward Thomas.

"Wow," he muttered.

"Kid doesn't understand the word *no*."

"Yep. You're wise to steer clear. You finished hiring?"

She scrunched her nose and dropped to her elbows, keeping her voice low. "I fibbed to get Jonn to back off. Do you know his father offered to buy me out the other day? Think he wanted it for Jonn?" She shrugged, wiping at an invisible spot.

Another man had pressed his will on Kick? Thomas caught a

growl stirring in his chest and held it back. She seemed to have the situation handled. "You know this guy already?"

"Jonn's dad? We're professional acquaintances. He played it like he was being charitable. He's cuckoo if he thinks I'll sell though." A wide yawn made her jaw pop. She fanned her face with her hand. "Woo. Excuse me."

The internal battle over concern for her well-being and his commitment to minding his own business resumed. But what the hell, he'd already erred on the side of butting in. Why not finish it? "Aren't you supposed to lighten your workload?"

"Trust me, I am. I'll clock out in about thirty minutes, after the five-o'clock dance-off."

"Do I want to know what a dance-off is?" He winked at her. "Need a partner?"

Kick's blush and laugh made his day. "It's unnecessary. Stick around and see for yourself. The afternoon homework time ends at five. The kids pick the song and shake off their studying stiffness." She tapped her fingers on the solid wood countertop. "In fact, Liam and his friend Jacklyn signed up to lead tonight's. They should be here by now. If they don't show, I'll teach you the cha-cha slide."

"What makes you think I don't know it?"

"You do? Then you can help me lead it," she said with a wink. "I'll be glad to get home and relax, though I still have to put in some time with my laptop. I'm almost finished with a marketing plan to repair the damage done by that newspaper editorial."

"What're you doing?"

"So far... I have an interview scheduled with the same paper, more advertising for the open-mic nights, and two Halloween parties next month. Oh, and a coupon too."

Kick's phone buzzed. "Excuse me. I have to take this." She stepped against the back counter. "What's up, Uncle Hugh?"

Thankful for the break, Thomas reminded himself he had enough to worry about with his own family. He added Joe and Toni to his list of follow-up phone calls. Dammit, he'd stopped into the shop to take his mind off his problems, not to take on more. The hum from kissing Kick did more than buzz his skin. It clouded his judgment. Yet Kick had no problem maintaining their established boundaries.

"You're kidding? What a bummer." The disappointment in Kick's voice grabbed Thomas's attention. "No, I see why you want to play poker with a full house. Ha. I was looking forward to Friday though."

Pay no attention. It's not your problem.

She swept some curls behind her ear. "It's fine, Hugh. We'll make it happen when everyone's feeling better."

Dammit. She sucked him back in. Thomas snapped his fingers and shifted to catch Kick's eye. "How many players do you need?"

"Hang on, Hugh." She put the phone to her chest and whispered, "He's out three, but Hugh's only found one new player. Friday's kind of late notice."

"Count Banger and me in for sure. It'll be fun."

"But you haven't asked him."

Thomas waved his hand. "He'll come." He'd fuss, but Banger would do it. The guy enjoyed hanging around older men as much as Thomas did.

Kick's face lit up like a sunny morning after a tropical storm, making the involvement worth it. There was the missing smile that made him jump into action earlier. Thomas meant it when he'd said Kick's smile was a treasure.

She went back to her call. "I think I found your two players." Her giggle tickled his ears and warmed his chest. "No, not my boys. You remember Thomas Harrison from Liam's open mic?"

Kick went over her list of loose ends for the evening, then ended the call. Her tongue peeked over her top lip and stalled in her cheek as she wrote a new item on a piece of paper. Christ, he was losing it, and he'd probably like it.

"Yo, fam." Liam entered the Perked Cup with a girl Thomas guessed was the Jacklyn that Kick had mentioned.

"Jax and Liam! Where've you two been? I thought your group planned to work here on AP Psych vocab this afternoon."

"We did, just not here. One of the girls told us her parents banned her from the café. I've heard other kids say the same thing. Don't worry about it though. They're just assholes."

"Lee," Jacklyn scolded.

Kick scrunched her nose. "Crap. Sorry guys. I'm fixing it."

Thomas dug his nails into his hand. He would not get involved in this. Playing poker with Hugh and his pals was enough.

"*StillWantUsToPickASongForTonight?*" Liam asked his mother in the way teens did. When a student did it to him, Thomas wondered if it was a trick to mess with his mind.

"*DoYouHaveASongPickedOut?*" Kick returned, her words a similar blur.

"Wha?"

"Ha. Gotcha." She laughed at her tease while the kids stayed nonplussed. "What d'you pick?"

"Oh." Jacklyn perked up. "'Cake by the Ocean.' We made up a dance."

"Sure you did," Kick muttered. Her energy appeared to have spiked with the arrival of both kids. "On the stage?" Both kids nodded vigorously. "Uh, Jax, what about the lyrics? I mean, your parents don't like certain—"

"You won't tell them, right?"

Kick shook her head. "Only double-checking. I swear they have spies or superpowers."

"True," Liam answered, rolling his eyes.

Kick turned toward the back. "I'll cue it." She pivoted back to the kids. "Oh, can you two come up with a dance for old-school song on Monday?"

"Like Matchbox20 or something?" Jacklyn asked.

Kick sighed as if her feelings were hurt. "I was thinking Motown or, hell, even Prince. But sure. Why not?" Kick raised her hands as she walked away, muttering, "That's what I get for asking *teens* about old-school stuff."

Kick stood at the food case, her chin propped in her hand, a somber expression on her face as she watched the pair perform on the tiny stage.

"Y'alright?" Thomas asked after scooching over a few stools.

She sighed. "They grow so fast. Sometimes it just hits me that my days with him are limited."

A distant memory popped into his head of a raven-haired sprite coaxing a horse to lower her nose by dropping oats on the ground. The girl was tiny enough to run under the animal's belly. And the mare treated her like an adopted filly. It became a ritual. Mabel, the horse, ate the treat while the girl hugged her neck, threw her tiny leg over, and slid down to her withers when Mabel lifted her head. Thomas remembered the bittersweet pain of how quickly life changed and shared a knowing smile with Kick.

She stealthily wiped an eye. "Rachel and her friends started this five-o'clock business. She's staying away thanks to the viral photo nightmare. But I miss her."

"Maybe you should go see her."

"I'm supposed to be resting, not driving across Wake County."

"Just sounds like stress talking. How's the meditation going?"

Kick turned her head and growled.

Message received.

<hr>

12

Dream On

<hr>

Kick

MICK & HUGH'S BUZZED WITH A FAMILIAR PARTY ATMOSPHERE ON Friday evening. It helped to have my body showing signs of improvement. Hugh arrived with Butch and Elliott, two of the old regulars. Each man greeted me with a bear hug and a cheek smooch. I sensed Dad's spirit settling into a corner of the room, waiting to check in on us.

I floated around the lounge, taking unofficial drink orders—everyone brought something to share—while Hugh and Butch divided up poker chips. I sensed a soft brush on my shoulder and a barely there whiff of my father's cologne. Hugh was across the room, so the scent wasn't his. I smiled toward my father's favorite chair and whispered, "Thanks, Dad."

The world quieted in a way it hadn't for months. My chest loosened with the comfort of being surrounded by surrogate fathers. Thoughts flitted to my last talk with him. "I never made your Ma happy. Help her find her peace, Katie Girl." *I hope the cruise is what she needs, Dad. I'm trying.*

"Where are the newbies?" Hugh asked.

119

Before I could answer, the doorbell chimed, interrupting the Herb Alpert album playing over the speakers. Thomas and Banger walked in, each wearing a scowl.

"Two of the newbies are here," I answered, turning toward them. "Evening, fellas. Everything okay?"

Thomas bent to kiss my cheek and handed me a six-pack of a local India Pale Ale. My hand rose to my cheek to feel the delicious hum. Were we officially greeting like this now? Again, it took me by surprise, more by how much I liked it than any question of boundaries. I didn't know why the simple gesture bewildered me. My earlier guests had squeezed me like a roll of Charmin, and I thought nothing of it. Thomas's simple, respectful hello had me contemplating the vapors. Not over his body but because it was him. Moreover, he took me in like *I* was a sight for *his* sore eyes.

Thank the heavens he answered my question before I could talk myself into a freak-out.

"Someone's grumpy because he didn't win our sparring match." I caught the humor in his soft accent and grinned like a silly schoolgirl.

As a child of an immigrant in a city with few natural-borns, I'd grown up around differing lilts and had an ear for them. Until Thomas, I'd thought I'd become immune to the charms of a soft accent. It was time to get a grip and focus. The future of Mick & Hugh's depended on it.

"Umph. Said someone's *you*," Banger answered with a grunt while handing me a fifth of a rare highland Scotch. Thomas made a point of rolling his eyes. "Thanks for the invite, Kick."

"Did you almost smile, Mr. McHenry?"

He shrugged and reset his face to its normal grimace.

I looked back at Thomas. "Were you two boxing?"

"Sort of. We belong to an MMA studio in North Raleigh. The sour face over there claims I cheated. He's just mad he didn't think of the move first."

"True," Banger conceded, rubbing his midsection, followed by a round of laughs from the rest of the room.

Thomas pulled me to the side after the introductions. "Y'alright? Don't mean to pry, but it looks like you've been crying?"

"Seriously?" I couldn't think of any reason for it. I entered the office and peeked in the mirror on the wall. "Oh hell." I looked like the love child of a raccoon and a Kewpie doll.

"What happened?"

"I can't wear my glasses while I apply mascara, but I can't see without glasses. Something *might* have smudged when I put the frames back on." It was a mess. I removed my glasses and swiped a finger under my eyes, smearing it more. "Lovely."

"Here." Thomas pulled a tissue from the box on the desk and stepped toward me, his wrapped finger leading the way.

I leaned back as far as I could.

"I won't poke you," he said, his brows furled.

"It's hard to tell without glasses."

He dropped the Kleenex into my hand. My memories rewound the past half hour, embarrassed by how I must have looked. "I need a magnifying mirror. No one tells you this happens when you get old."

"You're not old, Kick," he said over my shoulder, watching me. "It's fine, really."

I fixed my eyes by dabbing while holding my glasses at angles to help me see. "I'm glad you did, Thomas. It's what friends do." I turned around and smiled. "Thank you."

He gave me an awkward smile back and opened his mouth to respond when the doorbell chimed again.

"Hold the thought please. Hugh's guest has arrived." My hopes for the night took a turn when I saw the man walking through the front door. It was Big Jonn Graham. Maybe he'd at least buy a box of cigars. Or a case.

The man shook Hugh's hand. "Y'all's place looks great even if you used a competitor. But I forgive y'all." He leaned in and laughed heartily. "This time."

Then Big Jonn greeted me with an unusually friendly bear hug. "You look lovely, Katie." I didn't want to slug him in front of the guests. I figured Hugh had his reasons for inviting the man.

. . .

THE MEN TOOK A BREAK AN HOUR INTO PLAY. I'D SLIPPED AWAY TO properly finish my face clean-up, figuring a minimal look beat a demented anime one. I also checked in on Jake at the café a few times. For the first time, I left someone else in charge of the fall teen party and mentally patted myself on the back.

I laughed when he said, "Not to complain, but we know you're monitoring the camera feeds."

"I've peeked," I admitted and waited for Jake to finish chuckling. He had me. Banger's Angel Security system allowed me to monitor the café from my phone. It was my favorite feature so far. "The cameras don't tell me what you're thinking, so I figured I'd check-in."

No surprise, Jake made a great host. My confidence in the decision to give him more responsibilities increased. My grand scheme might work after all—eventually.

The men stretched their legs, refilling their plates and plastic highball cups. Jackets hung from the backs of chairs. I made a note on my phone to shop for a proper coatrack when I had time. It wouldn't be long until temperatures required heavier outerwear. My eyes traveled to Thomas's Mr. Rogers sweater. He had removed the fedora he wore coming in, and some hair fell onto his forehead.

Thomas and Banger shared an easy rapport with Hugh, Butch, and Elliott. Big Jonn did his best to command the room. My father had filled the role before, and Big Jonn slipped into the opening with acumen.

After Big Jonn's greeting, Thomas had played hot and cold for the next hour. As he made his way toward me at the makeshift bar, his brow lowered like Atlas's weight hung on his shoulders. Still, he made a handsome, albeit quirky, sight. He wore a short-sleeved, button-down, with black, silver, and cream vertical stripes. It looked like an homage to midcentury bowling shirts—high-end ones, but still.

"Another IPA?" I asked.

He handed me the empty. Our fingers brushed in the exchange.

The same sensation passed through my hand that had thrummed my cheek when he kissed it. He didn't acknowledge the interaction, so I ignored it too. *Hell, it probably came from one of my latest medicines, while he felt nothing at all.* "I'll take two fingers of Defiant neat this time."

"Snacks?" I tipped my head toward the half dozen bowls of junk food at the other end of the table.

"Big Jonn's an old friend, I take it?" he blurted.

I poured his Defiant and whispered, "Not at all. I almost walloped him for the Katie comment."

He looked confused. "But the other men call you that."

"Dad's *friends* call me Katie. That's all. He's the guy I told you about who asked about buying me out."

"The spoiled kid's father? Of course." Thomas nodded his head, looking like he'd matched the names and faces.

"Right."

"And he's single?"

The statement surprised me, and I answered with a chuckle. "I guess so. Why?"

He lifted a shoulder as I resisted the urge to snark. There was no way Thomas would give off jealous vibes. I had to be reading him wrong, which frustrated me. I wanted to be friends with the relaxed and attentive Thomas, but that man was hit or miss.

"He keeps tracking you. He's interested, Kick."

"Absolutely not." I squeaked a quick laugh. "He's strictly an acquaintance."

Thomas took a bite of a pot-sticker-looking thing, still frowning.

I thought about Big Jonn turning his ego *and libido* on me and shook my head. "I guarantee I'm too much trouble for a guy like him."

"A lot of men seem interested, Kick." He tipped his head toward the table. "Even Hugh and his buddies."

"What? No, no. They're happy to be together again. It's my job to be hospitable and accommodating, but I'm only your humble server." I scanned my outfit from my dark jeans to my lightweight green tunic sweater. Fun, but absolutely nothing suggestive. "They think of me as a niece."

The return of Thomas's frown said he didn't buy it. Was he jealous? Then why did he act like he was trying to push me toward Big Jonn too? Why was I explaining myself?

Thank goodness the rest of the men came over to refill plates and resume play.

"You two look deep in conversation," Big Jonn said with a goofy smirk.

Before I could answer, Thomas's phone rang. His brow lowered more. He showed the phone to Banger, who also frowned. He turned to Hugh and asked, "I have to take this. May I?" He pointed to the office.

"Be my guest," Hugh said, sending me a questioning glance. I shrugged a "no clue" in return.

He hustled to the room, answering the call on the go. "*Allo, Grand-père. ... Oui. Un moment.*" Banger followed closely behind.

Big Jonn leaned in and whispered, "Grandfather?"

"Beats Godfather," I said, jokingly, worrying my tongue in my cheek. "This has happened before. I think he's helping him with a project." I hoped. The amount of secrecy around the man sometimes woke my stomach butterflies. I hadn't known Banger was in on it though.

"I saw the newspaper article," Big Jonn said, his hand moving to my bicep. "Are y'all okay? Sure you don't need a loan?"

What was with him trying to give me money? I stepped back, not sure why. Big Jonn was friendly and caring, but I wanted to be off his radar for some reason. Maybe it was the last two encounters with his son. "The article is a nuisance, but we're fine, thank you."

He leaned into the table and lowered his voice. "Isn't business down?"

I supposed it was an obvious conclusion to bad publicity. "It's temporary." As long as the medical bills behaved.

"Good, good." Big Jonn raised his glass in my direction. "Like I said before, we entrepreneurs look out for each other."

Big Jonn was a third-generation contractor. I didn't think of him as an entrepreneur, but I wasn't going to call him out on Hugh's turf. I gave him a half grin for an answer and reached for a seltzer water for myself.

"So." Big Jonn bent his head toward the office. "I didn't know y'all were dating," he said in a soft voice.

Was Thomas right? Something was in the night air. I clarified. "We're friends."

Big Jonn slowly nodded as he stared toward the office. "Good. Good." His attention turned back to me. "You've been alone, how long now? Plus Leo's leaving soon, isn't he?"

"It's Liam, and yes, he's a senior."

"I can see how attention from a young guy like him might be flattering, but I'd be wary if I were y'all."

My nose scrunched as I tried to figure out why Big Jonn cared. "There's no need to worry. I'm a big girl, and I'll be fine there too."

"Maybe you're working too hard." He swayed his head lightly. "When's the last time y'all… had a little fun for yourself?"

"No offense, Big Jonn, but I don't see where it's your business. I'll consider dating when I'm ready. Frankly, life's swamped right now."

"You should tell the professor over there, because he won't take his eyes off you. But if you're not into him and want some company sometime, give me a call."

I knew about the way this man ran through women. We might have the love of our small town in common, but that was it. I put a fake smile on my face to psyche myself up for turning yet another Graham down, but Hugh saved me.

He touched both our shoulders. "Are we playing or gossiping? I want my chips back from that hustler in the office."

Banger and Thomas returned to the lounge as if on cue.

"Whining about losing, ye ole codger?" Banger asked, a surprisingly warm grin on his face.

"Sit down and deal, ya thief," Hugh called back.

I let out a big sigh, grateful to be out of the hot seat, and quietly laughed at the idea of jumping into the dating scene. I wandered into the office for some peace and to turn up the air filtration in the lounge. It had been a while since it had seen so many lit cigars at the same time.

I sat at the desk, counting the days until my doctor-imposed prohibition would end. I wanted to slam back two fingers of that Defiant like no one's business. The men weren't *trashed* per se, but the volume had grown loud enough to hear through the closed door, and it focused on Thomas. Elliot and Hugh were at the heart of it, but everyone joined in the rib over his wardrobe choices and subsequent nicknames. It compelled me to head back out there to be an ally.

"…wore one just like it in '63."

"…should have an old bowling team logo on the back."

I strolled in with a tray of water bottles and began handing them out. "For the love of Pete, gentlemen, stop the yapping and play. Shouldn't someone have won by now?" I set a bottle near Thomas's place.

"Got somewhere to be, Katie?"

"No, Hugh, but you're wearing me out and an excellent host never falls asleep on her guests."

"Big plans for tomorrow?" he asked.

"Some quick shopping and working from home." The first thing on the list was a magnifying mirror. "But I have strict orders regarding my sleep schedule." While I wasn't lying—I thought they'd have finished already—my goal was to take the heat off my friend. Only Hugh didn't take the bait.

He pointed to Thomas. "You should bring this one shopping with you. He could use a woman's eye."

"Quit picking on him, Uncle Hugh." I placed a bottle down by Butch. "A man has a little retro style, and you bunch go nuts."

"Retro?" Thomas asked, an eyebrow lifted in confusion.

"Nothing wrong with bringing him into the twenty-first century."

"Do I really need a new wardrobe?"

Oh crap, I had to backpedal quickly. I wasn't a mall-goer. An entire day spent buying a new wardrobe was my idea of time spent in purgatory.

"Liam says Thomas's stuff is—and I quote—vibin', fam. He says the thrift store look is in. That part's not a quote. He'd said something about it being spicy though."

"Thrift store look?" Thomas pulled his shirt away from his chest and looked down. "Maybe I should get a few things."

Like a sucker at the animal shelter, my heart cracked. "As long as we don't spend all day at the mall, I'd be happy to help."

Banger dropped his cards with a gruff. "I'm out."

Big Jonn ran his hand through his hair. "I'm out too."

Thomas's spirit perked up while Hugh beamed like a proud father.

What the hell?

13

Almost Like Being in Love

Kick

WHERE THE HELL ARE THE MAKEUP MIRRORS? I WANDERED THE aisles of Target for an hour with plans to meet Thomas at the inside coffee bar in fifteen minutes. I wanted to finish my shopping so he wouldn't suffer the torture of a typical Target list. The experience was scary enough for those of us who wrote them.

The place was a zoo, due to it being a Saturday morning. Happily, most of the items on my list were already in the cart. If I could only find—

"Can't believe y'all started without me."

"Jaysus, Thomas." No surprise, I jumped. I shot eye daggers his way while his sparked an amused silver. At least his mood had lifted from the night before. He didn't seem permanently damaged by the men's teasing either. The sight of him relieved my tension even if his methods could have put me in a cardiac care unit. "You're early."

"I am. You passed by, looking frazzled, albeit determined."

I scrunched my nose in frustration. "I can't find any high-powered makeup mirrors. You know, the kind that could reflect light into space?" I tapped the frame of my glasses. "To keep last night's fiasco from happening again."

"But you were beautiful once you took it off. You're lovely without makeup now."

Holy cow. Mr. Sweet was in the house, taking it to new heights.

"Thanks," I exhaled. "But even natural beauty is an illusion. A girl likes having the option to spruce up on occasion too. Turns out, a blurry mascara wand coming toward your pupil is as terrifying as a finger in a tissue."

A hint of a blush dotted his cheeks.

I raised my hands in frustration. "Anyway, they appear to be hiding."

We turned down the last aisle in the makeup area. "Ooh, there are some." I steered the cart toward one, with Thomas following. "Here's what I want." I bent to look in the first one. It reflected the normal side, so I flipped it over.

"Sonofabitch." I wheezed while jumping back. "What's the magnification of this thing… a thousand?" I turned my head to the side. I looked like an old hag, certain a tiny creature was mountain-climbing one of my pores.

"It thinks I'm Dorian Gray." I turned to Thomas, terrified. "Is my face really this bad?" I wasn't compliment fishing. This was an awakening. I'd caught a good glimpse of future Kick.

His eyes flashed with the universal male expression of *keep me out of this*. Smart man.

There was no helping it. Another check in the mirror and the unibrow shredded my last threads of dignity. "Why hasn't anyone told me my brows are a hot mess?" I squeaked. This mirror purchase was so overdue.

Thomas reached over and flipped the thing back. "Here. See? Gorgeous."

"On this side," I argued. I kept trying to calculate how long I'd walked around deluding myself that I looked okay. "I don't want any delusions when reality is a flip away. You can't fix what you can't see." I rotated the mirror back and winced. *Was that sun damage?* But I wore hats.

A wiry hair grew out of my neck. *Hell.* I tried to discreetly pull it out.

He sighed and shooed me out of the way. He stepped over and put his face in the view. The pores on his nose looked like tire-eating potholes too. "See? Everyone's frightening up close."

"Ha!" I pointed at him. "You *do* think I'm scary." I knew he'd been placating me.

"Christ," Thomas muttered, "walked right into it." He righted himself and turned to me. "No. I'm saying you're as human as me. I'm a scientist. You can take my word for it." He smiled and whispered in my ear, "Accept your beauty as reality. Age doesn't matter."

"You don't understand," I countered. "I'm not afraid of reality. Not being able to trust my eyesight is what's scaring me. I might as well walk around with the hem of my skirt tucked into my underwear."

He raised an eyebrow in response.

"Bet no one would say anything either."

With no tolerance for patronizing, I had to know if he listened. I turned my head to catch Thomas's gaze. My nose brushed his jaw and caught his scent. Sandalwood and lavender thrilled my senses. I closed my eyes and touched his hand. Lost in the moment, my mind checked out, leaving my foolish heart in charge.

I opened my eyes to find his closed jaw flexed, breath shallow. He turned toward me as he inhaled, his eyes squeezing as if in pain. I cracked. For a beat, I could picture more. But was it fair? Or proper? I'd captured lightning in a bottle once. No one did it twice. Besides, it ended up leaving me with a world of regret.

"Kick," Thomas pleaded, my name a rasp. The sound snapped me out of our what-could-be bubble and back to the real world of a crowded store. No matter how much I tried to fight it, reality kept biting me in the ass.

"What're you playing at?" Thomas asked, practically gasping as he looked at me again.

I searched his eyes gone dark—lust mixed with annoyance, maybe?

"Right. Sorry. Shit. I didn't mean to." I shook my rattled head, my breath hitching. Fortunately, his attitude lightened, telling me he wasn't angry. Perhaps he was as confused as I was. I touched the handle of the cart, and the thing zapped my hand.

To make matters worse, the mirror wasn't for sale. The Target people had attached it to the shelf for sampling products.

"What the hell?" I looked around and caught the flash of a red shirt and khaki pants from the corner of my eye. We chased down the saleswoman, an older lady with a sweet face. I pointed at the mirrors. "I'm looking for one of those to purchase."

"Sure, honey," she soothed. My exasperation must have shown. "Follow me."

Thomas and I fell into step like obedient children, past four aisles and around a corner to the hair-care area. *Huh. Who knew?*

Five different models sat on the bottom of the case, one exactly like the evil portal of truth from the makeup department among them. I should've known it would be the most expensive, but it also had the highest magnification. I scooped it up. *Mirror, mirror in the box… please be nice.*

"What's left?" Thomas peeked over my shoulder at the list on my phone.

"Dog food and treats for Macushla. One section over, I think. Then I'm all yours."

"Wonderful." Thomas carried a basket with a card in it.

"Aw. Who's the card for? If you don't mind me being nosy."

He looked at the basket and lifted a corner of his mouth. The partial smile was sweet and sad. "Someone in my family is going through a hard time. Her husband has Alzheimer's."

So that's what the calls were about. My suspicions suddenly cleared, I declared, "Your *Grand-père.*"

"What? No."

Another dead end with no explanation. Why was Thomas always so vague? Holy Hades, this nut was impossible to crack. I didn't know why it was so important to me, but the truth suddenly became essential. I gave it another shot. If it were for an aunt, he'd have told me his *uncle* was sick. "An older sister?"

Thomas's jaw flexed. He turned to me with a clear stare and said, "Yes."

"It must be hard to be away from her." Both my hands wrapped around his bicep, seeking some way to comfort. My brother was younger than me and back in Michigan. I couldn't imagine how hard it would be to support a sibling in her situation.

It also struck me how Professor Grumpy Pants had a heart of gold. Few siblings clung close to each other through their trials. People usually relied on parents for that.

"It's sweet of you to let her know you're thinking of her. I check in with my brother on the phone or with stupid texts, but we don't even do holiday cards anymore."

"Toni's not much into technology." A sad smile spread across his face. "I think she'd prefer corded phones with rotary dials."

"Then it's extrathoughtful on your part. I'm sure your act of kindness will brighten her day."

We kept our conversation easy as we shopped the men's department. I wasn't sure I wanted Thomas to change much about his look. Sure, the pleated, flowing pants might be out of style, but he rocked midcentury fashion. We'd planned to head down to the Village District after, where the real hunt would begin.

I figured we'd start small and casual. I parked him in front of a display of graphic T-shirts while I sorted through a clearance rack of button-downs.

"Why should I pay Coca-Cola to advertise for them?" His prickliness reared its head as he lifted a long-sleeved pullover.

"It's tribal identity," I called over my shoulder, shuffling through a few cute plaid shirts in a similar cut to the previous night's. I figured it would be easier to win him over if the general style were familiar.

"It's my go-to soda, but I don't feel compelled to yay team about it." The softly accented words were said by my ear, making me jump and sending a shirt flying. Thomas wrapped me against him with one hand and grabbed the rogue button-down with the other.

"Are you determined to resprain your ankle? You're like a spooked filly today."

The man had no clue. Our earlier interactions played on a loop in the background noise in my mind. He'd called me "gorgeous," "beautiful," and I think "lovely." What was with his thoughtfulness and attentiveness? I hadn't suffered through any horror show experiences with men, but I still knew it was a rare quality. Did he really notice as much as it seemed, or was I projecting? I'd watched the women I knew misread an interest plenty of times. I wanted no part of it.

"What are you doing?" I asked, breathless from the adrenaline rush.

"Keeping you from falling?"

"We're friends, right? We decided we'd be friends?"

"Believe so. Why?"

Surrounded by racks of clearance shirts, I let it out. "Friends don't call each other gorgeous or handsome, Thomas."

"They do if it's true." He smiled and added, "Alright, I don't write sonnets about Banger's eyes, but he couldn't care less about his pores or eyebrows. If he asked me, I'd tell him straight."

Thomas set the shirt in the basket. "Nice call." He dropped his carryall in the cart and placed both hands on my shoulders. "I'm saying this as a friend because it should be said. I can already tell you're ingenious as hell, caring to a fault, stunning inside… and out… fun, and you need to ask for help a helluva lot more."

Whoa, the man was trying to break me wide open in the middle of the men's department.

For no good reason I could think of, I dropped the pretension and the guilt. I let him see what his words did to me. I peered into Thomas's eyes and found his longing, his loneliness, and his desire to help others in an attempt to fix the first two. I glimpsed at how a soul mate might look. It scared the ever-loving shit out of me.

"Did you mean the things you said to Rachel the other day? About the magic coming from the connection?"

"It's in the who," I recalled. "You know I did. Why?"

"I can't remember the last time I had… the magic." Thomas grabbed the front of the cart and headed toward the checkout. "This is enough for today."

He'd gotten to me, but I'd gotten to him too. I saw it. He'd accidentally let me in.

And thought it a mistake.

"T-Thomas?" I sniffed, trying to keep the rude sound away from the phone, but my nose wouldn't stop running as I tried to hold off an ugly cry. The medicine swimming through my veins played with my emotions.

"Kick? Are you crying?"

"S-sorry. I shouldn't have called."

"What's wrong?"

I heard someone say, "Professor Harrison," before the sound muffled. I knew he'd be at work, but I'd hoped he might be in his office doing whatever academics do between lectures. "Shit. I'm bugging you. Never mind."

"Kick, tell me what's wrong or I'll call Banger, have him track you down, and come there anyway."

"Can Banger really do that?"

Thomas ignored my deflection. "Where are you?"

"Near campus." I let out a deep shudder. "I finished the first IV and my car won't start, and I'm exhausted from the medicine in the cocktail, and I can't think clearly 'cause I'm so sleepy and—"

"I'm on my way."

Guilt and humiliation flooded me. I should've been able to keep it together to call a tow and rideshare. "No, don't. I... I'll figure it out."

He inhaled deeply, reminding me of myself with my last thread of patience. "Already left the office. I'm glad you called. Let me help. Text me the address and I'll be there in twenty."

Text. *I should've texted him instead of crying like a damsel in distress.* "Oh. Okay. Thank you." The last came out in a whisper.

Forty minutes later, we were on I-85, heading to my house. Thomas had secured a tow for my Camaro while my brain floated around in the fog of the medicinal cocktail. As much as I hated to admit it, he'd been a white knight when I needed one.

He came alive in the helping. A soothing jazz playlist serenaded us as I held on to consciousness out of a sense of obligation and gratitude. Thomas tapped his fingers on the wheel to Chet Baker's sexy version of "Almost Like Being in Love." It hit a bit too close to home. I quietly scoffed at the way the trumpet seemed to tease my stubbornness, my vow, my survivor's guilt.

"What's wrong?"

I shifted to my left side so I could see him with half-opened eyes. "The chocolate and caffeine cravings have kicked in. I'd give a kid if I could have a frozen cola and a candy bar."

"There's a Sheetz at the next exit. We can stop and get them."

"No," I said through a jaw-cracking yawn. "I said *if* I could, as in, they're not allowed."

"Oh. Sorry, Kick. Must be hard."

"I'm getting used to it. My body's making steps in the right direction. I thought the cravings would've resolved by now though. Instead, they continue to call to me."

"Oh?" Thomas kept his eyes on the road while chuckling.

"Yes. And they speak with an accent, though not buttery like yours. Well, I guess so, but it's not Southern, it's Spanish... like Antonio Banderas." A blush formed on my cheeks, and I tucked my hands under them, hoping the chill in my fingers would stop the flush. "They whisper, '*Shjust* a *leettle* bite will be fine, *Keek*. One *leettle* square won't make you *seek*.'"

Thomas muttered, "She thinks I sound buttery?" missing my joke. "What about Antonio?"

I groaned. "He's a lying rat bastard. Lately all forms and any amount of chocolate make me regret it. It took an embarrassingly long time to admit, but chocolate is a bonafide dietary issue. Except... why wouldn't my body be *happy* it's out of my system if it doesn't like it? Anyway, anyone who says food cravings aren't real is *another* lying rat bastard."

He reached over and rubbed my shoulder. "How about I pick up a water instead?"

I couldn't help the audible yawn. "That'd... be... wonder...ful." Then the peace of sleep overtook me.

Thomas woke me after he parked and helped me into the house, grumbling at the lack of an alarm system.

As if trying to defend my honor, Macushla greeted us, circling my feet until she filled up on our scents and barking extra loud at Thomas until he crouched and petted her ears. The little traitor took thirty seconds to offer her belly.

"Tell me y'all have personal protection."

I glared at him through my half-mast eyelids. "You mean a gun, don't you?"

"Of course."

"This is a safe neighborhood, Thomas."

"For the love of—"

"A can of wasp spray stays on my nightstand with a baseball bat next to it." Another jaw-cracking yawn and a wince from aching muscles halted my steps. They had locked in my curled-up position in the Camaro's passenger seat. "Twenty-seven-foot straight spray and no holes in any bodies. Plus Liam leaves his shit lying around everywhere. I can't even walk through the house at night without risking bruises. If someone breaks in, they'll break their neck before getting to a bedroom."

"Christ, you're stubborn."

"I don't trust myself with a gun, Thomas. I know my limits." I'd made it to the kitchen counter, straining to lift the kettle.

"What do you mean?" he asked.

I lifted my gaze and stared him down before saying, "It's not easy living with autoimmunity, especially when it takes decades for a doctor to believe you."

He mouthed the word *Oh* and walked toward me. "Let me do this." Thomas finished filling the kettle and turned it on. "What're we making?"

"The ginger-green tea. The second shelf on the left." I pointed to the cabinet behind him.

Koosh began barking, taking two steps toward the door, whining, and then repeating.

"Oh hell, she didn't get her walk. My house manager, Carmen, is home sick." I carefully lowered to pet her. "And Mama forgot about your exercise."

"I'll take her."

I looked up at Thomas. "Do you remember where the greenway is?"

The corner of his mouth lifted in a secret smirk. "How could I forget?"

I flinched again, this time from the memory of him carrying me home.

"If it's not too much trouble, I'd be indebted."

Thomas laughed. "That's what it'll take?"

"Don't remind me, pal." It seemed my mortification knew no bounds. I stood and groaned from the aches. *Note to self: pound the water on IV days.* "Anyway, Koosh doesn't have to go far. A few pee squats will suffice."

He held his hands out to me. "Come here."

I obediently followed directions as he spun me around. To my surprise, he began kneading my sore shoulders until I practically purred. One particular hard knot brought on a blissful moan followed by Thomas's audible gasp.

He cleared his throat. "Can I ask you something?"

"Sure."

"How were you planning to drive home?" His fingers found a lump on my other shoulder. My head fell forward, breathing into the bliss.

"I wasn't originally. My friend Cyndi had planned to take me, but her own emergency came up. With no time to rearrange things, I decided to nap in my car, then drive home after rush hour. A rideshare was my next option if you weren't available, but it's an expensive trip."

"Doesn't your foundation provide rides to patients?"

I shook my head. "Not for me. I'd only take funds away from a client."

Thomas's fingers had found enough trigger points to make my shoulders relax.

"You're an excellent masseur."

He paused and cleared his throat again. "The next time your ride cancels, call me immediately. I get the feeling more water and a nap wouldn't have cut it."

"That's because it's the beginning. It'll get better with more treatments as long as my veins hold up."

"This is miserable, isn't it?"

I shrugged and let my head fall to the side. If the professor gig didn't work out, the man had options. "Depends on where you focus. It was worse when doctors didn't take my symptoms seriously… like there was no hope."

Thomas patted my back, indicating he'd finished. "Can you make it to the sectional?"

I looked over my shoulder. "If I couldn't?"

"I'd carry you."

"I'm fine."

"Go sit while I finish."

I followed his orders and sat on the sofa, focusing on my breathing, hoping to ease the last of the discomfort with a few minutes of meditation. My doctor's staff had shamed me, once again, for not taking the recommendation seriously. I counted on the muscle-relaxing effect of the medicine to keep me from "glowing" again, but I wouldn't have attempted it if I'd been in my right mind.

In the end, I didn't even see a spark. I woke up several hours later when Liam came home. The velvety comforter I kept on the back of our recliner had been wrapped tightly around me. Macushla had tucked herself into my legs. A large glass of water sat on a coaster on the coffee table.

I guzzled the water and made a trip to the bathroom. Koosh's food storage box had a note taped to it: I ate dinner (One scoop?). I found my phone and sent Thomas a text.

ME

I fell asleep.

THOMAS

Oh good. Thought you were ignoring me.

ME

Ha! Thanks for taking care of me and my dog. One scoop was perfect.

THOMAS

My pleasure, darlin'.

ME

I forgot to ask

Are you free Sunday evening?

14

Suddenly I See

Kick

I watched Hugh and Maggie Reynolds navigate the high-top tables in the bar area of Finnegan's Wake, my neighborhood pub. Hugh and Maggie had eaten dinner early and spent a few minutes with my gang before leaving for an event at the senior center. I hoped to give them enough positive experiences to keep them coming around after my *momster's* imminent return.

Then Thomas and Banger arrived. The four of them greeted each other and shared a few words by the host stand before the Reynoldses pointed our way. The bar's owner, Finnegan O'Dowd, was taking our orders, giving me cover when I accidentally sighed at the sight of Thomas. I indulged the secret pleasure of watching him weave the same path Hugh and Maggie had. Thomas wore the crisp, navy button-down we'd picked up in the Village District in Raleigh. It made his eyes glimmer as much as I'd thought it would. He also wore the jeans I'd found at the same men's shop.

Cyndi, sitting to my right, did a double take and whispered, "I heard that. I knew you were into him."

"Shush. You heard relief. I wasn't sure if he'd come. The man should get out more." It was why I'd also invited Banger.

"Get out more, eh? Sounds like someone else I know."

"Behave." Cyndi never missed an opportunity to nudge me back into the dating world.

The men joined our group, and Cyn piped up before I could make formal introductions. "Hey Professor." She sashayed in her seat until she noticed Banger and her back stiffened.

"Miss… Sendaydiego," Banger said.

I didn't know they knew each other.

"Ra—" A swift slice of Banger's chin interrupted her. "Mr.… McHenry. You may call me Cyndi."

"Are you two acquainted?"

"We've met," she answered vaguely.

Cyndi's tone told me to drop the subject. Banger's vibes reinforced the idea, and I didn't mind. I was happy to have so many friends and loved ones together. If Bobby had been in town, I wouldn't have done anything to celebrate, thanks to her way of making celebrations more trouble than they were worth.

"Gentlemen, you already know Cyndi, I guess." I moved to her right. "This is my Rachel and her roommate, Isabella."

"Bella's fine, Mrs. Mack." She waved and shifted back for the server to set a platter of wings on the table. The men dipped their chins in acknowledgment.

"Then we have Liz, who works with Hugh, and Jake, who you know from my team." I finished the other side of the table. "My oldest, Dylan, his roommate, Hen—" I cleared my throat. "I mean Dummy."

He flashed an impish grin. "You can call me Dum."

I shook my head and continued, "You know Liam and Deana. And last, we have Dee's handsome other half, Gordon."

"Hear that, sweetness? Kick thinks I'm handsome," Gordon said, joking, his deep voice resonating like an old-school disc jockey's.

Deana laughed as her hand brushed his shoulder. "The entire room knows you're handsome, G."

With plenty of space on the bench to my left, I extended my hand. "Have a seat. Grab some wings, and we'll add your orders ASAP." The enormous table Finn had reserved for us had bench seating on the long sides and room for two chairs on the ends. Thomas took the open space to my left, but Banger surprised me by scooching Cyn and me down and sitting on the other end.

Thomas reached his arm around my shoulder and gently squeezed. "Happy birthday. Quite the clan y'all have here."

"We don't do parties often and took advantage."

"Why don't y'all have parties?"

I raised a shoulder and answered, "Bobby," hoping it would be enough.

"Ah."

Finn's chef made sure our orders arrived at the same time, and we ate a jovial dinner. Finnegan's Wake was a rare kitchen that had my back when it came to my food issues. His chef, Randy, had recently been diagnosed with Celiac disease. Over the past year, I'd helped him tweak the menu to make life easier for folks like us, without being obvious for everyone else.

More importantly, the conversation at the table was a dream. Everyone joked, shared, and gave. I couldn't have asked for a better birthday. When the afternoon football game ended, leaving all the big screens playing the postgame analysis, Finn started a playlist Liam had passed to him with my favorite songs. Besides our easy mix of assorted conversation, we sang and danced in our seats.

Now and then, I'd notice a sadness in Dylan's or Rachel's expression. It was the only downer in our fun night.

After dinner, Banger, Dylan, Liam, and Dum left the table to shoot some pool. The friendly competition seemed to lift my oldest son's mood, but I knew what bothered him. His girlfriend, Suzy, had been a no-show for any family function since the funeral.

A similar thing irritated Rachel, so I reached across the table for her hand. "No Cody, huh?"

My daughter's look turned deadly. "He said he's studying."

I honestly didn't mind. "Isn't he? Dyl said Suzy is off with a study partner or something too."

She lifted a shoulder. "Homework didn't bother Cody when he went drinking with the guys last night or watched football this afternoon."

I turned away to keep from adding my two cents. I didn't care if either showed, but my disappointment for my kids could make me say something I'd regret. Thomas gave me a supportive smile, reminding me he'd overheard the talk Rachel and I had regarding her relationship. A blush crept over me, and I turned back to my daughter.

"Maybe he was hungover earlier?" Rachel growled in response. "It's not like he'd want to hang out with a bunch of old people, honey."

"Bella's here. So is Dum."

"Bella's a good friend, and Henry thinks I'm his second mama."

"You know Dummy doesn't let people call him Henry. Right?"

"It hurts my motherly sensibilities to call him that." I tapped my finger on the table. Another item for my to-do list. "A man about to finish his MBA shouldn't go by *Dummy*."

Cyndi placed her hand on my arm. "You can't fix everyone's issue, chica. Sometimes you have to let them figure it out."

Thomas leaned in and whispered, "She's right, you know."

Deana and Gordon nodded along. A nagging to the fourth power.

"I'm trying," I quietly answered. It was wearisome to see my babies sad. Their technical status as grown-ups didn't make it any easier.

A small roar rose from the pool table. Our group turned as one to see Dylan and Dummy giving high fives. Thomas bumped my shoulder. "I'm sure it'll be alright."

The opening bars of Luther Vandross's "Never Too Much" played, and Gordon stood, holding his hand out to Deana. "Let's dance to our song like normal people." He led his wife over to the corner where musicians played on weekend nights, enfolded her into his large frame, and lost himself to the song and their love.

Thomas, Jake, and Liz talked about school and the military while Cyndi chatted with the girls about her side business making jewelry. I barely heard a word as the Douglasses captivated me with their moves on the small dance floor. I wondered what it would be like to do that too. I knew it would feel as good as my friends made it look. But I couldn't think of a future when the past kept holding me back. Tears crept up to the bottom of my eyes as my secret birthday wish made itself known. To keep them at bay, I turned my head to one of the silenced television screens on the wall. Cyn tapped me on the shoulder and arched an eyebrow.

When the song wrapped, she stood and announced, "Come on, gang. Gordon was right. We should dance."

Stevie Wonder's "My Eyes Don't Cry" began as we approached. Deana raised her arms, declaring, "Let's Hustle, y'all."

I pointed at her. "If you yell 'Change steps' this time, I'm swatting you."

Deana laughed while making room for us. "You're bossy on your birthday."

"I'm bossy every day." Getting up had already changed my mood.

"True."

"Nice job, Professor," Deana encouraged, watching his smooth steps.

"Thanks." Thomas easily kept up with us like a pro.

In the meantime, I lost myself in the steps and rhythm. It was one thing I missed about my cut hours at the Perked Cup. My staff and I practically danced through our shifts. It was why Jake and Rachel knew the steps as well as we old folks.

When the festive opening of KT Tunstall's "Suddenly I See" came on, I was swaying toward the middle of the group. Thomas seemed to magically appear in front of me, raising my arms as he led me in a familiar forward lockstep, then paused.

He tilted his chin and asked, "How's the ankle?"

"Doing well." It was wrapped, safe in a moto boot and healing fast, actually.

He arched an eyebrow. "Trust me?"

I surprised myself as shock turned into a grin. I did trust Thomas, *darn him*. I liked this brazen side of him. He looked rakish, like he had a special secret only for me. I smiled my affirmation, daring him to go for it.

He held me both gently and firmly, carving out space for us to do a proper quickstep right there in the bar. The rest of the gang helped us by stepping back to the wall, giving us more floor space. The basic steps came back to me as if I'd never stopped practicing. It had been years since I'd thought of a progressive chasse, let alone *done* one. Thomas made it easy to follow his lead. He moved me with the precision of a seasoned dancer and the protectiveness of a lover.

And I wanted all his dances. I wished his hips were doing more than directing my moves in space. I wanted him to take possession of my will. I remembered him carrying me in my neighborhood and admitted my secret truth. I'd loved every second. I was starting to crave his arms around my body, no matter the circumstance, his scent filling the air I breathed.

Our bodies felt right, pressed together, shoulder to foot. Our hearts beat together, into each other, for each other. His hip shifted, and mine responded. His thigh flexed, and mine allowed him into my space. Each muscle told me what it would be like to be with him. He wouldn't push or pull me. We'd move together as a unit.

A part of me I'd thought dead reawakened on the dance floor before my friends and family. I couldn't stop laughing as I let this old life fill me. Like the singer, I knew exactly what I needed. My heart longed to start again. No, I craved it. As long as it beat with Thomas's.

This was joy, the purpose of dance and love and life. I would have stayed in his arms the rest of the evening, lived right there. But the song ended, though the gift would stay forever.

We stood together, breathing heavily, wishing we could be alone and take it to higher levels, and the bar broke out into applause. I caught the surprise on Thomas's face when I jumped up and threw my arms around his neck.

"I haven't danced the quickstep in *ages*. Thank you for giving it back to me." I kissed his cheek since it was an established practice in our tenuous friendship. "Best present of the night."

I slowly slid down his body, barely cognizant of the rest of the room, feeling how our dance affected Thomas as much as it did me.

"Oh hell. I'm sorry." I blushed and tried to hop back.

He refused to let me go and grunted, "Stop. Apologizing." He shook his head and continued, "What are you doing to me?" He took a step away and turned back. "Have dinner with me. Any night this week. Just us."

I couldn't answer him. Not yet. My head still spun with emotions. This was more than attraction, more than us. I'd caught a peek at who I could be. I wanted privacy to sort it out. At the same time, I wanted to shout my revelation from the parking lot.

I turned to my friends. Cyndi and Deana stared at me with smug grins. The action had also stopped at the pool table. My boys stared, their heads tilted like curious puppies. I laughed again at their confusion since the same emotion buzzed through me. For once, I didn't care. It was amazing to roll with the moment.

Banger glared. No surprise there. *Well, to hell with him.*

Thomas must have seen his friend's look as well because he headed straight for the foursome. The intense body language between the two told me someone wasn't in our corner, but I decided nothing would burst my glee bubble. It was my birthday, during a rough year. Grabbing Cyndi and Deana's hands, we brought the rest of the girls on the floor and shook our stuff, doing a mean Jerk to the song "Mercy," already half-done. Pink's "Raise Your Glass" followed—Rachel's signature song. She made her mama proud when she took it over like a pseudo-Karaoke, letting her stress go for a few minutes.

Gordon and Deana were the first to leave since the next day was an early workday for both of them. It didn't take long until it was just me, Cyndi, Banger, and Thomas.

"Go ahead to the car, man. I'll be there in a minute," Thomas urged his friend.

Banger said his goodbyes with a simple, "Kick." He gave Cyndi the manly chin tip and casually strolled out the door.

Thomas pulled an envelope out of his jacket pocket. "This is for you."

I slid a card out of the loose flap and laughed. "Who *doesn't* want a kitten shooting rainbows out of its eyes on their birthday?" Without thinking about it, my arms slid around his waist. My ear against his chest heard his heart tapping a rhythm as rapid as mine. "Thank you. Yet again."

Thomas's hand slid over my curls. I'd worn my hair down and hadn't been to the restroom since leaving the table. Heaven only knew how wild it looked. I stepped away, tucking a coil behind my ear, gathering my wits again.

"You still haven't answered my offer for dinner," he said. "I meant it when I asked."

How could I deny our pull? The least I could do was spend some more casual time getting to know him. "Sure. It would be lovely. I usually eat dinner alone on Thursdays. Would that work? I could cook or—"

"Thursday's perfect, and it's my treat. Let me take you to my favorite place."

The usual panic over a newly suggested restaurant sparked. "I don't know, Thomas. I'm hard to feed."

"Hey." He lifted my chin. "Solving problems is one of my favorite pastimes."

Afraid to be a pain in the ass, I nodded my head. "Okay. Let's do it."

Finn approached, giving Thomas a receipt. "Thanks, man."

"Can I settle the bill, Finn? I have to get Cyndi home." She'd drunk both our allotments of alcohol in exchange for my taxi services since I couldn't imbibe.

"It's settled." Finn's eyes flicked to Thomas.

"You're kidding?"

Thomas shrugged his shoulders. "It's nothing. Happy birthday."

The hell it was *nothing*. My boys alone ate enough for six people. But I wasn't about to make a fuss at Finnegan in his place. He received a flash of stink eye though.

Finn handed me a certificate.

"What's this?"

"Two free birthday drinks and a piece of flourless chocolate torte. When your moratorium, or whatever you called it, ends. I feel bad you didn't get to celebrate properly."

"Thanks, buddy." I gave him a quick hug. A few years older than Dylan, Finn had taken over the pub two years prior when his father had a heart attack. From what I could tell, he'd grown the business, like it was in his DNA.

"Hey, we entrepreneurs stick together, right? I mean, you bailed me out when you talked Randy off the 'my career is over' ledge after the Celiac news."

"Bless his heart. I remember the feeling."

Thomas shook his head, smiling. "Of course you did." He said his last goodbyes and left.

After giving Finn one more thank-you hug, I spun Cyndi toward the door too, refusing to look her way. I could *hear* the thoughts in her head the entire time I'd been talking to Thomas and Finnegan.

"Zip it, Sendaydiego. Not. One. Word."

So Nice

Kick

THOMAS SLOWED HIS CAMARO IN FRONT OF AN AWARD-WINNING Italian restaurant in downtown Oakville. His eyes lit up as he turned to me, telling me this was the place for our first date. The butterflies awakened in my stomach, as alarm bells clanged there. I didn't want to discourage him though.

I quickly opened the gluten-free restaurant finder app I used when eating at new places. The community rated it one star—not Celiac friendly. The autoimmune part of me warned this was a bad idea, but the part of me that craved normalcy told it to shut up and enjoy Thomas's company. Instead of politely asking if he had a second choice of cuisine, I let my insecurities over being out with a significantly younger, handsome man take center stage in my thoughts. Embarrassed and out of my league, I followed him down the sidewalk and into the foyer of Stefano's, second-guessing every decision I'd made so far.

Pulling my hair back in combs suddenly seemed outdated and didn't cover my pointy ears. The vicuna sweater dress I'd chosen to show off curves morphed into a frumpy sack in my mind. It also washed out my skin, the summer's kiss of color long gone. And surely he'd have preferred spiky pumps to my comfortable wedge-heeled boots.

Thomas, on the other hand, worked his light gray fisherman's sweater and black slacks like a film star. The color contrasted with his olive skin and raven hair while brightening his silver eyes.

The smell of garlic bread, sauce, and cheese represented trouble, but insecurity distracted me too much to pay attention. Thomas squeezed my hand. "The owner's a friend of mine. Stefano assured me he expanded the menu for gluten-free diners."

"It's sweet you thought of me." I sent a quick prayer to the universe for it to work out. I didn't want to burst his bubble, but low-FODMAP foods did not go with Italian cuisine. It was hard enough to eat on the autoimmune Paleo plan in this place. For me, eating had become about so much more than gluten. Finding an Italian place with both gluten-free and low-FODMAP knowledge would be a huge ask.

Thomas tensed and set his lips as he opened the door, his knuckles white on the handle. "Try it please."

I steeled my spine. Is this what dating would be like from here on? Hell, the last time I dated, we ate in a campus cafeteria. Fancy meals equaled a sub shop. It was time I grew up and figured it out. "Lead the way, Professor."

Stefano greeted us and escorted us to a reserved table. The two men shared about how they met when Thomas first moved to the area from Manhattan. The authentic food reminded him of his favorite place near Soho, so he ate here often. I smiled along, having had no clue Thomas had lived in New York. There was still so much to learn about the man.

"*Professore*, you don't visit me lately. At least you make up for it by bringing the beautiful Kick McKenna here." Stefano sent me a flirtatious wink.

With a polite laugh to hide my embarrassment, I answered, "It's good to see you, Stefano. I've missed the Chamber of Commerce group."

He lifted my hand to kiss it. "Those meetings are a bore without you." He pulled out my chair and asked Thomas, "Shall I bring a carafe of Sangria?"

Thomas placed his hand on his heart and said, "You know how I love it, but not tonight, my friend." He eyed me for a beat. "How about two club sodas with lime instead?"

Stefano didn't hide his shock. I feared we'd insulted him. "Certainly. I'll have Anita bring them."

"Thanks."

We spent some time with the menus. For me, it was infinitely torturous, trying to piece together a way for something to work. My thoughts raced through the list of approved foods. It was a shorter list than the restricted ones. *I should leave.* Maybe get an appetizer and go. I couldn't even order a simple caprese salad.

I wanted to flee but also wanted to hear more about Thomas's past in Manhattan and his current research. Every time his gaze lifted to mine, the relaxed excitement I found there kept me from saying anything. I bit my lip and scanned the menu some more until it blurred.

Finally the dreaded time to order arrived.

"I'll have the chef's special with a house salad and dressing," Thomas said.

"Garlic-mushroom risotto," the waitress, Angela, said as she wrote. "Any wine?"

I tapped his hand. "Please. Go ahead."

Thomas sighed and answered, "Sure. Your Nebbiolo, please."

"Yes, sir. And for you, ma'am?"

I took a minute to inhale deeply and dove in. "Any chance you can do the risotto without garlic?" I'd known for a while garlic bothered me, but until my last appointment, I didn't understand it had to do with being a FODMAP food.

Anita laughed in response. "It's already made."

Shit, shit, shit. My eyes flew over the offerings again, my tongue worrying my cheek. "Okay, I think I have it. I'll take a house salad. Hold the tomatoes, cheese, and bell peppers. Double the avocado, keep the olives, and add grilled chicken please. But no garlic or onion on the chicken. Salt and pepper will be sufficient. Oh, and absolutely no croutons. And I'd like the marinara side dish with the gluten-free noodles." My stomach could forgive a little sauce splurge for one night, right? At least authentic Italian cuisine didn't put garlic in a marinara sauce, and this place was the real deal.

Thomas rolled his eyes and arched an eyebrow.

Angela nodded. "O…kaaay." She took a moment to write everything out. "Any wine tonight?"

"The club soda's fine. Thank you."

"We don't want the bread basket either," Thomas added with a tense smile. I feared our night out might be over before it began.

Angela twisted her mouth. "As you wish."

And then we were alone again, staring at each other with so much to say, but no words would come.

"I'm sorry, Thomas. I embarrassed you in front of your friend."

His eyes narrowed for a moment before answering. "No, and stop apologizing. It's just… I don't understand. You weren't like this at the birthday dinner."

"Finn's staff knows me. You remember what he said about his chef?"

"But the risotto is gluten-free. I ordered it to show support, aside from it being the best I've ever had."

The sentiment gutted me. I reached for his hand. If I could have cried, I would have. "Garlic is a huge item on my *no* list. I don't want to risk the wine right now either, though it might have been okay since alcohol burns off in the cooking."

"I see." Thomas tipped his head back and blew out a long breath.

"I hear you." I scrunched my nose and added, "Maybe this is a good thing. This is my life, Thomas. It's intense now, but I'll always be high-maintenance. Aside from food, there are also rules for cleaning supplies, skin care, hair care, makeup. It's a never-ending life of rules." He could use a fat dose of honesty if he were having a tough time eating out. It also gave Thomas an out before our friendship went any further.

His gaze held mine for an uncomfortably long time. Finally. he said, "It's easy to forget. You don't look sick."

"My mother loves to hit me over my head with those same four words. And I don't know how to respond anymore. Should I feel guilty about it? Or grateful? You didn't know me before the diagnosis."

"What were you like?"

"Like I'd been drugged most hours of the day, only I couldn't sleep when I lay down. Lost hair at a frightening rate. My skin…" I shook my head. "And inflated. I told you about the weight and the boundary lines."

"The psalm."

I nodded. "It helps. The rules can be a blessing. You won't hear me apologize for the way I eat. And not because I'm in a more acceptable size but because I *feel* better. It lets me live again."

"Hey, we all have shit, you know?"

"Do I ever. You ever hear the quote 'Nothing tastes as good as skinny feels?'"

"Didn't a model say that?"

"Yeah. She got hell for it too. But I get it. Working in an industry where an added pound could lose her millions? Learning to hate fattening foods is a fantastic coping strategy, from where I sit."

"Like with the chocolate."

The memory made me smile. "Boy I hope it's temporary, but yeah." I took a long sip of my soda water and reminded myself why sugar was on hiatus. *This is healing, not a punishment.*

"I'm curious though. Can't they do anything for a cure?"

Laughing, I said, "Only if my genes change." Then I added, "Hey, maybe you can help with it."

Thomas coughed as his soda went down the wrong way.

When his throat settled, I asked, "Can we talk about something else? Your research, maybe? How's it going?" Unfortunately, he had to cough some more.

The restaurant interior ended up larger than it appeared from the outside. We sat in a solarium with sprawling chandeliers set to low light. Off of it were two additional dining rooms, characterized by dark wood, with burgundy tablecloths and candles on top. Against the window in the middle room was a stage occupied by a jazz trio composed of a pianist, a bassist, and a guitarist. Thomas leaned toward me and said, "I have a better idea. Let's dance."

"Well." I hesitated. "Where?" Taking over Finnegan's on a Sunday night was one thing, but I wasn't sure about it becoming a habit.

Thomas gestured toward the piano with his head. "You can't see it from our vantage point, but there's a dance floor in front of the musicians. Trust me, it's alright." He came around to my chair and pulled it out for me.

I took a deep breath and smiled, taking his offered hand. There was something about him challenging my trust. "They're not exactly playing a quickstep."

With his hand at the small of my back, he tipped his head toward my ear. "We can handle a little jazz."

"True." He led me by the hand to a tiny parquet floor. Three senior couples were already on it. Their cuteness put me at ease, as did being back in Thomas's hold. He kept us to the basics this time, with no attempt to clear the floor as the trio played "So Nice."

Miss Virginia, a regular from the café, was on the floor. My smile wouldn't contain itself as I watched her with her husband. Obviously together for decades, their bodies communicated with the slightest hip or shoulder gesture, anticipating each other's moves. They let me know Thomas and I had much to learn, though I enjoyed how well we already moved.

"Good to see you tonight, Miss Virginia," I said to her as Thomas floated me toward them.

"You too, dear," she responded with the warmest smile. "You're beautiful in your pretty dress. And such a handsome partner too." I giggled as she batted her eyelashes at Thomas.

Stefano's head shifting left and right broke my focus on our bubble, and I moved my hand to Thomas's chest. "Do you think he's looking for us?"

He caught my sightline and the restaurateur's gaze, then nodded. "Our plates are ready." Weaving our way back to our table, he leaned into my ear and said, "You know that couple?"

Nodding, I answered, "Her. From the Perked Cup."

"Sorry, Kick," he murmured.

"For what?" I looked up, confused.

"Everyone but me has commented on how beautiful you look tonight."

I blushed. "Thanks. I didn't tell you how devilishly handsome you are in your gray and black either. We're out of practice."

"Yes, we are," he answered with a sigh.

"Can I interest you in dessert?" Stefano asked us as he stacked our finished plates. "Our crème brûlée is marvelous and gluten-free."

"Perhaps another time. Thank you," I said with an apologetic scrunch of my nose.

As he walked away, Thomas leaned into me. "The dairy?"

"Yes. Nice deduction," I responded with a slight smile. "I have an idea. There's a dairy-free flan in my fridge. Let's dig into it. It's not Italian, but we can overlook that."

"I'd love to. Let's go."

The first flutter gurgled in my stomach halfway home. Sometimes I'd only experience a bit of bloating, so I ignored it.

The second grumble whacked me from the inside as we turned in to my sub. It felt like a bad science experiment bubbling in there. I grimaced, leaning forward and digging my fists into my stomach, hoping Thomas's attention to the road kept it off me. Activated charcoal could do the trick. There wouldn't be any dessert for me, but I could plate one for him.

As we walked up the path to my house, a monster cramp stopped me in my tracks. It took my whole will to keep from falling onto all fours. "Oh hell." No sense dodging the truth now; a long night was ahead.

"Y'alright?"

"No, Thomas. I'm sorry, but I have to give you a rain check." I sat on my front stoop when another cramp and growl twisted in my stomach. He frowned, looking confused. So I continued, "Something went wrong with dinner."

"But you grilled Angela on the ingredients." He sighed like he had doubts.

"It happens. I'm always at a chef's mercy. If the staff doesn't have the proper training…" I winced as another gripe rolled through me, trying to keep the groan on the down-low. "There are ample opportunities for contamination."

"But how?" There was an edge to his voice as another pain grabbed me on the right side.

"If I had to guess? The chicken shared the grill with something breaded. Or the salad prep person put the required croutons on the plate, realized there weren't supposed to be any, and flicked them out instead of making a new one. Or the noodles had buckwheat. I should've asked about it. Even though it's considered gluten-free, I react to it. I don't know, but… ahh!" Another cramp hit the left side, taking my breath.

"Can I do anything? Make tea?" His hand gently brushed my cheek. "You're flushed."

I nodded, too upset to answer, and handed him my house key. He eased me up and through the door before I took off running. I barely made it to the master bathroom, too embarrassed to use the guest one and risk Thomas hearing. I spent at least twenty minutes in the bathroom, fuming at myself for letting this happen. My stupid, stupid wishful thinking. Would this ever get any better?

When my body gave me a breather, I checked the mirror. My makeup was so smeared from sweat I had to take another minute and wash it off. By the time I'd changed into yoga pants and an MSU Spartans football T-shirt, my resolve had cracked. I sat on the sofa, my head in my hands, afraid to look for Thomas.

"Kick?" I jumped, not realizing he was so close. Thomas set the teacup on the coffee table. "It's mint."

"Thanks. Great choice."

He sat and touched my knee. "When we arrived at Stefano's, you wanted to leave, didn't you?"

"Yeah." The word stuck in my throat.

"Did I say something to make you think we had to stay?"

My head hung. I didn't know how to be a couple anymore. Hell, because of me, we were barely friends. Every time we'd try to start, something happened to me to shorten our time together. "He's your friend, Thomas. You were excited, and you *tried*." I turned to him so he could see my sincerity. "I wanted you to have this victory. I still appreciate what you did for me. Sometimes it's just not enough."

"I'm so sorry." He cradled my clammy hands in his, warm and tender. But his apology was also my last straw. None of this was fair. In my head, I knew no one promised me a fair life, but I didn't give a shit anymore, the brave face and fake strength vanishing.

Before I realized it, I recited the psalm as I rocked. "The boundary lines have fallen for me in pleasant places; the boundary lines have fallen for me in pleasant places; the boundary li—"

Thomas shifted on the sofa, closer to me. His hand gentled my back as he cooed, "It's alright, Kick."

"No, it's *not*, Thomas. We should be laughing and eating flan. I want to know more about you. I'm so high-maintenance I drive myself nuts!" I wasn't crying, but the waves of pain kept sweat running down my face.

"Are you giving up? Because I see it as a lesson learned for both of us. I defaulted to my *fixer* impulses and didn't ask your opinion. And you should feel comfortable enough with me to call me on it. It's a speed bump, but we'll get past it."

Molten lava raged. Every time I'd given him a way out, Thomas stayed, adding joy and lending a hand. It was like he was being punished for it as much as I was. I glanced at him and grunted, "The boundary lines have *not* fallen for me in pleasant places. There. I said it. You can tell him I said it too!" It would have come out as a screech if my voice could have stopped catching.

"Tell who?"

"God, that's who. I don't care if he knows I'm pissed. I'm tired of the three steps forward, two steps back cha-cha-cha that's my life. I'm tired of making plans and my body laughing at them."

I ran my hand through my hair, not caring if it frizzed. "The Psalm doesn't comfort. It judges. The words are a goddamn boot to the back of my neck, keeping me stuck to the ground, keeping me from taking care of my kids the way they deserve. My business. My friends. My body gets my best energy. They get what's left. And it's never enough."

On a roll, the anger continued, mocking. "You know what I've really given up, Thomas?" He raised a sympathetic eyebrow but didn't speak. "Spontaneity. I used to find a truce with my mother when I took her for drives to explore new towns. But she *insisted* we eat at local diners, which I can't do because I can't guarantee"—I pointed at my stomach—"this. She won't allow me to pack us a lunch either. It's her way or the highway, so we lost our last connection. I don't know how to help her be happy like my dad asked. When will my efforts ever be enough?"

As quickly as I vomited the words, they stopped. Gasping again, I put my hands to my face, hot from sweating, eyes wide and shimmering, but I didn't cry. I hadn't truly cried in years. My family trained it out of me as a girl, more so in the past eight years. Instead, my breath hitched. Annoying as hell, but it wouldn't stop. The tornado inside me had become a volcano and blown up.

Mortified, I whispered, "I'm so sorry. You didn't need to hear my crap. *Shit.*"

Thomas kept his gaze down and shook his head, his voice hoarse. He gently covered my hand with his. "Don't apologize. It sounds like this was overdue. Did it help?"

My throat locked as I lifted my head. Where was the silence a minute ago when it was imperative to shut the feck up? All I could do was croak and shrug.

He squinted at me and touched my forehead. "Hey now, darlin', you're warm."

Just What I Need

Kick

I SETTLED INTO THE TUB THE FOLLOWING AFTERNOON, MOVING THE detox process along. With headphones on, an audiobook playing, the chromotherapy lights cycling, and jets circulating sea salt and oils, I set my head against the bath pillow and blissed out. Salt water eased the rashes still burning in unmentionable places. It also renewed my perspective.

I loved my home, worshipped my bathtub, had the best friends and family (mostly) a girl could ask for, an engaging career, and I'd come a long way in the health journey. Nothing overpowered a gluten reaction like good news. Earlier in the day, I'd checked in with my contacts at the McKenna Family Foundation and discovered we could take on a new family. Despite my hurdles, I couldn't imagine navigating autoimmunity without decent finances.

Suddenly Deana burst into my bathroom, causing me to jackknife into a ball to cover up. My phone flew end-over-end, but I caught it at the last minute, saving it from a watery grave.

"What the hell are you doing?" I screeched, reaching for something to cover up with and only finding a washcloth.

"Let it go, shug. It's not like you have something I don't," Deana responded, sneaking a peek. "You could use some of mine anyway."

"Really? From where I sit, you still have your privacy and your dignity," I retorted.

"I rang the bell. You didn't answer. Can't a friend check on a friend?" She sat on the tub-surround. "What are you doing anyway, listening to that romance everyone's talking about?"

"Why are you here?" I asked, rubbing my eyes and jerking. Even my lids were raw.

"Why are you in the tub in the middle of the day?" Deana countered, not backing down from her perceived right to barge in.

I swept my hand over my body, hoping the washcloth would stay put. "Trying to relieve this lovely rash."

She bent down and studied my face. "Your chin's bright red."

I was tempted to show her my ass.

She stood, tsking, but softened her tone. "I brought you soup. It's the coconut thai you like, plus their nasty green juice. Liam said you had no food when he ate twice his weight at lunch. I thought you might be hungry."

I took a deep breath, willing my heartbeat to return to normal. "We have plenty to eat. My boy's too lazy to cook. Lee once told me there's a difference between *food* and *ingredients*. The soup sounds amazing though. Thank you, sweets."

Deana held a towel up as if I should let her wrap it around me like one of her grandbabies. I shooed her away instead. "You still complaining about me seeing your birthday suit? I don't see why you're stressing so much over a few extra pounds. The curves are cute."

"You're adorably petite and curvy and work them like a CEO, right?" I asked.

"You know it."

I knew from her tongue clicks and comments she viewed my anxiety over the recent weight gain as ridiculous. It took a second to come up with the words to explain.

"Remember back when you went on the big diet and you said

you felt trapped in the wrong body? You were glad to add a few pounds back on."

"I do. It taught me about gratitude for what the good Lord gave me."

"The opposite has been true for me. When I look in a mirror, I see an inflated skinny girl wondering what the hell happened—and before you call me ungrateful again, Dr. Chaddha doesn't approve of my BMI either. But the swelling, the aches, and the fatigue get to me." A glance at my pruney fingers told me it was time to get out. "At least the bloating stopped and I don't look pregnant anymore."

"Yeah, it's weird when you do that."

Deana dropped the subject as quickly as she picked it up. We'd talked weight so many times over the years. We both agreed there was more to health than numbers on a scale. It was nice to have a friend who'd been through most of my original recovery and didn't criticize me for the relapse. We each supported the other, and I loved her for it. I dropped my forehead to my knees. "Can I meet you at the dinner table?"

"Are you asking me to stay?"

"If you have time, I'd love it." While fundamentally different, Deana's schedule was as packed as mine. Between Gordon, her two children, and three grandchildren, she barely had time for her photography passion. The fact she made space in her afternoon for me didn't go unnoticed. She dropped the towel on the surround.

"I'll get the bowls."

"Thank you," I called out as the door shut, then quickly dressed in yoga pants and a THEATER MOM T-shirt Rachel gave me for my birthday. I made a quick readjustment to my hair from its high bun to a low one.

Dee saw me enter the dining area and said, "Are you wearing a bra?"

"Why?" I asked, looking around. "Are the boob police here?"

"No," she answered as if I were a petulant toddler. "I was going to ask how you're still so perky, but never mind."

"Oh." I sat in my chair and lifted a spoon. "Benign breast cysts. I'm full of Mother Nature's middle-aged implants."

"You don't say?" Deana looked at me like she was trying to figure out how to score some cysts for herself. "Gives new meaning to the Perked Cup, doesn't it?" She dissolved into laughter at her wisecrack.

"Have you *not* heard my boys make this joke? I almost changed the name in the beginning when Dylan wouldn't stop. He says I kept it out of spite." I took a bit of soup and set the spoon down. "Okay, what's going on? First the curves comment and now the boobs. You're up to something."

The perky joke hadn't fully fizzled, and she giggled again.

I sent her my best glare.

"Fine. I know how discouraged you get when"—she waved her hands toward my stomach—"you get sick. I thought you might like a reminder that it isn't *all* bad."

She was right. I did. "Aw. Thanks, Dee. Bobby's criticisms have been playing on a loop in my head. Wish you would live in here instead." I tapped my temple.

She patted my hand. "One of these days, we'll do an exorcism."

We spent an hour eating, drinking, and catching up on our staff and families. I poured Deana a glass of iced tea since nothing could get her to try the green juice.

Deana's visit lifted my spirits until she brought up Thomas. She snuck it in while she trounced me in two-player spades. "You going to see Thomas again?"

"I don't know. It might be too much. I mean, why would he want to put up with this? You know what Bobby says. How men don't put up with troublesome women." She took another trick while I laughed. "Are you going to wipe the floor with my yoga pants?"

"What would my family say if I let you win? Besides, your mama is a difficult woman, to put it nicely. Let me make this clear: you *are* going to see Thomas again." Deana bit her lip, holding firm, narrowed eyes staring me down.

I sighed. "You won't let the Thomas topic go."

"Um, nope. I knew you were sitting in this house, talking yourself out of a good thing before it even started. Let him make it up to you." She clapped the table with each word. She gave me another glare, the one which made unruly children behave on the spot. And me too, apparently.

"How small is this blasted town? Or is my house bugged?" I looked under the table for signs of a listening device but wouldn't know one if someone stuck it to my shirt. I'd only texted the team about being glutened and taking a day to recover. Technically, I wouldn't be better until Monday but was only on the schedule for Friday.

"He stopped in for a snack before my shift ended."

"Did you talk about me?" I didn't know what I thought about them gossiping, not as if it would matter.

"Aren't tomatoes on your forbidden list now?"

I hung my head, busted. "Yeah."

"Sugar, you had no business being in an Italian restaurant. Self-advocacy isn't only for you. It helps the rest of us too."

I dropped my head to my hands. "I know. You're right. How much did Thomas tell you?"

"You worried him. I think his waters run as deep as yours, if not deeper."

"How do you know? What did he say?" I'd suspected the same.

"You don't work in a coffeehouse without learning how to observe."

"You sound like a bartender."

She moved her hands up and down, as if weighing the two professions, telling me there wasn't much difference.

"I'll think about it. You mind if we call it a night? I'm already tired."

"Sure."

I walked Deana to the door and helped her into her sweater. "Thanks for giving up your photo-retouching time to set me straight." I had the feeling her talk with Thomas motivated her more than Liam's whining had.

"I couldn't let another day go by without setting you straight."

"Dang. How bad was your talk with the professor?"

She opened the door and stood in the space to keep the dog from dashing out between her legs. "Don't blow this, Kick. It could be good, for *both* of you."

Love for Sale

Thomas

Somber clouds shifted, allowing sunrays to filter through the trees on the campus paths, giving them a cathedral-like appearance. Thomas considered this appropriate as he slogged through the spongy trails to go sit in the chapel and disconnect during the pipe organist's practice session.

A panicked call from his assistant, Presley, had him rushing to the lab to work on Toni's latest tests. Fortunately, the grave error she thought she'd made was easy to fix. The panel he reported to at the university never pressured him as long as he showed consistent effort, but *Grand-père* and the Felidae Society members were a different story. They wanted results yesterday. As did Thomas.

After spending most of the night in the lab, he'd meant to get a few hours' sleep in his office. But a predawn storm kept him awake by blowing a tree branch against the window. Plus every time he closed his eyes, another pair like a spring forest appeared in the darkness. He couldn't stand the defeat he saw in them and the belief he'd put it there. For a reason he didn't understand, Thomas wanted to show Kick he was different, someone she could trust. But he'd tried to serve her in the way *he* wanted to, not in the manner she'd needed. He'd inadvertently forced her to pretend everything was fine. Until it wasn't.

So Thomas sought the peace of the chapel before his lecture. The organist was working on a César Franck chorale, which helped pacify his restless spirit any time it touched his ears.

Thomas stepped from the dark gray of the vestibule into the magnificent light of man's vision of a holy space. Stained-glass windows lined the nave's clerestory, projecting the welcomed arrival of sunrays as if Christ Himself rode on them.

The rainbow flood of colored and clear light lifted Thomas's mood to almost enjoyable levels. He hummed "Here Comes the Sun" to himself as he made his way to the middle, taking in the surroundings while quietly respecting those around him. His chosen spot in sight, Thomas turned the corner to his row, mindful of his case so it wouldn't make noise against the pew.

He stopped midstep. He couldn't believe his eyes. *There she sat.*

Four rows ahead, drenched in sunlight, her head bent in a book, Thomas knew her.

His case dropped on the pew before his knees gave out, his ass landing on the leather attaché.

After all these years, could she be real? How could she simply be sitting in a church?

Heads turned to glare at him for making noise, but not his angel. Her hair glowed in the sun the way it did in his dreams. Presently, it looked lighter, nearly platinum when touched by rays floating through clear panes. He chalked it up to the nearness and bright-ness of reality versus the haze of dreams.

Where had she been all this damn time? He thought of Kick and almost didn't want his angel to be real. The revelation took him by surprise. No. After waiting for so long, he had to see it through.

Thomas watched slim hands periodically turn a page. The rest of her remained doused in a vibrant mix of colored and clear light. She wore casual clothes. He hoped like hell she wasn't a grad student. No way would fate toy with his heart and make a relation-ship with his angel unethical once he'd found her.

He sat for a moment, preparing a greeting. Given the time he'd dreamed of this woman, why hadn't he ever practiced one? Did she dream of him too? What if the dreams were only one way? There was only one way to know for sure.

Thomas slumped in the pew. Should this be like the time he'd turned down meeting his blues guitar idol so he didn't have to risk disappointment? No. This was different, dammit. How could he dream of her for years—*years!* —and not say something when the chance presented itself?

He rose from his seat and took the fated first step, practicing his opening as he made his way to the side aisle. Thomas reached her pew, placed his hand on the endcap, and turned, "Excuse me..."

The woman adjusted her position and looked up. Only it wasn't his angel looking up. It was a young man. *On the effeminate side, but definitely male.*

Heat raced across his features, obliterating his thoughts. New words scrambled for purchase. Mortification had Thomas tongue-tied until... *Ted.* Ted was the name of the organist. "Have you seen Ted yet? Looks like he's running late. Do you know if he canceled?"

"I'm not sure. I don't come in here much. Just waiting on my girl."

Shock dried Thomas's throat as he croaked out a few words in reply. "Sorry to disturb you. Guess he's not practicing today."

"No worries, Professor. Have a good day." The young man's eyes returned to his book.

Thomas shuffled back to his pew in a whirl of anger, embarrassment, frustration, and despair. He fled the chapel as if someone had pulled a fire alarm, yelling at himself the entire way to the lecture hall.

Somewhere in his subconscious, he'd known it had been a fool's fantasy all along. She was nothing more than his mind wrestling with loss and loneliness, a result of his isolation. His "dream angel" was a delusion his mind made up to keep him moving forward when his psyche begged to give up.

In hindsight, the student looked wrong, even from behind. He was too light, too delicate, too sloppy.

By the time he set up his materials on the lectern, Thomas had a plan. No more relying on a goddamn dream. No more living like a hermit. He'd find the drive to expand his world or risk losing his faculties. Though music and the gym were essential, neither were enough to fill the void. He'd been ignoring the signs, believing personal entanglements were a hassle.

He remembered Kick's words to her daughter. *The magic's found in the connection. Not because of the how, the what or the why, but because of the who.*

Did she know then that she'd hit the nail on the head for Thomas? He'd find a way to reengage and keep his vows to the Felidae. Even if it killed him.

18

Take on Me

Kick

MY MYSTERY MAN VISITED ME IN MY SLEEP AGAIN. COVERED IN A sunlit haze, I recognized him by the way he made my heart flutter. I reached for him, but my hand filled with light.

"Where've you been?"

"Waiting for you," he answered.

Longish tresses floated through my fingers, though I couldn't see them. He turned his cheek into my hand, and the familiar gray strands at his temples caught the light. I closed my eyes, allowing the warmth and brightness to fill me. I inhaled the stillness he offered and exhaled my melancholy.

We floated down winding stairs to a secret sanctuary and walked a gardenia-filled path. When light beams occasionally broke around us, I saw his boots, pants, and a coat from a different time, but I couldn't identify when. My lack of interest in any history class not involving artwork, biting me in the ass, even in my dreams.

My dream lover touched my stomach where it still ached. The pain dissipated in an instant. He touched my jaw, and the rash there vanished too, leaving porcelain skin.

I placed my hand over his heart, sensing its slow beat beneath my palm. He sighed at the sensation. I'd never considered I could fill a need in this mystery man from out of time. But he craved my touch as much as I did his. As fast as he appeared, I knew he was leaving again.

"Please stay," I begged. "I'm better when you're around."

A rugged hand moved around the space, directing my attention to the porch we now stood on. The same gardenia bushes defined the outside edge, a gentle breeze making their fragrance surround us.

"This is all you, lady. I walked with you down here, but this place and everything in it is your doing."

I thought he was referring to meditation, and I remembered recent attempts and the subsequent glow they caused. My hands tucked against my chest for fear of discovery. "I'm not so sure."

My body lightened, and my feet felt like they could break free of gravity. But my dream man worked my hands apart, lacing our fingers. "Don't fear the light. It's you too." Then my body felt the welcomed pressure and presence of a hug without the sensation on my skin.

He added, "Come back here anytime you need to." Next came the sensation of lips gently pressed to mine. "Thank you for showing me around. If you don't mind, I'd like to stay awhile."

"But I want to stay too."

"No, angel. See who's at your door. Hurry."

19

You Do Something to Me

Thomas

"Hey stranger. Sorry it took a while to answer."

After three rounds of knocks and bell-ringing, Kick opened her door. Her wild hair and adorable squint gave away her just-woken status. An instant grin spread across Thomas's face. Then his thoughts turned to what it would be like to wake with her. He knew his sleep would be deep and restorative with Kick in his arms, the opposite of his solitary nights.

In his mind's eye, he wrapped a chestnut coil of her hair around his finger and kissed her perfect bow lips. He wondered if she ever smiled in her sleep.

But he didn't come to Kick's house to scratch an itch. Embarrassment chased his smile away. He wasn't used to losing control over his thoughts, or his heart, like he did around her.

"Everything okay?"

Thomas held up the bags he carried. "You're asking my question for you."

Kick stepped aside and swept her arm, permitting him to enter.

She yawned and said, "Sorry, I was napping. Are you…?" She leaned around a corner and checked a clock. "Yeah, you're early."

"My turn to apologize. I finished quickly and had spent too much time in my office this week. I was hoping you might be up for a walk and your Pokey-Go game."

When he said the word *walk,* Kick's dog barked and ran in circles.

"Shhh! *Chhtt.*" Kick snapped her fingers, but Macushla had keyed herself up and couldn't stop wiggling. "Crap. Settle down. He didn't know."

"Didn't know what?"

"The *W* word has *Harry Potter*-type magical powers over Koosh. When someone says it, she practically apparates to the person with expectations for an immediate… you know."

"Then how do y'all talk about going outside?" The dog resumed her vigorous barking.

"*Stop.*" Kick laughed. "She knows the *O* word too. We use ambulate, but Liam swears she's catching on to it. Anyway, it was nice of you to come by." Kick leaned in and sniffed the bags of food in Thomas's hands. "This smells wonderful. You said their kitchen is dedicated gluten-free?"

His smile returned, knowing he'd found a way to right his wrongs. He'd called earlier and offered to stop at the new café in Durham. "Thanks for taking another chance on my dining-out skills." Kick received the takeout bags so Thomas could hang up his leather jacket. He followed her into the kitchen.

"Thomas, don't be silly. You did nothing wrong. Not everyone is as sensitive as me. Plenty of people will appreciate the effort Stefano made with his food." She set the bags on the counter and placed her hand on his arm. "Please don't blame yourself."

He wished he could do more to fix things—use his connections to recommend a new doctor or a new study—to make life easier. But when he looked into it, he found Kick was doing exactly what she should. "How about I'm glad to have this do-over?"

She dipped her chin, smiling. "Do-overs are amazing. Do you

mind if I take a minute to freshen up? My head's still cloudy from sleep."

"Not at all. I'll set our places."

"Fantastic. Be right back." She padded off to the back of the house, muttering, "Bet I look a hot mess."

She had the "hot" part down, though Thomas was keeping his head in the friend zone. He might have given up on an isolated life, but he didn't have to get sucked into the whole shebang *even if Kick's feistiness captivated him.*

While plating their food, he laughed when her complaint reached his ears. "You've got to be kidding! What a fright."

With the food ready, Thomas explored the rest of the first floor of Kick's house. A bright, open space, the blue ceiling caught his eye first. It matched the sunny midafternoon sky, complementing large windows on three sides of the great room. The kitchen opened onto the dining area, with a rustic table in the center.

Opposite the window in this area was a wall of art, comprising three small pen-and-ink drawings of her children as babies. Kick's signature graced the corner of each one. Two large illustrations hung on the same wall. One illustration was a Cole Phillips piece he recognized from an old magazine cover. He liked the use of negative space, causing a young flapper to blend into the background. Or perhaps she emerged from it? The last piece was modern, a Malika Favre, playing with the same theme.

She returned and pointed at the Phillips work. "I can never decide if the girl is fading or emerging from the background."

"My thoughts too. What do you think's the difference?" Thomas asked.

"My mood," Kick answered. "For me, it's my mood."

She wore gray yoga pants with striped socks, a Hurricane's T-shirt, and a red cardigan. Slightly wild, the relaxed look fit her personality. The sweater ended above her hips, and he liked her form in the stretchy material. Her ass was another work of art. She'd clipped her hair loose at the neck, adding to her sexy, casual appearance.

"I still have the dairy-free flan. How about dessert?"

Anything for added time in this bubble he was seeing as a refuge. "Sounds perfect."

They settled on barstools and ate for a few minutes in silence. Bryan Ferry sang "You Do Something to Me" quietly in the background, competing with muffled dream barks from her sleeping dog.

Kick stared at Thomas, setting off his insecurity, suddenly aware there was more on the line for him than there had been when he'd made their plans. He raised both his eyebrows inquisitively, and she ducked her head with a shy smile.

Maybe they both felt a shift.

"Thanks again for the do-over." She swayed to the song as she ate. If music played in a room, Kick almost always found a way to dance to it. He guessed listening to it healed her, similar to the way it restored him to play it.

"Trust me, darlin', it's my pleasure."

They spent the rest of dinner listening to Cole Porter tunes, talking genres, favorite movies, and books. Their opinions overlapped in music—minus Kick's love for eighties alt-rock—and musicals. Kick sang along with some Broadway songs while Thomas joined in. His voice had never matched his ability to play an instrument. Kick called "uncle" when he tried adding his off-key voice to "Not While I'm Around" from *Sweeney Todd*.

She threw her fingers over his mouth, laughing and nearly falling off the stool into him. Kick's free hand landed on his thigh to catch herself. Caught up in her giggles, she didn't notice his muscle twitch or jaw clench. He didn't mind. Her company, her old soul mixed with youthful enthusiasm, meant more to him than any attraction. Hell, it *led* to the attraction. It was his motivation for keeping a smile on her face. He considered it a victory anytime he made Kick laugh, and thought himself a king for it.

"Please stop. I don't want to ruin my favorite Broadway tune. Rachel and I watch *Sweeney* at the end of every school year to blow off steam." Kick gasped through her laughter.

Thomas didn't hear a word as his attention focused on her fingers on his lips. Who was he kidding? Somewhere between her chewing his ass out and their first dance, he'd begun wishing for her mouth on his until it became a craving. He feared he'd lose his mind if he never knew how she tasted. He allowed a shiver to travel up his spine, hoping it would snap him out of his impending madness.

The music changed. Louis Armstrong's version of "La Vie En Rose" filled the space as the mood in the room also took a quick turn.

Kick closed her eyes and let out a deep breath. "We need to talk about something." She waved her hands around as if she didn't know where to begin. "This song… It's, well, it's all good, you know? Hell. Let me start over. The other night… my life… Things get hard, but I don't want you to think I'm not grateful for what I have. My break was only for a minute. It's not me."

Thomas rose from his stool and paced. The disturbance that sent him to the chapel in the morning seeking peace raced through his system again. His heart demanded he comfort her, but he didn't have the right, not the way he wanted. Something cracked in Thomas despite his plan to hold back. He slowly walked to Kick, pulled her off her stool, and wrapped his arms around her. She remained rigid at first, then like an ice cube on a hot sidewalk, she dissolved into him. And he glimpsed the part of himself he was missing.

Her lack of tears surprised him. Perhaps she'd cried enough in private. Her breaths hitched at first, so he held her until their breathing synced. He could have held Kick forever. There was a familiarity in her pain, allowing her to give back to Thomas as much as he gave her.

"Emotions aren't right or wrong, Kick. I don't judge you for them," he soothed, looking down at her. "We feel how we feel. I knew it wouldn't take long for you to find your brave face again, and here you are."

Kick stayed in his embrace for a long time without speaking.

"It's been a while since a man held you, hasn't it?"

She laughed out loud while she nodded against his shoulder. "Pretty pathetic."

"Not at all. I haven't truly held a woman in a long time. It's wonderful." Thomas let his cheek fall against her head, soaking up the emotion as his lashes drifted shut. "It's not weakness to show vulnerability. In fact, it can point to our greatest strength."

Thomas opened his eyes again, watching Kick study him from under her lashes until her mouth ticked up. "Why does it feel like I could tell you the same thing?"

He cleared his throat and returned her smile. "It's easy to recognize our desires in others when our souls share the same aches."

The dog broke their tension. She trotted into the kitchen, barked for dinner, and pointed at the cabinet containing her food. "Like clockwork, you are. Hold on." Kick eased out of Thomas's arms and filled Macushla's bowl, setting it in the mudroom.

She returned to the kitchen and filled two glasses with iced tea, herbal for her, and peach black for him.

"Can I ask y'all something?"

"Anything." She returned to her stool and gave him her full attention.

"Promise me you'll ask for more help." He raised a hand to hold off a response. "I know you've done it in the past, and folks bailed. I'm not running. Let me be a better friend. Let me in, Kick."

She shook her head with passion. "You don't know what you're asking. I mean, I know my friends love my kids and me. But some things are too much." A tear began a slow descent down her porcelain cheek. "Have you seen any other women in my life? Mothers in particular? I used to have a boatload of acquaintances through the kids and such. Each setback saw more fall away until there were none.

"Hell, Liam's best friend, Jacklyn's mother, and I used to be close. She has a different autoimmune disease, but we bonded over doctor's appointments and body aches. We supported each other in our illnesses. I thought we did anyway. Until my weight loss and I showed signs of remission. It was a shocker to get judged for doing too well, but there it was. When I suddenly became single, she dumped me altogether. Can you believe she acted jealous, like I might steal her man? Not that I blame her. Not really."

"Why the hell not?"

Kick rubbed her arms as she put together her answer. "Every

illness is different. What heals one person makes another worse. One thing they have in common is they mess with our heads. I'd forgotten about the loneliness. The recent appointments make me miss so much of my life and my crew."

Thomas leaned in, resting his hand against her cheek, brushing another tear with his thumb. "There you are. If nothing else, let the persona go when I'm around. Put the mask away." He wanted to pound on every person who'd let her down.

"What makes you say I wear a persona?"

"I remember the story you told me about your name. Kick. It's a shield. I get it, but I hope you can get comfortable enough to drop it around me." Thomas didn't miss the irony that his own life was a charade, but peeking at the man he used to be when he was with her gave him hope. He could let his mask drop in her presence even if she didn't know he did. "Kick can take care of the world and everyone in it. I'd like to see more of Kathleen."

She quietly laughed and fell into Thomas's shoulder. "You want me to fill up your hero complex quota."

Thomas adjusted Kick to meet her eyes. "Your strengths can lift my weaknesses too." Even if she wasn't fully informed.

"You're talking of more than friendship, Professor."

"Perhaps. Can't we test the waters and see Kathleen? Maybe there could be an *us*." Christ, who opened the door and let his heart run wild? He meant every word slipping from his mouth though.

"An *us*, huh?" she asked with a teasing grin.

He nodded. "Got to admit, it's nice having you to myself. We can go slow. Hell, we both have a boatload of responsibilities. We've no choice but to go slow."

"So what? Dinners? Workouts? Weekends?"

"We both eat. We exercise. I was serious about rides from your doctor."

"What exactly do you want from me, Thomas?" She sounded irritated and impatient, but her face darkened with sadness and doubt.

He answered the question by standing between her legs, bending down, and kissing her.

Hard. Desperate.

Thomas's mouth demanded she kiss him back, acknowledge his desire, and validate it. The longing to taste her shook him, creating a new vulnerability, begging her to be in the same place as him.

Kick responded by deepening their kiss. She moaned as she folded into him. Her desire announced itself as she wrapped her arms around his neck and stood, pressing her body into his.

Thomas whispered in Kick's ear, "Was that enough of an answer? What do you have to say now?"

A smart smirk lifted one corner of her sweet mouth. "The flan tastes better on you." She brushed a thumb over his mouth to wipe off her gloss, and Thomas gasped at the gesture. He didn't dare wish for a time where they could be a complete couple, taking care of small wishes along with the big ones. The thought made a pretty picture though.

"Who are you, Thomas Harrison?"

"Too many things. With you, I'm a man again. I'm me." He was swept up in a wave and riding the crest. He'd taken a chance, ready to backpedal if he'd gone too far. Kick's response made him want to celebrate each moment with her as the gifts they were.

"Um, what just happened to our friendship?"

Thomas's eyes creased as his mouth slowly formed a broad grin. "Let's say it's evolving."

"Do that again…," she said, her breath catching. "Now."

He eagerly obeyed. There might have been magic in their connection. More than magic if they'd been other people.

His lips kept smiling as they softly brushed hers, a blessed refuge from everything stirring his restlessness. This kiss was slow, warm, and delicious. She was right too. The flan tasted better shared between them. He took his time exploring her mouth and her lips, occasionally pulling on her lower one. He turned his back to lean against the counter while keeping her against him, content to stay right there. Their mouths opened, and their tongues learned how to dance together. They possessed as much rhythm in their kiss as they did on a dance floor.

Focused fully on each other, they didn't hear the engine of the car as he peppered kisses along her jaw. Or hear the dog trot expectantly to the mudroom when his lips traveled down her throat, curving her back slightly over his left arm. They didn't hear the door open or close. Thomas's senses focused solely on Kick's giggle and moan as he found a ticklish spot.

"The hell, fam?"

20

Secret

Thomas

"Then we sprang apart like we'd had a fire hose turned on us," Thomas told Banger.

"Have to say, brother, I'm with Team Kid. What the hell were you thinking?" Banger sat in a chair in the third-floor office at Thomas's house. His friend had come by to use Thomas's shooting range at the back of his property, then run the forest trails.

"It shocked Liam to see his mom kissing me, especially in their house. I'd expect it of a typical teen. He's a good kid though. Helping him with a physics assignment this week and then jamming on a couple of guitars was fun. I hope to find time to get to know Kick's other two better as well."

He stared at Banger a moment. "You, on the other hand, act personally affronted, and I'm not sure why."

Thomas set a box of folders and notebooks on a portable table and opened the top file. For a split second, he'd forgotten what he wanted with the box. His brain refused to focus on anything substantial, and it drove him nuts. When he looked out the window toward the trees, hazel eyes smiled at him. Leaves on the shrub near his kitchen door had already turned a dark brown with reddish edges and an overall burnished gleam, like her hair.

He'd had a hellish week. Still, he couldn't shake the possibilities whispering in his ear whenever his thoughts drifted to her. They'd only managed a coffee break and ride home from her latest IV treatment since their dinner do-over. Their conversations and quick kisses fueled a desire for more. Kick dazzled Thomas, and he had to tamp it the hell down.

What had him discombobulated all evening was the goodbye kiss after he'd settled her on the sofa with an ice water. He'd cradled her jaw in his hands, his thumb stroking her delicate neck before finding the pulse at the base. Then their beats synced up, as if their cells had declared them simpatico. When the kiss ended, Kick's lips turned a cherry red and stayed puckered for a second. He wondered if she was aware of it. Or maybe she missed his lips when it ended. He sure as shit missed hers.

And the buzz when he touched her? It became sweeter with each caress—like smooth jazz. It seemed Kick noticed it too. An idea bloomed that their meeting might be more than coincidence.

Dammit all, his thoughts had drifted again while Banger was speaking.

"Fuck all, you're not listening," Banger protested, running a hand over his buzzed cut. "The woman is fine, sure, but hanging out with her—and her kid—is trouble. Would your wiser, older friend steer you wrong? I see the 'maybe it could be different with this one' look on your face right now. I'll spare you the anguish and tell you it's not. Kick sticks her nose in *everyone's* business. You think she won't pick up on your secrets? On us? The Felidae will always be a problem."

Thomas opened his mouth to protest and swallowed it back. Banger was right. Plus the man loved a good pontification. Who was he to hold Banger back?

"I get you're lonely, but stick to the plan. Find another *bic*. You remember those—*disposable women?* They're a no muss, no fuss release. You haven't given it a real shot since you moved here." Banger walked to a credenza at the far end of the space. Thomas kept a small bar there, and his friend poured two fingers of Scotch into a tumbler.

Thomas spoke while he made two stacks of papers from the folders he skimmed. "I'm done with throwaway girls. Hookups work for you, but it's become a dreadful bore. And I've honestly never known a *bic* to be no fuss. They promise to be at first, then they beg for more. Next thing you know, they've gone psycho."

"You're talking about the blonde from Manhattan."

"She followed me here and showed up at my lab in nothing but a trench coat and heels."

Banger swallowed his drink and chuckled.

"She *took the coat off,* man. In front of my associates."

Banger continued laughing until he snorted, wiping his eyes. "Because *you* couldn't cut her loose."

"The hell I couldn't. She wouldn't take the cutting. She thought I was playing hard to get and almost got me fired."

Banger poured more whiskey but said nothing. Thomas took it as confirmation that maybe the games wore on Banger too.

"Kick's frankness is refreshing. She's sticky as you say, but she'd never pulled a bait and switch. We can be friends, even excellent friends, and still have our own shit since her schedule is as loaded as mine. Because, you know, she's actually grown. Hell, we had planned to hang out tonight, but I have to finish this stuff." Thomas raised the folder, then stopped to chuckle. "She acted *grateful* I canceled. Said she wouldn't feel so bad about the times her health or her schedule made her ditch plans too."

Banger returned to his seat and took a sip from his glass. "Naw, brother. Kick may understand moving slow, and I believe she won't play games, but she's a swan. She mates for life, and she's looking at you. Think about it. Why is her dating now such a surprise to her son? You had to have rocked her world to get her this far."

Thomas shook his head. "Kick's had a shitload on her plate. There's something I relate to. Stop worrying, man."

Banger raised his glass. "What about Vivienne? *There* was the perfect woman for men like us. You set her up so she could run her life while you went about yours. *Jings Crivvens*, I'd give anything for a find like her."

Thomas shook his head. "We lived that way before I met y'all. It was before my commitment ceremony to the Society. I was in a different headspace back then. The world was bigger too. There are similarities though. Kick has work, family, and her recovery to focus on. I have all this. It's probably what drew me to her, to be honest."

"If you say so. Don't forget I warned you." Banger walked toward Thomas and the box. "What are you doing anyway?"

Thomas ran a hand through his hair. "Trying to fix a crisis at the lab. Remember my first assistant, Presley?"

"Nigel's recommendation from Oxford?"

Thomas nodded. "That's her. Or it was. She died Monday. A hit-and-run while she was walking to her boyfriend's apartment. Police are still looking for the driver."

"Fuck, brother. I'm sorry. Did you tell Nigel?"

"Briefly. He's hard to get ahold of these days." *Grand-père's* cryptic warning came back to him, but he had more pressing issues to deal with. He'd do some digging when at the conference in Bordeaux.

Thomas continued, "I spent Wednesday with Presley's parents." It had been the hardest damn day he'd had in ages. It brought back memories he'd long buried—would've preferred they stayed so too. "Going through her locker contents now and sorting out what the lab needs from what could be shipped back home. The university has already lined up candidates to interview tomorrow. They're getting as pushy about my work as *Grand-père* is."

It helped to have Banger nearby while Thomas sorted through his assistant's things. The young scientist had shown so much promise, and Thomas had been fond of her. It would've been harder to go through Pres's desk contents alone.

Banger sat at Thomas's computer. "You good for me to update your machine now?" Thomas wondered if his friend sensed his need for companionship.

He answered while shuffling through another notebook. "That'd be great. Thanks."

Banger cracked his knuckles. "Since I'm here."

They worked in silence for thirty minutes before Thomas lifted a folder and a thumb drive dropped to the floor. A piece of tape with PROF. H on it piqued his curiosity. "What's this?"

Banger held his hand open and received the drive. "Perfect timing. Let me restart."

Thomas turned back to the box. The pile for Presley's family was half the size of the notes for the lab. Mostly, they amounted to duplicates of his own, but they were university property. The neatness and thoroughness of the work were indicative of his former assistant. He would miss having her in the lab.

"Uh, brother? You better come here."

"What's wrong?" Thomas moved around the desk to read the monitor. "Holy Christ."

His hands shook against his thigh as Banger clicked through a series of files and photos. The pictures were of Thomas in a World War I uniform. There was another of him in a double-breasted brown tweed suit with Vivienne at her dress shop's opening. Then came Thomas at Vivienne's funeral. A thick mustache with mutton-chops didn't hide his bone structure. Neither could the gray hair or the soft wrinkles around his eyes. Thomas couldn't deny the similarities between him and the pictures, but he thought he had buried them from the public. The Felidae should have destroyed them. They had people in governments around the globe.

Presley had made notations, speculating the photos were of the same man and not a set of descendants. He thought back to her comment about his strong family genes. A note commenting on how he appeared younger ended with a circle and underlined the word *mitochondria. Good guess*, he thought. He also thought the key to his situation lay with the ancient bacteria powering every cell. As freaked as Thomas was, he still admired her research. Yeah, she would've been a huge asset.

Thomas grabbed the back of his neck. Somehow he'd let his guard down.

Banger broke the shocked silence. "There's a folder in here on Nigel too."

Photos and notes on their European counterpart, dating back to his participation in the Boer War, popped up on the screen.

"It's a good thing she never saw the paintings and photos you have around here," Banger said.

Thomas ran his hands through his hair. "This isn't funny, man. She practically figured us out." He pointed to a text document. "This mentions the Felidae Society. How was she able to get this far?" Thomas felt himself grow angry with Banger. As the head of Felidae security, he kept the members hidden.

Banger focused too deeply on the computer screen to answer Thomas. Knowing him, the man was already chewing his own ass out. Banger clicked another file, opening a letter. He let out a low, "Fuck me," as he read.

"She planned to blackmail me?" Thomas croaked. So much for missing her. The letter was an ultimatum—make Presley a test subject, or she'd go public with her findings, starting with the dean.

"There's a folder in here with Toni's name on it too."

Toni's children didn't know she still lived. Releasing this information would've hurt them. Ruined lives. Blackmailing Thomas was bad enough, but screwing with Toni's life? He grew furious. "Dammit all to hell."

"You would've been. We dodged an armor-piercing bullet here."

"But did she tell anyone? Pres was a brilliant assistant. Capable and reliable. Do you think she would've blurted this out to a friend? Her boyfriend? I have a hard time believing she would, but—"

"You'll be leaving that to me now," Banger assured him.

With impeccable timing, Thomas's phone rang. "Shit. It's the old man. Did you send out vibes?" he said jokingly, looking for anything to ease the squeeze in his chest.

"Say nothing. Let me look into it." At some point, Thomas had to get to the bottom of Banger's recent pullback from the Felidae. He thought Banger and Alaric had resolved their bad blood.

"You sure?" Thomas answered the call. "*Oui, Grand-père.*"

Banger nodded his head while mouthing, "Not a thing."

Hold on Loosely

Kick

I SAT ON THE IMAGINARY PORCH IN MY MIND, SURROUNDED BY THE comforting scent of gardenias. My meditation practice had been taking me back here since I'd first dreamed about it. Unfortunately, my companion hadn't shown up again, but like he'd said, the place was mine. I learned to sit there anytime I wanted to refresh. Positivity and hope lived on the porch, filling me up with reinforcement. Boy was it a requirement presently. My mother had returned from her cruise the previous night.

Bobby wasn't allowed on my porch. The annoying voice she'd weasled into my mind stayed at the top of the stairway leading down to my precious space. It was a relief to maintain some headroom free of her. I didn't even mind seeing the cool glow around my skin when I traveled back up the steps and opened my eyes. Instead, I embraced the humming tingle accompanying the light, certain the glow would quickly fade.

My phone beeped a text alert. It took a minute to reorient and remember where I'd put it. I fished the thing out of a cargo pocket in my pants and swiped.

THOMAS

Will you be available in thirty minutes? It
won't take long.

ME

I'm at the Perked Cup all day.

THOMAS

I'd like to speak in person if it's alright.

ME

If you don't mind coming here. I'm
decorating for Halloween and meeting with a
sales rep.

Someone had broken my drive-through speaker the night before. The poor thing looked like they demolished it with a baseball bat.

THOMAS

You're not wearing yourself out, are you?

ME

No worries. Just finished meditating or
whatever. Feeling good.

THOMAS

Wonderful! Great job. I'll see you soon.
Finishing up notes for my new assistant.

ME

Sounds good.

I replaced my phone and walked out to the front of the café with a stupid grin on my face.

Cyndi stood at the counter, ordering from Deana's new hire, Crystal. Jake and Deana had both done a fantastic job filling our staffing holes. I hadn't been able to see our newest girl work on her own, so I stood back and observed.

"A flat white. Sub the steamed milk for half-heavy whipping cream and half water," Cyndi ordered. She gravitated toward the persnickety when it came to coffee. I think she enjoyed giving specific directions.

"Amazing. Any flavor?" Crystal prompted.

"Sure. Sugar-free lavender."

"Ah, perfect," she enthused. I'd heard Crystal's way of receiving an order was as unique as Cyndi's way of placing one.

I chuckled at the confused V on Cyn's brow.

"Hot or cold?"

"Hot please," Cyndi said.

"Definitely. Anything else?"

"Yes. The pumpkin scone."

"Absolutely. Fantastic." Crystal's encouragement bordered on orgasmic.

My hand jumped to my mouth to contain a snicker. From what I could tell, Crystal's zealous style came naturally. I shuffled to the drive-through.

Deana was working it without the squawk box but had a break in traffic. "I love your new girl."

Dee smiled at the comment.

"You didn't tell her to be more…"

"Exuberant?"

I nodded, trying my best not to giggle.

Deana shook her head and released her warm chuckle. "Naw. It's all her."

"I love it. She brightens the place with her coffee evangelism."

"What about you?" Dee asked. "You happen to sneak some caffeine in your office?"

"No. I'm being good. Why?"

"Oh, I see now. You have a Thomas gleam in your eye."

"Excuse me?"

"I saw you walk out here all smarmy. The professor looks good on you."

"Stop. And behave. He's coming by in a bit."

"This will be fun." Her laugh followed me as I finally reached the counter.

"How's the morning going, Crystal?"

"Wonderful, Mrs. Mack. What brings you back out here?"

My job? Then again, so much time spent away made it feel less like mine lately. Maybe I wasn't the only one. I hoped I'd be able to go back to normal and not have to make a new normal. I changed the subject. "This here is my bestie, Cyndi. She's part of the Perked Cup family. Thank you for taking great care of her."

Crystal's eyes opened wide as she shook her head. "It's fabulous to meet you, Mrs....?"

"Cyndi's fine, honey."

"Wonderful." Crystal turned back to me. "I try to give everyone their deserved service."

"I noticed. Thank you. Deana found a gem in you."

"She's chill."

"Yes she is," I answered, assuming she meant *awesome*. After giving Crystal instructions to refill the napkin dispensers and do the bathroom check, I made myself a cup of herbal tea and set it down opposite my friend's.

"Is she on drugs?" Cyndi whispered.

I laughed and the tea almost went down the wrong pipe. "I wouldn't ask that too loudly." We were still dealing with the fallout from the newspaper article. I shrugged anyway. "It seems to be all her though. Mmm. This is good."

"You mean fabulous?" Cyndi asked, imitating Crystal's enthusiasm.

"Sure. Who knew cardamom and cinnamon would be a wonderful midmorning pick-me-up?"

She leaned across the counter and sniffed the rim. "Smells delicious."

"I know. Deana hooked me up." I bent to my elbows, leaning on the counter. "What brings you in this morning?"

"Checking in. How did it go with the dragon lady yesterday?"

"Fine." My mother seemed happy to be back. For her anyway. She filled the ride home with anecdotes from her trip, telling me about the beautiful places she'd seen and how they contrasted with "those poor people's lives" who live near the excursion sites.

Cyndi wiggled in her seat. "How did she take the news of Thomas?"

The door chime rang, followed by my son, Dylan, rushing in, saving me from having to answer. I hadn't said a word to Bobby. To me, there was no news to report. We definitely weren't the kind of close that required sharing with my mother. I didn't know if we'd ever be. I still didn't think I'd want to risk my heart again.

I turned to my boy, his chest puffed, linebacker shoulders wider than normal, a peculiar strut in his step. "Morning, Lad. Would you like an Americano before work?" He was about fifteen minutes early for opening Mick & Hugh's.

"Sure. A double. Thanks, Mom. I have a question too." He bent down and kissed Cyndi on the cheek. "Morning, Aunt Cyn. Good to see you. This is more for you anyway."

"What is, honey?" Cyndi asked.

"Can I get a loan from my trust fund?"

I situated the porta-filter and turned around. "For the business launch? Your final project's far from finished." Not that I would know anymore. My kid's lips were locked tight regarding his thesis. "Isn't it early to be pulling money to finance it?"

He slid onto the stool next to Cyndi. "It is. I want the money for an engagement ring."

Hell-to-the-fecking-no. My hand shook so I nearly dumped the boiling water in the cup. Times like this made me want to curl myself into a ball and disappear. Or scream at the men who'd left us. Dylan benefited from men galore when he was a cocky little boy, and the stakes were *PBS Kids* programming versus *Nickelodeon.* Now when he really could use a man's ear and wisdom? He had me. *Thanks, guys.*

My boy needed a wife like he needed a hole in his head. Most *definitely* not a self-possessed-workaholic-med-student-with-her-own-family-dysfunction-issues wife. No way would I let him lay a finger on that money for a ring.

"Sweetheart," I started cautiously. "If you can't afford a ring from your bank account, take it as a sign to wait. Suzy has at least two more years of medical school."

Dylan turned from a twenty-four-year-old man to a toddler with puppy eyes in a heartbeat. He fixed his face on Cyndi, looking for help.

She raised her hands in defense. "Don't look at me, kiddo. I put the sing in single. I'm in your mama's camp."

My bestie. Loved her. We were definitely getting neighboring rooms at the old-folks' home. "You already live together, Dyl, and both your lives are intense this year. Why now?"

"Maybe *I* need it," he muttered.

I handed him his drink in a to-go cup. "Fine. What about asking one of your grandmothers? They both have multiple wedding sets, and they're gorgeous. The one Grandpa bought Bobby for their thirtieth anniversary is stunning. She doesn't wear it anymore."

"She has four grandsons. Don't forget Uncle Bert's boys."

"I haven't. You're her favorite by far." I held no delusions about Bobby's sense of fairness.

"Doesn't she still want it? Grandpa's death is so recent."

She all but threw it in the coffin with Dad. "I think she'd love a chance to be a part of your moment. Grandpa had amazing taste too." It had pissed me off when he'd given her the two karat ring as a peace offering. Another pointless effort to make her happy. After Bobby's icy response of "How nice. Isn't it odd how diamonds have no color?" I'd begged him to divorce her and finally seek his own happiness.

"I'll think about it. Thanks, Mom." Dylan kissed Cyndi and me on our cheeks and headed off to work. I swore he stood a little taller when he left. No small feat for my ginormous son who'd wanted a plan to feel secure. Perhaps I helped him after all.

"The first line of business." Thomas opened his arms wide for me to enter when we were safely in the privacy of my office. I stepped in, clinging to his waist, tucking my head against his chest, breathing in the sandalwood he probably used to wash or shave with or both. Thomas did more or less the same, burying his face in my mass of curls. I'd removed the scrunchie earlier to relieve a low-level headache.

Being together chased my doubts away. Since the first embrace in my kitchen, these stolen minutes filled me with hope and steeled my backbone as much as they turned me into a lust-crazed woman. We stayed like this until our heartbeats fell into sync. I was equal parts excited and terrified to admit I wanted more. Sometimes I wanted him every day. But we didn't have daily. So I pushed down the signs of clinginess and took what I could get.

Thomas peppered my jaw and neck with slow kisses. I flicked back my hair, giving him better access. His attention at the spot where my neck and shoulder met made me giggle, drawing a burly purr from him. "Discovering your spots is my new favorite hobby."

My hands trailed under his T-shirt and up across the tight muscles of his back. "I enjoy discovering you too." A desire to see him, to be with him fully washed over me until confusion set in. It was too soon, especially with Liam at home. I didn't even know if we'd *ever* become overnight people. The real problem was not knowing precisely what we were doing, what our goals were. If there *were* any. If I could ever get past the past.

Enjoy the now, eejit. You never know when it'll be gone.

Thomas scooted us to the edge of my desk and placed me between his legs. His lean made our heights match, so I took advantage. A flirty, teasing bite to his lower lip turned into a pleasant surprise when Thomas dove in, devouring me with an open mouth and his hungry tongue. His hand traveled from the back of my neck, down my arm, to my stomach. Jaysus. This. I'd missed it.

We both gasped and hummed like bees finding a favored flower when he pulled me closer until I brushed against his erection. Could he be ready for more? Or did he have the same apprehensions as me? We were moving a lot faster than I'd ever done, but I knew if Cyndi were in my shoes, she'd already know whether Thomas had any birthmarks and all that.

Without thinking, I took more, subtly giving Thomas's cock a grind until his movements froze. "I'm sorry darlin'. We need to stop."

"Wha—?" I breathed, the pull back to responsible Kick McKenna almost painful. My eyes swept him from head to toe when it hit me what was off when he'd walked in. "Hang on, why are you in a T-shirt and jeans in the middle of the day? Is everything okay?"

Thomas's cleft chin quivered with what could've been laughter at my undoing or unshed tears. I know I wanted to cry from the loss of his lips.

He tucked a curl behind my ear. "Time to talk."

In an instant, he masked up again; part of me was jealous of the ability. This hot-and-cold aspect of Thomas's personality wore on me too. From what I'd overheard in the café, it was the current way of dating. I figured I had to get used to it. Deep in my gut, a voice told me there was more, that he held back something big. But the truth wasn't always a friend. More than once, I'd considered it an enemy and would have gladly embraced self-delusion in hindsight. I wanted to be an easy place to fall, trusting it to be enough.

We each sat in a club chair before Thomas stated, "I'm leaving earlier than I'd planned for Bordeaux. Tomorrow, in fact."

"Oh." We'd made plans for… "The Raleigh State football game with Dylan and Suzy?"

"Yeah." He sighed, rubbing the back of his neck. "I have to cancel. It's about work."

I searched his eyes for signs of remorse, but as a person with plenty of experience canceling plans, I also knew the self-preserving value in distancing yourself from disappointment and moving ahead with the alternate course.

"Well"—I reminded myself to *be* the safe place—"we both knew things like this would happen." I leaned across the open space and grabbed his hand, lacing our fingers. I let the gentle hum roll through me even though it still startled me. His heavy calluses remained a mystery to me. It wasn't what I'd expect from the average professor and was another reminder we still had a lot to learn about each other. "It's about the research?"

Part of the mask lowered when he answered, "Yep."

"Can you get time for yourself while you're gone? I heard it's lovely there."

Thomas's hand moved up my arm to my neck, and he pulled

my forehead to his lips for a gentle kiss. "It is lovely." He let his head fall to mine on an exhale. "Your sweetness… I thought you'd be upset. This makes it harder."

I moved back to meet his gaze. "Thomas, we both have responsibilities. It's why we agreed to slow and casual."

"Yes, but…"

His work was a genuine passion, I wondered if he had any room in his head, let alone his schedule, for more. "Do you not want to go?"

He shook his head, found my hand again, and kissed my knuckles. "I hoped we could…"

I giggled. "Tell me about it. But I'll be here when you get back." If he only knew how many times I'd done this before. In my old life, I used to wait for weeks at a time before my husband would return. I often showed up alone for the kids' events. Hell, the last time I'd let myself think about dating again, I vowed never to get involved with a man who traveled for a living. Then again, I'd also vowed never to date a younger man. My breath grew shallow as my chest tightened. Here was my sign. We should let go and get out before we went too far.

"Thomas—"

"These past few weeks… you've been so good for me. I wish I could explain it better. Seeing you, talking to you, texting you. Hell, when you send me silly Pokémon notifications in the middle of my day and it's instantly better. Something in me is shifting." He lifted his head. I don't know what he found in my gaze, but his own suddenly filled with terror. "Damn, I've said too much."

But he hadn't. He'd said the words I needed to hear. "No, sweets. I feel the same. Please finish."

"Some crazy things have happened at work."

"Your assistant," I said, stroking his palm with my thumb. I couldn't imagine losing a protégé so tragically. My heart hurt for him.

"Yes, and more after. I'll get a lock on it. On me. I've been second-guessing myself at every turn. But you…"

"Me?" I waited and saw the words he couldn't say in his eyes. I wanted to keep him too. In whatever form we could find to work. Whatever it was we were doing, it helped. I kissed his palm. "Me too."

"You're making me want to whisk you away to someplace private."

His near pout made me smile. "Not very patient, are you?"

I received a sexy grin in return. "Normally, yes. Nothing steers me from my decided path. That's why I'm out of sorts over you."

"Ooh, flattery. Go on." I batted my lashes.

"I'm serious, Kick. Not upset, just confused. I don't know how to veer off my course, but it's all I can think about."

His words threw me. I wanted to help Thomas meet his goals, not interfere with them. "Maybe you should get a new compass?"

"Perhaps." Thomas tipped his chin like he took my words to heart. The words "let me be your compass" sat on my lips, itching to come out. I couldn't release them. While Cyndi's voice in the back of my mind egged me on, daring me to seduce and coax more from him, another one told me to be at peace with the present. That voice sounded a lot like Deana.

"How long will you be gone?"

"Ten days now. Since I'm going early, if I can leave the scheduled end, I will."

"Will you have time for calls? It's okay if you won't. I know how all-consuming business travel can be."

He stood and pulled me into his arms again. "I'll make time." He kissed my temple and said, "Can we get away when I come back? It doesn't have to be far. Maybe a simple overnight at my house?"

"I'd love to," I answered, unable to hide a grin, thinking of the things I'd like to do with him with an entire night's time and seeing the same thoughts reflected on his face. "But we already have plans for dinner with my kids next weekend."

"Right."

Based on the way he bit his lip, sexiness notwithstanding, I figured he'd forgotten. "Is it still on or should I—"

"No, no. I'll aim to get back for it. We can talk through the rest of our schedules while I'm gone."

"I'd like that too."

We sealed our plans with another thorough kiss, taking my breath away and almost making me beg to tag along on his trip to France.

"Y'all mind feeding me something to-go? I have to meet my neighbor soon." He held out the hem of his T-shirt. "The reason for casual clothes. My TA is teaching today."

I tsked and rolled my eyes in a sarcastic joke. "Make food for you? I suppose." I laughed and remembered something. "Do you have a ride to the airport? If you have an early flight, I could drop you off on the way to my IV appointment."

Thomas's shoulders dropped as he remembered what he'd promised me. "Dammit. I'm supposed to give you a ride."

My hand moved up his arm and stroked his back to ease his mind. "It's fine. Work has obviously demanded your attention."

"It would be great to see you again." He squeezed me tight and said, "Can you be at my place at seven thirty? I'll make breakfast."

"For me? Are you daft?" I laughed. Thomas had proven he took my food allergies seriously, but breakfast was a different animal.

"Only for you." He turned us away from my desk and whispered in my ear. "Don't worry, darlin'. I've paid attention."

What the hell. If I couldn't let Thomas fix a little breakfast, we didn't deserve to move forward. "Sure. Why not? I'll see Liam off to school and head over. You want me to bring anything?"

He kissed the top of my head and opened the door. "Just you. Thanks for trusting me."

My smile stayed broad as we walked out to the dining area, our fingers laced as Thomas followed me down the short hallway. Then we turned the corner, and my steps halted. My mother sat on a stool at the counter, staring straight at us. More accurately, she lasered in on our clasped hands, a shit-eating grin on her face.

22

Tainted Love

Kick

I DROPPED OUR HANDS AND BOLTED FOR THE COUNTER, ALL BUSINESS and service-oriented. Thomas didn't embarrass me, but until I knew for certain how to define us, we would be Bobby's new ammo of choice. Like a gun collector eager to fire a new weapon on a range, she would hungrily absorb this intelligence and shoot it off when it could do the most damage.

I quickly filled Thomas's order and sent him off with the friendly smile nearly every customer received, knowing exactly how cold I came off. I saw the confusion on his face as he pressed a quick kiss to my cheek, making it pinch with a sharp shock.

Deana watched it go down, taking a break from her inventory check to make sure I knew she saw me flinch. She told me how much I'd disappointed her without a word exchanged. Hell, I'd disappointed myself. I hated how my resolve crumbled when things didn't go as planned.

"I heard about… *him*." Bobby tipped her head in the door's direction.

"Good afternoon, Mother," I said as brightly as I could, ignoring shot number one while calculating which child had to die for blabbing. Probably Rachel.

"Regardless how much you deny it, you'll always be a bloody chip off the old block."

If I had a dollar for every time she'd said those words, or any other cliché for that matter. I deflected. "Aw, you missed the café when you left, didn't you? You should know, Hugh and Maggie have been stopping in again. They're doing well."

"*Pfft*," she answered, and I cherished the small win. I got her to answer my dig before responding to hers. Yes, it was petty. We were in danger of slipping straight back into our diseased habits.

"It's a wonder Hugh's chicken-shit wife goes anywhere other than the house and the senior center. Since he has a secret thing for me, it'll be fun to run into them now that I'm free."

Eww. Her words inspired an eye roll so thorough it was a wonder I still used glasses. There was no way I'd honor her ridiculous comment with one of my own, so I shifted back. "What brings you in? I thought you'd still be unpacking."

She jabbed her thumb over her shoulder, toward outside. "I have to get groceries. *Someone* left my refrigerator empty. I thought I'd see what your little group is up to before I go to the store. You sure you can afford the extra help? It's not like your father's around to make you more money." As if she honestly cared.

While working on the assembly line at General Motors, my father developed a side interest in stocks. He turned out to have a talent for it and grew his hobby into a side hustle. When I came into money, he turned it into enough to enable me to bolster the foundation and support trust funds for each child. Overall, I didn't hurt for funds but was aware of how quickly a café and an out-of-pocket doctor could soak up my bank account when not closely monitored.

"Kyle's keeping an eye on the money, and Cyndi keeps the books balanced. There's nothing to worry about." Before Dad passed, he'd taken Hugh's nephew, Kyle, under his wing. Kyle grew it into his own business.

Bobby checked her watch. "I don't like to shop when there's still a chance of a screaming toddler wandering the aisles. Get me a decaf cappuccino.”

One decaf latte coming up. Bobby always ordered a cappuccino despite her hatred of foam. I figured she simply found the word cool to say. She wouldn’t let me correct her anyway.

“I offered to have Carmen stock your kitchen before you came home, but you told me no.”

“No, you didn’t. You probably *thought* you offered but forgot to say something. You do that, you know. You should tell your fancy doctor about your poor memory. With what you pay her, the *least* she could do is fix it.”

Did I imagine it? I searched my memory bank and remembered our last phone call. I’d offered. If only she’d agree to email or text, I’d have written proof. Bobby proudly proclaimed an aversion to technology.

As I finished making her latte, three customers came in, giving me an opportunity for distance from Bobby, though her glare persisted. Crystal and I worked through another late-lunch group while Deana finished up in the back. The whole time, Bobby regaled tales from her cruise. When I could, I laid out the photos on the counter—actual photos. I admit, it was cute—admiring the gorgeous views from the Caribbean and South America. Every picture was filled with faces we’d never know, but the customer line and my crew learned their names, where they lived, where their grandchildren went to school, and whether their children were treating them right. Oh, and if said male children were married or single. Insert another eye roll.

At one point, Bobby leaned toward me, gossip-style, her favorite posture. She tipped her chin toward Crystal. “That one’s the village idiot.”

“The fu— Hell she is,” I whisper-yelled back. “She’s wonderful and you’ll leave her alone.”

“As long as she keeps away from me, we’ll be fine. Since you are here, get me another cappuccino. You’ve finally figured out how to make it right.” Bobby shivered and made a face. “No bloody foam. They never got it right on the ship.”

"Fine. I'm making it to-go. Then you can pop in on Dylan and ask him about his thesis project. It's coming along."

She waved me off. "I don't understand computer stuff."

"He'd explain it. Plus I think he has a question for you."

"Yeah? Is the shop still filled with smoke?"

Mick & Hugh's never filled with smoke. They invested heavily in air filtration, but she swore the store made her wheeze. "You'll be fine. It's slow this time of day."

She nodded her perfectly straight, limp, honey-blond bob thoughtfully. It highlighted her still crisp jawline and pert nose. A stunning woman, despite her consistent scowl, she was the opposite of me in virtually every way. "I'll do that. Thank you, dear."

"Have a nice afternoon, Mother." Happy to know we'd pulled it back from our usual cliff, my thoughts kept rerunning whether I'd offered to stock her kitchen.

Deana returned to the front, her purse over her shoulder, to make her usual end-of-the-shift to-go cup.

"Hey, Dee, did I offer to fill Bobby's fridge and pantry?"

She turned to me, her lips pursed. "I heard her, Kick. And yes. You offered to have Carmen do it though."

"Well, yeah. She's my house manager. She grocery shops for me." Lord knew I'd have no time or energy for it. Plus Carmen rocked. She'd saved my bottom many times.

"First, your mama thinks you eat weird food. Second, *if* she agreed, it would only be when a family member did it. Let it go, Kick. She's never gonna change. I heard her describing the local people in her pictures. That woman's a stone-chiseled—"

"So I didn't imagine it?"

She shook her head and laughed. "You're straight. You won't be in tomorrow, right?"

"Nope." We gave each other one-arm squeezes. "See you next week."

Liam passed Deana at the doorway. He beelined for me, a worried line running through his knitted brow.

"Something wrong, Weeman?"

"Have you heard from Snow?" he asked.

"No." As far as I knew, Rachel was safe and sound on campus. Thank goodness. I'd had my fill of family problems, but he gave me the feeling my plate was about to overflow.

Liam handed me his phone. "More viral shit about her went around school today."

23

Say it Right

Thomas

KICK JUMPED WHEN THOMAS WHIPPED OPEN HIS KITCHEN DOOR; HER fist stayed frozen midair, ready to knock one more time. He was still damp from a shower, jeans only half-buttoned, barefoot.

"Hey," he said, catching his breath.

"Hiya," she answered, worrying her tongue against her cheek. He was almost too distracted to remember he thought it a cute tell of Kick's anxiety. Almost.

"You're early. I just got out of the shower."

"So I see." Her hand opened and gently touched the nasty scar on his left bicep. "What happened here?" She'd seen him with a tank on when they exercised. And it was a large, ugly thing. How was she now noticing it? He didn't have the time, or the will, to tell the story of the scar. Neither the false one most people heard or the real one, not that he could tell her the truth.

He deflected. "It's chilly out there. Come on in." Thomas stepped back and watched her pass.

"Thank you." She stopped at the bench in the mudroom and laid her sweater down. Stepping into the bright kitchen, she spun in a circle, taking in the sunny space he'd updated first. He had done most of the renovations himself. "Oh, Thomas, this is beautiful. You did it?"

How did she conclude that without clarifying? He was beginning to think Kick could read him easily. Too easily.

Thomas covered her hand as it came to rest on the island counter, getting her attention. "I have to finish getting ready, darlin'."

"Darlin' still? So I'm not in the doghouse?"

"Pardon?"

"The last time we saw each other, I treated you like gum stuck to my shoe. Yet you still call me darlin'. Does this mean we're okay?"

Though he'd lived all over, he'd remained a Southern man first, calling any woman with friendship status darlin'. "Are you apologizing?"

Kick's shoulders dropped with her head, her shame screaming in her body language. "I am."

He sat in a stool at the counter, giving her his full attention. "Are you embarrassed by me?" He could relate to being hot and cold with an interest, though this was the first time he'd been the receiver.

"How do I explain this…?" Kick's head tipped back. She scratched at her temple before tucking a curl behind her ear. "It's best if Bobby hears as little as possible for now. I wanted time before she knew about us. If we… if we go our separate ways, she'll use it against me forever."

Thomas studied Kick's profile as the sun caught the curls at her crown, turning some a bright copper against the field of brown. He reached over and pulled back the one on her cheek. She'd given him a boatload of dysfunction to parse. One thing stood out though. "We'll be friends no matter what, Kick. We won't be going our separate ways."

She laughed and gave him her full gaze, a doubtful arrow or two shooting from it. "Really? Friends who kiss and grope each other into oblivion? Come on, Thomas. We're supposed to be planning a weekend away. I don't think it's for private cappuccino-making lessons."

Thomas shivered. "Good. I hate foam." For some reason, the comment made her belly-laugh. He was glad to lift the vibe in the room even if he didn't know why. "You know what I mean. We're friends with…"

Two of Kick's fingers suddenly covered his lips. "Don't say benefits. The phrase makes my stomach turn. Besides, I get we're going slow, but FWB is a total lose-lose."

Thomas turned his chin to kiss her palm. He knew slow. He did slow blindfolded with his wrists cuffed behind his back. He'd figure out the rest later. Hardened to the guilt that came from holding back, he said, "Don't worry about yesterday. You lost the ability to control what and how much a troublesome person knows. I've been there too."

Kick shook her head. "I can't believe my ears. Thank you."

"Still need to get ready. Mind waiting down here?"

"How about I make breakfast?"

Thomas glanced at the clock on the stove. Their delay made him run late. "Fantastic." He pointed to the fridge. "How do you feel about smoothies?"

"You kidding? It's the nectar of the immunocompromised. Your smoothie's in a master's hands. Now shoo." She waved him off with a smile. Thomas thought about her smile as he bounded up the stairs to his bedroom, his body humming with pleasure.

THOMAS HEARD KICK SINGING FROM THE UPSTAIRS LANDING. He couldn't help grinning as she danced at the kitchen sink, cleaning the blender. He stayed in the shaded area at the edge of the archway, watching her. Curls were bouncing, her pert ass swaying to Nelly Furtado's "Say it Right" while she sang along. She wore yoga pants and a T-shirt that fell to her hips. He'd learned she chose them for comfort and easy vein access—her IV day uniform. They did wonders to highlight her hourglass figure. She was a forest nymph, seducing him with her movements and sweet voice. Lost in the song and her work, he watched her lush lips move and eyes occasionally close from emotion in the reflection in the window. The need to adjust himself surprised Thomas. He wasn't a boy who worried about control. He was a man who defined himself by the word.

The words.

The words flowing from her mouth were the ones tapping on his soul for attention. They resembled the ones he kept locked away with his other impossibilities.

Seeing her in his space burned his heart more than the desire for a woman's touch. Outside of a cleaning service, Kick was the first woman to spend time here, and she didn't know the significance. Banger was the only other person who regularly visited Thomas's house, his sanctuary.

The room itself, gray cabinetry, black granite counters, and sage walls fulfilled his wish for a masculine, functional, and bright kitchen with modern conveniences. He designed it for himself; only Kick made the space look like a home.

He should have rushed breakfast and scooted them out, never to let it happen again, but he liked the view. He wanted more of it, feared it could become an addiction. As he glimpsed how life like this might work, the desire grew. Yet responsibilities to the Felidae pulled on him more than the weight of the luggage he balanced in his hand.

So he watched, frozen between his *musts* and his *wants*, knowing they wouldn't mix. *Screw it.* He left his suitcase and laptop bag in the hall, entered the kitchen, and encouraged Kick to finish the final bars of the song while he danced her around the airy space. The whole time, he contemplated the possibility of "what if."

Sliding into the passenger seat of Kick's Camaro, it struck Thomas how they'd gravitated to the same model vehicle—his almost fifty years old, hers about two. Like attracts like. For the first time since he'd received *Grand-père's* call, he was glad to get out of town. His mind and his libido kept wandering to places it had no business traveling. Trapped in her muscle car, reciting baseball stats in his head wouldn't help take his mind off the woman sitting next to him. He finished the smoothie she'd made. It tasted better than any he'd ever blended. *Damn her.*

Kick draped her left wrist at twelve o'clock on the steering wheel while her right hand caressed the shifter. It was another way she reminded Thomas of himself, driving like a champion rider bonded to a prized horse. He savored the feeling when he was alone in his own machine.

"For feck's sake."

"Wha-?" Her sharp tone jolted Thomas's thoughts.

She pointed to the SUV in front. "If this idiot's Rover can't handle the one-inch lip in the intersection's repave, he should take it to the sidewalk with the other Big Wheels. I mean, really? There's no reason he can't… oh, I don't know… drive over the tiny bump in his premium SUV."

He eyed her curiously. "I suppose." Fortunately, they maneuvered through town traffic quickly and eased into the twists and turns of a flowing country road again.

"Now look at this charmer," she complained about an oncoming car crossing the double line multiple times. "This one thinks her half of the road runs down the middle." She honked, and the driver's eyes lifted from her lap, then corrected the heavy sedan. Kick grunted. "Like I want to go another round with a texting bitch."

Thomas looked at her and laughed. Her eyes shifted to the side. "What tickles your funny bone?"

"I didn't peg you as a road rager."

Kick glanced over again. This time her jaw dropped, her posture defensive. "It's not road rage. Road rage is holding it in until you explode. I, on the other hand, say what's on my mind before it turns into a temper. So here I am, traveling happy as a bird because the bad juju flew away." She turned her head, a crazy, wide grin in place for emphasis.

Her eyes turned back to the road as she sped up. He needed this.

Focus on her flaws and get back to reality. She wasn't a mystical forest goddess. Kick was a typical, moody human.

She chanced another glance, and they erupted in laughter, Thomas shaking his head.

"Okay," she said, lifting her palm off the wheel in surrender. "I promise to be a lady for the rest of the ride." Her profile beamed. "But you know, Southern women can be nasty behind the wheel. Heaven forbid you meet one in a carpool line. Can't tell you how glad I am that those days are done."

"Banger told me something new went down with your daughter's harassment situation."

"Yeah." Kick brow creased. "The cyberbully attacked again. Unfortunately, Rachel has to keep the social media accounts for networking. Her boyfriend isn't supportive either. She should… Well, never mind."

"Why didn't you tell me?"

Kick glanced over. "I called the detective to make sure the harassment gets recorded. Since no one's threatened her per se… Well, Banger said he'd see what he could do."

"Y'all can tell me about these things, you know."

She shrugged a shoulder. "I wasn't sure you'd want to hear from me after the way I acted in the café, let alone hear me go on about my daughter's troubles."

Was his head really so far up his ass? He knew she'd screwed up in the coffee shop, but he'd been so focused on his own shit he'd barely given it a thought.

They fell into a comfortable silence, listening to music. Thomas resumed studying Kick's body as it handled the car. His eyes locked on her right hand. She was oblivious to the careful caressing of the grip as she harmonized with the singer on the radio. He could almost feel her hand doing the same thing to him. From the way she'd perked up, Thomas figured the song was a favorite. Soon she was equal parts driving and dancing. Thomas's breaths quickened, and he squeezed his eyes shut as he counted to slow his heart rate. The arousal became a given, but he didn't want to sport wood running through the airport or for the duration of the drive.

"You can nap until we arrive."

"Nap?"

"Your eyes keep closing."

"Oh. I was enjoying… the song."

She smiled brightly. "Yeah, 'Everlong' is great."

Thomas studied her profile, still swaying as she watched the surrounding vehicles. "You dance all the time, even here in the car. Did you ever take lessons?"

The morning sun through the trees edging the road striped her face in light and shadow like a strobe light. Her neck snapped to him. "What?"

"You're a natural dancer. You follow me like a proper partner. Even here, you've kinda figured out how to make a car dance." He opened his hands. "So I wondered if you've had formal training."

Kick nodded and chuckled, but not from happiness. Her stare traveled far into the past, the noise sarcastic. "I was Bobby's prized student at her dance studio growing up. Taught classes as a teen. She expected me to become a pro and do what she never had a chance to. Make her look good. She didn't take it well when I stopped."

"What happened?"

Kick bit her lip and focused on traffic instead of answering. When she finally did, the words came slow and deliberate. "No one alive knows the entire story. In short, there was a betrayal, and it killed my dancing dreams. I'd rather not say any more if you don't mind."

Thomas tapped her hand as it gripped to the shifter. "Alright. I'm glad you got it back."

A corner of her mouth lifted as her head tilted toward him. "No one's ever taking it from me again. And you make it fun."

The radio lit up with a jazzy song, sending Kick wild. He thought he heard Pee Wee Marquette speaking and shook his head. She cranked up the volume. "Come on, Thomas. You can't sit still for this one." She swayed and shimmied to the song. Her hands circled and crossed each other as she rapped along with the singer.

Thomas laughed and did his best car dancing to "Cantaloop

(Flip Fantasia)" until g-forces pressed him into the seat belt. At the same time, her hand flew to the stick, and she down-shifted to merge into a traffic snare.

Instinct made Thomas throw his arms out. One braced the dash for him, the other went to the side for her. And grabbed a handful of tit. He'd brushed fingers along the side of their softness already. But damn… the weight, the fullness in his hand… perfect.

Embarrassment swept through him, freezing him in place. Except his fingers twitched. Kick looked down, her previously panicked face melting into lust. Or embarrassment.

A guy in the car next to them flashed Thomas a thumbs-up. Then her nipple peaked between his fingers. They both gasped.

"I'm so sorry."

"Are you okay?" Kick breathed, sounding like Marilyn Monroe.

Thomas swallowed and almost choked on his cottonmouth. His hand flew to his lap. "Fine."

As they inched through the bottleneck, Kick quietly worked the car, biting her lower lip. When she chanced a glance in his direction, guilt, and possibly lust, filled her sweet face. "I let myself get distracted."

Adorable, feisty, vulnerable. The attraction he swam through wasn't just from holding the best thing his hand had felt in a long time. Her openness drew him in like steel to a magnet. Even when she kept information to herself, she was upfront about it. The word he couldn't shake, the one he was afraid to admit? *Sexy*. Christ, Kathleen McKenna was sexy as hell.

He couldn't take it anymore. "Spend the night with me when I get back. I'll have dinner with y'all. Then you can come back to my house."

The air between them stilled. Her posture slumped. "No, Thomas."

Why did he open his big mouth so soon? Oh yeah, he wasn't used to traditional relationships. They promised to go slow, and he'd pushed. "Right. Sure."

She reached across the console and squeezed his hand. "I want to spend time with you, and I want to have dinner with the kids."

Kick bit her lip and glanced Thomas's way. "It would feel weird to eat and take off."

"Weird how?"

"It's fast for me, though it's probably not to you." A pretty pink rushed up Kick's neck to her hairline. "Casual's new for me, Thomas. Spending the night doesn't feel casual. I'm trying to embrace the idea, but what if I can't?" She raced through the gears on the freeway ramp.

"You want to wait?" His tone asked, but his heart stated it.

Kick moved into the fast lane and purred, "I… I think so. But I don't always trust my head. I'm afraid of sending mixed signals."

He chuckled at her answer. "There's no way you could. You express everything you think, both verbal and physical." Didn't she see he was the one wrapped up in contradictions, not her? He slowly kissed her knuckles and bit his tongue to keep from confessing everything.

24

Riviera Paradise

Thomas

THOMAS RAN THE HILLS OF CHÂTEAU LONGÉVITÉ, ALARIC KRAUS'S vineyard and the headquarters of the Felidae Society. Crisp autumn air cleared his head as he set one foot in front of the other. Rows of harvested grapevines were the country version of a grid of city blocks surrounding Lord University. Steep hills comprising the grounds were definite cousins to the Piedmont neighborhood.

Since he'd arrived in Bordeaux, Thomas had traded one set of stressors for another. The tension at dinner the first night was thick enough to cut with a steak knife.

He'd spent the previous day in the drawing room, giving his presentation and fielding questions from his colleagues. Each team had mission parameters dependent upon the others, therefore the Felidae met regularly. Despite the space's opulent size, Thomas struggled to breathe freely by evening. The room had developed a thick, musty essence.

Thomas welcomed this morning's fresh air and solitude. His body had left Raleigh, but his thoughts stayed with the chestnut curls, porcelain skin, and sparkling hazel eyes back there. He'd expected pressure to produce would put her out of his mind. Smug, competitive comments from Nigel, the head of the Oxford team, didn't do the job either. Braggadocious reports on the man's progress with telomerase did nothing to poke through Thomas's indifference.

Thomas didn't seek glory the way Nigel did. Thomas only wanted to be sure his unique life had made a difference before he let it go. Last spring, he'd craved results like they were water. He'd been certain his theories were the ones to follow, where he'd find the genetic secrets of the Felidae members. He and Nigel worked the same questions from different angles, hoping it helped them get answers faster. Certain it would change the world, solve most, if not all illnesses, he wanted to help. He wasn't sure what had happened.

Lately his passion for research had lessened. He was desperate to help Toni back in Virginia. However, he wasn't so sure about anything or anyone else. He wondered if Presley hadn't been on the right track for the wrong reasons. Maybe they should study the genes of the Felidae against random people. Maybe he was making it harder to find answers.

Thomas almost ran into a crew setting up mechanical harvesters in the last fields with fruit as his head swam with his new idea. The crisp aroma of white grapes riding on a breeze hit his nose before he heard the commanding voices. He pivoted, taking a two-track lane up to the top of the hill. Alone again, he rested on a boulder. Many stones of varying sizes lay under an ancient tree. They'd been there for decades and were used to repair garden walls and such. He had helped the grounds crew with this kind of work plenty of times.

Hard work wouldn't bring the peace he sought though. He'd woken from a restless sleep with a tight throat like he was suffocating. Staying in Banger's family's airy corner suite overlooking the river didn't help.

Growing up at the base of a Virginia mountain, Thomas learned to find solace in his favorite vista near his family's land. High above the frenzy of life, he could reset. He let his eyes soften and did just that on top of the rock.

The heads of tall grasses gone to seed tickled his ankle resting on the edge of the boulder. Before he knew it, he transported himself to a familiar, inner place he hadn't been to in ages. His breath slowed, clearing tension from his body. He found serenity in the nothingness. Light winds continued traveling through the river valley, surrounding him like a blanket, tickling too-long hairs on his neck, welcoming him back with faint scents of vegetable canning, meat smoking, and leaves burning. He didn't know how long he'd stayed on the rock. He let go of the stress pressing on him, let go of concern for his family, said goodbye to Presley and her potential. He let loose the sharp ache in his chest whenever he thought of her family's pain—a pain he knew too well.

In the quiet, there were no microscopes to use or theories to prove, no algorithms to run, no blood to study. There was only an accord with nature and an occasional bird call with a suspiciously Midwestern, sexy chuckle. Kick found him, even in this space, but he welcomed it. His lips curved up at the sound.

Thomas opened his eyes and saw a bluish light, similar to the waters of the French Riviera, running along his skin. This, too, he welcomed like a long-lost friend. It hadn't happened to him since Uncle Theo had died.

He knew some Felidae manifested unique physical abilities. It was part of how he adjusted his appearance when needed. He hated calling them "powers" as some members did. He'd heard others had developed an aura, usually when emotions were at their highest. He'd never mentioned his capacity to do so to *Grand-père* or anyone else since it had stopped long before he met the Felidae. Thomas had figured he'd lost it. Until this moment, he'd viewed the experience like it reflected inner feelings. He'd never considered it could bring peace. He wondered if it could do more.

"THANK YOU FOR LETTING ME TAKE THE MORNING OFF." THOMAS said to Alaric. "The break helped." He'd struggled for half a minute with the perceived lack of support for the other teams. Well, until he asked himself what would Banger do? Five minutes later, he was out the door.

Thomas and Alaric met for lunch in the old man's office, dining away from the rest of the conference attendees. His mentor took a special interest in Thomas and the North American team while Alaric's partner, Eleanor, had charge of the European members. She worked closely with Thomas's counterpart, Nigel, and the others at Oxford.

"*De rien.* You appear… invigorated," he answered with a sentimental concern. Alaric had taken Thomas under his wing when Banger brought him into the fold. Therefore the term *Grand-père* held a dual meaning. Most used it out of respect. For Thomas, it was personal.

Sitting behind a regal desk in a dark-paneled office with towering windows, Alaric looked out of place at first. He wore a collarless linen shirt, a homespun wool vest, and worn jeans, preferring simpler fabrics and style. Steady energy defied his silver hair and beard, though it reflected in his amber eyes. Bronzed skin gave evidence of his work in the vineyard. He had recently spent long days toiling to bring in the harvest, only leaving the last few fields to the grounds crew when the Felidae members arrived.

Photos going back more than a century stood in front of books lining three walls. The wood in the room was rich, cared-for, and original. The flooring was wide-planked and as worn as the Aubusson rugs sitting atop it.

"The morning was… enlightening. *Merci encore.*"

"*Ce n'est pas la mer à boire.*" Alaric waved his wrist, indicating his favor was no big deal despite the dirty looks Thomas had received from more senior members as he headed out for his run. The old man took a sip of seltzer water and lime before saying, "Tell me about your Toni. *Est-ce qu'elle va mieux?*"

Thomas nodded. "She's doing better, yes." *Grand-père* raised his brows, waiting for Thomas to expand his brief answer. He chuckled at the old man who missed nothing. "I'm not hiding anything. Promise. Joe has Toni meditating twice a day and goes with her to the memory-care facility when she visits Ken. Still, it's her transition. Neither Joe nor I"—Thomas tipped his head toward Alaric—"nor can y'all for that matter, do it for her."

"*Oui,*" his mentor agreed.

"For my research? Toni's shown quantifiable changes in telomere length. As I mentioned during the presentation, we've found a new DNA variance," Thomas continued. "I'm anxious to see what comes of it." He rubbed his chin, still thinking about his revelation during the run. "I want to dive deeper into studying her mitochondria when I get back. It would be helpful if there were someone else to study—someone in a similar stage to Toni. Y'all don't know of anyone, do you?"

Alaric scoffed in his Gallic way. "Only you had the foresight to keep track of extended family. The rest of us were too eager to hide from them."

"It was easier to hide back then too. It's damned-near impossible to keep tabs on everyone now." Thomas settled back in the chair. He had asked the question, knowing it wouldn't go anywhere. He hoped by saying it, someone else would go digging. He would quietly spread the idea around with other members.

He resumed sharing about the lab, remembering Banger's direction about not mentioning the blackmail. "Losing Presley was a devastating setback, but I'm pressing on. Her replacement made a huge mistake the night before I left." Thomas chuckled, remembering the embarrassment on Bethany's face. Her face was green when he arrived, making him worry she was about to vomit from fear. He almost canceled the trip, but Banger was the only member he knew who could consider a summons to be optional. "She'll never forget her blunder and won't repeat it at least."

"I don't like you doing this work around the unworthy. Too much is at stake."

Did Alaric know about Presley's letter? "I didn't have the credentials to set up a proper lab when I first started. My people all sign NDAs when they start working for me." Thomas pinched the bridge of his nose, readying himself to confront his greatest annoyance. "Moreover, my associates aren't unworthy, as you put it. Plenty of people outside the Felidae are important and worthy to me."

Alaric scoffed at the comment. "You'll understand one day."

Thomas shook his head. He understood their prejudices, but he'd never accept them as his own.

Grand-père glanced at his door, seemingly to verify he'd closed it. "The thing is, dear boy, it's vital that we are the ones who find the answers. We must beat the Oxford team. *Now.*"

Thomas leaned forward in his chair, his elbows on his knees. "Aren't we all working toward the same goal? Finding out who or how we are? Along with changing the course of disease resistance in greater humanity?"

Alaric's gaze sliced to the door again, then back to his protégé. His normally warm expression chilled. "I'm not so sure. Update me personally from now on. Don't use the computer portal. I'll pass pertinent information to the rest of the members."

For as long as Thomas had been with the Society, he'd never known it to have factions. There were teams in the Western Hemisphere and sister societies around the world, but they worked together. This sounded like discord. The secrecy conflicted with his understanding of research culture. "What am I to say if another team contacts me for a consult?"

The icy glare warmed with a hint of admiration. "You double-speak like a master." The old man broke into a gravelly laugh. "As long as you don't use it on me. But I'll know if you do. I always find out."

Thomas swallowed hard and bit the side of his tongue. The château and the Felidae had been a refuge for him since they'd found him wandering the Mediterranean—a veteran with PTSD. Until this visit, he couldn't imagine holding anything back.

The sound of Alaric's voice pulled Thomas back to the room. "Tell your Toni I'm thinking of her. As soon as you have valid proof of her transition, I'll come for a visit. We're excited at the prospect of a rare female."

"She's not yet old enough to make it official."

Alaric stopped Thomas with a raised hand. "As technology advances, so should our policies. *N'est-ce pas?* Quantifiable proof she's one of us could override an age requirement for me. We didn't wait for Raphael after all." Alaric only used Banger's given name. He was one of three people allowed to do so.

"He was different," Thomas said. "Banger's parents were already Felidae when they made him their ridiculous experiment."

In this one instance, Alaric and Thomas disagreed. The old man had given his blessing to more or less "breed" the rare Felidae woman way back when. It had been an epic disaster, breaking Banger's mother and shining a light on his father's monstrous side. No one ever attempted it again.

Even though Alaric considered it water under the bridge, it irritated Thomas that he had never apologized to Banger for his role in his friend's disastrous upbringing.

Thomas leaned forward to stand, but Alaric stopped him by clearing his throat. "There's more."

He sank back, feeling like a kid. "What can I do?"

With his fingers steepled, elbows on the centuries-old country desk, *Grand-père* began tapping out a scale pattern. Thomas's eyes fixated on the fingers, watching their rhythm grow faster and started when his mentor spoke. "Using your original name again… I worry about what it implies."

Thomas opened his mouth to answer but shut it when the old man raised a hand. "I know melancholy when I see it. You're lonely, no? You might not believe it, but I remember the feeling. Trust my wisdom and cultivate more interests."

"I have work, the gym, music, renovating the farmhouse. I'm also thinking about moving my horse down. I visited my neighbor's stable right before leaving."

Alaric nodded politely. "What about a bit of romance?" He flashed his eyebrows. "Your arrangement with the Vivienne woman was good for you, no?" He resumed the tapping. "I thought the new assignment would recharge you, but you haven't been the same since her."

Thomas's jaw dropped open. "Y'all knew about Viv?"

A corner of the old man's mouth lifted into a mischievous smirk. "I had eyes on her. We told you we'd vet our new members for security reasons." His head gently tilted side to side. "It was obvious you kept your vow to us, so it continued. It's admirable how well you have separated your lives. You could arrange that again."

Thomas shook his head, incredulous. He should've known. What did Alaric mean by *let it continue?*

Kick was nothing like Vivienne though. Thomas and Viv were madame and client for years before he moved her to New York from Paris. Afterward, they still lived apart, spending time together but always keeping separate homes and agendas.

Kick was the anti-Vivienne. Involvement with her demanded a complete buy-in. There was his struggle. Hell, she gave everything to random customers. To a partner? She'd devote her soul. It would be beautiful. And he'd take it.

Thomas shrugged, unsure of what to say or do. "Life's different now, so are my needs."

Alaric's fingers stilled. He raised his hands in surrender. "All I ask is for you to find a way out of this mood. I don't worry about any… attachments you find. When the project's complete, I'll still need you. It'll only be the beginning."

Perhaps his mentor had a point, except… "You know you're asking two opposing things, right? It's nearly impossible to keep this tight schedule and maintain a social life. Hell, I had to stop coaching classes at the gym and rarely substitute anymore."

Alaric gave Thomas a distinctly French shrug. "You've handled more pressure with grace." He leveled Thomas with a piercing blue stare. "Maybe it's time to—"

A knock on the heavy door interrupted them. "Good afternoon, gentlemen." Eleanor Guillaume's voice carried from the other side. "May Chloe clear your plates?"

"*Oui.* Come in."

The elegant mistress of Château Longévité entered the room, wearing a concerned smile. She gestured for the maid to clear the desk, waiting with her hand across the back of Thomas's chair. Though she focused her daily efforts on the European team, she gave affection for each member without favoritism.

Thomas tipped his head to flash her a soft smile. She wore her tawny hair in a blunt bob and dressed as if she belonged in a sixty's movie with a Henry Mancini score. At first glance, she appeared maybe thirty, but her true age showed in her eyes and the way she carried herself. No one maintained the posture Ellie possessed—like a woman born to rule.

"The afternoon session begins in thirty minutes if you gentlemen are planning to join us."

He turned to Alaric, who nodded once, regal in his own casual way. Thomas pivoted back. "We'll be there *Grand-mère*. Thank you for the reminder."

Ellie brushed her fingers on his shoulders. "I know how you two lose time when you lock yourselves in here." She clucked her tongue and continued, "I miss the days when you could come and go as you please, Thomas... when you were Michael. Alas, you have a job now..." She took a step toward the door and turned back. "The clothes are new, no?"

Thomas shrugged, looking down at the jeans and button-down shirt Kick had helped him pick out.

"Everyone's casual these days—even the French." She shivered as if the thought equated Hades finally freezing over. "A wise choice, though I'll miss your formality. You were one of the few left to dress like a real man." She brushed her fingertips through the sides of his hair, the way a mother or aunt might. "I miss the gray sprinkles too."

Thomas made a note to himself to bring his old things the next time he visited. He hadn't planned what he'd placed in the suitcase. Outside of wanting to be professional at work, he didn't think about it much at all. His hands had practically reached for the new clothes on their own when he was packing. But if it made Ellie a little happier, he could remember for next time.

In the weeks since their afternoon shopping, T-shirts and a few other items had shown up in his mailbox with notes from Kick saying the item had been on clearance so he wouldn't fuss. That she thought of him made him warm to each piece.

"Thank you, Ellie," he said. "Your taste is impeccable, and your approval means a lot."

As she left the room, Thomas's cell phone buzzed with a text.

He hoped it wasn't the lab with another mishap. He swiped the device awake and frowned.

BANGER

911. Call. Don't text.

Too many possibilities could be behind those ominous words.

"You frown. Is something wrong?" Alaric asked.

"An emergency from Banger. I'll return it up in the suite."

"I ASSUME YOU FOUND SOMETHING," THOMAS SAID TO BANGER OVER their secured chat.

"Two things, actually. I'm certain there's a mole, but I haven't found him, her, or them yet. So, watch your back, brother."

Thomas stretched his neck. "Wow, you and *Grand-père* are on the same page."

"Not sure I'd trust him right now either, though it's doubtful he's a mole."

"If I can't trust Alaric, I may as well get out, don't you think?"

"Would that we could," Banger answered. "The Felidae is more like the Hotel California, brother. No one leaves."

Joe had left though. Thomas pinched the bridge of his nose, wishing the merry-go-round would stop. "You said there was a second problem."

"Right. How do I say this?" Banger only worked with the best equipment, so the resolution on his face was crystal clear when his face darkened. "There's reason to believe your assistant was murdered."

Thomas's head dropped with exhaustion before his gaze returned to the screen. "How? Why?"

"The accident wasn't your standard hit-and-run. Think about it, Thomas. There were only two people in her research file, and you didn't kill her."

Incredulous, Thomas laughed. "You think Nigel did though? Damn, man, I'm the better candidate. Besides, her ultimatum had implications for all of us. If she *had* come after me, you know you'd have taken her out."

"True," Banger agreed, his tone icy and factual.

"Fine." Thomas sighed. "I'll keep my ears open and my mouth shut." Desperate to change the subject, he added, "What about Kick's ordering box? Did the camera pick up anything?"

"It did. We found a partial tattoo on one of the perps. None of her staff recognized it, but we're checking local artists. She also agreed to adding another camera back there." Banger's tone grew irritated. "She won't let me run the system at her house though. You need to talk with her."

Confused, Thomas asked, "Did something else happen? I'm kinda removed from y'alright now."

Banger shook his head. "It's the violence of the attack on her squawk box. The smear campaign continues too. This is beginning to look personal, and she's acting like a petulant child. My people could keep her in a ring of safety, but she won't let us."

"You make it sound like you want to trap her in."

Banger's eyes narrowed. "Not you too."

Thomas ran a hand along his jaw, thinking. He didn't want to admit Banger might be scaring him. "Alright, are there other options? What if I can't get through either?"

"I'm working on it, but hate going rogue on a client, you know? Listen, I'm not asking you to fly your ass back here. Extra cameras probably won't pick up anything. But I can't do my job if I can't be sure."

"I'll talk to her, Bang."

"Make her agree."

Thoughts of research dissipated as he hung up with Banger and dialed the woman holding center stage in his thoughts again.

The call went to voice mail three times.

Dammit, they kept missing each other.

Control

Kick

At first, Uncle Hugh didn't see me standing in the doorway to his office. Or he acted like he didn't notice.

"You rang?" I asked in a failed deep, rumbly voice.

Without looking up, Hugh answered, "If Lurch had looked like you, I would watch *Addams Family* reruns." He gestured to my father's chair. Their desks had been on opposite walls. "Pull it over here."

I did as commanded and sat.

Still shuffling papers, Uncle Hugh dropped a bomb. "I want to make you an offer, Kick."

"One I can't refuse?" I asked, this time in a slightly better *Godfather* imitation.

He finally looked up. "You're full of jokes today."

I slumped in the chair. "I'm really in a bad mood and trying not to spread it around."

"Oh, well then, you better spill before I ask my question." Hugh rolled his hand as I sat in stubborn silence.

"Fine," I started, "it's Thomas. He's been a jerk ever since he left for Europe. I swear, a sense of foreboding had washed over me when I dropped him off at the airport. He's practically incommunicado when he promised he wouldn't be. Since I've heard all this before…"

"It brings up old issues."

I nodded. "Yup. Ones I swore I'd never allow again too. But enough about me."

Thomas had canceled our weekend plans for another emergency trip, this one to his home in Virginia, adding a week onto the timeline. He flew there straight from France. I understood responsibilities, especially when family needed you. I'd also spent too much time in the relationship limbo that came with a traveling man. It grew old quickly and only worked when there was a commitment to stay in touch. We hadn't though. It contributed to why I'd watched my patience slide through my fingers. One moment I'd wonder if there was a future for Thomas and me. In the next moment, I'd scold myself for thinking ahead when we were being casual, whatever that meant. Each day that passed made me doubt more.

"You two are an item then? I thought I saw sparks during the poker game."

I casually lifted a shoulder. "We're supposed to be *special* friends, I guess. Taking it slow. But this feels more like out of sight, out of mind."

Hugh clicked his tongue while shaking his head. "Young people… What the hell is a *special* friend anyway? In my day, when you knew, *you knew*. I asked Maggie to marry me after two weeks."

"Marry?" I almost yelled, certain I made a sour face.

"You don't want to marry again?"

I swiped my hand through the air. "*Hell* no. It doesn't mean I'm okay with living in limbo though." I also didn't want to dwell on my hurt. Most of my disappointment was in myself for the vulnerability that resulted in my bad mood. The last time we'd managed a solid minute of conversation, his voice was ice-cold, so I made an excuse and let him go. It grated. He knew I'd had enough of begging people to care, only to watch them drop me like a hot potato. He'd been the one to ask me to drop *my* walls? Let him in?

To add to the annoyance, Thomas and Banger had ganged up on me to have Angel Security install cameras with motion-activated mics at my house. My café participated in a beta group, testing the newest system, but Banger didn't have it in a residence and claimed it would be a favor to him as much as safety for me. The business was one thing, but hell if I'd agree to imprisonment at home.

I leaned on the front of Hugh's desk. "Can we skip my problems and jump to why you called?"

He inhaled a deep sigh, seemed to brace himself, and dropped a bomb. "I want to expand into cannabis…" My jaw dropping must have given away my shock. "Hear me out." Hugh cut me off.

I sat back and nodded, giving him the floor.

"Good. My contacts on the tobacco board are open to trying out a model where cannabis is sold in a smoke shop." He chuckled. "Most of the first round of licenses went to what they call the young hippie types. They think shops like mine will make it look more respectable. So I've been reading up on it."

Holy hell, I bet the cronies on the oversight board never even spoke to one of those "hippie kids." I'd been to a few dispensaries looking for pain relief. They had great intentions but tended to lack knowledge. I held up a finger and waited for permission to speak. "One, there's a lot—I mean a boatload—to learn about the product. People don't just smoke it anymore. Then there are the strains—"

"Like I said, I've been researching. I would hire someone to manage it." He leaned down like he had a secret. "Sylvie, next door, is letting her lease go in the spring."

"So you'd expand."

"Yes, it would be two stores in one."

I couldn't help thinking of the old video stores with the X-rated stuff in a back room. I laughed at the idea. Hugh's brow furrowed.

"Hell, I thought you planned to tell me you're selling. Are you sure you don't want to retire?" I asked.

"That's a big part of it. I'd feel better stepping back with bigger profit margins. It's night and day compared to what I do now. I'll be able to be an owner in name only."

That was practically his situation now, but I didn't want to sass. I said, "Well, if you and Maggie feel good about it, I say go for it. You'll have my support."

Hugh removed his hat, brushed it off, and set it behind him, signaling he wasn't through. "I want more than your support, Katie. I want your partnership."

"Wha-what? Why would I—" Did he not see my busy, crazy life?

"By the time we'd have our grand opening next fall, Liam will be gone to school."

"So I'll have enough time to run two stores? I love you, but are you nuts?"

He coughed and scratched his head. Sweat glistened on his forehead, and I finally saw Hugh's fear. He'd had my dad to lean on for this venture before. Now he was going it alone. I could relate.

Hugh sheepishly continued, "I see you as a consultant. Help me hire the right person to set it up. Some retail-oriented dispensaries have classes that help cancer patients and others with chronic pain or illnesses. You know, like yours. I thought you could lead one of those if you'd like. Or at least steer me in the right direction to find someone." He wiped his brow. "Mostly, I need your signature. Despite their prejudices, my general assembly contact told me there's a preference for women and minorities getting the new licenses. He liked the idea of giving it to a proven businesswoman attached to a smoke shop with a good reputation."

It encouraged me that Hugh hadn't brought up the rumors about the coffeehouse or me. It let me know the nonsense hadn't spread beyond Oakville.

I lifted the hair off my neck. "I wish Dad were here to talk to." From what Hugh just said, they both would still want my help.

"Me too, Katie. Me too."

I gestured toward the folder in front of him. "Is this your proposal?"

"It's a copy of everything I've gathered so far."

"Hand it over. I'll take a look."

•   •   •

I settled in at my dad's old desk, reading Hugh's notes. His ask still had me in shock. I couldn't believe he'd want to take on such a project. Then I looked at his numbers and wished he hadn't already gone home. They seemed too good to be true. I highlighted them and made an entry on my calendar to call him in the morning.

I also tried Thomas's phone again. It went straight to voice mail. I left a quick message and braced myself for another rejection. My thoughts drifted to the past and lingered there, wishing life had been different. My phone buzzing a text snapped me out of the unhealthy daydream.

LIZ

Are you free to talk to someone?

With a sigh, I resigned myself to dealing with the day. A new business opportunity could wait. So could my issues with Thomas. Maybe we were better off as friends. At least we'd only kissed.

ME

Coming.

Jonn Graham stood across the counter from Liz, in a situation reminding me of the one I'd found between him and my daughter. Did this kid never learn? "Do you like sushi?" he asked Liz. "I know the new bartender at the place up the road. I could pick you up later."

"What's going on, Liz?" I asked before she could answer Jonn. I didn't want her on his radar for rejecting him.

He turned to me and folded his hands at his chest. "Hey, Mrs. Mack. I didn't know you were here."

I nodded slowly. "I help Hugh out sometimes."

"Wow, you are Wonder Woman." He was unusually chipper.

"What can I do for you?" I didn't think he wanted cigars, but Liz could've sold him some anyway.

"I heard the old man here is hiring—" he began.

"I tried to tell him—" Liz interrupted before I held up my hands to stop them both.

"First, Hugh Reynolds owns this store. That's why it's called Mick and Hugh's. Calling him 'the old man' doesn't make a good impression, Jonn."

I stepped next to Liz and noted she had completed her inventory assignment. I gave the tablet back. "Why don't you finish up while I speak with Mr. Graham?" Despite his pleasant demeanor, I remembered his burst of temper the last time I turned him down. I wanted to put distance between Liz and us.

She did a double take to me. "Um, sure." Then she slowly made her way to the opposite wall.

I set my hands on the counter. "Jonn—"

He leaned in, his hands matching mine. "When we talked before, I may have had some bad bud. I apologize."

"Okay, but—"

"I'm serious, Mrs. Mack." He dipped his chin and looked through his lashes like my kids did when they were little. "You were right about the barista position, but I could do this. There's potential here, and I could help bring in a young vibe. I'd like to get real-world experience while I go to business school, then open my own store."

Shit. The kid made a good point. But Hugh didn't have the energy to mentor a kid like Jonn. He needed experienced help. Hugh really needed another manager, someone more like my father.

He leaned back on the counter. "What do you say? Can I fill out an application?" Before I could answer, Jonn added, "You told me before about going to school and finding my calling."

I nodded. "Yes, I did but—"

"You were right. *This* is my calling." Jonn moved his arm around the store.

I'll bet.

He continued, "It turns out I love business." He shifted and grinned. "I have my dad's talent for sales."

No kidding.

"I also hate construction. All those picky housewives..." The boy violently shivered for effect. "If I show serious interest in another venture, Dad will get off my ass—I mean case. Sorry."

I could understand him there. I might have loved dancing as a girl but not enough to do it professionally. The times Bobby and I butted heads after I gave it up made me shake too.

I stepped back and folded my arms, studying Jonn. This polite, humble version of him put me off. I'd never seen this side before. His cocky side still showed, but dare I say he possessed a delightful demeanor?

"Opportunities are also about timing. Mick & Hugh's needs people with experience. Maybe after you have some time in school." If he showed promise, minds could change. If we went ahead with the expansion, we'd have openings in a year.

Graham's eyes narrowed to slits, and he swiped a display off the counter before yelling, "So that's it? You won't even tell him?"

Ah, there was the asshole we all knew and avoided. My hands went up at the crash. "Whoa!" I caught Liz's eyes and tipped my head, telling her to move back to the counter. I wanted her near the emergency button in case Jonn wouldn't leave.

"That's not what I was saying," I started. Did it matter? Of course I'd let Hugh know about this, but Jonn's outburst changed everything.

The music switched right then to Janet Jackson's "Control." The words hit me like a sledgehammer to the gut. Since my dad died—hell, we could take it back to when I'd begun getting sick—the thing I'd fought the most for was control. Control of my body, of my world. The song gave me the push I needed to not back down.

"Mr. Reynolds receives notes on everything that happens when he's gone. It doesn't mean he'll have a different answer." My arm swept toward the door. "Now please—"

Graham's jaw flexed as his face turned red. "You McKennas are a couple of self-righteous bitches, aren't you? Dad and I wanted to help you. Make your bad publicity go away."

My temper was already on a short leash. I didn't want to lose it, but his words stopped me. "Excuse me?"

"My father is friends with the newspaper editor, plus he can put in a good word with the Chamber of Commerce."

I didn't know the kid knew the word *commerce*. I didn't understand what the Chamber of Commerce had to do with any of this. Nor did I see how the Grahams could make the sickening gossip go away.

Jonn snapped his fingers. "Poof. Everyone will love you again."

Sure, business was down and some of it had to do with the slander, but I had plans to deal with it. I had my own connections and figured it wouldn't be long until the spotlight turned somewhere else. I was more concerned about who was harassing Rachel.

I turned back to Jonn. "We've said our peace. It's time for you to leave. If you won't, I'll have Liz call the police."

"For what?" he spat out. "Tripping and accidentally knocking over a rack of cutters?"

He stepped at me, pushing me toward the walk-in humidor. My hands came up to block another advance, but they merely whooshed in a circle. Graham had vanished from my personal space, literally lifted into the air. By Thomas.

26

Send Me on My Way

Kick

"I'm not finished," Jonn Graham yelled.

"The hell you aren't," Thomas snarled. He took the kid by his collar and frog-marched him toward the door, leaving me equal parts stunned, infuriated, and turned on. My confusion returned.

Dylan arrived too, standing in the doorway; his eyes took a beat to settle on each of us. "What the fuck's going on?" He walked up to Graham, chest out and towering over him with as much menace as he could muster.

Thomas answered, "He's leaving."

Graham simultaneously said, "You'll see what happens when my father hears about this. Soon there will be two failing businesses."

Dylan opened the door, and Thomas pushed Jonn out with another growl of "You're done with the McKennas. If I hear you've been in the café or here, you'll deal with me."

Graham yelled from the sidewalk for anyone in earshot to hear. "Self-righteous assholes! Everybody knows you're sick." He pointed at Dylan. "You hardly work anymore. Mrs. Mack sells drugs to kids to keep the doors open 'cause no one's coming in.

Everybody knows it. You need our help or you might as well close."

I jolted at his words. Did the community believe we were on the verge of going under? Right as I thought I was making incremental progress with my mountain of stress, it slid back down, stress boulders piling up around me.

The kid must have known about his father's offer. It shouldn't have surprised me, but it rankled having him use it against me.

Thomas's hand came to my back, rubbing gently to release the tension, making it worse. He wrapped his arm around my shoulders and pulled me into his chest, kissing my temple. "Think nothing of it, darlin'. The asshat's trying to save face."

Still absorbing Graham's accusations, I followed Thomas back into the shop, my eyes connecting with his smile but not responding. I'd gone numb. Part of me wanted to throw myself at Thomas and welcome him back. Thanks to his radio silence, seeing him shocked me.

Once inside, Thomas gathered me into his arms. "I missed you," he whispered in my ear.

As I stood against his body, the numbness melted into heat but not the lust-filled kind. My hands slid from Thomas's waist to the front of his chest, zapping my palms as if electrocuted. I pushed him back, and saw red. I wrapped his tie around my hand, not giving a care that he'd worn one of his sexy suits again. Everything about him annoyed me now. I pulled him into my office, keeping my cool long enough to say to Liz and Dylan, "Excuse us."

The word *control* came back to me as I kicked the door shut. Thomas's darkened eyes beamed at me, filled with his own lust. To make matters worse, his sexy grin fanned my irritated flame. I'd give him action but not the kind he expected.

He wanted me to lean on him? To ask him for help. To be *more*. Then he left me hanging. That said way more than his sweet little heart-to-heart had. It was time I took back control.

"How. Dare. You," I growled.

Thomas stepped back, hands in the air, confusion replacing desire. "What'd I do?"

I paced the room, focusing on the hum of the air filters to pull my thoughts together. My emotions stood up and declared themselves, but the words came in spurts. "You… I had the situation handled, Thomas. You… you hadn't called or emailed. Hell, you barely texted."

"You haven't been easy to get ahold of either."

I walked into a corner and pivoted while Thomas watched, his feet planted, arms folded defensively across his chest. "One day. One day I had an issue and made you wait." I argued my case.

"You've been too tired to speak. Or a kid or an employee interrupted."

I ignored his arguments and kept on. "I've been supportive. Made sure I wasn't whiny. It's what you told me to do. So I asked nothing of you and stood on my own two feet."

"Who told you to ask for nothing?"

"Your unavailability shouted it loud and clear. Then you galloped in here like some white knight and tossed out the bad boy dragon. I'm not a damsel in distress. I won't hide in the shadow of a brave champion anymore. I can handle myself."

"Didn't look like it to me," Thomas bit back.

"Liz was ready with the emergency button. I'd already warned Jonn. He was just getting in a last word before he left."

"He pushed you!"

I stopped pacing, spun, and pointed at him. "You have a hero complex."

"And you don't?"

"No."

"Think about it, Kick." Thomas pulled his phone from his inside pocket and swiped the screen, like an alert had buzzed in his pocket.

"Am I keeping you from something?"

He grumbled, "I have a meeting."

"Then why are you here?" I mirrored his stance, facing off with him.

"Got back this morning and couldn't wait to see you. Figured fifteen minutes beat nothing at all. Was hoping we could make plans for tomorrow. Guess I was wrong."

I didn't want him to detract from my righteous anger. I pointed toward the front. "I can fight my own battles."

"Never said otherwise." He jammed the phone back in his coat pocket. "What did the asshole want anyway?"

"He came in here acting humble and friendly and asked for a job. He probably figured he'd pull one over on the 'old guy'," I answered.

Thomas took two steps toward me. "He was ready to hurt you, Kick. Hurt. You. What if he'd taken you out and turned on Hugh's girl? Huh? I had the means to make it end easily."

It didn't matter that he'd landed on my worst fear about the incident. Or maybe it mattered more that he'd read my mind.

"You don't get to play helpful hero when it's convenient for you, Thomas. Either you're someone's *something more* or you're not. Right now it doesn't even feel like you're much of a friend."

"You know I have responsibilities."

I looked up, exasperated with the word. "To hell with both our responsibilities."

He threw his hands in the air and turned toward the door. "This is ridiculous. I have to meet my boss. Next time, I'll remember to let the little bastard kick your ass."

"If that's what you take from this, fine." So my insecurities had come true. "It's a good thing we didn't go any further. Obviously, we're not right for each other."

His eyes narrowed as his chin tipped. "Obviously."

Thomas took a step, stopped, and looked over his shoulder. His eyes had gone to ice, the way they were when we'd first met. Part of me wanted to cry from witnessing their return, but I was too angry to take it all back. The fact he could so quickly go there with me told me more than any words. It was one thing if we decided we belonged back in the friend zone, but even my friends gave me time and respect.

Thomas beelined for the parking lot, a blaze of fury trailing behind him. And why not? Didn't they all leave eventually? It didn't matter. I was so over begging people to be my friend.

I entered the front of the store, shaken, sad, and fed up. Dylan and Liz stared at me. For the first time since he'd entered the drama, I studied my son's face. His hair was messy and tending toward fuzzy, his mouth turned down, and telltale dark circles rimmed his eyes. Something had been bothering him before he arrived.

"Let's call the day, Liz. You finished your inventory. I'll pencil you out for your scheduled hours. Hugh will understand." I remembered Graham's sleazy little come-on to her. "Dylan, let's go get some sushi." At least the jackass had one thing right.

27

Heartache Tonight

Thomas

THOMAS ANGRILY ZIPPED HIS CAMARO AROUND THE TRAFFIC CIRCLE in the center of Oakville and nearly took out an elderly lady gingerly navigating the turns in her tiny Nissan. "Damnit."

The precious live oak tree in the park at the top of the circle caught his eye. On instinct, he pulled the car into the municipal parking lot for the town hall, police station, and green area. He shot off a quick text to his assistant.

THOMAS

Running late. Can you stall the Dean a few?
Show him the project you're working on.

BETHANY

I'll introduce him to the mice. Everything
okay?

No, it wasn't. His heart wouldn't stop pounding, making him unfit to drive.

THOMAS

I'm fine. Just need about 30 mins.

When Bethany sent back a thumbs-up emoji, Thomas took a deep breath. At least he had competent students.

He locked the car and walked toward the old tree as if drawn to it like a magnet. It was the jewel of Oakville. The reason for the town's name. She—Thomas thought of it as a feminine entity—even had property rights to the park it "lived in" by way of some funky lawyering in decades past.

Since it was the middle of a school day, the park was virtually empty. As the oldest tree in the county, it had been fully grown when the first colonists appeared in the area. For some reason, no one chopped her down with the rest of the old-growth trees. She had survived the "big blow" that wiped out farms for eighty square miles, leaving the area rampant with poverty for generations. Locals had renamed the area the *Harricanes*. The name was spoken of as a warning down in Thomas's hometown. Some folks even made superstitious genuflections when the topic came up to ward off anything like that happening to them. Something about how much the tree had survived called to Thomas. It reminded him of his own life.

Thomas wasn't one hundred percent certain, but he'd bet money that the old live oak tree at the four-points corner of his property was the offspring of this one. He walked up to the mama tree and sat in the shelter of her long, sweeping branches. He rested his head against her bark and closed his eyes, forcing his breathing to slow. Being in the shelter of this grand old lady helped him calm down, helped him think.

If she could oversee the turnaround of an impossible situation, he could too. This juggling of experiments within experiments was getting to him. Banger had warned him it was a dumb idea. Back when he'd applied for the fellowship, he figured hiding his secret work in plain sight wouldn't differ from how he had always lived his life. But it had quickly become a burden this year. As the project accelerated, it became harder to hold back the aspects that should have only belonged to the Felidae Society. The animosity he experienced at the meeting in France didn't help. It left Thomas feeling very alone, like the old days.

Which was why he'd wanted so desperately to see Kick's smiling face. She had quickly become his light in the middle of the gray confusion. When he didn't know his purpose anymore, Kick's face appeared in his mind. What a joke.

An early-turned brown leaf blew into the tree's shelter, landing in Thomas's lap. The center of the oak leaf was a reddish brown, reminding him of Kick's hair. As Thomas closed his fist around it, the burned, rough edges made a crackling sound as it broke into bits, like his newfound relationship.

How dare she jump all over him that way she had. The whole thing didn't sit right. It pushed Thomas to do the thing he'd been avoiding. He pulled his phone out of his coat pocket and searched for Kick's name.

It took a minute to sort through the articles to find the right woman—until he added *Kick*. The first articles were local, featuring her coffeehouse and something called the McKenna Family Foundation. Going back farther, Thomas's breath became trapped in his throat. At first, he didn't believe it, then he found a photo of the five of them. The haze suddenly cleared.

The smiles, the closeness in the poses. *Happiness*. The perfect family. Kick hadn't accidentally left out a few details regarding her past. She'd deceived him. Like Thomas had her.

He clicked on a supporting link and gasped. The horror. His skin heated with anger. For himself. *For him*. How could Kick cover this up? Thomas's memories shifted back to the similar ones he'd experienced. He still couldn't justify what he'd learned. Maybe it was the residual anger from earlier. Or just all of it.

The tree rustled, like the old lady was reminding him of the importance of inhalations. His mind raced through recent memories, the odd questions answering themselves. Still, all he wanted to do was ask "why"? Why hadn't Kick said anything? Why hadn't she trusted him? As his anger shot into the stratosphere, Thomas's thoughts sorted themselves out. Wasn't she mad at him for keeping secrets? Here was evidence of what she held back. Evidence that this thing with her was too much, especially when his responsibilities were factored in. They were peas in a pod. Better off alone.

His heart ached—no, it was exhausted. Something had to give. *Fine.*

Kick had been right about them being over before they began. He could see that now.

Thomas scooted out from under the old oak tree and headed back to his muscle car, eager to open her up some as he high-tailed his ass to the meeting. The thing that actually mattered.

Except, the wind picked up as he marched toward the parking lot. The branches of the oak tree leaned his way, as if begging him to come back under their shelter. And listen.

28

I've Been Loving You
Too Long

Kick

THE SPEAKERS IN DYLAN'S BMW CAME TO LIFE IN THE MIDDLE OF Eminem's "Lose Yourself."

Oh, this song. For a moment I forgot about everything that happened in the cigar shop and revisited my longing for the past. I'd even take the parts that had annoyed me so much about those days.

The song also let me know where Dylan's head had been before everything at Mick & Hugh's went down. I avoided songs like this for a reason. The pain could be intolerable. The fact I'd been hiding from the same headspace hit hard. The past—the guilt—had poked at me for months, trying to get me to deal with it. *Holy hell.*

"You okay?" Dylan asked as he navigated our parking lot.

"No," I snapped, chest heaving, seeking a proper breath. Pounding beats fueled my angst with the past more than it did my anger with Thomas or Jonn Graham. I stared out the passenger window as the gas stations and strip malls rolled by. I saw none of it. I watched for a moment farther down Time's road, when I wasn't so alone.

"So… this song," I said to distract myself.

"Yeah." Dylan let out a sad breath. I hated how burdened he sounded. His life was only in second gear. He had miles to go before he was fully living his dream.

"You introduced Dad to Eminem."

"Yeah." The word shook with emotion. I turned my head to see why.

We pulled into a parking spot, and Dylan cut the engine before returning my gaze. The sadness in his baby-blue eyes sent my problems packing. "As much as he enjoyed teaching you fatherly stuff, he loved it when you brought something to him. Jaysus, Lad, he adored you." My body shook as I reached out and squeezed my son's hand. "I don't know what's wrong, but there's nothing you can do to ruin how proud we are of you. Both of us."

Dylan lifted his head, his eyes tearing.

"Hey," I started but ran out of words. I patted his cheek. "You sure you want to go inside?"

He blew out a slow breath. "I need a distraction."

You and me both. "Okay. I'll order a carafe of sake. One of those small cups shouldn't undo my progress. You can have the rest. Then you'll tell me everything."

The owner of Sugoi Sushi had a child with multiple food allergies, so he was known in the autoimmune community for accommodating customers like me. We greeted the hostess and found stools at the bar. I was on a first-name basis with the staff, but a new bartender approached. His nametag read Cole. He greeted us with a tip of the head and said, "What can I get you two?"

Dylan spoke first. "A carafe of sake." He turned to me. "Hot, right?"

I nodded and added, "And two glasses of water with lemon. We know what we'd like to order too."

"Sure. Go ahead."

"I'll have a Tokyo roll—with coconut aminos instead of soy sauce—and the seven-piece nigiri with salmon on a blue plate."

"That's for allergies, right?"

"It is."

Cole winked then let his eyes linger on my chest. I wanted to snap at him to cut the flirty shit but figured it was probably my lousy mood making a big deal out of nothing. "Sure. For you, sir?"

"I'll have the shrimp teppanyaki and whatever she leaves on her plate."

The bartender chuckled. "Sounds good. Be right back with your drinks." He left us to enter our order.

"New guy's a flirt," Dylan said.

"Eh." I shrugged. "If he knows what's good for him, he'll knock it off. Men are on my shit list today. I'm only tolerating you because you'll always be my little boy."

His eyes grew wide with surprise. "Is this about what went down at the store?"

I bit my lip to stop an emotion overload and nodded. The real reason for my anger with Thomas came into focus. "And other things."

Dylan propped his elbow the wooden bar top. "On behalf of my gender, what the hell did we do to you?"

Except, I couldn't tell him when I didn't have the words. The revelation in the car was still too new. I couldn't admit to my deepest angst about moving on, that I didn't think it was possible. That I didn't deserve it. So I deflected. "Tell me what's going on with you instead."

"Here you go." Cole set down the carafe and cups. "You're pretty cute together."

Before his words registered, Dylan chuckled. "What a moron." He blew on his cup and whispered, "I think the bartender thinks we're… on a date, Mom."

JaysusMaryandJoseph.

I closed my eyes and shivered. "Because why wouldn't I date a boy twenty-three years younger than me?"

Dylan's laugh grew. Well, he got his distraction. When he calmed, he said, "Plenty of people say you look younger than you are. I look older than my age, thanks to the beard. It's not so big of a gap then."

Big enough. I shivered at the thought. Then I shoved his shoulder and ended up moving myself instead. The kid was still built for a football field, like his old man. "It's not funny," I groused, creeped out. "Just when I thought today couldn't get any worse."

He looked up and caught my frown. "Aw, come on. It's funny as shit." Dylan's laugh eased into a snigger before settling.

"At least your mood has improved. If it comes at my expense, so be it." An empty cup stared back at me, tempting me to pour another. Remembering the number of doctor appointments still left on my calendar, I pushed it to the side.

Dylan threw his arm around my shoulder as I sipped on the water. "Anyway, we used to have mother-son dates regularly. What's wrong with doing it now?"

"Nothing, Lad." I snuck a pointed finger at Cole. "Not what he meant though, is it?"

"True." Dylan poured himself another glass. "Either way, this is the first *date* I've been on in ages."

His comment didn't sit well with me. School packed both Dylan's and Suzy's schedules, but it sounded like they might be taking their relationship for granted.

We welcomed the break created from the arrival of our meals. We ate while listening to Otis Redding's "I've Been Loving You Too Long." Lost in the melody and bleak lyrics, I sang along, letting the music say what my heart refused—that I was stuck.

As the song progressed, Dylan's chewing pace slowed until he was picking at his plate. Nothing came between Dylan and food.

I set my chopsticks on the plate, looked around to ensure no one eavesdropped, and said, "Time to talk. What's going on?"

He set his fork down but kept his gaze forward. "Suze and I fought all weekend." He ran his hand through his hair. It was getting long. "Truth is, all we do is fight. I don't know what I'm doing wrong."

"Then why did you ask me about money for an engagement ring?"

I almost got a laugh out of him. Almost. "I hoped it would make her happy. You know…" He shrugged. "Maybe if she sees I'm all in, she'll chill."

I could only think of one worse reason to get engaged but held my tongue. I disguise the wince. "Can you give me examples of what happened?" I folded my hands in my lap to keep them from shaking. A sense of dread had descended upon me.

"You know how we always have breakfast together because our schedules keep us out late?" I nodded, so he continued, "I usually make it, to… you know, spoil her some. Lately she claims it's because I don't like her cooking. So I didn't make breakfast today, and she called me neglectful.

"Everything I do is selfish, according to her. She yells at Dummy and me for being smelly, and we've no clue why. Suzy thinks the condo smells disgusting too."

"Medical school must be terribly stressful," I offered, my mind on alert.

"It's only going to get harder. Suzy hasn't started rotation yet. She acts like she doesn't want us around, but Dummy and I were roommates before she moved in. We aren't going anywhere." His soulful eyes turned on me. "I wish she'd just say she wants out."

"Did you ask her if she does?"

He gripped his raven hair. "Yes."

"And?"

"She burst into tears and locked me out of our room."

"Jaysus." I dropped my head into my hand, resting my elbow on the bar.

"What?" He turned to face me, eyes pleading like a worshipper seeking answers from his oracle.

I counted off on my fingers. "Let's see if I have this straight—sensitivity to smells, extreme irritability. Is she fatigued?"

Dylan blew out a breath and nodded.

"Any other possible medical issues? Like a virus? Pain?"

"Suze says she aches everywhere but doesn't want me to touch her." He took a sip of water. "Oh, she threw up a couple of times last week. Think she has the flu?"

Unfortunately, I didn't. "It's possible." I bit my lip, not wanting to ask. "Has she had a period recently?"

"How would I know? She's on the pill."

I shoved his shoulder. "Because you're supposed to be a responsible partner, knothead. Has there been any"—I circle my hand—"lady trash in the basket lately?" Being his only parent, this wasn't our first foray into the uneasy topic of Dylan's sex life. It didn't get easier.

Dylan whispered, his eyes wide, "I don't remember."

My head bobbed as I thought. "Well, Lad, I could be wrong, but it's possible—*possible*—your girl's expecting. It's quick enough to find out. If Suzy is, she might be confused, pissed, and who knows what all at the same time."

He lifted his chin quickly, finally catching on we were discussing a possible baby. He poured more sake and downed it in one. "Shit, Mom."

"Ask her, Dyl. But do it gently. And listen." I took hold of his face again to make a point. "Don't get ahead of yourself and pick out names either. It'll only make matters worse."

"Are you sure?" His voice cracked like he was thirteen. It took all my strength to not squeeze him and say it would get better.

"No. But I remember when a brutal bout with mono turned out to be… something else." The bartender walked by and did a double take.

Dylan lowered his voice. "You mean your autoimmune disease? You think—"

"No, son. I mean you. I'd thrown up so much with the illness, it didn't occur to me to get a pregnancy test. You didn't come along at a convenient time either."

"Why?" he asked with a shocked expression.

"Don't confuse inconvenience with being unwanted. That said, you were a surprise. Your dad had just landed a starting position. My job was all long hours and high stress as I tried to prove myself at the ad agency. We had recently bought a fancy-ass house because we thought it was what the NFL expected of us. Shit, I was younger than you are now."

"I miss him," Dylan blurted at the mention of his father, breaking my heart.

Rubbing his arm, the grief I'd felt in the car came back, catching in my throat.

"You never talk about him," he breathed out in frustration. "It's like he was never a part of our family."

My head hung. When moving on became excruciating, it was easier to pretend I'd always been single. It was also easier to make him the bad guy than deal with reality. "Oh, sweetheart." I dabbed at a threatening tear, thinking about Dylan's pain. "Guess you're right. Sometimes it was the only way I could get through a day. I think it became a habit. I'll do better, okay?" I took a drink of water to keep from crying in public.

"It'd be nice to talk about him."

"I made you think I don't want to?"

He nodded. My eyes squeezed shut at Dylan's honesty. In my efforts to dodge the pain, I'd hurt my kid. "Do you share your grief with anyone? Suzy?"

"Snow and I do, mostly. Lee, too, sometimes. But he also likes to shove it down like you. I think he gets mad about how much he's missed. Since it's his senior year, it's a touchy subject." Dylan dropped his head. "I know what the counselors said. It's just… If I'd hadn't been such a dick—"

"No, Lad." Tears long dried for my misery dropped for my son's pain. I scanned the bar again. As usual, the few people around paid us no attention. "Get this through your head… It. Wasn't. Your. Fault. No part of it was. Do you understand? You think I'd rather mourn you? No way I'd get over it."

"So you've gotten over Dad?"

No. Hell no. It's why the guilt kept kicking me when things warmed up with Thomas. I bit my lip, unable to say it aloud.

He gave me a pathetic attempt at a smile. "Snow, Lee, and I think you should date again, but maybe we're wrong. I don't know if I could ever get over it if it were me." Dylan's gaze returned to his plate and stared, as if he'd forgotten about it. He took a small bite. "We don't like the idea of leaving you."

I dipped a piece of sushi in my sauce and took a bite. It went down like sandpaper. That idea was fast approaching. "There are worse things than being alone."

Dylan furrowed his brow. "You're with Thomas though. Doesn't it mean you've moved on?"

A cynical laugh bubbled from my chest. How did one move on from a marriage that didn't end? Our journey together did, but not the marriage. Not for me. "Thomas was a mistake. Today proved it."

An expression looking a lot like a disappointed parent flashed across Dylan's face. "Over a little fight? Are you sure?"

Thomas and I started out with a fight. Maybe it was a clue. I took a pull of water and slid my plate Dylan's way. I nodded my response. I couldn't move forward when the past would always be unfinished. I could make a good life as a single woman. I'd figure it out.

"What if someone's trying to tell you to get back out there?"

I laughed at the suggestion. "I'm tired of trying to decipher what the universe wants for me. Every time I think I've figured it out, the universe"—I used the air quotes—"changes the rules."

"What about meditating? My friend—"

I touched his bicep to stop him. "Thank you, Dyl. I'm trying it, I swear. It's not a magic pill though." Argh that word! It was the secular equivalent of *Have you prayed about it?*

As I watched Dylan finish both our plates, my gratitude lifted to the universe for a kid who took a hint. I didn't want to talk about the future or the past anymore.

The bartender placed our bill where Dylan's plate had been, and my patience died.

I grabbed the ticket. "I'll pay for dinner with *my son*, thank you." A blush raced up Cole's neck. I pushed. "Don't assume. When a man assumes, it makes him an ass."

He took the bill and my card and disappeared. I watched for Cole to return, my face too hot for the minor offense.

Dylan leaned into me. "Are you still angry? Why don't you head to the car? I'll sign for you and apologize."

"Apologize for what?"

"Come on, Mom." He lowered his voice. "Cole may have been misguided, but he wasn't mean." He tipped his head, waiting for his words to sink in—I was the ass in the situation.

He added, "Go on, cool off."

29

Separate Ways (Worlds Apart)

Kick

AT HOME, MACUSHLA GREETED ME BY PERFORMING A PEE-PEE DANCE around my legs. Her doggie door had jammed, making her hold it in longer than she was used to. Fresh air appealed to my addled mind, so I joined her in the backyard. Dylan's situation mixed in with my troubles, competing for my attention like a tennis match of misery. Something told me his problems with Suzy were unfixable. Heaven help them if a child really was involved. I hoped I was wrong. I would've done anything for decent advice on what to advise him. After eight years of learning how to stand on my own, some days I'd still give anything to have my champion back.

My mother's favorite criticism—if I hadn't been whining about pain, I'd have kept my old life—buzzed in my head like reverb from a broken subwoofer. Then another one, also critical but voiced by many people, asked when I would move on.

Thomas and I had chemistry. It sparked whenever he entered a room. Plus he'd become a refuge. That would be the hardest part to let go, but I'd deal with it. The initial excitement to see him today irritated me because it felt so right. The guilt piled on higher, making me feel unfaithful. I'd rather lose Thomas than keep the unbearable guilt.

Another voice, sounding like Deana's, asked me if what Thomas had done earlier was so terrible. Wouldn't my friends have jumped in if they'd interrupted Jonn Graham and me? Hell yeah, but we'd have shown him the door together.

Fed up, I spun on the backyard patio to release the pressure, deciding some music would lift my mood and help me forget. Macushla did her zoomies around the yard while I opened up the house app on my phone. It allowed me to control the sound system and choose the outdoor speakers.

Desperate to silence the critics in my head, I paid no attention to which playlist turned on. Pink's "U + Ur Hand" perfectly fit my mood and I placed the phone in my pocket, giving myself over to the song. I spun, stomped, and pointed into the chilly night, singing about the men who drove me to madness. It was a karaoke performance to the universe, and I poured myself out, begging it to quit screwing with me.

Macushla joined in, wiggling her butt as she danced around my feet. Her blurry tail fed off my energy. Prince's "Let's Go Crazy" came on next, encouraging me to hang in there. Then I recognized the first bar of Gwen Stefani's "Hollaback Girl," squealing as the rebuke of the men in my life crescendoed. I finally laughed when Koosh did something looking like a doggy twerk, enjoying the release, wondering when I'd last laughed. Then she broke out into uncontrolled barking.

I looked down and glared my disapproval. "Shh! Spoilsport. We'll have to go in before someone calls the Po-Po."

Sufficiently tired from pouring out my pent-up frustration, I fell onto the garden bench when the opening bars to another song from the past came on. I patted the seat next to me for Koosh to jump up. Petting her helped my breathing return to normal as I watched her settle, placing her muzzle on my thigh. I told her my problems while singing along to Duran Duran's "Come Undone."

As Simon sang, I wondered who was there for *me*.

The question stung my heart the most. I'd had the perfect life until it tore me apart. We'd worked our asses off to make our life work, and it didn't matter.

My dirty secret? The one I admitted to no one? I envied my friends who divorced. Even those with messy ones. They didn't know how it was a privilege to fall out of love. Was I doomed to a one-sided fairy tale gone pitiful? Now *I* had to be the safe place to fall. The kids didn't have two parents to rely on anymore. So I couldn't afford to come undone. Instead, I waited.

The song peaked as ancient tears awoke and drenched my face. When it ended, I bent over Koosh, who licked me in an effort to soothe. Sobbing, I looked up at the sky. "Why'd you leave me, Shane?"

Crisp air touched the wetness, chilling my cheeks. My dog jumped from my lap and trotted to the sliding door to the master bedroom, staring in, her tail resuming a vigorous swish. I pushed the tears away, facing my future aloneness. "We done, sweet girl? Let's see if we can sleep."

I missed the glow as I slid the door open, stepped inside, and double-checked the lock. I moved toward the bed and stopped short. My heart leaped at the slightly transparent man sitting on the end of the bed.

Am I sleepwalking now? This wasn't the shadowed mystery with silver wisps in his hair from recent dreams. I'd known everything about this man and his body as well as I knew my own.

My man. The only one I thought I'd ever want.

He lifted his head and stared at me, becoming solid. Eyes the blue of the Caribbean Sea smiled as they perused me from head to toe. The room spun, and I stumbled, ending up on my knees in front of him.

"Shane?"

"Hi, Katie." The left side of his mouth raised, revealing that libido-stirring dimple, the one that thousands of young women drooled over twenty years ago. I'd been the only one for whom it came to life.

I scrambled back to my feet, retreating to a shadowed corner, my hands shaking at my lips. "H-how?"

Shane shrugged and clasped his hands, resting them on his knees. "From what I can tell, you brought me here."

When he first left, we'd met in my dreams many times. He provided the strength to get through the next day. He let me know he still loved and supported me. Sometimes I'd feel a light caress or sense a kiss on my lips. But it had been years since our last meeting. I figured my subconscious couldn't bear the pain of waking up without him anymore and abandoned it.

Macushla curled into Shane's side, no apprehension in her demeanor at all. "Hey little Koosh. Wow, have you changed." He thoroughly petted her from ears to tail until it became automatic.

"I don't understand."

Shane lifted his gaze and found my watery one. "Koosh isn't the only one who's changed. You have too. There's more out there than we realize, love."

His powerful voice soothed like the sound of waves on the shore. Shane had made me feel protected and secure. His heart was as big as his body. His wide-receiver frame towered over me by nearly a foot. He'd played football for Michigan State University when we met. He continued to play ball with friends after two knee injuries forced his retirement from a successful NFL career.

Ever the receiver, he'd said he'd always catch me. It was true. Until someone took him out.

"I've missed you, Katie." The words dripped with the same pain I felt.

I ran to Shane, falling to my knees, gripping him. My heart filled with warmth and electricity. Home again. Anyone who's known love knows home isn't a building. Home was Shane McKenna.

I gasped. "You're real? You're back?" It made no sense, but what did?

"Shhh." Shane stood, pulling me up with him, enfolding me in his big, protective body. It was different from what I remembered— cool to the touch. I didn't care. Life without my husband was too hard to sweat the minor details.

Shane's big thumbs lifted my jaw so my lips could meet his in a gentle kiss, purer than our first had been. Our tears mixed, became one as they slid down my face and neck.

With his right hand, Shane wiped away our tears. "Don't cry," he soothed. "Only smiles tonight." He dipped his head and smirked. "Let's just be. No questions. No explanations."

"I st-still don't un…der…stand." My heart pounded so fast I was afraid it would explode. I adjusted my breathing to calm myself and abide by his words.

"No one defines how or why we love. We just do."

"Sing for me," I begged. "Please sing our song." For me, Shane's tenor tone was the final confirmation of his return. Few knew Shane's passion was singing. Football had paid the bills and impressed the family, but he expressed himself with song.

Shane looked over his shoulder, tossed aside the decorative pillows, and sat against the headboard of our bed built for a king. He had me sit in his lap. "Everything here is the same," he said, looking around.

"I couldn't bring myself to change it." *I couldn't say goodbye.*

He wrapped an arm around my shoulder, kissed my nose, then he sang "Lovesong," by the Cure.

I closed my eyes, listening. It was a shock to hear it so real, so near, not a distant memory or old video. I pressed a kiss to his still perfect chest and listened.

I never realized how the song described those last eight years, loving each other from afar. This was my truth, why I stayed single. The song ended with me raw and reeling. The guilt overwhelmed me. "Shane, I'm so sorry. I've been—" I meant to confess about Thomas and how my heart had wandered, but Shane cut me off.

His eyes pinned me with a look of disappointment. "I get it, Katie. It hurts, but I get what you did."

"I didn't mean to kiss Thomas at first. It was just nice to have a male friend again. Then I guess I was lonely."

Shane shook his head while pressing his lips. "That's not what I meant. Do you still not get it?" He skootched over, and I got a better look at him, vibrating with emotions as he studied the ceiling. "You won't let go, and you pretend I never existed at the same time." The disappointment cut through me like a sword. "You're holding us both back, Katie. And you're hurting the family."

My dinner with Dylan came back to me, twisting my heart. The weight of the eight years fell on me, and my voice cracked. "Somewhere in my mind, I knew it hurt you." I studied Shane's face, looking for understanding. I continued through the hitches. "But they needed strength, not a broken mess. I wasn't anywhere near remission back then." I tucked a messy curl behind my ear, turned fully to him, and continued, "You died in my arms, Shane. How was I supposed to move on? I still freeze when I hear sirens and get furious at drivers who text."

He squeezed my knee, as I found the compassion I needed on his face. "You know I didn't want to go, right?" The dog rested her chin on Shane's thigh when his voice caught. "It was supposed to be a quick grocery store run. I didn't see the SUV, but when I think about how I'd asked you or Dylan to do the errand, I'm glad the woman broadsided me."

"I'm not," I cried, jumping off the bed and pacing. "Anyone with half a brain could see you were better suited to be a single parent." My outburst turned into a whisper. "I've screwed up so much. What if I've messed up the kids? Dylan… he's—"

Shane reached for me, but I couldn't settle. My heart and mind still raced. I found my respite in those deep blue eyes with their thick black lashes. That is, until they blurred from my own watery gaze. I didn't know if I could take what he'd say next.

"I've always been proud you were the mother of my children. I still am." He spoke with his head down, more to the dog, while he continued. "I used to work hard to give you confidence. I know some of that was your family, and some of it was your illness. But you're formidable now." His gaze met mine again, this time filled with lust. "Your body's stronger, but so is your mettle. Remember the depression you struggled with when you got sick and no one listened? My God, the day you confessed you were suicidal, it terrified me to my core."

"I didn't want to be an autoimmune warrior. I've barely survived it."

"No, Katie, you've thrived," Shane said with an awe I'd never seen or heard from him regarding me. There was a sadness in his voice too. He wiggled his fingers, pleading with me to return to him, this time for his comfort, not mine.

I obliged, settling on the edge of the bed. "I'll give it up. The shops, the house… everything. Anything. Please, just stay." Taking his hand and placing it over my heart, I continued, "There's a hole here I can't fill no matter what I do. Like I keep adding dirt to it and fall in anyway. With you here, I can be whole again. *We* can be whole."

He shook his head. "What's done is done. The one we became when we married is still in you, as it is in me. You… you absorbed me, which is why you feel different. You *are* different now." Shane sighed and continued in a hushed tone. "That's the reason your heart opened to someone else, Katie. Don't torture yourself over it."

"I won't let you go." With my future on the line, I made as clear a case as I could. "I've tried. Don't you guilt me into being with someone else. I'll tell you what I told him—I don't need completing. If you won't stay, I'll wait until we can be together again, wherever you've gone. I'll run the café, but I'll be killing time, waiting to be with you."

Shane kept shaking his head. "You don't understand."

"She ripped you away in an instant," I yelled, surprising myself. I bit my lip and whispered, "The love remains though."

"I know." He took my hand, turning it to kiss my palm. "It always will, and that's how it should be."

More tears fell as I stared into his face. He hadn't aged at all. But he probably wouldn't.

"You need to know I'm moving on." Shane stood and came around to my side of the bed, kneeling before me. "Don't stop living so long before you die. Don't piss me off." He added the last with a smirk. "You deserve happiness. Fight for it."

"Stop." A tiny voice, so different from mine, pleaded.

Sadness darkened Shane's expression. "It's because of you that we have tonight. Do you understand? You're becoming more."

"Not at all." I scoffed. "You're what's missing. So stay."

"You have everything I could give you." Shane moved to sit next to me and pulled me into his side. "You'll take it with you no matter what you do. So hear this, Katie. I *want* to go. And I want you to be happy."

"Where are you going?"

He let out a sad chuckle, running a finger against my wet cheek. "You wouldn't understand it if I told you. I think you'll see eventually. That's how different you are. Do you hear me?" He pushed the hair out of my eyes, tucking it behind an ear. "It doesn't mean I don't love you even if I still want you to love again."

I heard Shane, though I tried not to. I dug my fingers into his dark waves in case this was my last chance and kissed him thoroughly. His lips weren't the warm silk I remembered. His body didn't give off the perpetual heat it used to. Shane might look exactly the same, but he wasn't my husband anymore either.

His words were finally sinking in. "How long can you stay?"

The dimple I adored showed up one more time. "You need to use the bathroom."

"Among other things," I said, biting my lip. I couldn't wait to get into my pajamas, but I'd wear my torturous bra forever if it kept Shane around.

He smacked my thigh, chuckling. "Go on. I'll be here." To prove his point, he lifted the covers and settled in. The dog circled three times and dropped down by his feet. The way she used to.

Five minutes later, Shane kissed my shoulder as I spooned against his front. "I've missed this spot," he whispered.

I forbade myself from thinking about the goodbye, choosing to bask in gratitude for our night. Against my will, I fell asleep in Shane's arms, my head tucked under his chin. As time passed, I'd remember hearing him say, "I'll always love you, Katie."

A COOL BREEZE TICKLED MY NECK FROM LOOSE CURLS FALLING OUT of my ponytail. My gaze dropped to the warm sand under my feet. Salty air filled my nose. I looked up, confronted by waves from the Atlantic, caressing the shore. The tide was moving out.

Why didn't I hear it? The wind was silent too.

I turned around and stood before a beautiful beach house. It was the summer house on Emerald Isle Shane and I had planned to build come to life. I smiled at the memory of him picking the town because the name reminded him of Ireland. We were consulting with an architect before his accident.

The house sat on a spectacular bank with full views of the water. Tight plantings of Crepe Myrtles kept neighboring homes from seeing inside, making window treatments unnecessary. Shouldn't it have hurricane shutters?

A porch wrapped around the two sides of the house I could see. I remembered how the plans called for it on all sides. We both had adored porch life.

Before.

Beach grass grew so tall and thick I couldn't see where the access emptied onto the shore. I stalked the area, looking for a path to the house. Hell, any path. Before me lay nothing but large clumps of grass and sand.

The wind picked up, shuffling sand, making the dune shift. Grains of sand hit my face like glass. I slid down a foot but remained standing. I panicked at not being able to reach the house.

French doors on the top floor balcony opened. Shane stepped out and went to the railing. His wavy black hair blew gently with the wind, easier than it was beating my curls. Wearing only linen pants, he took my breath away. He stared at me while his arms braced on the railing. Despite the distance between us, I made out his brilliant blue eyes. They matched the color of the sky he stood under. I expected him to compel me forward, but his expression held a resolved sadness instead. It shifted to peaceful, and I knew.

The house was his, not mine.

I cried out but made no noise. He didn't try to speak, yet his eyes said what I probably wouldn't have heard.

A low sound finally reached my ears. It was a complete surprise. Our grandfathers conversed on the front porch, though no one sat in the chairs. As far as I knew, the two men hadn't met.

Our fathers had formed the original family bonds while working on the General Motors assembly line. We became friends at Michigan State when my dad asked me to tutor Shane in French. His grandfather was long dead by then. I only knew his voice from recordings. Shane's timbre was similar. And they shared the gift of singing.

My Grand-da Allen had spoiled me rotten. He was the rare family member who focused on my strengths growing up. He supported me instead of reprimanding my flaws. I'd clung to every generous, teasing encouragement as if it were a lifeline.

I looked through the picture windows to see if anyone stood inside. Instinctively, I knew it held the things Shane loved. Pictures of the kids, our parents, and his uncle Billy, rested on a mantel. A football-themed office occupied the northwest corner. His favorite dishes filled the refrigerator and freezer—the food I made before dietary restrictions became a thing. I touched my mouth to capture a giggle, and a sob escaped. Shane tilted his head and gave me a sad smile. It was the same sadness permeating mine. I finally understood what Shane had tried to explain. A blurry image of the love of my first life turned and silently padded into the house. It was time for us both to find something new. The gifted assurance he was at peace meant the world.

I turned away from the sight, walking up the beach, knowing I, too, was a new person. I didn't die that Labor Day afternoon, but I'd fundamentally changed in my core, my sinews, my soul.

At six o'clock, the alarm went off to Journey's "Separate Ways (Worlds Apart)." An icy chill had descended on my bedroom, making me desperate to share body heat. But there was only mine. I ached from the fresh scab over my heart and realized it could finally heal. Without glancing around the room, I knew Shane had left.

The singer's perfect angst reminded me how much I used to long to turn back time and trade places with my husband. It had never been possible to switch or follow him, back then or presently. It was his message in the middle of the night. We both had to go our separate ways. I came fully awake as the song wrapped to the anguished cries of the singer accepting the truth and saying good-bye. Finally, for me… the goads I'd kicked against for the past eight years had won. I cried tears of submission, then acceptance for hours.

I couldn't rise to make Liam's breakfast or see him off to school, something I only did when extremely sick. The reality I'd fought so hard, for so long, had gutted me. Shane and I were finished.

Yet the survivor's guilt, the guilt for trying to move on, for changing—all of it dissipated. It was time to start the new Kick.

30

Thieves in the Temple

Kick

"WHAT IN THE SAM HILL'S WRONG WITH YOU?" DEANA admonished, planting her hands on her hips in a power pose in my doorway. Thanks to Banger's security upgrades, I couldn't sneak into my office via the back door anymore.

I stopped typing midstroke, eyes wide. "Deana Douglas, did you pseudo swear?"

She scolded me through her teeth to keep our conversation private. "Don't play cute. I might think you've lost your mind. Check that, I already do."

"Excuse me?" My tongue worried my cheek, afraid of where her admonishment would go. The past few days had drained me, but Dee was in the dark about most of it. I'd spent the morning after Shane, wringing out the tears. Unlike before, these were good tears as I allowed myself to recall wonderful memories. Then the sun came out, both literally and emotionally. Getting to say goodbye turned out to be a gift. With a weight lifted, I surveyed my bedroom, the shrine to our past. The gigantic bed, massive en suite furniture, and worn-out comforter had to go. They never fit me.

I had padded into the kitchen with my phone in hand and called Charlie Rodriguez, my friend and carpenter. She had brought my designs at the café to fruition.

After a quick exchange of pleasantries, I said, "Ready to redo my master. How soon can you get me on the schedule?"

"Why the rush?" she asked.

I yelled into the phone, not giving her time to find a quiet spot at her job sight. "It's time."

Background noise buzzed and hammered for a beat before she answered, "No kidding. Tell me what you want." Charlie's cut-to-the-chase personality had been exactly what I needed.

I gave her a brief description of my vision for a room completely mine.

She blew out a loud breath. "Wow. Cool. And you're in luck. I had a cancelation that put a crew on the bench this morning. They'll be glad to work. Can you clear out the room by tomorrow?"

"Absolutely." The goal wasn't to erase Shane from my life. I knew more than ever it was impossible. It was time to build a respite where I could fully move forward. "Oh, and I want a legitimate meditation area, maybe a nook."

"Sure. Let's talk it through in the morning."

"Fantastic. Thanks, Charlie. This is going to help."

"I know. I've tried to tell you."

I'd canceled my appointments and spent the next two days clearing out my bedroom and working with Charlie's people. It was great to use all my muscles again.

Deana snapped her fingers in my face. "Are you listening?" *Not really.* I looked up with a guilty pout. She continued, "The professor stopped in here looking for you with his sad face. I told him to give you a little time to cool off, but this is silly, Kick. It's not like you to hide."

Little did she know. I was a pro. I'd been hiding more or less for eight years. Deana did have a point though.

She continued, "Put on your big-girl panties and fix this."

I lifted my hair off my neck, my office suddenly hotter than Hades in the bad way. "You sure he was looking for me?"

She looked at the floor and shook her head. "He scanned every corner of the dining room like he had x-ray vision and I also caught him side-eyeing my monitor. Then he asked, and I quote, 'Is Kick working today?' Yes, shug, he asked for you."

"I figured I ran him off."

She clucked her tongue. "You and Thomas have circled each other since the day he walked in here. Who cares if you weren't on the hunt? You should've been. It doesn't take a psychology degree to figure out why you went off on him the other day too."

She stepped inside and sat in a chair. "It's time, Kick. I wish I'd met Shane. The stories about him remind me of Gordon. I'll be the first to admit those men are as rare as a lightning strike, but he's gone. The professor isn't like those other fan boys trying to get up in your Kool-Aid. He *knows* your flavor. You know how precious it is to find it twice?" She tapped her fingers on the armrests, waiting on my reply.

"Circling each other, huh? Like dogs about to fight?"

"Or mate." She smirked before pursing her sassy mouth. "You light up when he's around. You stop wearing the Widow McKenna mantle and let yourself be you again."

I set my elbows on my desk, collapsed my chin into my hands, and took a couple of deep breaths before blowing her away. "You're right. Oh, put your eyes back in your head. You know you're right. But we were just friends."

I swear, Deana rolled her eyes three times. "Keep telling yourself that. Both of you are h-o-t for each other."

Really? Now I had a fresh fear. "But… if you're talking about a *future*, future… don't you think Thomas deserves someone who can have babies and grow old with him? I can't have more kids even if I wanted to, which I don't. What if I'm a distraction until he wakes up to what he really wants?"

Her face softened, often a sign she was going in for the kill. "Don't make decisions for him. Thomas is a grown man who knows what he's getting, right?"

For all the TMI I'd shared, my hysterectomy hadn't come up.

Then again, I wasn't sure if it mattered. "It's probably best to stay friends and no more."

She dismissed me with a *pfft* and continued. "He knows you're about to be an empty nester. Shoot, Liam's so busy you're basically one now. Doesn't take a genius to figure it won't be long until the word *Grandma* becomes a part of your vocabulary either."

"Bite your tongue," I grunted, grateful Deana didn't know about Dylan's situation. Her baby addiction would swing into overdrive. I rubbed my temples. "There's more, and it's embarrassing, Dee." After letting go of my grief for Shane, I'd been wondering if I should exorcise the ghost of my dream soldier too.

"Let's hear it," she said on an exhale, murmuring, "Should've made myself a latte. You require more caffeine."

"I've had a dream for a while." *JaysusMaryandJoseph.* Was I going to admit this?

"About Thomas?"

I shook my head. "No. The guy in it is fuzzy. He has long hair, tied back, with silver temples. A dark beard. Darkish eyes, I think."

Deana's brown eyes pierced my gaze with a skeptical one of her own. "Never call the police with this vague description."

I steeled my spine to overcome the embarrassment washing through me as I told her the rest. "The dreams have increased in frequency lately. They feel so…" I waved my hands in front of me, searching for words.

"You think he's real?"

"Well, wouldn't you?" I squeaked. "You talk about signs from God."

"Yes. Signs can be wrong. And shug, you've read this one *way* wrong. I promise you."

"You think so?"

"Unless…"

"What?"

"What about the Professor? Could he be the dream man?"

"No," I said. "Though it's misty in my visions—"

"As they are." She rolled her eyes again.

"One thing I know, the guy is older than Thomas. Like I said, his temples are a sexy silver."

"Newsflash, Kick. No one ages younger. For all we know, Thomas already colors away the gray."

I shrugged, confused. Having experienced an intense dream the night before, it lingered in my thoughts. Still, it could be another coping mechanism to get me through loneliness, like the denial I'd learned to live with regarding widowhood.

"It's just… Remember when I'd told you about the vision I had of Shane's funeral years before it happened? Then I'd had several nightmares about my dad having a heart attack?"

"Those are normal fears people have about family. I've had similar nightmares before."

I stood and walked toward the clerestory window, reaching my hand up to the dust motes in the sunrays, watching them float around my fingers. "They came to pass exactly as I saw them."

Deana rocked her hand and cut to the chase. "You didn't know they were visions until after they'd happened. Kick, I'm telling you, keep your heart and your eyes open to what—and who—is here *now*. Let the visions sort themselves out in their own time."

"Okay. Thanks for not laughing."

She stood and initiated a hug. "I don't want to make fun of a message from the Lord. Just don't get caught up in it, aight? It's already clouded your judgment about someone who's right here."

"I guess." Ready to shake off the events of the past hour, I followed her out to the dining room. "Maybe we can stop circling, as you eloquently put it."

"Thank you." Deana turned and patted my arm. "Take a leap and put yourself out there."

A leap. Such a frivolous word when the butterflies in my stomach seemed more suited to jumping out of an airplane.

I stopped in the hallway, pulled out my phone, and sent a text.

ME

Do you have time to talk today? About our fight? I'd like to apologize, but there's more I need to tell you.

THOMAS

Sure. When?

31

Falling for You

Kick

My anxiety was too amped to meet Thomas in the Perked Cup's dining room in front of all and sundry. As the clock ticked closer to his planned arrival, I escaped to my office again. I'd looked at his response at least a dozen times, trying to interpret whether it was good or bad. My knee wouldn't stop bouncing.

So much stress was ridiculous. Neither of us had enough skin in our game to be this jazzed. Yet viewing our fight through a different lens made me see our whole friendship differently. With the guilt removed—it never should've been there to begin with—I couldn't stop the sense my future hung on the next hour. I focused on the adage of hoping for the best and steeling myself for the worst. I closed my eyes and let my breath even out, falling into a trance.

Thomas broke it with a subtle knock on the doorframe and a clearing of his throat. His expression was unreadable, like the words in his text.

A green-blue light hovered around my fingertips, tucked under my desk. Shaking them helped make it go away and bring my head into the present. "Hey."

"Hey yourself."

Macushla had been curled up in her bed, napping ever since Carmen had brought her over earlier. The drywall crew had arrived at my house and unnerved her with their banging. She padded over to Thomas, greeting him with a nudge to a pocketed hand. He slid it out, rubbing her ears.

"Mind if we take Koosh for a walk? She and I have been cooped up back here."

He nodded, still giving me nothing regarding his thoughts. I feared I might scream, ruining any chance to get this right. I wanted to pin him down and immediately find out where we stood but didn't want to make a scene.

Macushla scurried, her nose to the ground, as we traveled the greenway behind my shopping center. She caught an animal's scent as she zigzagged through the grass. Then she skidded to a stop and filled her nostrils with another scent. I took my own cleansing breath. *Remember we're friends first.* The thought spurred me to speak.

"I don't exactly know how to begin this."

He stared into the waning light. It finally dawned on me what I had seen in his eyes from the beginning. I thought his stoic expression held ambivalence, but I knew—not sure how, but I knew then—it was regret. I wished I knew why. If he'd let me, I would suss it out.

"We've never spoken of my kids' father. And I think you may have the impression he…" My heart pounded. My voice shook. *Spit it out, Kick.* "He was killed eight years ago—broadsided in a car accident in front of our sub."

"I know."

There was a shocker. Most people who knew about me from an internet search announced it as soon as they found out, exclaiming it as if I didn't know my late husband was famous in certain circles.

"Google?"

Thomas nodded. "Some things didn't add up the other day. There were other times too, like the things that Jim guy said when he hit on you. With all the confusion and anger, I figured it was time for a search."

I let out a long breath. "So, you already know everything."

Thomas turned to me, his breath puffing a little on his exhale. We were finally in for a frosty night. "I read the articles, but we both know they're never the whole story."

My words tightened in my throat. I still didn't want to talk about the details.

He dipped his chin to catch my gaze. "Y'all up for filling me in?"

My head bobbed absently as I lost myself in time. "Eight years ago… on Labor Day… It was a harmless barbecue. Just the five of us since I was in the middle of a flare. We didn't notice we were out of hamburger buns until the patties were on the grill. My brain fogs up when it gets bad. Stupid, I know. *I know.*" I nearly cried at the words I'd exclaimed in my head a million times.

Thomas gestured to a bench a few feet away. "Sit."

Aside from a creek running along the greenway path, Southern pines surrounded the seat. The water provided enough humidity to pull essential oils into the air from nearby vegetation. I inhaled the pine scent mixed with wild dill, letting it open my chest and my heart. The bright, healing fragrance gave me enough of a boost to get through the hardest part.

"I asked Dylan to run to the store, but he didn't want to leave his computer game. Shane reluctantly grabbed the keys and took Dyl's little car since it was parked behind his. To be honest, I think Shane wanted a few minutes of peace from me. My health grated on both our nerves that day. We'd fought about who should run the errand." I watched water swirl around a branch in the creek running alongside the path.

My voice hitched as I continued. "I stood on the patio, tending the grill when I heard the ear-piercing crunch of a crash. I don't know how exactly, but in my gut, I knew it was Shane. Probably because I'd had dreams about it. Anyway, I jumped in my van and…" My voice broke and I whispered, "The car was a mangled mess. He was so broken. He… Thomas, he died in my arms." My voice gave out on the last five words.

I waited, watching the creek waters swirl, my fingers blanching from gripping the edge of the bench. And I kept waiting. Knowing your deepest pain lives just to the side of every memory, whether awake or asleep, is one thing. Telling your truth is exhausting. Loneliness became a bottomless pit as I readied myself to fall back in.

The tension pulsing off Thomas equaled mine, like I could touch it. I knew my story disgusted him. I should've been stronger. Pushed harder. My iniquities were too much, and we finished before we began. I braced for the words.

Thomas's inhale was a loud rattle before he turned to me. The mask finally dropped as he pulled me into his arms. "Come here."

I spoke into his shoulder. "Did you read about the bitch who was texting when she hit Shane? Local and national papers covered her trial. Former NFL heroes get coverage."

"Yes, they do." He pulled back to see my face. "Why didn't you tell me? Remember what you said in Target about the makeup mirror? You basically lectured me on facing my truth." He gentled his voice. "Was there a problem in the marriage? Some articles implied—"

"Trashy mags insinuate things about girls hanging around players, but no." I laughed before I broke. "The media knew him as Touchdown, but his teammates called him Reverend Touchdown because they said he lived like a monk on the road. The problem was… in the end, none of it mattered. We had a deep love and a wonderful family, and we still didn't last."

It came back to me like a flash flood. The explosive noise of the crash. Fear. Saying goodbye. The police holding me back when I tried to rip the driver apart with my hands. Sirens. Guilt. *Fecking hell, the guilt. It should've been me.*

Tears unleashed, filling my lashes, and Thomas crushed me into his chest. "Shh, baby." He nuzzled his nose into my temple while I collapsed into him, letting it all go. If he'd take the pain, I'd let someone else share it for a while. My soul ached from the weight and lifted with the experience. His strong body took my pain and my shame, telling me at least we were still friends.

I scoffed at another memory. "My parents made it clear I should keep myself tight for the kids. But I grew tired of my solitary grief. I tried to wish him away, but it didn't work. So a scenario opened in my mind where Shane left us, and I hated him for it. I convinced myself the fury would make me stop grieving. The grand delusion kept me moving. For better or worse. For the kids." I took a shaky breath and continued, my chin bobbing. "You should be upset for Shane though. He didn't deserve a dishonored memory. I still felt like I cheated on him anyway."

"With me," he said, not asked, blowing out a long breath. "Your reluctance with me. Your heart hadn't let go. It all makes sense."

Macushla pulled at her leash, nearly yanking me off the bench. She craved forward motion too. "*Chhtt!*" I corrected. Thomas grabbed the loop and fastened a tie-out to a slat.

"I'm not angry," he said. "Confused is a better word. It's out of character from the woman I've come to know."

I chuckled into his neck. "Self-delusion is highly underrated, sweetheart. I admit it freely."

"It didn't work though. You held on to him."

"I did. I'm sorry." I absorbed what Thomas gave, slowly figuring out he didn't judge. "Folks weasled up to Shane to be near someone famous. Imagine what they'd do to his widow. Deana, Jake, and my kids are excellent guard dogs, though Daddy was best. From day one, he'd spot a superfan with rotten motives and run him off."

"Like that Jim guy."

"Yup, except he's harmless."

"What do they want?"

"Some men think I'll give them money for their attention." I shivered and added, "This may sound weird, but there were men who wanted a chance to say they'd banged an NFL wife. And I used to think only girl groupies were so nasty." I blew out a long sigh. "It's taken years to be my own woman."

Thomas released a low growl, and I let out a surprised laugh. I clicked my tongue, and Macushla jumped into my lap, lending more support.

Thomas swung his arm around my shoulders and squeezed. "I understand some of the things you're saying."

"Really? How so?" I looked up to his gaze and caught sight of the North Star in my periphery.

"Well." He bent to pet the dog before continuing. "I'm a widower."

I straightened, tucking a curl behind my ear. Despite my talk of visions, I hadn't seen this possibility. "Wow."

"I don't speak about it much either. But it's easier here. No one in North Carolina knows besides Banger."

"You haven't said anything at work?"

"There's no point. I'd rather honor my wife by letting her be. It was hell at first."

"Yeah." I sighed, feeling the camaraderie.

"One of the worst things I've been through."

"I hear you. But you're good now?" He was so young. I wasn't sure I believed he'd healed. Maybe he was delusional too.

"I am."

"What was her name?" I asked as if the names of our late spouses would tighten our bond.

Thomas's voice thickened when he answered, "Alicia."

I looked away for a moment as I absorbed its significance. "What happened to her?" My heart broke for him, and I had to know.

He stood, pulling me up as Koosh jumped down, jerking hard on the leash. Thomas gently unhooked her from the bench and took the lead. "Let's leave it for another day." He put his arm around me again. "This talk is for you and us."

Seriously? After I'd vomited my secret all over him, he held back. For all the support and forgiveness he'd shown me, it hurt not to be allowed to reciprocate. I thwacked him in the ribs. "Typical male."

"What?"

"You're good to go when discussing my crap but lock it down regarding your feelings."

He chuckled and squeezed me. "My stuff can wait. I don't want to get off track with what's most important now."

"Which is?"

"Two things." My brows peaked, questioning as Thomas grew serious. "First, are you sure you've moved on now?"

I smiled into the dark path, proud of my new self. "Yes."

Thomas blew out a breath. "There's a relief." My gaze snapped to his. "The second thing is… well, us."

"We still have an us?"

"I hope so. I'd hate to think we couldn't make it past one fight."

"Right."

He nodded in the direction we'd come. "Should we head back?"

"Is it bad I don't want to?"

"No. I like having you to myself." We approached a ledge built into an underpass, and he stopped, settling me next to him. The sound of the water next to us and tires thumping overhead echoed off the underside of the bridge. It kept our conversation private. A couple jogged past, but we ignored them.

Thomas rubbed his bottom lip between his thumb and forefinger. "Let me make sure I understand." We'd spent several minutes rehashing our sides of our fight. "You felt ignored while I was away. You kept yourself together and handled business… as you do." He squeezed my shoulder at the last words. "Then I showed up unexpected, took over, and made you feel incompetent by throwing Graham out of the store without asking if y'all wanted my help. You know I was afraid he'd hurt you, right? I won't stand by and let someone do that. Ever."

"I would've been grateful for your help if you'd asked me. It's about—"

"Respect?"

I blew out a breath. "Yes."

"Tell me Graham hasn't been back since I threw him out."

"He hasn't," I said. "I was about to ban him myself." Enough was enough.

Thomas ran his hand through his hand. "I'm sorry, darlin'. I wish I would've asked before giving him the boot."

I bit my lip, remembering. "It was hot."

He barked a laugh, startling Macushla. "I knew I saw something in your eyes."

"Yeah." I blew at a curl the breeze teased. Cool air didn't keep my cheeks from warming. I let my head hang low as I continued, "Listen, I understand it's important to stay focused when you're traveling. It can bring you home faster too. I was disappointed by how hard it was to reach you but only because it sounded… intense. Shane's travel schedule was intense. It kept up after he retired and started his own company. Anyway, I figured you would fill in what you could when you returned. I mean, I have no real claims to your time or your thoughts—"

Thomas bent his knees to meet my eyes. "What if you had a claim?"

I chuckled before responding, "I've been back and forth on this question."

"Yeah?" He made a noise of affirmation. "What did you decide?"

"At first I thought it wasn't worth the trouble," I answered with a scoff. "But I cooled off."

"And now?"

I stared straight into his eyes and said, "I'd like you to have a claim on my time. Hell, you already fill half my thoughts."

"Only half?" He smirked, and we both laughed.

"Got me there."

My grin faded, thinking about the ways we could go wrong. "The thing is… I'd rather friendship than nothing, Thomas. If it's what's best for us, I'll be fine."

"What if you could be better than fine, Kick?"

It would be amazing. I was afraid to hope too. "I wasn't looking for a relationship," I muttered.

"Neither was I." He shifted his body to face me. "We're an inconvenience, but it could be worth it."

Thomas stepped away from the ledge, pulling me with him.

Then he leaned against the wall, bringing my body up against his. His lips met mine in an invasive kiss, telling me we'd interrupted each other's lives with equal audacity.

I challenged his kiss with a harder one, my mouth opening to his. The kiss became a duel—him punishing me for stubborn independence, me punishing him for cold indifference, both of us annoyed with the poor timing.

Yet we rejoiced in the possibility of more. We wanted each other, and the want alone could be enough to go to the next step. My toes and fingertips pleasantly buzzed, and I didn't care. I could've gone up in flames and taken us both.

I slid from Thomas's hold, elated. Not feeling one speck of guilt. Light from a streetlamp above wrapped under the overpass, catching Thomas's eyes in a striking silver. The cool bulbs bounced blue highlights off his raven hair, just this side of shaggy. A contrast to his usually crisp appearance, I took it as a visual confirmation of how hard his trip had been.

"*Jaysus*, you're handsome," I said, running my fingers through the hairs at his neck.

"Is this a new revelation?" he said teasingly, brushing his nose along mine.

Heat crept up my chest as I laughed. "No. But there's a difference between noticing the outside and what's in here." I placed my hand over his heart. "Without this, you were hot, smart, and a bit odd."

Thomas's chest rumbled against mine, sending electricity to my warming core. "I had the same impression of you."

"I'm not odd," I protested, indignant.

"Have you heard yourself order a meal?"

"It's not on purpose."

"I know." He kissed my nose. "It's adorable."

He reached down and grabbed my ass with both hands, pulling me against his erection. My body's response was instinctive. I ground against him and whimpered.

"Don't tell me you're not hot either. With an ass like this, I could walk behind you for the rest of my life and never complain."

He growled, and I laughed, remembering I'd thought the same of him.

Thomas's words made me feel something I hadn't in way too long… sexy. Brazen. If this is a glimpse of what we could be, it would be everything.

He began peppering my neck with kisses while I wondered what all this truly meant. In the middle of a kiss, he said, "I can hear you thinking."

"Does this mean we're…" My mind sorted through the possible labels. Each one came up unsatisfactory. Even Facebook's "in a relationship" sounded too clinical. Hell, we'd been in a relationship since we became friends. This was different, even from a few weeks ago.

Thomas's eyes creased to seductive slits as he slowly formed a smile. "Important?" He leaned in and whispered, "Maybe even essential?" His eyes flashed in mock alarm as if confessing a deep secret. "We're evolving, Kick."

"I like this," I answered, breathless.

"There she is." Thomas tilted his head, staring into my eyes. He ran his hands through my hair, brushing it off my face and catching his finger on a coil near my temple. I let it go. We'd talk about how to handle curly hair later. It was a sign. If he hadn't meant so much to me, the assumption he could mess with them would have irritated me.

"Who?" I asked.

"Kathleen. The woman who doesn't require a badass nickname to be strong. The woman who knows she's enough."

A tear fell down my cheek, realizing this was how Thomas saw me. In my mind, strength was necessary armor, not a trait. "I might like this woman," I confessed.

"She's amazing."

Wrapped up in each other, I treasured the warmth we created until a sharp breeze broke the spell, working its way between us. At the same time, a man ran by, catching Macushla's attention. She'd been curled up at my feet, having given up on us moving. She barked at the runner as if she'd asked him to rescue her from boredom.

We moved off the wall and turned back toward the Perked Cup, Thomas keeping an arm around me. "Let's get y'all back."

Crisp air filled my nose. The moldy-leaf-decay smell of early fall in the South was dissipating thanks to the incoming hard freeze. I shivered and tucked in closer to Thomas. The man practically emitted heat like a furnace.

"Your jean jacket is too thin," he said.

Words fled my mouth again as I confessed, "I'm afraid I don't remember how to do this and I'll screw it up."

"You know," Thomas began, scratching at his chin, "when you're trying something new, there's a good chance you'll have to do something you haven't done before."

"Are you patronizing me?"

His arm moved up my shoulder and draped my neck. He pulled me in for a quick kiss to my temple. My heart soared. "Only a little because I know your history. I'm in unfamiliar territory too, but we can figure it out."

We continued along the greenway, staying in a cloud nine bubble as I blitzed Thomas with questions about research and family. Wanting to know everything about him, eager for each answer.

He put his face in my hair, then whispered, "It's been a long day. Can we just walk?"

"Sorry," I said. "Some people get crabby when they're cold and tired. I talk."

"So you're exhausted all the time?" He laughed.

"Hey! You're lucky you're hot. Not to mention you have me buzzy and stuff."

Thomas stopped short, pulling me back and accidentally yanking Koosh. "Sorry, girl," he said, then turned to me. "Buzzy?"

After staring at me for several beats, waiting for an answer, I gave in. "Oh please. Like you don't know you can kiss me senseless, Mr. Magic Lips."

He laughed and resumed our course. His chest out, with a low, throaty voice, he said, "This is going to be fun."

"Buckle up, buttercup. I'm no picnic," I grumbled.

"Then, it's a good thing I'm a genius at solving puzzles. Sit back and relax, Kick. You have me now."

Thrilled and uneasy with his statement, I defaulted to what I normally did when panicked. I changed the subject. "Are you free for dinner?"

32

Thank You

Thomas

"This butterfly art is gorgeous," Thomas said while helping Kick slide out of her denim jacket. The mix of jewel tones in a Celtic design intrigued him and looked custom.

"I commissioned it from a local artist." She lowered her lashes and twisted her lips. A slight blush spread from her neckline. "It matches a tattoo I had done in the wrong place."

Thomas arched an eyebrow, surprised. He hoped like hell he'd get to see it soon.

"The tattoo came first." Kick gestured to her lower back. "I intended to put it on my shoulder but chickened out, afraid of Bobby's reaction." She raised her hands. "I know I'm grown. As you also know, I'm still working on giving up my fucks when it comes to her. Anyway, when I met the painter at an art festival, I asked her about commissions."

"It means something, yeah?"

Kick nodded and turned toward the kitchen area, speaking as they walked. "It's my Celtic zodiac animal. It's also the icon used most for thyroid disease since the organ looks like a butterfly. It fit my headspace at the time."

Kick reached Macushla's dish and fed her, the dog automatically sitting at attention while she waited for dinner. A sense of pride swelled in Thomas as he witnessed the discipline and trust Kick had built with her dog.

"You mean the metamorphosis imagery," he guessed.

"Call it cliché, but yeah. It still fits." Kick turned to the sink and washed her hands. A streetlamp to the left allowed anyone at the picture window to see passersby. She waved to a neighbor on the sidewalk.

"Be right back," he said, turning toward the guest bathroom, his mind mulling the butterfly imagery and Kick's life. He'd never thought of butterflies as a talisman. He liked the idea and decided to read up on it. He'd check on his Celtic sign too, for "shits and giggles," as his new assistant, Bethany, would say.

When he returned to the kitchen, Kick faced away from Thomas as she worked at the stove, her hair up in a high ponytail. The long line of her neck called to him, and he stepped up, placing his arms around her waist, peppering her neck with kisses. First they came soft and quick, then lingering and openmouthed.

She tipped her head back, giving him more access. "Mmm. This is nice."

Something was different about Kick. When he'd entered her office earlier, she'd had the weight of the world on her shoulders. Now that they'd cleared the air, she acted freer, looser. He smiled against her skin. Her skittishness had made some sense after the Google search. Knowing the whole truth presently, Thomas felt like a king. Kick came alive in his arms. This was what he'd missed with all those disposable women. He didn't know if it was a dream come true or a horrible idea. More importantly, he didn't care.

His hands traveled under the hem of her Perked Cup T-shirt until they skimmed under her breasts. Thomas took his time exploring, kneading them, delighting in their weight in his hand. He grew more thrilled with the way Kick's spine flexed and pressed against him as he played.

"You like?" he breathed into her ear.

"Hell yeah. I've missed this."

Thomas laughed into her shoulder. "I haven't even begun. Give it time." Movement out the window caught his eye, and he asked, "Should I stop?"

Kick turned the heat down and spun around. "Not unless you're starving. Why?"

He shrugged. "Anyone can see us in here. And you're—"

She cupped his jaw and kissed his chin, her tongue briefly teasing his cleft. Thomas chuckled in response but stayed firm in his desire to protect her. "What did you say earlier? We're important? The neighbors might as well figure it out now."

Thomas didn't want to reflect on her words too long, or he'd admit she'd already become essential. He wanted more, and he wanted it now, like a spoiled child. However, he'd also learned the value in waiting.

Kick tapped his shoulder. "Let's plate up. Dinner's ready."

They ate at the kitchen island, listening to Sarah Vaughan. Halfway through "You'd Be So Nice to Come Home To," Kick's brows drew together. She stopped eating. Her fork seemed frozen, hovering inches above the plate.

"Something wrong?"

Kick settled her fork on the plate and sighed. "Before we go further… I should tell you something."

Thomas set his fork down and turned toward her. "I'm listening."

"*ICan'tHaveMoreKids*," she blurted in a breath, reminding him of the way Liam often spoke. "You should know."

He blanched, not because he'd thought they might have any, but because the prospect never crossed his mind. He'd assumed she was done, medically or otherwise.

"Also, I wouldn't want any more if I could," she continued, slower this time. "Pregnancy made my autoimmune condition worse, and motherhood—though worth it—didn't help my body at all. I'll never stop being a mom, but I'm ready to finish raising children. Anyway, I had a hysterectomy, so even if I did, it would be moot."

"Why are you telling me this?" When he allowed himself glimpses beyond the present, Thomas saw only his work, his hobbies, and recently, Kick. He suspected where she was leading though.

"You're in your prime, Thomas. You should have full disclosure, especially after you told me about already losing a wife."

"Thank you, but I don't want children either. I like your kids… but I also like how they're housebroken, in more ways than one. Well, almost for Liam." He smiled at his joke but didn't get it returned.

"What if you—"

"Dumped you for a hot coed? Is this where you're going?"

"Don't act like it's never happened. The odds aren't good for women in relationships with our dynamics."

Thomas wrapped an arm around Kick's shoulder. What could he say when he was sure every fool who'd entered such an arrangement probably also swore the same words he wanted to promise her? But they weren't him. None of them shared his secret.

"Is this why you've been hesitant with me?"

"Partially."

"There's more?"

She adjusted her ponytail and turned to face Thomas. She muttered, "I'm done with secrets."

Thomas cringed and covered with a nod.

"When I was a teen, I caught my mother with a much younger man at her dance studio."

"The reason you quit." He didn't realize he'd thought out loud until Kick jolted.

She lowered her head. "Yes. It led to a shitstorm I couldn't have imagined. If I could do it over, I would've kept my mouth shut."

"Who did you tell?" Thomas was afraid he knew the answer.

"My dad," she whispered, blinking her eyes. "He pulled it out of me two weeks later because I wouldn't stop acting out. I remember feeling like I was boiling inside. Being a kid, I didn't know parents did this to each other. If I'd kept myself together, Dad wouldn't have known. It broke him, Thomas. Then he had his own affair, to retaliate, I guess.

"To make matters worse, Bobby announced his affair at my graduation party and turned it into her personal martyrdom. She never let him forget it."

"And her affair?" Thomas asked indignantly. Nothing surprised him when it came to human behavior. He wished he could find a way to punish Kick's parents for dragging her into their mess, dead or alive.

"She blamed Dad for it too."

"I still don't understand why this made you hot and cold."

Kick pushed her plate away. Thomas hated seeing her struggle, wished he could give her his truth to make it easier, but his vow always came first.

"Bobby knows I blame her for everything that went down. I'm the only one who has, other than Shane. Hell, even Dad drank her pity punch. Apologies aren't in her DNA, you know. She responded to me with a certain… wrath. Anyway, if she can prove we're alike, her actions would be justified, and I would need to shut the hell up now and forevermore." Kick shivered like something terrifying had crawled on her. "If you haven't figured it out, I've made it my life's mission to be the Anti-Bobby."

"Even I can see you're nothing alike. Darlin', she's gaslighting you."

"I know." Kick waved off the words. She stood, paced around the island, then sat back down.

"Have you considered it might be healthier to cut her off?"

Thomas didn't know which was sadder, Kick's heavy sigh or her chin quiver. "In his last hour, Dad convinced himself she'd find happiness with him gone. He asked me to help her find it, and I agreed."

What a horrible burden to place on a daughter, he thought, but he knew well the desperate things a dying man would say to find comfort.

"Our circumstances aren't like your mother's and…"

"Juan," she gritted out.

Incredulous, he raised an eyebrow. Could there be a more stereotypical name?

"He did the Latin classes at the studio."

Bet he did. Disgusted, Thomas continued, "We're nothing like them."

Kick's eyes flashed with panic as he drew her into his chest. "I'm serious. Don't let your mother dictate who's important to you."

Thomas kissed her pretty, pouty mouth.

"You mean essential?"

"It would be nice, wouldn't it?"

She nodded. "Okay. If she brings it up, I'll tell her to shove off."

Thomas gave Kick a squeeze. "Thank you." He finished his meal while she cleared her plate and loaded the dishwasher. He'd believed their schedules were their biggest hurdles, but this might end up harder than expected. He liked the possibility of putting Bobby in her place though.

She picked up Thomas's plate and asked, "Whiskey? I have a twenty-one-year Redbreast I bring out for celebrations."

"You're spoiling me." He smiled, anticipating the smooth drink. "Thank you."

She reached up on tiptoe and moved books around in a cabinet. Other liquor bottles waited patiently on a lower shelf. "Big cube?"

Thomas chuckled. She had designer ice cubes. Kick's attention to detail was turning out to be thorough in scope and intention. He'd see to it she knew he noticed. "Perfect."

She gave him a good pour, set it in front of Thomas, and replaced the cork top.

"Not going to join me?"

Kick patted her belly and scrunched her nose. *Adorable.* "Still on lockdown. The doctor doesn't want me drinking grain alcohol for at least six months either. We've had differing opinions on what the word 'distill' means, but I figured I'd capitulate this time. However, I'm not telling the family in Ireland." She laughed at the last sentence.

"Why not?"

"Uncle Billy... Shane's uncle and the McKenna patriarch. He

teases me for not liking Jameson's. I only get a pass because I drink Redbreast and Bushmills. If he finds out about this, he'll take my Irish card away."

Kick filled her electric kettle and turned it on. She poured a small glass of what looked like pink iced tea from the refrigerator and brought a pillbox to the island. She sat on her stool and spilled the night's allotment, swallowing four at a time.

Thomas inhaled deeply, taking it in, still getting used to how much of her life was under constant supervision. "How are you feeling now? Is your program working?"

"I think so. Thanks for asking. The IVs are improving. I get an immediate boost—long enough to get home and crash. I have all-day energy the next day." Kick rolled her neck, the stretching making it pop. "It's better in small steps each day. I call it the autoimmune cha-cha. It's the kind of improvement I've learned to appreciate because it sticks."

Thomas chuckled at the phrase. "Autoimmune what?"

"Three steps forward, two steps back. It's still one step forward in progress." Kick shrugged. "The health journey isn't a straight upward climb. As long as there's improvement over time, you're hanging the moon."

Thomas thought it a fitting image of life in general.

Kick finished her medicine and put the pill organizer away as the kettle blew, ending with a cup of mint tea. She took Thomas by the hand and said, "Join me in the living room?"

They settled into the corner of her leather sectional and caught a few minutes of a sketch comedy. Pictures of the kids adorned the built-ins surrounding the fireplace. Pumpkins, witches, and other seasonal decor dotted the open shelves.

"Your Halloween tchotchkes are adorable, but I'm curious why you don't have any photos of your late husband," Thomas said.

Kick answered absently, "Everything's upstairs in the den. It's a veritable shrine to Shane up there." She looked up at Thomas. "It was too hard to keep the past in every corner, so I put it in one place."

He could relate. A miniature portrait of Alicia sat in his reading nook. It was the only surviving image he had, but he could imagine how oppressive it would be to keep a houseful. Alicia's presence still inhabited the rooms at his home in Virginia. He liked keeping her in designated spaces too.

Thomas looked down at Kick and gave her a soft smile. "I'd love to see it."

She finished her tea and sat up. "Sure. But before I take you up there, I have another question."

"Shoot…" He smiled, kissing her on the forehead. Like someone had opened a dam and he couldn't get enough. He didn't know where this emotional, mush-ball side of him was coming from.

"Halloween. Any chance you could help me with the party we throw in the afternoon? It's from three to five. It started for our high school regulars, though little kids have started coming, along with young adults who've graduated and stayed close. The neighboring shops join in now too."

"I can be free. I'd love to help. What would I do?"

"Pass out the candy as people enter." She flashed a cheesy grin. "And wear a matching costume."

His eyes narrowed in suspicion. "What kind of costume?" She'd lassoed him in like a sucker.

"I'm going as a fairy."

Thomas laughed and rubbed the pointy tip of her ear. "Of course you are. There's no way I'm showing my face in public in fairy tights. Sorry, not sorry."

"You don't have to wear tights. Liam's Renaissance Faire pants could work. And there's still time to pick up manly fairy wings."

"*There's* an oxymoron." She faked a pout, but he wasn't falling for it. He raised an eyebrow to challenge. Kick may have to turn in her Irish card, but he'd damn sure keep hold of his man card.

"Fine." She sighed. "What do you have to wear?"

"I have a Bela Lugosi as *Dracula* shirt."

"Sounds scary."

"I could… smile? Without bloody teeth."

"I don't know. You have resting grump face, and mothers will yell at me from the middle of the store if their kids cry."

"For Christ's sake. I'll think of something. Speaking of RGF, I should get Banger to stop by. It'll be *my* entertainment for the afternoon. And good for him to be nice to little kids."

"Are you sure? He scared me when I met him. He sports more of an RAF?"

"Uh… angry?"

"Asshole."

Thomas barked a laugh at Kick's accurate description. Still, he planned to mention it to Banger. He found himself surprised to admit he looked forward to the afternoon. He had shrunk his world too much over the years. Thomas rarely spent any time talking to young children.

They were halfway up the stairs when Kick asked, "Do you follow football at all?"

Thomas shook his head. "I'm more of a UFC, boxing, or martial arts kinda guy."

"I thought so, considering you had to Google me to find my connection to Shane."

Thomas reached the top step and took in the loft. A hallway to the left led to doors he assumed were bedrooms. A full bathroom lay straight ahead. A big sitting space composed the open area to his right. Another U-shaped sectional anchored the room with a large-screen TV on the opposite wall.

"Whoa." Thomas crossed to the shelves surrounding the television. Shane's photos, trophies, and other awards filled one side while the children's accolades covered the other. He was in many of these photos too. In one, Shane lifted a young Dylan, larger than the other kids in the picture. He beamed in a photo next to a smiling Rachel with a tennis racquet and first-place ribbon. He spent time with each relic, taking in the essence of life as a McKenna, overwhelmed by what they'd lost. No, whom. No, both.

It gave him a sense of why Kick worked so hard when he got the impression she didn't have to, why she didn't move the family to an easier living situation when she'd practically described the house as being haunted. He knew hauntings could comfort as much as cause upset.

Kick stood in front of a photo of a tiny Liam raising a football in an end zone, his gleeful face offset by everyone else in the frame. Some people grabbed their heads, brows furled. Others were bent over, laughing. A sad smile filled her face as she traced Liam with a forefinger. "He was so excited to get the ball; he never heard us yelling he was running in the wrong direction. The score went to the other team. Lee cried until Shane promised he'd still take him out for ice cream. He figured the boy deserved a celebration since he had caught a boomer of a pass and ran three-quarters of the field… against his own teammates." She shook with laughter by the time she finished.

Thomas wrapped an arm around Kick and kissed her temple. "It pleases me to know y'all were loved."

"Thanks," Kick whispered. "I'm glad my secret's out." She stood on her toes and placed a soft kiss on Thomas's lips. "When you're comfortable, you can tell me yours."

He bit his lip and stepped back. "I told you about my late wife."

Kick shook her head, moving closer, drawing his forehead to hers. She whispered, "I promise not to press, but there's more. I might figure it out though." She tapped the side of her head. "It's like a sixth sense I can't help. Secrets have a way of revealing themselves to me."

"Oh really?" Thomas lifted an eyebrow and smirked. He hoped Kick didn't honestly believe she had magical powers.

"Better believe it," Liam scoffed, standing at the top of the stairs. They both jumped at his words. "If I were you, I'd spill now. She's figured out every secret the three of us kids tried to hide. Fam's a McKenna legend. The Irish cousins say she's part Fae."

Kick looked between the men, a deep blush trailing down past her collar, her head shaking.

33

Lovely Day

Kick

I stood outside Thomas's office, my hand shaking, hovering in midair. It shook from hunger mixed with hopelessness. Setbacks are normal, but my doctor hammered me on stress, which only added more. It was wrong to come here after my disastrous follow-up appointment.

I practically ran to Thomas's office, eager to get away from everything wrong in my life. I'd fixed my issues over Shane and enjoyed my time with Thomas, though I still had a ton of work to do. Instincts led me to his office because I was needy, discouraged, and weak—all the consequences I hated about being autoimmune. I decided too late that he shouldn't have to deal with me dumping this on him.

"The glass in the door may be striated, Kick, but I can tell it's you," Thomas called from the other side, a smile in his tone. "Your hair gives you a specific silhouette. Door's open, darlin'."

I stepped inside, my fake-it-till-I-make-it smile plastered on. "You busy?" My gaze swept the office. Stacks of folders occupied every available surface, even a love seat. "You are. I'll leave you alone." I hoped Thomas would take them out. It was a mistake to stop in. The *old* Kick ran to her rescuers. Where'd the lessons of the past eight years go? My biggest takeaways had been that happiness is fleeting and only I can control my joy.

He tipped his head, studying me. "What's wrong, baby?"

This is wrong. I should've gone to University Gardens and meditated. I waved my hand to indicate everything was fine.

"If you wait a few minutes, I'll go with you to the Gardens." He took another step and kissed my temple. "But it's never a mistake to come to see me."

Shit. I'd voiced my thoughts. My shoulders slumped on an exhale.

He gestured to two library chairs, lowering me into the second one and taking the first for himself. "Doctor's appointment didn't go well?"

"How did you know I saw Dr. Chaddha?"

"Wouldn't you be at the Perked Cup otherwise?"

"Touché."

Thomas pulled my hand into his lap, stroking the top with his thumb. I tipped my head back when my vision blurred. "Yeah, it's the appointment. Mixed with stuff going on at the café."

"You mean the shiner Liam sported the other night?"

I nodded. Once my son finished cluing Thomas into my "voodoo-secret detection skills"—his words—I spotted his black eye and cut cheek, then proceeded to "lose my shit"—also Lee's words. I maintained it was justified. Thomas calmed us both and drew out the story of the fight in the coffeehouse. He kept me from marching up to there in a panic too. Instead, I called Jake, hearing his side, getting assurances they limited the damage to a broken leg on a chair. It happened when a boy said filthy things about Rachel. According to Jake, the kid riled Liam on purpose.

"It doesn't help our reputation in the community… There was another opinion piece on the neighborhood website yesterday."

"What did the doctor say?"

"She nailed me to the wall. Diet, medicine, and extras like supplemental IVs or massages can't make up for staying stressed."

The frightful state of Thomas's office increased my unease. "I'm sorry to bother you when it's obvious you're swamped. I shouldn't be dumping this on you. I'll go… meditate."

"Hang on." Thomas squeezed my hand, the connection a sweet hum. It worked its way across my limbs and to my core, pushing back negative emotions. "Are you referring to this mess? An ancient file cabinet broke yesterday. The new one's out for delivery." He pulled me into his lap, bringing me into a tight hold, allowing the stress to take a short hike. "I'm thrilled you came to me. You weren't weak to stop by. It takes strength to show vulnerability. Plus strength is *facing* rough news, not ignoring it." He tipped up my chin with a gentle finger and pressed a kiss to my hopeful lips. "It's damn inspiring. I've had my share of setbacks lately. They make me want to punch the wall sometimes. You remind me setbacks are part of the fight too."

I soaked up his encouragement, appreciating what he offered. Fearing it too. It would be easy to lean on Thomas, but I was afraid to cross the line into becoming a burden. The little nagging voice in my mind kept taunting me, telling me this was too good to be true. My setback was proof I would never deserve another chance at happiness. The menacing voice had quieted with early progress, but it currently shouted at me with each additional problem.

And why was this the first I'd heard of Thomas's setbacks? Openness couldn't be a one-way street.

"How about lunch and a walk in the garden?"

Could he use the break as much as I could? I lifted my chin and studied his face, handsome as ever. But there were shadows under his eyes. Yeah, maybe we could lift each other up. The possibility of helping Thomas with his troubles made mine dissipate. "Sounds perfect," I answered.

Thomas helped me stand and moved to a coatrack in the corner. A quick knock caught our attention, and a gorgeous honey-blond coed stepped inside.

"Oh, sorry to interrupt, Professor. Thought you might be ready for my wicked hex key skills."

A corner of Thomas's mouth ticked up. "Sorry, Beth. The

cabinet hasn't arrived yet." He turned to me. "Kick, I'd like you to meet my new lead assistant, Bethany. Beth, my… Kick."

I chuckled at the awkward introduction while extending my hand. "Nice to meet you, Bethany."

"Beth is fine." She shook my hand, her eyes a pretty peridot, bright with curiosity.

"You could've texted," Thomas said.

"True. I also thought you should see this." Beth pulled a folder from her backpack and handed it to him.

Thomas's forehead drew into tight trenches as he perused the sheets inside the folder. "This is the latest data?"

Beth's face also darkened as she nodded.

"Dammit all."

"I don't know how the original sample is doing so well when these others have telomere issues," Beth said.

My eyes flashed at the word *telomere*. I'd read about them and was expecting a report on my own soon.

"How do you feel about setting up for the next step, Beth?" Thomas asked.

I barely caught her panicked expression. My mind was busy watching them together—a ridiculously handsome, young professor with a devoted ingenue at his side. How was he *not* seduced by the scenario? I didn't doubt Thomas. He showed complete respect for their instructor-student boundaries. But I looked at Beth and saw my flaws—the autoimmunity, infertility, gray roots, extra weight, half my life already finished. I was the Anti-Bethany.

"Can you give us a minute?" Thomas asked.

I turned for the door, and his hand around mine prevented me from going any farther. "Thank you, Beth." She stepped through the door, closing it behind her.

Here I'd thought Thomas had been dismissing me.

His eyes perused my face before he pushed a curl behind my ear. He looked pained as he said, "I have to get to the lab. I'm sorry."

I tried to reassure him with a small smile and head tip. "Sure. I should've gone to the park anyway."

Thomas's thumbs stroked my neck. "I'm glad you didn't. Come

by or call me anytime." The twinkle in his eyes matched the brightness of the sun streaming in his south-facing window. But it couldn't extinguish the festering darkness in me. "I wish I could join you."

"No worries, handsome. I understand."

He kissed my temple. "I know you do. Thank you."

"Will you still be able to do the Halloween party tomorrow?"

"Wouldn't miss it."

"Figure out your costume yet?"

A sexy grin filled his face. "You'll see."

Great. I batted my lashes. "It'll help my stress if you tell me."

He tapped my nose. "Not like meditating will." Thomas lowered his mouth to mine in a soft, slow kiss. "I hope our visit helped. You sure made my day."

I stood in the hallway, watching the two walk in the opposite direction as my car. I couldn't help but think I was watching Thomas's true future or something like it.

I was such a lousy waste of his time.

34

Holding Back the Years

Thomas

ANOTHER DEAD END. THOMAS SLAMMED HIS HAND IN THE DESKTOP. It was late, but he couldn't go home. Not until he figured out the block. His finger hovered over Alaric's number. He'd spent the past twelve hours working on a setback he couldn't fix, but he couldn't place the call. Not yet.

Desire boiled in the pit of his stomach. It started the first time his lips met Kick's and grew with each encounter. Did he want out of the Felidae? Or would he settle for more autonomy? The choice wasn't clear yet, so he waited. He'd mastered waiting by necessity. If Thomas could snap his fingers, he'd get his break, proving the genetic origins of the Felidae members and others like them, and he'd hand the next phase off to someone else. Hell, he'd give it to Nigel even if Alaric protested. They might not be best buddies, but they were allies in the work. Right?

Thomas let his mind wander to the morning with Kick. It might be easier to keep her off the Felidae's radar if he returned to real estate. He'd been a developer before going to school. If he talked to his business manager, he could slip back into the game.

He'd grown fond of Liam too. Both Kick's boys, really. He didn't know Rachel well since she was staying in Raleigh. Banger hadn't tracked down the source of the girl's online harassment yet. Still, Thomas wanted to know her better too.

He enjoyed encouraging an anxious Liam the other night, already upset from defending his sister's honor. The boy had been anxious over physics. ADHD made it hard for Liam to focus, but he was whip-smart. Thomas knew the frustration of trying to work when your mind was elsewhere.

He hoped her kids would give him and Kick their approval before things went further. Wait, was he honestly contemplating a serious commitment? He thought back through their last two meetings and texts. They were growing close fast. Perhaps too fast. But damn if his every cell didn't respond to Kick when she was near.

Thomas ran his hands through his hair, grabbing at the roots. How had his calm, collected demeanor wandered off? He hated not being able to see a clear path. Now it was obscured, both personally and professionally.

Thomas spotted Banger from the parking lot of the twenty-four-hour diner, the only customer sitting alone in a booth. Other couples and groups sat around tables on the other side of the space. Knowing Banger, he'd probably paid the waitress to keep the section empty.

Thomas joined him, a chin tip from each for a greeting. He wordlessly perused the menu, noting how nothing fit in Kick's diet. The waitress stepped up, coffeepot in hand, and took their orders. Thomas made sure he chose as few carbs as possible. He needed energy to get through another long day.

Banger's eyes followed their waitress back to the kitchen before breaking his gaze and addressing Thomas. "Why did you drag me out of my house in the wee hours?"

Thomas muttered, "You were awake."

"Not the point."

He gripped the back of his neck, swiveling it from side to side in a futile attempt at a stretch. He filled his friend in on the issues at the lab. Thomas hoped Banger's logical brain could help him look at the problem from a different angle.

"Not to be Captain Obvious, but you freak out when you're on the verge of something big. Since I'm not in a hand-holding mood, I'll say congratulations. I knew you could do it."

Thomas took a sip of weak, tepid black coffee and slumped. "Fuck off."

The overly bright lights gave Banger's pale skin an unfortunate, ghostly appearance. He lifted his hands in surrender. "It's not about wanting to help. If you had a hardware or software issue, I'd be right there even if it went against the university's protocols. Based on my understanding of what you do, it sounds like you're on track. Have you considered calling Nigel?" Banger's nose flared at the name. For as long as he'd known the man, they'd shared an animosity.

"Considered? Yes. But Alaric and Ellie are trying to pit us against each other for a reason they won't share. It makes no sense."

"Not to you."

"Something going on I should know?" Thomas asked. "There were more closed-door meetings than usual back in Bordeaux."

Banger shook his head. "Don't know, brother. But with each day that passes, I'm convinced there's a bonafide traitor in the Felidae."

"Christ, I never thought about it like that."

Banger casually lifted a shoulder. "Make sure your lab stays secure twenty-four seven. Let me do my thing. I want to know ASAP if anything seems off."

Thomas agreed as the food arrived. They ate in silence, Thomas scarfing down his eggs and sausage, leaving the toast and jam.

Banger set his coffee cup down abruptly. "What else is going on? You're holding so much tension you're making my TMJ ache. Have you banged Kick yet?"

Thomas dropped his fork and scowled. "Come on, man."

"I'm serious. What's taking so long? You look like a man who wants to blow out his carburetor. Get it over with and let her go." Banger took a bite of pancake and circled the air with his fork. "Or make another Vivienne arrangement."

Thomas shook his head. "It's not so simple. I traveled more back then. A similar arrangement wouldn't work when I'm in town most of the time." He didn't want to add *he* was different too. Thomas didn't want the distance, physical or otherwise, again.

"Sure it could. Tell her you're available on weekends and leave it at that."

Thomas tried to school his reaction to the idea souring his stomach. Between the kids, the people at the Perked Cup, and Mick & Hugh's, he'd been accepted into the fold by everyone. He liked them all. This wasn't only about Kick.

"Oh hell." Banger dropped his fork. "Bad idea, brother. Stay the fucking course." He pointed at Thomas. "Still don't know why you won't stick with the pretty little bics. Consider yourself like a stud dog. If the animal doesn't blow a few times a year, he gets unreasonable—even violent. He gets some? He calms the fuck back down. We're the same way. A disposable woman is the perfect solution. A few weeks of bump and grind, we're happy, they're happy. We move on."

"You know…" Fatigue made Thomas irritable. "With you, everything's disposable."

"You wound me," Banger said, dramatically touching his heart. "And you, my friend, hold on to everything. How long have you had your car? *Jings Crivvens*, get a new one already."

Thomas's bubbling emotions made him get real. He exhaled an exasperated breath. "Don't you tire of living outside real society? I thought the Felidae would help me finally belong, except I don't live on the vineyard full time."

Banger scoffed. "Who wants to?"

"Exactly. We're still on the outside, man."

"I like to think of it as moving between two worlds. I get to choose." Banger shoved a chunk of pancake in his mouth, speaking around it. "It's about perspective." He chewed and swallowed.

Thomas looked at Banger's plate again—four plates, actually. Lord, when would their breakfast end? This had been a mistake.

"I've thought about it, and everything *is* disposable. As soon as it's not useful, it has to go."

The words made Thomas want to hurl. But he grew tired of talking. He craved the connection he'd already cultivated with Kick. Something deep down told him sleeping together would grow their spark, not quench it.

Banger let out a long sigh. "You're worse than I thought. You still making music? My piano fills the lonely spaces late at night. I was working on Ravel when you texted."

Thomas arched a brow. "You already play his stuff better than the man ever dreamed of it. Anyway, I'm moving Eddie down here soon. Not that my horse will fix this."

Banger muttered while stabbing a sausage, "Don't know, brother. He's a good horse."

Thomas held in a laugh. "Eddie's coming because I'd like a piece of home nearby. I also don't want him thinking I've abandoned him." Thomas hoped to share Ed with Kick too.

Banger shook his head, then slapped the table. "I know what's going on. I recognize it now. This is a midlife crisis. I had a major one about a year before we met. Hell, I'm surprised you haven't had one already." He drank the last of his coffee in time for the waitress to refresh the cup. He sent a flirty wink her way before continuing, "I fell hard for a dark-haired feisty miss for a minute." Banger snuck a wistful glance out the window. Darkness wrestled with the dawn, leaving the sky a tortured gray. The emotion was universal then.

They turned back to each other. "We had a rare connection. Then reality slapped me in the face. I couldn't grow old with her. So I left. I'll admit ghosting was hella easy then." He made a wiping motion with his hands. "It was better for her. Then I banged my way from Europe to Australia. Ended up surfing in Polynesia for months. Tourism was taking off, and the ladies were more than happy to have a lesson and a screw from 'an exotic ginger'." Banger waggled his eyebrows.

"Bet they were," Thomas said. He could see it too—Banger's usually buzzed blond hair long, his face constantly sunburned. The women would've eaten it up.

"As I said, man, I can't just leave. I have a contract with the university." Thomas drank from his warmed-up cup. "I could stop going to the café, but we still might run into each other." He didn't want to admit a future with Kick excited him, but it was the picture forming in his mind. He didn't care about growing old with her. He'd do what he must. Thomas wasn't sure how far they could take it. He just knew he hadn't felt this good in forever.

Then his phone rang. Thomas checked the caller and said, "It's Alaric. You mind?"

"Go right ahead." Banger pretended to zip his lips shut.

"*Oui Grand-père*. Thank you for returning my call."

"Certainly. Do you have news?" Alaric asked.

"It's not good. The general population samples keep failing. Toni doesn't want me to use her family's DNA, and I won't break her trust."

"I thought I impressed upon you how urgent progress is now," Alaric snapped. The man cleared his throat and changed his tone. "I'm a patient man. I have to be. But now isn't the time for caution. It's time to push."

"Isn't trust more important for the long game? We can't have Toni running away… or worse. She's more than potential Felidae. She's family."

"*We* are your priority and your family. I can't have you conflicted, my boy."

Thomas remembered his induction ceremony. The vows were easy since Joe took them at the same time. The pull of loyalty began when Joey left the group, calling it all bullshit. Thomas had never parsed out exactly what had ticked him off. Joe refused to say. Maybe he'd ask again the next time he went home.

"I haven't forgotten my vow."

Banger rolled his eyes and looked up at the ceiling.

"Focus is everything," Alaric urged.

"Understood." Thomas's hand shook as he set the phone down.

"I can get the DNA sample for you," Banger offered.

Thomas's hand found the back of his neck again. "I might take y'all up on it," he answered, distracted.

From the moment he'd made his vow, the Felidae came first. Why did it sound like Alaric had spoken about more than family ties with his warning? More than once, Thomas thought Alaric had the gift of sight.

Perhaps Banger was right. The timing for him and Kick wasn't right. He shouldn't let himself get caught up in their newness. He should back off.

35

Thriller

Kick

OUR HALLOWEEN PARTY BEGAN EARLIER THAN EXPECTED WHEN moms of preschoolers stopped in for lunch after class. My crew didn't mind since the candy bowls were ready. We had color-coded buckets to make it easier for kids with allergies. The regular bucket was refilled twice before the high schoolers arrived. If the pace kept up, the day would've been our most successful by far.

Jake and Deana ganged up on me, insisting I ditch the fairy wings since they kept knocking into the staff. I'd barely missed poking out Deana's eye twice. Thus my fairy costume became an elf's.

I didn't mind. I was flying high on the joy of my second-favorite holiday, my bedroom remodel was due to finish soon, and I'd made peace with my doctor's earlier admonishment. I'd even meditated and worked out first thing in the morning.

"You look oddly happy," Bobby commented from her perch at the counter.

"It's Halloween," I answered. "The sun's shining. Pumpkin spice fills the air." It wouldn't be long before I could add decaf coffee back into my regimen. I marked it on my calendar. "It's a good day, Mother." *Wow, Bobby's presence didn't bother me.* I shifted my shoulders, searching for tension. Nope. My spine was set but not tight. Hell, I was on a roll.

"It *is* a good day." She'd handed out candy when I sent Crystal to get more from the grocery store. Plus she didn't stage-whisper mean things about the children or their mothers. "Are you enjoying your time with that younger man?"

"Uh, I am." She didn't need to know about our fight or making up. She also didn't know about Dr. Chaddha's comments and most definitely wouldn't hear about my insecurities over seeing Thomas with a more suitable woman. Bobby and I worked best when we took the British approach to conversation and kept it to the weather.

"Well, good." Bobby nodded into her cup. "He looks like the kind of man who can help you lose your extra weight."

I paused midwipe during my counter-cleaning ritual. On a great day like the present, it was easy enough to let the comment roll off, so I said nothing and kept to my work until the wood sparkled.

"You know," she added with a defensive tone, "he's fit. I bet he'll be fun to work out with." My non-comments often startled her more than arguing back did.

"He is fun to walk with, but the good doctor didn't clear me for anything harder than lifting small dumbbells and bodyweight exercises."

"Which explains the tummy," Bobby said.

Jake handed off an order, shaking his head.

"I suppose it's better than when you had no curves at all. Poor thing." She backpedaled. "When your doctor lets you run again, you'll return to a proper size."

I knew Bobby only saw her flaws when she looked in a mirror. So I chose to view her words as positive and moved on to serve a customer. In some ways, I preferred her clueless warnings to the outright jealousy she'd shown when I'd lost the hundred pounds.

As high schoolers sauntered in dressed in costumes, Deana still passed out candy. She always left by three so she could pick up her grandchildren at the bus stop. With a smile on my face, hiding my concern, I approached her. "Not to scare you, Dee, but shouldn't you scoot now?"

I held my hands open to take the bowl from her, enabling a quick escape. A grin washed over her before she responded. It turned out she wasn't freaked about being late. "I forgot to tell you… my Maceo took the afternoon off and went to the school parties. He's bringing Genesis's kids home too. I want to stick around and see which big kids dressed up."

"Aw. Mace is such a wonderful dad." Looking out the window for approaching teens, I added, "Hope my kids turn out like yours."

Deana's smooth laugh rumbled from her chest. "If they don't, I'll discipline them myself."

"Hey, do you have any photos ready to hang in here? If we get some up now, you could schedule holiday sessions next month." Deana had recently set up an indoor studio in her house. I hoped she'd take the leap and turn her side hustle into a full-fledged venture. I'd miss her face around the café, but she had talent and had proven her business savvy as my manager.

"There's a handful left to frame. I'll bring them on Monday."

"Perfect."

"Is Cyndi stopping by?" Deana laughed. "She sure knows how to put together a costume."

I moved my chin from left to right. "Cyn's booked, and she's doing the grown-up party thing tonight," I added.

Dee opened yet another bag of candy, restocking the buckets. She looked over her shoulder at Bobby and turned back to me, talking low near my ear. "You and the professor aight now?"

"We're good," I started, checking over my shoulder as well. "I'm taking everything one day at a time. Enjoying each moment." Something stopped me from opening up completely about my concerns. I wasn't sure how to take the insecure feelings from yesterday. Were they related to my emotions from the doctor's appointment, or did they happen congruently? Or maybe I didn't want the words released into the same air Bobby occupied, fearing they'd magically find a way to her ears. It was Halloween after all.

Liam's arrival interrupted us. He came by straight after school, wearing his brother's old practice football gear with zombie makeup added.

"Hey, Weeman." I circled my face with my forefinger. "Please tone down the makeup before more littles show up. Don't want to scare anyone."

"Fine, fam," he grumbled. "Yo Grams," he said to Bobby.

She returned it with a "Hello, pumpkin. Have you grown?"

Liam and I both did a double take her way. We weren't used to her saying anything close to complimentary toward my youngest. She'd decided Liam would be my scapegoat child from day one. From what my brother Bert told me, she did the same with his youngest. He had two boys and no girl. Bert's saving grace came from living in the Detroit area. Our mother only visited them twice a year unless they traveled down. Thankfully, she planned to be there in December. I'd thought spending the first Christmas without Dad with her favorite child would ease any pain the holiday might bring.

"You look just like Dylan," Bobby said.

Liam lifted the practice jersey by the collar. "It's his old football gear."

"Ah. I see," she said, taking a sip of coffee. "Can you refresh me?"

"I'll get it," I said and reminded Liam to clean up.

Lee came back from the bathroom, looking more dirty than scary, and walked straight to me. "When am I going to get my parking space in the garage back? The morning frost is getting thick on my car. It's not *my* stuff filling my spot either."

I cringed, watching Deana and Jake eye me suspiciously. "You're right, sweetheart. You can have my space until the furniture gets moved. We'll be ready for it in a day or two."

"Thank you." He sighed.

Deana arched her eyebrow, wordlessly demanding an explanation.

I laughed before saying, "You know about the remodel, right?"

She looked to Jake, who shrugged. "How could we not?"

"Well, I bought a smaller bedroom suite. Hugh and Maggie are downsizing and had a mint-condition Stickley set. It's a queen sleigh bed and perfect for me. Some guys from the crew moved it a couple of nights ago for side money. Since the room's not yet ready, it waits in the garage."

"I see. Were you planning on saying anything?"

"Dee, I see you so little lately we spend most of our time catching up on business. You can come see it when everything is done." The corner of my mouth lifted, happy with my self-defense.

Bobby tsked and shook her head. "You had a perfect set before. I don't know why you had to get a used one. From the *Reynoldses* too."

"It suits me, Mother. Did you hear me say it's mint? I've loved that style forever. Plus they practically gave it to me when a dealer would've paid them beaucoup bucks. Besides, the old one's in storage for Dylan."

"Oh," she said, seeming appeased by the notion it waited for her favorite grandchild. She didn't understand my son was on the verge of success greater than anything his father or I had dreamed of at his age. Since she didn't understand computer science—hell, I barely did—I let it go too.

We spent a half hour busting through a busy line. It was like old times except for the two people missing—my dad and Rachel.

Deana was wrapping up her shift when she looked out the window and said, "Thank heavens he's here. I was hoping I'd get to see his costume."

I sidled up to her. "Who are you…?" I spotted Thomas walking away from his Camaro. "Oh. Wow." I shook my head, laughing at his costume. Silly, but scorching hot.

You could hear Thomas's spurs ting against the floor as he entered the Perked Cup. They wrapped a pair of well-worn cowboy boots, followed by perfectly broken-in jeans, an empty, albeit worn, gun holster, a sheepskin vest, poncho, western hat, and a cigar nub. He swaggered better than Eastwood himself and looked like he could be comfortable roaming a desert. On a horse. Hunting bad guys.

My face turned red as my knees weakened, and my underwear

dampened from the sight. A grin split my face as he neared. I didn't even care if Bobby picked up on my vulnerability. The man looked too scrumptious for words. I wished my bedroom were finished so I could convince him to spend the night and play cowboy and… elf something. *Whoa, where'd that come from?* Okay, I wouldn't, really. Not until I knew Liam was comfortable with him, but *Jaysus*, I wanted to.

Thomas was my icing on a fantastic cake of a day. He stepped up to me and placed a kiss to my cheek, keeping the cigar nub in place. "Hey beautiful."

"Hey yourself." I tipped the hat, still grinning. He'd let his stubble grow since yesterday. "Don't you think you're a little dark for Blondie?"

"Look again, darlin'. He isn't exactly a sunny surfer boy."

"Good point. It's an awesome costume, actually." I stood on my toes, kissed his cheek back, and whispered, "Sexy too."

Thomas's eyes flashed with amusement and lust. "Think so?"

"I do."

Thomas bent and whispered, "Enough for a feel-up in the office?"

My knees weakened more from the offer. "How about after the party?"

He pretended to pout before his mouth curled up on one side. "Can't wait." He touched my shoulder. "What happened to the wings?"

I jutted my chin toward Jake and Deana, who was saying her goodbyes and waving out the door. "I bumped into them too much." I spread my Celtic embroidered tunic out at the hem. "I'm an elf now."

He touched the tip of my ear and grinned back at me. "An elf suits you better."

Bobby choked on her coffee, taking a few coughs to resettle. My pointy ears were another of her embarrassments.

"When's this party happening?" Thomas asked.

"It should start in earnest in about thirty minutes. You want a coffee before it picks up?"

"Sure."

"One of the famous pumpkin spice lattes?" Liam asked from the order area.

Thomas scrunched his face, his nose getting an adorable crease I'd never noticed before. "Christ no, kid. An Americano is fine."

"Well said, my dude."

"Was he testing me?" Thomas asked me.

I shrugged. "You never know with him." I tapped Thomas's chin. "You should lose the stogie, pal."

"It's not lit," he argued. I answered with a sigh and squint. "Mothers yelling in the middle of the dining room?"

"Among other things." I held out my hand for it.

His face scrunched in disgust. "No, darlin'. I'll take care of it. Go see to your customers."

Thomas went to the bathroom, came back minus a cigar, then talked Bobby into handing out the allergy candies. It was the lightest bucket. There were plenty of us behind the counter to handle the crowd once it kicked in. Parents of the elementary school kids brought them by after school for heavy snacks and early trick-or-treating before heading home.

The inside became standing room only, causing customers to hang around on the patio too. The afternoon was perfect for alfresco partying but made it impossible for us to keep track of everyone. The café filled with Hogwarts students of all ages and houses, gruesome monsters, pretty princesses, and superheroes from the year's blockbusters.

I was in my element, as was the rest of the crew. We even danced a few steps to Michael Jackson's "Thriller" and other Halloween songs while waiting on customers, enjoying the buzz of the crowd.

I rang up an order for a mother in desperate need of a large pumpkin spice latte, with a juice and cookie for her kindergarten-aged Batman. An earsplitting series of bangs filled the dining room, erupting near the windows. The sound deafened like rapid-fire gunshots.

36

Once in a Lifetime

Kick

Jake flung himself over the counter with a fluid jump before I registered what had happened. The bangs, the screams, and the stampede all blended together. I looked down at little Batman, his face filled with shock and terror, tears already streaming down his cheeks. I grabbed him, his mother, and two nearby teens, brought them behind the counter, and made them stay down.

Someone cried out, "It's a mass shooter!"

Another voice shrieked as if hurt. The space filled with smoke and a sulfur smell. Liam grabbed a fire extinguisher and sprayed a smoking object on the floor.

Panic filled me. "Liam!"

"It's out," he called back over his shoulder.

I pulled the first aid kit from under the counter and shoved it at our new girl. "Crystal, take this and help Lee."

People held their phones above their heads, filming. Thomas had his phone raised, and I stepped to him, fury boiling over and skewing my judgment. My anger toward the person who'd done this channeled into a rage at him for adding to what I feared would become a media frenzy.

Charging forward, I yelled, "No!" and slapped the cell from his hand. Despite the unrelenting noise, his phone seemed to clang as it hit the floor, shattering the screen. The sting to my fingers came next as the reality of what I'd done set in. We both stared at each other for a beat, equally shocked by my response.

"What the hell?" he growled, his jaw flexed, nostrils flared.

"Some motherfucking asshole set off firecrackers to create a panic. And it worked. If your video gets on tonight's news, it could shut me down."

"Come on, Kick." Thomas oozed disappointment. "I was calling 911, then Banger. If the alarm hasn't gone off at the Angel office, they need to know. They should be looking at the feed right now."

My chin quivered when his words set in. I'd let my temper override logic again. "I'm so sorry."

Little Batman had been peeking over the counter, his eyes wide. He'd watched our interaction and heard me swear. "Sorry about the yelling and naughty words, sweetheart. I'm really, really upset." His mother's eyes sent evil daggers my way. *Jaysus, I had to rein in my temper.* I patted little Batman's hoodie ears before his mother batted my hand away. "It was only a mean prank. No one shot anybody. The scared people are saying things they don't understand."

"Don't you touch him," the woman snapped. My guilt grew for my part in the spread of panic.

"I want to go home, Mommy," he whimpered. "I hate Ha-wo-ween."

Lovely. I turned my attention to the mother. "Take the back hallway to the rear door." I told her the code to open it and looked at the teens hovering by her. "Take the girls too."

Giving little Batman's mom a job helped her settle. She moved the kids out efficiently.

Liam called 911 while Thomas and Crystal triaged a few teens who'd been near the attack—now a smoking, shredded backpack under the front windows. Both panes suffered spider cracking, and one had a small hole burst in front of the bag. Teens on the patio were helping another with cuts in her leg.

"Send an ambulance to the Perked Cup, please. We have three burn victims and others with cuts as far as I can tell," Liam said. He wasn't the only one calling in our attack either.

I turned away to gather ice and clean rags.

Quickly what looked like the entire fleet of Oakville PD cruisers skidded to a stop in front of the café, in full tactical gear. Half remained outside, taking charge of the crowd. The other half came inside with weapons drawn. More screaming ensued.

Scanning the room, I made sure everyone kept their hands up. The collective terror on my customers' faces made my knees buckle in despair. I murmured under my breath, "We can't go down like this. We can't."

Gaping at Thomas, a defiant tear dropped down my cheek. Not only was my festive day ruined, my business might be too.

I yelled to the officers, "It was firecrackers, not a gun."

The lead one looked in the direction I'd jutted my chin and turned back. "Still need y'all's hands up, ma'am. Anyone see who did it?"

"I think my barista went after him."

Everyone around me kept our hands raised until the police decided the scene was secured. Liam, Thomas, and Crystal were allowed to continue assisting the wounded until the EMTs showed. I shuffled around the space, giving reassurance to shocked kids as best as I could. I hated that they had to have their party ruined by someone. *Oh hell. What if this was related to the harassment?*

During the entire calamity, Bobby sat on her stool, watching it go down. When my eyes finally landed on her disapproving expression, I couldn't help but laugh from relief. I counted my family members. Staff too. They were safe. It appeared the burns, though painful, were second degree.

I wanted to puke from the sulfur smell still in the air as I made my way to my mother. "You okay?"

She pointed to her cup. "Someone knocked over my cappuccino." I burst into an inappropriate belly-laugh, grateful she hadn't tried to leave during the stampede and hurt her weak knee. Jayz, they could've crushed her.

"I'll get you a new one."

One officer cleared his throat. "Detective Ross is almost here, Mrs. McKenna. He wants you available for questions when he arrives." He turned to my mother. "He'll want to talk to you too, ma'am."

"Not until I get a cappuccino," Bobby sassed. At her age, she expected respect from law enforcement but didn't hold any for them. I raised my hand to intercede when the officer opened his mouth to argue.

"May I make her a quick cup? Please. I can make one for you too, Officer…" I checked his name tag. "Taylor."

He let out a long sigh and frowned. "Make her the drink, but no one else. If you haven't noticed, you're done for the day… at the least."

Oh, I'd noticed, but I said nothing. I sent him a grateful grin and dutifully made my mother a Bobbi-ccino, also known as a latte.

Right then, Jake and Dylan approached the crowd outside, man-handling Jonn Graham, of all people. He wore a Dumbledore beard minus the robe, wig, and hat.

"Get your goddamn hands off me," he yelled, twisting and pulling to get away.

With the crowd quieted and sitting on the ground, I watched officers speak to the trio. Jonn spit in one's face and tried to donkey kick anyone near him.

Someone inside shouted, "There's the guy!" An officer inside moved to the boy to get his statement.

In a matter of minutes, they cuffed Jonn and hauled him away, but not before they bumped his head against the doorframe. I knew his father would make the department pay for that one.

Dylan cautiously stepped through the crowd and embraced me. "I'm glad you guys are okay," he said.

"We're not, Lad." I gasped. "We're so not okay. How did you know?"

"Was working in the window and saw the asswipe sprinting, shedding his costume as he ran. Then the screams and chaos. Instincts kicked in and I took off. Caught up to him in the woods behind us and tackled the fucker. Jake reached us then and showed me how to secure him and keep him from getting away." He gave me another hug. "Don't worry, Mom. The cops have him now."

Thomas appeared at my shoulder. I turned in to his arms, my breath hitching, holding in a sob. "I'm so sorry," I said into his chest.

"Shhh." He comforted me. Over my head, he asked Dylan, "Can you get us water?"

"Sure."

"We're not supposed to se-ser-serve anymore," I said.

Thomas tipped his chin down to me. "It's bottled water. It'll clear your head for the detective. Mine too. In fact..." Thomas caught Liam's attention and crooked his fingers so he'd come to us. He asked me, "Why don't the boys see to handing out water to those still here? It'll help everyone settle, especially your sons."

"What's wrong with my boys?" My head peeked around Thomas's shoulder, panicked they may be hurt.

He cupped my chin up to hold my attention. "You're rattled. So they're rattled."

"Oh." I sank into a chair, and Thomas took the one next to me, setting his arm around my shoulder.

Detective Nick Ross arrived and eased into the chair across from me. I couldn't believe it was my fifth statement to him this fall. Since he'd been the lead in Shane's case, we were sort of friends. "Detective." I exhaled on a shaky breath.

"We must stop meeting like this, Kick." He sounded both concerned and annoyed. I wasn't sure which emotion applied to me.

"You know, as much as I like to spoil you and your fabulous colleagues, I hate talking to you too. Professionally speaking, I mean. No offense."

He chuckled, pulling a tablet out of his jacket to begin our interview.

"What am I going to do, Detective?"

He lifted his gaze to mine. "You'll let us do our jobs. We have a suspect, the backpack, and remnants from the firecrackers. At least you have cameras now," he said. "Tell me everything you remember."

My mind swirled with faces, some laughing, some crying. I couldn't reconcile the cheerful beginning of the day from the smoky, panic-stricken end of it. I turned to Thomas. "Maybe you should go first."

Thomas pressed a gentle kiss to my temple. "You can do this. You're the only one who was here the whole day. Start with what you remember last. Before all hell broke loose."

The vision of Thomas in his spaghetti Western costume, strutting across the parking lot, flashed through my mind, making me smile. "I remember you."

"Good." Nick nodded approval. "Go from there. Don't forget, we have a suspect in custody. The kid's been making trouble around town for a while. Give me as clear a picture as you can, and it'll go a long way."

He helped me with memory-jarring questions: if anything unusual happened—*it was a party*—if anyone new stopped in recently—*the place was packed and most wore costumes*. Plus I'd been in and out this fall for appointments. I didn't know for sure if there were new customers or new delivery drivers for that matter.

Thomas did a great job giving a clear and concise account of what he remembered. For the first time, I envied his nearly robotic, calm disposition. His statement added a lot to mine. Still, the evidence against Jonn Graham was circumstantial. I was grateful he resisted arrest.

One by one, witnesses told their stories and left. Dylan drove Bobby home with her car while Jake and Liam followed in Jake's truck. Then they went to the hardware store and picked up supplies to board up the front windows. I sent the rest of the crew home and cleaned the equipment. We were shutting down for a few days. The OPD took off as soon as they could. They asked the morning crew to come down to the station to make sure they fleshed out the details from the day. I couldn't help feeling like I'd ruined everyone's day.

I wanted to think we'd made it out lucky. There wasn't a shooter.

The windows didn't crash down on the crowd outside. The newspaper articles would report some ankle and wrist sprains, cuts, and abrasions, along with the few burns, but everyone survived.

Except scared little eyes haunted me every time I closed mine or even blinked.

37

Integrity Blues

Thomas

THOMAS WAS HELPING BOARD UP THE PERKED CUP'S WINDOWS WHEN Banger arrived.

"Took y'all long enough," he grunted, holding a corner while Jake drilled a screw into the opposite side. Thomas couldn't shake the feeling someone watched them. He believed he could keep Kick and her family safe, but Banger possessed an almost mystical sense regarding danger. For the first time that evening, Thomas took a deep breath.

"My team and I went over the feeds. Made other arrangements too."

"Yeah? Like what?"

"Let's talk inside," Banger directed. When his tone had this edge, bad news usually followed. Except Thomas didn't care. News couldn't get much worse, and he wanted answers now. Watching the whole thing go down, seeing what it did to Kick, rattled him too. Hell, he wanted to wring the neck of anyone involved in this, especially Jonn Graham.

Plywood at the large span of windows darkened the usually

bright and cheery interior of the café. If it hadn't been for the row of windows over the prep counter, it would have resembled a cave. The café felt dark and sad anyway.

Kick didn't turn around when they entered. She vigorously scrubbed the espresso machines, her hands a bright red. Thomas approached, clearing his throat, and she jumped, the rag and brush in her hands flying in opposite directions.

He caught the panic in Kick's eyes and raised his hands. "It's me darlin'." Thomas tipped his chin to the table where Banger set up. "Bang's here. He wants to talk."

Kick scrambled to pick up her supplies, placing them on the counter. She kept turning her head away from him, biting her lip, then worrying her cheek with her tongue. For all the shit she'd put up with since they'd met, she'd never been this out of sorts. He hated it.

Then again, Thomas kept finding himself pumping his fists at his thighs to keep his hands from shaking. He wanted to stay calm and do better for Kick, though part of him wished he'd put Graham in the hospital when he'd had the chance. His lawyers would've taken care of any charges.

He grabbed her by the shoulders and dipped his head to catch her gaze. "Y'alright?"

A sarcastic "Just dandy" left her lips before she winced. "Sorry."

Thomas pulled her in for a hug. "No. It was a dumb question. I know you're upset. I want to say it'll be fine tomorrow, but I can't. We are working on it though."

Kick stroked his back, returning comfort. "Helping me clean is huge."

Banger cleared his throat, waving them over. "Can we start?"

Kick answered, "I'd like the fellas to hear this if you don't mind."

"Suit yourself," Banger answered.

"I'll get them," Thomas offered. The guys were already packing up outside. They set the toolboxes on the now empty floor space by the front door, then gathered around Banger.

As he typed on his laptop, he asked, "Have any of you seen the footage yet?"

They all shook their heads.

"I can't. Not yet," Kick answered.

"And the rest of us have been busy with the cops and clean-up," Jake added.

Banger glared at Thomas and Jake, tapping the screen as he turned it around for everyone to see. "This should've come first. Especially for you two."

Thomas's back bristled, thinking of how it would've looked to abandon Kick and her family to run to the back, but Banger was right. He'd been letting too much slip lately. He had to get back to directing his life instead of letting life happen to him.

Banger played the video of the outside cameras. The spiderweb shatter made the crowd jolt even if the window hadn't disintegrated. So did the explosive sounds of firecrackers. Everyone on the patio suddenly ducked in the footage. Kick gasped and jumped, watching.

Thomas pulled her to his side and rubbed her arm.

She kept an intense gaze fixed on Banger and the screen.

"Here's our suspect." Banger followed the running form with his finger. "There goes Dylan." Jake was out the door a second later.

"He's good at avoiding cameras." Banger cued up the interior feed, and Kick raised her hands. "Can I have a day? One day… before I see it? Just tell me what you know, Banger."

He stopped the video. "Fine. It was brilliant on his part to do this on Halloween." Kick's shoulders fell at his words, and Thomas glared. Banger showed indifference, keeping himself about the business and getting shit done. It was why Thomas pressed him into helping Kick initially. "The wizard getup helped our suspect keep his face away from cameras."

"Then how do we know it really was Jonn?" Liam asked. "The guy's an ass, but he's also a wuss. Maybe the noise scared him."

Jake cleared his throat. "Dumbledore never ordered. I figured he was waiting on friends. Then the explosions came from the area where he stood."

Banger continued, tracing the running trajectory with a pen tip.

"He didn't run toward the smoke shop even though the closest exit is near there. Makes me think he knows about the new cameras. Good thing you talked Hugh into using my team too."

"Why today?" Kick squeaked before her face pursed with indignance. "Hurting *me* is one thing, but the café was crawling with kids. The little ones…" Her voice broke. "Their eyes. I know what it's like to have a real-life horror show on a loop in your mind, and I'm a grown woman. If the windows had waterfalled on the kids outside…" Her voice hitched, and Thomas's vision went red. "Don't get me wrong, I'm thrilled the injuries were few and minor. But we altered those lives today…" Kick beat her breast, and another defiant tear let loose despite her tight jaw. "In my place. *My. Place*. If this is Jonn, I'll kill him."

Jake, Dylan, and Liam shifted in their seats, reminding Thomas of hungry predators. Everybody tensed, poised to beat the shit out of the boy at the word.

"If you don't mind…" Banger opened up some still shots. "The cameras caught two details." The first one showed a partial tattoo on the lower part of a bicep. It was a still from when the boys turned Graham over to the police.

Thomas said, "This looks similar to the tattoo you showed me before."

"It does."

"You mean the tattoo from my vandalized squawk box?" Kick asked.

"But this isn't the same man." Banger cut in.

They were a group of some kind then. Christ, he hoped this wasn't a gang.

"The other guy was shorter, stockier." Banger clicked on the second still. It showed the suspect's ear as he left the café. He had turned his head, leaving a clear shot of a stud earring, though not a run-of-the-mill diamond. This was a sapphire stud.

"Well, fuck me sideways. There it is." Dylan shoved open hands toward the screen, shaking with violent anger.

"Holy shit. We got him," Liam said, his face scrunched in fury.

Thomas looked around the group. "Fill me in please."

Kick' head fell on a deep sigh. "The boys are right. Jonn Graham wears his mother's sapphire stud as a memorial to her." She pointed to the screen. "But why not remove it when we know this?"

"The guy's a moron, Mom," Liam explained.

"He wore a disguise. The hat fell off as he left, remember? Plus he's cocky. I bet he got off on the idea of doing this right under our noses. His calling card in plain sight, so to speak," Jake added.

Kick slammed her hand on the table. "But why? What does he want?"

"He's pissed about being thrown out of the store?" Dylan guessed.

Kick's jaw sliced to the side. "The drive-through tattoo thing suggests he's been up to something for a while."

Banger stopped her speculating with raised hands. "Let my team work on it. Graham's in custody. OPD's already going over the evidence. These tattoos are my primary concern right now because Kick's right. The tattoo connection suggests he's done more."

Thomas made sure his friend caught his disapproving glare. Banger often took freelance work outside the confines of the law. It left him to conclude the police were optional. But law enforcement was already involved. Thomas wanted to make sure Kick's family kept the police on their side.

Banger stared back a beat before reluctantly adding, "I'll pass the information to the cops too."

Thomas mouthed, "Thank you," and let his friend finish.

"In the meantime, we need to make changes. Will any of you be working tomorrow?"

Kick nodded. "I'm meeting with the insurance rep, the window repair company, and who knows what else."

Banger continued, "Then I'm posting a security guard here." He raised his hands when Kick opened her mouth to speak. "For now. Until I can upgrade you again. Plus we're installing the *full* Angel System in your house." She opened her mouth again, but he cut her off. "Yes, it's necessary."

He closed the shot of the earring when she wouldn't take her eyes off it. "You're in shock. Trust me. You'll think clearer after some sleep."

Kick scoffed, "Like that'll happen."

Banger's visage changed. He stared at the five of them for a lifetime of seconds, his jaw pulsing. Then he leaned forward and vowed, "I promise to sort this out, Kick. If it's just a hateful kid, we'll still make sure he goes away." He tipped his chin to Thomas. "We'll both take care of you."

Kick sighed with relief. "Thank you."

Thomas wondered if she understood everything his friend had done. Banger was taking the McKennas under his personal protection, and Banger McHenry's fealty didn't come easily. Thomas swallowed hard, remembering his friend's words about commitment at breakfast. Promises were vows to Banger, and he'd been clear-eyed serious when he'd said everything was disposable. Could he be changing his mind in this regard?

Banger went on. "You and your boys should take shooting lessons with Thomas. He's built a range on his property."

"What?" Kick screeched, her face pivoting to Thomas.

He knew where Banger was going with this and agreed.

Banger pointed at Dylan and Liam. "Look at them, Kick. Their tension and anger are palpable. You want to kick ass, don't you two?"

"Abso," Liam answered.

"Fuck yeah," Dylan said.

"You have a range?" Jake asked.

"Don't y'all have a place to keep your skills up?" Thomas asked back. He assumed a veteran like Jake would want to shoot with his buddies.

Jake lifted a shoulder before a slight blush formed. "It gets expensive after school bills."

Thomas raised a hand. He didn't want to add guilt over an employee's debts to Kick's list of burdens. He guessed she'd already paid her staff more than average. "Say no more. You're welcome to it. We'll set up a time for us to meet. Then I'll only have to explain the safety system I've set up with my neighbors once."

"Sounds good," the men said.

"Fuck me." Kick dropped her head into her hands. Thomas didn't know how much more she could take. She'd been such a source of sunshine earlier.

He rubbed circles between her shoulder blades, murmuring, "I swear it will be good soon."

Banger didn't seem to know when to shut it. "One last thing: I don't want you staying at your house tonight. I have a relationship with a hotel you can check into."

"What about the dog?" Liam asked.

"No. Come with me," Dylan offered. "Koosh knows my condo and does fine with the fenced patio."

"But Graham's in jail… and Liam's school—" Kick started.

"It's a teacher workday, remember, fam? The first quarter ended today."

Banger added, "Until your upgrades are made and I'm certain how many people are behind this, I don't feel comfortable about you and the kid staying at your house. What if it's being watched?"

"Well, hell." Kick dug her fingers into her hair. "But Dylan… after everything we talked about… you honestly think Suzy will agree to two extra McKennas and a dog? We'll fill up the living room."

He shrugged and sighed. "Your safety comes first."

Banger typed on his phone. "The crew will be at your house first thing tomorrow."

Thomas asked Dylan, "Do you have two guest rooms?"

"There's a futon in the office, and the living room sofa is big enough for a night."

Thomas said the words he'd been thinking. After his talk with Banger at breakfast, he thought they might send his friend over the edge. But hell if he cared anymore. Something had shifted in him when Jonn Graham dimmed the light in Kick's eyes. He turned to her. "Send Liam and the dog to Dylan's. You're staying with me."

Banger flattened his mouth in a tight line and sighed a sound of reluctant acceptance. No one else caught it. Thomas told himself he didn't care.

. . .

THOMAS SETTLED KICK ON THE SOFA IN HIS FAMILY ROOM. A FIRE warmed the room, and an old *Animaniacs* episode played on the television. She looked like she belonged. Thomas designed the room for his comfort—a place to unwind after a long day wracking his brain. Kick softened and brightened it with her presence. It didn't matter if she was strung out and still in shock. She'd relaxed too.

He'd set up one of the guest rooms and left her to change clothes when they arrived. When she descended the stairs in a sweater and lounge pants, her face washed and hair in a clip, he'd never seen anyone prettier. Kick's posture stood taller than it had walking up the stairs. She wasn't the bright star she'd been before the Halloween party, but she reminded him of the warm glow of light when dawn first broke, promising more. Jonn Graham had dimmed the light, but he couldn't extinguish it.

However, when Kick reached for her cup of mint tea, her fingers shook.

He beat her hand to the cup and passed it over. "Something wrong?" He bit his lip. Another dumb question. "I mean, is there anything else I can do?"

Kick's mouth rose in a shy smile. "No. Thank you." She moved the cup to her left hand, flexing the fingers on her right. "It's silly, but they tingle whenever I remember smacking your phone out of your hand. It's the ghost of remorse, I guess. I'm sorry."

Thomas took the hand in his and kissed her knuckles. "No more apologies. I'll get a new phone tomorrow."

"But my temper—"

"Shh." He set the teacup on the coffee table and pulled her to his side. "Everyone was upset."

"It's just… It's how my mother would've reacted. Hell, it's what any of the Sullivans—Bobby's family—would've done. They're a shoot-first-aim-second kinda bunch." She was quiet for a beat before she laughed. "I still can't believe Bobby sat through the whole thing without a scratch. It was so unlike her."

It took a moment before the tears fell.

Thomas wrapped his arms tighter. "Let it out." He lost himself in the dancing flames while she cried, the only noise occasional sniffs. He often sought clarity in a fire. They were incredibly wise.

Kick finally spoke in hushed tones. "Thanks for all you did today."

Thomas kissed her temple, still contemplating the flames. "What did I do?"

She took his face in her hands and turned him. "You stood by my side, but you didn't treat me like a delicate flower."

"How so?"

"Well, you knew I could give my statement to Detective Ross when I didn't think I had anything left. I wanted to run and hide under my desk. But you steadied me. When you said it, I believed it too."

Thomas had to catch his breath. "First, you're not frail. You're one of the strongest people I've ever met. They knocked you down, but look at you…" He squeezed her shoulders. "When you came down the stairs, you already stood tall again. No darlin', you're a *precious* flower, but not one too delicate for foul weather. You're a bloom that opens as soon as the clouds clear, stretching toward the sun."

She sniffled one last time. "You really think so?"

"I do."

The corner of her lips lifted. "You're right, I am. I'm grateful the damage was limited too." She tipped her head back and sighed. "It could've been much worse. There's a lot to be grateful for. But I'm not ready yet. I'll focus on it tomorrow."

"Sounds perfect, baby."

"Baby?" she challenged, mischief back in her eyes. "You've used the term before. Is it a thing now?"

"Have I?"

"Let me guess… it's an ironic dismissal of our age difference?"

Thomas smiled. "Sort of." The breadth of the joke stayed with him. For now. Maybe forever. It was the last hurdle he had to jump. Until he could put it behind him, his cards—and thoughts—stayed close to the vest.

To change the subject, he kissed Kick thoroughly. The heat generation in the room switched from the fireplace to them. Thomas moved to the corner of the sectional, bringing Kick half alongside him, half on top. His hands drifted down her back until they were cupping and kneading her perfect ass. She writhed on him, creating magnificent friction for his erection.

His lips worked their way across her jaw and down her neck. He was about to take a bite when Kick stilled. He sensed hesitation from her and mentally smacked himself in the head. Dammit all, she'd been through hell this day, and he was taking advantage.

He pulled away as they both said, "I'm sorry."

Thomas placed his fingers over Kick's mouth. "You don't owe me a damn thing tonight. You've had a hellish day. Literally. You're staying here for your safety and comfort." He took her hand and pressed a kiss to her palm. "The company's fantastic. But I'm one hundred percent honest when I say we will go upstairs to our separate rooms and it'll be fine."

She scrunched her nose. "So you don't want to…"

"Hell yes, I do." He swept a curl out of her eyes and tucked it behind an ear. "I want nothing more than to carry you up to my bed, strip you down, and have a proper introduction to the most perfect ass and prettiest tits I've ever seen." He grabbed her bottom again to make his point, his fingers lazily trailing up the seam of the yoga pants.

She acknowledged her desire with an honest-to-God whimper. He didn't know he could get harder. The switch in blood flow made him dizzy, or it was just Kick? Her voice was dark and grave when she asked, "Is… is that all you want to do?"

So his feisty lady liked kinky talk? Good Lord, she'd be the death of him—a sentence he'd gladly pay. "No…," he continued, his words a primal rumble. "First I'd pin your hands above your head and take you hard and fast as punishment for what you're doing to my safe life. I'd nip your body with my teeth because I don't know if I can keep my cool around you. Then I'd taste you. No, I'd *feast* on you."

Kick's breath caught in a gasp, her lust a squeak from her lips.

"You like that?" Thomas adjusted her body in his arms.

Wordlessly nodding, her eyes wide with possibilities. He couldn't lose his cool. Not now. *Not yet.* With every throb of desire, he felt like the world's biggest asshole.

He kept his lips against her cheek as he spoke. "I want you, baby, but I don't think tonight's the night. When you're here because of want, not protection, then I'll do those things and more. I'll show you what your body does to me."

A slow gulp descended Kick's throat. "You're not making it easy."

"Good. It sucks to be the voice of reason right now."

Kick sat up, catching her breath. She downed the rest of her tea and stood. "You're serious?"

"I am. The timing isn't right."

Her head bobbed slightly several times. "Sure. Okay." She wrapped her arms around her chest, retreating into her thick sweater. She pivoted around, stopping her gaze at each landmark on all four walls. "I love your house, Thomas."

"Thank you." He walked to the fireplace and turned it off, shut off the television, and led Kick back to her room. He stopped them in the hallway and kissed her on the forehead. "Go to sleep, darlin'. Forget about today. We'll talk in the morning. And we'll make plans."

"Well, good night." She reached up and pulled his mouth down to meet hers in a long, sweet kiss. It was nothing like what he wanted from her. But he damn well wouldn't be a selfish bastard.

Thunder rolled quietly in the distance as Thomas paced his large, empty room in the opposite wing of the second floor. He feared it would be another sleepless night, only this time it wasn't worry over loyalty or research keeping him up. A sexy, curly-haired woman down the hall had him bothered.

38

Dancing in the Dark

Kick

"Door's open, Kick." Thomas's voice sounded like slow tires crunching gravel. My nerves amped up as I cautiously opened his door. A crash of thunder made me jump into the black void of his bedroom. The night light in the hallway behind me kept my eyes from adjusting. Plus I'd fled the bedroom without my glasses, thinking only of my need. They didn't make much of a difference late at night anyway. A quick flash of lightning hinted at Thomas's form in the bed, staring at the ceiling.

"Need something?" Compared to his warmth in the family room, his distant voice sent a chill through me. Hope forced me to speak the truth.

"Yes." I stood in the doorway, my arms folded around my torso, shuffling my feet, not so much from the cold wood floors as from the wanting. My new self craved his attention. I'd paced through at least two songs on my playlist before the little voice sounding like Cyndi's convinced me to take a leap. I kept kicking myself for agreeing to let the mood fizzle earlier. I'd never been good at telling a man what I wanted. It was time to learn. "I can't sleep."

Thomas scoffed, "Join the club, darlin'."

The same Springsteen song playing in my room filled his dark space. "I was listening to 'Dancing in the Dark' too." It was part of the problem. I'd put on my lusty playlist and tried to take care of myself, only to end up making things worse. I was a live current drawn to the one who could help me find myself again.

"I know. After pairing with Angel System, it can play in any room."

"Right." Grateful for the dark, my face heated. Did he know why I had it on? He had to. If it were possible, it turned me on more.

"Why 'Well, You Know'?" Thomas asked. "It's an odd name for a playlist."

"It's an inside joke between my brother and me. When we were teens..." I steadied my racing heart with a cleansing breath. "My father didn't trust Bobby to say anything nice about sex... during our talk... about it."

"Alright. And..." Thomas pushed. I hated his impatient tone.

Lightning flashed, and thunder followed soon after. It wouldn't be long until it was overhead.

"So... Dad took me out for a burger. He asked me if she'd said enough to me about, and I quote: '*Whale... ye new.*'" I imitated my father's lilt. "In our twenties, Bert and I realized Dad had used the same words with him. It's been our euphemism ever since."

A small chuckle floated to my ears. "Cute."

I turned and shut the door, blinding me outright. I took a determined step toward the sound of Thomas breathing.

Struggling to figure out his abrupt attitude change, I asked, "Are you thinking about work?"

A sarcastic scoff followed. "No."

My swallow hit my ears louder than the rain. "Then why are you brooding?"

Another thunder roll filled the silence. "Physics. The laws of attraction."

"So, you mean... me." I took another step. "I've been thinking about you too."

"Kick," he warned. "Don't do this. We admitted the timing isn't right."

"Why? Because today was horrible?" Lightning flashed again, followed two seconds later by a bang. Thomas's lump showed on the side closest to me. I glimpsed a sitting area near the window before everything returned to black. "What if that makes it the perfect time?"

"I won't take advantage. I want this to be… well, different." This time his tone changed from cold to disappointed.

"You were in the café too. Besides, it's not in you to take advantage."

Another strangled grumble laced with sarcasm.

I sighed, frustrated. "I can tell there are hard things bothering you, but you're also young, Thomas." How could I tell him to stop wasting time, like I had done, without sounding like a horny teenage boy just wanting to get some? I was afraid I'd already patronized him. I moved to sit on the edge of the bed but couldn't find it in two steps and didn't want to ruin the moment by falling.

I started over. "The past eight years have taught me to be strong on my own. Today I saw what it could be like to be strong with someone. Strong with you." I let my hands drop, and the robe opened. I wore a basic satin button-down nightshirt, nothing fancy or seductive. I'd packed fast in a hurry to get to safety.

"Stop." Right. Thomas's eyes were adjusted to his room. "My restraint's at its limit. Come closer, and I don't know…" The intensity in his voice communicated more than his words, shivered through me.

"Maybe I'd like to see you lose control," I confessed. My body ached for the things he'd suggested. The robe dropped off my shoulders, and I undid the top buttons. A deep intake of breath let me know Thomas could see me.

Lightning and thunder met directly over us, shaking the house and illuminating the room through another set of flashes. As if pushed by the storm, Thomas sprung at me, pulling me to him. His loud growl drowned out my surprised squeal and the remnants of thunder. Then I found myself straddling Thomas's abs, his deft fingers finishing the last of my buttons. His hands ran up the sleeves before pushing it off and into the night, leaving me exposed.

Gentle hands caressed my skin from my knees, up my thighs to my apex. A rumble of approval as nimble fingers explored the folds there, making me shake as they tested my clit. A quick press set me to rumbling myself, like the storm outside.

His hands stalled, and I feared he'd stop as he had downstairs. "Why are you fighting this?"

"The things I want to do with you..." His timbre turned to sadness. "This should be a celebration."

I shook more than my head. "After the day we survived, it is. Or are you scared?"

Thomas's hands met at my breasts and cradled them. My head fell back, and we both moaned as his fingers rolled over my nipples. He was exploring, seeing where I ignited.

"I'm terrified." His fingers continued to play, feeding my need, distracting me from his answer. "Alright. I'll take what you're giving, baby. I'll take it all."

The storm bellowed again, seeming to cheer us on. Thomas pulled me down to him, joining our mouths in a devouring kiss, releasing the day's emotions. Two people who had spent the day terrified found peace in the storm's violence. He opened my hair clip, throwing it into the abyss, and shook out my curls until they surrounded him. "I've wanted to do this for so long." My shivers almost broke our spell. I shifted my legs and Thomas hissed, "Damn, your feet are like icicles."

I giggled as he palmed my arch. I'd been too distracted to notice the cold. "They're always freezing."

Thomas lifted the quilt and arranged us so I was on my back while he lay alongside me, his fingertips making long sweeps of my body. I found the remedy for what my soul longed for under his covers, surrounded by his scent—sandalwood, citrus, him. I shifted until my hand touched his hard cock, barely contained in pajama bottoms.

He hissed in pleasure as I said, "I wouldn't mind an introduction either."

The bottoms disappeared, and we set to discovering each other in earnest. His hard abs thrilled my fingers as they traced each muscle. They traveled farther down until I squeezed his erection.

"I knew you'd be impressive."

I treasured the sound of Thomas's smile in the dark. "What do you mean?"

I peppered his pecs with quick kisses. "Everything else about you has impressed me. From your retro suits…" A flicker of licks around each nipple received rumbles of approval. "To the way you instinctively knew how to lead me in a dance…" More kisses across his abs. "To the way you've befriended my kids, my crew." I scooted down his body, taking note of the source of my praise. I ran my tongue from his base to tip and through the pre-cum weeping from his cockhead, licking my lips and humming my approval of Thomas's taste.

"Fuck," he gritted, pulling me back up the bed despite my protests.

"Let me take care of you tonight." He bit down on my breast, easing the sting with eager flicks of his tongue, then asked, "What do you want, baby?"

I pulled his ear toward my mouth. "I want you to fuck me, Thomas. Hard."

His sexy growl of agreement curled my toes, made my skin feel like my internal electricity might become real. There was power in my honest words. And in his approval.

Thomas granted my request, beginning with a devouring kiss, exploring my mouth with aggression. His intensity equal to the weather outside, my core matched it with thrusts against his erection. He showed his appreciation by grabbing my wrists. A flash of light caught his playful, spectacular smile. "You trust me?"

"You know I do."

He stretched both hands over my head and placed them under the bottom of the headboard. I remembered what he whispered in my ear downstairs, and my pussy throbbed with anticipation. "Don't let go until I say."

"I won't be able to touch you."

"Touch me later. Let me feast while you feel."

"Oh, okay," I gasped into our dark refuge. Without the light, I may as well have been blindfolded. My senses heightened by Thomas's direction. Each passing minute made my pulse pound like a drumbeat. It drowned out all sound until my moan from his magic tongue filled the room. I scissored my feet, begging for more.

"Uh-uh," he scolded. "Keep still."

"It's torture."

Thomas dropped his lips to my folds and spoke against me. "You make torture fun." He pinned each thigh with his hands and licked up one side, then the other. "Christ, you're soaked." He added a finger, then two, inside and went to work on my clit with his exquisite mouth and fingers, slowing as I neared the edge of reason. He relented with a laugh when I growled.

"You like this." He observed with quiet awe. "How you grip my fingers."

"Thomas… I want your cock. Or I'll let go and make you give it to me."

He laughed, reaching for the nightstand. The telltale crackle of foil drowned out the rain, heightening my anticipation. "Don't worry, Kick. I want to feel each squeeze of your pussy until you force me to come inside you."

I reached for the latex. "Let me?"

Thomas thrust himself through my hands as I rolled the condom on him, hard and soft, like silk covering steel.

Another crack of thunder exploded directly above the house. This one rattled more than windows and walls. I felt it in my bones.

"Y'alright?" Thomas checked in, stroking my lifted thighs. But I wasn't scared by the weather or by what we were doing. We were finally here. On the precipice of everything we'd chased for weeks. I took the storm above as the sign I'd once sought. The universe was cheering us on, shredding the baggage we carried, washing our slates clean.

We'd become our basic elements, electrical currents sharing our energy, restarting our hearts. Instead of answering, I chanted, "Fuck me, Thomas. Fuck me. Fuck me…"

He stood to the side of the bed and grabbed my ankle, spinning me, pulling me to the edge. "Like this?" Thomas lined himself up as I nodded, too lost with lust to speak.

He braced and thrust in, filling me until he was seated to his balls and froze again, hissing a sigh of relief. "Perfection. *Christ*, you feel good."

So did Thomas. It was more than a cure for a lustful want or forgetting a bad day. He fixed the ache in my soul. Thomas wasn't a replacement for what I'd lost. He uniquely filled the new me. A tear slid down to the mattress, rejoicing as a new peace set in.

He brought my hands over my head, taking my mouth as he filled my pussy. His emotion-filled moans were bringing me to the edge. "I choose you, Kathleen." Thomas's gritted declaration sounded angry, like he was rebuking the night.

"What?" I didn't understand. The fire of lust we'd lit grew again. I cried out, "More."

He bent and drew a nipple into his mouth, sucking and pumping and starting the countdown to my orgasmic launchpad. My body responded to the luscious sensations of his pulsing. I adjusted my angle to catch my clit on his inward slides, squeezing on the way out.

The bed slid with each powerful thrust. "How can I say no to you?"

He picked up the pace, surprising me with more to give, creating a delicious friction. I climbed to heaven and jumped off at the top of the steps into the bliss of letting go, chanting, "Yes, yes…"

"That's it, baby," he encouraged. "Beautiful angel."

I met his thrusts with equal fervor until Thomas lost himself with his own yell.

I arched my head back into the mattress, overwhelmed by the fervor of my climax. Aftershocks continued running through us, sparking more lust with the slightest shift. Our union was more than either of us dared hope.

After cleaning up, we lay together in bed with me wrapped around Thomas's side. "I feel so alive," I whispered, sliding my fingers through his chest hair.

"We're *definitely* doing that again… after I fortify the bed." He laughed at the same time kissing the top of my head.

After the buzz of ecstasy wore off, reality returned to my thoughts, and I said, "What did you mean you choose me?"

"Umm…" Thomas let his answer hang in the quiet.

It stung to have him still holding back after what we'd just done, but we couldn't discover all our secrets in one night. I snuggled deeper into Thomas, letting him know he could keep his answer to himself. *For now.*

My jaw cracked on a loud yawn. "Can I stay here with you?"

"You'd *better*." Thomas turned me, spooning behind, pulling me right into him, murmuring. "All the things I could do to you. You're a sexual muse." He kissed the back of my neck. "I'm already addicted."

"Thank goodness." I sighed and confessed, "I was afraid your hesitancy earlier was from… disappointment with my body."

He let loose a low growl. "I'm such an idiot." He turned my chin and kissed me deeply. "I'm sorry, beautiful. Everything about you is amazing, including your body. But there's a shit ton to do tomorrow… I mean later today. Get some sleep."

One of his hands absently kneaded a breast while the other nestled between my thighs. The storm settled down, becoming a quiet rain cleansing the land and our hearts for the rest of the night. I dozed off with his lips against the back of my neck and didn't dream at all.

Thomas moved one of the sound protection muffs from my ear and said, "Nice job, darlin'."

"That's lit, fam!" Liam cheered.

"*Noice*, Mom." Dylan patted my shoulder.

"Very pretty, Mrs. Mack," Jake added.

"You certainly *irritated* the target." Banger said, rubbing his chin. I took it as high praise.

Giving in to my desperate need for progress, I threw my hands in the air and did a victory dance, after placing the gun back on the table, of course. I heard P!nk in my head and wiggled my booty for the sheer joy of it for the first time in days. It didn't matter how much work we still had to face or how many unanswered questions we waited on. The McKennas were okay, and I was enjoying having Thomas by my side even if he was often one of those unanswered entities. All new, important relationships had their mysteries in the beginning.

Everyone continued gushing about the well-placed shot pattern I'd made on the target with Thomas's .38 revolver. In my mind, it was beginner's luck. I admit to being shocked at holding a six-shooter at all. I thought today's badasses used semiautomatics. Thomas wanted the boys and me familiar with all his handguns since the police had found a revolver in an ankle holster on Jonn Graham when they patted him down.

When Thomas first brought it out, he told me criminals liked them because the casings stayed with the gun, meaning fingerprints on said casings also remained inside the gun. I didn't know what to make of a geneticist's knowledge of such a thing. I found myself staring at him a minute too long yet again wondering about his past.

Graham was still at the police station, the camera footage and identifying marks making it hard for his father's lawyer to keep the authorities at arm's length. Banger's people continued to work their magic, so we cleaned up the café and waited. And took firearm lessons.

It had been three days since my night with Thomas. My time since had been packed with fixing up the Perked Cup. Restoring its reputation would take longer. Thomas had also worked late at the lab each night. While I agreed with him about spending time with each of my kids before he slept over, the ensuing nights had been long and lonely.

Since Banger and Jake joined us, we had three marksmen for three trainees. The boys had run through the paces with Banger and Jake while Thomas and I made lunch at the house. Thomas's agreement with his neighbors regarding the range involved making sure only one person fired at a time. He also raised an orange flag on a tall pole for visual confirmation the noise had Thomas's permission without them having to leave their property.

We'd walked the peaceful path from his garden to the range when it was my turn. I thought the boys would hear the word *food* and take off for the farmhouse, but everyone stuck around to watch me shoot.

I held the Sig Sauer the way Thomas showed me, stood in what I knew as mountain pose—a yoga term fitting the instructions he'd given me.

"Remember your breathing," he coached.

Breathe in, aim; breathe out, squeeze. It was empowering, really. Knowing I could shoot a gun, *several actually*, boosted my confidence. I emptied the clip and did the same thing with his Glock.

Dylan had the best patterns of the three McKenna newbies, but mine were a close second.

"Well done." Thomas kissed my cheek, mindful of our company. He stood behind me like a mental spotter, fortifying me while I went through the paces with each shot.

Thomas shut us down when a few dogs began uncontrolled barking. It turned out to be the longest he'd ever had the range active. The poor pups had had enough. We packed up the gear and decided to do our lessons individually from now on. We lowered the flag and walked back to the house for lunch.

Sitting at Thomas's table, around a platter of subs for the men, my gluten-free sandwich lay plated in front of me. My body relaxed for the first time since the night I'd slept over. Having to wear the mask of strength at work became a burden I welcomed. My staff needed Strong Kick. Hell, *I* needed her when I was there, sorting through the mess. In this setting, each man eased a little of the burden, giving me a chance to recharge.

I cut my sandwich in half. Thomas took advantage of me wiping my hands and grabbed my left one under the table, holding it in his lap while we ate. I already missed him something fierce. Though my bedroom suite was finished and Banger's team had completed their upgrades, I'd woken each morning from either a nightmare or a spicy dream about the handsome professor currently stroking my palm. My eyes flashed to his at the memory of a yummy thing he'd done with his tongue right before my alarm woke me in the morning.

Thomas arched an eyebrow, his eyes bright with amusement. I wondered if he'd been dreaming of me too and couldn't help my grin.

We sat around an oversized rustic table filling the dining room. I adored the contrast of regal and casual. Southern-exposure windows flooded the room with sunlight. An antique dry sink-turned-sideboard sat against a creamy wall. The color in the room came courtesy of a striking painting of a woman and a horse, hung above the sideboard. Vivid colors in the style of Marc Chagall electrified the room. My head had done a double take as I passed by the painting, my eye catching the signature. My degree had been in fine art, not art history, but it looked like the real deal to me.

"Holy shit," I'd muttered, forcing myself to stop thinking about the probable cost. I had a feeling this one sat at the high end for a real Chagall. It left me wondering again about this man who managed to carve some space for himself in my heart. What else would I find here? Or in his head? The rumination would wait though. There was a crew to feed, more plans. Discoveries could come later.

Banger ate in silence for a while before saying, "How is Angel-at-Home working so far?"

I blushed, wiping my mouth to hide my embarrassment about having put him off. "Better than I thought it would. Thank you. I haven't minded having sound in limited areas. And the extra security helps me sleep." My eyes flashed to Thomas's, the heat of a scarlet tint spread across my cheeks.

"Good," Banger continued. "From now on, listen to me the first time."

"Yes, boss." I rolled my eyes.

"My team will be finished with the upgrade to your café by the end of the day too."

"Yippee," I fake-cheered. "Does this mean the security guards can go?"

"Well, now——" Thomas started.

"Kick." Banger dropped his sandwich on a sigh.

I held up my hands, certain I wasn't a petulant child. "The Perked Cup's reopening is tomorrow. I didn't think our reputation could be more smeared, but the neighborhood website found a way. People are posting en mass about how they won't come back. Don't you think big burly guys… nice as they are… lurking in the corners will scream, 'We're not safe'?" I refreshed my throat with a pull from my LaCroix. "Adding an array of monitors visible to the public was genius, Banger. I think it'll be a perfect deterrent."

Dylan lifted his shoulder. "Mom has a point."

"Thank you, Lad."

Banger and Thomas stared at each other, sharing a silent conversation like they were siblings.

"Fine." Banger let his shoulders drop. "Make sure your staff is up to speed on the panic buttons… *and* they must install my panic app on the home screens on their phones."

My gaze moved to Jake. "Can you be in charge of this? It would mean coming in early to train Deana and Liz, but I could take your shift."

"Kick," Thomas warned. He had the disappointed professor look down pat. *And it worked.* By saying my name, he reminded me I was overscheduling. Plus we'd managed to set up a lunch date.

Jake bailed me out. "How are you feeling, Mrs. Mack?" Jake was the only non-McKenna at the table who'd been with me before my health setback. He'd witnessed the descent without the personal attachment of a son fearing something was wrong with his mom.

I chewed my sandwich bite, using it as an excuse to self-check and answer honestly. We'd experienced unbelievable stress in the past week, but I hoped I'd become better at letting it roll through me. Since my flare, I'd learned stress's negative effects could be attributed more to the attitude of the person in question. If I believed stress would hurt me, it did. I'd made sure to meditate every day and got my movement in by helping set up my new room.

I rolled my shoulders. "Feeling well, all things considered. Thank you, Jake."

"I wouldn't mind working a double if I could take an extra day at Thanksgiving."

I ran the preliminary schedule through my head. "It should work. Thank you."

"Appreciate it, man," Thomas added.

I grinned wide and caught Thomas's eyes, twinkling silver this time. I felt fantastic. The McKennas were down but on their way back. Again. Thomas had told me the lab was making progress too. And I held tight to our promises of more.

The boys made the table laugh with their banter and tales of Dylan taking Liam and Macushla home to Dyl's girlfriend, Suzy, and roommate, Dummy.

The last drops of my LaCroix traveled down my throat when the doorbell rang.

A curious expression crossed Thomas's face as he rose to answer it. He disappeared into the entry, his smooth voice rising and nearly cracking when he greeted the visitor.

"Tess? Hello. What a surprise!"

Thomas returned, leading a stunning young woman with the kind of tan I'd never achieve. As she looked around the room, her eyes landed on Banger. It shocked me when she said in a sharp, albeit breathy tone, "Hello, Raphael."

Banger dropped his head into his hands. "Fuck. Me."

To Be Continued...
Turn the page to read the exclusive cut scenes.

39

Bonus Cut Scenes: Like to Get to Know You Well

The following scenes take place on the morning after Kick and Thomas' big night together.

Kick

It was the first morning in a long while I didn't fight waking up. I couldn't tell if it was the light on my eyelids that brought me to consciousness or the gentle caress to my shoulders. I stretched and smiled, keeping my eyes closed on the chance this was one of my lucid dreams. A dream had never surrounded me with such a delicious cedar-and-citrus scent though—in the sheets, the quilt, and especially potent from behind me. This was definitely real. A wonderful, new reality.

A stronger ray of sunlight pried its way through my lids, startling me. It was too bright. I bolted up to a sitting position.

"Whoa." Thomas chuckled, raising his hand. "Bad dream, darlin'?" His tone shifted from surprise to concern.

He had to stop it before I fell hard. We may have taken the next step by sleeping together, but we had made no commitments. We'd certainly hadn't declared any vows.

I reminded myself to slow the hell down as I shook my head. "No, sweets, I'm late. Liam—"

"Has the day off and stayed at Dylan's."

I let out a long breath. "Right. It's a teacher workday." The previous day's disaster washed over me like a flash flood—the Halloween party, the panic, Jonn Graham. Thomas too. I turned fully to him as a smile stretched across my face. I couldn't help it. He'd been... everything. Darn him and his chin. Oh hell, the shoulders too. And other things. A big, beautiful...

"You're adorable." Thomas's hand slid up my arm and took hold of a curl. A fuzzy one.

I let out a squeak and grabbed my hair, trying to squish the mess down. "Jaysus, I must look a fright." No one saw me before I'd fixed myself in the bathroom. Not anymore.

"Did I not say you're adorable?"

"Thomas," I scolded, then figured I should explain. "I forgot to bring a silk pillow or a head wrap. Hell, I didn't even put it up in a pineapple." I pulled my curls over my shoulder but could only see the ends. Messy, fuzzy ends. The curly police would arrest me for hair abuse.

I slid my leg out from under the covers and quickly swept my toes over the floor, hoping to grab my nightshirt. Thomas noticed and stretched across me, his brow lifted in the way it did when I confused him. So much for being stealthy.

"Don't cover yourself around me." He nudged the quilt and let his eyes sweep over what he revealed. "I like the view."

"I planned to wrap my hair in it."

Thomas reached for my temple and pulled his fingers through the rat's nest. I squealed and gasped at the same time. It was a sound of equal parts surprise, pain, and anger. I grabbed my head. "You broke curly girl rule number one, pal. Plus, ouch!"

He blushed and rolled back to his side, contrition already in place. "I'm sorry. I've been wanting to do that forever. Guess I got carried away."

He had the nerve to grin at me like a little kid about to descend the stairs on Christmas morning. He had told me no other women had spent the night in his home. Something about that made me want to grin too.

"Will you want to shower?"

"Now that you've turned me into a backup dancer for a disco band?" I laughed. "Yeah, I could shower."

Thomas's head tilted like a puppy's. "A backup dancer, huh? Should make you perform for those bathroom privileges."

It was then I noticed Thomas wore a T-shirt and pajama pants. His hair was also damp. I grabbed his jaw and turned it to the side. "You're shaved. And showered."

He lifted a shoulder. "I woke early and worked out. Wasn't about to slip back into bed all sweaty."

"Oh." I bit my lip. "Thank you. You didn't wake me."

He kissed my forehead. "Not on your life. Yesterday sucked. Plus, you looked too peaceful to wake." He whispered in my ear, "I may have felt bad for keeping you up late. I was afraid you might be… sore."

My eyes flashed wide with embarrassment. I hadn't thought of that. I managed a discreet stretch. He had a point.

"A little. My bladder's hollering though. Would you mind getting my scrunchie while I use the bathroom? It's on the hope chest at the foot of the bed in the guest room."

"How the hell do you know that?" Thomas chuckled. "I don't even know where my wallet and keys are."

I shrugged. The kids always called me their LoJack. "I guess I'm just a mom. You left your stuff on top of the dryer in the mudroom, by the way."

He bobbed his head and laughed. "Impressive, darlin'. I'll be right back."

Thomas

Thomas tapped a knuckle on the door to his bathroom. He carried a mug of coffee for him and a glass of lemon water for Kick.

A gentle "Come on in," lifted his spirit. Since he'd woke, his emotions had run the gamut. Initially, Thomas freaked out to the point of a near panic attack. Thank Christ for a fierce workout to set that straight. Anytime he returned to Kick, his heart soared like a lovesick kid, something he'd never been.

He'd loved his late wife, Alicia, but their relationship had started off as a beneficial arrangement. He had considered her pretty face and pleasant personality a bonus—luck, really. When she died, Thomas discovered how much he'd truly lost.

Thomas straightened his spine and figured he'd simply been alone too long. His mind returned to his early-morning meditation when he determined to focus on the moment. It was all anyone could count on.

He stepped onto the tiled floor and quickly shut the door to keep the heat in. "Here's your lemon water."

Kick's face lit up. "Ooh, thank you. I'm parched." She took a long drink, and Thomas watched the muscles in her throat work. His own mouth went dry as he thought about licking her there. Her neck had to be one of her sexiest parts. He took a deep inhale to settle himself.

"Mind if I sit?" He tipped his head toward the covered commode.

"Not at all. It takes a few minutes to bring my curls into submission…" Kick giggled as if she'd made a joke. "Like this hair ever submits. We should plan out the day anyway."

Thomas sat and took a sip of his coffee, fascinated by the sight before him. Kick made a simple satin, cream bikini and bra set look like goddess attire.

She bent her head into the shower area and squeezed her hair with a T-shirt. He'd never known anyone to do that unless no towels were handy, but he'd given her a stack. She pressed and squeezed two different products through her hair, then stood, moved to the sink counter, arranging her gelled curls over the T-shirt and intricately wrapping everything up on top of her head with a clip of some sort.

She caught Thomas's gaze in the mirror and smiled. "What?"

He blinked himself from his stupor. "What the hell did you just do?"

Kick pointed at each of the bottles. "One's a filler. The other is a fabulous flaxseed gel. It seals more or less." Her finger tipped up to her head. "I plunked everything into my hair T-shirt to let it set while I finish getting ready."

"A hair T-shirt?"

Kick bit her lip. "A regular towel frizzes my hair with one touch. I guess your gorgeous, straight locks couldn't care less, could they?"

"A vigorous scrub and comb and I'm done."

"Wow." She studied Thomas with what looked like envy.

"How did you figure all this out?" he asked, after taking a long pull of his coffee and absorbing the new information.

"Ah, well. Bloggers, mostly, until they became fanatical. Then I experimented on my own. My hair is super porous. Not all curlies are. Those lucky ducks. At least the humid part of the year is over."

"Must be hell," Thomas muttered.

Kick shrugged like it was the least of her problems. Considering everything he knew about her, Thomas guessed it was. "Great products and a good cut are my friends."

She stepped in front of Thomas and sifted her fingers through his hair. If he'd been a cat, Thomas would've purred for her. Kick arranged his hair, putting it back the way she'd found it, like she was careful to respect the way he'd styled it, though he'd never been a man who'd styled his hair. Or he hadn't been in a long time. Her fingers slowly slid along his jaw as she eased away from him and over to her open suitcase on the bed.

After Thomas had left to grab her hair thing from the guest room, he'd brought everything back with him. Not only didn't he want Kick running back and forth between rooms, but he also liked the idea of her living in his space with him, even if only for a few hours. His constant delight at entering the room and seeing her there was changing something inside him, though he couldn't admit it.

Thomas sat in a wing-backed chair by the big window and watched Kick dress in a pair of jeans and a Perked Cup T-shirt with a plaid flannel over it. As much as he'd enjoyed every second of her striptease the night before, watching her move into clothing pleased him too. He'd liked watching her do pretty much anything so far. Damn, he might've been in trouble.

He stood as Kick removed the clip and T-shirt from her head, then hung it up in the bathroom. She returned with perfectly formed coils gently framing her face.

"Think I'll let as much of it air-dry as it can while I make us breakfast, okay?"

Thomas shook his head. "What?"

"Is it okay? With the long day ahead, I don't know when I'll be able to thank you for… everything." She dipped her head and blushed. "Breakfast isn't much, but I want to do something."

Thank him? Thomas should show his gratitude for the best night he could remember. He should've been bowing down and kissing her bare feet in supplication. She'd opened her heart and soul, gave Thomas everything while previous commitments forced him to hold back. He was so used to it that only a part of him cared. That part cared a helluva lot though.

Kick added, "We'll need a proper breakfast today."

No doubt. The day would be long and hard. Thomas made a mental note to see if he could have dinner delivered to Kick and Liam and anyone else helping her sort through the chaos at the Perked Cup.

Kick moved some items around in her suitcase. Thomas's brow pinched. Part of him wished she could place it all in the closet. Permanently. He pushed the thought aside. No matter what, his commitment to the research couldn't stray.

"What would you like to eat?" Kick asked. "Or maybe I should ask what you have."

Just then, Thomas's phone buzzed with a text message. He stopped and swiped it open. It proved his point… "This is the lab. I should call in."

"Of course."

Thomas shooed her on. "The kitchen's yours to peruse. Anything you make will be wonderful."

"I don't know, professor. I make some weird shit nowadays." Kick's laugh sounded like an angel's, or his head was loopy from the orgasms.

She was out in the hall before he could answer her non-threat. Thomas chuckled as he dialed the phone. The check-in with reality was exactly what he needed to keep his head—and heart—from getting caught up in her.

Kick

A gallery of old photos on the second floor slowed my progress to the kitchen. The wooden frames varied in size, texture, and tint, but they all enhanced the black-and-white pictures. One photo was in the nineteenth-century style, where the subjects had to stand perfectly posed for several minutes and didn't smile. The men in it looked like legit miners. I wondered if they were from the California gold rush.

Another photograph showed a gorgeous woman standing in front of a boutique in a big city. Based primarily on my recollection of art history and design, I guessed the time frame to be around World War II. I wondered who the woman had been to Thomas. A great-grandmother, perhaps?

The pictures told a story of time, moving all the way to the 1970s, given the size of the shirt collar on the last one. What a treasure. These had to be members of Thomas's family. I wanted to ask him about it, but he paced in front of his bedroom window, deep in conversation with whoever had texted from his lab.

I hoped someday to have walls done like this in a future home, though my pictures couldn't go back farther than the one Bobby had of her father in his World War II RAF uniform, looking proud and defiant for his controversial service.

My stomach grumbled, reminding me of my mission. I hoped I could have breakfast ready by the time Thomas came down.

.   .   .

"Surely this isn't all for me," Thomas chuckled as I set a frittata on the kitchen island. Still sizzling in the cast-iron skillet, I sliced it up and served him a piece.

"Eat as much as you want and save the rest for later." I sat in front of my plate with a boring omelet on it.

"Kick," he drawled. "You didn't have to do all this, especially when yours is so…"

"Wanting?" I laughed. Once again, I reminded myself that a little dietary pain now would pay off soon enough if I could keep making progress in my health journey. I waved off Thomas's concern. "I used some of the same veggies in your frittata for my plate." I shrugged. "The other things simply aren't allowed right now. Don't worry about it."

"Well, hell," he mumbled, then took a bite. "Good Christ, darlin' this is amazing. Now I feel like a heel."

"Stop," I warned, then laughed at his pinched brow. "I'll have the rest of my life to eat cheese and ham. As long as they're organic, of course."

Thomas must have put together how his ingredients didn't meet the organic requirement and grimaced. "Well, shit."

I bumped his shoulder, still smiling at him. "Just shut up and eat."

A buzzing from Thomas's jeans pocket caught our attention. "Oh right." He pulled the phone out—my phone—and set it on the counter. "You received a few alerts while I was talking to my assistant."

I swiped it awake and saw several texts from Cyndi, each one more manic than the last. "Crap. Cyn's freaking out about yesterday."

The last one said:

CYN

If you don't text soon, I'll hunt you down!!

Sorry, chica! Finishing b'fast. I'll call ASAP.

I shoveled the last two bites of omelet and said, "I need to call her."

"Go. I'll clean up here." He leaned over and kissed my cheek. "Thank you for making all this for me."

As if I hadn't spent years making separate meals for the kids and me. I mean, as much as I could, I made one meal for all of us, but autoimmune diets aren't something you just subject to healthy, growing kids, especially when they're teens.

I caressed Thomas's jaw and bit my lip, fighting the pull to fall hard for his concern. It wasn't who we were. To avoid the gratitude in his eyes, I threw it back at him. "Thank you for all *you've* done for me." I placed a quick peck on his nose. "This was nothing."

I fished my earpiece out of my purse and said, "I'll call Cyndi from the bedroom while I pack."

"WHAT ON EARTH HAPPENED YESTERDAY? I CAN'T BELIEVE I HAD TO learn about it on the community page this morning."

I winced at Cyndi's words. "Do I even want to know what's being said on there?"

"No," she clipped. "Stay off the site. In fact, just wait until I tell you it's okay again."

JaysusMaryandJoseph. "There went my joy bubble. I guess real life had to break it soon anyway."

"Yeah, about that," Cyndi started. "The boys said you're at the professor's."

"Mm-hmm."

"Annd…," she prodded, but I kept mum. "Come on, Kick. Is it a 'love shack' situation?"

"What? No. It's a rather pretty farmhouse—"

Cyndi's timbre changed to what I imagined a phone sex worker might sound like. "Chica, I want to know if the tin roof's still rusted." Keeping with the B-52's theme, her meaning finally clicked.

"Ah, no. I guess it's not." I collected my shower items and dried them with a towel.

Cyndi's squeal over the phone nearly burst my eardrum. "Woo-hoo!" Thankfully, she resumed her normal tone. "How are you doing?"

I dropped the bottles into a Ziplock bag. "Fine? Why?"

"Kicky…" She chided me. My name from her mouth told me everything she'd been thinking. Whether I'd been overthinking and planning a life with Thomas. She knew me enough to run the gamut of my emotions without my saying them.

Still in denial, I lightened my voice and deflected while placing the bag in my suitcase. "I swear everything's fine." I almost believed it.

"Shit. You've gone off the deep end." I opened my mouth to respond, but she jumped in first. "Just listen. You're in my territory now. I'm super proud of you, by the way. Anyhoo, make sure you keep your head. Don't make any big declarations—you haven't made any, have you?"

I gathered up my discarded nightshirt. "No, but—"

"Good. Keep it that way."

I threw it on top of yesterday's clothes and dropped into one of the wing-backed chairs. I wanted to sink inside its comfort, and I swore it would have let me. To be honest, I could see myself living with Thomas in his farmhouse, with his handcrafted furniture, beautiful photo galleries, and his gratitude for a simple breakfast. My heart had already jumped, as Cyndi put it. "I'm confused," I confessed.

"I know, chica," she soothed. Then, as if she were imparting a lifetime's worth of wisdom, which I guess she was, she said, "You two have such an easy chemistry, it's probably hard to understand how rare it is. I really wish you could go on a string of crappy online dates, but we can't turn back time. So, no matter what, keep your feelings to yourself for now. Trust me."

"You know how much I hate games." I stood and resumed packing. Her words made me antsy.

"I'm talking about your heart, Kicky, not games. You've moved fast physically, for you. It's perfectly fine to keep your heart at a slower pace. In fact, I insist upon it. You've been meditating, right?"

JaysusMaryandJoseph. Why did everyone care about my meditation habits? "Yes," I grumbled.

"Then you understand living in the moment. Practice it with Thomas. Don't look down the road, just keep your eyes right in front of you, so to speak. And receive as many orgasms as that man wants to give you."

I laughed at the advice, though it made a world of sense. It calmed the butterflies in my stomach too, meaning it hit the spot.

I folded my suitcase over and zipped it up. "Thank you for talking me off a cliff I didn't know I stood on."

"Anytime, chica. Call me when you get home? I want to know all the things about the attack. The professor too, unless you'll be having another sexfest tonight."

"No." I laughed. "I'll be home. I'll call."

Thomas

"I wish you'd have let me bring that down for you," Thomas said as Kick rolled her suitcase over to the mudroom.

"If it had been too heavy to carry, I promise I'd have asked. I'm no martyr, Thomas." She walked to the kitchen and opened the cabinet doors.

Good to know, he thought, but simply nodded. "You're looking for…"

"A water bottle. You have any? I left mine in my office." Then she mumbled, "I'd kill for an Americano right now."

Thomas didn't know what to do with the uncomfortable feeling he had anytime Kick brought up her eating restrictions. He hated the idea of her watching others eat—or in this case drink—something she couldn't have. Yet he also knew she'd notice if he dumped his thermos of coffee in the sink just to show solidarity. He moved to the cabinet below the coffee station and pulled out a stainless steel bottle. "I only use it for water."

She sighed in relief. "Thank you so much." She filled it with ice, water, and a squeeze of lemon before sitting on a barstool next to Thomas. He was checking the lab schedule on his laptop, hoping he could get more time with Kick. "Shit, it's getting late," she muttered. "I don't even have time to swing by the house for a quick yoga session."

Thomas gestured toward the stairs. "There's a workout room upstairs. You could do it here."

She rechecked her phone. "Nope. There's still not enough time. Thank you though."

"Anytime." He turned his chin and flashed Kick a quick smile, not thinking about how much he enjoyed having her in his house. *Nope.*

Kick took a long pull from the water bottle and sighed, looking refreshed by the water. Maybe she wasn't craving caffeine as much as Thomas had thought.

"Speaking of upstairs, I love your photo gallery."

Thomas jerked at Kick's words, then hoped she didn't notice. After the close call with Presley, he'd thought about taking the pictures down, but he'd been too busy. Plus, no one ever saw them except the cleaning crew. Until now. "Thanks."

"I loved the one of the woman in front of the boutique. Was she a grandmother? Great-grand? I mean, I presume the photos are of family, right?"

Thomas closed his eyes, not knowing if he'd dodged another bullet or not. He didn't want to talk about the photos. They were on the walls for him. So he wouldn't forget the past. They pushed him forward too. He definitely hadn't thought about them when Kick needed his support and safety.

Thomas cleared his throat. "She was a family friend."

"When was it taken? And where? The store looks glamorous. Was it hers?"

Christ, he almost bit her head off, regretting ever putting them up. They lived in the part of him he couldn't share. "Late '30s, I think. New York, I believe. It was her shop." There. He answered and hoped like hell Kick would let it drop.

"What about the Depression?" Kick asked, her brow pinching.

Damn her curiosity. "Money wasn't an issue." Thomas shrugged. "She could afford to wait it out. The war too."

"Huh. Fascinating." She smiled and shook her head. Kick got up and refilled the bottle.

Thankful she hadn't pressed. Thomas returned to his laptop and powered it down. He'd hoped to sneak up to the third floor and message *Grand-père*, but figured he shouldn't risk it. Kick's poking-around habit would probably lead her right up to his sanctum. He had to stay mindful of security. The Presley thing made him jumpy.

Or he'd become too complacent, thinking Banger had everything handled.

Or he wanted an excuse to think about anything other than the woman in his kitchen. He knew better than to let his heart run amuck, but Christ, how it wanted to. The damn thing was annoying him. He didn't want it pitting him against his commitments to the Felidae.

Kick sauntered over to Thomas and stepped in between his legs. She wrapped her arms around his neck, sifted her fingers through his hair. "Before we head out and go our separate ways, I wanted to do this one more time." She leaned in and kissed him. Her sigh did him in.

Without breaking the kiss, Thomas stood and lifted Kick onto the counter. He set one hand next to her thigh, the other at the back of her head, and kissed her thoroughly. It was all he'd meant to do. The next thing he knew, he'd removed the soft, pink-and-gray flannel and Kick's T-shirt.

She didn't complain, so Thomas unclipped her bra and slid the straps down with his nose. His hands were busy with her jeans—and his own. For a brief second, he noted their location and knew he'd never see his kitchen the same way again.

Kick didn't protest though. Her forest-green eyes hazed over with the same lust he figured shown in his. Her soft lips and sweet gasps quieted Thomas's noisy thoughts. This was what Kick did for him. He hoped he did the same as he pressed into her. Her back arched as a sweet smile spread across her face. And his weary mind finally rested a while.

.   .   .

*****

Thank you for reading! You can sign up for my newsletter and also find information on *Kick Back*, the second book in the Oakville Obsessions series using the following QR code.

Follow Kallyn

Thank you for reading *Kick Start*. It would make my day if you would review it at your preferred retailer or review site. In the crowded world of fiction novels, reviews—even short ones—are the best way spread the word about Kick and Thomas to other readers like you. From the bottom of my heart, thank you. XO

To keep up with my newest books, teasers, and sales, follow me here:
Website: kallynjones.com
Facebook: KallynJonesAuthor
Instagram: KallynJonesWriteNow

Did you notice the chapter titles are song titles too?
Songs are a big part of the Oakville Obsessions series. You can find the public playlist on Spotify. Enter Tunes for Kick Start in the Spotify search bar or click through the link on my website.

Author's Note

Dearest Reader,

You probably noticed some speculative elements in this book. The science aspects will be explained as the series continues. Promise.

Please note that at this time of Kick Start's printing, cannabis is unfortunately not legal in North Carolina. That's where the "this is a work of fiction" disclaimer comes in. You would not want to plan a roadtrip to Raleigh to visit a dispensary at this time. There aren't any. Odds are you'll pass through other states where cannabis is legal anyway.

Because of this, I imagined which tack a reluctant NC General Assembly might take in regards to a federal legalization law. It's based on the unique way this state approaches the sale of tobacco and alcohol. In real life, I have no idea how a hypothetical comprehensive law would play out. Sadly, our politicians are currently pushing hard against legalization for medicinal purposes.

XO, KJ

Kick Back: Book Two

A LATER IN LIFE ROMANTIC MYSTERY

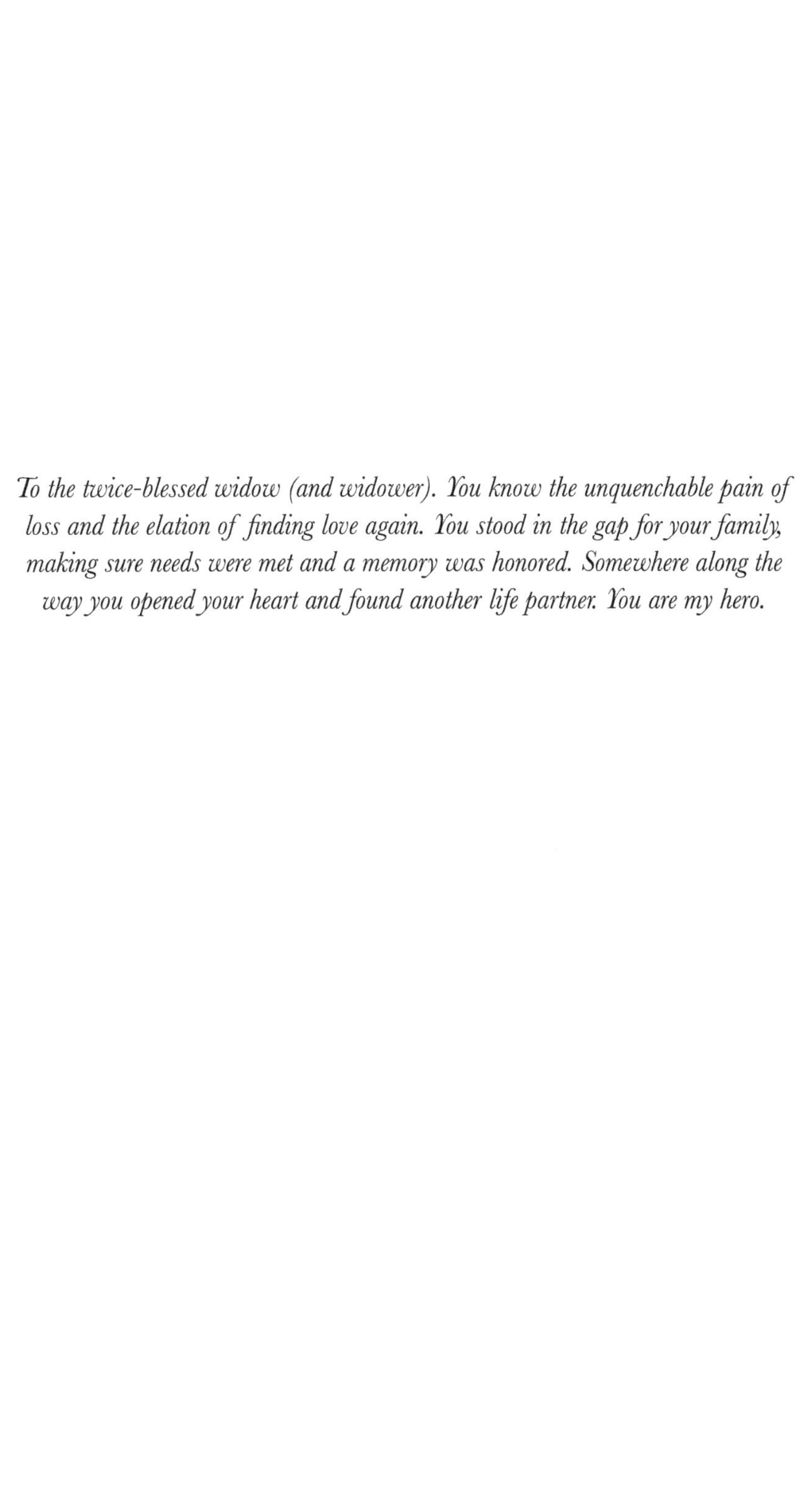

To the twice-blessed widow (and widower). You know the unquenchable pain of loss and the elation of finding love again. You stood in the gap for your family, making sure needs were met and a memory was honored. Somewhere along the way you opened your heart and found another life partner. You are my hero.

1

I Feel the Earth Move

Thomas

A PERFECT AUTUMN DAY FOR THOMAS HARRISON INVOLVED TIME
outside on his property, the sun illuminating leaves at their peak of
color, his new lady, and a tightly formed pattern of bullet holes in a
target. He would accept three of the four.

"Open. Your. Eyes." Thomas said through a tight jaw, his
patience thinning with his love, Kick McKenna, though he'd never
admit it. Kick's opinion regarding beginner's luck on the shooting
range the other day turned out to be right. It was their third time
practicing with his handguns, and he swore she made the bullets
curve around a target.

It looked like more than a mental block to Thomas. He caught
the flashes of panic Kick tried to hide since her coffeehouse had
been attacked on Halloween. She couldn't shake her fear and
soldier on when at the shooting range.

Kick set the empty Glock on the bench, the dummy sporting a
few new holes—for some reason most were in the arm area. One
bullet had landed in the intestinal region while the rest punished the
trees behind it.

"I flinched."

And then some. "Yes."

"Why are we doing this again? I have faith in you, Banger's team, and the police." Kick muttered something else under her breath that Thomas didn't catch.

Thomas leaned against the bench, folding his arms. "I can't stay with you all the time. None of us can. It's driving me crazy. So I'm making damned sure you can hold your own if somebody comes after y'all again."

"You think there'll be an again?"

Thomas reached for Kick's hand and stroked it with his thumb. "What's going on?"

She took a step back and crossed her own arms, squeezing the biceps until her fingertips blanched.

"The first afternoon was exhilarating. New." Kick stared at the dummy. "When I look at the target now, I see Jonn Graham's face. As mad as I am, I can't kill him."

"Well, hell, baby." Thomas stepped closer to Kick. "I can change the target from a body to a bull's-eye." He drew Kick into his arms, absorbing as much strength and affection as he gave. Her tenacity still held. He should've known she'd struggle with the identity of her harasser. A part of her saw every young customer with a mother's eyes.

If Thomas was honest with himself, he'd admit he sensed the boogeyman making his neck hairs tingle. The feeling of *when* not *if* things would escalate kept his jaw clenched at night and sore during the day.

"I've missed this," he whispered into Kick's ear. A quick hug and kiss on the temple hadn't been a proper greeting, and he knew it. They'd rushed to their shooting lesson when she arrived. Banger was due in an hour with an update on his investigation. The Oakville PD stayed stuck in hands-tied mode, and Thomas required the answers that only Banger's security wizardry could provide.

"I've missed *you*," Kick returned. "I haven't slept well since… we were together." She bit her lip and looked away.

"Yeah," he said, his gaze fixed over Kick's head, watching ducks paddle in the back pond. "Same here darlin'."

"I don't want to shoot anymore. It feels too serious now, and a target change won't make a difference."

Thomas frowned. "This is *serious*, Kick. The night we met, your coffeehouse had an attempted break-in and was vandalized. Then someone threw a brick into Hugh's window. Yes, I think it's related. Later, your squawk box was damaged. All *before* the Halloween attack. There's been a media campaign against you. I don't like the online harassment of your daughter any more than y'all do." Kick shivered at his last comment, and Thomas gave her a squeeze. The Rachel issue had always bothered her the most. "Think of this as part of your self-defense lesson and another way to take care of your health."

Kick chuckled. "That was low." After a thoughtful pause, words tiptoed out. "Why are you trying to scare me?"

Thomas lowered his voice. "If you're just now frightened, you haven't been paying attention." He ran a hand through his hair and around his neck. "Want me to settle down? Prove to me you can handle yourself when I'm not around."

Kick stepped back with a stomp and wrapped her fingers around her neck. Her skin heated neither from a blush nor embarrassment. Thomas had pissed her off. Good.

"You can't be serious," she growled. "*Handle* myself when *you're* not around? Where the hell were you when I had to tell my children their daddy wouldn't watch any of them go to prom, graduate, or get married? Where were you the first time I got seriously sick after the funeral and still dragged my ass out of bed to take the little ones to school and practices, fighting a fatigue so deep I was afraid I might fall asleep at the wheel?"

Her body vibrated with fury, but Thomas didn't regret waking her up even if he'd insulted her.

"You think Jonn Graham is the first kid I've had to throw out of my store? Hell, Thomas, I'd been *handling* myself for eight long years before you came along." Kick tipped her head back and looked up at the clear sky, her hands planted on her hips. "Longer when you consider the twenty years it took me to get a fecking autoimmune diagnosis. There were times it felt like no one believed me."

Kick turned and frowned when her eyes landed on Thomas's smile. "What the hell's so funny?"

He lifted his chin. "Not laughing, baby. It's good to see your fire back."

"You tricked me?"

Thomas raised his hands and shook his head harder. "Not at all. Unfortunately, I'm an idiot, but your demeanor has had my nerves on edge as much as the idea of someone hurting y'all. So I put my size twelve in my mouth."

He dipped his knees, ducking his head to meet Kick's gaze. "Graham is more than an annoying kid. Since his father's lawyers shut down the boy's questioning, we still don't know why y'all were targeted. So, you can learn to use these"—he pointed at the guns on the table—"or you can accept the bodyguard offer." Staring at the guns, his mind went back to their first session. "The boys are eating this up. If you think I'm overprotective and pushy, how do you think *they'll* act if you stop?"

"Jaysus." Kick stared at her boots. The breeze blew several curls into her face. She finally straightened her spine and took several deep breaths while flexing her fingers. "Let's do this."

Thomas picked up the empty Sig Sauer—he had her working with his Glock, Sig, and Colt revolver until she picked one to keep—and passed it to her. "First, your stance is straight and loose, and your grip is perfect. So, keep those going. Second, practice firing the empty gun. Watch it work as you pull the trigger. Observe it from different angles as you point it forward. Then get back to targeting. Convince your brain to keep the target in your sights. Without bullets, it'll be easier."

"It'll make you feel better if I get this?" She stepped up to the bench and blew a curl off her face. "It should make *you* feel better." Thomas pressed up against Kick's back, moved her hair out of the way, and kissed her neck. "Can't deny seeing you like this turns me on though." He made sure she felt his desire against her fine ass.

"Okay then," she breathed, tossing a flirty smile over her shoulder.

He backed away as she reached for the Sig. "Work on my suggestions while I run up to the house. I have another idea."

Kick stood stock-still, staring down at the weapon, her tongue worrying her cheek.

"Kick?" he asked. He was getting familiar with her tells and guessed something else bothered her.

Her head stayed bent as she asked, "Since we're clearing the air and I want to clear my thoughts… When Banger comes… will Tess be with him?"

Thomas exhaled a weary breath. Appeasing Kick's insecurities in the past week might have been harder than handling her fears with the guns. "Doubt it. But it wouldn't matter if she was. She's like family, darlin'. Hell, when I went to Bordeaux last month, I stayed in their suite."

"You're not helping," she said through gritted teeth.

"I stay there because I've been more or less adopted by them."

"And you've never been with"—Kick pointed her finger at his chest—"or even had a crush on Tess?"

Thomas shuddered at the thought. He wasn't kidding about her being family. It had never crossed his mind, though he couldn't tell Kick why. "I swear."

Kick lifted her eyes. "Does she know this, Thomas? Because Tess was awfully familiar and downright possessive of you when she showed up at lunch."

Again, family. To Tess, Thomas was another kid, like Banger, but he had to keep his damn mouth shut.

"Hey." Thomas pulled Kick in for another hug. Her lower lip gave the slightest wobble. "I think you're confusing protective instincts with possession. It looked to me like you surprised Tess as much as she did you. He rubbed Kick's back. "Where's this coming from?"

"Are you kidding?" Kick almost looked angry. "Tess is gorgeous, young, and happy-go-lucky. I'm a mess, old, and have all this"—she pointed to the guns on the table—"shit happening." She sighed and stepped away, digging her fingers into her scalp. "It's too much for me. If it's too much for you, I'd rather you bail now, then…"

Thomas's laughing stopped Kick in her tracks. He had never wanted to spill the whole truth so badly. *He was afraid she knew too much already.* As Kick's brow drew into a deep furrow, Thomas quieted and raised his shoulders. "You don't see what I see."

"And what is that, exactly?"

Christ, he needed to get her safe. He longed to see more smiles on her face. "Maybe you've cast a spell on me." His fingers brushed her pointy ears, currently showing between the loose curls falling out of her barrette. "You're an elven queen after all."

Kick swatted his shoulder and scowled. "I'm serious."

"Fine." Thomas schooled his features and gave serious thought to why he was drawn to Kick. "You're smart. You care deeply. You're f—"

"Don't you dare say fierce. I'm not special. I do what I need to do to make it to the next day and hopefully, the next year."

Thomas reached toward her. "*That* is the definition of a fighter. Please let this Tess thing go. She'll probably jet off to Bali as soon as some mystic invites her to his retreat." He wrapped his arm around Kick's shoulders. "I'm not going anywhere, baby. Not sure what we're doing, precisely. I damn sure want to see where it goes though. Alright?"

"Sure."

"Something needs to be done about your stress," Thomas murmured.

Kick tapped his ass. "I have an idea or two."

The smack did more than get Thomas's attention. It made his skin hum, going straight to his cock. He shifted his hips to fix the tightness while taking note of the buzz. As gorgeous as the day was, he couldn't wait for the night to begin. He'd planned the perfect evening for them. Business first though.

He took a deep breath and stepped back, picking up the Sig again. "Dry fire this while I run up to the house. The sooner we're done, the sooner you can show me those *ideas.*" He waggled his brows and grinned.

"Right, handsome." She kissed his chin and took the weapon.

Thomas walked backward a few paces, rubbing his chin. Kick kept fussing over the cleft like it had magical powers. Not that he minded the attention. He'd soon get to pay attention to the parts of her he enjoyed.

He watched Kick at the bench for a beat. Her stance still looked good. *Too* good in her moto boots and dark jeans, curving in all the right places. The denim jacket with the Celtic butterfly on the back ended at her waist, highlighting her exquisite ass. Her straight spine and lowered shoulders highlighted her graceful neck. Relief washed through him, seeing the fiery woman he'd first noticed still in there.

Yeah, her courage wasn't going anywhere. Kick may need to wear the "happy armor" around her crew, but the warrior was still inside. If he ever got a chance at Jonn Graham for doing this? At least he had Banger on standby to take care of the body.

Thomas smiled and called out, "You got this, baby. Remember your breath. Be right back."

Kick let her hair sway out of the way as she adjusted her stance. She eyed the gun and said, "I'll be here."

Thomas cleared the top of the trail from the house, carrying an airsoft gun. He figured lightening the recoil and removing the "danger factor" would help Kick acclimate to the act of shooting. He heard Kick before he saw her.

"*What's* over, Snow?" Kick was talking to her daughter on her cell phone, pacing the worn earth in front of the firing range. "You haven't flushed four years down the toilet. … But you're only twenty-one."

She pulled the phone away from her ear, flinching at the female sobs coming from the speaker. "Hold on a sec, Snow." Kick set the phone next to the Sig and quietly did a happy dance. Thomas rarely watched football, but he knew what a touchdown performance looked like. This rivaled the elaborate ones.

Kick took a cleansing breath and picked the phone back up, mouthing "Rachel" to Thomas. "Okay. Thomas is back. No, it's fine. … No, I never hated Cody." She rolled her eyes. "I've watched you two grow apart for a while though."

Kick's shoulders slumped, and she squeezed the bridge of her nose. "You do?" No two words had ever held more disappointment in them. "Of course you can come home. Lee's out for the evening, so it'll be you and Macushla. She'll be thrilled for the snuggle time. … Sweetie, I can't understand. … That's the electrical issue. Do what I showed you."

Kick stared at Thomas, her face scrunched as if on the verge of tears. Her head dropped, her posture both exasperated and resolved. In a small voice, she said, "Be there in an hour. … It… it's fine. … Love you too."

Kick let the phone fall from her hand to the table. She leaned her weight against the edge as Thomas approached, wrapping his arms around her once again. He began to think his main purpose in their relationship was to make up for Kick's dearth of hugs. She responded to each one like it was a transfusion.

"I'm sorry, but I have to go."

He buried his face in Kick's neck. "What happened to Rachel?"

"She broke up with Cody, the Boy Wander."

Thomas raised an eyebrow in question. "Pardon?" He wasn't sure if he'd heard her right.

"Yes. Rach caught her boyfriend cheating. Wouldn't surprise me if he's made a habit of it."

"We'll clean this up and go."

Kick placed her hand on Thomas's chest. "It'll be better for Rachel if it's only me. Besides, Banger's coming by."

"He could meet us at your house. Then I can look at Rachel's car."

Kick reached up to his neck and pulled Thomas's mouth to hers. He liked how their kisses were becoming common. "I've already planned to take the car to our mechanic over her Thanksgiving break. If it's truly dead, I'll have it towed next week. Besides, you have enough on your plate right now. I'm sorry, handsome."

"I see." A term for the McKenna children began forming in his head, something like the *McCock-blockers*. He wouldn't take it out on their mother though. Hell, he regularly dropped everything for his family *and* the Felidae. He'd be damned if he let his libido drive his emotions all because Kick had responsibilities too. "You can't stay to talk to Banger?"

"Cody's apartment—and more importantly, his bedroom—is directly over Rachel's. She can hear them going at it." Kick laced her fingers behind her neck and stretched. "Hell. I want to hear what Banger has to say."

Tempted to ask if there weren't any coffee shops the girl could escape to, Thomas held his tongue, fearing Kick would jump on him in defense. Focusing on an understanding attitude seemed like the best route to go for both women. "Do you think she'd be alright if Bang and I brought dinner over? He could fill us in afterward, in private. Would that give Rachel enough time to settle?"

Guilt tried to wash over him for being a selfish bastard when a daughter needed her mother, but Thomas pushed it down. He couldn't shake the niggling feeling Kick's safety was on the line, as well as her family's.

Kick's eyes glistened as she raised her hand and cupped Thomas's jaw, catching him by surprise. "Where have you been all this time? Dinner would be wonderful." She stood on her toes and pressed a slow kiss to his lips. "Once she calms down, she'll probably study in her room. Still, I don't think they're ready for—"

"Me staying the night." He deepened the kiss before letting Kick go. He didn't mind so much either. A part of Thomas thought of the house as Kick's late husband Shane's. Thomas didn't know if he'd be comfortable staying there, especially with two of the children at home. He'd lived as a bachelor for too long.

Another lingering kiss and Kick ran off to rescue her daughter in distress. And she accused *him* of having a hero complex?

"Looking pretty, brother." Banger sniffed in Thomas's direction, walking into the kitchen. "Mmm. You smell like heaven too." He teased with a Cheshire cat grin, peering around Thomas's shoulder. "Where's Kick? Is she up in the bathroom?"

"What?" Thomas started when he heard his friend's words, then walked into the kitchen to get a beer. He wore only jeans and a new button-down, his hair still damp from a shower. He flexed his hand to keep from hitting the wall. "Dammit all. I forgot to call. Knew I was forgetting something." He'd been more upset than he let on with Kick. He'd worked off his frustration with a hard weight session, losing track of time.

Banger checked his phone. "Nope. No calls. What's wrong? Where's Kick? I assumed you were"—he waved his hands in Thomas's direction—"otherwise *occupied* until the last minute."

"In my workout room, not my bedroom." Thomas sighed.

Banger lifted an eyebrow. "You dumped her already?"

"What? No. Her daughter called with an emergency."

"Ah, the little princess."

"Sure." Thomas couldn't remember the last time he'd felt so vulnerable, like he wore it underneath his shirt. It irritated him.

"Are we still meeting?" Banger asked.

"Right. Shit." Thomas opened the fridge and grabbed two IPAs, offering one to his friend. "I'm sorry, man. I meant to call and see if we could meet at Kick's house. I told her I'd get dinner while she gets Rachel settled."

Banger rubbed his lower lip. "It could work. I'm supposed to take Tess to dinner after this. Let's call her and have her meet us at Chez McKenna. I'd appreciate diffusing Tess's undivided focus for an evening."

Thomas tipped back the bottle. Would more time around Tess help Kick or make things worse? He took a long pull and decided. Tess was family and Kick spending time with her would convince her. "I like it. I'll check with Kick and make sure it'll work. Then you can call Tess. Sorry again for wasting your time. Maybe you could help me with the security update on my computer while I finish getting ready?"

Banger sighed dramatically as he fell into step on the way to Thomas's office. "I knew you were only using me for my brilliant mind." He sat in the tall desk chair. "This helps me too, brother. I want to talk to you about something."

"A Felidae something?" Thomas sat in a wingback chair across from the desk.

"Sort of."

"Well?" Thomas finished the beer and set it on the side table near his guitar stand.

"Fine. What the fuck's wrong with you?" Banger surprised Thomas with his change in attitude.

"Excuse me?"

"The last time we spoke alone, I thought you'd decided to cool it with Kick. Next thing I know, she's spending the night—not that I'd blame you. But the lessons and children and problem fixing and… and *cologne*."

"Is it too strong? I don't want to aggravate any of Kick's allergies."

"*Jeeves Crimmins*! Since when do you care about fucking allergies?"

Thomas tapped a finger on the beer bottle. "It's not a bad idea. Maybe we should pay more attention to the immune system in the lab." Research ideas popped into his head at the oddest times. He wished he'd brought his phone down from the bathroom and looked around for a piece of paper to write it down on, further distancing himself from Banger's lecture.

Since becoming a professor, he no longer tolerated dating younger women. In his rule book, they were now students or mentees, and he wouldn't cross the line.

"Are you even listening?" Banger pressed his mouth together as he waited for Thomas to signal he was. He jabbed the air with his index finger and declared, "You're hooked, brother. I told you not to let her reel you in, and you let her anyway."

Thomas shrugged. "I recall the words 'do something new.' I am."

"I suggested you buy a new fucking car. Or get a new hobby. But you won't let anything go. How old is your Camaro anyway? You look at Kick the same way you look at your car though. Don't you ever miss new-car smell?"

"Christ, you're all over the place. You'd think I was threatening *your* happiness." Thomas leaned toward his friend. "My Camaro is mint, and it's better for the planet than buying a new one would be. Now, I don't know what's going to happen with Kick. Presently, she's good for my soul. No one's made promises, and I certainly don't have any intentions to. As for a hobby, I told you I was looking at places to board my horse Eddie. He'll keep me busy soon enough. Maybe we should find a horse for you too."

"Mmphf." Banger grunted. "I never had to get up before sunrise to water a motorcycle. I'll stick with them. Besides, *how* is an ancient muscle car good for the environment?"

"The Camaro's regularly updated. Carbon emissions from making a new one outweigh the lifetime footprint of any vehicle."

Banger rubbed his lower lip. "Is that true?"

Thomas waved his fingers. "*Hello.* Scientist." He stood, deciding he was done with Banger's counsel. "Like I said the other day, I'm tired of the usual dating scene. Kick makes me feel like myself again, but it's still casual. However, it would be *exceptionally* nice to sort out this harassment of her so she and I can see what a simple relationship looks like."

Banger nodded, then shook his head. "Fine. But I don't see how anything regarding Kick McKenna is simple." Banger cut off Thomas's response, saying, "Finish getting dressed, you bumpkin. I'll get your update going and call Tess."

"Thanks, man. I don't know why I couldn't get it to work last night." When he was halfway up the stairs, the ringtone from the house in Virginia shrilled from the bathroom. Thomas ran the rest of the way to catch it.

2

Why Worry?

Kick

"Hello handsome." I threw open the front door without checking the sidelight.

Tess smiled brightly. "I don't think I've ever received that particular compliment. I simply *love* history-making days."

I hoped my face didn't blanch along with my obvious wince. Then again, with my pasty complexion, who would know? It was no match for the olive-skin, perma-tanned beauty standing before me. "I'm sorry, Tess. I thought you were Thomas." Taking a step back, I welcomed her into my house, giving her a quick hug with air kisses.

She whispered in my ear, "It's fine, dear. I'm thrilled to see Thomas taking an interest in someone more..." She looked me up and down and shrugged. "Well, more."

Dear? Was I entering the circular stage of adulthood where young women speak to their elders like they are children? I thought I had a decade or more to prepare.

I placed Tess's jacket on Dylan's hook in the mudroom and showed her around the first floor before putting the kettle on.

Rachel padded into the kitchen, her head on her tablet. "Did I hear dinner arrive?"

She stopped short at the bar where Tess sat. "Oh, hello. I thought you were Thomas."

"That seems to be going around lately." Tess lit up as she perused Rachel and turned to me. "This must be your daughter?"

"Yes," I answered. "This is Rachel. Sweetheart, meet Tess McHenry. She's Banger's sister."

Tess violently flinched at the mention of Banger's name and said, "It's Tess Sanchez, darling."

"Oh, my apologies. You and Banger don't have the same father?"

Tess jolted again, as if Banger's name physically hurt her. I then remembered Tess had called him "Rafael" when Thomas first introduced her in his dining room. Maybe she didn't like his nickname? He clearly hated being referred to by what I assumed was his given name, not that I'd ever thought his parents had named him Banger. I felt a bit of kinship with the man, guessing we might have similar family dynamics.

"We don't." Tess abruptly changed the subject, turning to Rachel and wrapping her arms around her. "Delighted to meet you." She sat back and declared, "You're stunning."

Rachel dipped her head. The redness in her face had eased while a touch of puffiness lingered from her tears. She had been a mess when I picked her up, and she'd cried on and off the entire drive up to our house, breaking my heart into countless pieces. Her voice cracked as she said, "Thank you. So are you."

"Aren't you a doll? Tess held Rachel's chin and turned her head left and right. "You must take after your father. Though the curls could be from your mother."

I wanted to jump up and down or wave my hand in front of her face and yell, "Hello, mother in the room." *Jaysus*, was I becoming invisible too? I'd heard about how menopause made women disappear, especially to the young. Thanks to my surgery a while back, I couldn't be certain when this infamous time would descend upon me, but I guessed it was close.

Rachel answered with a light chin tip and a half smile. She'd always loved being called the "female version" of Shane, since they shared the same raven hair, ocean-blue irises, and a single dimple. Aside from the curls, she'd outwardly only received my nose, which looked like a cute button on her. On me, it disappeared. Maybe I was becoming invisible. I hoped I could use the power for good, though doing evil sounded fun too.

"Do you model?" Tess asked, still assessing.

Rachel lifted a shoulder. "Occasionally. I'm studying to be an actress and such."

"She plans to go to Broadway," I added, proud of her ambition and talent, if not also terrified for her.

"Ooh, I see it." Tess beamed. Then her lip formed a pout. "You've been crying, haven't you?"

Rachel's eyes shimmered as she nodded. Another tear slipped out, racing down her cheek.

"Oh my darling, come." Tess wrapped her in a big hug. "I can tell this is about a boy. No one knows more about messy relationships than I do."

I blew a curl off my cheek and worked on our tea. Part of me had had enough. My baby needed *me*, not this interloper. Who was Tess anyway? Something was odd about the way she and Banger never came right out and said they were siblings. If they didn't have similar strawberry hair and strong cheekbones, I would have doubted they were related or assumed one was adopted. Except they also carried themselves in an aristocratic manner, despite Tess's exuberance and Banger's sharp broodiness.

"How old are you?" Tess asked.

"Twenty-one."

"Pfft." She waved off Rachel's answer. "You're too young to settle with a boy. We *are* talking about a boy, right?"

If you asked me, Cody Dalton would always be a boy. Rachel simply dropped her head in acknowledgment.

"Do you even know what you want? What if it's not a man at all?"

My eyes flashed wide, watching Rachel blush. *There* was something I hadn't considered, though Tess had a point. My daughter had plenty of time to explore what life offered her. I hoped she had her fill before she settled down and wished like hell she never "settled" when she did.

That sent my thoughts toward my oldest, making a mental note to check on Dylan's relationship. He had informed me that my suspicions of an impending pregnancy were wrong, thank goodness. But practically every minute of my days since the Halloween attack on the Perked Cup had been focused on the investigation. I had no idea if his relationship with Suzy had improved.

I distributed the three mugs of tea and took a sip of mine, thinking of the next morning. After a long two months, which seemed like years, thanks to this crazy autumn, I'd be able to add decaffeinated coffee back into my diet. Finally the barista could partake of her product again, albeit caffeine-free. I had to survive the entire holiday season before the full moratorium was lifted. I dreaded planning the Thanksgiving menu.

The girls, as I now thought of them, lost themselves in conversation, so I headed over to the garage and dug out two containers of salted caramel cashew cream from the deep freezer. I figured we could do dessert first while we waited on the men, and girls in the movies always ate ice cream after a breakup. Since Rachel and I didn't eat dairy, this would do.

As I padded back to the kitchen, I overheard Tess ask, "You know you can live without him, right?" I bit my lip to keep from scoffing but rolled my eyes.

Did Tess think she was being wise? Rachel knew about life moving on better than most girls her age. Her dad had been our world. Shane had certainly filled mine. I shattered—Hell, we all shattered when he died. But we found a way to move on as a foursome. For the first five years, it took all my energy to put one foot in front of the other, feeling like I wore cement shoes as I did it.

Rachel's voice broke. "I do. It just… feels weird, you know? I thought life would be one way, and now it's not."

Tell me about it, kid. I placed the containers in the microwave and set it for thirty seconds so it could be scooped.

"Now darling, you're only at the starting line of life." Tess patted Rachel's hand, then rubbed her bicep to soothe my daughter. Why was the woman so touchy? She'd been the same way the afternoon she showed up at Thomas's. She'd been overly familiar with him and wouldn't have surprised me if she'd grabbed his ass.

"Would anyone like some cashew cream while we wait for dinner?" I asked.

"Salted caramel?" Rachel asked. "It's my favorite."

"Which is why I buy out the store when it goes on sale."

"Cashew?" Tess asked, scrunching her nose. "Not ice cream or gelato?"

Rachel saved me from growling. Her face lit up, and she leaned toward Tess. "Mama and I can't have dairy. But you *must* try it. It's hype. I like it better, to be honest."

Tess tipped her head to the side as if she were deciphering my daughter's slang. I watched, waiting to see if she sought any clarification. Instead, she smiled and said, "Lovely. I'll take some too, thank you, Kick." Tess's accent was the only thing I moderately liked about her so far. It didn't sound fully French, though Thomas had told me she lived at the estate in Bordeaux. Her accent sounded more Spanish to my ears, especially when she called me "Keek," the way my house manager, Carmen, did. It was a cute quirk. The revelation of her last name, Sanchez, helped seal my conclusion.

I scooped out the cashew cream and set the bowls next to the mugs.

Their conversation continued without me, so I jumped up on the kitchen counter—an old habit from when I was a kid—and ate my bowl as if I were invisible. Tess asked more detailed questions regarding Rachel's future plans. It turned out my daughter had auditioned for the Lost Colony summer theater company in the Outer Banks. That was news to me.

As the words and encouragement flowed between the two, my temperament grew surlier. The floodgates opened on my insecurities when it came to Thomas. Tess's faux wisdom had a point. If what he and I had started soured, I'd move on. I'd done it before, so I knew I could do it again. Therefore, the question mulling around presently was did I even want to take a chance again, knowing it could all be gone in a snap?

The frozen dessert had soured in my stomach, my hands had the jitters, and my chest felt squeezed, making breathing difficult. I checked to make sure no one noticed and slipped off the counter, quickly placing the bowl in the kitchen sink. I needed privacy before I made a fool of myself.

"Excuse me. I'll be…" I raced across the open space to my bedroom.

My rudeness went unnoticed though. I vaguely heard Tess ask Rachel, "Do you have supplies for a facial? They always help…"

I closed my door on girl time and paced my room. It smelled wonderful, not from the new construction—we'd used low-VOC materials besides having a whole-house HEPA filtration system. No, the suite smelled wonderful and settled me because it was finally mine. It wasn't that the ghost of Shane had been exorcised as much as he'd moved on, bringing both of us peace.

Except a current of questions flowed from me like a riptide, dragging me under. Everyone lives with the possibility of being alone. I mean, all relationships come to an end at some point. I didn't dare think of anything long-term with Thomas, so would it be better to stop before it started?

I moved into the bathroom, took a deep look in the mirror, and asked myself if I honestly thought I could keep my feelings for him in check. I suspected my near-panic attack rooted itself there. With relationships, I wasn't sure I possessed the keep-it-casual gene. Instead of a straightforward answer, my reflection stared back, clueless, sad. Scared.

I took a few more minutes in my meditation corner, sitting on the window bench, and traveled to the porch in my mind. This time it was attached to a pretty mountain home overlooking a river, the kind you wade into to fish. The solitude quieted my mind until there was certainty I could wear the robe of reality again. I figured disappointment sat at the core of my issues. My stress amped up on the gun range, then dove headfirst into mom mode to take care of Rachel. I'd been looking forward to Thomas's comforting presence all week, stuffing my stress, rolling it ahead to today. It hadn't been fair.

The past eight years had taught me to stand solidly on my own feet. The past few months even more so after my father's death. I couldn't throw that all away when a man came around offering a shoulder. I didn't want to either. I liked the woman who stood on her own power. A cleansing breath sealed the deal as I rose to those feet and left my bedroom, grateful for the time to get my shit together without the drama of dumping on Thomas.

The ladies had disappeared though. I looked around the first floor and only saw the dog sleeping in the recliner. Half a cucumber lay on the kitchen counter. A faint laugh told me Tess and Rachel were upstairs, probably in Rachel's bedroom.

The guys parked in front of my house as I was wrapping up the cucumber. I opened the front door to see Thomas approaching the steps, a large bag from Finnegan's Wake, my favorite neighborhood pub, in his hand.

"Mmm. Gimme. Gimme," I said, reaching for the bag.

Thomas grinned and held it behind his back, leaning in for a kiss. "Gimme first."

"Sure. Fine. Whatever," I returned, reaching my hand around his neck to bring his lips the rest of the way to mine.

Banger walked past us with a "Mmphf," holding a growler from Finn's.

I tipped my head in his direction and asked Thomas, "He okay?"

Thomas tracked Banger to the kitchen and turned back to me. "He's great. You heard a happy growl." Another quick kiss touched my cheek. "You'll get used to it. He's actually grateful y'all took Tess off his hands for a bit."

I blew a curl from my face and shrugged. "Wasn't me. Rachel's having a great time though."

"Really? That's fantastic."

I followed Thomas to the dining table and might have made a growling noise myself.

"Isn't it good?" He checked. "You're not still feeling weird about her, are you?"

"No," I answered, meaning it. Still, it stung to have someone else ease my daughter through her crisis, especially since I'd dropped everything to help her.

We sat around the messy dining table after finishing our meal. The fellas drank the IPA Banger picked up. The ladies opened one of my bottles of Malbec. I had club soda with lime. I sat back in my chair, content and happy to see leftovers for Liam, though he wouldn't be home until late. If I didn't know better, I'd swear Thomas bought one of each item on the menu.

My gaze moved to him and fuzzed out. *Jaysus.* I needed to tighten up, or I'd end up addicted to him. The man oozed care and competence without even trying. He made plans with Tess and Banger regarding the places she wanted to visit before she left for a retreat in Boone. The thoughtfulness in his eyes—currently bright gray—the way his cleft chin tipped as he searched his memory for unique places in the Triangle. It had me swoony, threatening to turn me into a lust ball, demanding everyone get out *now*!

Keep it together, Kick. I took a deep breath and suggested, "The art museum is currently running an exhibit of Frida Kahlo's work. Reviews of it have been quite favorable."

"Ooh, I loved her," Tess said. I found her response odd, as if she'd known the woman instead of the work, but I smiled in response.

"I do too. She's one of my faves. I've been meaning to see it."

"You have?" Thomas asked. I couldn't tell if his wheels were turning to plan a visit or if he was upset I hadn't said anything. Cyndi was my go-to museum buddy, so I hadn't thought about asking him about it until that moment.

"Yup. Well, until…" I waved my hand in the general direction of the Perked Cup. "I probably won't get over there until Christmas break now. Which reminds me, you're all invited for Thanksgiving dinner. I'm hosting and doing a big one before the kids scatter to points unknown. Deana's bringing her traditional dishes, so it won't be all my food—though I swear my stuff is tasty." I ended with a self-deprecating smirk. Years of putting up with my family's comments on my diet and cooking habits had trained me well. Thomas squeezed my hand at my words, the crinkles around his eyes giving me reassurance.

"Oh no. I don't know when I'll be back," Tess said, looking genuinely disappointed.

"I have plans as well, but thank you, Kick. It's nice to be considered," Banger added.

"Is this the only time I'll see you? It can't be," Rachel protested. "I was hoping to introduce you to my Gran." Thinking of how Bobby would take Tess gave me the shivers. The woman could find fault with a heavenly angel.

"You'll see me again, darling." Tess reached toward Rachel and squeezed her hand. "Just maybe not for a little while." My daughter gave her a sad smile accented with a tiny pout. "We'll text and make phone dates as soon as my time at the ashram is over. It's a silent retreat."

"It sounds amazing." Rachel's sapphire irises glowed with admiration. I swear, the drama in this girl. She'd chosen her major well.

"Anyway," Thomas started. "I could come early. Joe called last night, and I plan to go up to Virginia for a late supper. He and Toni have early plans." He leaned in and murmured in my ear, "I could be your sous-chef." The idea made me want to float above the table. Naturally, I tamped it down, mentally stomping as hard as I could.

"Will you spend Christmas in Virginia or in Bordeaux this year?" Tess asked him. She knew his family then.

"I'll split my break between here and Virginia. I have a project I'm working on."

"Other than the research?" I asked.

"Yes."

I wondered if he'd have time for me but didn't want to bring it up in front of the others. Banger still gave me the feeling he didn't approve. I'd accepted he'd finally warmed to me, but I didn't think he liked the idea of *us*.

Dream a Little Dream

Kick

I wiped down the dining room table, stretching my shoulders as I set everything to rights. They were sore from the combination of target practice and worry. Thomas and I finally found our alone time, more or less. Banger and Tess had left for a movie, and Rachel retreated to her room to finish a paper.

Banger, Thomas, and I had met in my office after dinner to go over updates on the Halloween attack while Tess hung out with Rachel a while longer. Avenging Angel Security—Banger's firm (now that I knew his given name was Rafael, it made me chuckle)— was still working on it. His best people hunted down strong leads. One of the security team members had "persuaded" a tattoo artist to admit he had recently done multiple insignia like it.

They were sure the person wearing the sapphire earring had been Jonn Graham, leaving me crestfallen. I accepted it in my heart too, but I hated the confirmation, hated the idea of someone I knew scaring so many children. Next to injuring one of my own children, it had to be the worst way possible to get to me. We all figured that was why he'd done it.

After that, I checked out. My chest grew tight again, making it painful to breathe. For a minute, I wondered if my food was cross-contaminated, but Thomas had assured me he'd let the staff know my order was specific for me. Stress caused me to struggle again.

In the end, I had let Banger's resolve and Thomas's reassuring tone lull me into a sense of security and forced the rest to roll off my back.

I snapped my cleaning rag, dropped the sponge on it, and wiped my brow with my sleeve. Thomas stared at me from across the space, coming from the guest bath. He dipped his chin and stalked directly to me. My half smile sped him up. He moved on me until my back hit the island counter.

I gasped. "Do you want more food?"

"No. I'm stuffed from supper."

Holy hell, his eyes had turned to navy and his brows drew together. I didn't know his lust face well yet—it was too dark when we were together—but we'd done enough for me to guess this was it.

My words came out breathy. "Then why are you looking at me like I'm a grass-fed, medium-rare filet with sautéed mushrooms on top?"

"Am I?" His mouth hovered over my ear. "You *are* rare."

My breath strangled delightfully. Then he stepped into me, pressing our bodies together. I rested my head against his chest and let myself relax.

"I've been wanting to do this all evening. I'd hoped Banger's update would ease your mind. Rachel seems better. So why do you look like someone kicked your dog?"

"Oh." I waved off the question. "It's stupid. Let's go find a movie." I moved to take a step toward the living area. His hands locked around my biceps, keeping me in place. "Would you like a whiskey?" Another round of deflection.

"No, Kick. Tell me what's going on. I won't think it's stupid."

I took two ragged breaths and steadied my temper on the third. If Thomas hadn't been around, I might have lost it. "I dropped our plans to rescue Rachel, but it was Tess she needed. Hell, once they got to talking, I was invisible. I put her before you for nothing."

Thomas set me on the counter and stepped between my knees, allowing him to hold me close and meet my gaze. "Is there more?"

"As I drove to Snow's place, I had flashes of girl time, giving her motherly wisdom, being needed. Tess bogarted it all—nice as she was—and there was the problem."

Thomas blinked and shifted his head left and right, letting me know he didn't comprehend.

I blurted on a deep exhale, "I thought I was ready for an empty nest, okay? Hell, I have all kinds of plans for when Liam goes to school. I figure I'll finally have the time required to truly feel better, you know."

"Among other things."

"Right? Lately I don't know. Every day leads to a series of lasts I'm not sure I'm ready for after all. In September, Liam had his last Homecoming, but it was mine too." I paused a beat, letting my words sink in. "Like I said, it's silly."

Thomas pressed me to him this time. My legs squeezed his waist, clinging like a koala. It felt… too good. Not for the lust factor but for the way his whole body and soul settled mine.

"Christ," he muttered and stepped back, running his hands through his hair. "Here I wanted to thank you for sharing your daughter today."

"You did?"

He nodded. "Yep. Tess is a natural nurturer. She thrives on it. Kind of like you." He chuckled. "She drives Banger nuts with it, but I think she's lonely."

"Then why doesn't she have her own kid?" I grumbled.

"It's… complicated."

Aw, hell. I'd lived long enough to learn to not judge someone's parental status. Looking fit and fertile didn't mean everything was copacetic on the inside. For all my health issues, I'd managed to make three healthy babies, but assuming others could was a huge mistake.

He pressed a long kiss to my forehead. "Maybe you could rest easier now? No one will ever replace you as Rachel's mother."

"No, but you and I still didn't get our day."

"I'm here now. We'll have more too. Soon."

I agreed, smiling with new resolve. He'd said some things I already knew and all the things I needed to hear.

We took a walk to stretch our legs and allow Macushla to burn up some energy before bed. Liam was supposed to have run with her earlier, but he'd had a band emergency. Already filled to the brim with drama, I didn't fuss at him. When we returned, I changed into lounge pants, a tank, and a waterfall cardigan as a reward for making it through the day. I made popcorn, drizzling it with melted ghee and nutritional yeast to make it "cheesy." We settled on the living room sectional with the bowl and drinks, watching *Tombstone*. We'd discovered we both loved the version with Kurt Russell and Val Kilmer, et al., while strolling the neighborhood.

During the opening credits, I turned to Thomas. "There are a couple more events I'd like to talk to you about."

"What's up?"

"Well, Liam's birthday is next weekend. We're having a party at the Perked Cup so his band can play. I was hoping you might like to go?"

"I'd love to." He flashed me a shy grin. "Are you sure he wants me there? Who else is coming?"

"Lee does." I tapped my chin. "As far as grown-ups go, the regulars will be there. The café will be about half his friends and half adults."

"Sounds great. What else?"

"Well... do you usually attend the Winter Gala at Lord University?"

Thomas wrinkled his nose. "The stuffy dinner where faculty is supposed to mingle with the old-money blowhard donors, then they give speeches about the amazing things they've done together?"

I swallowed a suddenly dry lump in my throat. "That's the one."

"What about it? Are you going?"

I gave him a sheepish grin and wiggled my fingers. "I fall into the blowhard donor category of your scenario. Though I'm not old-money."

"You?" Thomas's brow furrowed, incredulous. I almost laughed.

"Remember when I told you about the McKenna Family Foundation?"

"Oh shit. Right."

Reluctant and nervous, I sighed and said, "I'm giving our speech this year. I could use a friend in the audience if you wouldn't mind."

"Mind? I'd be honored. I'm sorry I sounded like a spoilsport." The hand wrapped around my shoulder rubbed my arm. "Have you done this before? I've only been once, but I don't remember you being there." Thomas's fingers traveled to the tip of my ear, and he smiled. "I would've noticed."

I shivered from the contact, not knowing what to make of his appreciation of a feature of mine I'd always associated with yet another genetic failure. "It's been a while. Even in good years, December tends to be a hard month for me, so Dad and Dylan were probably there when you attended. They've always been the speakers too. Dad could charm the room by simply standing at the podium and smiling. And don't get me started on my son. Women trip over themselves to talk to Dylan. He inherited the art of speaking from his father and grandfather. Anyhoo, Dylan has an event the same night, and Dad… well. It's up to me now."

"I'd love to escort you. Thanks for asking. You don't want me to speak, do you? As a faculty member, I'm not sure it's protocol."

"No, no. My foundation manager and I are working on a speech. Thanks, sweets. I'll get comfortable with it after some prac-tice. Having a handsome face to find in the audience will help more than you know."

"Happy to oblige." He squeezed my shoulders. "Any more upcoming command performances for me?"

I smiled at his snark. Teasing Thomas was a hell of a lot of fun. He also had a brilliant smile—often reminding me of a middle school boy with a dirty secret. "Nope." I set the empty bowl of popcorn on the coffee table, and Thomas grabbed me before I could settle back in my previous spot. "What are—"

He arranged us spooning on the sofa with me in the front. He pulled the quilt off the back and spread it over us. "Your arm candy wants a better snuggle."

I chuckled at his joke and happily settled in. We stayed that way for a long while, saying our favorite lines from the movie while his hand absently explored my belly. The simple gesture would be the highlight of my day, relaxing with a brilliant, devilishly handsome man who mysteriously found me interesting enough to hang out with too. It was fun, natural, and terrifying.

Eventually his hand worked its way under my tank, grazing my breast. "Mmm. Way better. Thought I caught the telltale signs of bralessness."

I looked over my shoulder and smirked. "You make it sound illegal."

"Never." He deliciously rumbled into my ear, "It should be required." His hand alternated between massage and rolling my nipple between his fingers, setting off my arousal meter.

"Thomas, you know we can't—"

"Shh," he whispered in my ear before lightly touching the tip with his tongue. "Don't worry. Promise we won't put on a show. Relax, baby." His strokes slowed down and lengthened until I followed his command. As my breathing synced with his, my eyes nearly rolled back into my head, lost to the bliss of Thomas's touch. "Your body drives me crazy."

Chuckling at the sentiment, I almost reminded Thomas he hadn't really seen anything yet, between the dark and currently being under the blanket. Words scrambled in my lust-fuzzed out brain though, dissolving them into a mix of moans and hisses.

Thomas rolled me toward him, his hand thus drifting under the waistband of my pants. His irises flashed a midnight blue now, and he made his own buttery gasp at his discovery. "No underwear, Kick?"

I managed a throaty, "I take lounging seriously," eliciting a toe-curling, rumbly laugh from the man rocking against me.

Taking advantage of my new position, my hand meandered into Thomas's sweatpants, finding him equally commando. When I'd declared my desire to get cozy on our walk, he told me he kept a gym bag in his trunk, then joined me in the comfy-fest with Adidas sweats and an LU T-shirt. "Great minds think alike?" I asked, running my hand along his length from tip to base and back.

Thomas did his best to pull away. "No. Not me. Not now."

"But—"

"I have to wear these home. Don't want a mess."

"Don't you have shorts in your bag?"

"Kick," he warned. The middle school boy spark on his face died for a moment, and I almost apologized. For what, I didn't know. I just wanted the moment back.

"Please. Let me..." He finished his thought with a deep kiss, his tongue diving in for a taste, a dance, hell, a swim. My brain officially scrambled. His mouth traveled down my neck and settled at my collarbone. All thoughts and words surrendered to wonderfully electric sensations. His fingers resumed their pursuit of my pleasure, making the current grow until I vibrated with my release.

Each breath puffed through my nose and gritted teeth as I fought a fierce battle between the need to let go and the impending scream I feared would accompany it. Thomas fixed my dilemma by kissing me again, capturing my moans with his mouth.

I was trying to remember how to inhale and exhale when the front door flew open.

"Yo doggo." Liam greeted Macushla, whose nails did a tap dance on the tiles in the foyer.

My eyes flashed to Thomas as my heart took a roller-coaster dive. The handsome bastard winked, mouthed a shushing noise, then grinned at me like he'd won the biggest prize in the world. I narrowed my gaze and scowled. This wasn't funny. I didn't want to act like a teenager hiding from her parents—I paid the bills, after all—but it felt like it had done back then.

Thomas bit his lip to keep from laughing and snorted anyway, leading to a low chuckle.

"Fam?" Liam walked straight to us, though I knew he couldn't see us. Then again, the television was still on, airing the late news. "Oh, hey." He dropped into the recliner perpendicular to our position on the sofa. Fortunately, I'd already sat back up, facing the screen, and propped my head in my hand on the armrest.

"Hi, Wee Man. Aren't you early?" He had a midnight curfew and always texted if plans changed, especially if he wanted to stay out longer. Not that I knew where my phone lay at the moment. I chastised myself for dropping yet another parenting ball.

"Mr. Moore made Jax come home early when he found out she was the only girl at practice. Apparently, the guys and I planned to jump her instead of working through the harmony on our last song for my party."

"Liam," I scolded even though I mostly agreed with him.

"Come on, fam. Why would we go to the trouble of making a band and do something so horrible? Plus why would I wait until eleven p.m. to do it? We'd hung out most of the day. It makes no sense."

"Calvin doesn't see your band the way you do, sweetheart. To him, it's a hobby."

Liam dropped his cheek into his hand, making him difficult to understand. "He also assumes we males can't control ourselves."

"Mm-hmm." He'd tapped into one of my major pet peeves. The man had always been weird about our kids' friendship. He initially tolerated it because it got him close to a famous football player. I made a note to ask him what had been going on between his best friend and her parents. His frustration sounded like it had been brewing for a while.

Thomas rubbed small, soothing circles on my hip under the quilt. I appreciated the show of support.

"What do you think, Prof?" Liam had begun using Thomas's title as a nickname instead of an honorific. It was kind of cute.

"How old is Jax?" Thomas asked.

"Seventeen."

"When's her birthday?"

"March fifteenth."

"Well"—Thomas exhaled—"there's your answer, pal. Don't get between a girl and her father, especially when she's a minor. Trust me."

"Tragic." Liam slogged over to the fridge, warmed up leftovers, and sat with us, eating while we watched the rest of the movie. It didn't take long since my boy inhaled food like a starved puppy. He set his dish in the sink and stretched while bellowing a yawn that sounded somewhat like a moose call.

"I'm whipped and heading up. Will I see you in the morning, Prof?"

Thomas shook his head, but I answered, "We're waiting to catch the *Saturday Night Live* cold open, then calling it a night."

"Okay." Liam bobbed his head. "Night, kids."

"Good night, sweetheart."

"Night, Liam." Thomas stretched his arm around my shoulder and squeezed me into his side, like we were when we started the movie. He leaned into my hair and chuckled.

I swatted his abs and huffed.

"Hey." Thomas turned to face me. "Are you upset with me? Do you regret—" The look on his face was so pained he couldn't finish the thought.

"No." I let my forehead fall to his. "It's… I regret nothing. You're… amazing. It's not like I'm going to ask the kids' permission to see you. But if they were little, I'd keep you from them until we knew for sure what we're doing. Having you sleep over with them in the house feels more… well, more than what I think we are. Am I being silly?"

Liam asking if Thomas planned to stay the night stuck with me though. He obviously didn't mind, but I needed to make sure. I saw it as a respect issue. Unfortunately, I hadn't found any more alone time with Liam than I had with Thomas since Halloween. All our lives were pretty hectic.

Thomas took a while to answer my question, his voice thick and thoughtful when he finally said, "No. You're not silly. You're a mother." Thomas spoke quietly into the space between us. "You know I only wanted to make the troubles of the day disappear, right? It's hard to see you upset over so many things. I'm going to make damn sure the pressure on you eases. Promise."

I sat back and cupped his cheek. "You really are the sweetest man." I kissed Thomas's lips, holding mine to his for a long moment, wishing they were a conduit to my thoughts and I could let him truly see what he did to me.

Yes, people had my back. Also true that some didn't. It had been a long time since someone wanted to put me first. I smiled, unbelieving. I didn't want to become addicted to Thomas's heart any more than I wanted to be reliant on his help.

Thomas must have sensed my mood shift and changed the subject. "Can we spoon a little more? No hanky-panky. Just want to hold you longer before we call it a night."

We stretched back out and arranged the quilt over us, catching the weather report. "Besides, this couch is so big and comfortable it's easy to get lost in."

"You can thank Shane there. He insisted most furniture was too small for him. When we saw this piece, he declared it man-sized." I chuckled at the pleasant memory. "Truth is, I agree with you on the comfort factor. I love stretching out on it too."

Thomas grunted and his body stiffened.

I looked over my shoulder. "You okay?"

He answered, "Mm-hmm," but his warm, attentive gaze had shut down.

"You sure? Did I say something wrong?"

He pecked a kiss on my head. "Everything's fine."

I knew he wasn't, though I wasn't comfortable enough with him to push the subject. I feared the possibility of making him angry and let it drop.

Thomas stayed quiet the rest of the night. Even during the cold-open sketch. His bottom arm stayed under me, but he moved his top hand from my hip to his own.

. . .

My stuffy nose woke me in the middle of the night. An obnoxious voice on the TV preached nonsense to insomniacs and had infiltrated my dream. I turned off the television and fluffed the throw pillows, stealthily maneuvering into a more upright sleeping position. I could've moved into my bedroom, but Thomas still snuggled beside me. I didn't want to disturb him. Okay, I also wanted every minute with him I could get. Until the preacher—which I turned off—invaded my head, my sleep had been pleasantly dark and empty.

Once resettled, my breath evened out as I absorbed the peace of the night. Faded light from the streetlamp illuminated the ceiling through the clerestory windows at the fireplace and in the kitchen at the other end of the open space. Staring up at the faded light hovering above us, I embraced the sensation of sinking into the dark bottom of the room. It was a warm, cozy retreat from my worries and other things that might go bump in the night.

As the drift began, Thomas shifted, laying his head on my chest. He made a soft, agonized sound, which broke my heart and left me to wonder who chased him in his sleep.

I brushed his hair off his forehead, my nails lightly massaging his scalp, my fingertips barely touching the sad furrow between his brows. His face relaxed, and my breath caught on his beauty. Full lashes lay against angular cheeks, softening them. His sculpted lips lost their tension, barely parting.

Thomas's arms wound around my waist and tightened as he snuggled deeper. I continued to barely stroke his hair as I whispered, "Shhh. You're okay." His body stilled, and it occurred to me he might require more.

I continued whispering, "Let's walk down the stairs to my favorite spot." I shared the secret porch from recent meditations, wondering if any part of him heard me. I believed words spoken into the dead of night were said to the soul without the judgment or influence of a conscious mind.

I hoped sharing my special place would scare off whatever affected Thomas. I also hoped it would encourage his subconscious to open up and know his secrets were safe with me. In my heart, I pledged to hold on to them like the treasures they were. His breathing evened as he clung to me for support.

When finished, I couldn't stop thinking about what might haunt him. My struggles seemed to either tattoo themselves to my face or they blew up into a flare—lately, literally. This man rationed out his private thoughts like they were needed for a war effort. Then again, maybe they were. The one-sided nature of our evening hadn't set well with me. Perhaps with this, right here, his heart showed me what he needed most. Maybe there was a way I could ease his burden too and could be useful to him after all. It might also mean I could become his essential person—like he was becoming mine.

Though I didn't dare whisper my desire into the night. Instead, I turned my lips toward his ear, whispering, "Dream a little dream of me." I drifted off to the lyrics swimming in my head.

THE NEXT TIME MY EYES OPENED, I WAS WEDGED BETWEEN THE SOFA and the coffee table. I slowly stood, extracting one limb at a time, noting how the suspect in my couch-ousting had snuggled into Thomas's side. Macushla had already resumed dreaming—running and growling in her sleep—but I was sure it was a ruse. I knew the second I entered the kitchen, she'd practically apparate at my feet, asking for breakfast.

The clock read six in the morning, and I didn't feel like dozing. Once Thomas had relaxed and I conked out, I'd slept better than I had in days. The couch was comfortable, but I knew the reason had more to do with my company. I padded into my bathroom to take my thyroid medicine and go through a quick get-ready routine.

True to my suspicion, Koosh appeared in front of me as soon as I started filling the water kettle in the kitchen. The smart little shit threatened a bark, like she knew I was trying to be quiet and let Thomas sleep. I fed the blackmailer before taking a moment to open my brand-new bag of decaffeinated coffee. The time had finally arrived to give coffee another go. We called it a "challenge" in the autoimmune world. I fought the urge to rip the bag open, choosing to savor each moment, smelling the fresh grounds. Nutty, rich, with a hint of vanilla and spices. I couldn't wait. Catching the kettle before it boiled, I let the water drip through my brand-new pour-over carafe, opting for simplicity from my first cup.

I poured the finished liquid gold into a thermos and filled my favorite mug with the rest. My eyes drifted shut on the inhale, and my mouth watered from anticipation.

4

Timeless

Thomas

Countless years of waking up in strange places kept Thomas from freaking out when consciousness came back to him. He opened an eye and checked his surroundings. Kick's living room. He'd spent the night on her sofa—no, on *his* sofa. Thomas hated how much the thought irritated him, but he couldn't deny it either.

He sat up and spotted Kick in the kitchen area, her hands wrapped around a mug. She took a sip and tilted her face to the ceiling, her eyes closed. She appeared to be right on this side of orgasmic. He cleared his throat, partly to keep from scaring her but mostly to distract himself from the amorous lust she inspired.

Kick started and set the mug down, a guarded smile on her face. "Hey handsome. I didn't wake you, did I? Sorry if I did."

Thomas answered with a gruff morning rasp. "No. But who were you talking to?"

A warm blush spread across Kick's face as she lifted her mug with both hands like it was the Holy Grail. "My coffee. Again, I'm sorry. I was trying to be quiet, but the excitement over my first sip got the best of me."

Thomas studied her bashful demeanor. He had meant what he said to Liam the night before about planning to go home. He also couldn't deny how good it felt to sleep with Kick in his arms again. Once his frustration with himself passed from being pissy over Shane picking out the furniture, he had to admit how nice it was to be in her space. Her late husband might haunt it here and there, but no one could deny how she inhabited every square inch of this home. He didn't mind waking up to the sound of her voice at all even if her words were kooky.

He pushed away any further thought of going down that trail, unsure how far he could get while under the Felidae's radar. From their first interactions, Thomas had envisioned them maintaining their own homes no matter what happened. He'd learned to love his space and his projects. Since the morning he saw Kick fixing breakfast in his kitchen, he wasn't so sure anymore.

He rubbed his face and shook his head, smiling. He could honestly get used to this. "Don't worry about it, baby." He padded around the living room furniture and into the kitchen, gave Kick a kiss on her cheek, mindful of his morning breath. He said a slightly foggy, "Morning."

A wide grin spread across Kick's face. "Good morning, handsome." She ran her hands through his hair. "You look like you're about to go on stage with the Cure."

"Who? And why?"

"Oh, come on." She giggled. "You're not that young. *Surely* you know who the Cure is. Anyway, your sleepy head and face are cute."

Thomas lifted a shoulder. "I'll take your word for it." He tipped his head to the side. "Mind if I use your guest bath?"

"Help yourself."

"Can I have one of those when I get back?"

"Like you have to ask at the barista's house?" Kick raised her mug. "This is decaf though. Would you rather have an Americano?"

"If it's no trouble."

"None at all."

"Thanks darlin'." Thomas entered the bathroom and took care

of his morning routine. After a quick shower, he dug out fresh underwear and a T-shirt from his gym bag. He paired it with the jeans from the day before and headed back into the kitchen, eager for his espresso.

Kick had everything waiting and put the cup together as he walked over, handing it to him with a twinkle in her eye. "You know"—she ran her hands through his wet hair—"your hair is about as straight as mine is curly. It fascinates me."

Thomas took a sip, savoring the smell as the cup neared his nose, the bitter, nutty flavor mixed with the crema as it slid down his throat. "Fascinates? Isn't it boring compared to yours?"

"Uh-uh," Kick said. "There isn't any sign of porosity. I bet your hair never frizzes on you."

"Can't say it has."

"Absolutely incredible," she remarked, as if awed, carefully sifting a piece away from his forehead.

Thomas took another pull and grinned. "Don't you mean apoplectic?"

"What?" Kick's eyes flashed with mirth and annoyance when she realized what he referenced. Ever since their acquaintance became a friendship, Thomas had occasionally teased her about the note he'd found attached to the smoke shop door on the day they met—how the staff at Mick & Hugh's was apoplectic about being closed. It was so Kick and made Thomas chuckle inside any time he thought of it.

She swatted him on the bicep. "Smart-ass. I might put you to work for that."

"It'd be my pleasure either way, baby."

Since there were four for breakfast, Kick made a full meal. She asked Thomas to sauté loose sausage while she chopped up mush-rooms, bell peppers, and spinach. She planned to put them all in a frittata. As soon as Thomas had the sausage done and drained, she put him to work on two packs of bacon. Apparently, Liam could down a pack by himself.

Kick had just placed the frittata in the oven when Rachel came downstairs. "Hey guys," she said with a jaw-cracking yawn.

"Good morning, Snow," Kick said in a perky, motherly tone. "Feeling any better?"

Like her Disney Princess namesake, Rachel floated to her mother with a dancer's grace and bent to kiss her cheek. "Much. Thank you. Good morning, Thomas. I didn't realize you were spending the night."

"It wasn't planned," he sheepishly said over his shoulder.

"We both fell asleep on the sofa watching *Saturday Night Live*," Kick explained.

"Aw"—Rachel snuck a piece of bacon—"how cute. It's like you're teens or something."

"Um, thanks. I think." Kick chuckled. "Which do you want to do, sweets—make your own latte or finish this guacamole I'm making?"

"Ooh, are we having breakfast burritos?"

"Frittata."

"Even better. I'll make a latte. Thanks, Mama."

"Snow, when you're done, would you mind waking your brother? This pan's about ready to come out of the oven."

"Lee's up. He's in the bathroom— Welp, never mind. Here he comes."

Macushla ran up the stairs, barking and chasing her favorite person down the steps to the living room. Liam picked her up and placed her around his neck while walking into the kitchen. "Mmm. It smells great down here. You should stay over more often."

"Liam," Kick scolded, looking embarrassed.

Rachel handed her latte to her brother. "Here, squirt. You can have mine. I'll make another even though you should make both since I had to put up with your face pubes in the bathroom."

"Rachel," Kick warned again. "We're about to eat."

"No kidding. I almost lost my appetite. They're stuck in dried-on shaving cream droplets." Rachel shuttered dramatically. "Disgusting."

Thomas finished the last of the bacon and turned off the burner. He took the stool next to Liam and watched the McKennas in action.

"Do you know how spicy it is to be an only child now?" Liam retorted.

Rachel answered, "No, Lee. As a matter of fact, I absolutely do *not*. How spicy is it?"

Liam pressed his elbows into the quartz counter and leaned forward for emphasis. "It's big. Heaven."

Thomas bit the inside of his lip to keep from laughing out loud. The boy had his mother's sense of snark.

Kick finished preparing the bowl of guac and placed it on the island counter. "Here I thought it would be nice to have two of my children home for breakfast. Silly me." Thomas let his head hang and laughed.

"Some things don't change," Rachel said.

"Nope," Kick agreed. "Do you think you two will still argue like this in front of your future children?"

"Yep," Liam answered. "I'll make sure to have the most kids so we can gang up on their aunt and uncle, and I'll finally win."

Thomas broke into a belly laugh while Kick and Rachel rolled their eyes. Kick looked at Rachel and said, "A clown to my left"— she turned her head toward Liam and sighed—"and a joker on my right." Then she gave Thomas a huge, gorgeous grin. *There* was something he could eat up every day.

An hour later, breakfast was finished, the kitchen was cleaned, the pleasant sound of the kids playing *Smash Bros* floated down from the loft, and Kick ran around the house like her pretty ass was on fire. Thomas had repacked his gym bag, set it on the bench in the mudroom, and presently stood watching her fret from the hallway in front of her office. Kick carried a loaded basket of what he assumed to be dirty clothes into the laundry room.

"What's wrong, darlin'?" He followed her down the hall.

Kick shook her head as she sorted the clothes, loading the darks into the washing machine. She unsuccessfully flipped her hair out of her face before sighing and tucking it behind her ear. "Rach wants to go home sooner rather than later, but Lee can't drive her because he has a test tomorrow. So I'm cramming as much work in as I can before I chauffeur again." She paused her work. "I'm sorry I'm such a poor host."

"The last thing I want to do is pile on your to-do list, baby. What if I took Rachel home?"

Over her shoulder, she said, "You're heading out to the gym."

"I'm not teaching. Sundays are informal, so I can arrive any time. Plus it would give me a chance to peek under the hood of her car."

Kick stopped again, turning around. "Why would..." She sighed, tucking the hair back again. "You really want to do that? You know it's unnecessary, right? I don't expect you to take us all on. The kids act like children sometimes, but they're mostly out of the nest. Hell, they've been practicing their flying skills for years now."

"It doesn't mean an older bird can't show them a thing or two, does it?" Sure, he had a family, but Thomas had missed this part of it, the care, the imparting of wisdom, even learning from a bright, young mind. His students were never close enough to count. Not like this. He practically champed at the bit to help.

Her eyes narrowed and she huffed a breath, murmuring, "It feels like a big ask."

Thomas stepped into Kick's space, gently pushing her hair back yet again. "I have the time. It's a simple favor, and it would ease my mind to know what's going on with Rachel's car."

Kick's eyebrows raised. "It would ease *your* mind, huh? So I'd be doing *you* a favor by having you relieve my impossible day?"

Thomas answered with a big smile. To be completely useful, even to a few? She had no idea.

"You're slick."

"Thank you. You can pay me in kisses."

"Um, okay. As if I wasn't going to. Which reminds me, let me give you the name of the towing company I use. If you think it needs it, call them and put it on my account."

Thomas cleared his throat. "Give me the name of your mechanic again. If I can't get Rachel's car working, *I'll* have it towed there. My dime."

"Thomas..."

"Kick." He raised his voice in a squeak to imitate hers.

Her lips pursed to keep from laughing. It didn't work, and she giggled. "Okay fine. Thank you." She let out a sigh of relief. "I do have a lot on the list today."

Thomas tapped his lips. Kick was still smiling when she pulled his head down to meet hers. He took advantage of her open mouth and their privacy, deepening the kiss. His fingertips adjusted her jaw to fit the angle he sought, and he let his tongue dance and linger with hers. She still tasted like coffee. The comforting, spicy flavor of it fit her.

One hand drifted down to her ass, pressing her into his erection. Her sweet moan traveled from his cock up to his heart, and he broke their connection. "*Now* you're welcome."

Kick's hazy gaze took a moment to clear. Her smirk returned when it did. "I swear you're twelve."

He tapped her button nose. "Which means I keep you young. A kiss from you will sustain me for the rest of the day."

"That's all it took?"

Thomas patted her fine ass and left a relaxed Kick to her chores as he called for Rachel.

Rachel sat in silence for the first quarter of their drive into Raleigh, and Thomas let her, giving her some space to ruminate. Every so often, his eyes sliced to the passenger seat, and he saw her face morph through the five stages of grief. He thought he also caught worry for family and possibly—probably—something to do with school. The girl seemed to let all her emotions show on her face, like her mother.

Thomas considered tuning the radio to an easy jazz station, thinking it would keep his brain engaged without disturbing Rachel. Before his hand reached out, Rachel spoke, her head turned toward the passenger window. "Do you think it's strange how you and Mama have the same car… the make, I mean?"

"Strange?"

Rachel shifted her body to look at Thomas. "Do you think it's fate or something? Like kismet or serendipity?"

"Ah. I see." They came to a red light, so Thomas took a moment to look at Rachel and found her returning his gaze. "Like attracts like, so it makes sense your mom and I would be drawn to the same model car. Nothing more went into it."

"Like attracts like, huh?"

"Not the woo-woo stuff about money and intentions, in case it was confusing. Socially, people of like minds have migrated together since the beginning of our species. It's mutually beneficial for survival and helps make the days more pleasant if each party has a mix of similar interests. Does that make sense?"

Rachel turned back to her window. "So she's safe with you?"

Now he understood. Thomas's back straightened as he immediately answered, "Yes, Rachel. As much as it's in my power, Kick is safe with me. Do you worry about her?"

"A bit. Since Granddad died, it's… difficult again."

Thomas's professor instincts kicked in. He'd learned the hard way how a struggling student could look like they lacked motivation when, in reality, they were drowning with worries. "You can rest your mind about your mother. From what she's told me, it's been a rough year, but remember her progress too. Hell, she had her first coffee this morning. Make sure you celebrate her victories, alright?"

"Okay. Sure."

Now fully in professor mode, he figured he'd press on. It was another way to help Kick out and get to know her little clan. "It won't be long before we reach your place. Are you ready for it?"

Rachel's quiver reached her chin. Still, her voice stayed steady. "Tess and Mama helped me see that what's bothering me isn't the loss of Cody so much. We weren't ever a 'together forever' kind of couple. I think he hurt me because he didn't know how to say goodbye. I didn't either, to be honest."

"I'd love to give him a piece of my mind. Maybe accidentally pop his nose in the process."

Rachel laughed, which meant Thomas had achieved one of his goals. "If it were necessary, my brothers are totally qualified. Shit, I wouldn't be surprised if Dylan shows up when he finds out. Did you know he ruined my first kiss?"

"No. But I can imagine."

"It happened during the Homecoming dance after Daddy died. My crush before Cody had asked me. Dylan saw him kiss me in the courtyard outside our school gym and rushed him. He gave the boy a black eye. It was my brother's first of several suspensions after the accident. I think Dylan blamed himself for it and decided he'd fill Daddy's shoes to make up for it. He thought he was defending my honor." She stared straight ahead for a few blocks, then quietly murmured, "It was a sweet kiss too."

Christ. Thomas knew all about people in intense pain tripping over each other despite their mutual love. He mulled over what to say next when she said, "The thing is, Mom was engaged to Dad by the time she was my age. She planned their wedding during her last semester of college. Her last semester. Then she immediately moved across the country to settle in before Dad started training camp in San Francisco."

Thomas shook his head at the thought. "That's nuts."

"No. It's romantic."

Thomas turned to her and sighed. To him, it showed Kick's life-long struggle with boundaries, as if her eventual health issues were nature's way of getting her attention and teaching her to put herself first once in a while. He knew better than to talk so intimately about Kick to her daughter though. "I know, she's badass."

"She had her shit together, okay? She knew what she wanted and went for it." Rachel hung her head. "I've been too scared to let Cody loose. Fuck all, half the time I can't decide what to eat for dinner, especially since my teacher wants me to lose weight."

What the hell? Currently, Rachel wore a large, plaid, flannel shirt over leggings. Her shirt seemed to swallow her, but he'd seen her in fitted clothes before. She had the expected dancer's body. Lean, toned, and flexible. She'd demonstrated the last after break-fast when she lifted her leg to the kitchen counter and folded her body over her knee, then switched to the other side. Kick responded like it was a common practice. She'd huffed, swatted her daughter on the leg, and told her to use her barre upstairs in the workout room.

An odd feeling stirred in Thomas's gut—a fatherly one he didn't want to acknowledge. Some fierce desire to chase down this so-called instructor and chew his or her ass out traveled from the growling pit in his stomach up to his heart. Damn if it didn't scare the shit out of him.

Rachel sighed, stretching in her seat. "Anyway, my point is, this Cody thing is a big reminder that it's taking me too long to grow the hell up."

"Well, it's not a good idea to compare yourself to your mother, darlin'," Thomas drawled, tipping his head to consider. "I mean not only because of different times and different generations. Your life circumstances are different too." They waited in a left-turn lane, so Thomas let his gaze linger, making his next point. "It's not a big extrapolation to guess why your mom took on so much pressure in her senior year. It might have been a crushing amount of work, but it got her away from her mother in the end. Hell, she put half a country between them." Thomas's mouth tipped at the corner at the thought. "It's a wonder she stayed on the same continent."

"She loved Daddy."

Thomas winced. He didn't understand why he'd suddenly become so sensitive to the topic of Shane McKenna. He'd been serious when he'd told Kick it pleased him to know she'd been loved. "She did. They also could've eloped, had a small wedding, settled in California before getting married, or several other things. My point is y'all should grow up the way that works for *y'all*."

He was about to ask Rachel about plans for the summer when they pulled into her parking lot. Thomas spotted her car near the fence and frowned. He parked as close as he could and jogged straight over to investigate.

"Dammit all." All four tires had been slashed.

"What the hell?"

"Were your tires fine yesterday?"

As she opened her mouth to answer, her head turned, her eyes narrowed, and she tracked a male leaving the apartment building.

Thomas guessed who it was by the low growling sound she made. "Is that Cody?"

Rachel nodded.

Thomas stalked over to him, intercepting the young man before he reached his Dodge Durango. "You do this?" He pointed to Rachel's car.

"Do what, and who the hell are you?"

"Rachel's friend." Thomas stepped into Cody's space. The boy's face flashed with fear. Through gritted teeth, Thomas slowly snarled, "Did you slash her tires?"

"What? Fuck no."

Rachel caught up to them, keeping a distance. Cody lifted his chin in her direction. "Didn't take you long, did it? I *knew* you had others."

"He's seeing my mom! But of course you'd go there. Makes you feel better, doesn't—"

"Look at me, asshat," Thomas warned. "You swear you didn't touch her car? We already know you don't mind hurting Rachel personally."

Cody tried to move away, but Thomas pinned him to the truck.

"I didn't do shit. She ain't no innocent bitch neither," Cody squeaked.

Thomas's nostrils flared, his hand clenching into a fist.

Rachel placed her hand on his arm. "Please, Thomas, let it go." She turned her glare toward her ex, who was panting from the fear-fueled adrenaline rush. "The twat-waffle isn't worth shit."

"Cute—" Cody started but was cut off by Thomas.

"Not another word to her, do you hear? If you see Rachel, you politely smile, but you never say another word to her again. And the next time you fuck a girl, do it in silence. Better yet, do it at her place. Got it?"

Cody's face busted into a wide grin, and Thomas's stomach dropped. He'd said too much and let the little fucker know Cody had gotten under Rachel's skin. "Sure." Cody waggled his eyebrows at Rachel, and Thomas almost hit the kid then. He held back, knowing an assault charge wouldn't bode well with the university.

Thomas almost didn't care since he had a crack lawyer. *Kick might care though.*

"I never stepped out on you."

"Not what I heard."

Thomas growled, wondering if there was more to the social media shit going on with the girl.

Rachel stepped between the men and pushed Thomas back with the poise of a young lady who'd done this before. She turned around and asked Cody, "Can you just tell me if you saw or heard anything from the parking lot last night? You and Kierra must have come up for air sometime, not that she got off, I'm sure. Maybe I should text her. I bet she needed something to keep her distracted."

"I'm not supposed to talk to you."

Rachel folded her arms over her chest. "You can nod for yes or shake your head for no."

Cody shook his head, turned around, and climbed into his truck. It roared to life, and he revved the engine. He lowered the window before putting it in gear. "Are you wearing my shirt? Give it back!"

Rachel shouted back as he pulled out, "Hell no! It's the least you owe me."

Thomas reached into his pocket and pulled out his phone. He couldn't believe he'd almost punched his girlfriend's daughter's ex-boyfriend. He thought back to Rachel's story of Dylan running rough-shod over her crush. *Christ,* he was devolving into a boy. He had to rein in the protective, fatherly instinct ASAP.

After yelling, Rachel turned around. "Who are you calling?"

"I'm texting Banger. He needs to check this out." Thomas met her gaze. "You should call the police."

"I was going to call Mama."

Thomas sighed and looked at the sky. "Absolutely do *not* call her. She has enough going on. We'll fill her in when we have answers." He pegged Rachel with his professor's stare. "You want to grow up? Now's a good time to start. Filing a police report is simple."

His phone rang, and Thomas answered it, walking back toward Rachel's Honda Accord. "Hey, man…"

5

Tightrope

Thomas

Tess bounded through the doors to Thomas's lab with more energy than she should have. She'd always had this annoying joie de vivre, as long as she kept herself away from her dark spaces. He thought time spent with her gurus and daily yoga practice had done Tess a world of good. For now, Thomas appreciated it. He hoped some of it would rub off on him.

Her attitude hadn't transmitted to Banger though. Thomas's friend pulled up the rear of their trio. Banger usually checked on the lab a few times a year, after hours to run security sweeps. The university did their own, but Banger trusted no one's authority or talent more than his own. Regardless, Thomas's team knew his friend, and they'd all passed another thorough analysis into their backgrounds after the near miss with Presley. Thomas still couldn't believe his talented protégé had almost blackmailed him.

When Thomas mentioned a new lead showing a link between mitochondrial performance and an area of "junk DNA," Banger asked if he could check it out. They'd made it a group visit when Tess began citing recent studies from universities around the world having nothing to do with Thomas's or Nigel's facilities. She'd shocked the men with her interest and questions regarding where the science was leading.

"Well, friends, meet the gang," Thomas said, sweeping his arm across the space. They greeted Spencer, the day's lead; Jules and Charon, two of his undergrad assistants; and his new right hand, Bethany. Thomas turned to Tess. "My other team members aren't on today's schedule." The trio turned a corner. "Ah, here's Gautam."

After they all exchanged greetings, Thomas explained to Tess, "G is probably the most important person in the lab. He's our data collector and helps us interpret our shenanigans."

Tess made a namaste bow, greeting Gautam while Banger dipped his head, looking embarrassed. Thomas dipped his chin in a tight smile. He understood Banger's irritation with Tess, but she'd always made Thomas laugh. "How delightful. Have you had any interesting recent finds?"

Gautam gave her a shy, thoughtful smile. "As a matter of fact, many." He turned toward his computer monitor and clicked through a few folders. "I'm not sure how much Professor H wants to share."

Tess tipped her head up at Thomas, a proud grin across her face. "Professor H. I'm still not used to hearing it."

Thomas shoved his hands in his pockets. This was the closest he'd probably get to showing his family his work in action. Presentations in Bordeaux didn't really count. He turned his attention back to Gautam before he lost his cool points—at least that's what his students had called them. "Don't worry about it, G. I plan to introduce them to our current stars." He couldn't believe how much he wanted—no, needed—Tess's approval of his work. Most of the Felidae cared about results, not the details on how they'd been achieved.

Thomas led them around the corner to a work area with a rodent rack. He figured plates with smears wouldn't matter much to Tess. The cage he had in mind was already on the counter, as

Charon had just removed the top and was taking notes. "Come see our new mice."

Tess oohed and aahed over the mouse pups while Thomas explained, "We'll check them soon to see if any were born with the genetic variance my assistant, Bethany, recently discovered in their parents." He hoped at least a few from the litter had what he was looking for. So far, following this route proved more fun than trying to track Toni's progress. He believed the two tactics would meet and merge soon.

"Are you certain you don't want to retest Rafa and me?" Tess asked. Stalwart in her refusal to use Banger's preferred nickname, Thomas stayed equally stubborn in his desire to stay out of their standoff while his friend walked away.

Thomas studied Tess while she added, "We have much in common with these babies, don't we?"

He nodded. "You may be right. I'll let y'all know if I need it. I still have a sample from you and two from—"

"Who's with Gautam?" Banger asked in a low-voiced huff, jabbing his thumb over his shoulder. "I haven't met him."

Thomas peeked around the corner and turned back to the group. "That's Drew. He works at the lab next door. Gautam's probably running a sequence for him." When Banger's scowl wouldn't ease up, he added, "We do it all the time when G is slow here. The professor Drew works for is studying genetic variances in colon cancer, and they don't have the resources I do." Thinking some food and a dram might lighten his friend's mood, Thomas said, "Why don't we go eat?"

As the trio passed Gautam's station, he and Drew looked up from their work. Thomas put a hand on Drew's shoulder. "How are you holding up?"

"Taking it a day at a time, Professor. You?"

"The same." Thomas hoped the young student was telling the truth. "If you need anything, let me know."

Drew nodded slightly. "Thank you."

"What was that about?" Banger asked as Thomas reached him and Tess, who were waiting at the door.

Thomas sighed and said, "Drew was Presley's boyfriend. They'd met while studying in the lounge at the end of the hall. I don't mind letting him borrow Gautam on occasion, and it probably helps him to deal with his grief. One of my students told me Drew had already bought Pres a ring."

Banger stared down the hall toward said room, his jaw flexing. "Shit."

THE TRIO SETTLED INTO A DARK WOODEN BOOTH AT THE BACK OF Thomas's favorite pub near campus. He knew Tess would've preferred Garam Masala at a local Indian place, but the interior architecture here lent itself to more private conversations. Not only did the booth they shared come with high-backs, the entire pub was divided into small, themed rooms. It kept the noise down and allowed for quiet conversation. Plus Banger's mood lightened when he discovered the pub offered the largest selection of whiskeys in the Carolinas. He ordered a flight of rare Highland scotches.

Tess let a soft smile brighten her eyes. "This is nice, Michael—I mean Thomas. Thank you."

Thomas dipped his chin to acknowledge her mistake, then lifted a questioning eyebrow. "I haven't been Michael for a while."

She patted his hand. "I see you so rarely that I still forget. *Pardon*."

"If you didn't jet-set so much, you might see me during the meetings in Bordeaux."

She scrunched her face and took a sip of water. Then Tess stilled and seemed to consider his words. "You're right. It's been hard there lately. I can visit here more often. You and Rafa are family, no? I can trust you."

Thomas wondered if the same suspicions he had were on Tess's mind, while Banger mmphf'd at the inference to his given name, as usual. Tess leveled Banger with what Thomas thought of as a European growl. It was part Spanish, part French, and fully continental. "I will *never* refer to you by that vulgar name."

He muttered, "It's never been about what you think it is."

Tess flicked her wrist, dismissing him. "No matter. I must speak with you two. I have your sworn secrecy, yes?"

Thomas shifted his gaze between his tablemates. "You know you do," he said. Banger huffed and nodded.

Tess leaned into the middle of the table. "Well, the definition of *loyalty* as we know it may be changing."

The waitress arrived right then, setting down a sampler of boxty, Scotch eggs, and a selection of potato-and-cheese croquettes. Banger reached for the first glass in his flight, a settling smile stretching across his face as the first sip went down. Thomas kept with a local bourbon called Mystic and savored the smooth finish. Tess picked up a glass from her own flight of Highland whiskies— the same one as Banger's—and sniffed it.

"What?" she asked after taking a drink. "Some aspects of life in those mountains weren't so bad."

To distract him and keep his mood easy, Thomas said, "You go first, Banger. Tell the server what else you want."

"Is your name actually Banger?" the waitress asked. Thomas cringed, wishing the topic of his friend's name would drop already. After the man himself affirmed her question, the girl continued. "Is it possible it's in reference to a legend? My grandmother used to tell me old stories when I was little."

Tess scoffed, and her demeanor soured.

The corner of Banger's mouth lifted in a defiant smirk after he finished the first glass. "Which one? There are many legends in the Highlands."

"Right?" the server asked, for no reason Thomas could figure. "My grandmother grew up there. She told me one about a laird from a long time ago who loved to hurt girls." She blushed and didn't continue.

"It's not my favorite of the stories, but I've heard it," Banger said grumpily, nearly growling.

"Oh, no matter." The waitress waved her hand. "I'm sure it was only my gran's way of warning me about troublesome boys, like the Laird Mackendrick or something."

"Did it work?" Banger asked while Tess turned shades of red Thomas didn't know she could achieve.

The young woman laughed. "I've always had a soft spot for bad boys, so I guess not."

"Your gran had sight then." Banger leaned toward her. "Bad boys need someone to believe in them anyway. And remember… folks say the *men* of the village started that harsh tale. I think they were jealous of the laird." He winked at the server and gave her his order.

"Tess, Banger and I have picked up on the weird stuff happening with the Felidae too." Thomas wanted to take advantage of the quiet time before their meal arrived. He hoped Tess might have actually seen or heard something that could help him get to the source of the discord.

"That's because you're both smart."

"Well, the old man shut down communication between Thomas and Oxford," Banger grunted.

"No?" Tess asked, her eyes pinned to Thomas.

"Yes, he did. The atmosphere at last month's meeting was tense at best. The only person from the other team who acted relaxed around me was Ellie."

"I bet she did," Tess muttered.

"What's wrong?" Thomas downed the last of his bourbon, wishing he'd ordered a second.

"She's been sneaking… secret calls, texts… meeting with staff in the barns."

"Sounds like she's helping to run the vineyard and the Felidae," Thomas said.

"The vineyard is Alaric's." Tess bit her lip, leaned into the middle of the table, and continued in a low voice. "She runs the estate, not the wine. No, boys, something isn't right."

"I picked up as much from *Grand-père*," Thomas said, his throat dry. He'd never known Tess to be so keyed up.

Tess pointed at him and wagged her finger. "Get those mice strong. Find your answers fast."

Thomas ran his hand through his hair. "That's pretty much what *Grand-père* said too, but the mice are secondary. My real hunt is with the DNA. We won't know much about the mice for a few generations."

Tess nodded vigorously. "I can relate."

Thomas reached across the table and grabbed Tess's hand. "I wish I could change what happened to you." He turned his head to Banger. "To both of you."

Tess's face darkened a moment before shaking it off.

"Is your lab secure?" Banger growled.

"Why?" Thomas looked back at Banger.

"I don't like Drew having access to your equipment. My team needs to run him," Banger added.

"Because of Presley?"

"Who is Presley?" Tess asked.

"My former right hand at the lab."

"She was killed in a hit-and-run in September," Banger told Tess. He pointed his third snifter glass Thomas's way. "She was planning to blackmail Thomas. She knew about *us*. We found it all when we went through her stuff. Brother-man, here, should've thought about this before now." Banger turned a hard glare on Thomas.

Banger was right. Kick had already softened him. If she hadn't distracted him, Thomas would've kept his focus on the research. He probably wouldn't have been blindsided by Presley either. He hung his head guiltily.

Tess's brows drew together in a furious V. "I have money. Let me fund the rest of your research."

"Tess—" Money wasn't Thomas's hurdle. Legality and credibility were.

She raised her hands. "What? Then you can control all the facets of your work. This is good, no?"

"For once, I agree," Banger added.

Damn it all. Thomas enjoyed teaching now. He couldn't say that though. The research had to come first. Before anything. Or anyone. Why did he desperately wish he could let Kick in on this? She didn't need more on her plate, but he sure could use her instincts.

"I have wine. It's vast, and some important cases are going bad. Wine doesn't age like my whiskies or cognac. The cases are suited for collectors who simply want old things. It's rare, see, worth millions—hundreds of millions."

Of course it was. *Christ*, Thomas wasn't an unbalanced nut case who jumped at every anxious scare. He'd worked too hard to fall prey to someone else's emotional whims. Until Kick, he couldn't remember the last time he'd found himself out of sorts. Kick was nothing compared to this though. He had to understand the discord within the Felidae before he made such a big decision. Deep in his heart, Thomas figured it would probably happen soon. He made a mental note to call his lawyer just in case.

Thomas turned to Banger. "Go ahead and run any check you may or may not need. Just… please don't tell me about it." Dammit, this had to be as illegal as hell. Not that he worked completely aboveboard either. "Not unless y'all find something I must know."

Between the McKennas and the lab, he wondered if the intrigue would ever end. What the hell might happen next?

6

I Hope You Dance

Kick

CYNDI SENDAYDIEGO, MY DEAREST FRIEND, PAUSED HER WORK, hanging the decorations for Liam's birthday party. She snapped her fingers in front of my face. "Are you breathing, Kicky?" She had me imitate her deep inhale and exhale. "Why are you so stressed? More than usual, I mean." She looked around the room. Lee and his band were setting up while Thomas oversaw the sound check. My other two kids had arrived early and were setting up the finger foods Carmen's daughters had delivered.

Carmen was my house manager and had developed some of those typical health issues many women contend with in their middle years. Earlier in the year, she'd begun experimenting with her favorite Puerto Rican recipes, adapting them for my autoimmune issues, and they accidentally helped her. It wasn't long before she'd finagled her whole family into eating this way. Her girls had taken up the mantle and were developing a catering business.

"The morning's gone smoothly, chica. You did good." Cyndi's voice was soothing.

My gut told me this would end up being one of the easiest of the kids' birthdays I'd thrown except for the wild card that terrified me.

"What you see on my face is dread. The day's been too smooth. I'm waiting for the 'Bobby shoe' to drop."

Cyndi's face lit with recognition. "Why'd you invite her anyway?"

"She's technically Liam's grandmother"—even if she didn't want to be—"and she won't stop reminding me how she missed my birthday."

"Didn't you plan for her to be gone?"

"I didn't set the ship's schedule. It was a beautiful coincidence though. I took it as a birthday present from above." I chuckled.

"There's my pretty bestie." She pointed at my face. "Stay like this the rest of day. No matter what."

My laugh deepened, then fizzled out like a balloon with a pinprick. "Whatever. What if… Maybe I'm too much like my dad… or Charlie Brown? I keep hoping she'll let the mountain of shit go, but the most I've ever gotten from her are crocodile tears. Still, Dad asked me to keep trying. I can't stop now."

Cyndi set down her tape and gave me a quick, tight squeeze. "Can't say I can relate. My 'rents are fabulous and across the country. You've done a great job with this though. And a shit ton of us love you. Count me at the top of the list."

"Thanks, sweets."

She helped me finish the decorations, and as we carried the step stool and supplies to the back closet, she nudged my shoulder. "Thomas fits in well over there."

"You think so?"

"Dylan's hard to read, but the rapport is there with Snow and Lee."

"He's spent some quality time with them. No complaints came in from any side, not to me anyway. Also, Thomas is not the type of man to give me a piece of his mind about what's wrong with my kids. They speak well of each other though."

We returned to the front and stopped to watch Liam and

Thomas finish up with the rented soundboard. I turned to ask her about work and discovered Cyndi had been staring at me, a smarmy grin on her face. I did a double take and furrowed my brow to ask *What?*

"You're gone for him."

"I'm… No." I waved her off and walked behind the counter, my safe spot. I felt an urgent need to make certain the regular restaurant napkins had been swapped out for the birthday ones. Cyndi settled across from me and stared until I insisted, "We're casual. We're doing *casual.*" I emphasized the point with a curt nod.

"Bull," she scoffed. "Make me an ice tea please. Caffeine's in order if I'm to believe you."

Her snark tempted me to tell her to do it herself. It wasn't like we were open to customers. In this case, I welcomed the distraction. Even while talking about Thomas, I kept looking over my shoulder for Bobby, wondering what kind of mood she'd be in, whether the quiet mouse or the worked-up snake would show up. Whether she'd allow the party to be fun.

I made us both iced teas—mine decaf, of course—and passed Cyndi's across the counter. "Who's the giant piece of candy hanging out by the door? I'd love to lick his stick," she said, working her straw like she was the lead in an eighties teen film.

I hissed when she made googly eyes and tapped the solid wood surface to get her attention. "His name is Zach. He's a friend of Jake's, and he's our security guard for the party. So leave him alone, missy. He can't be distracted. Not that he would be. Zach's a professional. He's thinking about going into law enforcement."

Cyndi sat taller and shimmied, sending Zach a wink. "I do love a man in uniform."

"He could be your nephew," I snapped. "Besides, what about Manu?"

She finally turned to me and set her cup down. "I know how to 'do casual,' Kicky dear. Which is why I know you and Professor Dad Jeans are fooling yourselves." She turned and watched Thomas walk over to us. Before he rounded the corner, she leaned in and muttered, "I thought you were dressing him now. What happened?"

I whisper-snapped back, "I only bought a few things. For all we know, he needs to do laundry. You better zip it though. I've already been to a party where the guests had fun at Thomas's expense. Let him be, please. It's Liam's day, not ours."

"You're no fun." She pouted. "Can't flirt with the young ones, and yours went and covered his cute ass with baggy denim. How am I supposed to get my entertainment?"

"Oh, I don't know, the band maybe? They'll play soon."

Thomas scrubbed his hands and stepped up to us while Cyndi continued, "But who can I dance with? You won't let me have any fun." She turned her attention to Thomas. "Will you save a dance for me, Professor? Or does Kick have all your slots?"

I sighed in defeat. How could I deny Cyn a little fun at my expense? She had held my lonely hand for so long. This was new for the both of us. Thomas's mouth lifted at the corner, giving me the impression he knew what we'd been discussing. "I'll check my card, Cynthia."

"Cyn," she said. She loved being able to pick up men and greet them as 'Sin.'

Thomas's smirk grew. "I noticed."

I wanted the subject changed ASAP, so I asked Thomas, "What would you like?"

"I've got it. I came over here to relieve you. Why don't you go greet the guests and make sure Liam's ready. Settle any nerves he has with your magic."

Who was I kidding? I was a goner. My brain fritzed on the sweetness overload, but friends did amazingly sweet stuff for each other. Even friends who might be more than friends, though not sure how much more. I caught myself grinning and sighing when Thomas leaned down and kissed my forehead. It didn't matter if his jeans were a little baggy. I liked how he chose function over fashion. His striped button-down hugged his strong shoulders and made my mouth water if I thought about it too long. Plus I'd picked out the shirt.

Regardless, I couldn't be hot and bothered on my son's eighteenth birthday. I had to be the responsible mom and hostess and keep my cool.

It didn't help that my favorite nightstand toy was currently recharging from a sudden overuse. Frustration masturbation was no fun. Between an important research lead and a goodbye dinner for Tess on Thomas's part, and sick employees on both our parts, we'd spent the week infrequently texting or talking on the phone. I'd taken to sending him "gifts" via the *Pokémon Go* app, if only to annoy him while letting him know I thought about him too. It beat sitting by the phone.

"Go on," he encouraged. "If it gets crazy back here, I'll call you over."

I caught Cyndi grinning like she'd discovered the world's largest stash of Lick-A-Sticks.

"Thanks," I said, poking his solid six-pack and feeling like an awkward idiot. But Cyn had rattled me. I moved around the counter as she tracked me, mouthing "Casual" and lifting her eyebrow.

I shook my head as she belly-laughed. Maybe we were kidding ourselves, but I couldn't afford complete honesty. Not yet. Like I'd told Thomas after our first fight, self-delusion was highly under-rated. There were times it was the only thing keeping me going.

"Mama." Rachel intercepted me as I was about to pass Cyndi, preventing me from swatting her arm. "Gran texted me."

"Oh?"

"Yep. She's not coming. She said she couldn't reach you."

I fished my phone out of my back pocket and swiped it awake. No missed calls, texts, or emails. "What did she do, send up smoke signals?"

Rachel threw me her disappointed-parent glare. "Gran said she doesn't feel well. It *is* November after all." When it came to the dysfunction between Bobby and me, Rachel grew more impatient with me by the year. She didn't know the complete story though. Hell, she didn't even know as much as Thomas knew about what had gone down between us. So I couldn't fault her. Plus Bobby worked overtime to make sure my daughter had all the details on her side of things. It was easier to be the occasional bad guy in their scenario.

Still. I rolled my eyes. "It's November in North Carolina, not the Midwest. The temperature's going to the upper sixties today, but whatever." I knew Bobby wasn't sick. *I* knew *she* knew I knew she wasn't sick. I also knew she used Rachel as a messenger to keep from having to tell me. Well, Bobby's games worked in my favor today. She hated not being the center of attention, so fine, stay home. No way in hell would I call her and beg. For the first time since I'd unlocked the café in the morning, I took a lung-filling inhale and completely relaxed on the exhale. Now this could be the best birthday party I'd ever thrown.

My gaze met Cyndi's and knew she was thinking the same thing.

"Thanks for telling me, Snow. Want to come with me and greet guests?"

Rachel bumped my shoulder. "I've already welcomed most of them, but let's go anyway."

Liam's band played a forty-minute set, then broke for refreshments and adoration from the teen side of the Perked Cup's dining room. I sat at a table with Thomas, Cyndi, Deana and Gordon Douglas (who'd stopped by between grandkid events), Hugh and Maggie Reynolds, and my friend Charley Rodriguez.

After doing a stellar job on the construction of the Perked Cup, my dad and Hugh had hired Charley to remodel their store. Along the way, she'd become my friend and my go-to for any carpentry needs. Her company had recently redone my master bedroom.

Liam tapped the mic to get everyone's silence. He cleared his throat. "Thanks for coming to my party. Y'all are the best."

He turned to the kids at his table. "To the band, thanks for your support and trust in my crazy ideas. We've come together and are finding our flow. We're more than Metaphorical Chemistry. We've got the real thing, and it's big."

My eye roll over their name was an automatic reflex, and I

hoped it went unnoticed. I'd made a case for Second-time Toddlers when the kids were naming the band. For some reason, it didn't fly.

Lee raised his cup in a toast, then addressed the crowd again. "We can't wait to play another set, and if you need a live band in the future…" He held out his hands and grinned while the room laughed. "You know my mom's number."

He continued, "Speaking of Mom… you get to be last." I narrowed my eyes at him with a warning glare.

"Settle down." He chuckled. "You know you get your own shout-out. Things have been tough lately, but I honestly can't remember the last time our life was easy. Thank you for all the shit… oops, I mean stuff"—the room laughed at his gaff, more at him recognizing it than him correcting it—"you do behind the scenes. It may look like we kids think the world revolves around us… since, you know, it does." He flashed his darn dimples. "But we see what you do and how hard it can be. Or at least *I* see it. Rachel and Dylan are probably oblivious."

"Shut it, dimp," boomed a recognizable baritone from the middle of the crowd. They laughed again while I shuttered at my oldest son's new nickname for his little brother.

Liam raised his mug. "Thanks for this party. More importantly, thank you for being our mom and dad wrapped in one squeezable package. We love you."

Not once, when planning this day, did I think he'd do something so special for me. The tears dropped steadily as my baby recognized my often futile efforts to make sure my kids turned out okay, despite the loss of our family's glue.

I dabbed some tears with my sweater cuffs and met Liam in the middle of the dining room. We hugged for a long time or until he lifted me off my feet and made the room laugh again at my protests. He set me down and kissed the top of my head.

When he was born, I immediately bonded with him over the brown curls like mine. Bobby noticed them too, and I think that solidified her dislike for my youngest on sight. Then Liam sleep-smiled while I held him, and his daddy's dimples showed up. I was a goner and knew he'd always be my special little buddy.

What no one ever acknowledged as my body fell apart in his first few years was how my little buddy lightened the dark moments with goofy grins and precious cuddles. Liam had never been the reason for my autoimmune disease, despite Bobby's claims otherwise. Hell, the symptoms raised their heads *years* before my son was born, even though doctors told me they were in my head. No, Liam wasn't the reason I was sick; he was the reason I didn't give up. More than once, I'd convinced myself my family would be better off with a different mother, a better mother.

Back then, I couldn't imagine how this tiny human would eventually kiss the top of my head. Presently, he seemed to love doing it to make a point—like he'd achieved a life goal. He still made me laugh on a daily basis. Knowing he was currently one inch taller than his father had been and would never share the experience of exchanging that first, knowing glance over it, I let Liam gloat as much as he wanted.

"Thank you, my Wee Man," I said when I squeezed him back. "You still have several months before you head down your path, but always remember: 'whistle, I'll be there.' No matter what." I kissed his cheek and watched him walk away.

Liam moved through the crowd, chatting and back-patting his way to the stage. The band played their version of "Somebody That I Used to Know," with Lee and his best friend, Jax, singing leads. It was the first time I heard it in full and I was captivated, standing still in the middle of the crowd. It's a sacred gift to see your child become the person they're supposed to be. I had no clue what Liam wanted to study in school and suspected he didn't know either. It didn't matter. He was showing me who he was right on the stage.

To my surprise, when the members of Metaphorical Chemistry put their instruments down—everyone but Liam— Thomas jumped up on stage with my son. He picked up a guitar that rested in a corner and placed the strap around his neck. Then he and Liam played a duet of Stevie Ray Vaughan songs. They continued for two more songs before calling it an afternoon. Both men—it was hard to think of my baby as a man, but it's what he'd been since 8:33 a.m.—received a standing ovation as they high-fived.

"Jesus, your man is in the wrong profession," Cyndi said, leaning into me while we clapped.

My sentiments exactly. I stood gobsmacked next to my friend, unable to do anything but clap. Thomas played like he'd been a member of Double Trouble himself.

How was it possible? Moreover… "How did I not know about this?" I asked Thomas as he stopped in front of me for a proper postperformance hug.

We sat in our seats, and Thomas took a long pull from his waiting ice tea. Then he turned his middle school smirk on me. "You saw my guitar in the first-floor office."

Did this imply there was a second-floor office? Or was it where the third-floor stairs led to? What else didn't I know?

He leaned into me and kissed my cheek. "You know the important stuff." A buzzing energy radiated from Thomas, and I was a heel for not amplifying it. On the other hand, I'd let everything out of the box—Every. Thing.—stuff my *kids* didn't even know. Thomas, obviously, still held back. My face slid into a scowl despite my attempt to mask it, or it must have given Thomas's reaction.

"Hey, now"—he slid his hands along my back—"we're busy people. It'll flesh out in time."

I couldn't rectify how an ability like that didn't ooze from him. I'd known plenty of people with talent outside their professions, and the discovery of their other expertise always came up right away. We'd also been distracted by so much—too much—since we'd met.

"I suppose. You promise you weren't hiding it from me?"

A sexy chuckle rumbled from Thomas into me as he drew me tight and kissed my head. "If I wanted to hide it, I wouldn't have played in public now, would I?"

His answer, though true, did nothing to reassure me. My instincts yelled he hid something, and it often felt like multiple things.

"Fantastic job with the party, darlin'." He held his gaze on

Liam's group. Seeing him command his table, having the time of his life, lifted my spirits. I had done a fantastic job. One day at a time was what mattered in my world.

However, despite my hatred of ultimatums, it seemed like Thomas and I were heading for one soon. While I enjoyed his interest in my mind and my life, an ache sparked into being in my heart.

7

Girls Just Want to Have Fun

Kick

"Whatcha doing tomorrow night?"

I jumped, almost dropping a gallon of milk. No one ever snuck up on me while I rearranged items in the cooler.

"What the—" My adrenaline still ran high after the Halloween incident, sending an overwhelming urge to strike out until my mind registered who had spoken. "Rachel... what're you doing here in the middle of the morning?"

"My professor canceled class, and I wanted to see you. I'll get a latte and study for a while here too."

Right. Rachel went to a small college, so I could see where getting away to Oakville for a couple of hours could be a fun break from reminders of her recent ex-boyfriend.

I set the jug of milk in its place, then kissed my daughter on the cheek. "It's always lovely to see you. Go ahead, make yourself a cup. You don't need Deana or me, sweetheart."

"Mom." When I didn't respond appropriately, Rachel rolled her eyes. "I asked you what you're doing this weekend?"

"Oh." I'd missed it thanks to my blood pressure spike. "Ah,

making and freezing pies for Thanksgiving. Why? You want to spend the night? How's the rental holding up?" Thomas had arranged a tow to the mechanic for Rachel's Accord and rented her a car. I didn't know what to think of that, to be honest.

"What if you and Aunt Cyn went to the eighties club with Bella and me? I have the week of Thanksgiving off. I can help with the food then."

I crossed my arms. "Why do you want to take two old ladies to the club? Is this a trick? Because Cyndi still knows how to party. She might dance even you under the table, Miss Snow."

Rachel nudged my shoulder. "No. Geesh. After Lee's party, I realized I miss you. Bella and I are planning to blow off the stress of school and the Cody stuff. I thought you might want to do the same. It's been crazy around here though."

"No kidding."

She leaned her head down to mine. "What do you think?"

I tapped my lip. "I'll see what Cyn's up to."

"You can invite Thomas too, if you want."

"He's busy, but thanks. He's my ride to and from my IV appointment on Friday. We'll have breakfast."

She bounced lightly on the balls of her feet, an easy smile spreading. "He's a good guy, Mama. I'm glad you're finally moving on."

"Thanks, sweetie," I said. It felt more like we were stuck, but it also seemed like I'd been challenged to be patient in every area of my life. It wore thin. A night out would do me some good. Since Rachel had turned twenty-one, we'd hung out at the pub to catch a live band, but I'd never considered going to a club with her. Why not? It probably helped her to use me as an excuse to not hook up. My motherly instincts told me she wanted time before taking a new direction.

I smiled up at her. "Sounds fun."

"You two look adorable," Rachel said, fingering the lace hem of my tunic. "Love the hippie dress."

As if I'd ever wear this as a dress. The slightest wind and "hello cellulite."

"When you're forty-seven, it's a tunic, sweetheart."

She giggled at me, but could I blame her? Rachel didn't have a single dimple or jiggle where it shouldn't be. "Your girly combat boots go great with the moto leggings." She stepped to the side to greet Cyndi and compliment her black leather ensemble, complete with platform boots. For my tiny friend, all her shoes came with platforms. The best part of her outfit, though, were the beaded earrings resembling a peacock's tail she'd made. Cyndi fed her creativity with a successful side hustle making jewelry.

We had met Rachel and her roommate, Isabella, out front of Ducky's, an eighties-nineties-themed nightclub in downtown Raleigh.

Cyndi squeezed both girls. "You're so considerate for arranging this." She grasped both girls' hands and pulled them out of the long queue. "We're blowing this line though."

"But—"

She walked us to the bouncer and looked back. "Consider it an early holiday present from Aunt Cyn." She scanned the bouncer like she was picking out a dessert. Her head tipped back, index finger pinching her bottom lip in approval. "My, my, aren't you a prime one?"

"That's why he's a bouncer," I murmured. "What are you doing?"

She shooed me away and popped her caboose. "Cynthia Sendaydiego. I reserved the Spyder."

The bouncer skimmed his tablet. "Yes, you did. Show me those IDs, ladies, then you're all set."

Before it registered, the four of us were lounging in the best spot in the house, like we owned the place. A low-banked booth, it resembled the Ferrari from *Ferris Bueller's Day Off*. It took up prime real estate on an upper level and overlooked the dance floor.

Ducky's interior design was based on John Hughes's films. Whoever came up with the concept possessed an eye for detail. Other half-moon booths filled out our level in a plush material the color of Molly Ringwald's hair. They filled quickly as the same hostess who escorted us dropped off each group.

The bar on our level occupied a long wall. One bartender looked exactly like John Bender from *The Breakfast Club*, including the same ripped plaid shirt and fingerless gloves. His partner looked like Iona from *Pretty in Pink*, with a platinum wig and a fantastic cat eye. I danced in my seat, like a giddy toddler on her birthday.

I turned to Cyndi. "This place is fabulous. I hope there's a Molly Ringwald doppelgänger around here."

"She's the manager," Cyndi answered, reminding me she'd been here plenty of times. Despite having each other's back, our lives had been very different. Sometimes we were more like siblings than friends.

A server, dressed as Ferris himself, arrived. "What can I get y'all?" He flirted shamelessly with the girls. Seeing Rachel slowly come out of herself boosted my mood more. We both knew she'd done the right thing in letting Cody go, but it was good to see her posture return to its default of dancer-perfect again.

"You're getting *crunk* tonight, right? You promised. You deserve it," Cyndi said, pulling my attention from the girls.

There was the hard part. The hard work never took a day off. The bruises still covering my arm and the time away from my business all flashed before me. I couldn't live in fear of setbacks either. I laughed, pointing to my heart. "*Crunk* in here? I promise. With *my* liver? Two drinks max."

"Oh, my liver!" she bellowed, bumping my shoulder.

Had I forgotten how Cyndi made the joke whenever she over-imbibed in college? Wow, it had been too long since we let loose.

I turned to Ferris. "Do you serve Herradura?" No matter the progress, I was keeping to the six-month experiment with naturally gluten-free liquor. Fortunately, there were plenty.

"Yes. Do you want a round of shots?"

"No." I'd made good progress but not shot-drinking progress. "How about a Horseshoe Margarita? Just a splash of agave."

"Can do." Ferris turned to Cyndi.

"Sex on the Beach, honeybuns," she said with a wink.

"Schnapps? Cranberry juice? I thought you were working on a low-glycemic index plan. That's a lot of sugar," I asked by her ear for privacy after the server moved to the girls.

She tapped my arm. "No mothering on Girl's Night Out. You're not supposed to bug me about a cheat day."

I jolted, embarrassed for calling her out. Normal people had cheat days even if I couldn't. I still wasn't completely convinced my indulgence was a good idea. "Sorry, chica."

Cyndi stretched out her arm and pulled me into her. "It's all good. Promise you'll loosen up even if you can't get plastered, okay?"

I gave her a big smile. "Promise."

Rachel ordered the same drink as I did, and Bella chose a local IPA. This was the first time my daughter ordered something other than beer when with me. "Branching out, Snow?" I asked after Ferris moved on.

She shrugged off the question. "I'm staying away from gluten." Since when? I hadn't noticed her plate at Liam's birthday party.

I studied my daughter, hoping the low light would keep her from catching my scrutiny. Rachel seemed a little pale, more like me than her father's golden tone that she usually had. She shivered and rubbed her hands over her arms. She wore a dancer's shrug over a plaid, sleeveless skater dress. I didn't like this. She'd never been easily chilled before, like me.

"Are you cold, Snow?"

"It's fine." She sent me a small, fading smile, which failed to reassure me. "I'll warm up as soon as the drinks come."

Cyndi elbowed me and pointed to one of the half-moon booths across the balcony from us. It was filled with men who looked to be in their twenties. They were put together, like new professionals. "Two of those cuties are eyeing our girls."

Boy, was I out of practice. I didn't know what to do. "Should we leave them alone or something?"

"What's wrong?" Rachel asked after laughing at something Bella had said. With the music pounding, it was hard to hear across our little table.

I tipped my head toward the men. "You've caught someone's eye. Do you want us to go?"

Her laugh came at my expense now. "Why would I want that? It was my idea to bring you here. I thought you'd like the atmosphere."

"I do; it's fantastic. Won't I cramp your style though?"

The laughter grew. "You speak appropriately for this place. No, Mama, I came here to dance and make sure you get lit. For as much as you can." She winked at me. Even though it was a sarcastic comment, it set me at ease. "Strangers never believe you're my mother anyway. I don't think it'll keep anyone from coming by." She paused and waved her fingers at the table. A cute blond fella waved back, and it was my turn to laugh.

Our drinks arrived, and I raised my glass. "To the McKenna women and the sisters of our hearts."

They all returned the toast, and we let ourselves sink into the booth for a bit, absorbing the vibe of the crowd and enjoying the music. We each ordered a refill during our catch-up fest while flirting continued across the balcony.

Hanging out with Rachel and Bella came naturally—a pleasant surprise. I'd never, ever have considered partying with my parents. Here, we were simply grown women of varying experiences, enjoying a luxurious night out. Admittedly, it helped to not be squished into the general population downstairs. I could lose myself in the music on the dance floor, but squishing around tall tables with a young crowd? It would have been uncomfortable, to say the least. Once again, Cyndi had my back.

Eventually the pull of my favorite songs grew too great. Slightly tipsy and ready to let loose, I stood, adjusting my blouse and shaking out my hair.

Cyndi and I made our way down the steps to the dance floor while the girls said something about the bathroom. The centerpiece of the enormous dance floor was a black-and-white mural of the namesake, Ducky from *Pretty in Pink*, hanging behind the DJ's area. It was backlit, so the white areas changed colors. As we descended toward it, the music changed to a Prince tribute and Ducky glowed purple. The light shining from it bounced off a big disco ball, turning everything the singer's signature color.

We entered the fray as "Delirious" finished, transitioning into "I Would Die 4 U." The dance Cyndi and I did included the requisite hand gestures as we pointed at each other for "U" and dissolved into laughter. "Little Red Corvette" finished the set without Rachel or Bella joining us. I wondered out loud what kept them when Cyndi pointed up toward our level. The young men from the half-moon had left their group and sat with our girls.

"Looks like tonight was good for both of us."

Cyndi nodded, rubbing my arm.

"Is it weird I'm glad for her?"

"Why would it be weird?"

I didn't personally know any mothers who wanted to meddle in their children's love lives, but I knew there were plenty who did. Not wanting to go into it, I pulled Cyndi back to the music and kept dancing.

When the tribute finished, we poured waters from the stand near the dance floor. I downed my little cup and finally said, "I've always felt like I had to hide my male interests from Bobby." I chuckled. "Even after I was married."

Cyndi shook her head. "Bobby's never been a normal mother, Kicky. Sometimes I forget how much you've had to figure out on your own." She took our cups and threw them in the trash. "Miss Thing has a brilliant head on her shoulders, thanks to you. The girls will come down when they're ready. Let's shake what our maker gave us."

The floor pulsed to La Bouche's "Be My Lover" as a black light shone from Ducky again. It made my skin glow purple, courtesy of my ghostlike quality. The beat fit the vibe of the crowd, who spent most of their time jumping up and down.

Cyndi and I managed more than that and worked up a sweat. The girls joined us then, bringing the entire group of guys with them. After swaying and rocking to the songs and briefly showing the youngsters variations on the Running Man, the music slowed to give us a break.

I recognized the live version of the song from the audience's cheers alone. The sultry opening bars to one of my all-time favorites made my heart leap as my skin embraced the cooling sensation of mellowing out. I closed my eyes and shifted my shoulders as the lone guitar was joined by other instruments. My hips hit the two beats of the drum and the story of the "Hotel California" began for me. As I moved with the crowd, I let the song consume me as it had so many times over the years. It simultaneously haunted and healed my soul.

I spun to Cyndi, who wore a conspiratorial smirk. My gaze tracked the group, counting, wondering why it felt bigger. Or was I so in my head I didn't notice the crowd move?

"Need a partner, darlin'?" A leg melded behind mine when I stepped forward, my body recognizing the owner and automatically following when his hips shifted back. A huge smile spread across my face as I glanced over my shoulder. "You didn't jump." Thomas's Southern baritone warmed my ear.

"Nope. What do you think it means?"

"Maybe you sensed me watching."

"You were?"

He leaned over my shoulder and purred, "Sexiest sight in the room."

Holy hell, he smelled good. The crisp notes of a peaty Highland scotch on his breath touched my nose as his lips grazed my cheek. A hint of his sandalwood and citrus stayed with me when he pulled away.

It had only been a day, but I'd missed him. As expected, I'd passed out on the way home from the doctor's office. Thomas had settled me in my room for a nap and left. His presence currently made my knees weak. And my sex stir. My head fell back in a giddy laugh as he took hold of my fingers and spun me, then held me tight before I recognized the direction change. He lowered his head and raised his eyebrow, seeking permission the way he'd done when we danced at my birthday dinner. Cool, navy eyes bore into mine as passing light from the disco ball flashed a speck of silver, revealing the mischief there.

Still trust me?

A thrill slowly traveled up my spine. A corner of my mouth lifted as I winked. *Bring it, handsome.*

He began a slow-paced Salsa, matching the sexy tempo of the song. The achingly easy pace of the dance differed from any I'd ever performed when competing. The steps committed to my muscle memory, Thomas only needed to shift a hip for me to know what came next. As he changed our hold, he had me duck and sway with him in an arm loop. It felt as if we'd been dancing together for years and like we could do this forever.

Thomas pulled me in, and his dark button-down shirt brushed where my billowy sleeve had bared my arm. The silkiness caressed my skin, sending a shiver that had nothing to do with the room's temperature. Butter-soft jeans barely shielded strong thighs, brushing against and between my legs as we moved. The surrounding space opened as our group stopped to watch, then a larger crowd paused to give us more room. Thomas refrained from adding in flashier moves, yet something about us drew attention. For me though, the crowd disappeared. His shoulder shifted, and I was seduced by another cross-body lead.

"Thomas," I pleaded, but for what, I wasn't sure. To be alone? To melt back into the crowd?

"Shh. Don't think. Feel." He rasped quick breaths across my cheek. He pulled me back in, perhaps taken by the moment as much as me.

It all became a drug unto itself while the keening guitar vibrated through my bones. Here was the part of the song which always threatened tears and a longing for what my life could've been, as it reminded me of the trap of chronic illness. How there was no hope for a cure, no breaking free. This, though, felt like a celebration, a desire fulfilled or one promising more.

I didn't want the intoxication to end, and the chase of notes to the finish brought a slight panic. I wanted to dance forever. When the song concluded, we fell into each other's arms in shock, but the sound of clapping broke us from our trance.

I threw my arms around his neck and jumped as Thomas

finished the work, bending his back and planting a hard kiss to my lips. A piercing whistle burst our bubble.

"I only told you Rachel and I were hanging out. How did you know we were here?"

"By accident, really. Rachel mentioned it to Banger's assistant when they called her with some follow-up on the cyber harassment."

I cringed at the mention, not wanting reality to taint my beautiful reprieve.

"Sorry, baby. I didn't mean to dampen your fire."

Thomas pulled me off the dance floor, resting his back against a column, pulling me against his body. "Y'alright?"

I gave him my best smile. "I'm fantastic. You didn't dampen anything." I went on my tiptoe and teased him. "Well, nothing you don't want dampened."

Thomas growled and kissed my jaw. With the bubble gone, we were both painfully aware of the crowd. "Can we get out of here?"

My voice caught in my throat, boiling with need. "I'd love nothing more. But—"

Thomas tucked some hair behind my ear, stroking the tip. "The elf queen can't leave her people, can she?"

I cleared my throat. "It was Rachel's idea to come here. To cheer up both of us." It would've been different if Thomas and I had made a commitment, but abandoning the group, my family? I was never the girl to ditch her friends for a quick lay, even one that could be more.

My hesitance proved how much was still unsaid between Thomas and me. We had feelings so hot they scorched, but the constant cancellations on both our parts, the dropping of everything for someone else, it showed where we really stood.

"How about a drink instead?"

"I've had my tequila quota for the night, but I'll take a club soda and lime."

"Look at you"—he grinned—"behaving while being bad at the same time."

In a snap, our heat lowered back to friends-who-might-be-more.

I bit my lip and shrugged. The boundaries were helpful when they were reasonable. They helped me have energy for a night like this. I hoped there'd be more. Many more nights out with great friends, a grown child, and a deliciously sexy man. This glimpse into how the next phase of life could work turned out to be a gift I'd never expected.

"Meet you at the bar? The ladies' room is calling." A minute away would also help to clear my head.

8

Modern Love

Thomas

A BARTENDER WITH FAKE PLATINUM HAIR MADE TIME TO DANCE around her space but couldn't manage to get it in gear enough to shoot up a Jack and Coke and a club soda. *Maybe her wig is on too tight?* Thomas turned his back to the bar. It kept him from glaring at the woman.

He didn't see the appeal of the garish club. It celebrated a time when people had terrible taste. It made Kick smile though, so he liked it. He never paid attention to the movies the place supposedly enshrined. Thomas could tell how much she adored them by the way her face lit over each additional detail she discovered. For that, too, he gave kudos to the management. Not so much for an efficient staff.

A too-young woman slinked down the length of the bar toward him. Normally, this would've been the beginning of a game to distract him. Lure her in, play the pursued, set the terms for the night. Women who approached first rarely looked for long-term relationships.

"Hey handsome, what're you doing alone?" In a skimpy top

revealing nothing, tight ripped jeans, and hooker shoes. The visual enhanced her "playing grown-up" vibe.

She insisted on touching his arm, making his skin crawl. When Kick had stroked his shirt, it made Thomas's skin hum. "I'm not."

Where the hell was the damn bartender?

"Get a girl a drink and I'll listen to anything you want to say."

She stepped into Thomas's space, stroking his chest. He caught her wrist as he shifted back and hit the bar's edge. A wild-haired brunette caught the corner of his eye. *His* wild-haired brunette.

"My name's Lili." The girl ran her tongue over her teeth.

She should never do that again. Christ, he'd bet she was no older than Rachel. The problem with being the pursued? The pursuer discouraged no as an answer. "Help a guy out here?" Thomas called over his shoulder.

Kick stepped closer, a smirk on her face. "You looked like you had everything under control."

"We were talking," Lee-whoever snarled at Kick.

"The conversation's over, sweetheart," Kick answered with the familiar disciplinary tone and stony stare he remembered from the first time he'd laid eyes on her. Like then, it stoked his fire.

"Tried to tell you… was waiting for my lady," Thomas added.

"Her?" The girl's face contorted. "She's *ancient.*"

Kick slid her arm across the back of Thomas's shoulders, and he finally took a deep breath. He liked bars with history. And regulars. He couldn't relax here at all.

"The word you're looking for is *grown,*" Kick said with a devilish glint in her eye. She waved her fingers. "Shoo now, little one."

Thomas happily shrugged.

"Fuck off." The co-ed wobbled away on her too-high heels, scanning the room for another sucker.

"Guess we're even now?" Kick asked.

"How do you figure?"

"You bailed me out. Now I've rescued your pretty face." She kissed his cheek for emphasis.

"I had to ask for your help."

Kick's brow raised as a corner of her mouth ticked up.

"Touché." Thomas surrendered. He pulled her in close and kissed her quick. "Made your point."

Kick scanned the bar top. "Where are the drinks?"

"We've been abandoned." Thomas raised his hand once more, snapping his fingers to get Platinum's attention.

"Hey Iona!" Kick bellowed. Platinum's gaze shot their way, an apologetic pout on her face.

"I'm sorry, guys."

"No worries. Can you have Ferris send our drinks over to the car?"

The bartender nodded. "Can do. Sorry again."

"Isn't this place great?" Kick asked as she swayed toward a booth resembling a Ferrari Spyder. "She looks just like Annie Potts from the movie. They've thought of all the things."

"What movie?" Thomas stared at the booth while Kick slid in first.

"*Pretty in Pink*, Professor. Didn't you pick up on the club's theme?"

"I heard about it. Don't know any of those films by name though."

Kick clicked her tongue. "What rock have you been sleeping under? Do you even know why we're sitting in this car? It's one of the signature features here."

After Thomas settled next to her, shaking his head, Kick explained *Ferris Bueller* to him, along with some vital aspects of eighties pop culture he'd missed.

"I'm sorry we couldn't duck out earlier," Kick said, absently teasing the drink straw with her tongue.

Thomas swallowed hard. He still craved getting her alone. The heat they'd created on the dance floor hovered on the edges of his control, waiting for permission to blaze. He took her hand into his lap, rubbing Kick's palm with his thumb, tracing her lifeline.

"Do you ever do something just for yourself?"

She chuckled. "Do you?"

"You're my *just for me*," he answered, feeling the grin spread, hoping every muscle contraction would tell her the truth he had sworn to hold in.

"And you're sweet." Kick turned in to him, draping her free arm across the back of the booth. Her thumb mimicked Thomas's as it stroked his neck. "Rachel picked this place for me, knowing how much I love eighties music. Then Cyndi pulled her magical strings and reserved the VIP spot. She mentioned another group has the second time slot or something."

"So, y'all don't plan on closing the place down?"

"Are you kidding?" Kick let a sexy chuckle roll through her body into Thomas's. "I don't know about you, Professor, but it already feels like two a.m."

He finished his drink with his free hand. "Would you want to come back to my house after?"

Kick's eyes lit up as a smile spread across her face. "Liam is spending the night at a friend's house." She scooted closer, enough for Thomas to peek at her purple satin bra and how well it embraced her perfect breasts. He bit his lip. Could they finally get their much-needed alone time?

She kissed his jaw and purred, "Your wish can be granted."

Thomas picked up the tumbler to distract his shifting in the seat. Whether she gave him an eye twinkle or growling frown, each minute with Kick was doing the impossible. She cracked the safe he'd locked his heart away in, one slow tumbler tick at a time.

"Thank you, Genie."

"No problem, sweets. Let me text Lee." She let out a deep sigh, chuckling. "The kid thinks he's my guardian now."

Thomas couldn't say he blamed the boy.

"There you two are," Cyndi called out, moving toward the Ferrari.

A fit, middle-aged man hung out on the edge of Thomas's vision. He stole quick glances over there to see if he recognized the guy and make sure he meant no harm.

"Where else would we be?" Kick chuckled. Cyndi leaned in and whispered something, causing a loud gasp from Kick. "That's how you roll, not me."

"Only saying…" Cyndi tucked a few strands of hair behind her ear. "I would bless it."

Kick bumped her friend's shoulder, and they fell into each other, laughing. It didn't take a rocket scientist—or a geneticist—to figure out that Cyndi had half expected to find them banging in a dark corner. As much as he would've accepted the offer, he was proud of Kick for rejecting the idea. He didn't want any part of their relationship to be cheap.

Cyndi swayed too much in her seat, as if the room spun for her.

Rachel and her roommate dumped themselves into the other side of the booth. The server Kick called Ferris brought out a platter of wings she had ordered for the group, guessing everyone would return soon. As the kids dug in, Kick pulled something out of her purse, then unwrapped it.

"What do you have there?"

She bit off a piece of what looked like a Slim Jim. "A Paleo meat stick. I keep them around for emergencies, like needing extra protein to soak up any remaining alcohol." She managed a sassy smile while chewing.

Thomas couldn't resist the pull of the words. "A meat stick?" He waggled his eyebrows. "Save room for my meat stick when I get you home."

Kick blushed and ducked her head. "Another reason for some extra energy." She tapped his thigh. "Nice middle school joke, by the way."

"Always." Thomas winked and took a sip from his glass. The guy he'd kept his eye on stepped out of the shadows.

The man bent over the booth to speak to Cyndi. "Hi, I'm Randy. I loved watching you dance."

"Ooh, I bet you *are randy*." She batted her lashes, extending her hand for a flirty shake. "Muscled as well. I'm Cyn."

Thomas chuckled as Kick turned toward him, rolling her eyes, mouthing, *She loves being able to say that.*

Randy grinned like he'd hit the Powerball jackpot. "No way. You look too much like an angel. Can I buy you a drink?"

"Mind if I disappear for a little while?" she asked after scooching out of the booth.

"If you must." Kick feigned annoyance, but she squeezed Thomas's hand under the table. Not for the first time, Cyndi reminded Thomas of Banger, who was conspicuously absent at the moment. It also didn't take a PhD to figure out where he'd wandered off to. All those young ones downstairs? Hell, maybe the high-heeled princess had preyed on the man. Thomas laughed to himself at the thought.

"She'll eat him up," Kick muttered in Thomas's ear. His brows shot up until he clued in that Kick was speaking of her friend and not his.

"I bet." He took some wings for himself.

"Aren't you having any, Mama?" Rachel took advantage of the empty space and slid next to Kick, who shook her head.

"The sauce isn't safe. No worries for you though. They're grilled, not fried." Kick glanced over her shoulder. "I thought the fellas you found might like some."

"They went back to their booth." Rachel dropped a bone and wiped her fingers.

"We could take what we don't finish over there," Kick offered.

"Relax, please. You don't have to be a mama all the time."

"Wait until you're one."

Rachel shivered briskly and wiped her forehead. "The guys went their own way when Bella made it clear we didn't want to do anything more than dance." She placed her head on Kick's shoulder. "We came here for a girl's night." She leaned around her mother and addressed Thomas. "No offense. It's cute you hunted her down, actually."

"It wasn't hard," he said. "You told us where y'all were."

"I did, didn't I? Yay me." She beamed and Thomas melted yet again, his memories flashing to another similar young smile. Why did they all seem to fit each other seamlessly? He reminded himself this wasn't like back then. Times had changed and so had he.

"…tell me you were in love?" Thomas overheard Rachel whispering to her mother.

"What?" The alarm in Kick's voice set Thomas into action. He wanted no part of their tête-à-tête.

"Excuse me, ladies." He leaned into Kick, who was studying the dance floor and seemed as eager to get away from Rachel's misinterpretation. "My turn for the men's."

She nodded at Thomas, then grabbed his hand to keep him in place. "Snow, ready to hit the floor again?"

"Sure. This place is so fun. I haven't danced like this in ages."

Kick did a double take. "The school bills I pay claim otherwise, you know." She tipped her chin up to Thomas. "Meet us downstairs when you're done?"

He leaned down and kissed her cheek. "It's a date."

While he walked away, Rachel told her mother, "This dancing is for me."

In the men's room, Thomas bumped into Banger. "Find yourself a *bic*?" Not long ago, he'd found his friend's code word for a hookup—a disposable woman—appropriately funny. Most of the women had the same attitude toward them anyway.

Banger adjusted his shirt and rerolled his sleeves while checking himself in the mirror. "You know it." He sighed. "It's all about the carburetor, brother." Thomas waited at the door, knowing Banger itched to say more as he washed his hands. The man could never resist. "Surprised you let your woman out of your sight after practically nailing her on the dance floor."

"Don't," Thomas muttered.

He raised his hands. "Civilized fucking is still fucking. That's all I'm saying. Speaking of, when are you taking your little show to its natural ending?"

Thomas opened the door. "Later. At my place. Civilized, you know? Besides, you're the one who suggested we come here."

Big hands clamped down on Thomas's shoulders. "If my stud buddy's given up bics, I should facilitate his own carburetor maintenance when I can."

Thomas looked at the ceiling, chuckling. "There's no hope for you, but thanks, man. Where're you headed?"

"To the bar to wet my other whistle." Banger smacked his lips. "Seems my throat's dry. You?"

"Meeting the ladies back on the dance floor. Listen, they reserved the Spyder booth upstairs. No one will mind if you relax there a spell. We left some wings on a platter if the staff hasn't bused them."

"Naw, I'm good. I'll get a drink and find you. Then again, you'll probably have another audience soon."

"Don't worry. No more big scenes tonight."

9

New Sensation

Kick

THE GIRLS AND I BUMPED INTO CYNDI ON THE STAIRS.

"Are you going to dance?" she asked.

My voice never carried in loud places, so I answered with a nod and a smile.

"Good. I'll come."

As we reached the bottom, the music changed to something slow. "Well, hell." Cyndi grabbed my bicep and gestured toward the bar. "Let's get a drink."

I told Rachel and Bella we'd catch up and pivoted with my friend. "Where did your dance partner go?" I asked Cyndi.

She scrunched her face like she'd tasted something rotten. "He kissed like a plecostomus. I cut him loose."

I shuffled to keep up with her swift little feet. Cyndi must have been very thirsty. "You kissed him already?"

She slipped her arm through mine as we reached the bar line. "My sweet, amateur Kicky... I test drove the important stuff first. I'm too old to waste time getting to know someone first."

Okay then.

We were next in line, so Cyndi asked, "What do you want?"

"A club soda and lime."

"Perfect. I should dilute my blood alcohol level too. Pace myself, you know?"

"Exactly." We both stepped up to the bartender, but Cyndi ordered for both of us. I moved over to make room for those behind us and watched the floor. Rachel and Bella were easy to spot, dancing with a mixed crowd of people their age. A couple of kids looked familiar.

"Here you go." Cyndi handed me a tumbler with the lime wedge already floating.

"Thank you, chica." I took a big drink and had to keep myself from doing a spit take. I made the same face Cyndi had done a few minutes earlier. "This is tonic, not soda. I can't have it." Cyn took it when I pivoted to take it back to the bar. "Give to me. I'm parched," she said.

"Fine by me." It didn't solve my dry mouth though. "I'll go get some water from the station."

"I'll be right here."

It took several minutes to make my way through another line, but I filled two of the tiny cups and slammed them down. As I squeezed through the milling bodies to find the trash can, the smell of all the cologne ever made threatened to knock me off my feet. Unfortunately, it masked nothing. I caught a glimpse of the gray receptacle when the paper cups went flying out of my hand. A big monster had grabbed me from behind, smelling like ten packs of cigarettes. I felt his sweat soak into the back of my tunic.

My fight-or-flight response hadn't abated since the attack, and it jumped into action immediately with the added thought of *Where the hell is Thomas?*

"Here he is! Here he is!" Cyndi waved wildly with one arm at Thomas while the other stayed around my shoulders. A small crowd had gathered, thanks to the show my bestie made when she found me fighting off Mr. Big and Hairy.

Thomas rushed to us. "What's wrong?"

"Kicky beat up a guy."

"What?" His gaze rapidly swung around the group.

"Cyn…" I gave her a warning look and turned to Thomas. "Some big guy grabbed me from behind. The asshole said he'd watched us dancing and wanted his turn. Before I could tell him to buzz off, he tried to take me toward the door. I think he meant for us to leave here."

"Dammit." Thomas jammed his hand through his hair, then pulled me in.

"I'm fine." At least I was now. I couldn't stop the post event shaking, but it made all the difference being in his arms.

"Fine? You were awesome," Cyndi added, smacking her lips. "I came up at the end, thinking our girl needed an assist, but she put those platform boots to good use. On the Sasquatch's foot and balls."

Thomas growled, now looking farther out. "Sasquatch?"

Cyndi shrugged. "He was huge and furry. Not in a fun way, either."

"And smelly." I added.

"I see." He lifted my chin with his thumbs. "Where is this guy now?"

Cyndi tapped his pecs. "Sorry, Professor, the Sasquatch got away. He took off when I shouted and security came over."

He sighed and growled again. "Y'all want to leave?"

My flattened palm traveled up Thomas's chest, stopping at each plane change until it reached his neck. I needed to feel him to stay calm. Plus something else was happening to me. My body felt like it was waking up, like each cell wanted to touch and experience as much as it could. "No. We came here to dance and relieve stress. Let's do it."

Cyndi took a step and stumbled forward. Both Thomas and I grabbed an arm.

"Alright there?" he asked.

Cyndi giggled. "I'm just still *intoxth-icated*. I need more water. Or dancing."

Our group moved back to the edge of the dance floor. Back in the shelter of my people, my body relaxed and became inspired. Cyndi and I showed the kids more dance moves from high school and college. I could swear the crowd cheered us on until I stumbled into Thomas. He deftly righted me, but I couldn't stay on my feet.

"The room's spinning," I complained, my nose scrunching in confusion.

With his arms holding me up, protecting me from the crowd, Thomas guided us to the downstairs lounge area.

"I'm okay. Swear." I protested his movements, thinking they were a show of power or disappointment in my behavior. But the room wouldn't stop swirling, and I couldn't figure out where I'd screwed up. Clearly I'd become a complete lightweight this fall, thanks to the detoxing.

Thomas turned to me with concern on his face when I'd been expecting judgment. "Tell me exactly what happened while I went to the restroom."

I smiled, happy he wasn't mad at me. At the moment, I would've told him anything. I filled him in on meeting Cyndi on the steps and the tonic water mix-up.

"What's wrong with tonic? Don't you like it?"

"Uh-uh." I leaned into the railing surrounding the dance floor. "I can't have the high fructose corn syrup."

"Ah. I see."

I continued, "So I went to the water station and downed two of those smallish cups." My hand swept through my hair. It didn't occur to me how crazy it might make my curls look. I didn't like my hair sticking to my head and had to make it stop. "The guy came up behind me—like you do sometimes—only, I hated it immediately. He was slimy and smelly and all over me. He didn't want to dance."

"Doesn't sound like it," Thomas said in a rough, angry tone.

"My boots came in handy." I smiled, then frowned when the man's face flashed through my memory.

"Kick?"

I stared at the floor, suddenly fascinated by the mix of black and purple swirling into a pattern—anything to take away the image of his face. I wanted to force it away, rub it out of my synapses.

"I probably need more protein. Some carbs too."

Thomas gave me a gentle shake. "Let's go since there's nothing you can eat here."

"What's going on kids?" Banger asked, appearing out of nowhere.

"Hey, hiya, security guru." I didn't know why I said something so dumb. Thomas had mentioned arriving with his friend, but this was the first I'd seen him.

"We need to leave," Thomas answered.

My head tipped up fast, and I took a step to compensate. "But the girls—"

"Should go home too." Thomas said soothingly. He bent his knees to meet my eyes. "Please. I have to get Banger going on this guy."

"What guy?" Banger asked.

"Someone tried to take Kick against her will. Obviously."

"The hell? Why didn't you come get me?"

"Sorry man. Was making sure she and Cyndi were good. At first I thought the guy had made a free grab. It doesn't sound like it now."

Thomas repeated what I'd told him to Banger, making me cringe with embarrassment. The girls arrived before we could retrieve everyone.

"Mama, we need you to do more of your kick-ass old-school moves," Rachel half begged, half whined.

Thomas raised an eyebrow to let me speak. I didn't want to think about how good it felt to not have him step in. Cyndi had Bella's hands and did a sloppy jive in the background, ignoring our conversation.

"You two are so funny!" I called out while fanning the hem of my tunic, suddenly scorching hot. Not the best place for my first hot flash, but what did I know? I turned back to Rachel. "What did you say, sweet girl?" I brushed some wisps of hair behind her ear. "Such a good girl."

"Well fuck. Yeah, we're out of here," Banger said for me.

Rachel's face fell, but she didn't look surprised, only resigned. "Are you still driving us home?" she asked me.

"Of course—"

"No." Thomas interrupted.

"I'll take the girls," Banger said.

By now, Isabella and Cyndi had joined us properly.

"Another thirty minutes of dancing and I'll be sober enough to drive Mama," Rachel insisted.

"No. Let's go, princess." Banger said, his arm extended toward the coat check. Bella frowned at both of them.

Thank you, I mouthed to him.

He passed me a tiny grin and said to Thomas, "I'll speak to the manager on our way out."

"Because of the guy? Isn't it common in places like this?" I protested.

"Let me check," Banger insisted, and I snapped my jaw shut. He walked away with his hands around the necks of Rachel and Bella. I frowned but just as quickly couldn't remember why.

I turned to Cyndi for help, but she was studying the light from the disco ball, her hands up as if she were trying to catch the rays coming off of it.

We followed behind Banger and the girls to the front of the club. Rachel and Isabella retrieved their coats while Thomas and Banger spoke with people at the desk. One of them was the security guy who let us in.

I tapped Cyndi on the shoulder. "You okay, chica?"

She'd been swaying next to me with her eyes closed. While still moving to the music, she said, "I'm f-faba… aw-thum, mamacita. I swear I can *feel* the music inside me." She shimmied in a circle and fell into my side.

Thomas returned. "Did you get your coats?"

I looked at Cyndi. Did we have coats? I couldn't remember. Rachel and Bella had disappeared from the coatroom window.

"Can y'all stay here while I check?" he asked.

"I have to pay the bill," Cyndi and I said at the same time.

"I invited you," I told her.

Before Cyndi could make her case, Thomas butted in. "It's taken care of."

"What? The tab?"

"The whole bill."

"Again?"

I was about to pout when Cyndi elbowed me in the side. I came this close to falling over. My amazing platform boots saved me again. "Thank him properly," she ordered.

Thomas dipped his head. "It's my pleasure. The four of y'all were... a fun diversion."

"Yeah right."

"He likes you...," Cyndi stage whispered, getting some spit on my cheek. I wiped it off with the neck of my top.

Thomas dropped his head between us. "Promise me y'all will wait here while I get your things."

I held up three fingers but couldn't remember where the gesture came from and shrugged. "Someone's honor."

Thomas laughed lightly. "Be right back."

Another wave of heat swept through me, making it hard to breathe. I slid my arm through Cyndi's. "I think I'm getting hot flashes of all things. Let's get some air."

The current bouncer bid us farewell as he held the door for us, the cold air relieving my unbearable heat.

"We're waiting for your fel-le-la," Cyndi sang for no reason other than a lack of sobriety.

Jaysus, she needed to stop swaying. Or was it me? I said to no one, "I need my re-remedy." My tongue started failing me.

"How're you ladies doing?" Two of Raleigh's finest approached. They looked way too young to be cops. "You don't plan on driving tonight, do you?"

"Well..." I looked at Cyndi and back at them. "I s'pose we can walk, oci-ociffer," I answered while swaying. "Is that the right word?" I asked Cyndi's nose, after missing my aim for her ear.

He grabbed my arm. "Easy there. Do you need help? Why don't you come with us?"

I yanked my arm out of the policeman's grip, anger arriving from nowhere and at the wrong time. "Listen here, lad. You look no older than my son. So, scram!" I flapped my hands in his direction and almost fell over. "Fly away and leave us old ladies alone."

"No." He took my arm again. "Let's not cause a disturbance."

"If there's a disturbance, you made it. Who says we *need* taken care of? Because we're women and you… you're… men? Is that why?" My tone rose with each word. I draped my arm over Cyndi's shoulder and bellowed, "We don't need no damn men!"

"Yeah." My feisty friend jumped in. "S'right. We don't need any goddamn men! Even ones with badges and… and… guns and… shit." She paused, pivoted to me, and whisper-yelled, "They have guns, Kicky."

The two cops stood back with folded arms like they were watching a street performance, which they more or less were. In the back of my mind, a tiny person tapped on my shoulder and tried to tell me something wasn't right. I'd sensed it for a while, but a disconnect kept the voice mute.

I flung my free hand, almost making us fall again. "Stay strong, s-sister." I shooed at the officers again. "We pay our bills, we get ourselves off, we don't *want* to pick up your shit around the house *and*… We. Can. Get. Ourselves. Home."

"Now there's a visual." An amused Southern drawl filled my ears, and I remembered why we were freezing our asses off in the first place. "There a problem, officers?"

"Are you with these two… ladies?"

"I am." He bent to us. "Sorry, it took a while. My phone went missing, but I found it in the Ferrari."

"Have you been drinking?"

Thomas put his hand to his heart. "I promise, I'm sober as a saint."

My eyes popped wide at him. "You are? How wonderful."

Thomas's warm smile buckled my knees. He wrapped an arm around my waist and kept me steady.

"We could stay at the Sher-Shery— the hotel," I told the air.

Thomas slid my jacket around my shoulders as he answered, "No. You're staying at my place after we drop off Cyndi."

I popped up on my toes. "How wonderful. You were so fun last time."

Thomas's warm chuckle melted the parts of me that were frosting, literally.

"Good fun," Cyndi agreed, as if she'd been there. "You two deserve your time. I won't even bother you about the threesome."

Thomas froze, his brows raised almost to his hairline.

I leaned toward the young officers and sweetly said, "Thank you, *ociffers*. We're fine now."

The front one raised his hand to his hat and said, "Have a good night, Mrs. Mack."

I flinched, nearly falling over. "I knew he looked familiar."

"Friend of Dylan's?" Cyndi asked.

"In his grade," I whined.

"Sucks to get old," she moaned.

Thomas put his arm around us both to steer. He checked me over and frowned. "Don't understand why you're acting so sauced."

I stood up straight. "I'm not pithed."

"You're slurring your words."

"Ith's not slurring. Ith's schpeaking in curthive. Ith's an ancient art." I leaned around him and fist-bumped Cyndi.

"We can prove it. Say the magic drunk word," she said.

"Oh yeah." For some reason, the code word we'd used to check on each other in college easily popped into my memory. "Sup… super… oh shlit." I giggled.

"What's this magic drunk word?" Thomas asked with a smile in his tone.

Cyndi answered, "Sup-floos. Shit. I can't do it either."

"Super… are y'all trying to say *superfluous*?"

"Yay! You can drive us home." I clapped in relief. Until then, I had no proper way of knowing if Thomas truly was sober. Plus I could feel my body fading as fast as my mind.

Thomas stepped forward, a tighter grip on our shoulders.

"Right. Any chance either of y'all can tell me where the car's parked?"

I pointed to the deck catty-corner from us. "Fourth floor." My eyes raised to his. "Hey, I remembered."

"I'm so proud," he mused.

"You spoke sarcasm. That's so cute." I tucked my head into his shoulder. "I knew there was a reason I liked you."

10

Where Dirt and Water Collide

Thomas

THE WOMEN CONFIRMED THEIR LACK OF SOBRIETY WHEN HALFWAY across the street. They began singing the Irish drinking song "Whiskey in the Jar"—with clapping included, but not necessarily at the correct times. With an amused headshake and wondering what he'd gotten himself into, Thomas coaxed them forward.

Kick urged, "Sing, Thomas. I'll teach you the words."

"Everyone knows the words, darlin'."

"Come on then."

"No." At least she sounded nice. He couldn't carry a tune if it meant his life. Still, by the time they stepped off the elevator, Thomas's ears rang. He steered them through the garage, wasting five minutes before Cyndi remembered they were parked to the right of the elevator and not the left side. He opened the driver's side door, pulled the seat forward, and helped Kick's friend out of her platform boots. As soon as Cyndi hit the leather seat, she curled into a circle, reminding him of Kick's dog.

He let the seat fall back, stood and found himself alone. Kick had disappeared. He ducked back into the car to turn on the engine and heat, then went to find her.

Kick sat on the garage floor against a column with her head on her knees. Thomas crouched down to better check on her and rubbed her calf. "You okay in there?"

She groaned, and her breath hitched.

He shifted his body to search her eyes. "Is there something you need?" He hadn't looked for water in the car, but they'd passed a vending machine on the first floor.

"Huh?"

"Do you need anything?"

Lifting her head, Kick's mouth pressed into a line as she stared off. In a faraway sound, she said, "What do I *need?* I need to let myself jump off the cliff and dive deep in love." Her finger made a circle over her heart. "I need a hole right here because desire burns so hot it leaves scorch marks, but s'okay since love fills in."

She stroked the butterfly charm around her neck. "I need to stop being transformed by disasters and have love transform me instead. I need to be forever chased even though I'm fiercely faithful. I need chemistry, so alive it's sentient."

She crossed her arms and rubbed her biceps. "I need to drift off to sleep and awake to skin on skin, with no need for an extra blanket. I need no doubts I'm the most important person on the planet." She lifted her head and met his gaze, point-blank. "I need extraordinary, and I won't settle." Then she exhaled a shaking breath and laid her head back on her knees.

Thomas fell on his ass as if pushed. *I'll be damned.* He ran a hand through his hair and took a couple of deep breaths to slow his racing heart.

Shit. Fuck. Hell. "She's right."

She deserved all of it. *Christ*, she'd earned it. Could he be this person though? She'd laid out the stakes in detail. All his other shit was simply that. A slow exhale whistled painfully from his chest.

When Thomas lifted his head, Kick hadn't moved. He shifted to his knees and jostled her lightly. She either slept or had passed out.

A couple of harder squeezes and she jolted, lifting her head to see who'd done it.

"Everything's spinning," she complained.

He moved some curls out of her face. "Can you make it to the car? It's getting cold. Or do you feel sick?"

She smiled and brushed an errant piece of hair out of Thomas's eye, mimicking him. "It's getting long." She let her fingers run through it. "Like silk." Thomas sighed, wanting nothing more than to let her continue the simple caress. Still in a distant voice, she declared, "Ever since the curls tightened, you can't do this with my hair. It's the only thing I miss about not straightening it."

Throat dry and mind clouded, he croaked, "Why can't you?"

With a quiet chuckle, she said, "I told you. I end up with a head of fuzz, silly."

Entranced, he couldn't stop himself from demanding, "T-tell me again—how to do it."

A sleepy smile stretched across her face. Her eyes remained closed, making her face angelic. Her hand lifted to the back of his neck to demonstrate. "You come from underneath. It's okay to grab and scrunch or gently tug, but don't pull through. As soon as there's resistance, stop. Or it's Janice Joplin time."

Thomas dropped his forehead to right above hers. Irresistible. He craved to see what happened next, like he needed his next breath.

He reached toward her nape and slid his hand to cup the base of her skull.

"Mmm." She purred and nuzzled his hand, kitten-like.

He moved his fingers slowly back until reaching the resistance she mentioned. His hand returned to her neck, fingers curling, turning it into a light massage.

"Yeah. Perfect." The ethereal tone remained and her eyes never opened. His angel if he allowed it. "I miss this."

A bitter breeze ruffled her curls, snapping Thomas out of his trance. He reluctantly stood and pulled Kick up with him.

Thomas moved her closer to the light fixture and lifted her chin, checking her pupils. The improved illumination from their new height confirmed his suspicions. If he hadn't thought so before, Kick's "true confessions" session settled it. Brown flecks in her irises were completely absorbed by enlarged pupils, and they didn't respond to the brightening. "Can't believe I'm saying this, but I think y'all were drugged, baby."

"What? Why?" Her head lobbed slightly.

"You're certain you had no more alcohol tonight? No vodka in your soda?"

"Uh-uh." Kick shook her head and tilted, falling into the cold cement column. She stuck out her tongue. "Only yucky tonic water. Then real tap water. I filled the cup."

"You were slipped something somewhere." He drew her in tight and growled.

"'S impossible." She mumbled as if she were only half-awake. She nestled into Thomas, melding her body to his, unconsciously swaying, rubbing on him.

"Can we go to your house now?"

Damn. Now she was horny? Thomas welcomed the crisp wind gusting at his back.

He pried himself away and opened the car door. It wasn't hard to shut himself down. He'd never do anything with her in this state. Thomas buckled Kick in. "We're going somewhere alright."

When he found out who'd drugged her—he guessed both women too—there'd be hell to pay. Thomas texted Banger his suspicions and asked his friend to double-check Rachel and her roommate. He stretched into the back seat and checked on Cyndi. Out cold but breathing. Her pulse seemed fine, but he wasn't a doctor. He put the car in gear, livid at how something like this happened under his nose.

"Cyn's address is on my phone," Kick mumbled, her hands unsuccessfully trying to work the zipper on her purse.

"She's coming with us to the Emergency Department."

Both women were out when they pulled up to the emergency department's entrance. Kick ended up walking in with his assistance. The staff brought out a gurney for Cyndi.

. . .

BANGER CALLED WHILE THOMAS FILLED OUT PAPERWORK FOR THE women. He considered it an absolute joke since he knew so little about them, but he didn't want to upset Kick's kids. They'd been through enough in the past few months. They were all probably sound asleep anyway.

"The girls showed no signs of drugs, just drunk and pissed at me for waking them," Banger reported.

"Kick will be happy to hear it."

"Are you sure you don't want me to bring them in?"

"No," Thomas answered. "Let them sleep. Are you going back to the club?"

"Almost there. That bartender better still be on duty."

"What about the guy who grabbed Kick?"

"From what you told me, it doesn't fit the timeline. I haven't forgotten him though."

"Thanks, man. Sorry to make you stay out so late."

Banger chuckled. "Your woman's a menace—a good one, but still a menace."

THOMAS SAT IN THE CHAIR NEXT TO KICK'S BED, WATCHING HER sleep like a peaceful Sleeping Beauty with an IV and a heart monitor quietly announcing each beat. What the hell would he do? Both women had been drugged, so the bar staff was suspect. No one had manhandled Cyndi though, and she'd clearly felt the effects first. He remembered the Randy guy she'd disappeared with for a time and texted the info to Banger.

Regardless, at least two had been involved, which probably meant another planned attack. Thomas craved breaking someone with his bare hands. He wanted to join Banger and help his friend find the answers to his questions, but he couldn't leave Kick. Thomas couldn't even let his phone or the lab distract him. He kept going over the way she'd spoken with her heart in the garage. He wondered if she'd be mortified by what she'd said even though they were the prettiest words he'd ever heard. More than anything, he wanted to give her everything she wanted—no, deserved.

Kick finally stirred, and she sat up with a start, her hair hanging down like a veil shielding her face.

"Hey there." Thomas shifted to the bedside, but she didn't look up. "How are you feeling?"

With the same out-of-it voice, Kick said, "I have to take my detox pills so I don't get sick."

"It's alright—"

"Will you get it from the car? The stuff called… you know… when you want to cook a steak outside? You use… oh, what's the stuff…?"

"A grill? Propane?"

She shook her head so hard the monitor beeps increased.

His own memory of older remedies clicked in. "Are you thinking of charcoal?" Thomas asked.

Kick's shoulders sagged in relief, and she finally looked at him. "Yes. Activated charcoal. Thank you. If you hurry, it should still work."

Thomas pointed to the IV in her arm. "You've had medicine for about a while, darlin'. It'll be enough for what happened tonight."

Kick's head shifted from the line to the half-full fluid bag, then around the bay they were in. Her brows furrowed in confusion. "What did happen?"

Thomas took her free hand in both of his and rubbed Kick's knuckles. "What do you remember?"

She leaned back into the pillows as she ran her IV hand over her hair, getting it caught. "Jaysus, I'm a fright. Can you get a scrunchie from my purse?"

She already sounded more like herself. Relieved, Thomas reached for Kick's purse, unzipped it, and set it on her lap. He found himself impressed with how she could pull it all into a bun while attached to an IV and not fully sober.

"I remember seeing Banger."

Thomas didn't expect this. "What about him?"

"He took the girls home."

"He did."

"Banger put his hands around their necks like he was steering them. He was disrespectful."

Thomas snickered. Of all the things her currently beleaguered brain could remember, she took the mama bear route. "True. Do you remember waiting for me outside?"

"No. Wait… cops?" She reached for her forehead. "Oh hell. The kid knew Dylan. We yelled at him."

His laugh grew. "That's right, occifer."

"Where the hell were you?"

Between laughs, Thomas said, "Getting our coats and finding my phone, remember?"

"Nope."

"Do you remember the parking deck?"

"Uh-uh. Should I?"

He held his tongue and looked down at his shoes. Thomas longed to talk to Kick about what she'd said, but he figured she'd feared the feelings in those words as much as he did. It was a good thing she didn't remember them. Her lack of memory also fit with the information he'd read about the drug's effects. "No. Just curious. You sang pub songs."

"Oh *jayz*. Were we loud?" She shifted against the pillows. "Par for the course, I guess. Songs and booze go together like bangers and mash when you're from an Irish family."

Thomas flinched at the mention of liquor. "Kick…" *Christ*, he didn't want to dump more bad news on her, but the nurse would be in soon and catch her up, regardless. He decided then. Nothing would come before keeping her safe anymore. He didn't care if the Felidae objected. He couldn't ignore this feeling pulling him in. She wouldn't be his last priority, his emotional retreat from everything about his life he hated. She needed him, and he'd be there.

"You're not in the emergency department because of two cocktails from hours ago."

11

Fly Me to the Moon

Kick

My face scrunched up when Liam walked into my medical bay with Thomas. It had nothing to do with the night's events either. I should've been happy that my son had someone to rely on besides me, but I felt my forehead crease deepen. The fecking damsel-in-distress situation—yet again—made me prickly. I'd grown used to being ghosted when I needed people and accepted the reality of taking care of business alone. Thomas's helpfulness messed with my head even if I *had* asked him to call Liam for me.

Adding to the matter, the two of them didn't look like friends or a teacher with a student. They looked like a father and son—granted, a young father. I should've overflowed with appreciation. Instead, I found myself in a torrent of confusion. On the rare occasion I had let myself envision finding another life partner, I'd pictured it as something personal. I'd never thought a new relationship could help my family.

Oh, who was I kidding? There wasn't a family for Thomas and me. We were special-friends-who-might-be-more at an indeterminate time. Boy, did I miss the days where a girl would get a varsity jacket or class ring to let her know precisely where she stood. Maybe our timing simply stank.

I held my arms out to my son, and he rushed me for a hug. "I'm okay, Wee Man."

Liam sat on the bed and dropped the duffel bag of clothes and things for me and Cyndi as Thomas took the chair. I brushed a curl out of Liam's eyes, and a hint of doing something similar flashed through my memory, only I couldn't see the face. "You don't mind me having Thomas wake you at Collin's?"

"Naw, we were up." Liam answered with the enviable energy of an eighteen-year-old. "I'd have been mad if you walked through the door in the afternoon like nothing had happened."

Oh. Right. I was supposed to spend the night at Thomas's house. I caught his gaze, and Thomas passed me a slight, knowing grin. Yup, bad timing.

My nurse slid the door open. "Only one family member at a time allowed in here." She held up a tablet. "I also need to do a run-through on you."

"Again?"

Thomas and Liam stood. My son moved to the door, but Thomas leaned down and kissed my cheek. "How about I take the boy to get a coffee? Promise it won't hold a candle to yours."

"Flatterer," I grumbled, though a smile pulled at my lips. "Will you check on Cyndi too?"

"Of course."

I turned to my nurse. "Do I have to pee in a cup again? I'm sure I can get you a quart now."

She smiled and shook her head. Her face filled with the kind of empathy that made a nurse great. "We're done with specimens. If you can stand, I'll help you to the restroom. After I get your vitals, a detective would like to speak with you."

As the reality of another attempt to hurt me settled in, I started shaking.

Alone in my room again, my mind raced through the night's events, desperate to remember anything. It stubbornly remained a kaleidoscope of fuzzy images and happiness. The contrast to what Thomas told me about what happened made the shakes worse.

Tony Bennett's "Fly Me to the Moon" tiptoed gently from the speaker in my patient bay. It soothed the restlessness as I leaned back, closed my eyes, and sang along. No invisible monster would beat me. There was a moon to see after all.

"You sound nice, Kick," Detective Nick Ross said, quietly sliding open the glass door, Thomas following closely behind.

"Only one visitor allowed," I warned.

Thomas put his finger to his lips and winked. "Shift change."

Okay then.

Thomas settled on the foot of my bed while Nick took the chair. "Can I get your statement?"

"Why you? We were in Raleigh last night."

The detective flushed, fuming with anger. At least that's what I assumed. "It's not illegal to drug a drink and the grabbing you experienced is common behavior, given the setting. So there's nothing for the RPD to do. I'm here as a follow-up to your previous events."

Events?

Thomas grunted, and I reached for his hand.

I adjusted my ponytail and let the detective's words sink in. "This wasn't illegal?"

Nick shook his head. "It would be special circumstances if you were hurt or… worse. There's a bill in the general assembly to fix this loophole. From what Mr. Harrison told me, you're only here because of your medical history and his insistence. Odds are, you would've slept it off and assumed you'd had too much to drink."

Jaysus. "What about Cyndi?"

Thomas cleared his throat and answered, "She's getting IV fluids with some extra medicine in the bag. She took it harder, but she'll be fine."

"We were drugged then?"

"The preliminary assessment suggests so," Detective Ross replied. "I'll go over the tapes with your security team soon," he added.

My… Oh, Banger again. I blew out a shaky breath.

Thomas jumped in. "From what I gather, Cyndi took the brunt of it."

"Given her high blood pressure, it's a good thing your boyfriend brought you two in," the detective added. "She could've been in big trouble if left at home."

I flinched at the knowledge someone might have really harmed my best friend. The ridiculousness of the entire situation seemed to slap me in the face.

"And you think this is related to the other harassment?"

"I don't believe in coincidences." The detective's voice dropped. "Honestly, people don't have this much bad luck, Ms. McKenna. First I need your account of events. Then we wait—for the final toxicology reports and for the footage to show us anything."

"Where's Liam?" I didn't want to risk him overhearing anything even though I couldn't remember much.

"Sitting with Cyndi," Thomas answered. He brushed loose wisps of hair from my forehead.

Again, my boy was witness to the fallout from an attack on me. "How is he, Thomas? Is he scared shitless? Lee might never let me out of the house again." My breath hitched.

A corner of Thomas's mouth lifted. He continued to play with my curls. Maybe he was scared too. I sure didn't know what to make of it all. I only knew I didn't plan to go away quietly.

"He'll be alright. I talked him down. Made some promises." Thomas glanced at Nick and back at me. "Stop stalling and tell Detective Ross what you can even if your memories are still fuzzy."

What promises?

"Fine." I shifted in the bed. My hips hurt for some reason. "I remember the inside of the club, the Spyder, the bartenders—"

Detective Ross lifted a finger. "Tell me about them."

I closed my eyes to picture them better. "One dressed like John Bender from *The Breakfast Club* and the other like the woman from my favorite Molly Ringwald movie. Shit, I can't remember the name." I squeezed Thomas's hand. "You surprised us... our dance. Chicken wings on our table. A meat stick."

Thomas affirmed my memory with a broad smile. An image of

a girl clinging to him came to mind, and I frowned. "A child playing grown-up called me old."

"That was all before. What do you remember after Cyndi bought the sodas?" Thomas asked.

"Iona…"

"What?" both Thomas and the detective asked.

"The other bartender cos-played as Iona from…" I snapped my fingers a few times. *Pretty in Pink.* I sank back into my pillow, relieved to have the words off the tip of my tongue.

Detective Ross tilted his head like a dog hearing a weird whistle. "Which means…?"

I stretched my neck. Why did IVs always seem to tighten my muscles? "Let's see… Platinum wig, cat eye makeup, black-and-white dress. She had a button nose."

He typed away even though I only remembered the superficial things about her appearance.

I turned to Thomas, remembering what he'd asked me. "Cyndi bought tonics, not sodas." I bit my lip as a confusing image came to mind. "Why do I see a werewolf attacking me? I kicked him. He howled. I think he tried to bite me. He was mad."

"Cyndi said he was large and hairy and called him Sasquatch," Thomas reminded me.

"Good. So this suspect looks wolfish. Do you remember anything else about his appearance?" Nick typed on his pad.

I continued my trip through my foggy memory as it appeared. "I couldn't find my way back to the dance floor or to Cyndi. It's like a labyrinth formed around me out of nowhere. There were bodies and flashing lights."

I continued for several more minutes, trying to bring up any image from the night, but they grew murkier with each successive word. The images contrasted with an overwhelming feeling of joy and love I remembered. To keep from crying over the contrast of my feelings and reality, I bit my lip and held it together. I wouldn't let my head travel to the place where my night almost ended up.

Detective Ross sighed. "You might not think it's much, but you helped, Kick. I'll let you rest and call you when I have an update. If you remember anything else—especially any new, distinctive features of the man who grabbed you—call me." He gave me his business card, though I already had two at home. "It's fine to leave a message."

The nurse entered with release papers. All necessary samples were squared away, and since I could move around on my own, there was nothing else for them to do for me. I dressed and stepped out into the hall.

Detective Ross turned to Thomas. "Thanks for your help, Mr. Harrison. I'll call you if anything needs clarifying."

"Please do."

To me, he added, "I'll check in to see if your missing pieces come back."

I shook his hand and watched him leave. As my nurse passed by, I tapped her arm. "May I see Cyndi Sendaydiego?"

"Sure." She pointed to a treatment bay two doors to the left. "In there."

I scanned Thomas for a hint of his plans. "Right behind you," he answered my unasked question.

I slid the door open and stepped around the curtain. Cyndi looked up and smiled through tears. "Hey, chica."

"Jaysus." A few steps more and I scooped her into a squishy hug. "Oh, sweetie."

She pulled back, slightly annoyed. "We were drugged."

I scrunched my nose. "So they say."

"Kick—" Cyndi's chin quivered.

"You won't blame yourself."

"They said it was the tonic and—"

"Shh." I hugged her again. "It doesn't mean *you* spiked them. Besides, you ended up with the worst of it." I leaned back and studied her warm brown eyes. "Feeling any better? Can I bring you home with me?"

She shook her head so hard a tear flew off her cheek. "No, chica. Lee's so freaked. He'd probably spend the day watching me breathe. That's no way to get my beauty rest."

"But—"

She tapped my knee. "I texted Manu when my fingers started working again. He'll be here soon with a change of clothes. He agreed to play nurse too." She waggled her brows and gave me a Cheshire cat grin.

I sighed and tried not to smile. "Leave it to you."

"Me? Look at you. *The Unsinkable Molly Brown.*"

"So you think I was the target?"

Cyndi gave me a pity nod. Her face turned serious, contemplative. "Did I go off with a man?"

I swung my head to Thomas. I didn't remember a man.

He cleared his throat. "He said his name was Randy. If the cameras were working, he'll show up by the booth at least."

Cyndi ran her hand through her hair, and I watched it fall back into shape perfectly. "The staff pressed me hard to do the whole rape kit enchilada. But I said no." She shivered. "I would know about that. And I would *remember.* I do remember a man grabbing my ass and pulling me up against him, but I think it was this guy. He was harmless." Something like recognition crossed her expression, and her hand flew to her mouth. "Shit. I didn't mean like your grab. It was—"

I pulled her hand away from her face and squeezed it with my own. "I know." I chuckled to push down a threatening tear. "Hell, I remember so little. It's like Thomas told me a story about a woman who sounds like me."

"I hear you. After the drinks, all I have are feelings instead of memories." Cyndi closed her eyes and sighed. "They're amazing though." A smile spread across her face. "I *felt* music. Did you know Prince feels incredible?"

"I wouldn't expect any less from him."

My knee hiked up on the edge of the bed, and I moved my hand to Cyn's forehead, running my fingers through the silky bangs of her perfect bob. Another flicker of a memory flashed, then disappeared. "You look better. I think."

She lifted her arm with the IV. "It's a magic potion. Thomas said you only needed the basic fluids. I told you, you're unsinkable."

She turned her head to Thomas, who was texting in the visitor's chair. "With your handsome entourage to boot."

Cyndi dropped her head, and her breath hitched.

"Hey now." Careful of the IV line, I wrapped her in a hug and said into her ear, "We're okay."

She cried into my shoulder. "Take my mind off this, Kicky." She sat back, dabbed at her face with a tissue, and rearranged her blanket. "Tell me something embarrassing about you to make me feel better."

"Why? No."

She faked a frown face. "You owe me for taking the hit."

I flinched at the word *hit*. I dropped my gaze. If this was about hurting me, Cyndi had been collateral damage. Her high blood pressure could've turned the night into a tragedy. I caved in to the guilt. "Fine. I can't seem to grasp anything today. It took me forever to get dressed because my hands wouldn't work."

Cyndi waved a hand in dismissal. "That's expected. You can do better."

I peeked over my shoulder at Thomas, who had his nose buried in his phone. *What the hell.*

"Okay. You know those nipple hairs that pop up out of nowhere—like an inch long overnight?" I checked back. His head stayed down, but his brows had raised high.

"Sure. Everyone gets those. You pluck them, you move on. So?"

"One grew out of my neck," I murmured and plopped my head in my hand, wishing I could sew my lips shut.

She clapped her hands together like a goofy seal. "Oh, fabulous. It sucks getting old."

"You suck."

Cyndi waved a casual hand. "That's nothing, chica. Is your pudendum balding yet?"

"Excuse me? No."

"Just wait."

Thomas jumped in his chair and sounded like he choked.

I tapped Cyndi on the shoulder. "Stop messing with him. As if you have this problem."

"Who says I don't?"

I rolled my eyes, feeling like my daughter. "Knowing you as I do, you'd convince someone from the Hair Club for Men to bend the rules and do a transplant down there. You wouldn't give in to aging so easily."

She pressed a finger to her chin. "You may have an idea for a new business… Genital Hair Transplanting. We could call it the Pussy Club."

"Sounds like a place I know of in Tampa." Thomas snickered.

I snapped my fingers in his direction. "Please. You're encouraging her."

He grinned and returned to his reading. I knew they both messed with me while I sought to be a comfort.

I turned back to Cyndi and found her staring at Thomas, her head tilted to the side like she was evaluating him. "He makes a pretty picture. The accent though? In the deep timbre? I don't think I'd ever want him to stop speaking. It's like butter."

"I know, right?"

"Right here, ladies." Thomas exhaled. "Besides, y'all are the ones with the accents."

Cyndi fanned herself.

"Oh, for Christ's sake. You feel better." I laughed. "Stop screwing around."

"I guess I am." Then she tsked me. "Humility is good for you though, Miss Unsinkable."

As if I had no experience being publicly humiliated. *Firecrackers in a café, anyone? How about graffiti with impossibly poor grammar? Or a lying newspaper article?*

"Did you get the magnifying mirror I told you about?" Cyndi continued, snapping me out of my mini pity party. "They are a godsend for your neck situation."

Thomas snorted behind me. I turned and glared, though he dared not look up. "Keep looking at your phone." He coughed another laugh. I knew he remembered the whole Dorian Gray fiasco in Target last month. I returned my attention to Cyndi, who watched our interaction with curiosity.

"I found one. Thanks for not telling me how bad my brows were, by the way. You're supposed to have my back…"

Her chin quivered again.

"No, no, no. That's not what I meant."

"I didn't have your back, Kick. We could've done the water cups like you wanted."

I hugged her again. "Who's paying dearly for it, eh?" Tipping her chin up, I added, "It's not on you."

"Okay." She turned away as the tears dropped.

"You want us to go?"

She wiped her eyes while nodding vigorously. I kissed her on the head and touched Thomas's shoulder. "Are you taking me home, or is Liam?"

He stood and lifted an eyebrow. "Are you joking?"

"Right." Of course Thomas would see me home safe. I welcomed this protective side now. I didn't know what had come over me.

"We're getting food first. I heard there's a burger joint near here that serves gluten-free bison burgers and fries. They have a dedicated fryer."

He knew about dedicated fryers. I almost swooned.

Liam had been napping in the waiting room while we visited with Cyndi. "Can Liam join us?"

Thomas looked confused as he answered, "I assumed he would."

There was my problem with the man: I didn't feel like I had the right to assume anything. Should I though? Did it matter?

For the first time that day, I noticed him. Without definitions. Not a protector or even a friend. With no qualms about age differences. I *saw* Thomas Harrison. The man with a sexy cleft in his chin, a Cary Grant stare, and a giant heart. Some of the bliss I had experienced the night before came back.

Just him. Just me.

I grabbed Thomas's bicep and let my head fall on his shoulder. "Thanks, sweets. For everything." I looked up into his reassuring silver irises. "You think life will get quiet now?"

Thank You

Kick

MY DOORBELL RANG TWICE BEFORE IT REGISTERED IN MY BRAIN. THE roasted-till-golden Thanksgiving turkeys rested on a rack. The dressing, sweet potatoes, and gluten-free Hawaiian rolls were currently baking. And I was in gravy mode.

Of all the items on the menu, the fecking gravy put me on edge. To me, making gluten-free gravy was tricky at best. I had two boxes of store-bought sitting in the pantry in case it backfired. Since they had garlic and onion on the ingredient list, going that route would mean no gravy for me.

"I'll get it," Deana called out.

I mentally retraced the previous arrivals and remembered Cyndi had yet to show. The last we'd spoken, she was still recovering from what we called "our night out" in order to avoid the word *drugging*.

I glanced at Thomas, who vigorously mashed a giant pot of potatoes. He laughed and said, "Looks like the clan is complete."

Clan? Oh, this man. He'd lightened everyone's mood since walking through the door. I really liked this version of him.

The house was pleasantly full—a rarity lately. It pleased me as much as the sweet and savory aromas filling the space. Deana's daughter and son were at their respective in-laws, so she and Gordon had arrived with multiple desserts and what smelled like an amazing mac-and-cheese side.

Cyndi sauntered in, looking well and gave cheek kisses to each of us. She set up a charcuterie board, featuring a mix of German sausages her mother had made, on the sideboard in the dining area. A tray of lumpia with multiple sauces sat next to it for our appetizers.

"Can I do anything?" Cyndi asked as she washed her hands in the kitchen sink.

"Nope. Pour yourself some wine and join the others for some football. We won't be long."

She practically swayed at the word *wine*, and I immediately apologized.

"No worries, chica." Cyndi waved off the apology. "I'm just not ready yet. What else do you have?"

"I'm trying out a lychee-flavored sparkling water if you'd like. I've only had one, but I liked it. It's in the cooler on the screened porch."

Cyndi's eyes lit up. "Now we're talking. Thanks, Kicky."

She passed by my friend, Charley, my son Dylan and the Douglases, who were watching the game in the great room, on her way to the cooler. Like a second hostess, she gave out hugs and kisses as she went by. It was a surprising coincidence so many had accepted my invites, but I buzzed with the joy of hosting a crowd like in the old days.

Back then, Shane would insist on hiring a caterer or renting a room in a restaurant to keep me from wearing out, but the kids were also little and required all my energy. Now they'd become a tremendous help. Each took a turn either cooking or zhushing up the house in the past week. Plus I didn't know any chef who wanted to handle my diet issues on Thanksgiving.

Along with the game downstairs, an epic *Smash Bros* tournament could be heard with occasional roars from the loft upstairs. My other two and Dylan's roommate, Henry—he insisted we call him Dummy—kept trying to lure Dylan up to join them.

My gaze landed on Bobby's sour visage as she sat by herself at the kitchen island. She had been at the center of activity when Rachel and the boys were chopping and setting up, but their services weren't needed anymore.

I didn't know if the crowd bothered Bobby, the noise did, or both. There wasn't much I could do about it, so I kept her vodka tonics weak but flowing. She finished her current one and set it down. "Are any more *strays* showing up?"

I gave the gravy another stir. It was almost ready. "No. We're all here."

With a snide tone, she said, "Good, 'cause you're making me eat with some damn rude people today."

Apparently, her first comment had been a rebuke I'd missed. I set the spoon on the stovetop and turned around. "What's wrong?"

Bobby tipped her head toward the great room. "These people can't even say hello."

I'd sworn everyone had. As I slowly scanned the room, Cyndi caught my eye and piped up—Bobby had spoken loud enough to be heard over the TV. "There you are!" Cyndi strolled over to my mother and forced a kiss on her cheek. "Between my trays and these giants, I didn't see you sitting here. We petite girls need to stick together, don't we?"

Cyndi stood in Bobby's blind spot and mouthed *battle axe* while Bobby shot full-tilt laser beams out of her eyes at me. My mother hadn't wanted a kiss or a hug from my best friend. They hated each other. Bobby had simply been back to pushing random buttons to see if one would upset me. Well, I wouldn't let her. It was a day of thanks after all.

I fixed Bobby another vodka tonic. Mostly tonic—the corn syrup didn't bother her. "Here. Why don't you have some appetizers? Cyndi's mother made the sausages."

"Pfft." She waved me off. "I won't spoil my dinner. You're almost ready, right? Or will we have to eat cold turkey?"

I'll give you cold turkey.

Thomas jumped in. "Speaking of… my potatoes are finished, and I can carve the bird now. I'll grab a beer first though." He walked toward the door to the screened porch. "Can I get anyone something? Gordon?"

"Please." Gordon jumped up and joined Thomas. I figured both of them required a break from the tension, and I couldn't blame them. It took a lot of energy to deal with Bobby Allen. I'd taken a couple of days off after the girl's night out, but my energy wasn't all the way back.

"Since you're heading that way, can you turn on the heater too? It'll be easier to set up the summer table out there instead of trying to finagle another one inside."

"Yes, milady." Thomas flashed me his cheesy grin, and the stress melted away.

"You're not seriously making a kids' table, are you?" Dylan asked from the sofa, his love for football still overruling his need to dominate his friend and siblings in all things Nintendo. Football connected Dylan to his father. He was my only child with genuine memories of the years Shane had played on Thanksgiving Day.

"You'll be more comfortable as a foursome out there than crammed around the one in here," I answered.

Dylan waggled his beer can. "This disqualifies me from kid table status." He tipped his head toward the porch. "I say *that's* the adult table and in here is the geriatric one." His challenging smirk reminded me of his preteen years when the hormones showed up, bringing the cocky grin along for the ride.

I shook my head, laughing. "Whatever gets you through the day, lad."

No matter what happened with Bobby, it would be a good day. Hell, it would probably be the last big feast for a while. My heart ate up the buzz, the intergenerational camaraderie, the extended family. I'd worked hard for this.

Deana and Cyndi collected the things needed to set the second table. "Thank you," I said to them as they passed. Bobby groaned loudly.

"What's got your underwear in a twist?" I leaned down and quietly asked. I'd thought the weak VTs would've set her at ease by now. Instead, they turned up her volume. One of her brows lowered, and her face fell into a maniacal smirk, like she was about to impart a terrible truth I'd been too stupid to realize for myself. "You're living the life of Riley now, aren't you? Your world will fall apart next year when your boy toy finds someone his own age. You'll have run the kids off too. Next year, it'll just be you. And me."

"Aww, thanks for caring, Mother," I said, tapping her hand, my words laced with sarcasm.

"I promise you, Ms. Allen, this boy toy has no intention of going anywhere," Thomas said from behind us. His voice held a clear warning in it. My heart sank and jumped at the same time. *Shit, shit, shit* ran through my head. Talk about rude guests. Bobby held the honors there.

He handed me a cold LaCroix. "Thought you might need this."

"Much appreciated." I mouthed the words, *I'm so sorry*.

Thomas's phone buzzed, and he pulled it from his pocket. "Can I take this in your office?"

"Of course." I watched him hustle to my study, wondering who it could be, pretty sure his grimace at the screen matched the one I gave Bobby. As I stared at the closed door, a scorched smell reached my nose.

"No, no, no!" The gravy. I only tolerated arrowroot for a thickener, but it was tricky. It didn't take much to end up with a gelatinous goo.

OUR DINNER STARTED OFF WITH QUIET NICETIES. SITTING BOBBY AT the opposite end from me—the place of honor—served mostly to keep her as far away as possible while allowing me to monitor her from under my lashes. More than once, I wished she had stayed home, like she had for Liam's birthday.

I cleared my throat, determined to be the proper host, directing the conversation when called for.

"Charley's brother lives in Spain, Thomas."

"Did y'all grow up there?" he asked Charley.

She shook her head. "We were raised in New Mexico."

"No kidding?"

"Yes. Teo normally visits this time of year, but he's on assignment."

"And Charley is the first woman to head a premier construction firm in the Triangle."

"I remember," Thomas graciously said, pausing to study me. "The work you did for Kick is fantastic. I've made extensive renovations in my house and would love some woodworking tips."

Their conversation took off after that, and Deana leaned into me. She, too, had begged to stay as far away from my mother as possible. "You don't have to work the conversation so hard. Relax, shug." I gave her a smile to let her know I'd heard.

The gravy boat passed to me, and I raised it, not being able to partake myself. Having burned my attempt, I'd heated up the store-bought. "Anyone need more?"

"Wonderful job, Kicky," Cyndi cheered from her end of the table. Everyone chimed in as I added butter to my cornbread dressing. It wasn't the same without gravy, but I'd be darned if I'd eat it dry.

Thomas clinked his wineglass, getting our attention. "A toast to the hostess. Thank you for opening your warm home and serving us this magnificent feast. I still don't know how you pulled it off with the substitutions." He waited as my friends laughed. "What did you call it?"

"Well..." It took a moment before his question registered. "Oh, it's gluten-free, dairy-free, low-FODMAP and soy-free for Rachel and Liam."

"Amazing." His bright face turned to the rest of the table. "I thank the rest of y'all for bringing side dishes, desserts, and drinks. Mostly, thank you, Kick, for showing us your enormous heart and beautiful smile. You're the embodiment of what today is about."

The volume rose with a chorus of "here, here's," "cheers," and a loud "damn straight." Thomas's *slainte* rose above the rest and made me smile. He even pronounced it correctly. It was the toast my father and Shane had always used. Though I'd long become used to holidays without Shane, this was the first Thanksgiving without my father. Is this why Bobby misbehaved?

"That's what my family says," I told him.

"I figured."

Everyone took part in the toast except for Bobby. She scrunched up her face like she'd tasted something rotten and mouthed a mocking *y'all* to everyone and no one. My brows pulled down, and I opened my mouth to tell her off, but Thomas patted my hand and murmured, "Let it go."

The table returned to a buzzed grouping of conversations of twos and threes. All except for Bobby, but by that time, I didn't care. There could be no way she was missing my father when she had treated him so terribly while he lived.

My gaze instead drifted to the table on the porch. Fortunately, the day was warm enough for alfresco dining with the addition of the warming lamp. But Dylan looked as quiet and out of place as his grandmother did at our table. I hoped it didn't have to do with being out on the screen porch.

He entered the dining area and asked, "Mind if we start one of the pumpkin pies?"

"Where's your gorgeous fiancée, dear?" Bobby called out. She turned to Gordon and announced, "He's about to start a computer company, and his wife will be a doctor. Isn't it fantastic?"

"Yeah, well… RIP," Dylan muttered. As he cut the pie and reached for a server, he added, "We're not getting engaged after all. I'll get your ring back to you, Gran."

"Don't worry about it boy-o. It's probably a simple quarrel." Bobby turned a heated glare on me. "What did you do? You've never liked his girl."

Nothing. And there was the problem. I'd let my troubles take over my thoughts and forgot about the possibility of being a… nope. The G-word wasn't welcome inside my head. I also noticed Bobby couldn't remember Suzy's name. *Ha.*

"Not a thing. I agree. Suzy's lovely." And she would make a fine wife for someone else.

"It's not like that, Gran," Dylan warned, crossing the room. "Drop it please."

"Crap," I murmured under my breath.

Thomas, Charley, Deana, and Gordon all stared me down with questioning gazes. I shrugged and shook my head. Dylan had left the door open and the table outside erupted in laughter, with Liam at the center of attention.

Bobby tsked a response. "That boy's a troublemaker and a show-off. Like his father and this one." She nodded toward Thomas. "No wonder you gravitated to him." My jaw dropped as she stunned me speechless. She added, "Just wait. That's all I'm saying. Just. You. Wait."

"Mother—"

"Enough," Thomas said, deep enough to make everybody stop eating. "Ms. Allen, I've heard enough."

I covered his hand. "It's okay, Thomas."

He gentled his voice for me. "Let me. Please." He turned back to Bobby. "You don't like me. Fine. There's one thing I've learned over the years and that is that family is a treasure. No matter how short or long y'all's time together, taking it for granted is a travesty. To stomp on it the way you do is criminal. No matter how you feel about me, you will not speak to me with disrespect. Moreover, I won't listen to you put down your daughter or any of your grandchildren."

"Are you going to allow this?" Bobby pushed hard against the table, her chair scraping the floor, looking at me. "Well, I *never*." She stormed out of the room and slammed the door to the guest bath.

Deana and Cyndi beamed as they watched us. Gordon wore a smirk too.

Thomas raised my hand and kissed the back of it. "This is bad timing, but I'm afraid I've got to head up to Virginia now. I don't want to take my family for granted either." He rose, and I followed. "It was nice seeing everyone."

As Thomas sorted out his jacket from the others sharing the same hook, I asked, "Can I give you anything to take?"

He shook his head. "Joe and Toni have it covered. It's more about having a few days to spend with them anyway."

"Right." My heart wouldn't stop racing after the confrontation with Bobby, knowing round two was imminent. "What do I do? About you know who?"

He gently lifted my chin. "Boundaries, Kick. Tell me"—he tipped his head toward the dining room—"would your father have intercepted the scene back there?"

I nodded, adding, "Shane too."

"Darlin', despite your promise to a dying man, your father wouldn't want her speaking to y'all like this. It's high time your mother learned about boundaries." He leaned in and kissed my cheek, whispering, "It has to come from you."

I thought of the Psalm I'd gone to pieces over in front of him. I couldn't imagine a scenario where Bobby would ever consider a boundary to be pleasant.

"Was it Joe who called earlier?"

"Huh? Oh yeah. They were running late. Now I am." He pressed a kiss to my lips like he was transferring courage and confidence. "Hold on to the good parts of today. You've got this."

At that moment, I knew I did. "I'm fine. Don't worry. Thank you for being my sous-chef."

"Had fun being your sous-chef." His thumb stroked my cheek. "I loved watching your face light up as the meal came together. Simply gorgeous."

Lord almighty, his eyes were smiling for me, making those little creases that weakened my knees.

Thomas called goodbyes to the house and left me wanting more. Missing him already.

As soon as the door shut behind him, the one to the guest bath opened.

"Well, good thing he's gone," Bobby declared with a sweet smile. "I don't understand what's so wrong with our family that you had to invite them. It's your deep-seated desire for attention, isn't it? Your father and I worked long hours and you've never gotten over it." Bobby sighed in disgust and took a step to move past me and back to the dining table.

My hand around her bicep stopped her, my tone unusually calm, a small smile on my face. This wasn't a ploy for attention or an emotional outburst. It was what we both needed me to say.

"Oh, hell no. I'll send a kid over with leftovers, but you're leaving now."

What About Your Friends

Kick

A PLATE SLID THROUGH MY HANDS, CRASHING INTO TWO ON THE floor. My fingers weren't the only part of me that wouldn't stop shaking. Yes, I'd stayed cool-headed while I told Bobby she had to leave. I was proud of myself for holding my ground without blowing up.

Since she'd left, memories flashed through my mind as my friends—my true family—helped me clear the table. The first scene coming to mind was my wedding reception. Bobby had flirted shamelessly with Shane's Uncle Billy, the McKenna patriarch. My mind's eye watched one of the sweetest men I would ever know wearing a tuxedo covered in chocolate sauce. Bobby had scooped some into a glass from the fountain she'd insisted on and dumped it on Uncle Billy after he'd put her in her place. Considering her usual reaction to being told no, I'd gotten off easy with a house-shaking door slam earlier. Who knew a tiny woman in her late sixties could manage such force.

I'd nearly tripped with a pile of dishes when a memory from Dad's funeral appeared. Roberta Allen, "devoted widow" wearing bright yellow, huffing from boredom and loudly smacking gum while the rest of us were blubbering messes.

"Go sit down, sugar," Dee soothed, taking the next dish as it dangled from my hand.

"How about a coffee?" Cyndi asked.

I shook my obedient yet reluctant head as I slid onto a barstool. "Remember? It's not allowed right now. It would be too late for me anyway."

"Not even for special circumstances?" Cyn persisted.

"No sweets. I'll take an herbal tea though. Can you put the kettle on?"

She filled it and took my place in front of the dishwasher.

"You may be upset, but I'm proud of you," Deana encouraged.

"Me too," Gordon said, sliding an arm around my shoulders. "It wasn't easy, but you did it."

I smiled up at him. I was proud of myself too. It irritated me how much doing the right thing didn't stop me from physically reacting to the confrontation. I tapped my collarbone to calm down, making sure I didn't hyperventilate.

"Any chance the hot water's for coffee? It would be the perfect accompaniment to Dee's sweet potato pie," Gordon asked, rubbing his hands together.

"Shoot. You're right." I jumped up to make a big pot, but two enormous hands on my shoulders pressed down, settling my ass back where it belonged.

A deep chuckle came from above me. "Stay. I'll get it."

"I'm the barista, remember? You're the drug developer," I said, accompanied by a grin. Gordon worked in testing for a local pharmaceutical company.

Gordon was already at the french press, chuckling and checking with Deana to make sure he had the right number of scoops. "I've learned a thing or two from you ladies"—he kissed Dee on the cheek—"especially mine."

"You sure you don't want an espresso? Or foam?"

Dee laughed. "Wrong man, shug."

"Okay, fine." I settled in my spot, taking in the smells of pies in the warming drawer and newly brewed coffee. It didn't matter that I couldn't have any. The comforting aroma was enough. The prohibition was temporary, and my full belly wanted nothing more. My heart filled with my friends' encouragement. This was the purpose of family. It didn't matter whether we shared DNA.

Rachel sat on the stool next to mine and spread open the newspaper. "Lee and I plan to do Black Friday tomorrow. Want to come? We asked Dyl, but he's not vibing."

"At four thirty in the morning?" Rachel nodded vigorously. "Absolutely not." I kissed her cheek. "Thank you though. What are you buying?" I leaned over to see what she had circled.

"This blender's a great deal."

The grown-ups in the room all cooed like we were watching a toddler try to walk in heels. Over the years, we'd all had our fill at battling the predawn cold and the cranky, grabby crowd.

"Why would you do this when you don't have to? The world's changed, Snow. Order the blender online. I bet you can get this exact one."

Liam slid onto the third stool. "We want to say we did it once."

My gaze stopped at each of my friends. They each rolled their eyes, smirking. I knew, like me, they were thinking, *Oh, to have their kind of time and energy*. Me? After two days of chopping, brining, spicing, and stirring, I planned to sleep in and rest my body—especially my right arm. I hoped for a dreamless night and didn't know what I'd do if Bobby haunted me there.

"Holy shit." Rachel gasped and slapped the paper closed.

She and Liam both looked like they'd been caught being naughty.

My brows drew together. "What now?"

"Nothing," they said in unison.

I held my hand out, wiggling my fingers. In an instant, they were both six and three again, caught putting my makeup on Rachel's dolls. Mouths gaping in surprise, as if the dolls had wrecked their own faces. "What's in the paper?"

"Trust me, Mom, don't look," Liam pleaded.

Rachel knew better and slid it over.

On the opinion page was a piece about my coffeehouse: A Visit to the Perked Cup: A Lesson in Lies. All the warm fuzzies left the room. This person claimed to have been a regular who was disappointed in our "irresponsibility on Halloween." My defenses went up. At the same time, I recognized my disappointment, but how could I have expected something so public? Graham had been allegedly messing with *me*. I didn't think he'd take his anger out on random children. But if he wanted to make my life difficult, he'd succeeded. My fingers were crossed that the holiday shopping season could turn the business around.

True to its word, the opinion piece was a lesson in lies. It started out reaming my former employee, Madison, for being rude. I'd give the writer that one. Maddie's parents wanted her to quit after the attack. She'd fought with them over it without my knowing. Then she became hell on wheels for it. I let her go, telling her she could come back if her parents changed their mind or when she turned eighteen.

The next item involved complaints about the new camera installation. It claimed, in a vague, "sources say" way, that the cameras invaded privacy by listening to every conversation in the café, which wasn't true. Video coverage had improved along with clarity, but the mics were by the counter where any dangerous encounter would happen. The thought still gave me chills.

The last two claims made me laugh out loud. It said someone on the inside "verified" cameras in the bathrooms. It wasn't only a lie, it was illegal. As much as I'd have loved to know the identity of the weasels who regularly made a disaster area of my restrooms, I'd never.

Then it declared Jonn Graham innocent, saying he ran from the scene because he was frightened, like the rest of the crowd. It argued he hadn't been in the café, though my cameras caught otherwise.

I folded the paper back up and set it as far away as my reach allowed. "Nope. If Herself can't ruin my day, this sure won't."

"What's up?" Deana asked, holding out her hand.

"A piece in the paper telling readers to boycott the café. It also claims we're picking on poor Jonn-Jonn Graham. It's not worth your thoughts."

Ever the protector, Gordon picked it up and read it. His gaze passed between Deana and me. "It's lying, right?"

"Most of it. Maddie let her argument with her parents bubble up on the customers before I let her go."

Dee clicked her tongue. "Poor thing."

"Are you going to sue?" Gordon asked.

"I might threaten it, but opinions are free speech. Plus the editor doesn't like me." I tapped my chin, landing on an idea. "The business section reporter loves his free Friday coffee though. I wonder if Banger's team can help me with a rebuttal. It should help if someone at Angel can send reassurance that we don't invade our customer's privacy. I might be able to get the paper to advertise a new sales campaign too—for free—to make up for this mess." My eyebrows popped as a sneaky grin spread across my face. War could be fun when I wasn't battling my mother.

"You mean the study-hour plan?" Liam asked.

I nodded, loving the idea of making the paper eat its words.

"What's this?" Deana asked.

I pointed toward my office. "Marketing flyers I'm working on. Half-off drinks between three and five with a school ID. Like happy hour for a coffeehouse."

"Great idea, Kicky." Cyndi beamed.

"Thank you." I motioned toward Liam. "Wee Man helped."

"I've got a box of beaded bookmarks ready for holiday sales if you want them."

"Fantastic." I said, grateful for the help and hopeful my ideas could counteract this smear campaign. My energy hadn't returned, but I'd be ready when it did. Active support from my friends went a long way too.

I'D GIVEN THE COUNTERS A FINAL WIPE AND STARTED THE dishwasher for the third time. Our guests had rolled themselves out the door about half an hour earlier, stuffed like the birds they'd eaten.

Thomas had texted that he'd arrived safely at his family home. I dimmed the kitchen lights and rolled down the new shade over the kitchen window.

Dylan sat alone on the sectional, watching the evening football game. The other kids had resumed their Nintendo marathon with *Mario Kart*.

I plopped down next to my son, passing him two fingers of Defiant. I sipped herbal tea with a pink hue, reminding me of a warm flower. "Okay, lad. I've been a shit mom, but I'm here now. Fill me in. I was obviously wrong about a possible baby."

He scoffed and tasted his drink. "No, you weren't."

The tea caught in my throat. "She's pregnant?" I sputtered and checked my tone, whispering, "Suzy's having a baby?"

A sad squeak came from his usually deep voice. "She was."

I set the tea down and wrapped my arms around my son. "I'm so sorry, lad. Miscarriages are rough, but you can get through it. Stay close to her."

He shrugged me off, bending over and grunting. "Suzy didn't lose the baby, Mom. She aborted it and told me after the fact when I asked her if she'd missed a period." A sad keening escaped from his chest, punching straight through mine. How could I have missed that?

"How did I miss it?" He whimpered. "You keyed in to the clues as soon as I told you."

I rubbed his back, my tears matching his. The light from changing commercials reflected off falling tears, shining diamonds dropping for a life never known. "Oh, sweet boy. Any idea why she didn't come to you first?"

"She said she didn't want me ever to know." His throat caught. "I would've taken care of it, Mom."

"We all would've helped you. Gladly." I pulled him back and started rocking him while patting his shoulders. "It'll happen in due time."

"But I still love this one."

I grabbed his chin with a firm hand. "Listen to me. He or she would've adored you, but it does you no good to think of it as alive. It was a potential life. Did Suzy tell you how far along she'd been?"

Dylan shook his head, his eyes wide as he tried to absorb my words. I hated the bluntness, but motherly instincts told me it would help him move on. "You have no way of knowing whether the fetus would've made it to the end. It's the tragic truth of every pregnancy. What happened after she confessed?"

Wiping his cheek with the sleeve of his flannel, he said, "She left. We're done. Not because of the ba—procedure, but because her doing it without a word to me says everything I needed to know about us as a couple. Suze is staying on her best friend's couch. When Mai's roommate graduates next month, Suzy will officially move out of the condo." Dylan's tears resumed their descent down his rugged face. A shadow of his toddler-self sat before me, softening the masculine edges so much like my father's. I pulled him back into an embrace, wishing I could do anything more. I would trade my health gains in order to take away his pain.

He spoke in a scratchy rasp into my shoulder. "I don't know what's more painful." He sat back, running the sleeve over his face again. "That's not true. I was so numb when Suzy left. It seemed like the next step, like we'd been heading there since the summer. The dreams about a little boy or girl wake me up in the night, not her."

My hand cupped his jaw, thumb stroking his cheek to soothe. "Your dad would have been thrilled to know how much you want to be a father yourself."

"I didn't realize it until it was too late. Maybe if I'd said something?"

"I can't believe she wouldn't give you a reason she did it."

"She did." Dylan lifted a shoulder. "Medical school. Even if I took responsibility for it after, Suzy would have to take leave to deliver and recover. She never asked her adviser about it though." He shrugged. "Add in the terror of having to tell her parents, I can almost see things from her perspective. It's still no excuse in my opinion."

"They placed the weight of the world on her shoulders."

"I'm mad as hell over her doing it without talking to me."

"You should be." I took a sip of tea, trying to settle my nerves. I envisioned the situation from Suzy's perspective. "She probably felt so alone."

"Alone? She had me."

Shit. I hadn't meant to say it out loud. I took another sip. "Says a lot about where you fit in her world, doesn't it?"

"That's what I mean," he scoffed. "Her parents' wishes came before mine. I can't believe I almost asked her to marry me."

I squeezed his knee. "Don't beat yourself up over a first love. Learn from it and take small steps forward. It's a good thing finals are coming up. You can focus on them and rest over the holidays."

"God, finals." Dylan ran his hand through his hair. "I can't focus on school. I feel stuck."

"Maybe I can help. Go pour a couple more fingers of the whiskey and meet me on the back patio. Leave a tiny sip for me. We're going to need it."

"What are you doing?"

"You'll see."

After tearing apart my closet until I remembered I had stored it in the office, I located an old Chinese lantern, grabbed my jacket and fire stick, and set it up. A few minutes more and Dylan lifted the lantern until it warmed enough to take off on its own. I held his hand as we tipped our heads back, watching it catch an updraft and float toward the stars. We both sniffled as we said goodbye in our hearts to the one who wouldn't be.

Watch over him or her, Shane, I silently prayed. Then I took a small taste of Dylan's Defiant, observing my family's tradition of toasting their dead. Some things overrode doctor's orders. Dylan knocked back the rest of the amber liquid when I handed the tumbler to him.

The sliding door rumbled as it opened. "Whatcha doing out here?" Rachel asked, wrapping her plaid blanket around her.

"Saying goodbye," I answered in a hushed tone. The golden blaze grew smaller by the second.

"To Suzy?"

"Sort of," Dylan answered, clearing his throat.

"It's beautiful. Can I say goodbye too?"

"Sure, sweetie." I opened my other arm and wrapped it around her middle. I didn't tell her about the little soul we wouldn't meet. Dylan could share when he was ready.

A light breeze stirred our hair as we watched the fire drift from sight.

A MUG OF WARM WATER AND LEMON STARED AT ME FROM ITS PERCH on my desk. It was a poor substitute for the black gold from the Perked Cup, but it kind of worked. Dr. Chaddha, my physician at the functional medicine clinic at Lord University, had recently given me some encouragement to hang in there with her detox program. Thanks to Thomas's quick thinking, the setback from my night at Ducky's could be managed quickly. I might not even need to extend this strict regimen beyond what we'd planned. It motivated me to see the protocol through.

I should have followed her protocol and meditated to clear my mind of the previous day's "mama drama." Instead, I stared out the window in my home office, rehashing everything Bobby had said and done. She would still be livid, and she'd find a way for me to pay. Lemon water couldn't stop the growing anger, but one thing could. If the stress Bobby loved to cause could lift, I knew my head would clear, and I wouldn't drop the ball with my kids again.

My hand jittered while dialing my brother.

"Kick?" His voice was raspy, and I scolded myself for calling him so early.

"Hey Hubert—" My joke of a nickname.

My little brother's actual name was Robert—as in named after our mother, Roberta, not our father, like other boys. You could say he was named after our Grandpa Sullivan, who was a Robert and never forgave Grandma for only birthing girls. But we knew better.

Bobby either didn't notice or didn't care how it looked. Only those who knew my middle name knew she'd named both her children after herself.

"Cute. What'd she do?"

"Sorry to wake you." Bert had started out "Robby" until the neighbor kids noticed how much it sounded like "Bobby" and started calling him a mama's boy. He'd made sure "Bert" stuck instead.

"No, we're up. I have the boys today. I haven't spoken much yet, is all." It sounded like he took a pull of coffee. Lucky dog. "Spill. We were about to start the season off with a *Die Hard* marathon. Since you're distracting me, the guys went back to their *Switch*."

"*Die Hard* isn't a Christmas movie," I protested on behalf of the true classics.

"The hell it isn't. And quit stalling."

My quiet laugh filled my office. As much as she'd tried to pit Bert and me against each other, we eventually admitted we were the only members of an elite club of crazy. Our support for each other overtook the initial resentments until it ran deep. At least I hoped it did.

"Where to begin?" I filled him in on Bobby's antics since she'd come back from her cruise.

"She threw out the Curse of Cromwell shit on Lee? God, I haven't heard that one in decades."

"It was my fault. I thought a vodka tonic would calm her down. I forgot that booze makes mean people meaner, not nicer."

"Geez. What did Liam do?"

"He's so amazing, Bert. He brushed it off, went upstairs, and started a *Nintendo* tournament. I've never understood how a grandmother doesn't like her own grandson. Wasn't my big crime not being a boy? I gave her two."

"No," he replied. "Your crime was being first. Girls come second in her world."

My breath hitched from being so keyed up. With everything else, I'd forgotten about what a shit she'd been to Liam when she'd first arrived.

"What can I do?" I could almost hear his fingers rub his temple as he hesitantly asked the question.

"I may have kicked her out of the house, but I need Bobby out of the state. Please take her early. I need a break."

"Won't it cost you extra to change her ticket?"

"Don't worry about the fecking ticket," I snapped, then took a deep breath. "In fact, tell her you received a bonus and asked about changing it. If she thinks I want her out of town early, she might turn us down out of spite."

"Uh… you *do* want her to leave early."

"You don't have to tell her, Bert. Please." I was so desperate, I resorted to whining. "For your big sister."

"The same one who poured hot sauce in my cocoa? It was spring by the time I figured out Swiss Miss wasn't supposed to make me cry. *That* big sister?"

"I paid for it too. Bobby used the Shillelagh on me. The bruises lasted into summer."

"I'll pay for this."

"Are you kidding? The golden boy does no wrong. She'll clean and cook and spoil your kids rotten."

"They don't need her mind games when their parents are in the middle of a divorce?"

I sighed, defeated, and admonished my selfishness. "You're right. Never mind. I'm sorry."

"No." He stopped me. A long sigh followed. "You're right. She's coming down anyway, and you need to get better. I still feel bad about having to cut the funeral trip short." Bert's ex had planned to take the boys on a trip to the Grand Canyon when Dad passed. She pitched a fit over the inconvenience. "What's a few days early?" he added.

"For real?" I squealed and tapped my toes.

"When should I expect her?"

"The tenth?"

"A few days before the original date? How about next weekend?"

"For real?"

"Of course. It'll be my Christmas present for you. Don't expect a package in the mail."

"I'm paying for her ticket." I laughed.

"The best presents are from the heart, right?"

"Yes, they are. Thank you, little bro."

"Yeah, yeah. Make the flight for Sunday, okay? I have a date Saturday and plan on having her stay over."

"Ooh. Keep Bobby far away. She'll demand proof of fertility."

"No kidding." He laughed this time. "I'm not looking forward to her annual 'when are you having a girl' pester either."

"Wait, you're getting a divorce. How are you supposed to get a daughter from the woman she hates more than me?"

"Kick," Bert groaned. "She doesn't hate you."

"Bobby had to marry Dad because of me. Plus I was born with curly brown hair, while she has perfect blonde hair. It's practically the same thing. You have no idea how much it helped you to favor her."

"What does your hair have to do with it?"

"That's what you took from my spiel? Today's products weren't around when we were little. To her, the stubborn, frizzy mess growing out of my head was proof of my obstinance."

"Damn. You two deserve a permanent separation."

Don't tempt me.

"Text me the flight info when you have it," he added softly.

My voice hitched, making me unable to speak.

"I know. Promise me you'll have a great December."

"Mm-hmm," was all I could manage.

"Love you too, sis."

As the Proverb said, my brother was born for adversity. We didn't come by it naturally, but I could breathe again with this burden about to be lifted. I could deal with the *momster* for a week.

I padded into my bedroom and sat in my new meditation corner. Instead of settling onto what I'd thought of as "my mind porch," my mind continued to race. Twenty minutes later, with my Christmas shopping list worked out in my head, attention drifted to Thomas, hoping he was having a pleasant visit.

Rachel tapped on my doorframe. She held up my phone. "Sorry about interrupting, but it's Thomas. I thought you might want to take it."

14

She's Always in My Hair

Thomas

THOMAS RELUCTANTLY ENTERED THE COFFEE SHOP IN DOWNTOWN Raleigh. He ordered a pour-over black and took in the Día de Los Muertos decor. The place had atmosphere. He'd give it that. Young professionals bustled about, giving it the opposite vibe of the Perked Cup. All the lower-level tables were filled by people with laptops. Thomas saw the staircase and guessed Banger was upstairs. He'd already sent a text stating he'd arrived. His friend sat at a corner table, and they spotted each other immediately.

"Hey man," Thomas said, feigning indifference. He pulled out the chair on the opposite side of the table with his foot and sat. A significantly smaller, albeit quieter, crowd hung out here. "Okay Lucy, 'splain."

"What? The location? The last-minute summons?" Banger inquired, looking ragged and gaunt.

"All of it. Is everything alright? How's Tess?"

Banger took a sip of coffee and blew out a slow breath. "She's safely settled at her retreat outside Boone. I don't want anyone knowing I'm back, which is why we're not meeting at Kick's. I'm trying to stay away from the north end of the county—officially anyway."

What the hell? "What's going on? Is this about Kick's attack?" It's what he had assumed when Banger left the urgent voice mail. Thomas's foot tapped double-time to the Latin music filling the space.

Banger nodded once. "Partly. I'll hold the details until she arrives. I have a question for you though. It's a completely different topic."

Thomas's foot paused. "Shoot."

"I've been going over the footage from Kick's. Liam's birthday —this Charley Rodriguez—"

Thomas tapped the table lightly. "Yes. She was at Thanksgiving. What about her?"

Banger lifted a shoulder as his eye narrowed. "I've known of her since some of our work overlaps. Anyway, something struck me as familiar and I didn't know why. So, I did some digging."

Thomas rolled his wrist to get Banger to move on.

"Her background checks out the way ours do."

"What's wrong with our background checks?"

"Not a thing, unless you know what to look for."

"And you think this woman is…"

"Not who she claims to be. Possibly one of us," Banger finished.

"Impossible," Thomas mused, rubbing his chin. "We'd know, wouldn't we?"

Banger shook his head. "Not necessarily. Look how long it took to find you."

"That was decades ago. Completely different times. There's no proof. Right?"

Banger raised his eyebrows, letting Thomas know he'd keep at it.

"Do you want me to do anything? Arrange a meeting? The lab is on the verge of—"

Banger raised his hand, cutting Thomas off. "I've got it. Just keep your girl close, okay?"

"Planning to." Thomas knew all of Banger's reservations about

Kick, still he couldn't hide his grin. It almost sounded like his friend was giving a blessing, despite them.

"Good. I don't like the weird coincidences happening around her."

Thomas thought he heard his friend mutter "menace," but Kick approached before he could say anything else. It didn't matter since Thomas's priorities shifted the night they went to the club.

"Mr. McHenry, are you trying to send a message about my coffee?" she asked as she sat between the men. The glint in her eyes told Thomas she was teasing his friend.

Banger actually gave her a little smile. "No. I have my reasons for meeting in a neutral place."

She took a sip of something Thomas assumed was decaf coffee. "I'll save you my 'don't you know how busy I am' rant since we all are. I assume this is life-and-death important."

Banger let out a cleansing breath. "There's news about who drugged you and your friend."

Kick's shoulders dropped. "I was kidding." She took another pull from her cup and leaned in. "Okay, let's hear it."

Thomas braced. Cameras were notoriously unclear and often turned off. If they didn't have answers soon, he might lose it.

"The main camera at the upstairs bar had been mysteriously turned off."

Kick tilted her chin. "Cyndi bought our drinks downstairs."

Banger tapped the side of his temple and pointed at her. "And there's footage of him adding something to those glasses. Both drinks were tainted, which is why your friend had it worse than you. Plus she drank more alcohol before it happened."

Kick scrunched her nose and Thomas couldn't tell if it was from anger or guilt. He reached under the table and squeezed her hand.

"There's more," Banger added.

"Lovely."

Banger slid a still photo in front of Kick.

"Here's the John Bender look-alike." Thomas leaned over her shoulder and agreed, not that he knew the character. He recognized the bartender.

"Right. Do you know the other guy?"

She shook her head, but her back stiffened. Her gaze whipped to Thomas as her brows drew together.

He rubbed her arm. "You're safe now."

Banger continued. "This was before Cyndi bought the drinks." He slid the photo to the middle of their four-top and laid two new ones in its place. "We think this is him with you, Kick."

She gasped and looked away. "It looks a lot like my messy hair." She inhaled deep and turned back. "The last photo showed the same man near the front door. It fit with Cyndi's description of him storming out of the place when Kick didn't cooperate."

"His grungy beard and effect is quite lycanesque. Looks like Detective Ross correctly interpreted my odd memory of fighting off a werewolf."

Without thinking, Thomas leaned forward and growled. "Dammit! Who is this guy?"

Banger whipped his head around and shushed him. "The management at Ducky's has fully cooperated. They're pissed. Your detective questioned the bartender. Turns out he's young Graham's cousin, but—"

Thomas interrupted. "Daddy Graham's lawyer is his lawyer now."

"Ding, ding, ding." Banger finished his coffee and leaned back in his chair. "It ties him to Halloween, so he's a person of interest, but he's not in custody. He admitted knowing your wolf-man."

Kick shivered. "Please don't call him mine."

"Right. Sorry." Banger tapped the table while Thomas gave Kick's hand another squeeze. "Anyway, my people dug more and found out where Wolfy works. Any guesses?"

Thomas ran his hand over his face. Could it be this easy? "Graham Construction?"

"Give the man a prize."

"No." Kick gasped, her eyes wide. "Does Big Jonn know about this?"

"Working on it. The guy's in the wind though. Since the

bartender is family, how could he not know? Oh, I almost forgot the best part—"

Kick's hand went to her forehead. "How can there be a best to any of this?" Banger stared at her for a minute, so she rolled her hand. "Lay it on us."

"The cousin has the same tattoo as young Graham."

Kick's brow furrowed. "Does that mean he beat up my squawk box?"

Banger and Thomas shrugged. Thomas knew the answer before he heard it. "He's still a person of interest. Thanks to counsel, he's not saying anything."

"JaysusMaryandJoseph." She tucked some hair behind both ears, then grasped her hands behind her neck, letting her elbows fall to the table.

Banger lifted a shoulder. "My sentiments exactly." He tapped the table again, getting Kick's attention. "My team's on it. *I'm* on it. In fact, I'm leaving after this to chase down a lead."

Thomas brushed a curl off Kick's cheek. "You're my priority now too."

She frowned at him. "You don't have to choose."

"Kids," Banger said. "Deal with this later. I have a request before I go."

"Anything," Kick said, her face determined.

Banger turned to Thomas. "This is for you, brother. Will you feed my fish? I ran out of those vacation feeding tablets. If you pick up some and stop by once, my assistant, Siobhan, can do the rest when she gets back from her own mission."

Kick pursed her lips. "How long will you be gone?"

Banger collected the photos and answered, "I don't know." He looked back at Thomas. "I'll probably fly directly to France for the holidays. But I only need this week."

Wherever this lead came from, it must have been moving quickly. Banger rarely ended up hanging like this.

Thomas nodded his support, but Kick said, "Could Rachel help you?" She lifted her hands as the men's mouths opened. "She's coming up on finals and could use time away from—"

"The breakup drama," Banger guessed.

The corner of her mouth ticked up as she agreed with him.

Banger pinched his lower lip. "If the princess wants, she could stay at my condo. I'll give you the code."

Thomas tried to study his friend without him or Kick noticing. Where was this coming from? It took years for Banger to take on Siobhan as a right hand. "Bang—"

The man made a swiping motion as if he knew Thomas's concerns. "She's a good kid and could use the peace. Besides, I don't like how often the brats in her building prop open the exterior doors. They have no sense of responsibility."

Kick winced and frowned at Banger's words. She didn't ask for clarification, and Thomas chalked it up to her motherly worries. He didn't think she already knew Banger had cameras of questionable legality pointed at Rachel's building. Then again, she also didn't know they'd been on her street for weeks too.

"Aren't you taking the kids to the mountains for Christmas?" Thomas asked her.

Before she could answer, Banger said, "Have your daughter call my assistant when she doesn't need the place anymore."

Kick gave him a grateful, slightly adoring smile. Thomas knew it well. He wanted to know it better.

Banger's chair scraped the floor as he stood. "Well, guys, I'm off. If you need anything, you know to call Siobhan. She's me while I'm gone. I'll check in with her when I can."

Thomas grabbed the sleeve of his friend's jacket. "Thanks, man. I don't have to tell you to stay safe."

"I'm always careful." Banger shrugged. "No guarantees on safe." He took a step and turned back. "See you in Bordeaux?"

Thomas shook his head. "Just Virginia this year." He patted Kick's hand. "I have other plans for the break."

He adored Kick's pretty pink blush.

Banger dropped his chin, pivoted on his heel, and took off down the stairs.

Thomas moved to stand, and Kick cleared her throat. "Wait a minute."

He scooted back in and waited for her.

"Why do you act like you have to choose between me and your career—like it's one or the other?"

Thanks to the Felidae, it was. He sighed.

"Thomas," she soothed, "this isn't an either/or. We don't have normal dates, unless you call greenway walks, shooting lessons, and rides home from IV appointments dates." They both chuckled. "You've been good for me and my family. Why can't I be good for your career?"

She rubbed his forearm, which made her sweater run up and expose her bruises. The added IV from the emergency department meant her usual arm hadn't had time to recover. He hated how she looked like she'd been beaten. Had he been good for her? It didn't feel like it. At least Banger's team had made progress.

Thomas made himself focus on her words. "You are doing better with the airsoft gun. I want you to move back to the Sig the next time we practice."

She clicked her tongue. "That's what you took from my speech?"

They both laughed as Kick swatted his bicep. She made a sweet, swooning noise he'd noticed she did when his rumbly laughs stayed low in his chest. How he liked the sound *she* made.

Thomas rubbed his neck and said, "Alright, darlin'. I'll think about your speech."

"Good. I want to see you succeed, Thomas."

"You do, don't you?"

Kick blinked at him a few times. "Of course. I hope one day you'll be able to tell me all the details, because it sounds like you're working on something huge."

He hoped like hell he could tell Kick everything too. The real question was, how would she take it?

15

I Melt with You

Kick

THOMAS PARKED HIS CAMARO IN FRONT OF MICK & HUGH'S, walked around the passenger side, and opened the door. I growled as he bent down, like he intended to pick me up. Then I almost laughed as he jumped back, leaving me room to step out of the car.

His concern touched me. Deeply. But having had the "stiff upper lip" drilled into me from an early age, I couldn't get past the visual of being carried into the smoke shop. Once again, Bobby's admonition about how nobody wanted to hear (or see) my sob story came to mind. As I had already told Thomas, as cruel as her words had been, they were also right. Add the harassment of me, my family, and my business, and it also felt like eyes were following me wherever I went. Someone on the community social media page had already posted a photo of my bruised forearm, implying it was proof I used drugs. I uninstalled the app from my phone right after seeing it.

"I'm sore and stupid tired, but I'm not an invalid, Thomas." *Jaysus,* how I wished I could curl into my sweater and take a nap in his front seat. I stuck a foot onto the asphalt and pushed up. "Thank you, though." When I took a step, I swear my foot refused to work, forcing me to reach for the roof of the car. I sighed in frustration. Maybe I should've brought a cane with me. "I suppose a girl might use an arm."

Thomas smiled at me in the same way I used to smile at my toddlers, who didn't enjoy asking for help. Without a word, he wrapped an arm around my waist and propped me up against his side as if we were simply walking into the smoke shop like a devoted couple.

"Katie, you came," Hugh called out after Thomas opened the door. "Dylan told me you had one of your appointments this morning. I was about to call and make sure you still planned on decorating today."

No surprise to anyone I'd overbooked. The IV treatments had been easing up when it came to knocking me out, until I'd been drugged—yeah, it was time I stopped dancing around our girl's-night-out fiasco and called it what it was. My doctor had added something to the medicine bag to help my liver recover, and my body felt like it was back at square one. I hoped it would go by quickly.

There were also multiple reasons I wanted to stop by the smoke shop. After kissing Uncle Hugh's cheek, I told him, "I'll decorate for you after I take a nap in Dad's recliner. I have some samples for you too. Remember?"

"Oh right." He followed Thomas and me to the office as the three of us passed Dylan behind the counter. I smiled at my son, both from gratitude that he hadn't left Hugh hanging in order to finish his thesis and to reassure him I was fine. Dylan had cut his hours significantly, but it still helped Hugh. I was sure he would have sold the shop outright if my son had left him all alone.

Before dropping into my father's raggedy yet comfy chair in the back office, I pulled some CBD ointments and lotions out of my tote bag and spread them out on his old desk, gesturing for Hugh to look them over.

Thomas took the blanket from the back of the chair and opened it. He tipped his head, silently commanding me to sit. I gladly obeyed this time.

He tucked the blanket around me. "Why are you recovering in this ratty thing?" he asked with a chuckle, sounding both confused and sexy.

My jaw cracked on a yawn. "Carmen brought in extra help today so they can deep clean. If I tried to sleep, they would tiptoe around the house and struggle to get it done right while I worried about making them mess up their big job." I smacked my lips together, hating the cottonmouth the treatments caused. "And I promised Hugh I'd decorate the shop for him."

Uncle Hugh looked down at me sheepishly and quietly said, "You have a better eye for it than I do."

I reached for and squeezed his hand. I'd done the holiday decorating since the store opened and had a system. "I know. After my nap, I'll be good to go." My tongue practically stuck to my cheek, and I turned my focus to Thomas. "Would you mind getting me a water bottle from the fridge? It's in an alcove in the back hallway. Hard to miss."

He kissed my forehead, and my sore body relaxed. "You got it. Be right back."

"Okay, Hugh, check out this stuff." I pointed at the jars and tube on his desk. "I think you should stock these, but try them out first. You know, like you do with cigars."

"You don't want me to smoke these though."

I ignored the bad joke and opened one of the jars of the salve instead. I held it up and demonstrated. "Scoop out a small bit and rub it into your hands. Pay special attention to your arthritis spots." Hugh did as told with an open curiosity.

"It's a little warm." He sniffed his hand. "Smells nice too, Katie. Not girly."

I nodded as I finished rubbing mine into my elbow. "You could sell it now since there's no THC in it. Your notes suggested an interest in focusing your expansion on using cannabis for health issues over recreation."

Hugh's eyes lit up. "That's the idea."

"Around here, it's a good tack. You'll want recreation products, but you could still emphasize aspects like relaxation, energy, and such." I held up the jar. "I've been using this for years—ever since my doctor told me to stop taking acetaminophen. I use it on sore muscles too. Mostly my back."

He smiled widely. "I knew you would be the perfect partner for this."

Hugh asked about the other products, and I filled him in on terms like full-spectrum CBD and CBG, among other things. I thought the lotion would be perfect for his wife, Maggie.

"You think this will help us get the license?"

"Absolutely." I screwed the lid on the jar and put it back with the others. "Take them home and try them. Hell, you and Maggie should take notes. I'll email you some websites you can study for more information. The board will appreciate it. Knowing them, though, you'll go far if you have a ready-made clientele who love these and might be curious about trying stronger things."

As I wondered where Thomas had disappeared to, he returned with three bottles. I opened one and chugged half of it. I set it on the desk with an audible sigh of relief. "You're my hero."

Hugh tapped my foot. "Are you sure you're set to decorate later?"

I did my best to give him a confident smile, hoping he couldn't see through to the truth. "It'll be ready tomorrow."

"It'll be perfect." Hugh placed the jars and tube in his briefcase on the opposite side of the office. He zipped it and took it with him. "Thank you, dear." He strutted out of the room with more pep than I'd seen him have in a while.

Thomas's gaze followed him out. "What did you give Hugh?"

I lifted a shoulder. The little movement hurt, and I wished I had more of the salve in my bag. "A CBD-CBG salve for his arthritis."

"It must've been a miracle."

"Naw." I laughed. "The hope did that." I switched to a whisper. "I think Dad's death scared him about leaving Maggie alone. He's betting on setting her up with the cannabis profits."

"Can it work?"

I shrugged. "Possibly. Other than a medical issue, Hugh and Maggie have little overhead. Not like someone raising kids."

"Like you," Thomas suggested.

I closed my eyes and leaned back, thinking of how many more years of college tuition payments I had ahead of me. Then I wondered if Liam would ever get around to applying anywhere. "Don't remind me." At least my family had the buffer of our inheritance. My mind drifted to the families the McKenna Foundation helped. I hoped we helped them enough to ease their worries.

My aching feet finally yelled at me loud enough to get my attention, and I shifted in the chair.

"What's the matter, baby?"

I shifted the blanket, hoping it would help. I scrunched my nose. "Would you mind helping me with my feet?"

"Are your shoes too tight?"

I shook my head and ended up stretching my neck. "No. The more the medicine works, the sorer my muscles get."

"Sure." Thomas wheeled an office chair over by the footrest. His hand traveled along my calf, gently squeezing, resulting in one of those sensations of pain that feels so good.

I opened my eyes when his massage stopped and saw the grin spread across his face.

"What?"

Thomas's face filled with warmth, showing me the real him. "You and your boots."

"They're moccasins, not boots." As comfortable as crocs without the hideous style. "They're usually comfortable." I shifted farther as he removed them. "Nothing's comfortable at the moment."

"How's this?" Thomas rubbed small circles along my Achilles tendon and over the top of my foot.

"It's heaven." I smiled at my weirdly dreamy voice, barely recognizing it as my own. Thomas's touch transformed something in me, especially since the attack. When we found common time to be together, he seemed to make sure he touched me as much as possible even if it only meant holding hands.

To distract myself from an entirely inappropriate arousal—why hadn't I rescheduled the deep clean? I asked him, "What took so long getting the water?" I finished the first bottle and dabbed at my mouth with my sweater cuff.

Thomas sighed as if he had to steady himself. "Dylan cornered me about us—I'm a bit shocked because I thought it was obvious we were together."

"Well—" I could relate to my son. I guess we both wanted formal declarations. The lad probably thought more about his own pain, though, and wanted to make sure I was settled. He'd taken on too much after his father died—of his own accord, but I could see where he would need reassurances.

Thomas kept his focus on a troubling spot on my instep. "You know you're my priority now, right?"

"Sure, sweets—" He hit a potent spot, making me groan. The pleasure raced through me, almost as intense as an orgasm. It took my breath away.

I looked up, and Thomas's eyes had glazed over. *JaysusMaryandJoseph*, why hadn't I had the foresight to be doing this in my bedroom or his? Because I was a distracted, overthinking idiot, that's why.

Thomas's thumb stuck on a spot I'd swore felt like a rock under my skin. I gasped and might have done more, but my brain fuzzed.

"Seriously?" Dylan stuck his head through the doorway and scolded us. "I can hear you. You're creeping out the customers. Me too."

Thomas's hands sprang away from me as if he'd been shocked. His eyes dropped to the floor as he panted, like he was struggling to catch his breath.

Hell. Would I ever get "me time" that didn't involve a nap? I bit my lip. "Sorry, son. The medicine is wreaking havoc on my body. Thomas's foot rub helps the pain, but I'll be good. I promise."

Dylan squinted but nodded and shut the door.

"I should stop," Thomas said, though he had resumed stroking my shins.

I shook my head. "I should've known the spot would be tender.

My hands don't have your strength, so I've never had such an intense reaction to it."

He switched back to small circles with light pressure. "What do you mean you should've known?"

"It's been a while since I dabbled in acupressure, so my memory of the foot map is a bit faded, but I think you hit the spot for the liver. The liver area is always tender." I sat back and let out a cleansing breath. "I promise to behave."

"Christ, darlin', you kill me," he said with a slight laugh and exhale of his own.

"How so?"

Thomas rubbed my foot over his jeans, letting me feel his entire erection. He closed his eyes and shifted in the chair while I flexed my toes, wishing I could do more. So much more.

"Damn, baby."

"That's my line," he rasped with a smile in his tone. "I wish I could take you right to my bed right now, but I'm going straight back to the lab from here."

Despite our desires, it sounded like neither of us had figured out how to work the other into our lives yet.

"If you took me anywhere in your car, I would fall sound asleep before we arrived anyway."

"Then I should probably go." He rolled his chair closer to me and kissed me long and gently. It made the desire worse, but it helped to be on a similar page. "Is the pain better?"

Was he kidding? I might have been floating above the chair. "Much. Thank you." My jaw popped again on a long yawn. "I swear it isn't you."

I reached for Thomas's neck to give him a hug, and the gauze bandage I'd forgotten to remove pulled on my sweater sleeve. I rolled it up to unpeel everything. "Can't wait until these are through."

"What the hell happened now?" Thomas exclaimed. He grabbed my wrist and examined my entire forearm while I wished hard to be invisible. The embarrassing paparazzi-like photos came to mind. This was worse than those had been.

I dropped my arm and my shoulders. "A new tech worked in the treatment room today." When he simply stared at me like my explanation said nothing, I continued, "In some ways, starting a line is like an art. My vein blew out with half the bag left. She had to"—I didn't know why this embarrassed me so, but I hated it and took a deep breath to continue—"thump my arm to make another vein surface. My regular arm is still healing."

"Goddammit." Thomas pulled my hand to his lips and kissed along the bruises, reminding me of Gomez Addams. Only I wished I had Morticia's badass confidence.

"I didn't mean to whine," I said. "I might only need four more."

"Is it helping?"

I nodded and thought ahead to when I could have all-day energy again.

"Good. Let me tuck you in."

I sat back and drank down the second water bottle as Thomas made quick work of my other foot. I made a break for the restroom, then let him wrap me back up in the blanket, ready for an hour of peace.

He gave me another panty-melting kiss. When Thomas pulled away, he was flushed as he dropped his forehead to mine.

"I feel like a tease," I confessed.

"Whatever for? I initiated the kiss and the foot rubs. I like it when you let me take care of you."

"Well, I don't like leaving you frustrated."

"I'm not."

Right. I could see the bulge. Hell, it looked Photoshopped, even though I knew it wasn't.

I let my gaze travel from Thomas's face to below his waist and back, then raised my brows to let him know I didn't believe him.

"I'm a grown man, not a boy, darlin'. I'll be fine when I walk out of here. In fact, I'll float, thanks to you."

I'd almost run out of my last bit of energy and needed to get on with the napping. I lifted my hand to Thomas's chin and gently stroked the cleft in his chin. If I dreamed about anything, I hoped it would be about his kisses. I smiled against his mouth as we kissed one last time. "You're like an early Christmas present."

"Then I'll wear a bow the next time I see you."

Please let that be code for we'll have sex again soon.

I SAT ON THE MEDITATION PORCH IN MY MIND, CLEARING AWAY THE naptime cobwebs. In real life, I was sitting in my father's recliner, legs crossed under me, hoping I did meditation correctly. It relaxed me. Energized me too. I considered both a victory. One of these days, I'd look into finding an actual meditation coach. Or a guru. In the meantime, whatever this place could be called, it worked. At least it did until the noise level on the other side of the door disturbed my peace.

I opened my eyes to find the glow had returned. However, multiple colors shifted around me instead of the light blue color it had been. I didn't have time to ponder what it meant since a commotion had clearly been growing outside. I flapped my hands and shimmied my body, willing it to fade. It had long stopped frightening me, probably because I always felt better after it appeared. As long as I was alone when it happened, I usually let it flow because it also reminded me of a warm, friendly hug.

Someday soon I planned to get an energy reading. Someone in that line of work should help me understand it all. At the moment, it stayed another item on an unending to-do list.

I stepped into the salesroom, ready to complain about the noise in a mom voice but discovered a literal crowd staring me down. A half dozen customers—then again, reading their frowns, probably not—stood in the center of the space, holding signs and chanting, "Don't buy from immoral businesses." Someone else threw in "Jesus is the reason for the season," which seemed oddly random.

I wanted to reply that axial tilt was the actual reason for the season but thought better of it when I saw my clearly exasperated son. Dylan had his hands in front of him, trying to push the crowd back outside without touching anyone. Thank goodness he'd kept his head. My son had a history of fighting and winning. He was a big man, which sometimes meant hotheads tried to provoke him to prove their own manliness. Given our present circumstances, I didn't want him dragged into the fray.

I moved to the area behind the counter, seeking some distance. I whistled, then called out, "Let me guess: this has something to do with the opinion piece in the paper? If you have questions, I'm willing to—"

A familiar woman with a pin-straight, bleached, stacked bob pointed at me and declared, "Look at her arms. I told you she shoots up."

My gaze dropped to my forearms. Sure enough, I had pushed up the sleeves, probably from warming up while sleeping. Well, hell. I hastily pulled my sweater sleeves down and bunched the cuffs into my fists. I wanted to tell her an actual addict is better at hiding the track marks, but I wasn't sure if it was true. It wouldn't have mattered anyway.

I stared at the countertop, wishing I could clean it. *Inhale for four. Hold for four. Exhale for five… Again.*

In my periphery, I saw someone outside edge onto the sidewalk, carrying a long gun. *Oh, hell no.* I really should have rescheduled Carmen and her crew. I might've been able to convince Thomas to stay with me for the afternoon. Murphy's Law struck again.

Moving to the end of the counter, I planted my feet and crossed my arms, my jaw set. "Lock the door Dylan." The last thing we needed was someone bringing a rifle into Hugh's store.

"You can't hold us against our will!" Blonde bob yelled. I thought I recognized her from Liam's track meets.

"No one's keeping you here. You folks refused to leave when Dylan asked you to leave. Now, *that* is illegal, plus you're turning my friend's store into a fire hazard." I pointed to a sign over the door. "The shop also has a no-gun policy. I'm not about to let you risk a good man's livelihood over lies in a newspaper."

The man next to the blonde said, "I told you this place was immoral too. I heard the big guy's her son. Bet he does drugs too."

I rolled my eyes and took a cleansing breath, afraid to move anything else. Dylan's high school football record was still spoken of around town. I wondered if these people lived in Oakville, aside from blonde bob woman. *Jayz*, I wanted to hit someone. I wiggled my fingers to make them relax.

This group definitely didn't want to hear my sob story. Without letting my gaze leave the crowd, I ignored the accusations and said, "Anyone who wants to leave can go out the back with Dylan." I tipped my head toward the front. "This door stays locked for now."

The noise volume ticked back up with the theme of me infringing on their rights, not the other way around.

I pulled my phone out and texted Jake at the Perked Cup.

ME

A hyped-up crowd won't leave Hugh's. Can you spare anyone to help? By anyone, I mean you.

I loved having a strapping young veteran in my corner. This kind of situation didn't faze him. He texted back quickly.

JAKE

Sorry, Mrs. Mack. The same group sent people in here first. I pressed the emergency button when someone broke a coffeepot. You should do the same. OPD will be here soon.

More hell. I jumped up to see over the crowd. Sure enough, a mob actually picketed in front of my coffeehouse. My blood boiled at the thought of someone marching behind the service area and scaring my staff—again. Plus why the hell did people consider breaking my stuff a viable option?

I texted back.

ME

Will do. However, if Liam's there, don't let him explode. Lock him in your office if you have to.

Jake texted back a thumbs-up. I worried about Lee more than I did Dylan.

After pocketing my phone, I pressed the button under the counter, then stood on a nearby chair and yelled, "The police are on their way, so I suggest you get the hell out now." I pointed at a camera. "We already have evidence of who's done what this afternoon."

Instead of scaring them off, the people resumed chanting, "Don't buy from immoral businesses."

Like clockwork, I heard the police sirens. The added honking told me they were at the intersection near our shopping center. All but three in the crowd rushed toward the back, and Dylan urged them to stay calm while he opened the door.

The remaining people faced me while the crowd outside stopped pounding on the windows and turned around, holding up their signs as the police cruisers arrived.

My hands dropped to my waist as I took in another long breath.

"Stay strong," an older, portly man said to the other two. "We'll shut her down soon. Cara, you'll have the coffee shop by the New Year."

My head snapped up. "Excuse me? On what grounds? You clearly don't understand the concept of a lease agreement." Or how good my lawyer was.

Old portly held up a hand and counted off. "We know you broke the agreement. You dealt drugs there. They were found in your diner."

"I called the police myself when I found them. And it's not a diner."

"Exactly. Y'all serve weird food, not American stuff. What's a scone? My granddaughter said it's European."

I threw my hands in the air. "It's coffee, pastries, and sandwiches. If you don't like excellent coffee, go somewhere else. No one's forcing anybody to use my café… or Hugh's shop."

"There's my point." He held up a second and third finger. "You lure our children into unholy thinking. It's bad enough you put them in danger on Halloween. You teach them your wrong ways every afternoon."

"The kids do their homework in a safe, monitored environment… if they want to."

"We have issues with their homework too." The man moved his index in a circular motion. "You're all swirled together. In cahoots."

For feck's sake. A thought sparked, cluing me into what might've been the source of their rage. "Are you upset over me caring about kids who aren't my own? Or is it the diversity tutoring after school?"

An exceptional children's teacher at the high school had started the group in September. It had something to do with the school not being able to sanction a program that would only benefit a minority of students. An off-campus group could zero in on disadvantaged kids who would benefit from time with a peer tutor. It had to do with economics more than race, but there was an overlap of both. Of course I'd jumped all over sponsoring it. It had the added benefit of helping kids from different backgrounds get to know each other better than they would have while surrounded by their normal peers.

"It's not natural."

I inhaled sharply as the man hit my last nerve, but a team of officers knocked on the door and saved me from chewing him out.

Grateful for the reprieve, I stepped over to the door and flipped the lock. I hoped this wouldn't affect Hugh's ability to secure the cannabis license. I wondered if it was why he'd been dragged into my harassment. The crowd wouldn't object to selling cigars. Hell, we lived in tobacco country. Our neighborhood was built on former tobacco fields, and yet drive five minutes in any direction, and you'd pass land still growing it. Cannabis, however, was a different story.

What I wouldn't give for Thomas to show up and save the day like he'd done with Jonn Graham. I wouldn't yell at him. I'd kiss him in front of anyone. Well, what do you know? In the middle of the chaos, I realized Thomas had become my safe place. His new declarations about priorities had done the trick.

At least I had the upcoming Christmas gala to keep me hopeful.

Spending time with the McKenna Foundation families and Thomas together would fill my spirit bucket that this crowd threatened to drain. Add in my plans for some sexy times at my house after the presentation—Liam was spending the night at a friend's—and I could forget all about this afternoon.

16

King of Pain

Thomas

THOMAS COLLAPSED INTO HIS BED, EAGER FOR THE SERENITY OF sleep. He'd spent many nights sleeping cramped up on the love seat in his office, pulling his weight with round-the-clock shifts in the lab. The only time he took for himself was the hours spent with Kick, making sure she made progress with her health, getting to know her and her family better.

The anger over her drugging, right under his nose, hadn't lessened. Thomas hoped Banger's silence equaled good news. His friend had a way of disappearing only to return right before a major story broke around the world. The last time he'd done it, a prominent drug lord turned up dead. Then Banger pulled into town with a smile and light step. It's why Thomas trusted him to get Kick out of danger, and he allowed himself to be the one comforting her when a riled-up crowd caused more trouble like they'd done the day before.

He fell asleep to the memory of her laughing after dinner. Knowing he could lift her spirit—and Liam's—did the same to his own. The next thing he knew, Thomas found himself back in the trenches and smelling the noxious gas. Instead of trying to breathe it in like he usually did, he pinched his nose and ran to get away from it. He didn't care about the angel he used to wait for anymore. He ran to find Kick, realizing she'd become his safety. As dreams often do, in the next instance, Thomas sat on a veranda in the desert, his Uncle Theo next to him, pride in his eyes.

Thomas dropped his head, unable to keep looking at another person he hadn't protected. As if Theo knew Thomas's thoughts, the man gave his shoulder a good shove.

"Get over yourself, boy. I'm not here to yell." Theo dropped his voice to a soothing, fatherly tone. "I want to tell you I'm proud."

Thomas had respected his father, but Uncle Theo had been the father of his heart. When he'd searched Thomas out during a very dark time, their bond had become unbreakable, even when Theo would take off for years at a time. But did he forgive Thomas for what had happened?

Before Thomas could ask, Theo said, "It's my fault a cannon ball killed me, not yours." The old man chuckled. "If anything, I blame myself for stepping in front of the damn thing."

Thomas blew out a deep breath in relief. "Thank you." So much weight lifted with those two words. Thomas had spent enough years with the Felidae to know some of the members carried enough energy to travel between the physical and the metaphysical world. He'd always hoped Uncle Theo possessed that freedom, but this was the first time they'd spoken since the horrible night he'd died.

"I needed this, Theo."

As if reading his mind again, the old man said, "I know. That's not why I'm here though."

Thomas wondered if someone was in trouble, his breath catching on the intake as Kick flashed through his mind.

Theo shook his head and reached for Thomas's shoulder. "Untwist your britches, son. Your work… your cousins can help."

Thomas's brow furrowed. "Cousins? You mean you…"

Theo smiled and tilted his head. "Yes, boy." He looked out over the expanse. "I believe we're on my old balcony—well, my wife's family's veranda—the way the house was built into a hill. It's a bit of both."

"Y-you had more children… after—"

"Yes." Theo dipped his chin. "They're like *us* too."

How was that possible? He had never mentioned children back then.

Uncle Theo lifted a shoulder. "I didn't feel worthy of raising them. I couldn't handle seeing another family age without me."

So, there were more subjects to study? Thomas rubbed his forehead, both excited and perplexed. *Where would he find these people? Did they have families?*

Theo spread his arms wide. "Start with this estate, I guess. Sorry, son. I'm new at this."

If Thomas did his math right, Theo had been gone for years. How many were there?

"Two."

Christ. He jumped at the words. So Uncle Theo could read thoughts. The last thing Thomas wanted to do was yell at the father of his heart. He missed the man dearly.

Theo's big hand raised up and dropped onto Thomas's knee, squeezing. "I agree. Let's say we sit quietly and rock for a spell."

At the moment, Thomas wanted nothing more.

The next morning, Thomas rang up the house in Virginia. This wasn't a call to make from the road. He wanted to keep his head in case he didn't get the answer he hoped for.

"Hey, Joe, how are y'all holding up? Are we doing the holiday open house or going low key this year?" The Harrison estate was part family home and part historical landmark. He and Joe used to cater brunches for the locals during the holidays. Between his progress at the lab and with Kick, then seeing his uncle—he'd been surprised to discover he remembered it all—Thomas felt like he was walking on a cloud.

"Let's go low key. Toni's not ready for the hoopla. She found out she can spend Christmas Day with Ken. It lifted her mood tenfold when his caretakers passed on the news."

Thomas shared the joy. Watching Toni deal with her husband's battle with Alzheimer's felt like witnessing a slow-motion crash. His heart perpetually broke for them and soared for their small victories, like this one. "Wonderful news."

Some silence passed before he found his courage. Joe had become quite the homebody. "Hey, I called to ask what y'all would think of coming down with me for a few days after Christmas. There's someone I'd like you to meet."

"What kind of someone?"

Thomas didn't blame Joe for making him spell it out. He hadn't even introduced Vivienne to the family.

"It's a woman, Joe. Someone I've grown fond of. She's—"

"What has your precious Alaric said about her?"

Thomas's eyes squeezed tight. This was why he'd made the call before heading out. "He said to pursue other interests and—"

"There's no way he'll allow this, Thomas."

"As long as I keep my vow, it's none of his business." Thomas walked out onto the back deck to cool off. He watched the sunrise through barren trees. The warm, vibrant colors mixing with the foreground reminded him of Kick's hair. He had to find a way to make his worlds exist in peace.

In a clipped, gruff voice, Joe warned, "I won't run interference this time."

"What are you talking about? What interference?"

"Can you honestly tell me you didn't know they watched her the whole time? Alaric was obsessed with it." Joe cleared his throat. Thomas sensed his emotion growing, like he wanted to yell, but reined it in. "Why do you think I left the Felidae anyway?"

"I don't know, Joey. You won't tell me."

"The Felidae made orders to kill Vivienne if anyone found proof you'd broken your vow of secrecy. They protect the Society above all else."

Thomas fell back into an Adirondack chair. *Did it matter? What did they think would happen if my research was successful?* He thought back to the early days in the Felidae. No one ever asked him about his personal life, and he didn't see the need to volunteer anything. "You can't tell me they expect me to live like a monk." Of course not. *Grand-père* practically told him to go find a girlfriend.

Instead of answering his question, Joe laid it all out. "They ordered me to spy on Vivienne and kill her if I found evidence she knew about the Society. Or about you. So I left. I made sure she was safe. Then I told the old man to fuck off."

Thomas pressed a hand to his chest in a sad attempt to stop his heart from pounding so hard. He wondered out loud, "What do they think will happen with my research? If it works, everything will come out."

"I don't know, and I don't care," Joe snapped back. "As long as y'all leave me and Toni alone. The horses and the estate are all I want from the world now. If everything goes public, leave us out of it. At least until Toni is stable enough to make her own decisions."

"Hang on." Thomas redirected. "Do you think the Felidae will harm Kick—that's the name of the woman I wanted y'all to meet." Apparently, he had already changed his mind. "I mean, without confronting me first?"

An exasperated exhale came through the phone. Thomas's hands started shaking, so he pulled his Bluetooth out of his pocket and activated it, hoping to finish the call without dropping his phone. He had enough to worry about.

"I love you, man," Joe began. "You've had my back for as long as I can remember. You know I begin and end with family. I don't give a shit about changing the world. But you've always had an arrogant cluelessness about you. I just didn't know how deep it went. I figured you *knew* about the surveillance and that was why you stayed away from Viv so much."

Thomas scoffed. "We weren't a close couple. Not sure if you could call us a couple at all."

His voice much softer now, Joe said, "To answer your original question, I would like to meet this woman who seems to have miraculously found a way into your heart. It'd be nice to meet someone normal for a change. It'll be better for everyone if y'all come up to the estate though."

"She's taking her kids to the mountains for Christmas and can't get away after either. She runs her own business."

"Kids?" Joe barked a laugh. "Now I know you've gone off the deep end. Tell me something. Does Banger know about this woman?"

"He does. His company is in charge of her security." Thomas hadn't explained it right, but he was too frazzled to fix his meaning or to explain further. "Why?"

"Who do you think took the Vivienne assignment after me? It didn't end with me. It never ended."

Dammit all.

Suddenly chilled to the bone, Thomas went inside his house and poured himself two fingers of bourbon. With as few words as he could manage, he ended the call after assuring Joe he'd be there for Christmas dinner.

He watched the backyard descend into blackness along with his mood. His cluelessness about Vivienne was arrogance, as Joe had said. He hadn't loved Viv enough to protect her at all costs. There was the indictment.

Was all this effort to protect Kick and her family a waste? Was his frustration with how long it took to get intel on the drugging simply folly? The harassment played out like a stupid, public frenzy with Kick as a scapegoat. If needed, she could move. She'd done it before. He knew, without a doubt, Banger would make the bartender and his accomplice pay even if the police couldn't.

But did Thomas put Kick in more danger? He obsessed over the possibility he might be the downfall of the woman he'd fallen for. Yeah, he knew he loved her already. What would he do about it though?

Diamonds and Pearls?

Kick

"SETTLE DOWN SO I CAN FINISH THIS UPDO." RACHEL CLUCKED HER tongue at me. "I don't remember you ever being this fidgety." She worked an asymmetrical french braid around the right side of my head and rolled pieces of lower curls into a loose bun at the nape. The result made small bits of curly fringe edging the look. I loved the romantic style.

"It's her hawt daaate," her roommate, Isabella, sang with a cute, throaty flutter.

"Right," I protested. "It has nothing to do with giving a ginormous, super important fundraising presentation for the first time in years." I sighed to release the stress and smirked. The talk wasn't the source of my nerves. Sharing about our foundation families came easily, and I wished I could take the floor longer to highlight all of them. If I had to deal with a handsy director to help them, it was worth it, especially with Thomas at my side.

No, I itched for alone time with Thomas. At this point, our first night together seemed like a dream, given the circumstances of throwing us together after the attack. Tonight would be different.

We were different. I'd been planning our own after-party for days, and I wanted it to be perfect.

Rachel secured the last bit of hair to the bun and spun me around to face my mirror as I grabbed my glasses to survey her work. For the first time since I'd picked up the progressive frames, I wished I'd ordered contacts. I silently cursed my eyes for getting older. The blurriness was harder to accept than cracking knees and thinning eyebrows. I thought about Thomas's perfect vision and deflated some.

"Are you listening, Mama?"

I shook my head, embarrassed at being self-focused when Rachel had given up her last Saturday of the semester to help me get ready. "I'm sorry, Snow. What'd you say?"

She tilted her head as if trying to decipher my thoughts. *Let it go, sweetie. You're too young to understand.* "I said it's time for makeup. Are you sure you don't want to get into your dress first?"

"No. My dress is a wrap, like my robe. I'd feel better leaving it to the end."

"But I can't remember where to have the makeup stop."

I looked down. "I'd say do the whole décolletage. The neckline is open." Very open.

"Okay, then." She turned to my kit and pulled out products, then set to work, gooping me up. "What's this stuff?" she asked, a tiny vial held between her fingers.

"Dab a little on the under eye, and it deflates the bags while lightening dark spots."

"Huh." She squinted to read the ingredients. Maybe it wasn't only me. "Can't wait to see how it works."

I settled back into the chair and closed my eyes. "Remember, this isn't a swanky awards show."

"Shush. Photographers will be there. They always are." Her voice dropped in the way it did when someone focused on two things at once. "You and Thomas will be in all the area newspapers, along with Lord University materials, I'm sure."

"Good point," I whined, already imagining how bad my photos would look. Add in Thomas next to me, and I wanted to cancel the whole thing. *Humble yourself for the families*, I reminded myself. "Come to think of it, you should go for me next year."

The product smearing and dabbing ceased, so I opened my eyes to find Rachel staring at me with a rebuke on her face, looking a lot like Deana's. "You do perfectly well with the presentations. Hell, if Dylan's wasn't on the same night, you'd join him too."

"I like the presentations fine," I agreed, settling back in the chair. "It's the media. I take the worst pictures."

She laughed. "True. I can teach you how to pose though. It's easy when you understand the mechanics."

I sighed again. "I'll always be more comfortable behind the lens. You, sweetheart, take a beautiful photo with your tongue sticking out and your face screwed up."

Bella barked a laugh. "She's right. You do."

Rachel returned to the makeup and picked up blush and a brush. "Hush, both of you, and let me finish."

Not long after, I stood in my closet, wearing sexy undies with the loose bits caged in. Literally. To me, modern shapewear felt like trying to go to the bathroom in a wet, one-piece bathing suit, then pulling it back up. Panic attacks in those situations might have ensued multiple times.

I'd chosen a full-coverage garter with boning to hold my stomach in. Despite my best efforts, my tummy pooch stubbornly refused to be tamed.

The dress was amazing. I stared at it a moment, letting the soft velvet sleeve slip through my fingers.

The shopkeeper of Cyndi's favorite boutique scored a vintage DVF velvet dress for me. I had seen it a few years prior and saved the picture as a "maybe one day I'll splurge" kind of thing. In my wildest dreams, I didn't think Debra would locate the actual dress.

A forest-green velvet, the dress matched my eyes and complemented my hair, after I'd pumped up the auburn highlights with red rinse. It flowed like liquid to my ankles, with the designer's signature wrap style, a high slit, and deep bell sleeves. The belt and sleeve lining were done in silver, which I matched to my shoes.

Debra "happened to have" a pair of 1920s reproduction dance

shoes perfectly matching the dress. Knowing Cyndi, she had mentioned to her friend how much I hated stilettos. When I had met her at the boutique, these curvy little beauties were the only chunky-heeled Mary Jane's in the shop. They offered plenty of comfort for walking and dancing. When I spun in the dress, the sides opened, showcasing the silver beauties.

After dressing, I sat on my new bed and soaked in the moment. This night was so different from the stressful NFL parties requiring my presence.

My thoughts brought me back to the worst one. Overweight with no explanations for why and crushingly tired all the time, I dreaded each minute getting ready.

Some of my friends had pretended to support me, but their actions told a different story. I could tell they were caught between judging me for my inability to lose what everyone called "baby weight" and rebuking themselves for thinking that way.

The NFL wives didn't pretend though. They flat-out ignored me. Some also had kids and paid beaucoup money for their gorgeous bodies, either with a personal trainer or plastic surgeon. I guess, to them, I needed to "get with their program."

I didn't blame them anymore. Many had been under their own pressures as they ignored the common-knowledge philandering of their husbands. Many times I asked the universe how I'd found a husband who stayed faithful to a woman in my messed-up circumstances while other players strayed so easily. We were a rather medieval group of noblewomen with our happiness levels dependent upon whether we had hit the relationship lottery.

Presently, I ran my hands over the plush velvet again, sending out a thank-you for having friends who supported me. I looked around my room and smiled at the space I had recently remade into mine alone. We were both ready for a future with new memories. I thought of the man who was on his way to escort me for the night. We'd come a long way in a short time, and it lifted my heart to have someone who would walk by my side again. Thomas took my weird lifestyle in stride—actually seemed to find it fascinating. The rumor mill surrounding my family didn't scare him off either. If the upcoming articles in our town paper didn't fix my PR problem, Thomas promised to bring in a team to turn it around. I believed he'd do it too.

I stood and moved to my new, full-length mirror, turning from side to side, checking for lint or wrinkles. Rachel knocked on my door and peeked her head in.

She gasped. "You look beautiful, Mama. It's like I'm little again and you're going to one of those swanky parties of Daddy's." The best part of those evenings had been Rachel sitting on her own stool, pretending to get ready next to me. She would chatter nonstop about the colors I used and how to do my hair. I guess not much had changed there. It was nice to hear she had sweet memories of those times too.

In my new shoes, Rachel and I stood eye to eye—such a contrast to those old, insecure days. She approached quickly. "Let me do one thing…" She gently coaxed a couple more curls down onto my neck and one tiny loose wave from in front of my ear. This act felt familiar too.

I snapped my fingers. "The jewelry!" Cyndi had surprised me with an early Christmas present when she dropped off the dress after picking it up from the tailor's. She'd made me a beaded necklace and matching earrings. The neck piece was more like a neck sculpture. A butterfly rested on budded branches moving from my collarbone down to the top of my cleavage. The colors were maroon, silver, and black, with splashes of green. Drop earrings with the same beads and tiny buds hung in a delicate thread down to my shoulders. I adored everything about the set. I set it in place and turned around.

"His jaw's going to drop."

"Thanks, sweetie. Speaking of… I need to fix my purse before Thomas arrives. And Snow?"

She looked up from cleaning the makeup.

"Thanks so much for helping me." I touched my heart. "Especially since it's the last Saturday of the semester."

Rachel pinched her brows and waved it off. "Don't worry about it. Since you hooked me up with the fish-sitting for Banger, life has been nice and quiet. I made major gains in finishing up." She squeezed me as tight as she used to when she was a toddler and whispered in my ear, "I'm happy for you."

After arranging my purse with the necessities and placing just-in-case medicines in my cape pockets, I paced my room, singing along to pop Christmas songs. Rachel insisted she answer the door when Thomas arrived so I could make an entrance. *Love my girl.*

At five on the dot—late for Thomas, but he probably didn't want to rush me—the doorbell rang. Rachel knocked on my door to make it official. I handed off my cape to her and entered the living room, walking around the staircase to meet him. As I turned the corner and he came into view, I don't know who was more stunned. My jaw dropped, making it feel the way Thomas's looked.

He stood in the entry in a three-piece navy suit by Tom Ford. I recognized the cut and fabric since I was contemplating purchasing the same one for Dylan's upcoming angel funding meetings. Tapering slightly from the shoulders to hips, it fit Thomas like a dream. My dream. My scorching-hot dream. This was so unexpected.

His midcentury look had grown on me to the point I liked the quirky sophistication. But this? The man was fire wrapped in fine fabric, threatening to burn me while I begged for more.

In the years I had attended this event, I had only witnessed a few faculty members looking this put together. All of them were independently wealthy. *Oh boy.*

"You went all out," I said to him, but he didn't hear me.

Instead, a low wolf-whistle floated past Thomas's lips. "Wow! Is this for me?"

I nodded slowly, aware it was the first time I'd ever heard the sound without my hackles raising.

Thomas moved with purpose across the entry to me. His eyes picked up the suit color, showing a deep navy as he approached. He gently lifted my hand, making me feel like a treasure. He held it high over my head as he slowly spun me.

"I love your hair up," he said near my ear. Before I could say anything, he added, "Christ, Kick, you're stunning," letting me know the dress and Rachel's work had done its job. He kissed me on the temple, which I took as a sign he didn't want to mess up my face. "I'll be the envy of the men at this thing. Ready?"

I smiled as my answer since my tongue momentarily glued itself to the roof of my mouth. He reached for the cape in Rachel's arms.

"No, you don't," she called out, handing it off to Bella. She pulled her phone from her pocket and raised it. "You don't leave looking that amazing without a photo."

"You're kidding?"

She planted her feet in front of us. "After enduring all the pictures for Homecoming, prom, and yada, yada *I* had to pose for? Bet your ass you're taking a picture. Hell, you made hors d'oeuvres and invited the neighbors over one year. You're getting off lucky."

I lifted my eyebrow in acquiescence. "Touché. But no posting it to Insta, okay?"

"Oh, it's getting posted," she retorted. "I don't have to tag you though. Now skooch together. Good. Remember what I said about posing? Take a step back and pop your knee out… There." I thought she pressed the photo button a dozen times. "Now have fun and behave. No, wait… you used to tell me that. Be bad and don't behave."

I noticed Thomas's tie was slightly askew and straightened it. Really I needed an excuse to put my hands on him. I blew out a long breath to steady myself. His chin caught my eye like a magpie with anything shiny. Unable to help myself, I ran my thumb in it and noted the contrast between his soft, freshly shaved skin and the solidity of his jaw.

He chuckled as he approached Bella. He took the cape from her and laid it over my shoulders. The left side of his mouth lifted into his sarcastic smirk. "You have an opera cape."

I fastened the buttons and pulled the satin-lined hood over my head. "Problem?"

He shook his head once. "Not at all. It's real. I mean, the cape doesn't look like a reproduction."

"Nice catch, Professor." I shrugged like it was nothing. It had been a big deal for me to buy something so extravagant. As the wife of a professional athlete, it had been expected and was another thing I'd been failing at. "I have a thing for art deco and picked this up at an auction in the midnineties." I slowly turned in it and tried Rachel's pose again. "It does something to the soul to walk in one. The satin won't frizz my hair either."

I held it out at the sides, admiring the soft silver velvet and the butterfly appliqué wrapping both sides. The design caught my eye when I'd first seen it, but the hand of the fabric had sold me and had motivated me to engage in a bidding war over it.

He dropped his head slightly and checked me out from the top of his midnight-blue eyes. "Let's go darlin'. My chariot awaits."

Rachel waved and giggled. "Have fun! We'll finish cleaning and get the hell out before you return."

For the first time that night, Thomas frowned.

18

Quando, Quando, Quando

Thomas

THOMAS WISHED LIKE HELL THEY HAD ENOUGH TIME TO STOP AT THE hotel bar for a drink before heading into the gala proper. But a head-on accident on a two-lane road made them run late. They arrived just in time for Kick to meet with the event coordinator. She sent off a text of their arrival as they walked past the doorman. The sound of the band warming up drifted into the lush lobby. A new presence in downtown Durham, the hotel boasted a modern look with a two-story waterfall quietly flowing over crackled glass, greeting guests as they entered.

He watched Kick glide up the staircase with a dancer's grace to the central hub and gathering area of the hotel. The sight irritated him as much as it fed his desire. A tiny honey blonde with a bright smile strode over to her.

"My goodness, Kick, how lovely you look." The two women enthusiastically embraced, and the newcomer held Kick at arm's length. "It's been a while since I've seen you." She bobbed her finger in her face and feigned a disciplining scowl. "Too long, missy."

"Good to see you too, Anna Leigh. You never age. And I love your dress."

"This old thing?" The woman Thomas pegged as the coordinator laughed. "I'm on duty tonight. But look at you. Go check your gorgeous cape so we can go over the details one last time. Someone called out sick, so you're bumped up."

Kick sighed as she unbuttoned the cape. "Of course."

Thomas felt his phone buzz inside his jacket pocket.

When she made introductions, Thomas said, "Why don't y'all get up to speed? I need to make a call and can find you after." He turned to Anna Leigh. "Will y'all be in the ballroom the whole time?"

"For as long as I need her," she answered in her perky, Southern accent. "Afterward, I make no promises."

He kissed Kick quickly and took a step toward the desk. He felt her pull his hand and turned back.

"Everything okay?"

Thomas's life had been a distracted blur since his talk with Joe. He wanted to close her up in a tower like a treasure, but what did it matter if he ended up being her biggest danger? He wasn't about to blow her night with his stupidity though. "Sure. See you in a few." Thomas presented his best grin and kissed her temple.

As he moved to the check-in desk, he heard Anna Leigh ask, "What's your dreamy Dylan up to these days?"

Kick gave her a hesitant laugh and moved out of earshot before he caught her response. Another perky voice asked, "Good evening. May I help you?"

He looked up, realizing he reached the desk clerk. Before he could answer, the sound of a stampede stole his words. A large group of teenage girls, each carrying equipment bags and dressed in warm-ups, jogged past him with a handful of women taking up the rear. They passed, and his reason for being at the desk came back to him.

"Right. Is it too late to book a room? I'm attending the gala." If he couldn't keep Kick—and he'd concluded he needed to let her go for her safety—he'd give himself and her one beautiful night.

The clerk's mouth drew down. "I'm so sorry, sir. We're booked solid." She pointed in the direction the mob had passed. "Lord U is hosting a girl's travel Lacrosse tournament this weekend. We don't have any rooms available. All the hotels around here are booked. We can schedule a cab if you'll need one."

He shrugged and sent her a half smile. "Won't be necessary. Thank you." His phone buzzed again. "Where's the bar?"

She pointed to her right. "Around the desk and down the hall a few steps. You won't miss it."

He tipped his head. "Thanks again." Finding the lounge was easy. A handful of what looked like exhausted parents had already pulled together bistro tables and settled around them. He took a stool at the bar and ordered a double Laphroaig. The text was from his assistant, Bethany.

BETHANY

Third time running this protocol and it's a success again. Congratulations, Professor! We have our breakthrough. Do you want me to run it one more time?

THOMAS

No. That'll do. Thanks.

BETHANY

You should be excited. This is huge!

THOMAS

You're right. I am. Excellent work! Y'all have been invaluable. Thanks again.

Thomas tucked his phone back in his pocket and took a swallow of the whisky. He lifted his eyes and noticed the bartender studying him.

"Bad news?" the young man asked.

He shook his head. "No. Great news, actually. My team made a historical breakthrough." *One giant leap for humanity. One disaster for me.*

The bartender tilted his head. "Then why do you look like your aunt died, man?"

Thomas let out a ragged breath and answered, "Good question." He fired off two texts, then finished the rest of his drink. He set the glass down on top of his payment and a hefty tip. Thomas nodded at the bartender and stood. "Thanks, man. Have a good evening."

"You too. Congratulations."

CROSSING THE OPEN LOBBY, THE NOISE GREW LOUDER AS GUESTS arrived. Thomas sent a text to Alaric, keeping his promise to be a good Felidae soldier. *Christ,* the old man will probably want him flying out to Bordeaux. He hoped they wouldn't try to keep him from his family for the holidays. How did he end up regretting success with his life's work? The phone buzzed back almost immediately, but Thomas couldn't bring himself to read it.

He checked his coat and finally stepped into the ballroom. Designed with the typical modern tricks, it used mirrors and lighting to make the room appear larger and airier than it was. He spotted Kick at a curving bar in the far corner.

Thomas kept his eyes on her while he traversed the room. The man next to Kick was too friendly. Her body language roared discomfort yet with an air of politeness. She'd once mentioned not liking a sleazy department head, and Thomas guessed this was the guy, based on his overindulgent demeanor.

Time to put the big-boy pants on and let the worries go... the research too. She needs you now.

Weaving his way around the dining tables, he stepped right up behind her, pulled her into a tight, one-arm squeeze, and kissed her temple. "There's my lady. Who's this gentleman keeping you company for me?"

Kick relaxed into Thomas's arms, and he swore she let out a tiny "Thank God" under her breath. With a crisp smile, she said, "Professor Thomas Harrison, this is Dr. Ted Drummond. He's the head of the Center for Integrative Medicine, and his office is the first point of contact for the McKenna Foundation."

"Pleasure to meet you." Thomas offered his hand to the man, who looked ready for retirement.

Dr. Drummond studied Thomas closely, then turned back to Kick. "I see you've hooked a young one. Didn't know you were one of those feminists." He stared directly at her cleavage and cleared his throat before adding in his drawl, "Well, *Mrs.* McKenna, wonderful as always. Looking forward to your presentation. Lord knows I adore those women you find for us, considering the exposure brings in more private pay clients. My favorite kind of woman." He raised his eyebrow and cackled like Yosemite Sam. He lifted Kick's hand and kissed the top of it as she stood board stiff. Drummond walked away, calling out to another colleague near the dance floor.

"*Jaysus*, that man," she exhaled. In a cartoon falsetto, she said, "You're my hero."

"A guy can try." He kissed her properly. "Have I told you how beautiful you look?"

Kick tapped her finger on her lower lip. "Hmm. Maybe. It never grows old though." She giggled. "Can you believe Dr. Drummond? I swear, in one breath, he ogles me like I'm his future mistress. Then he basically accuses me of cougaring and acts like he's disgusted by it." She shivered. "It makes my skin crawl. Did you know he's older than my father if he were still alive?"

"No surprise, he looks it," Thomas growled. "Tell me you don't have to speak to him anymore."

"I will on stage. He behaves when a spotlight's on him. Don't worry."

"He better, or there's going to be an added feature to your presentation."

"Are you cave-manning?" She ran her fingers up the side of his sleeve, across his shoulder, and down the lapel.

"Am I imposing on your feminist sensibilities?"

A smirk escaped, and she peered up at him through lowered lashes. "I'm torn because I find it nice." Her hand slipped inside his jacket and around his waist. "And it might turn me on."

"This tears you up because…"

"Because I want to do the same. If a woman waltzed over to us and catted all over you, I think I'd lay her out."

"You're right." He pulled her against him. "It's a turn-on."

Kick raised her hands and wiggled her fingers. "Don't make me ruin my nails, okay?"

Thomas chuckled while shaking his head. "Can't always hold in this magnetism." As usual, he thoroughly enjoyed focusing on Kick and letting the rest of the world go to hell.

"Have y'all decided on an order?" a kind-faced, middle-aged woman asked.

"Jaysus. I'm sorry we've taken up the bar."

The bartender laughed softly. "No problem, miss. Glad y'all chased off the doctor before he grew more hands. I've worked at events he's attended before. There's always one or two ladies he zeros in on."

"I'm glad too." Kick blew out a breath, making a few curls bounce on her forehead. "I'll take a club soda with lime. The soda though. Not tonic water."

"Sure. Are you the designated driver tonight?" the bartender asked.

"No. Maybe?" Kick's nose scrunched in the cute way Thomas liked, but he could tell she wasn't over the shock of their night at the club. "I don't want alcohol tonight."

"What if I made you a cocktail without spirits… mix some juices with club soda? It's what I rely on when I'm working."

Kick's face lit up. Thomas took a moment to commit it to memory. "As long as it isn't tonic water, it sounds fabulous. Thank you."

The bartender turned to him. "What about you, sir?"

"Do y'all have a local bourbon?"

"Mystic?"

Thomas hummed. "A double with a big rock."

"My pleasure." The bartender turned away to fill their orders.

By this time, the ballroom had filled, and Anna Leigh announced it was time for the guests to take a seat.

Thomas accepted his glass and led Kick by the hand to their table. They were in front of the stage since she was speaking. He pulled out the seat for her and heard a woman call out, "There you are, Mrs. McKenna. I've been looking everywhere for you." The stranger hugged Kick and was introduced to Thomas as Eveline Boggs, the patient whose story was featured in her presentation. "Honey, the photographer wants our picture for the paper. Can you believe it?"

"No," Kick whined. "I hate being in front of the camera and had planned to hide from them."

Eveline's body posture deflated. "He said he needed both of us for the story. I told the reporter about all you did for me and my family. I swear, Mrs. Mack, he only wants the photo. They can get the rest when you're on stage."

Kick inhaled and turned to Thomas.

"Go." He shooed her on with his hands and gave her a tight smile.

"You can come too," Eveline added. "We'd love some man candy in our picture."

Kick giggled and lifted her eyebrow. "Magnetism. Can you join us, Mr. Candy?"

He stood and followed the women to a fireplace in the lobby. The photographer and Eveline's son were waiting in chairs. The little group was arranged with the men behind the women. While the photographer checked the light, Kick chuckled some more and turned her head toward him. "Definitely chocolate."

He leaned over and asked by her ear, "What's that?"

"If you're my man candy, you're a fine chocolate."

He snickered at her side. "Thought you can't have chocolate."

"It's not a loss if you're the substitute. While I'm standing on stage later, I'm going to contemplate finally getting to have my chocolate later tonight." She covertly ran her tongue over the edge of her top teeth. Thomas shivered with desire. He could play. For a night.

"Only if you do a good job," he purred and discreetly patted her bottom, getting a hop and a squeak from her.

They smiled for a half dozen shots, shook hands, hugged, and set off for their salad courses.

Toward the end of their dinner, Thomas leaned into Kick and asked, "Everything alright, baby? You've only eaten the vegetable, and you didn't touch the salad or soup."

She lifted a shoulder and smiled apologetically. "Croutons were in the salad. Bisque soups are made with flour and the same with the gravy. But it's okay. I ate a large, late lunch and snacked while the girls primped me. The steamed broccoli is fine." She patted his thigh to reassure him. "I'm used to it. Don't worry."

"There's nothing I can do?"

"Don't bother the staff. The kitchen isn't set up for someone like me. Cross-contamination is a real risk back there."

He grimaced, and she tapped his leg again. "Happens all the time. Call it motivation to leave early." She flashed him a flirty grin and batted her lashes. "There's a protein bar in my cape."

Of course there was. "Alright, I'll leave you alone." He tapped her knee in return and finished his dinner, feeling bad for pressing her and frustrated at not being able to fix it. It made his irritation come back too. If anything happened to her, he already knew he'd lose his mind.

Kick finished the vegetables and turned her attention to the woman sitting on her right. She was the wife of a doctor at the clinic. She fussed about how long it had been since Kick attended a gala, which had been a common theme for the night. He overheard the older woman tell her, "It's wonderful to see you've finally moved on, dear." Thomas turned his focus to the man on his left, a friend of his boss.

The time finally arrived for Kick to speak. Dr. Drummond introduced the segment and a short film featuring Eveline, her family, and how the McKenna Foundation helped her move from a patient without hope of living a vibrant life. In the nine years since she'd met Shane in a waiting room—inspiring his idea for the foundation—Eveline had thrived as a single mother and had become an entrepreneur who offered a service to other foundation clients.

Dr. Drummond introduced Kick, and she rose to a polite

applause. She moved with her dancer's grace, long neck held high, a serene smile on her face as she stepped on the stage and crossed to the podium. She maintained her dignity as Drummond grabbed her in an inappropriate hug, his hand resting on the top of her ass. Kick's eyes barely flashed as she kept her brave mask in place while Thomas's hands fisted as he rolled his shoulders.

"There's a saying about chronic disease I can attest to," she started. "A healthy person has a thousand dreams while a sick person has one. The McKenna Family Foundation has been honored to work with the Center for Integrative Medicine at Lord University Medical Center for the past nine years. Each year, new names are added to our roster of beneficiaries, and we know those names are more than medical files. They are ten women and one man, seven spouses, twenty-three children, and five grandchildren. When a person is sick with an autoimmune disease, every relationship is affected, every activity must be considered..." She leaned into the mic. "*Every* aspect of life was radically changed."

"Work shifts are shortened because there isn't enough energy for a forty-hour week, 401Ks get cashed out, beautiful houses are sold to pay for medical treatments, vacations vanish because there isn't enough money left over once the bills are paid. Insurance won't cover many treatments, so a patient who barely meets rent and food will often go without medical intervention and watch their health deteriorate for a lack of options. Such was the life of Eveline and our other foundation friends."

Kick tucked a curl behind her ear. "To be blunt, the rate of suicide among the autoimmune community is astounding. The blood-brain barrier is often crossed with the diseases, radically affecting mental health. Moreover, the pain of having family, friends, and dreams ghost your life as an illness takes it over can be too much to bear."

"You know this already though." Kick looked out at the audience and paused. "My apologies for beginning on a downer. I only wanted you, our beloved research teams, to remember how high the stakes are in our community. Mostly, you know about the difficulties surrounding the quest for the elusive diagnosis and the 'oh shit factor' that sets in once a patient receives it." The audience laughed while Kick lifted her gaze to wink at Eveline.

"It makes my heart soar to see our clients and their families improving in all areas of their lives. Because of their progress, the whole family dreams again. You'll hear about some of these life changes in a moment, changes you help bring to fruition."

Kick checked her notes and sighed. "What continues to keep me up at night is knowing how many more families out there need your help. So tonight I've gussied up and squeezed my hiney into a fancy dress to stand before you and share about the changes coming next year—the tenth anniversary of the McKenna Family Foundation.

"Thanks to the efforts of the Annual Fund Campaign, we will take on five new clients next year and for each of the following five years." A robust applause filled the room.

Thomas's jaw dropped. He sat in awe of her poise, her command of the crowd and the way she charmed every attendant. Kick shared about partnering with a cab company to give clients vouchers for rides to and/or from treatments, which often left a patient unable to drive afterward—something he knew well.

Eveline went back on stage to share how her daughter opened a drop-in daycare center around the corner from the clinic. It was another partner, using vouchers so clients didn't have to cancel appointments for lack of childcare. She spoke of help with food— partnering with local markets, and vouchers were a common theme —and job placement once a client had improved their energy.

Pride filled his heart, along with a sense of unworthiness. Thomas saw how far Kick and the others had come. He was moved by her determination to pull up as many others as possible. He knew he had to keep her safe at all costs. Hers wasn't the only life on the line. He wished he hadn't made his last call home. A drop of sweat fell down the center of his spine.

The segment finished with Kick bringing up the foundation's executive staff and Eveline's family, who handed each grant to the researcher receiving it. She stepped back while the rest of the group received a standing ovation, but it was Kick who received the applause.

Thomas stood with the audience and beamed. His phone buzzed with the fifth text since the speeches began. One side of his heart burst for the woman who received more of his adoration by the minute. The other side hardened with a sense of dread.

The last presentation was half-finished by the time Kick made her way through the crowd of well-wishers and she returned to his side. He hugged her tight, not wanting to let go. Adrenaline boosted the lavender and exotic floral scent at her neck, making it smell like passion. He could coat himself in it if they weren't in public.

"I'm so proud of you," he whispered. "How did I not know the extent of this?"

"We're still getting to know each other, remember?" She smiled demurely, placing her arms around his waist and tipping her head back. "It only *feels* like we're old friends."

Kick was right. Despite their natural rapport, they were totally, painfully, new. He reached over and rubbed her back, afraid his hand might be too sweaty to hold hers as emotions ran wild.

The band eagerly played upon completion of the dog-and-pony shows. Kick leaned into Thomas and asked, "Please dance a couple of songs with me. I need to release this nervous energy."

"You didn't get it all out on stage?"

"No. Mine let go after the fact." She pouted as a thought crossed her mind. "I should've thought to reserve us a room."

Dammit all.

19

Don't Let Go (Love)

Kick

THE BAND PLAYED A HOLIDAY SONG BY DEAN MARTIN AS THE GUESTS stepped away from their tables. The university always hired a full-sized jazz band, and I practically buzzed as Thomas and I made our way to the dance floor. I longed to be in his arms. Since we had to wait a bit to be alone, dancing would serve for a nice appetizer.

Several people stopped us on the way to the dance floor to congratulate me and the work of the foundation, which meant we missed Dean. The brief time the band took between songs gave us a chance to find a spot on the floor and get into hold. They began a sultry version of the song "Quando, Quando, Quando." It fit my mood and the mood of our time together so far.

Thomas opted for a Latin-like sway with subtle steps and occasional turns instead of a formal ballroom-type display. As much as I loved the fun we'd had before, I appreciated his instinct to stay low key this time. He basically took us around the floor in what I'd call a lover's hold, with near, full-body contact. Caught up in the evening's success, the beauty of the song, and the feel of this man, I sang the words into his ear.

Then I felt his phone buzz.

"Do you need to answer it?"

He set his chin and sliced the air briskly. "Later."

The band moved immediately into "A Kiss to Build a Dream On," and I continued to sing. Since the song was slower than the last, Thomas kept me in a tight hold for the entire song even as he lazily spun us. At the end of the song, he kissed me deeply. A small group near us quietly clapped when we came up for air, and I blushed. Thomas was waking something in me, and I longed to celebrate it.

I was proud to be with him and proud of him. I might've felt the spark of L-word feelings for him and savored the revelation without the pull to rush anything. It was a treat to enjoy each moment with Thomas as they came.

His phone buzzed again.

"Sounds important," I said.

He nodded, and we exited the floor. He swiped his phone and frowned.

I brushed his shoulder. "Tell me what's wrong."

He looked at me with a confused expression, so I explained, "Your smile hasn't reached your eyes all night."

"I'm sorry, baby." He sighed and glanced down again, then back to me. "I need to return this."

I reached behind his neck and rubbed the newly clipped hairs there. "Feel what you feel, Thomas. I only want to help and support you." Taking mysterious calls out of the blue had already become a routine for the man anyway. I didn't mind.

He flexed his jaw and gave me a grin that still didn't reach his eyes. "It won't be long."

"Take as long as you need. I'll head to the restroom and fish my protein bar out of my cape."

His brows drew together in a way I recognized in myself. It always equaled my resting bitch face. Despite my attempts to lighten the mood, it wasn't working. "Any chance we could leave after I make this call?"

I smiled and ran my thumb across his chin. "If you hadn't asked, I might have begged."

We left the ballroom for the lobby, traveling in opposite directions.

I guess I took a wrong turn. When I found a bathroom, it was blissfully empty and stayed so the entire time I used the facilities. It gave me a chance to process the evening so far—how happy Eveline looked, how much it filled my soul to make a difference in someone's life, how far the medical treatments had come since I first fell sick. I also imagined what the rest of the evening would hold. I wasn't ashamed to admit what I saw excited me even more.

After retrieving my cape, I found a nearby love seat to perch on and fished out the protein bar. I asked the universe to let me snack in peace. As fun as peopling had been, I'd had my fill. I was needy for my alone time with Thomas, hoping we could finally take the next step to "something more."

I finished the last bite and stuffed the wrapper back into my pocket, wondering where the hell Thomas had gone. He still hadn't returned. I worried something had gone awry at the lab. He'd told me about some crazy mishaps already this semester. Then there was the tragic accident of his first assistant.

When we danced though, he'd been the attentive man I knew and desired. Then I realized what was wrong—his sexual tension was probably worse than mine. I'd been distracted by the stress of recovering from the drugging and preparing for my speech. I hadn't had time to give in to lust. Add in our opulent surroundings, the attention, our gorgeous clothes, he probably yearned for alone time more than me. Poor guy.

Why hadn't I thought to book a room? I'd overheard someone earlier say the rooms were filled.

I stretched my spine from side to side and looked up to see Thomas finally returning, his face blank. Well, he was simply steeling himself for the crowd. I didn't think he liked the spotlight-like attention either.

I stood as he approached and asked him, "Is everything good?"

He gave me a tight nod for an answer, so I reached up on my

tiptoes and purred into his ear, "I can't wait to be alone." I hoped it would lift his mood.

Half his mouth lifted. Again, it didn't reach his eyes.

"Quando, quando, quando," I sang.

Thomas's jaw flexed, and his nose twitched.

I gave up and placed my head on his shoulder. "Tell me about it in the car?"

"Sure."

THINKING IT MIGHT CHEER HIM UP, I PRACTICALLY ATTACKED Thomas when he shut the door to his Camaro. Leaning over the shifter, I kissed along his jaw, slid my hand under his jacket and began unbuttoning his shirt.

It didn't matter if the parking garage was cold or that we hadn't ordered a limo. I didn't want to wait.

His eyes hazed with lust, but his hands stayed at his sides. "What are you doing?"

"I'm still keyed up. I need you."

Thomas growled, wrapped his arm around my waist and pulled me on to him as the split in my dress exposed my legs and garter.

"Ah, damn." He groaned. "Black satin."

"Hate lace," I said for no reason other than the loss of my mind to lust. My lips worked the other side of his jaw, but I couldn't kiss the flex away. He wouldn't relax. Still, his fingers stroked the material, hugging my ass. Working his way under the material, he slid it aside and trailed his fingers through my folds.

"Dammit all. You're soaked."

"Please, Thomas." I fisted my hands in his shirt, took a moment to stroke his abs, then worked on his belt, my body pulsing along his erection.

His free hand found my jaw and angled it for a deep kiss. I lost myself in his aggressive tongue, the taste of a peaty scotch there, and his sandalwood scent in my nose. Amped up on adrenaline, I didn't notice his tongue was dueling, not dancing.

"Yes." I slid my hand into his pants, wrapping my fingers around his length, coaxing the heated gasp I wanted. Thomas went stock-still. He pulled away—his mouth, his hands. I even felt his body try to sink into the seat.

His no came out gruff and firm.

Out of breath and still not in my mind, I whined, "What the hell is wrong?"

"I spot at least two cameras with perfect views inside the front seat..." He looked around frantically. "Need to keep you safe."

Safe? There wasn't a soul around besides us.

"I'm sorry." My core ached from need and continued a slow pulsing along his thigh. "How did you know?"

His hands moved up to my shoulders and flexed. "You hang out with Banger, you learn things. We're getting out of here."

I hoped the drive home would settle Thomas and help him open up, but the tension continued to emanate from him. Every minute or so, he inhaled a long, sharp breath and released it violently.

"You're angry."

"Yes."

"Is it the phone call?"

"Let me get you home."

"Did I do something?"

"Christ, no." He exhaled again. "You're perfect. It's..." He never finished his thought, and I didn't know how to help. We sat in a keyed-up silence the rest of the drive, the air in the car so electric with words longing to be said and need dying to be filled it could've propelled us the rest of the way if the Camaro needed it. I opened my mouth to speak several times, but words caught in my throat. The tip of my nose tingled and my chin quivered.

We entered my house with Thomas still woefully tight-lipped. I removed my cape, strode to the liquor cabinet, and retrieved the Redbreast for him. I poured it neat and offered him the drink. He accepted it on an exhale, deflating his warrior's posture. Then I turned on my sound system, hoping music would help ease whatever caused this mood.

"I'm sorry, Kick."

"The phone call," I acknowledged while walking back to Thomas.

He shook his head. "Yes. And no. It's me." He downed his whiskey in a swallow, ran a hand through his hair, and barked an angry "Shit!"

I reached for him. "Please let me help. Is there a problem at the lab?" As a mother, I'd learned early on about twenty questions and pulling answers from the reluctant.

His shoulders bounced as he heaved a cynical scoff. "Not at all. We hit it huge today. Made a repeatable breakthrough, which makes it official. This might be the beginning of a fundamental shift for… people."

"Oh, fantastic." I wrapped my arms around him, genuinely thrilled for his accomplishment. A hesitant pause preceded his reciprocation, then he held me so tight he wouldn't let go.

The air in the room took on an ominous feeling. A knot formed in my gut. I thought, for the first time, the night might end differently than how I'd planned. "You're not happy about this? Or did I actually do something wrong?"

Thomas sighed while clinging to me. "I've been summoned to Bordeaux. Immediately. It means I'll be gone for the rest of the month. I had planned to turn the work over to someone else once I hit this milestone. I didn't expect it all to happen so quickly. It was supposed to be my trigger to leave."

Leave? I leaned back to catch his eye. "You're shitting me, right? Thomas, if you knew you were out the door in a few months, why'd you start with me? Or have you changed your plans?" My breath caught, and I inhaled deeply to dampen my temper.

"I thought there'd be a couple of years before I had viable results. And… and I don't know what I want," he admitted gruffly while stepping out of my space, leaving me aware of his absence. And scared.

I held on to the island counter and let my head drop, taking my eyes off him so I could think this through. "Have we had an expiration date all along? I thought you wanted to see where we could go.

You're the one who said we would have more. We're set for it tonight too. Rachel's back at Banger's, fish-sitting and studying. Liam took the dog with him to a friend's house. I was more excited about this than I was about the gala. That was mostly an excuse to splurge on a dress"—I lifted an eyebrow—"and buy sexy underthings."

He iced me out and stared at me with his shitty mask in place. So I tried harder. I took a step toward him and purred, "*Quando*, Thomas?" Another step. I ducked my chin. "*Quando?*" I pressed against him and ran my hand around his neck and put my lips up to his ear. "We're finally free. If not tonight, *quando?*"

He made a low, frustrated rumble in his throat but only moved when he flexed his jaw.

I stepped back and leaned into the island countertop. My brow furrowed. I was still processing the signals, not believing what I saw or heard.

"I don't get it. You're going to sit at my table, so to speak—one I've worked hard to set—and tell me you have no appetite?" I untied my dress, letting it fall open, and swung my arms out to my sides. "It's an all-you-can-eat buffet, Thomas. What am I missing?"

"We'll never work," he murmured.

I jolted as if struck by his words. I reached for his hand to reassure him, but the contact zapped me. "What the hell?" I curled my hand into my stomach. The pain sparked more anger, and I hissed. "Maybe you're right. The commitments you made to me a couple of weeks ago meant the world to me. But I don't know about this hot and cold with you."

Thomas's masked face gave me nothing. He looked at me like I was a stranger, and I couldn't figure out why.

"You know it, don't you? You know I don't throw my heart or my body to just anyone. You know exactly how important you've become." I silently begged for a quiet resolve to stomp out my panic and temper. I wrapped my hands around my neck and whispered, "You *know* me."

He scanned the living area, refusing to look at me. Several times his face lifted toward the den space upstairs. Yet he stayed silent, stewing like the hours before a hurricane arrives, when the clouds quietly swirl together, their spin deceptively slow and beautiful.

I repeated, "Everything is set. We can finally let go."

He kept quiet except for an exaggerated exhale. Why wouldn't he speak? He'd already become the one I confided in. *Jaysus*, I told him everything. Why didn't he feel the same?

I couldn't wait out the silence. I had to open my mouth, had to say something. My temper woke up with a low rasp. "I wasn't looking for you." My eyes narrowed as my composure crumbled. "I stayed away from the bar scene and… and those swipe apps. I didn't need this." I pointed my finger in his direction. "But you needled. With your charming smile and hypnotic accent. You convinced me you cared. You made me care. You offered your security connections and defense lessons. *You* made me feel like I was important."

The energy unleashed, and I stomped around the island in my underwear and heels. I stopped and squared off with him, my hands on my hips. "I'm not disposable, Thomas. If that's what you wanted, you could've found a 'bic' like Banger does." His gaze snapped to me while mine narrowed again—confirming my guess. "That's right. I figured out your icky bro code term. I told you, I puzzle things out. You made me think we'd be important." My last-ditch effort expressed, I slumped against the counter, confused. Beat.

Finally words rumbled and rambled from Thomas. The ones I picked up were, "I can't have you in another man's house. It's *his* home."

A relieved giggled burst past my lips. "Seriously? Sweetheart, I'll pack a bag. We can go anywhere. I adore your house. We can talk about your issues with my home later."

Thomas shook his head. "My plane leaves in a few hours. I have to pack."

I folded my arms and assessed the truth between the lines. "There's more to this. If this were about a plane to catch, we'd waste no time with a silly fight. We'd enjoy each other and celebrate the time we had."

His nostrils flared, and his gaze struck me full-on. "Silly? You jerk me around for weeks, pour yourself out to everyone but me, then bing! You decide you're ready now. I'm supposed to just hup to, and *I'm* ridiculous?"

My head spun with his false interpretation. "That's not how it happened, and you know it. What's really wrong? I've told you feelings are neither right nor wrong, they simply are. Something else must be going on here because it's all very wrong right now."

"Want to know what I feel?"

"Yes. Please."

"I *feel* like I'm out of here." He stormed over to the hook where he'd left his coat and jacket.

"Fine. Get *ye awa*! But you walk out my door, you don't come back." The heat from my face told me it was blood red. My chest heaved, only not in the way I had hoped.

"You were going to leave me eventually. I might as well make it easy." He punched his arms into his beautiful suit jacket as it hit me how upside down the night had become.

"*Me* leave *you*. It looks like the other way around from where I stand. You're the man-child running from something good. At least it's done before we took it too far."

Thomas threw his coat over his arm and yanked on the front door. "Small favors." He stormed out, icy mask in place. I heard the Camaro thrum to life, then roar down the street as if the car were furious too.

I paced in circles, pulling out the pins in my hair, letting them lay wherever they fell. My breath puffed like a bull with no one to charge. With an ironic timing, En Vogue's "Don't Let Go (Love)" began pounding from the speakers. Perfect. The house now seemed to mirror my angst. I moped back to the island and collapsed onto a barstool. My head dropped onto my folded arms. Fecking hell, his earthy scent lingered on my arms like I'd been marked. My heart sure had, but why? It didn't feel like Thomas had purposefully duped me.

Too stunned and exhausted from the day, my body trembled as I sobbed. I only had the energy for a single tear though. It stealthily slid along the bridge of my nose and onto my forearm as I failed to comprehend what had happened. My heart felt like it shouted through the Bose speakers about how I had a right to lose control… *bet your ass I did*. Then the ladies urged me to not let go… *Oh hell*. It was too late. Thomas had gone. Now what?

20

Solitary Man

Thomas

Ever since Thomas had landed in Paris at noon on Sunday, he'd been physically and emotionally inoperable. He played the dutiful protégé for Alaric. At times, he even let himself feel proud of his work, but moving through the days reminded him of slogging through a cold bog. He gave himself credit just for functioning in the meetings at all.

Finally free for an afternoon, Thomas escaped to Tess and Banger's quarters for a nap. He hoped his near exhaustion would help keep away any dreams of Kick and her destroyed visage as he walked out on her. He sank into a comfortable winged-back chair and stretched his feet out onto the hassock. Thomas spotted a cashmere throw nearby and pulled it over himself.

As he waited for sleep to set in, he watched the river flow by outside the window and thought about drowning. He didn't want to do anything so drastic though. Not anymore. Part of his problem was he couldn't be sure what he wanted. Thomas considered the possibility he might drown in his own heartbreak. The one he'd caused. Once again, he'd have to get used to being alone. Only this time fate hadn't changed his course. Thomas had done it all by himself. He powered off his phone and placed it on the side table after deciding to own his cowardice and let the wound fester. He deserved it. One thing he knew, he didn't deserve the McKennas. He sure as hell wouldn't put any of them in danger.

Dammit all. His head was fucked, and he ached for it all to stop.

ELLIE WOKE THOMAS UP FROM HIS NAP WITH AN ASSERTIVE CALL OF his name from the main hallway. Then he heard a round of fast raps on the door to the suite. *So that's where the noise came from.* He'd heard it in his dream. Kick had been calling for him, locked in her bedroom, and he couldn't open the door.

"One second, *Grand-mère.*" Thomas rubbed his face to wake up and caught sight of his azure-blue aura glowing full tilt. Funny how his dreams of Kick brought it out. He inhaled deep into his diaphragm and squeezed his fists, making the energy draw back inside him.

Ellie's exasperated sigh on the other side of the door made him wince. He took another breath to steel himself for whatever bothered her, and something did trouble Ellie. She wasn't a woman to hunt someone down personally. She'd lived too long with staff.

He eased the door open. "What's wrong?"

Ellie clicked her tongue. "You are, my dear."

Thomas gestured for her to enter, then saw his little mess in the sitting area. He cleared off Tess's prized Bergère. "I'm sorry, *Grand-mère,* I haven't been feeling well." He folded the blanket and placed it on the back of the divan. When he resettled in the winged-back and regarded Ellie properly, she looked like a disappointed mother.

"How old am I, Thomas?"

He chuckled. "Surely you don't want me to answer your question. Not sure I know anyway."

She leaned forward while keeping her back posture perfect. "We both know we don't succumb to viruses beyond a small sniffle. I might not know our origins…" She tipped her head in Thomas's direction. "That's your job—yours and Nigel's. This much, I do know."

How could Thomas tell her he was heartsick? Second-guessing his actions had been keeping him up most nights.

Ellie reached over and squeezed his hand. "I'm proud of you. I've been trying to catch you to tell you in private, but you spend most of your days closed off in here. You missed breakfast this morning too. So now I'm concerned. This is not you. Focusing on Europe doesn't mean I don't care about the other teams."

Thomas rubbed his brow. He wasn't comfortable talking about Kick with Alaric, so there was no way he'd want to seek advice from Ellie. Not with the mysterious warnings from the past few months. He had to get his shit together and fake it till he made it at least.

"You should be floating off the floor—dancing and playing music like you usually do." She raised her hands in the air. "You won! Celebrate it."

"It's not a race, *Grand-mère*." He put on a smile and hoped it looked real. "I am happy about the work." His thoughts traveled back to where the idea came from—his former assistant and a conversation about Paleo cookie recipes. "You know, we found these genetic variances thanks to Presley's suggestion back in September. I know there are more too."

Ellie's face lit up. "How is Presley? She's a lovely young woman."

"Oh no." Thomas's shoulders fell. "I'm sorry. I thought Nigel would tell you. Presley died in October. She was hit by a car. She…" He almost mentioned the suspicion it wasn't an accident, but he'd promised Banger he'd keep the information secret. Damn the Felidae and their vows.

Ellie's hands flew to her face. *"Quelle horreur!"*

Thomas nodded. "It was awful. I'll make sure her name stays with the work though. Presley was a brilliant scientist." *Even if she was a blackmailer.*

"You've had a terrible season. No wonder you're out of sorts. When someone becomes used to disappointment, they rarely know how to respond to achieving their heart's desire."

If only Ellie knew he'd let go of his "heart's desire" to save her. Because of them. He didn't think Ellie would understand. Or, really, she understood too well. Thomas had heard rumors about her past and knew Ellie could be more ruthless than any in the Felidae, despite her elegant, gentile appearance.

"I know you and Nigel are working on separate aspects of our secrets, but can you explain how your variances differ from his work? In the meeting with Alaric, the barrage of science terms lost me."

Thomas rubbed his chin. He wondered if the actual rift lay between her and Alaric. Surely *Grand-père* would have kept her up to speed on all the projects. "You know Nigel studies telomere length… why ours stay long without the health risks associated with artificial enhancements, right?"

"Of course."

"You could say my work goes back farther. To live as long as we do, there have to be variances in our DNA. I think the genetic differences affect several systems in our bodies. It's also why some of us have special… talents, as you call them, and others don't." At some point, he hoped to study the reappearance of his aural energy.

Ellie dipped her chin to let him know she followed his logic.

"My team and I found some anomalies that keep our mitochondria from atrophying over time, the way most people's do," Thomas continued.

"This is from your granddaughter's samples?"

"Twice-great… yes."

"How do you know it isn't isolated to your bloodline?" She gave him a knowing smirk and raised an eyebrow. Ellie had been following along the whole time. He wondered why she hadn't asked the question during the team meeting. "Wonderful instincts keeping tabs on your extended family, by the way. I wish the rest of us had your foresight."

Thomas patted her hand. "Making sure everyone prospered and lived happily kept me from feeling so lonely. By the time I met y'all here, the system was in place. It's nothing special"—he shrugged—"other than being lonely."

Ellie gave him a curt nod. "This is a nice way of saying you didn't abandon your family once they turned on you, like the rest of us did. I appreciate how you understand, and you are special." She closed her eyes and sighed—a peaceful, hopeful sound. "Another female Felidae would be… a dream come true."

Before Thomas could say anything, Ellie tapped his hand and stood, ending their tête-à-tête. He mirrored her, following her to the door as Ellie spoke. "Cook is preparing beef bourguignon for supper. It's your favorite, no?"

This smile came easily. Thomas appreciated family in whatever way it came to him. As the matriarch of the Château Longévité, Ellie knew when to slip out of her business role and into a mothering one. Since most Felidae members were much younger, she embraced the intention.

"Sounds wonderful. Thank you." The bright sky drew his attention outside. The sun had cleared away a drizzly day while they'd been talking. "I think I'll go for a run. Promise to be back in time for dinner."

Ellie kissed both his cheeks and pinched one for good measure, making them both laugh. "You better."

AFTER DINNER, THOMAS SAT IN THE FIRE ROOM, THE OLDEST ROOM in the château. The cozy atmosphere reminded him of the oldest rooms in his homestead. It was also where Alaric kept the instruments for evening gatherings. The old man had been dispatched to the distillery for an emergency though. Despite Thomas's appreciation for his favorite of the cook's meals and his earlier run, his dark mood returned easily. Sitting alone sipping cognac didn't help even if it was from one of the vineyard's prized bottles. He took Ellie's pseudo-advice and picked up his favorite guitar. Playing his emotions would be a better solution than drinking them. Besides, it took too much liquor for him to get drunk enough to forget.

Halfway through his song, Banger entered the room, surprising him. The man wore a huge grin. "You're the man of the month around here. Congratulations, brother."

"Thanks, man." For a minute, Thomas absorbed the praise. Ellie had been right about getting too used to disappointment.

Banger poured a dram of Ardbeg whisky, picked up a bodhran that he kept by the fireplace, and sat across from Thomas. "What should we play?"

Thomas lifted a shoulder and chuckled. "Don't ask me. I don't even know what I was working on."

Banger frowned. "It was a Prince song." He tipped his head from side to side. "Something else going on with Kick? Siobhan filled me in on the mob at the coffeehouse and the smoke shop. I thought it had been handled. Did Kick tell you anything else?"

Thomas's blood ran cold. His heart might have skipped. He slammed half his cognac. "What mob?"

"What…" Banger rubbed his lip. "Is something wrong with you two? Is this why you look like a lost puppy when you should be sitting here with your chest puffed out?"

"Why does everyone keep telling me how I should feel?" Thomas snarled, then finished the liquor. "I left her, alright? The night of the gala—when the test results came back too—I walked out. Then I flew here."

"What about protecting her? After the drugging, I thought Kick became your priority over everything else."

Thomas rolled his neck, then rose to pour another drink. "She still is. Kick's in more danger from *me* than whatever the hell her neighbors are up to." Once the glass filled, he turned and glared at Banger. "Isn't she?"

"What—?"

Thomas looked around to make sure they were alone. "Joe told me about Vivienne. All of it. Finally."

"I see." Banger rubbed his brow and took another sip of scotch. "What do you need me to admit?"

"Joe said he was assigned to watch Viv and kill her if I told her about the Society. It's why he retracted the vows so quickly." If Thomas hadn't been staring at Banger, he would have missed the head tip.

"That's Joe's story. What do you want from me?"

Thomas set the glass on the bar and folded his arms. "He said you took the assignment after Joe told Alaric to shove it."

Again, Banger confirmed with a nod. Thomas's head fell, but his friend jumped in before he could express his disappointment.

"I knew it was too much for Joe and volunteered to take over as soon as he stalked out of the old man's office." He raised his hands. "Before you work yourself up more, sit and listen."

Thomas shuffled back to his chair and sat, studying the way the spirit clung to the sides of the glass.

"I was tasked with taking her out if necessary, but I wouldn't have done it."

Thomas's head snapped up, confused.

"Need I remind you? My wonderful sire killed my one true love to teach me a lesson. I did it to another Felidae not long after, believing the lie." Banger sighed as he dropped his gaze to his own tumbler. "Time has a way of smoothing us out, like this liquor. It distills us until we're transformed." He turned his eyes on the dancing fire, and Thomas watched them darken. "If she had put anyone in danger, I would have followed the order, but I volunteered to make sure Viv survived. I thought the paranoia was idiocy. Still do." He swirled his glass, took one last swallow, then pointed at Thomas. "I did it for both of you. There are others who would've finished her immediately. It's the easy way."

"To teach me a lesson."

"Precisely. You weren't fully vetted when you made your vows. The old man changed the rules after you."

Thomas's hands rose to his neck and squeezed. "Here I thought your father was just a diabolical asshole."

"No arguments from me there."

"I feel like an idiot for not noticing. What else have I missed?"

Banger waved the glass in front of him and sent Thomas a sad smile. "When I found you, I was so happy to have a potential friend in this crazy existence I left some things out. You were too happy to see the dark side or to even consider one. You see it now though, don't you?"

Considering everything that had happened these past few

months? He saw a lot now. Thomas stopped swirling the cognac and took a sip. It settled on his tongue before he swallowed it, similar to how reality was settling in his head, but it refused to travel to his heart.

Banger refilled his tumbler, walked over to the door, and closed it. He was halfway back to his seat when he said, "On to Kick. I understand you being over the bics, and you can't take off to get away from her, thanks to your job. So, is there a way you and she could work out an arrangement? Like you had before?"

"Not if y'all plan to kill her." He raised his hands to hold off Banger's comeback. "Besides, I didn't want an arrangement this time. I wanted it all with Kick—her friendship, her family, her friends—not just her body." Thomas ran his hands over his face, coming to grips with the truth. "She inspired me at the gala, Bang. A nurse from the clinic took a chance and asked Kick to help with an injustice going on at the clinic regarding pediatric patients. You know Kick. She had to help even though this was outside the focus of her foundation. So I volunteered—"

"Fuck." Banger gasped and squeezed his eyes shut.

"I don't mean me personally. It's a real estate and legal issue. The people who handle my assets can look into it. It's mostly a matter of money and contacts. I have plenty of both."

"Okay. Good." Banger sat back and took a sip, settling himself.

"But don't you see? The actual results of my research are far into the future. I can do good now with my resources. That's how Kick lives her life. She does as much as she can with each minute she's given. It's—"

"Well, fuck. You're gone for her after all." Banger blew out a slow breath, and Thomas sat up, ready to take the blow. "You did the right thing. Don't look back. If I were you, I'd spend as much time away as possible. Since you still have the university commitments, consider renting a place near campus. Mostly, stay away from Oakville. Don't read the paper. Stay off social media. Let me handle the McKennas. I promise I'll make sure they're okay. You have my word."

Thomas sank back in the chair as if Banger's words had hit him.

His friend continued, but Thomas barely registered the words. "As soon as you can, find another position, or let me set you up with a private lab in another state. Whatever you do, don't look back."

Thomas let Banger's words sink in. They made sense, but what did logic have to do with any of this? His mind kept going back to the phrase "like attracts like."

Way Down We Go?

Kick

DARLENE LOVE SERENADED THE CAFÉ WITH HOLIDAY CLASSICS WHILE I filled coffee orders. I had opened for Deana, and the rush gave me a bit of an energy lift. Thanks to stress and the lack of sunlight, sleep had more or less taken its own vacation since Thomas had walked out on me. I took a second to sip from my decaf almond-milk latte. The americanos would have to wait until I could reintroduce them after the new year. Until then, I drank the decaf while inhaling the rich aromas surrounding me and pretended.

When Ms. Love pleaded with her baby to "please come home" for the holiday, my energy nose-dived. *Stupid Christmas songs.* This particular song hadn't bothered me for years. Then again, it wasn't Shane I pined for presently.

I told myself I was perfectly fine. He-who-must-be-forgotten and I had dodged the bullet, not going any further. Still, I missed his touch, his fine ass filling out a pair of jeans, his arrogant saunter, his gentle kiss. I wanted the rough, demanding kisses he'd given me too.

I missed our conversations most of all, the way his accent had sounded like home in such a short time and the way he made me feel like the only person in a room. Then there was the dancing… *Jayz*, I loved dancing with someone again.

After Darlene Love made a run of "pleases" and a last beg to come back, I set a filled cup of coffee down on the counter a bit too hard. Actually, I slammed it down and splashed it over one of my regulars.

"Ack! Mrs. Salmaan, I'm so sorry." Grabbing a rag, I dabbed at her ruined sleeve. "This is so embarrassing. I-I never—"

She leaned in to catch my wild gaze. "It's alright, dear. I'm fine."

I filled a fresh cup and gingerly passed it to her, then took a twenty-dollar bill from the register. "Here, no charge today. This is to clean your pretty blouse."

"No, Mrs. Mack. Keep your money. I can fix it myself, no problem."

I tried to check on her skin under the cuff. "Are you sure you're not hurt?"

"I'm fine. Truly. We all have man troubles from time to time." Mrs. Salmaan lifted her cup and blew into the opening.

"Excuse me? You don't think my jitters have to do with"—I lowered my voice and leaned in—"those articles about me?"

"Pfft." She waved her free hand. "No one I know believes such nonsense." She gave me a wise, gentle smile. "In my experience, a woman in your state has a man on her mind. Whatever it is, you should fix it. That's all I'll say." She dipped her chin at me. "I hope your day improves, and don't worry about the spill."

Mrs. Salmaan shuffled out the door before I could explain there was no fixing my situation, which was a good thing. I didn't want to argue with her, and I didn't know if I could hold my tongue either.

But hey, I didn't go from Professor Jekyll to Mr. Hyde at the gala. I didn't give up and walk out without a decent explanation. I hadn't gone radio silent either. Okay, maybe I did, but in my mind, it was up to Thomas to make the extra effort. I deserved one fecking great apology. No… a grovel. I'd take an amazing grovel. Hell, I gave him all my cards when I had come clean about Shane's accident. Yet Thomas had the nerve to still keep his tight to his chest.

There was one positive thing to take from the experience. I was pretty sure… No, I was certain my desire to love again had been stirred. *Stirred?* More like an outboard motor dipped itself into my lake of desire and let her rip. So if Thomas wasn't the right man for me, *universe, show me the honey.*

Such was the mantra running on a loop in my head. Still, my heart had a new hole—a roughly six-foot-tall hole, with a fabulous ass and sexy cleft chin.

My next customer stepped up to the counter. Before I could ask for her order, she gestured toward the door with her thumb. "Mrs. Salmaan was right, you know. No one believes those ridiculous rumors. In fact, I think some protesters were paid."

"Sure." I chuckled and tucked a curl behind my ear. When I looked up, the rest of the line was nodding their heads along with my customer. "Thank you, Mrs. Tan."

Come to think of it, business had picked up since my rebuttal interview and afternoon promotion had been printed. The editor had done everything but retract the opinion articles. According to my contact at the paper, my lawyer had done a great job threatening them with a libel lawsuit. I hadn't contacted a lawyer, however. I'd bet money on who did though. Blast that man. I hated him for thinking he could dump me and take care of me at the same time. "For my safety," my ass.

"You should know I come by here every time I go out so those bastards won't shut you down. Our neighborhood needs you. Shoot, our whole town does."

I bit my lip to keep from crying. When I looked at the line again, their heads kept bowing. Some added in an "I do the same thing," along with other words of encouragement. I think I inhaled deeply for the first time in several days.

I called out, "You people are the best. As my thank-you to this town, I declare today a free coffee day. It's all on me."

I checked with Crystal in the drive-thru. "Make sure drive-thru orders receive our gratitude too."

"Absolutely. You're fantastic, Mrs. Mack."

I laughed at Crystal's enthusiasm. The girl didn't need caffeine in the morning. She made her own energy.

. . .

Shortly after the rush, Deana sauntered into the café, singing a gospelly carol. As much as my customers had lifted my spirits, I couldn't believe someone who had just had her girls smashed until they were practically see-through could be gospel-Christmas-song cheery. I did a double take as she walked up to me after taking a minute in her office.

"You look dead. Still not sleeping?"

I answered, "Nope" as I wiped down the counter.

"Why don't you spend some time in the back? Get a little rest. You're not supposed to come back full time for another two weeks."

I rubbed at a spill on the bar as if I could also make the pain go away by scrubbing the cloth hard enough. "Okay, Mahalia. But I'm off tomorrow for my last IV treatment. I'll be fine."

"Kick, sugar, don't wear yourself out and get sick before your trip. You'll be mad at yourself if you can't enjoy those kids."

"No worries." Even I could tell my soldiering-on smile didn't reach past my upper lip. "It's all good."

"Who you convincing?" She clicked her tongue. "The professor hasn't reached out, has he?"

"Not since the voice mail about the protesters. I guess someone at Angel Security told him about it. I don't think he'll call again."

"Heyyy"—she drawled until it was a six-syllable word—"stop this pride."

Pride? Was she kidding? I shrugged as I continued wiping. "Thomas had a point, Dee. Granted, I'm not sure what his point was, but he did both of us a favor."

Deana carefully took the rag from me and placed it over a towel bar to dry. "You don't need this added stress. It's been a challenging enough fall."

I laughed at her last words. "I should've known though. It's been so long since I had a man in my life. I thought it'd be butterflies and rainbows if I ever jumped back in. I had forgotten how a relationship is mostly stress."

She reached for my shoulder and squeezed it. "Have a little

faith. I believe in you two. There's magic in the air when you're together."

I growled, not wanting to think about our *magic*. "The only thing I know for sure is it takes both parties to be in a relationship. Only one has to leave for it to be over."

"A fight isn't necessarily the end, Kick. Even a big one."

My hands needed something to do, so I adjusted my ponytail, then folded my arms, hoping it made me look stronger than I felt. She was right about the nap. "It wasn't a fight, Dee. It was a blindside." I vigorously shook my head, trying to make the memory of his cruel words go away. A hard shell had erected around my heart since you-know-who had walked out. Unfortunately, it numbed me out to everything, but it beat crying. Besides, he walked out, not me. Feck all if I would get on my knees.

"Call Thomas tonight if you don't hear from him first. Do it for me. Gordon thinks you should too."

I laughed. Deana knew the depths of my fondness for her husband. "Well, if Gordon says so…," I drawled. "I'll think about it after the nap."

"Promise?"

I rolled my eyes and sighed my acquiescence. Anything to get her to stop talking. "Pinky swear." I probably wouldn't have any energy anyway—

"Not good enough. You need to Oprah swear."

"Seriously?" I leaned against the counter. Only ten minutes in the café and the woman exhausted me. The nap didn't whisper to me. It screamed in my head like a cranky toddler in a department store.

Deana answered with an evil side-eye that I was sure still terrified her children. For a moment I was afraid she'd fire me if I didn't obey.

"The man was adamant about his desire to break up."

"Pfft." Her hand plopped on her hip like it had its own mind. "Men are emotional creatures."

I barked a laugh at her turn of a usually misogynistic phrase.

"Truly." A customer came in, saving me from the grilling. "Go," she ordered. "We'll finish later."

I couldn't wait.

Deana did pick it up later. After a power nap, we buzzed through the lunch rush, keeping the free coffee going. Word must have traveled fast because we worked almost right up until the high school let out. We had about fifteen minutes for a lunch break and ate in our favorite corner of the dining room to monitor things.

In between bites of a chicken wrap, Deana picked up the conversation as if it wasn't hours later. "You know, you freaked out on him because you had unresolved feelings for Shane. I'll tell you, Thomas hung in there. He knew something was wrong with you, and when you called to explain, he practically came running."

I sighed, fearing she'd finally found the one argument that could work.

"Gordon thinks his voice mail was a 'man's apology'."

"Does he?" I sipped on my iced cardamom tea. "Dee, I begged him to tell me what was wrong. It's obvious something ate at him. But he wouldn't budge. What about my self-respect?"

"Granted, it sounds immature." She took a long pull on her drink and snapped her fingers. "Is this about your age differences again? I swear, you may not feel like it now, but you look as young as he does."

"No," I snapped. *Jaysus*, would anybody listen? "Since you brought it up—sort of—what about my illness? Maybe the days apart got me thinking—"

"Lord Jesus—"

"Stop. I'm serious." After wiping my hands, I brushed back a curl. I didn't want to admit it, but truth was truth. "Maybe it's better to not tie him down with my illness. I didn't know I had an autoimmune disease lurking when I dated Shane."

"But you're doing fine. You've made so much progress this fall." She pointed a finger at me. "How do you know it isn't on account of meeting the professor? At least a little."

I nodded my head, considering the merit of her argument. "I'm doing better—now and hopefully for a long time—but I can't stop the clock. Healthy or not, aging has its own problems. I don't want to take away Thomas's best years with him saddled as a caregiver."

"You think Thomas won't age? What if you get better and end up having to take care of him? Hmm? Plenty of young men get sick."

"You're not helping."

"Because all I hear are excuses."

Aw, hell. Was she right? Thoroughly confused, I didn't know whether to cut a latte or pour a piece of cake. I craved peace. I thought it would come from Thomas, but…

"Give me time to think. If I don't hear from him before the holiday, I'll call Thomas in the New Year. Something preoccupied his mind during the gala, and his emergency trip had to be part of it. At the very least, we both need time to cool off." I lifted a hopeful shoulder. "Maybe we can salvage something when he gets back."

I knew I couldn't handle hearing the coldness in Thomas's voice again, and I hoped the downtime would help me grow a pair of ovaries by the time he returned.

22

I Wish I Was the Moon

Thomas

"Do you have free time soon?" Banger asked Thomas. "I have news about Kick."

Thomas sat in the solarium off the kitchen, finishing a café au lait, a croissant, and sausage. He had been enjoying spending time with the chef and sous-chef—the only kitchen staff who worked at the château this time of year. Lately he'd kept his visits to the big gatherings, keeping interactions with the servants short and formal. He missed the times spent chatting and helping around the property. Now that he saw those memories through a different lens, Thomas wondered if he'd ever have the moments back.

He checked his phone and rubbed his forehead to finish waking up. He couldn't get the dueling thoughts of Kick and his research out of his head.

"I have time now," Thomas answered Banger. "About to get some air. Want to join me? Otherwise, I could cut it short. Are you working in the suite today?"

"I am, but I'll join you. We'll need the privacy."

Christ, now what? "If you're trying to upset me further, it's working." Thomas spent a few minutes staring at his research notes while Banger ate a quick breakfast staring out the wall of windows. His brain refused to focus as he worried about what Banger might have to say.

He set his tablet and phone to the side and told his friend, "I'll be in the garden when you finish."

As Thomas stepped outside, clouds drifted away from the sun, warming his face. He peered up and wondered if it would shine for Kick today. It wouldn't rise in Oakville for a few more hours. The distant fields had a beautiful, sleepy quality, like an army of plant soldiers at rest. Voices traveled across the quiet fields from in front of the winery. A small crew unloaded a delivery of barrels for the new wine.

It hadn't snowed yet, but frost lay thick on the land. Small spurts of breath steam puffed from Banger's mouth and nose as he approached.

Anticipation got the best of Thomas. "Spit it out, man."

He waved off Thomas's impatience. "Need to pick these words carefully. You know my freelance work is a secret."

"You know I'd leak nothing you tell me."

"True. The thing is my two jobs for you have accidentally over-lapped. Only, I'm not sure how closely they're tied."

Thomas's brow furrowed. He gestured for Banger to lead the way onto the lane running up field two. It would take them to the highest part of the property. He yanked down on his knit cap, though he wasn't cold. It was nervous energy. "Go ahead. I'm listening." He couldn't imagine anything making him feel worse about what he'd done to Kick. Then again, when didn't Thomas feel guilty?

Banger cleared his throat. "Brace yourself, brother. I have more questions than answers right now."

"Sounds ominous." Right then, a loud crash floated up the hill, followed by yelling down at the winery. The commotion assured Thomas they couldn't be overheard. "Let me have it."

"First. The bartender's in the wind. Law enforcement had nothing more than grainy camera footage of a legal gray area, and the guy's lawyer wouldn't allow questions. So, his passport hadn't been confiscated."

"Where did he go?"

Banger sniffed and shrugged. "Whoever sponsored his trip is good. The kid played charter plane hopscotch. He added in a couple of boats for good measure. We're working on it."

Thomas hoped the boy stayed as far away for as long as possible. He figured Kick was safer that way.

"We do think we have Kick's werewolf—one Taylor Johnson."

"Where is he? Why aren't you with him?"

The men watched an owl take off from a nearby tree. It circled the field, hunting for mice and other vineyard pests. Thomas knew this bird. It had lived on the property for years and had become a vital part of the ecosystem.

"Siobhan's working on a connection. It's the main thing I wanted to talk about. When she sends me the signal, I'll interrogate him from here. You can sit in on it if you'd like."

"From here."

"My office in the suite. Yes," Banger said as the owl made another pass, taking it closer to the winery. Thomas guessed the bird had a better shot at finding a mouse closer to the building thanks to the cold. "I know you trust me to do what I have to, but I thought it might ease your mind to see it for yourself."

The owl adjusted its wing feathers, threw out its legs, and grabbed a mouse with ease. It landed in an area behind the winery and appeared thrilled with itself as it dove into the meal with gusto. Thomas envied the bird. No matter how much he did with his life, he would never know the freedom of flying and the joy of living so basically. He appreciated the perspective check.

When did his life become so complicated? He couldn't blame Kick for it. Thomas had been frustrated with his life long before her.

"What do you know already?"

Banger raised his hands over his head and stretched. "Johnson, Young Jonn, and the bartender all worked together on a crew last summer. As you might guess, no one liked Graham Jr."

"Makes sense. Anything else?"

They turned to make their way across the field, closer to the château. "How about the tattoos go back to this particular crew?"

"This is interesting. The attack on Kick's squawk box."

"Most likely goes back to these men. I want to ask him about why they have them. I'm sure it wasn't because of a fun club thing."

"Yeah." Thomas stuffed his hands in his pockets. "I'd like to know too." On the one hand, Thomas was grateful for Banger's progress. On the other, he hated how dark Kick's circumstances were becoming. He ran his fingers through his hair and searched for the owl, but the bird had gone.

"She's vulnerable right now," Banger said, staring in the same direction.

"How so? And why are you telling me? You were crystal clear about cutting my ties last night."

Banger sniffed. "Maybe I felt bad about the Vivienne thing. I kept information from you. This time I think you should stay fully informed." He stepped away from the fence and continued on their path across the field.

The air had warmed enough that it stopped biting Thomas's nose when he breathed. His body grew antsy, and he longed to run even if it had to be a small one. He was about to tell Banger he'd meet him in the office when he realized Banger hadn't answered his first question.

"You haven't explained why Kick's vulnerable." Thomas froze in place and waited for his friend to continue. He dreaded the answer if it was worse than what Joe had told him.

"My team has intercepted multiple death threats on her specifically, but nasty shit is said about all of them. Every time she's harassed, with an article or the protesters and such, the crazies who buy into it come out."

Thomas's gaze fell to the ground as his shoulders slumped. "How many threats are we talking about?"

"At least a dozen."

He spun around. "I left to protect her. Who is her biggest threat? Them or me?"

Banger chuckled—actually chuckled while Thomas freaked out

—and turned his head up to the sky. "That's not even the weirdest part of these past few weeks." He stopped beside Thomas and dropped his voice. "The overlap I mentioned? Turns out the bartender's phone records show a couple of calls to a number in Oxford."

Thomas swallowed hard. "England?"

"Not the one in North Carolina, brother." Banger turned in a circle as he spoke.

Thomas's hands wrapped around his neck. Friend or not, if Banger was messing with him, they were throwing down. "You've already told me you suspect Nigel in Presley's accident. Are you implying he also wanted to kidnap my girlfriend?"

"I thought she wasn't your girlfriend anymore."

Thomas growled again as the knot in his stomach grew bigger. "Slip of the tongue. I'm upset. What are you getting at?"

"There's a lot of work to do yet. I just don't like what I keep finding."

"When does your work lead to good news?" Thomas muttered.

"When I can simply go ahead and take out the bad guys. Spread a bit of chaos among the demons of the world, so to speak. I'm afraid the baddies won't be strangers this time."

Thomas shook his head and heard his neck pop. This didn't make sense. "Kick's problems started before our friendship. Plus the nut jobs who keep stirring the shit around her have nothing to do with my research."

"You might be surprised. This Graham fellow—I mean, the dad —is wily. He's as connected as they come. Family goes back to Oakville from before the Revolution. Like yours does in Virginia."

Thomas couldn't follow the logic. Moreover, he couldn't stand the thought of not being able to help Kick. "It's like you're telling me two plus two equals five."

"Then let me work on the math." Banger clapped him on the shoulder. "As I said before, I only want to keep you informed."

"What should we do?"

"Siobhan's trying to convince Kick of the benefits of a qualified bodyguard."

Thomas broke into a nervous laugh. "Lots of luck there. At Christmas, no less."

"It's the best option we have right now."

Thomas couldn't take much more. Not in the mood for self-analysis, he shoved his stomach knot down, gave it a mental stomp, and said, "I have to go think. Meet you back in the suite?"

"Sure. Siobhan should ping me any moment." Banger took off for the château at a quick clip.

Empty of mental capacity for more worry, Thomas took off running across the ridge and over the fields, going down to the river. He ran as fast as his legs would allow.

Thomas entered Banger's suite and immediately heard the man on the phone. He popped his head into the office doorway to check in and see if he had time for a shower.

Banger rolled his hand for Thomas to come in as he spoke. "Hold on, Von, he's back. Turn the camera on now."

So much for washing off his run. Thomas removed his running jacket and set it, along with his gloves and hat, on the credenza before taking a seat. Banger had pulled a chair behind his desk, next to his own. A man's image filled the center of the laptop screen, already beaten significantly. He sat in a small, sparse room that looked like it was on a ship.

The women had been right about the man who attacked Kick. He was a wolfish son of a bitch. Dark hair in need of cutting seemed to cover him everywhere. The man must not have owned a razor or scissors. Thomas couldn't quite place his age but guessed at under thirty.

"Wake him up."

Thomas did a double take at Banger's words and realized the man's eyes had been closed as his head hung to the side. Long bangs had obscured them.

A young man, Thomas assumed he worked for Banger's company, stepped into view. He jostled the tied man, making him start.

"Hello there, Taylor."

Taylor jumped as much as one can while tied to a chair. He did his best to twist around, looking for the source of the voice. "Who are you?"

"I'm no one, Taylor. At the moment, I'm simply a camera placed six feet away. I could be your savior or your destroyer. Your future depends on how you answer my questions. Understand?"

Taylor's head swung back down.

"Do. You. Understand?" Banger reiterated in a sharp tone.

"Yes." By the way he dragged out the word, Thomas clued in that the man had probably been drugged.

"Good." Banger checked his notes. "My friends tell me you confessed to attempting to kidnap my friend, Kick McKenna. Smart choice, fessing up. It saved you some pain."

Taylor's head snapped up, and Thomas saw exactly how much pain the man had already been put through. *Christ*, it had been so long since he'd been in a battle mindset Thomas second-guessed whether he should've been there. He'd gone soft since he'd become a scientist.

Then Taylor said, "Kick" and laughed. It was lascivious and menacing. Thomas's blood pressure spiked in anger, and he suddenly longed to be on the boat.

"Yeah, my manager hired me to take her. Said I could do whatever I wanted, as long as she was delivered to the address alive and mostly unharmed. Paid well too."

Mostly? Thomas growled and Banger placed a hand on Thomas's shoulder, reminding him to keep his shit solid.

Banger spoke into the mic. "This was your manager at Graham Construction?" After Taylor nodded his affirmation, he checked his notes again and continued. "This guy is nothing to the McKennas. Started pouring concrete and moved into drywall five years ago. He's nothing. Who's behind your boss, Taylor? Who wants Kick harmed?"

Taylor shrugged, then whimpered. "I… I can guess is all. We do odd jobs all the time. Sometimes they're for the big boss. Other times they're for his shit kid."

"By big boss, do you mean Big Jonn Graham?"

"Sometimes." Taylor coughed, then asked for water. His lips were cracked beyond being chapped.

"Soon." The team member with Taylor told him. "You're doing great. It's almost over."

Taylor's responding smile almost looked angelic, encouraged. He licked his lips and continued. "Most jobs come through the fore-man. Some through the project manager. A few come from Mr. G. I learned fast to stop asking though."

Was everyone in this company corrupt?

Banger inhaled and chuckled. "I bet you did. You listen though, don't you?"

Taylor answered with another smile. This one was filled with pride. Thomas shook his head at the waste.

He wrote *ask him why?* on a nearby pad of paper. He slid the note to Banger.

"So, you don't know who wants Kick harmed. Do you know *why* someone wanted her kidnapped?"

"Like I said, dude, I don't ask."

"What did you hear?" Banger questioned.

Taylor's voice became agitated. "My driver—Wade from my crew— said we had to take the bitch to the address in the warehouse district, keep her drugged until our relief came. He figured they'd either let her go after the weekend or traffic her. I thought she was too old to traffic. Figured she'd be toasted for good."

Thomas couldn't take it anymore. He stood and paced the office, away from the screen. He hated what they were doing but hated this kid more.

"Hit him," Banger said flatly.

Thomas heard the dull thuds and smacks, along with the corre-sponding grunts and cries, as Banger's associate carried out his orders.

"Mind your words when speaking about the lady, Taylor." Banger finally spoke again. "In fact, how about you don't mention Ms. McKenna at all?"

A tinny groan flowed out of the laptop speakers. "Y… mfph… uk… mfkr."

"What?" Banger asked innocently.

Thomas walked back behind the desk and stood off to the side. He'd never taken pleasure in this kind of work, and he didn't know what to think of the way his friend obviously did.

"Clean off his face and give him some water."

The associate did as directed, then told Taylor to repeat himself.

"You should grab Young Jonn. He's a little mother fu—" His lips caught around his teeth.

"Tell me all about him, Mr. Johnson."

Banger's invitation seemed to perk the kid back up. Apparently, Jonn Graham Jr. had made plenty of enemies at Graham Construction. No surprise there. Taylor told them how the kid was obsessed with Rachel McKenna and had been for a few years. Thomas remembered back to the first time he'd entered the Perked Cup and saw how the boy leered at her. "Could've told you that," he muttered to himself.

Banger sent him a warning glare to keep his mouth shut.

Then Taylor volunteered information on the tattoos. "My boss came up with the idea. Those of us who do the side hustles have them. Then Young Jonn goes and gets one last summer. Only, he wants it to be like a gang thing, see."

Taylor asked for more water. When the man with him looked into the camera, Banger said, "Go ahead. As long as you talk, Mr. Johnson. You talk, you drink. Capiche?"

The associate held out a cup with a straw.

Banger turned to the side and stretched out his legs as if he were on a friendly business call. "Tell me about John-with-two-n's gang, Taylor."

"Obnoxious, ain't it?" The young man chuckled. "Remember how the big cartel was busted up last spring?"

Banger laced his fingers behind his head. "I've heard of it."

"Well, dipshit—that's what we call Young Jonn behind his back, 'cause if we said it to his face, he'd cry to Papa and get our asses fired, right?—anyway, dipshit wanted to start up a cannabis-selling venture and fill the hole that had opened up."

"But cannabis is legal now," Thomas said. He winced as Banger shot up and slapped the desktop. He'd been loud enough to catch the mic. Fortunately, Taylor didn't seem to notice. Thomas slowly settled down into the chair he had originally been in, hanging his head. Banger had gone out on a limb for him in several ways. The least Thomas could do was to respect the process.

Taylor shook his head and winced again. "The legal stuff is expensive, dude. Licenses take time and cash. Lot of it. Dipshit is cleaning up with a new black market. No taxes, no cartel to dodge. I wanted to do it, but the rest of the crew didn't want the commitment. Hell, I taped the bag to the sink in the coffee shop."

Banger leaned in. "Wait. You mean the Perked Cup?"

Taylor laughed. Pride filled the eye that he could open. "Yep. I taped it up to the sink. Jonn was supposed to take his share, put the bag back, then call in a tip."

"Why the hell would he go to so much trouble?" Banger jotted some notes on his notepad.

"Who knows, dude?" Taylor tried to shrug and groaned in pain. "I figured it had to do with the Rachel girl. Jonn's butt hurt she won't pay him any attention. The bitch has an asshole boyfriend too, so it's not like he's out of her league. He thinks more money will catch her eye. Anyway, her mom owns the place."

"Her mother is Kick McKenna, dumbass. The one you tried to kidnap. Didn't you notice their last names are the same?" Banger asked with an almost smile.

"Oh, right." Taylor inhaled as best he could and let it out. "My head's fuzzy, dude."

Christ. Thomas figured if all the men involved in this were swirled into one being, they might end up with a decent IQ. Might. He wrote down *what's the endgame?* and passed the note to Banger.

His friend read it and mouthed *wait* back to Thomas.

"Any chance you had anything to do with the attack on the Perked Cup's ordering unit?"

"You mean the drive-thru?" Taylor hissed as his face twitched.

"Yeah, we did it. Payback for the pot, right? I'm mean, she took all of it. Dipshit only wanted to sacrifice some, not the whole thing."

Banger wrote some more, then leaned close to the mic. "You've done well, Taylor. I appreciate it."

"Thank you."

"Certainly. One more question. Think hard. Does this go back to Young Jonn or his father? See, I still don't understand why the McKennas are being picked on." Banger clicked his tongue and tapped the desktop. "As you know, it's my business to protect them now. Someone—you—try to take Kick at a club right under my nose, it makes me mad. I need to find out who and why."

"I wish I could help you more… mister," Taylor said earnestly.

"Again, appreciate your cooperation. Unfortunately, wishes don't help me either."

"Young Jonn would know. His old man is too hard to get to, but the dipshit would know. He runs his mouth more than me."

Banger laughed as Taylor rambled on more about the youngest Graham. Thomas wished he'd bashed the kid's head in when he had the chance in October. His lawyers were involved now though. Plus the boy was under house arrest. His side would have to stage a kidnapping of their own. One the police would actually notice too.

Thomas stood and rubbed his neck, stretching it from side to side. *Christ*, he needed a shower more than ever now. He had to wash off more than his run. The knot from earlier had returned, too, threatening to make him vomit. He still didn't know who was a greater source of danger for Kick—Jonn Graham, et al., or him, by way of the old man who reigned over the Felidae? Thomas still didn't know what to do.

As he walked out of the office, Banger called out, "Don't go far. We still need to talk."

23

Love is a Battlefield

Kick

THE CHRISTMAS TUNES DIDN'T BOTHER ME THIS AFTERNOON. NOT much did, in fact. I bounced around the work area, chatting up our customers, convincing myself my heart wasn't broken. Anytime a sentimental song came through the speakers with a longing for a loved one at Christmas time, I thought of the new year. I even had to put off thoughts of *him* every time I made an Americano black. I would get through the holidays first, enjoy the time with my kids, and worry about my heart second. The T-man could wait.

Placing a few drops of a cannabis tincture under my tongue helped. I'd done it as part of the product testing for Hugh's new venture. I had read up on a line that gave caffeine a run for its money when it came to focus. Should I have added it to my regimen without consulting my doctor? Probably not. But I waited two hours after taking my morning pills and was reasonably confident it would help, not hurt, my performance. I made sure there was nothing in the mixture to cause impairment, surprised by how much research was being done on the stuff.

Presently, it was time for Deana to end her shift and collect her grandbabies after school. It felt like old times and gave me another reason to look forward to January. Not much longer until I could reintroduce foods in earnest and begin the ending of my detox protocol.

Deana gave me a hug and air kiss before pouring herself a travel mug to go. With no customers currently waiting, she said, "Can you save some time for me tomorrow?"

"Will lunch work? I plan to do next month's schedule and get ahead of paperwork before I take my time off."

"Sounds perfect."

I studied Deana for a moment, trying to decipher what she wanted. She never made mysterious appointments with me. Her visage gave nothing away though I suspected she planned to bring up Thomas and someone's pride. I gave her my sweetest smile. As long as we discussed how proud he was, I didn't mind. "Have a great evening."

I had switched the holiday playlist to punk Christmas songs—I couldn't take the heartstring-pulling anymore—when the door chime announced a new customer.

"And here's the delinquent star of our recent chamber of commerce meetings." I heard Big Jonn Graham before I turned around and saw him. He always played life that way. He leaned on the counter as if he was getting ready to tell me a secret. "Been wondering if you were hiding."

Considering he found me in my coffeehouse, the man hadn't looked hard or for long. He spoke with his grandiose, old-timey, politician-like accent. I almost laughed but behaved. I knew it for what it was—a harkening back to a certain age when former Yankees, like myself, didn't occupy all the empty farmland around town.

I gave him a half-assed grin and waited to hear his order or what he really wanted. However, Big Jonn simply stared back like he expected me to explain my whereabouts. If he wanted to throw me off-kilter, it worked. Plenty of people were members in name only. Not to mention, after what happened on Halloween, I didn't think

I'd see a Graham walk through my doors anytime soon, if ever again.

I held a sharp gaze on him and calmly said, "I've had doctor's appointments. I'll attend meetings after the new year when they're all through." Shit. A shiver of disappointment traveled down my spine. I should've simply said appointments or meetings. Looking weak in front of this man had never been a wise thing, especially now. I didn't blame him for his son's behavior. Hell, my oldest had jumped into a world of trouble in response to Shane's death. In the past, I'd felt empathy for Big Jonn's plight. Not anymore.

He reached out and touched the top of my hand, making me flinch. I mentally slapped myself again, hoping it wasn't noticeable. I knew he caught it by the sad smirk on his face, and I almost missed his next remark.

"I came into y'all's shop, hoping to make a peace offering. I'd like to buy gift cards for my crew. From all the to-go cups dotting our job sites, I can tell they love y'all's coffee," he said, then lowered his voice. "Then our families can put the messiness of our disagreements behind us."

His face looked so sincere I kind of believed him. A part of me desperately wanted this all to be over and ached to believe him. But was he crazy? I mean, come on.

I picked up a new rag and wiped at the counter. "The situation of your son's house arrest makes it a tad hard to drop. The police wouldn't stop the process if I asked them to anyway. Young Jonn broke laws. It'll go a long way if your lawyer allows him to confess to the attack on my shop though. I wouldn't care if he pleads to lesser charges as long as it ends quickly too."

"Attack?" He tsked. "My boy's been a handful since his mama passed, but this?"

"Mr. Graham…" It struck me how a man my age could success-fully have me feeling like a mindless girl. Then again, growing up with the hostility in my mother's family, I knew how to spot the buildup of a gaslighting. Downplaying the attacks on me and mine, as if I'd blown things out of proportion in my head, was a classic move. I wouldn't argue the merits of the evidence with him.

"Jonn, I don't think you should be here." I moved my hand toward the under-counter alarm and hovered my finger at the button. He raised his hands in mocked surprise. "Ho there, darlin'. Aren't you jumpy? I'm starting to see where you're coming from now."

"What're you talking about?" I clipped.

"My apologies for prying, and I honestly hope I don't sound rude…" I raised my eyebrows, waiting for him to continue. "I heard about the breakup." He rubbed his stubbly chin. "It's a bad time of year to be alone. Bet it's got you edgy."

Edgy? He had no clue and almost had me laughing again. I smiled as I shook my head, determined to keep him at bay while not wanting to anger him. It wouldn't help my case if I threw another Graham out of my store.

He thumbed through a display of beaded bookmarks Cyndi had for sale by the register. "You and I have a lot in common."

"True, but—"

"Let me take you to dinner. One dinner, darlin'."

I didn't like the way he used the same endearment Thomas had. Big Jonn made it sound condescending instead of endearing.

Before I could turn him down, he continued, "A while ago, I offered to help you get your diner back on its feet."

"Coffeehouse—"

"Sure. Anyway, I can still speak with the editor at the *Oakville Mirror* for you if it helps. We could strategize a plan over Italian." He patted what I admit was a very fit stomach. "Nothing like great lasagna to let a man think, right?" Big Jonn laughed and winked at me. This man was built as if he worked right alongside his crew members, though I didn't see where he'd have the time with all the schmoozing he did around town. Still, he couldn't hold a candle to Thomas—well, the Thomas who cared. There was more to handsomeness than physical attributes.

I didn't realize he had continued speaking. "…No matter what my son witnessed, the success of our town is still important to me. And… I have to say… you look a little overwhelmed."

I closed my eyes and inhaled. Wiping the counter had lost its therapeutic aspects. "I can appreciate where you're coming from, Jonn—"

"Big Jonn."

"Right. Still, I don't think the Assistant DA would approve of you being here. Young Jonn isn't allowed near the Perked Cup or me, but I can't remember if it applies to his family. I could call…" I reached for my phone, thinking Big Jonn might go quietly if he watched me dial.

"Well, now," he purred and smiled sweetly. "There's nothing to worry about, is there? I'm simply doing some last-minute Christmas shopping and prefer to spend my money locally."

The bell rang again, and a young couple entered. They queued up patiently, waiting their turns to order and laughing at something on his phone. The addition of two potential witnesses relaxed me, and I let out a loud exhale.

"Okay. How many gift cards should I ring up? It's a thoughtful idea, Mr. Graham."

With a sigh, he gave me the number and muttered, "Here I was hoping to start fresh in the spirit of the season. Let the shenanigans become water under the bridge. Maybe talk more about a partnership."

His words were smooth, but *Jaysus*, he made the hairs on my neck stand straight up. "The thing is"—I looked down at my feet—"from where I stand, my toes are still soaked by your bridge water."

Graham paid for the cards and tucked them in his coat pocket. "Then I'll say an extra prayer for our families. It's our Lord's birthday after all."

"Go right ahead." I hung my head and shook it, relieved to see him finally step away from the counter.

He turned and sauntered out the door, humming "Baby, It's Cold Outside" when it wasn't even playing in the coffeehouse.

My body shook from the pent-up adrenaline. *Breathe, Kick. In for four… hold for four… out for five.* I lifted my head and smiled at the young couple.

"Hey there. What can I get you two?"

· · ·

As if my adrenal glands hadn't been through the wringer already, the fight or flight response spiked again a while later. Alone in the dining room again, a group of kids approached and rushed through the front door. They wore their hoodies up with sunglasses and bandannas covering their faces. A group of unabombers had descended upon my café, and I was sure this time would be the end. My heart pounded out a dirge as I checked the drive-thru area, making sure Crystal was safely out of sight.

My finger hovered over the emergency button as the kids all dropped their hoods in unison. Next came the bandannas and glasses, and I let out a long exhale. They were some of my high school regulars.

My hand flew to my heart to calm the staccato beats. "Hi guys. Why the hell are you dressed like robbers?"

Each one turned to the next, then back at me. "We didn't think about that," the first boy said with a shrug. "We're in disguise."

"We couldn't be seen coming in here," another added.

I blinked at them as I tucked a curl behind my ear. "Whyever not?"

A third explained, "Yeah. Our parents think you're brain-washing us, but we like studying here. Gabe here"—he pointed at the first boy—"is our tutor. He toots really good. And the school librarian is a bi—"

A fourth one—a girl—jabbed the boy in his side. "Tutors don't toot, dumbass, they tutor."

The boys scrunched his nose. "You make absolutely no sense."

The first boy—Gabe—smiled and said, "She's right."

"Tragic."

The girl jumped back into the conversation. "Anyway… It's easier to study here, Mrs. Mack. My grades tanked after we were grounded from you. Please don't tell anyone we came by. Can we get drinks and stay in the corner if we're quiet?"

Grounded from me? The words wouldn't make sense even though I knew exactly what she meant.

"Of course you can study here. Can't guarantee you won't get in trouble, but I won't say anything. You know I work hard to give you guys a safe place to study."

"Exactly," the second boy said. "We told our parents the same thing, but they think we've already been… what's the word?"

"Indoctrinated," the girl answered.

JaysusMaryandJoseph. Counting breaths wouldn't help this one, so I raised my arms over my head and stretched my back. Time to roll with it. I stood at the register and swung the tablet around. "I assume your numbers are in here. Want to enter them and I'll get your orders going?"

Ha! Take that, Thomas and Siobhan. I had two huge hurdles and handled them myself. Thomas had sent more messages about the protesters, but I knew better than to let myself get strung along. The whole breakup-and-stay-friends thing never flew with me. Like slowly removing a Band-Aid one hair at a time, it not only prolonged the pain, it magnified it.

And Siobhan? She had been bugging me, stressing the need for a bodyguard. When I pressed her for a reason, she gave me vague answers about the investigation from the club. Well, missy, I had proved I didn't need one. The protesters did their worst and it backfired. The people who mattered knew me and my business. Okay, Siobhan had mentioned online death threats, but what woman hasn't experienced horrible behavior on social media? Case in point, my daughter. I shivered with anger at the thought of what she had recently been through. If she wanted to go to Broadway, though, she'd have to toughen her skin too.

Most of my after-school kids paid for their orders with credit cards, so it surprised me when they all placed cash on the counter. I tilted my head in question.

The first boy said, "Our parents track our purchases."

Right. Smart kids. Adjust and shift.

Wasn't that what I was doing too? Again, I'd thought about how my life plan had been heading one way and hit a dead end. Well, I could do some adjusting too. I took away one big lesson from my experience with Thomas: I knew I could move ahead with someone else. In fact, I looked forward to it. But maybe this time next year, after Liam left for college. When I had time for myself.

24

Kick

Thomas

"Sorry about blowing the interrogation," Thomas said to Banger. A shower had been exactly what he needed to clear his head and focus.

"Fortunately, our guest was too nervous to notice your faux pas." Banger kept his eyes on his computer screen, his fingers typing away as he spoke. A few more clicks, and he closed the laptop. He sat back and stretched his legs. "Besides, it's my fault. I forgot you've softened since becoming a scientist. I should've expected it."

The bluntness rankled. Thomas wrapped his hand around the back of his own neck. "I wouldn't go that far—"

"Stating a fact, brother. It's best you own it."

Damn. Leave it to Banger to set him straight. Thomas dropped into the chair in front of Banger's desk. "Is it possible to put bodyguards on the McKennas even if Kick won't change her mind?"

"It's more like surveillance, but sure. Consider it done."

Thomas relaxed some and exhaled.

"Where's your head at now?"

Thomas rubbed his freshly shaved jaw. "What's your take on Big Jonn Graham?"

"The papa?" Banger opened his laptop and double-clicked on a file. "Family status has risen and fallen multiple times. The original Jonn was a prominent lawyer-turned-politician. This one sought the almighty dollar, used father's seed money and contacts to start his construction business. No questionable contracts. Nothing out of the ordinary anyway."

Thomas couldn't believe he was innocent with as many corrupt employees as he had. "What about his character? Give me your gut, Banger. It's bailed me out countless times already."

"The man's fifty percent charisma, fifty percent ruthlessness. Behind his Andy Griffith routine is a cutthroat. From what I can tell, family's everything to him."

"Goes the same for just about everybody."

"Don't be so sure," Banger muttered. He stood slowly and waved for Thomas to follow. "I need a drink. Let's go to the sitting room."

Thomas spoke as they moved. "Did the interview give you any new clues whether he's behind the attempts on Kick? She's what matters."

"Interview?" Banger chuckled. "Tell yourself what you have to, brother. Taylor Johnson went on a fishing trip with some of my people. Anyway, we're still watching the son. His motive compounds with each mistake he makes, like interest. My team's working on it though." Banger tilted his head to the side, studying Thomas with that intense, icy stare of his. "I promise, I have her back. No matter what. You can rest easy."

Thomas fell onto the divan as Banger poured two cognacs. "Is this Tess's prized stuff? I thought she planned to sell it." Thomas didn't know how much it was worth, but millions would have been a low-ball number.

"She's selling the wine—"

Before Banger could take his seat, the door flew open with a loud creak. A pile of packages, suitcases, and perfume pushed their way into the main room before Tess did.

"Did you have to say her name? It's like she's *Beetlejuice*," Banger muttered in disgust. Thomas wished he had it in him to put these two together until they hashed out their differences. It's what Kick would have done.

She had her sandy-brown hair in one of those pixie cuts and wore a complete yoga ensemble, including one of those long, drapey cardigans like Kick often did—a real contrast with Ellie too. Tess dropped her accoutrement. "I thought I heard talking. Hello, boys." She looked them both over, saw their drinks, and smiled. "Good idea." As Tess poured herself a drink, she declared, "I'm thrilled we'll have three for Christmas, but Thomas, dear, I thought you would be in the States by now. What about your lovely lady?"

The question made Thomas want to puke.

"Tess…," Banger warned, causing her gaze to flash between the two men. Her eyes drew down in understanding and sympathy. "No? Oh, my dear, Thomas. You didn't send her away, did you?"

Almost at his limit of emotion, Thomas took a long pull of the spirit to steady himself. "It was for her own good."

"*Pourquoi?* She's wonderful for you." She downed her liqueur in one shot and turned to Banger. "Did you not see how much he brightened around Kick?"

Banger shrugged sheepishly and shifted his head from side to side.

Tess took a seat across from Thomas on the divan and reached for his hands. She cast a disappointed glare at him, then said, "Do you even know you love her?"

"I…" Thomas's face warmed. "Well…"

Tess let her head hang for a moment. When she looked back up, her visage was both faraway and sorrowful. "Don't let this place stand in the way of her." She jostled their hands as if it helped her think. "When you treat love like glass, you'll either put it away in a storage case or break it. With the first, you turn a useful vessel into a wasted work of art. With the other… well, it's destroyed, isn't it? Neither help anyone." Tess's brows drew together as she turned her attention to Banger. "Did *you* do this?"

Banger threw his hands up. "Why am I always the bad guy in your scenarios?"

"I *know* you."

He took a drink and rubbed his face. "Not anymore, you don't."

Tess pivoted back to Thomas, tipped her head, and sighed. "Fix this."

Thomas let his head fall. "What about my vows to the Felidae? What if I put her in danger because of it?"

"Fuck them," Tess declared with a certainty that had Thomas's head snapping up and his eyes popping wide. He'd never heard defiance from her. Banger, of course. All the time. Did this animosity run in their blood? Thomas turned to his friend and found him smiling, like he was proud of Tess. It must be genetic.

"Banger and I will protect you two. You deserve happiness."

When had happiness ever been a goal for him? The answer was simple—never. Thomas did his best with his unique life to make a difference. He didn't ask for more.

"Won't we?" Tess had turned her attention back to Banger, who lifted a shoulder.

After a sharp, Gallic growl from Tess, he added, "Yes. Okay?" He pointed at Thomas. "He knows this."

Thomas wrinkled his nose. *Did he?*

"Don't you?"

"I…" He sighed.

Banger asked, "What's going on in your head?"

"It's swimming with what's right and what's wrong." Outside, the golden hour had arrived, reminding him dinner would be ready soon. Thomas wondered if Alaric would eat with them tonight. With their business finished, *Grand-père* had spent the day with the winemaker. It struck Thomas that Alaric pursued passions outside the Felidae. Maybe he could follow the old man's example and get away with it. If they were all together, should he say something?

Banger broke into his thoughts. "When someone makes a tactical error, it's best to admit it, then correct it as soon as possible. Pussy-footing around with it prolongs the fallout."

"I thought you wanted me to leave Kick alone."

"Thomas…" Banger scratched at his head and sat up. "It's written all over your face. You miss her. You hurt her. It's tearing you up. I don't think it's only the guilt eating you either. You cut a hole in your own heart."

"What do I do?"

Tess tapped his knee like she was scolding a nephew or little brother. "Figure out what you want. Then proceed accordingly until you get it."

Thomas turned to Banger for clarification. He shrugged and said, "What she said." Then he clasped his hand around his neck and sighed. "Things are about to get interesting."

"Say nothing to Alaric or any other Felidae—especially Ellie," Tess warned.

"She's right," Banger added. "Don't mention what you know about Vivienne either. As far as I'm concerned, it's a 'better to ask forgiveness than permission' situation. Alaric will never change his mind about protecting the Society, so nothing good will come from confronting him on any of this. With him, stick to the lab and Toni. Nothing else."

Thomas could see their points, but had they just formed a faction? If so, how many were there? His head swam with questions. One of the biggest blurted from his heart through his mouth. "What if I've burned this bridge?"

With wisdom too old and refined for her youthful features, Tess soothed him. "You won't know until you find out, will you?" She stood and walked over to the bar. As she poured more cognac for each of them, she said, "You might have to be patient, persistent too."

Banger nodded along with Tess's words, and Thomas wondered where his friend's optimism had come from. He reluctantly asked, "Why the change of heart, man?"

"Tess. She has me thinking. You have changed a lot since you met Kick. For the better too."

Thomas leaned forward and placed his elbows on his knees. If the three of them were about to form their own conspiracy, he might as well bring them in on everything. He allowed himself to voice what had been quietly niggling in the back of his mind for weeks.

"My aura is back."

Tess took a sip of her cognac and lifted an eyebrow. She handed a glass to Banger, who took a long swallow.

He said, "I never knew you had the ability."

Tess passed the last glass to Thomas. The spicy warmth settled his resolve. "It had faded by the time we met. I figured it was long gone."

Banger and Tess let their heads bob in understanding.

Thomas took another pull from the tumbler, readying himself to share what was really on his mind. "I think I've glimpsed a glow coming from Kick." He smiled at the memory. "It was a warm light. Not too bright. Also, I think she tries to hide it."

Banger waved his glass and sat forward. "Well fuck, brother. Why didn't you lead with *that?*"

25

Missing

Kick

My neck popped as I rolled it while sitting in a deceptively sturdy rocking chair. The things looked to be at least one hundred years old and lacked the loving care usually given to an antique. I breathed in fresh sea air mixed with fresh-cut grass from the rolling fields before me as a curl stubbornly plastered itself to my cheek. When I rolled my shoulders, they immediately relaxed, allowing me to settle into the woven bark seat. For a dream, this place impressed me. I hoped I could come back here again.

The low whine of another rocker caught my attention. I tucked the wayward curl once more and turned. My eyes watered at the sight of my dad. "This is where you grew up, isn't it? I had no idea how I knew this piece of family history. I'd only visited Ireland with Shane, and we stayed around Dublin, visiting his side."

He sighed in the stoic way I missed so much. "Minus the heartbreak and fighting, aye."

"I thought you lived in a city."

"As an older lad, we moved." He stopped rocking and leaned toward me. "What's on your mind, Katie girl?"

My gaze traveled around the worn-out porch. Normally, a building this damp and unkept would have my mold allergy on high alert, but my lungs never protested. I breathed in deep and smiled. "I want peace, Daddy."

He reached for my hand and squeezed it.

"Everything's fallen apart since you died."

"You said the same thing after Shane, and you did fine. In fact, you flourished. You learned how to stand on your own."

Disappointed with myself, I looked at my lap. "I had you to rely on." I thought about how much my little community—from my friends to my loyal customers—encouraged me and didn't understand why their support wasn't enough.

He pressed my knuckles to his cheek, showing more affection in these few minutes than he did when living. A hug from my father had been rare—hell, anyone in my family. "You miss your man."

"No." Dad used to have a sixth sense about my thoughts—it's where I inherited the same understanding about my kids—but he was wrong this time. I inhaled deeper, feeling like it was the first chance my chest had to relax all month. "Shane and I made our own peace. I've moved on."

"I mean your new man," he said with a melancholy chuckle.

"Oh." I scrunched my nose and flicked away another loose curl clinging to the breeze. "You know about him?"

"I do. All of it."

Despite being a grown woman, I blushed at the thought of my father knowing all about Thomas. Dad's chuckle grew uncomfortable too, as a deep pink crawled up his neck, certainly matching my own.

He sniffed and rubbed his nose. "Give him another chance, Katie."

"But—"

Dad's reason surprised me. "Look how quickly you bounced back. Where do you think it came from? It's not from the newspaper articles or the sales you're running at the café."

JaysusMaryandJoseph. Did he see everything?

"I would've agreed a few weeks ago, Dad." I touched my sweater over my heart. "The ache, here, says otherwise now."

My father scooted his chair closer and tapped my knee. "Listen to him. That's all I ask. Listen."

I had a looming sense my father had spoken his peace and was prepared to go. I couldn't let him leave without saying my own. Thomas Harrison didn't matter at that moment, Mickey Allen did. "I'm sorry my promise isn't working, Dad. I can't make her happy." To keep a threatening tear from escaping, I stared at a flock of sheep in the distance.

His chuckle grew to a laugh before dissolving. "Aw lass… I couldn't either, so how can you? In my heart, I knew I asked the impossible. I should apologize myself. It made me feel better in the moment, but it wasn't fair." He lifted his cap and ran a hand over his brown waves before setting it back. "No, she's a grown woman who is so committed to her misery the whole concept of happiness scares her. Never mind her. I want you to make yourself happy, Katie. No one else will do it for you. Trust me."

The tear escaped as I nodded, seeking understanding and acceptance. "She's in Michigan with Bert. You think she'll be happy?"

"Does it matter? The point, Katie dearest, is she's grown. It's not your responsibility to puzzle it out. I should never have tasked you with the impossible." He scratched at his nose again. "I'll tell you this much, happiness could slap your mother in the face, and I'm not sure she would recognize it. Leave it, lass."

"Okay, Daddy."

With those words, my alarm went off. There would be no chance to say goodbye or receive the hug I craved. I fought waking, hoping I could finagle a proper send-off, but it was futile.

I finally rose and padded into my bathroom to start the day. It didn't mean I was ready to call Thomas though. Back in reality, the muscle aches and tightness from physical exhaustion lingered. I craved "me time" so I could recover and prepare for whatever came in the new year. I hoped the mountain trip would help.

Before I left the sanctuary of my bedroom, I made a promise to my father to find the cottage where we met… and soon.

I SAT IN MY OFFICE, WATCHING A KALEIDOSCOPE OF COLORS DANCE on the ceiling and walls. While submitting myself to yet another Deana lunchtime lecture about you-know-who, a package arrived from France. Proof of how far off the deep end my mind had wondered, I thought it was a new french press I had purchased and ripped the box open. Inside were a dozen glass, Celtic-styled butter-flies. A note simply read FOR YOUR OFFICE WINDOW. My confused frown over this new collection had been met by a smug grin from my dear friend. "Did you know about this?" Dee simply shrugged and bused our table.

Of course, the newly acquired rainbow made it hard to read my monitor, but my brain wouldn't focus either.

"Know how I knew you were back here?" Cyndi asked as she strutted into my office.

"It's where I work?"

"Ha. You're hit-or-miss lately." Oh, true. She dropped into a club chair. "No, chica. Barbra Streisand's 'Jingle Bells' is playing. You're the only person I know who still keeps it in a queue." It was my second-favorite Christmas song, though I didn't see why we had to limit it to holiday listening since the lyrics were about winter fun. I had also dropped the hammer on all the heavy-duty emotional tunes when Deana played "The Christmas Shoes" song.

"How are you holding up?" Cyndi kicked back and noticed the ceiling colors. Pointing up, she said, "Did the kids do this?"

"Nope. We're taking our presents to the mountains." I tipped my head toward the box sitting on the credenza.

Cyndi rifled through it and held up the note. "Thomas?"

I let out a confused and frustrated sigh instead of an answer.

"Oh, honey." She came back to the chair and settled on the edge. "That's why I wanted to check on you before we both leave town. What do you think?"

"They're handblown. And not flowers."

Cyndi sat back, crossing her legs. Her foot swung in time to the frantic beat. "He's never been a typical man. Are you going to call him?"

I blew a curl off my forehead and tucked it behind my ear. "In the new year, I think. I need time to rest and recover before I do it. Besides, a new collection—as pretty as it may be—isn't enough of a grovel. Can you make him get on his knees, Cyn?"

She tapped her chin and grinned. "From the looks of his gift, I'd say he's about to all on his own. But don't you think you deserve someone who's drama-free?"

I shrugged. "He doesn't have a psycho ex. That's a rarity at our age. Plus he's been a trooper about my family baggage."

"True." Cyndi recrossed her legs, this time bopping her toe to Tom Petty and the Heartbreakers. "I want it clarified that while I'm super disappointed in the professor's behavior, I'm so proud of you for standing your ground. If you want to try something new, I'll be happy to set you up or help you with a dating app."

I exhaled and smiled, happy to have a release from Deana's guilt trips. "Thank you, roomie. I know I'm ready emotionally. I just don't know if I'm ready for the dating game physically right now."

"Either way, I've got your back." Cyndi bent over the tote bag she'd brought with her and pulled out three packages. "You received your present early with the butterfly necklace, but these are for the kiddos." She set them on my desk. I couldn't wait to see what unique thing she'd come up with for them. "Maybe next year we could go away together."

If I could arrange for Bobby to head up north again, that could be fun. Before I could answer, the sound of someone clearing their throat caught our attention.

"Excuse me, ladies."

The familiar baritone made my body yearn for him again. His soft voice soothed my nerves in a way liquor wished it could. I wanted to hate him for it, but couldn't.

Great. I knew then I wasn't ready to make any decisions about us. As long as I put it off, our future wouldn't be finished. But the universe delighted in throwing me curve balls before I was ready for them. Cyndi jumped up like she'd been poked in the ass. She leaned across my desk to give me a kiss on the cheek.

"Merry Christmas, chica." Before she pulled away, she added in a whisper, "Give him hell."

Cyndi scurried away as I braced to face Thomas.

26

All I Want for Christmas is You

Thomas

THOMAS'S HEART POUNDED A HARD BEAT AS HE STOOD IN THE doorway to Kick's office. It didn't matter if Deana's face had lit up when she laid her eyes on him. Despite the buzz of activity, she had stopped working and run around the counter to hug him. "I knew you would come to your senses," she had said in his ear.

Word must have traveled about the coffeehouse's owner because some customers frowned as he had crossed the dining room. Then Cyndi passed by and muttered, "I suggest dropping to your knees now and waddling on over."

His eyebrows ticked up in question, then he saw, really saw Kick's drawn face. Pretty as always, anyone else might have missed it. His regrets hit him full force.

Thomas took a tentative step into the office, but Kick's words stopped his small progress.

"I've been doing well. I mean since you left."

"I know. You've been great. I saw the exposé on you and the café. Your honesty about the flare was inspiring. Bet it helps many women who read it." *Christ*, how he wanted to hold Kick and tell her with his body how proud he was of her.

Kick muttered something like, "Blast him and his voice."

"What?" He took another step forward.

She folded her arms across her chest. "Thomas, why are you here?"

"Maybe I'm not well. Maybe I need you to save me."

"How?"

Dammit all. What didn't she do for him? Thomas ran his hand through his hair. "By listening. Making me laugh. Showing me the world from your point of view." He tipped his head back and closed his eyes. He had to take a chance and trust her with the locked parts of his heart. "By letting me bury myself in you. Lose myself as I wrap my arms around your body."

"Well, hell." Kick planted her hands on her hips. "You're playing dirty."

"I know. Told you that you have a hero complex too." Thomas felt the corner of his mouth twitch. Even now, he couldn't help but tease her. He lived for their banter.

Then the first tear fell. "Do you know how much you hurt me?" Kick pointed to the butterflies she'd already set up on the windowsill where he'd imagined them. "Did you actually *want* to do something special for me, or are they a part of your game too?" She walked toward the window, staring up at the little glass pieces. "You more or less told me we were a game the night you left. Well, I wasn't playing, Thomas. I won't be anyone's joke either."

The moment he had been bracing for had arrived. It was as bad as he'd feared. Then again, he'd known exactly what he was doing to get the maximum effect. It was time to fess up. "It wasn't a game or a joke. I said what I did so you wouldn't fight me, and I needed you to let me leave. But you were, and *are*, real. I had to go because of how real you are."

"To protect me," she clipped with an icy tone.

Thomas's spine stiffened. He took another step forward. "Damn straight."

Kick held out her hands to keep Thomas from coming closer.

"Then why are you here now? As far as I can tell, nothing's changed."

"I was wrong."

She stared up at the window. Thomas had the impression she was purposely trying to keep her gaze off of him. "I'm tired, Thomas. I need time to think. That's why I haven't returned your calls."

He sighed heavily, afraid he might have been too effective when he left her. "I know. I'm sorry. As soon as I realized how wrong I'd been, I had to see you. It couldn't wait."

When Kick finally turned toward Thomas, her face was wet and her nose had pinked. He wanted to stomp on his own heart the way he'd obviously done to hers. He reached for her.

"No, no, baby. Please don't cry."

"Don't." Kick gave him a wide berth and sat on the edge of a club chair, sitting with her spine tall and shoulders back with pride. "I won't tighten my emotions for other people's comfort anymore. Hell, you're the one who told me it takes strength to be vulnerable. These are tears of strength. Deal with it."

"I hate being the reason for them though." Thomas fell to his knees in front of her, brushing the tears off her cheeks with his thumbs. "What can I do to make it better? How can I make this up?"

Kick's breath hitched as she sniffed and dabbed at her face with the neck of her T-shirt. "First tell me what happened at the gala. From what I can tell, there's a disconnect between what I experienced and the truth. I need the whole truth if we're going to move forward."

"Well, I thought—"

"Stop." She raised her hand to go with the directive. "Thoughts are judgments and all I saw back then. Tell me how you *felt*. I promise to not contradict or condemn you."

Thomas sighed, resolved. "I was angry about being summoned to Bordeaux right before finals."

"You didn't have an option to finish the semester?" Kick's brows drew together, and Thomas watched her try to make sense of the situation. How could Thomas explain it though? He couldn't. Not yet. Her commitment had to come first.

"I didn't, but I can't say more. Not yet. I'm so sorry. Which leads me to now. Like then, I'm still afraid you'll tell me to go to hell."

"Hold on. What?" Kick's brow furrowed. "You make it sound like it's a given."

"Sometimes I *feel* like it is. Definitely did then."

"You doubt me?" She looked up at the ceiling. The angle of the sun had changed, and the butterflies no longer made their prismatic display. Kick turned back, and her eyes widened as if inspired by a thought. "This is about your secret, isn't it? It's about what happens in Bordeaux, and this is separate from teaching at Lord."

He inhaled audibly, on the verge of crossing his point of no return. "Yeah."

"The truth wouldn't send me away, Thomas, but secrets will. I might be shocked and angry, but I know who you are on the inside. At least I thought I did."

The tension wouldn't leave Thomas's shoulders, and he rubbed at them. He finally sat in the other club chair, pulling it as close to Kick's as he could get it. "I don't… can't say. Yet."

"I should warn you, I'm close to figuring it out."

He laughed at her preposterous assertion. "What makes you think so?"

"My da— Ah, intuition." Kick touched her heart. "Here. Liam and I both told you how I figure things out. Your secret is so close I can sense it." Her smile was a warning and a promise. Somehow it eased Thomas's muscles. Her voice softened. "I'm not worried, but I am concerned for you. It's better if you would trust me and just leap."

Thomas's heart deflated again. Trust wasn't his issue. He knew Kick would keep the secret. His gut told him one thing at a time, and the first thing was winning her back.

"I also hate myself for the temporary comment during our fight. I did plan to turn my work over to someone else. It wouldn't bother me to do it, if it were in the right hands. You are not my research." He reached over and cupped Kick's cheek. "I can't walk away from you though. You've awakened a part of my heart that I thought had died."

"I could say the same thing about mine."

Thomas shook his head. "You weren't dead. You were too busy to grieve."

"You hit the nail on the head, though, didn't you?"

"I don't understand."

"We've bypassed all the usual dating steps. Our only official date ended up with me glutened. We're busy, don't you see? At the same time, it's also deep—maybe too deep." Kick spoke with her chin down as if she were thinking aloud. She looked up with resolve in her eyes, turning him on. "I told you I'm struggling with the casual thing, but you need it, don't you?"

"Well—" He absolutely didn't. Not anymore.

"It's okay." She nodded, more to herself than to him. "We both know lifetime vows are a joke to the one who gets left behind." Kick leaned into the chair arm, setting off her breasts perfectly. Thomas seriously considered kicking himself in the ass. She continued, "Today's all we have, so I'll only ask you for the moments we can get. That and no lies."

"You know you've brought the light back to my life, right?"

She smiled shyly. "I used to think so."

Thomas ran his hand through his hair and declared the absolute truth. "You've never been disposable to me." She was breaking his heart. "I don't need dates either. They'd be nice, but our outside commitments haven't changed." He took her hands and raised each one to his lips. "It would be my honor if you'd let me back into your heart the way you still occupy mine. I promise we'll figure out the rest later." He'd make damn sure Banger and Tess held up their promises too. "Tell me what else you need."

"Will you stop with the loquaciousness?" Kick smiled widely and slugged him in the bicep. "I needed a good grovel to make up for your blindsiding." She tilted her head from side to side. "You've come close."

Thomas moved back to his knees and between her legs. Eye to

eye, he paused, wanting to get lost in them. Hell, he was a goner. "How's this?"

"It could work, especially since you didn't send me any flowers."

Thomas narrowed his gaze, letting her see his disdain, hoping she'd see everything now. "Flowers are for cheaters who only want to look like they're sorry."

"Right?"

"Now what?"

Kick moved forward and gave Thomas an eyeful of her cleavage, fritzing out his brain. She'd be the death of him. She tapped her lips. *Yes, ma'am.* Thomas moved over her, pressing her back into the chair and kissed her with all he had—his hopes and promises. Kick moaned and squirmed under him, giving back as much as she took. Then she tapped on his shoulder.

Thomas lifted his head and looked into Kick's eyes. Hers traveled to the camera in the corner on the ceiling. "It's on?" he asked.

"Always."

Christ. He sat back on his heels, both hands gripping the edge of the chair. "Think Deana's been watching?"

Kick giggled. "I bet she had a part-timer go buy popcorn."

He hung his head. "I need you so badly."

Kick ran her hand through his hair, stopping to cup his jaw as her thumb caressed the cleft in his chin. He kept his eyes shut and relished the moment. He thought of the time she'd done it in the parking garage, speaking her truth with the help of a drug. With the clearest of minds, Thomas said, "Let me give you the extraordinary. I'm trying to figure out how to do it."

"And I'm the last person to ask for perfection."

The intercom broke their spell, and Deana said in a quiet tone, "Sorry to bother you, Kick. The boys are here."

"Why is she whispering?" Thomas asked.

"Oh, she definitely saw us. She's probably corralling them in the dining room for our sakes." Kick grinned broadly—dazzling him—then bit her lip.

He kissed her again and asked, "What's up with the boys?"

"They're leaving Dylan's Beemer for Rachel and me to take to the mountains. His car does better in the snow than either of ours. I also have stuff to put in Liam's Jeep."

Thomas growled. "Why are y'all driving up separately?"

"Rachel is finishing up an incomplete this afternoon. We'll be fine. I'm the best driver on snowy roads anyway. Remember I grew up in the Midwest?"

He stood and offered a hand to Kick. When she was on her feet, he pulled her into a tight embrace, hugging her with his whole body. "You've given me the best present today."

She narrowed her eyes in a warning before exhaling and relaxing. "As long as you tell me everything. Soon."

"I will."

After helping load the cars, happily apologizing his ass off to the boys and enduring another round of threats from Dylan, Thomas settled in at the bar for a quick coffee and snack. He'd been drained when he entered the coffeehouse. Now he was practically dead on his feet, and he still had to drive to Virginia.

Before he could make his last ask of Kick, her friend Charley walked in. She greeted him politely, making him wonder if Charley had been out of the loop on their fight. Since they had made up, he wouldn't call it a breakup. Something struck Thomas as she stepped up to the register to place her order with Kick. The back of his neck itched and his eyes burned, like his mind fought hard to place where he knew Charley. This wasn't about Thanksgiving dinner either. Things like this occasionally happened to the Felidae members and others like them. When a person meets so many people in a lifetime, they're bound to run into doppelgängers of old friends. Sometimes it turned out they were the descendants of these people. Such was Thomas's sensation now. If he hadn't been eager to finish up with Kick, he would have casually worked up a conversation with Charley about her history. It wasn't hard to do when you ran a genetics lab. Instead, he let the women catch up for a few minutes while he searched his memory for old friends of Mexican or Spanish descent. Unfortunately for this task, he'd had many. He was still going through names as Charley passed. She placed a hand on his shoulder and said, "Merry Christmas, if you celebrate."

"Thank you. I do," he said, tipping his head. "Same to you. Do you have plans?"

"My brother is finally coming into town. Can't wait."

"Sounds wonderful."

Charley had been at the end of the line, so Kick made her way over to Thomas once her friend had left. "Why do I feel bad that Rachel's on her way up from campus?"

"There's no need to be conflicted." Thomas squeezed her hand. "I have to leave soon." He kissed her knuckles, not caring if any of the customers saw it. "Sure wish I could bring y'all with me. We need time together."

Kick leaned onto her elbows, leaving them eye to eye again. Thomas reveled in having her full attention on him. "I feel the same, but we wouldn't get much time alone in either of our scenarios. We have obligations, Professor."

"What about New Year's? Could you take another long weekend so soon?"

"With you?" Kick winked, then smirked. "Deana would move heaven and earth to make it work. Yeah." She nodded briskly. "I might not get a day off in January, but I'll make it happen."

"I'll be back on the morning of the thirtieth. Think you can come over around noon?"

Kick's eyes rose, and he practically saw her working out the schedule in her mind. "It should work."

"And stay through the first?"

Her grin turned into a wide smile. "I like this plan, Mr. Harrison. I'll see if Liam and the dog can stay with Dylan. He could use the company too."

"Good. I can travel safely, knowing we have time tucked away for ourselves." Thomas kissed her nose. "Then we can figure out how to make all this into something looking more normal."

Kick's lips parted with excitement. "You mean like a regular couple?"

He returned her earlier wink. "Exactly."

27

Have Yourself a Merry Little Christmas

Kick

OUR QUIET FAMILY TRIP TO THE MOUNTAINS TOOK A ROCKY TURN ON day two. After a late arrival and a morning of cross-country skiing, our nerves were as sore as our muscles. The boys had to share a room, which should've been no big deal for three nights.

However, little brothers forever remained little brothers when the big one was in a bad mood. With Dylan and Suzy officially over, I thought getting him away from the condo where they lived would do him some good. Instead, he'd been acting like a rabid wolf and Liam was a fresh ankle. After a howl, a scream, and a hard crash, I yanked their door open to find them wrestling on the floor in their skivvies.

"Boys!" After they ignored me, I took off my shoe and threw it at the wall where it bounced off and landed smack in the middle of them. You don't spend twenty years with a professional football player and not learn how to throw awkwardly shaped objects. I had a particular talent for short passes.

The boys sprang apart like they'd been electrocuted. I removed the other shoe. "There's one more here for whoever speaks out of turn. Dylan… you want to begin?" Despite his terrible temper, he was my go-to because I could usually make him see reason quickly.

"Sorry, Ma. I just need space," he huffed, raking his hands through his hair.

"And a fucking punching bag." My second shoe bounced off Liam's head. "Ow!" I had warned him.

I squeezed my eyes shut, quickly thinking about the correct way to mitigate. "You know, there's a reason I never became a judge, right?"

"We know," they said in unison. Yeah, it had often been the opening words to a long rant about kids expecting mothers to be cops, lawyers, and judges and the impossibility of it all.

"You two separate. Liam, join me in the living room. You can help me figure out why my laptop won't sign on to the Wi-Fi. Dylan, you have an hour in here, then I want your help cooking." Both boys grumbled and rose to their feet.

I continued. "As for sleeping, the last one up has the option of using the second bed in here or the sofa in the game room. Keep in mind, I won't enforce quiet hours once the rest of us wake in the morning."

"Gotcha," Dylan said.

"Sure, fam."

After signaling for Liam to follow me, I turned back to Dylan. "You know, son, Lee might have a point about the punching bag. There's a gym downstairs. And an indoor pool. Maybe you should try out the facilities, burn off some of the anger."

Dylan dropped his head, pinched the bridge of his nose, and broke my heart. "Sure. Sounds good," he whispered.

I set a hand on his shoulder. "Please don't sneak out though. I need your help later. Give me a heads-up before you leave."

"Gotcha," he repeated.

I turned back to Liam, jumped up slightly, and grabbed him by the earlobe—not the easiest thing when he was nearly a foot taller than me.

"God, fam." He fussed. "What the hell?"

"A young man acts like he's five. He gets treated like he's five."

"But he started—"

"Keep talking. You'll dig a deeper hole." I let go and took him with me into the kitchen where we unloaded the groceries I'd purchased.

"Dylan's in the middle of his first big breakup, Liam," I said. "Your sister is too. The least you and I can do is to be a soft place for them to land." I tapped him on the temple. "Use your noggin. If they snap at you, it doesn't mean you have to snap back. It's usually best to leave the room and give them a minute to decompress."

He whined, "This is going to be a long four days."

A WHILE LATER, LOUD MUSIC BEGAN BOOMING FROM RACHEL'S room, playing the same song over and over, and it wasn't Christmas-y. Initially it amused me to see the way the boys' eyes went wide at certain lyrics from Lily Allen's "Not Fair." By the fifth go-around, I actually winced and my sons grew ornery.

Dylan stood next to me in the kitchen, slicing sweet potatoes, while I prepped the chicken. Liam chopped broccoli at the table. The boys had taken up growling when the song would start over. At least they agreed on something. When the song rolled over a sixth time, Dylan dropped his knife with a sharp wrist flick and took a hard step toward Rachel's room. I reached for his arm, stopping him.

"Let me speak to her."

Dylan turned to me with fire in his expression, then exhaled and slumped his shoulders. "Yeah, okay." He resumed his potato job.

The knob on Rachel's door didn't budge, so I banged on it. Hard. "Rachel! You don't get to lock your mother out of a room in her own house. I don't care how old you are."

The music stopped, *thank Jaysus*. Feet padded across the room. A click sounded, and it opened. "This is a rental."

"I'm footing the bill."

"Right. Sorry." She scratched her nose. "I was thinking."

"Your brothers and I noticed. We need to talk."

She tilted her head, looking truly puzzled. "What about?"

I moved into her room, shut the door, and sat on the ski-themed bed. "Snow, you're not the only one of us who's upset about a breakup."

She waved her hand. "I'm fine—"

"You've played "Not Fair" almost six times in a row." I laughed, remembering the uncomfortable grimaces on the boys' faces. "It doesn't take a degree in psychology to figure out the song's appeal." I lowered my voice and tried not to giggle. "Your usually thick-headed brothers figured it out, and they're kind of freaked out."

"Oh." Her eyebrows lifted. "Oh! Shit… but… don't you think they know I'm not a virgin?"

"Of course they know. They also try very hard to not think about it."

She sat up indignantly. "How is this my problem?"

I sighed, exhausted from the drive and my own emotional roller coaster. "If Dylan were blissfully happy, I might tell him to get over it. Right now you're both on edge. Can we all try to keep our problems in Oakville though? I want us to have fun with each other. Okay, sweetie?"

Rachel almost shrugged, but it dissolved into shakes. "He gave her the present I had asked for. You know what that means? Cody gave that bitch *my* present!"

I tucked a curl behind my ear. "How do you know this?"

Rachel's phone seemed to appear out of thin air. She held it out for me. "She posted it on the Gram."

"Oh." I let my head drop into my hand. Then I grabbed her phone and abruptly stood.

"What are you doing?" Rachel reached for me, but motherly indignance must have sped up my reflexes.

"Blocking them." I worked quickly while Rachel objected. "If you're going to pursue this Broadway thing"—I blocked the girl—"you're going to need social media to advance your career." I found Cody easily enough. His new girl had tagged him. "But you need to learn how to be the boss of your accounts. Don't let anyone get it over on you because of some stupid Gram tag." A few taps and Cody was gone too. I handed the phone back over.

"Sweetheart, I know you can undo this later, but please don't. I also know you understand the illusion all this crap is. Curate it so it makes you happy, not sad." I tipped my chin back at her feed. "It should be filled with pretty inspiration images, not stupid taunts."

"Yeah." Rachel blew out a long breath. "I guess so." She brought the phone to her face and yelled, "I Marie Kondo'd you, *bitch!*"

We both laughed and hugged. "There's my girl." I gestured for her to follow me.

My phone buzzed with a text alert from Thomas. They had been arriving at regular intervals since we made up. In need of a distraction, I swiped the phone awake and found a link to a song. I told Rachel to help her brothers in the kitchen and I would join them in a few minutes. After closing the door to the owner's suite, I opened the attachment.

Using the endearment "baby" made Al Green's "I'm So Tired of Being Alone" feel like it was written for me. Thomas tugged hard at my heartstrings with it. His attention pointed to an honest penance, as he'd been pouring his heart out through song lyrics. It was like he'd given himself permission to feel. The songs were my favorite present so far. I sent a message back.

ME

Wow! Putting it all out there. I needed it.
Thank you.

I added an attachment: Pink Martini's "Dream a Little Dream."

ME

Hope your holiday is going well.

The ping back arrived immediately.

THOMAS

Tomorrow will be rough.

ME

I'm sorry. It's been emotion-central here, too.

THOMAS

The 30th will be our refuge.

ME

Can't wait to breathe you in.

THOMAS

You kill me. I'll dream of you. Do the same,
baby.

ME

With pleasure.

I left the room and joined my kids in the kitchen for a little chat. "Listen up, crew. Half of us are happy, and half of us are hurting. Can we all make a promise to tread lightly?"

"Guess so."

"Sure, fam."

"Yes, Mama."

"Thank you. Now, how about we also promise only to play Christmas music? At least until the twenty-sixth. I especially don't want to hear any sad songs or breakup songs. We'll save them for when we get back to Oakville."

"Aren't there sad Christmas songs though?" Liam asked.

"Not this year," I answered. "If one comes up, skip it. Remember our theme for this holiday?"

In unison, they said, "To have ourselves a merry little Christmas," in a drone I'd expect from little kids, not my grown ones.

"Jaysus. There's an enormous chasm between *Elf* enthusiasm and you three." They each chuckled, making me think there might be hope for our trip.

I gripped Rachel's and Dylan's hands, looked them in their eyes, and said, "This will probably be our last holiday together as our foursome." Squeezing the hand to my left and my right, I continued, "It might not feel like it right now, but you will add new loved ones to our table. Littles might even show up if we're so blessed." I caught Rachel's vigorous head shake out of the corner of my eye, but the center of my focus was Dylan. "In the right time."

Liam grinned but stayed quiet. The other two almost seemed amused too.

"I'm not only talking about Thomas." I bumped shoulders with Dylan. "You already moved out." My head tipped to Rachel and Liam in turn. "My empty nest days are right around the corner, regardless. You may not appreciate the brevity of it, but I do."

Rachel asked, "But we can always come back home, right?"

"My house is always open to you guys. I'm not sure if I'll stay in our big house though."

A cloud of fear and sadness descended upon the room. I tapped the table. "Hey now, these are good changes, not bad. You're supposed to grow up and have your own lives."

I took a deep breath and addressed the elephant in the room. "Dylan and Rachel, it turns out your relationships were practice ones. You've both learned important lessons at a young age. I, for one, can't wait to meet the people you're meant to be with."

A micro-smile reached Rachel's face. Neither of the kids was ready for an official move-on pep talk, so I didn't dare go any further. Dylan looked to be near tears.

"All done with the motherly sermon," I told the younger two. "I need to speak with your brother now."

"What should I do?" Rachel asked.

Liam saved the day when he said, "Want to help me with a song?"

"I guess." I glared at my daughter, warning her to listen to my words and enjoy her little brother. They went down the hall to the media room.

I turned to Dylan. "Doing any better?"

"The workout helped a lot. Thanks for the idea." I couldn't believe he still had energy to burn after our cross-country skiing outing earlier, but there was a major, physical difference between us. Dylan walked over to the fridge, pulled out a soda, and popped the top. "Teach me how to be strong, like you were after Dad died."

"I don't remember being strong, lad." Dylan drank from the

can, then returned to his chair at the table. I rubbed his shoulder, remembering those horrible early days. "You can start by learning the difference between strength and resilience, like I did. Focus on strength and it's easy to go cold, to numb out. Resilience though? It acknowledges the pain, feels it all, and moves forward anyway."

Dylan sighed. "I want to get back to normal me."

I grabbed his chin as I inhaled deep, preparing for a hard truth. "This *is* your normal now, lad. *This* you loves deeply. You can move ahead with the knowledge and believe one day the right person will be at your side, loving you and being loved in return. It'll be beautiful, son."

"It's embarrassing. Aside from my wrecked heart, the investors look at all areas of my life to see if I'm a stable risk. How am I supposed to build a successful startup when I can't make one person happy?"

"I think the word you're looking for is humbling, not embarrassing. And let me tell you, there's no better leader than a humble one. That person understands forgiveness. Service too."

"So what do I do?"

I wished I had something strong to drink, but I hadn't touched any alcohol after the attack. "Here's what I did: I set the alarm every day, no matter what. Each morning, I woke up shocked to find myself alone and was afraid I wouldn't get out of bed if I didn't have to turn it off."

Tears threatened as I found myself back in that headspace. I blinked several times to keep them at bay. "My toothbrush still worked, so I used it—even if it looked lonely in the cup."

I reached for Dylan's soda and took a sip. "The point is, I took tiny steps to get through the day. Then one morning, I woke and noticed the sun filtering through the drapes and thanked heaven for it. At the time, it felt like for-fecking-ever to get there. Now it's a memory of the lowest low, mixed with the highs of you kids and life-changing lessons."

"Can't wait," he scoffed.

"You'll get there. I promise." Still not sure if he believed me, I stood and leaned against the counter. The smooth chill helped take the edge off my sad memories. "Do you know where Suzy is now?"

He clipped out acerbically, "In Greensboro with her precious parents. She's moving her stuff into Mai's apartment on the thirtieth."

"Will you be there?"

"I won't lift a thing. It's on her to get a crew, but I will make sure she goes."

"That's the day Liam and Koosh are coming over."

"It's fine. She'll be done by noon. Dum and I have already ordered the replacement stuff—mainly a new television and couch. We'll be ready by the time Dimp and the dog show up."

"Dylan…" I swear, these kids were born to get on my nerves. Here I'd been pouring my heart out too. Still, I laughed before schooling my face into motherly disappointment. "Don't call your brother Dimp. I feel bad enough abandoning him for New Year's Eve."

"You serious? Mom, stop." He paused so long I didn't think he had more to add. "When Dad was alive, didn't you guys do it big every New Year's Eve?"

I smiled at the memory. "Yes, usually. I haven't thought about it in ages."

"I remember. You'd both dress up in fancy clothes. Granddad and Grandma kept us. Or didn't we have a couple of neighborhood girls one year? Yeah. They were nice to us. Nicer than Gran anyway. Do you want pretty boy hanging out with Gran by himself?"

We shuddered in unison at the thought.

"God no. She'll still be out of town anyway, and he's eighteen. I mean, I trust him not to burn down the house. But I don't want him to feel like he's cramping my style. I still want him to feel special too."

Dylan raised his hands like he couldn't take any more. "Chill. Please." He put his arm around my shoulder and squeezed. "Have you considered the possibility that Liam's dicking around with school and college decisions because he's afraid of leaving you alone?"

"Uh…" *Hell, really?* Had I missed another thing? I thought Liam was the kid I didn't have to worry about, other than how his college prep test went.

Dylan smirked at me. "Didn't think so. In pretty boy's mind, if he dinks around at community college, he won't have the guilt of going away. With Thomas around, he has permission to figure out what he actually wants to do with his life."

My spine straightened. "What does Thomas have to do with anything? I'd never hold you kids back."

"Sure. Doesn't mean we wouldn't feel bad about leaving you alone though."

"We?"

"Yeah. We don't want to see you alone. Something from a psych class has stuck with me. What was it exactly?" He snapped his fingers. "Oh right. 'Nothing is a bigger burden on children than the unlived life of a parent.' Was it Freud?"

"Seriously doubt it," I murmured through my shock and guilt.

He snapped again. "No, Jung. Definitely Jung."

I dropped my head into my hands. "Kill me now. Should I write checks to all three of you or make one big one you can divvy up?"

"For what?"

"Therapy. All this time I thought focusing on you three would fill in the gap your father left. Now you tell me I've screwed you up anyway."

"No. Shit. That's not what I mean." He patted my head and chuckled. "Look at our extended family. You were doomed to fuck us up with or without Dad."

I groaned and fussed with the curls hanging in my face.

Dylan's laugh grew. At least I'd cheered him up. "I'm kidding. All in all, I'd say we're fairly functional. It's quite an achievement." He bumped my shoulder. "Well done."

"Are you serious?" I looked up, hopeful yet cognizant of his penchant for messing with me.

Still, I was stunned. Dylan had chosen a university close to home, but it was one of the best in the country for his major. I thought staying nearby had been as much for him as for me. It had been so close to Shane's death that I didn't think any of us were ready to lose another family member. Had I been wrong? Had I kept him from living his true dream? It hit me hard how we hadn't talked enough about the important stuff.

Over the years, I noticed a common trait among kids whose parents had chronic health problems. While the parent often went out of their way to pretend everything was hunky-dory so their kid could have a "normal" life, the child also kept problems from the sick parent to lighten the parent's daily burden. *Shit.*

As usual, Dylan paid no mind to my tune out and continued on about his plans for Liam. "He can help us get the condo back in shape the first night. Then we're having a guy's poker night on the thirty-first. There's a chair with Liam's name on it. PB will be fine. I'll make sure he has fun."

"PB?"

Dylan tossed his mischievous side-eye my way. "You don't like Dimp, so I'll try out Pretty Boy."

"Seriously?" Honestly, my kids could exasperate me so easily.

"It has a ring." Dylan kept his eye on me, challenging me to yell the smirk off his face.

"The boy has always been insanely gorgeous," I quietly admitted.

"I know, right?"

"It's the dimple."

"The curls too." It was good to see a spark of mischief in Dylan's silver eyes. The corner of his mouth twitched.

"He'll beat you up one of these days though. I hope I'm there to video it."

He puffed his chest out as if he were invincible. "Bring it, Mom. Bring it *on*." After what he'd just told me, it lifted my spirit to see evidence that he wasn't completely crushed. Dylan would move past the pain of both Suzy's betrayal and their breakup with the efficiency that came from being young.

Something he said earlier gave me pause. I pulled away and gave him a stern look. "Hey, you're not going to make Koosh stay in the house all day, are you? Her bladder can't hold it in forever."

"I'll put PB on Macushla duty. It'll be his hotel fee."

"Way to make him feel like an honored guest. Glad I raised you right."

He squeezed me again and added a couple of pats for good measure. In a surprisingly accurate imitation of my late father-in-law's accent, he said, "But you've done just grand, me darlin' mudder. A grand job indeed."

I wondered how long it would take to know if Dylan was right.

28

Merry Christmas, Baby

Kick

MY BLADDER WOKE ME CHRISTMAS MORNING BEFORE DAWN. I HAD decided it would be a good time to reintroduce caffeinated coffee. The genuine stuff. A present to myself for working hard and not giving up despite the setbacks. "My precious," I said in a Golem voice as I watched the water flow through the paper filter into the carafe.

The condo's main living area faced east. There was something about watching the sunrise from the top of a mountain on Christmas morning. It called to me. With my coffee in hand, wrapped in a thick fleece blanket, warm slippers on my feet, I slid the patio door open and slipped into a deck chair, closing myself up tightly to ward off the chill.

Memories of the magic of Christmases past flooded in. Of the time when babies and small children were the stars of the holiday. Each child had taken a turn bounding into our bedroom to wake us up for presents. One did it at three in the morning. I searched my visual memory bank for a face on said menace and glimpsed long, black ringlets bouncing on my side of the bed, yelling, "Waffles,

Mama. Izz Kwiss-miss. Make waffles." Rachel—the little imp. Liam had been a newborn, and after only three hours of sleep, I snapped back at her, making her cry on Christmas morning.

There lay the reason I tended to lose those memories—they were intricately bound to the pain of undiagnosed illness, misunderstandings, and the false accusation of being lazy. When it came to the kids' childhood moments, my brain couldn't recall a sweet memory without an ugly one popping up alongside it. It was a major part of the reason I'd clung to the adage of living in the moment. The only problem with the plan was how quickly children grew.

I had done my utmost to keep my illness from ruining their childhood. Still, instead of enjoying what was supposed to be my best years—the magical time as a young parent—I was often robbed of the joy. I wiped away a tear as the sky changed as quickly as my kids had grown.

Blink and the horizon was red.

Blink again, it turned pink.

Another blink and there came the orange.

Tip the mug, swallow some liquid energy, and the sky had turned to yellow.

So be it.

It was time to make peace with the madness of the past. Christmas breakfast before dawn had become a leisurely brunch at eleven. Nothing was wrong or right about any of it, it simply reflected the state of our family. Plenty of people had shitty holidays. I decided against lingering in self-pity and regret and dissected the beautiful memories from the diseased ones. If my body was doing better, it was high time I whipped my mind into shape, starting with the holidays.

It didn't take long before thoughts turned toward what the future would be like. I couldn't believe I'd almost become a grandmother already. I wouldn't have freaked personally. Plenty of my girlfriends had grandchildren. I knew Dylan wasn't ready yet. None of my kids were. I wondered how Thomas would've reacted to the hypothetical. I took another sip from my mug and envisioned him with us next Christmas. Would it happen? Would we travel to

Virginia with him? To Bordeaux? I couldn't take the speculation any longer and sent a text in case he was up. My phone rang almost immediately.

"Merry Christmas," I whispered upon accepting the call.

"Are the kids still asleep?"

"Yes. But I am outside. I don't know why I'm whispering."

"I like it. It makes me feel like you're in bed with me."

"Shit. You weren't up. I'm sorry."

"I'm still in bed, but I've been awake for a while. Don't apologize."

I grew concerned by his words and asked, "Is everything okay with your family? In Bordeaux?"

The low laugh rumbled through the phone, laced with a morning rasp. Hearing the sound was another gift. I chided myself for feeling too much, too fast. I had promised Thomas one day at a time, and I'd meant it.

"It's all of it, baby. What has you roused so early?"

"I usually am. The opportunity to see the sunrise from the top of a mountain was something I didn't want to miss."

"Mm. You're facing east then?" he rasped some more.

"The balcony is. We have views on three sides, which spread for miles. It's so beautiful up here. I could stay forever."

"We'll have to go back together. I love the mountains. In fact, I think I'll get up now and go for a hike before we leave for the nursing home. Thanks for the idea. I've been laying here wondering how to fix things I have no control over and kicking myself for wallowing in self-pity."

"I did the same thing. I sat on the porch thinking I'd find peace and ended up in a pity party. After chastising myself, I remembered this must be a tough day for you too."

"A party for two then?"

"No. Sorry. I've always cleared away the ugliness in my head by placing my focus somewhere else. I honestly wanted to make sure you were okay."

"I know. It was only a tease. And stop apologizing. We both have more problems than Cracker Barrel has biscuits." There was a rustle in the background, like sheets shifting. "Your call will be my favorite gift this year. It's helped more than you know."

"Your chuckle is mine."

"You like my morning voice?"

"Very much. It's my new drug, and I'd gladly get addicted." He rewarded me with another demonstration of his low belly rumble. "I never thanked you for the butterflies."

"You were distracted."

I laughed into the phone. "That's one way to describe it. Seriously, were they handmade?"

"Yep. A glass blower in the village by the vineyard has a big one in the front window. I asked him if he did smaller ones in various stages of flight."

"You commissioned them?" I didn't know what else to say. Until this moment, I thought Thomas's first set of messages had been about appeasing his guilt. I didn't think he had an actual change of heart until right before he'd left France. It sounded like I was wrong. My breath caught, making my words come out breathy. "I love them."

"You're welcome. Don't get too flustered though. You have more gifts coming."

"I do?"

"Absolutely. When you come over on the thirtieth. Expect to be wooed."

"Wow." I was filled with a childlike wonder, thinking about what he had planned. "It's a good thing I didn't send your present back."

"You didn't?" He sounded almost smug about it.

"No. I ordered it before the gala, but I've been too swamped to deal with the postal service. So you're one lucky fella."

Thomas inhaled and let out a long "hmmm" over the line. "No kidding."

Our conversation lulled, and I saw two predator birds catch a vertical draft, their wings outstretched as they circled each other and let the current lift them. It looked like such a peaceful gift to be able to let go and give the wind control. Then it occurred to me they were probably on the hunt for breakfast. A breeze snuck around the sides of the balcony and caught my breath from the iciness.

"I should go in. I'm getting chilly."

"What are you doing the rest of the day?"

"Shower, dress in holiday yoga gear…" Thomas laughed. Oh, to make him laugh all the time. It lit me up to hear it. I continued, "A light snack until the kids wake. A brunch casserole is cooking in the Crockpot. Between now and then, I'll read. That'll be another gift for me. One of my favorite authors released a Christmas novella for her motorcycle club series. I can't wait to dig in."

His chuckle deepened. "Christmas at a motorcycle club?"

"Why not?" I laughed too, making sure I kept the noise down. "Honestly, I'm tired from skiing and looking forward to vegging out. You should go so you can hike."

"Can I call you later? Our lunch with Ken will be hard for all of us. Your voice lifts my spirits." Thomas's tone dropped and grew serious. "Damn, baby. When I walk through the rooms of my house here—both the newer areas and the original ones—I wonder what your reaction would be to them."

"Oh." I imagined him telling the historical significance of each cubby and corner. "I would love all of it. You know, I might take a nap later, but I'll have the phone nearby. Please call anytime."

"Alright. Bye, baby. Thanks for thinking of me."

"Merry Christmas, sweetheart."

My kids surprised me by waking up early. Rachel turned on an old ceramic tree I'd inherited from my grandmother. It sat on a table in front of a picture window overlooking a ski trail. The presents had been stacked under the table. When I had packed it, my only concern had been for its cuteness and convenience, so it was a joyous gift to feel the history and memories the little tree represented. I felt the warmth of the family members I had loved my whole life as I made new memories with my kids.

As usual, they had unwrapped their gifts in no time.

My favorite present from them was a photo. They had re-created a Santa picture from when they were one, four, and seven. Stranger shy, Liam screamed the entire time on Santa's lap while Dylan frowned at me for not helping his baby brother. Rachel's fake smile, head toward the camera and gaze out of the corner of her eyes, gave away her own nervousness. It's so classically awful it always made me laugh. Their grown-up version, with Liam faking the same scream, was a hilarious surprise.

"You guys know me so well. Thank you." Their grins and pride in pulling off a group present made my heart swell. There might not be silly family movies and magical presents anymore, but this day with our little unit would be a treasure. My last gift to them was ultimately a gift to me—new snowboards for each. Within an hour, they were fed, dressed, and off for an afternoon on the slopes. And I took my nap.

THE PHONE RANG WHILE I READ A BOOK AND LISTENED TO MUSIC, comfortably tucked into the love seat in the living room. "Hey, Thomas." What the hell was with my voice? It had a wispy Marilyn Monroe vibe.

"Hi, baby," he muttered, adding in a sad sigh.

"That bad?"

"I'm toast. Guess I don't do emotions so well."

"No kidding?" I bit my lip, wanting to take back my go-to sarcasm. I tried to lighten it by adding a giggle. "I hadn't noticed."

He sighed again into the phone, his anguish crystal clear.

"Sorry, sweetheart. I didn't mean to make light of it. Do you want to talk about it?"

"Not really. It won't change anything. Toni's living the nightmare. I'm left watching it happen while trying to support her."

"But I want to help you while you help your family."

"Alright. Tell me what y'all are doing right now." I should've guessed Thomas would deflect. I wished I could tell whether it was to distract himself or me. Was this about emotional overload or more of Thomas's secrets? Then again, maybe he simply didn't feel comfortable talking about other people's business. I respected that, especially since mine seemed to be plastered all over town lately.

When I considered the ridiculousness of what I had been doing, a belly laugh erupted from me. "I've been listening to 'Have Yourself a Merry Little Christmas' for the past two hours. And reading."

"One song?"

My chuckle continued. "No. It's Liam's idea of a gag present. It's my favorite Christmas song, and I made it the theme of this year's celebration since we only have the four of us. Mr. Smarty-Pants hunted for every version of the song he could find. I'm required to listen to it this afternoon so I'll finally get it out of my system."

"Sounds like torture."

"It's fine." I shifted and shook out the back of my hair. "The ones I don't like, I remove. It's been fun comparing them. I have definite opinions about each version."

"There's a surprise. You have opinions about everything."

My eyebrows furrowed as insecurity took over. "Is that a bad thing?"

Thomas's tone returned to its soothing purr. "Not to me." I heard a ruffle of material that was lower than a squeak and softer than a creak. I guessed he was in a leather chair.

"Where are you right now?"

"In the library. It's relaxing in here, looking out at the stables and woods. Joe's upstairs napping after working with the horses. So there's more privacy here than in my rooms right now."

"Wait. You have horses?"

"It's Joe's business, but our family has bred them for generations. He's pared it back from what it used to be. Most of our current horses are boarders."

I sighed in approval and fished for an invitation. "I had no idea. I'd love to ride one sometime."

"Sure. Didn't know you could."

"It's been a while. I ran out of time for it in college."

I sensed his mood turning dark again and heard the longing when he remarked, "I wish you could drive up here now."

My heart broke for Thomas's circumstances at the same time it lifted me to know how much I mattered. "Any chance you could come home?"

I heard another sound like material rubbing on leather. "There's still three big meetings to attend regarding the running of the estate, then a delivery to oversee at my farmhouse. It won't be ready until the thirtieth, and I'm driving down with it first thing in the morning."

"Interesting… What is it?"

His voice lifted, and I could see a smile on his lips in my mind. "A surprise."

I played along and flirted back, hoping to encourage a better mood. "Ooh. I like the sound of this. When do I get to see it?"

"It'll be ready when you arrive. You're planning to spend the night, right?"

"Yes. We're set with the boys."

"Excellent." He grew quiet again. I reminded myself my new beau was a brooder.

"I don't like this gloomy tone, especially not today. No one should be sad at Christmas. What can I do?"

"What if we sexy-Zoomed?"

"No." I laughed at his request. This man and his middle school mind. "As part of your penance, you get the goods in real life or not at all. The Wi-Fi here is sketchy anyway. It would probably end up looking like a trailer for a horror movie."

He clicked his tongue and sighed in a way I knew chastised my joke. Then he paused so long I thought the call had dropped. Finally Thomas demanded in the raspy rumble I adored, "Tell me what you want me to do when you come to me."

"I'd like to see your surprise and then play it by ear. I can't wait to hang out."

"Kick…," he growled.

"What? Oh." I giggled, cottoning on to his meaning. "Well, of course I want to do *that*."

"Tell. Me. What. You. Like."

I reached for my glass of water to quench a sudden dryness. "All of it, I guess."

"Everyone has preferences, Kick. Tell me yours now so it won't take so long to puzzle out. Then I'll spend the next few days dreaming about doing those things to you."

My knees would've folded if I hadn't already been sitting. I racked my brain to find honest, sexy, and seductive words. I hated being hopelessly out of practice. "It's been so long—"

"Kick…"

My breath disappeared, and I blurted, "You know how people talk about the pleasure of pain?"

"Yes."

"It doesn't work that way for me. Pain is and forever will be only pain. I've spent too much time living in—and with—it for it to be sensual."

"Alright. Go on," he drawled.

"With what?"

"What do you mean? Make me picture it."

"Seriously?" I sucked at phone sex. He laughed at my reaction. "Fine," I said defiantly, grateful he couldn't see my good old Celtic blush. "Biting is pain. Pulling is pain. Pinching is pain. I don't know."

"What brings you the greatest bliss?" Before I knew what was happening, Thomas pulled deep truths from me.

A memory from the early days of my treatments came to mind. "A while ago, I tried all the massage techniques out there, especially the aggressive type." I chuckled lightly. "I thought I needed to live by the scripture, 'I beat my body and make it my slave.' Only it didn't work."

"Did anything work?"

I would have told everything to his liquid-smooth voice. The sound brought back images of lying in his bed the morning after we'd been together.

The western sun rays penetrated my eyes, making me sink into the sofa for refuge until they passed. I focused on the light particles dancing overhead as I explained, "I tried this popular Rolfing expert. When she walked into the room, she declared I needed something different. She called it light-touch. Thomas, I relaxed like I couldn't remember ever having done before."

"Fascinating."

"Apparently, my body tightened in a protective response to rough contact. Her light strokes allowed blood to flow into my muscles because they released the tension—like a physical sigh. That's what I want."

"A physical sigh?"

"Yes."

"Hmm."

"Now what are you thinking?"

"I'm thinking about how I'm going to make you physically sigh."

I literally sighed in pleasure over the phone. Thomas's sexy burr meant I'd achieved my goal to lighten his spirits. "Am I helping your mood?"

"I need to go up to my room," he muttered. "You?"

"It's plenty warm in here. Did I say enough?"

"You're killing me."

"Sorry. Too much?"

"Stop apologizing. It's perfect. I knew the answer to my question would get heated, but I didn't expect to be this bothered. When you're back in my bed, I'll have to figure out what it will take to keep you there."

"You already know the answer."

I watched the light particles some more as I waited for Thomas.

"Working on it, baby."

"I know."

"Thank you once again for your honesty and vulnerability. I'm not worthy of it, but you're teaching me how to do better."

Again, the man threw Kryptonite words at me, turning me into a lusty mush ball. "I swear, if the kids weren't here, I'd hop in my car."

"My turn to apologize now. If honesty is what you need, I actually miss them too. I loved Thanksgiving, Kick. All of it."

"Keep letting me in and you can have it."

Thomas shifted again. This time I heard the creaking of floorboards. "I'll figure out a way. I promise."

I stood, too, and watched out the picture window. I loved his new determined inflection. Thrilling to think it was for me. "You know, I'm beginning to believe you. The kids are due back soon though."

"Nice hint." He chuckled again, and it pleased me to hear him continue to do it. "Will you think of me throughout the day?"

I laughed at the challenge. "Yes, and your smooth, sexy accent too. It might make me miss you more."

"Think of me imagining you."

Careful, Kick, you're about to leap off the cliff. Defensiveness seeped into my thoughts as fear of his other side unfairly crept in. I'd been burned harder than I had admitted, but he deserved his chance at forgiveness too.

"Since you ask nicely, I will."

"Yours is the only face I see when I close my eyes lately."

"Careful, Thomas. We're keeping it casual and in the present, right?"

"Yes," he drawled. "We are."

"I don't want to scare you anymore."

"Don't worry about me."

"Thomas, what you said a second ago… Do you mean you've… pleasured yourself… thinking about me?"

He cleared his throat and teased. "I do believe I have, Kick."

A wide grin spread across my face, and I made an unladylike—definitely not sexy—sound. "Awesome." Pride tickled my insecure inner girl.

"Did you just chortle?"

"Is that what that was?"

"You're proud of yourself."

"Maybe? It's a new concept for me."

"Kick…" The liquid honey way he drew out my name almost set off an orgasm. The man should've been in radio. Before

Thomas could finish his thought, another muffled voice traveled through the phone.

"Be right there, Joe." He turned his attention back to me. "Been summoned, baby."

"I hope my kids stay as close as you three. Your parents would be proud."

"Thanks. We haven't always been, but we're working on it." Thomas's words caught, and he cleared his throat. "Knowing y'all, the McKenna kids will always get along."

I scoffed. "Hell, I've already broken up a fight between the boys and negotiated the oddest of music compromises between the boys and Rachel."

"Tell me all about it when I see you," he said, laughing. Then his tone turned serious again. "Thanks for cheering me up."

"I'm so glad it worked."

"You know it did. I'll be pestered about my perma-grin, but it's worth it. Have yourself a merry little Christmas, baby."

"You too, Thomas," I whispered. I wished I could keep him on the line forever.

29

Delirious

Kick

I parked in the circular drive at Thomas's farmhouse, pulled my suitcase and some bags from the trunk, and followed the path to the side door. My feet practically floated above the pavers. In a few seconds, those weeks apart would be nothing more than a memory. I worked hard to stay in the moment and cherish the good without expectations for more.

Thankfully, Deana had been a godsend when I told her about taking more time off. "Are you kidding me?" she had said. "Go get yourself some of his man-meat right now, shug." Of course, Thomas had still been in Virginia. So she volunteered to cover everything over New Year's with the promise that I feast myself on "the professor's prime rib until you can't walk straight." Calling her Thomas's biggest fan would be an understatement. As a thank-you to Dee and the staff, I declared New Year's Eve and Day additional vacation days. We all deserved it.

Thomas opened the door as my foot hit the steps on the small porch. When he pulled me into his arms, it felt like home. Without ever completely letting me go, he deftly discarded my bags and walked us into the kitchen before hanging on some more.

I could've spent the next three days right there, doing nothing else. Okay, maybe not, but his presence, his woodsy scent, and his heartbeat had enough power to sustain me. The rest added up to dessert—the best kind.

Thomas tucked his nose in my hair and inhaled deeply. It was pulled loosely into a scrunchy, and several pieces had fallen out in front. He peppered light kisses down my neck, back up, and along my jaw, warming me up. It didn't help that I had worn my heavy winter jacket. Straight-line winds had dramatically announced a cold front in the morning. Right then, one gust shook the kitchen window, but my ski-weight coat made me sweat.

"Thomas?"

"Hmm?"

"I'm getting hot."

"God, baby, me too."

I laughed at him, off in his own lustful world. "Can I have a moment to take off my coat?"

He paused his veneration long enough for me to slip out of it and hang it in the mudroom. I turned around to find him staring at me. The butterflies in my stomach took flight, only they were not the kind to fly because of anxiety. These were the good kind, the happy kind, like being a teenager with my first lover again.

"Well? What?"

A warm smile filled his face as he extended his hand. "Come."

I glided with him as if caught in a trance, around the kitchen island, to find he'd been in the middle of preparing our meal. "You were fixing lunch. What can I do to help?"

He moved toward me and said, "Just this." Then he leaned down and kissed me with all the emotions we'd built up through the numerous texts and phone calls over the past week. The softness of Thomas's lips, his tongue, and his citrusy, sandalwood, *him* turned me to liquid by the time we came up for breath.

I placed my hand on his cheek and said, "You can kiss me anytime. Now what?"

"Sit. Let me serve you."

The idea excited me, but I was too familiar with the consequences of throwing culinary caution to the wind and didn't want our time together to end after another awkward start. Sure, he'd managed successful takeout and the sous-chef time at Thanksgiving, but they weren't home cooking. Most people didn't understand the details and substitutions of eating my way. It seemed cruel to expect him to have it down already.

"Are you positive you don't want help?"

He kissed my temple and eased my concerns. "The soup and flatbread are from the gluten-free restaurant in Durham. Bacon crumbles are uncured. Hard-boiled eggs and nuts are organic. Rachel gave me the recipe for your salad dressing—which is fantastic, by the way. Now let me finish chopping the lettuce."

"Okay, okay." I raised my hands in surrender. "How about I get the plates and silverware?"

"Fabulous… after you read this." He wiped his hands on a towel, then handed me an envelope sitting on the island.

I looked at Thomas curiously, finding no clues as to the contents in his expression. I removed the papers, unfolding them.

"Medical papers. Yours?" My eyes lifted but only found his back. He'd washed his hands and was chopping up cucumbers. "What's this about?"

He looked over his shoulder. "You haven't been with anyone in years—except for me, of course." I blushed at the statement, feeling like an amateur even though I could have numbered off countless reasons why I'd lived my life the way I did. I also knew Thomas didn't intend for me to defend myself. He continued, "This is proof I'm clean too." He padded over and kissed my temple. "I can't remember the last time I didn't use a condom, and I haven't been as active as you think I have. Anyway, would it be alright to ditch the barrier? Just us?"

"But this means we would be exclusive and a bit more than casual."

"It better. Are you planning on seeing anyone else?" Thomas's face flashed with something like jealousy.

"No." I tucked one of those curls behind my ear. "Jaysus, I had to rework my schedule to be with you. When would I get time for another?" My voice quieted when he growled and I realized my blunder. "That's not what I mean… I don't want anyone else," I confessed. "I promise. I thought you wanted us to wait on making any big decisions."

Thomas tipped his head toward the papers. "This is what I want."

I slid my arms around him to let him know how much his declaration meant, and he kissed me again. "It's settled then?"

I nodded, too moved for words.

"Good. Now, would you set our places?" He pointed to the cabinet above the dishwasher and the drawer next to it.

I spotted a napkin holder nearby and set plates for two on the far end of the island. I poured myself a glass of water and moved closer to Thomas to watch him work. I hopped up on the counter, intending to chat with him and sip my drink. I sat with my hands on the edge, my head hanging down as I stretched my neck, working out kinks from nerves and the previous long days. Whether for good reasons or bad, any form of jitters had a way of locking up my neck muscles. I was forever taking moments to stretch this or that limb to keep pain at bay.

The chopping sound stopped, and I looked up to see Thomas staring at me, his eyes dark and heated. I raised my eyebrows in inquiry.

"What are you doing?" he asked, almost sounding incredulous.

A blush bloomed across my face and chest as I looked around. "I didn't feel like moving a stool over here. I-I hopped up on the counter to be close to you and to speak with you while you work. I—"

He took a step toward me like a predatory animal. "Not what I meant. You don't know, do you?"

"What?"

"I caught your movements out of the corner of my eye, turned around, and you were writhing like a cat on a sunny patio. Then the way you bent over—Kick, I can practically see down to your navel. It's like personal porn. You really don't know?"

Suddenly parched, I took a sip of water and shook my head.

He stepped into me and slid his hands, open-fingered, into my hair at the base of my skull. Pulling my mouth to his, he took my lips with a wonderful, claiming force.

He remembered not to tangle his hand in my curls. He listened and touched my hair the way I liked it. He gave me his respect and vulnerability when he took what only I could give him. This might be heaven.

"You're wearing the sweater I asked you to and a skirt. Your hair… it looks exactly how I pictured it. Don't know if I can finish making lunch. I had planned to make sure you had enough energy for later, but… would you mind if later is now?" As I answered with a shake of my head and a devilish grin, Thomas fingered the bow at the waist of my wrap sweater. "May I?"

My head buzzed with desire for this man. When our eyes met, cohesive thoughts flew out the window. All I knew was lust and heat. I nodded, barely cognizant of the meaning of the gesture. He gently pulled my glasses off and set them out of the way. Then he tugged on the bow, watching it easily slide open. The two sweater halves fell away, revealing a lavender satin bra, chosen for the way it showcased my cleavage. My lids fell to half-mast, overwhelmed by the knowledge Thomas would soon see all of me. This wouldn't be like our first time in near pitch-black.

On a sharp inhale, he gently ran his fingertips down my neck, pausing at my collarbone, then continuing down the valley between my breasts. The lightness in his touch caused me to sway as if he were playing an instrument.

"What are you thinking?"

I kept my eyes closed and smiled. "The song 'Delirious' started playing in my head. I guess I was dancing to it as you touched me."

"Do you do that a lot?"

"Walk around with a personal soundtrack in my mind? All the time."

He laughed and resumed delicately stroking the edges of my bra cups. "Is this what you want? From our phone call?"

"You remembered."

"Have thought about little else. Is this what you meant?"

I flashed him my sassy grin again and answered, "It's a start."

He undid the front fastener, and the cups fell away. His hands swept over each breast and held the weight of them from underneath. We both gasped at his touch.

"This is even better." I breathed, watching his response, pleased when his head bowed in appreciation. My skin prickled with the need to be touched everywhere.

Thomas nuzzled into my cleavage, startling me when he inhaled audibly and moaned in delight. Who knew breasts actually heaved? I'd read about it, often mocking words. I chuckled in embarrassment, realizing what I'd done. Then he licked down the center and under my left side, eliciting a moan from me, and all thoughts of foolishness vanished.

"This is the *best* start." I ran my hands along his biceps, getting the feel of my own new landscape.

"Christ, the way you respond to me—"

"Shut up," I countered.

Thomas's smile pressed into my skin as he repeated his ministrations on my right breast. His tongue continued laving the areola, then flicked rapidly over my nipple. My head dropped back as my toes curled. I leaned forward, propping myself with my hands near my hips. It wasn't a conscious move, but it had the effect of shoving my nipple even farther into his mouth. I shifted on the counter as my body came alive from his sucks and flicks. I was wet and coming undone. Thomas unlocked my body with his touch, and I couldn't wait to fly.

He released me with a small pop and took a step back. "Damn," he said, his eyes glazed as if he were in a trance. "I imagined you upstairs again, but I need more now." He took hold of my ankle, sliding down the zipper on my boot before removing it, then the other.

He picked up one of the hard-boiled egg halves and said,

"You'll need energy. Eat." I closed my lips and held the egg with my tongue while sucking his fingers as they slid out, then chewed the egg, a slight grin on my face.

Thomas tsked. "Minx." He put the salad bowl in the refrigerator and moved back to me. Taking hold of my hand, he eased me off the counter in front of him and spun me around. The sweater slid off my shoulders, then my bra, leaving only my butterfly necklace and my skirt on, but I could tell where this was going.

Instead of spinning me again, he pulled me against his body with one hand wrapped around my waist. My back melded to his front. His other hand ran up my neck, causing my head to tip and give him easier access as he kissed and sucked, traveling down one side, shifting my jaw, and back up behind my ear.

"It pleases me how much you respond," he whispered. "What if I add more?"

Thomas bent enough to gather my skirt with his free hand and explored my thighs with his fingertips while the other hand moved up from my waist to my breasts once again. He paused long enough to say, "I promise not to pinch, but you said massage was good, right?"

I answered with a long moan and a slight buckle of my knees because his fingers found the apex of my thighs at the same time he spoke. "That's it, baby. *This* is a proper start."

Thomas kicked open a lower cabinet door, lifted my knee and placed it on the shelf edge. Then his fingers slid up into me, and we both purred. On an upstroke, I jolted as if sparked and bucked up on his erection. He stopped his movements and, through heavy breaths, said, "Damn, lady. If we don't move upstairs, we're both going to come in this kitchen."

"Would it be so bad?" I asked, my tone wispy.

"Yes. Said I dream of you in my bed. It's happening. But…" His fingers traveled back up to my neck. "Before we head up, I want to" —he unclasped the necklace and placed it on the counter—"find something." He unzipped my skirt and let it fall to the floor. His hand immediately moved to my right hip where I had a Celtic butterfly tattoo in the same design as the necklace. They were identical to the one on my jean jacket, only much smaller. "There it is," he declared.

I bit my lip to keep from laughing. "Been wondering, have you?"

"Didn't get to see it in the dark before." Rubbing circles over it with his thumb, then tracing the lines of the interlaced design. "Don't hide it anymore." He bent and kissed it. "I'm getting you a bikini to show it off. My butterfly."

Hell, I hadn't worn a two-piece in, maybe ever, but Thomas made me feel like I could do anything. Knowing he understood how the art symbolized the way events can change us so fully we become completely different people—like a new species—meant the world too.

He cupped my ankles, sending a shiver up my spine, and ran his hands up my legs, under my ass—in a similar way he'd done with my breasts.

"You're stunning, Kick," he said low and reverently.

What a humbling thing to hear. After years of working out and yoga practice, I knew how to maximize my posture to appear as svelte as possible. Add in extremely clean eating, and I knew my skin looked good for my age. It was still hard to believe his words. The exact number of pounds I'd yet to lose to make the desired BMI raced through my mind.

I chased the doubt away by turning my attention back to Thomas. I spun around and smiled. "I appear to be at a disadvantage."

"How so?" His grin said he knew my meaning but teased anyway. "You hold all the cards, baby."

I moved my finger up and down. "Still… you're still fully dressed."

He shrugged his shoulders. "It makes me want to worship you more." His grin grew as his eyebrow arched. "My feet are bare."

I crossed my arms to feign prickliness. It only managed to prop up my breasts, making his eyes blink as they stared.

"They are handsome feet, but you should, you know. Tit-for-tat."

"Since you have all the tit—" He tweaked one of my nipples and I flinched. "Dammit. Sorry."

"It's okay," I said, moved by how much my comments about pain were part of his plans.

"And you have the tat—"

"Fine. I'll do it." I cut him off and unbuttoned his top button on one of the plaids I'd bought him while he backed us out of the kitchen. His shirt finally came off in the upstairs hallway, thanks to being out of practice with cuffs and his continuous chuckles. Thomas Harrison turned out to be very ticklish.

I paused to appreciate his body. My eyes couldn't get enough. He was blessed with a lean build, defined waist and shoulders. Athletic without being overly bulky. My hand glided up his chiseled abs and across a deep scar on his left bicep. The muscle underneath flexed as I traced it with my finger. "I didn't notice this before. What happened?" Of course, it had been a crazy day and dark night when we were first together. Then again, the man had a way of distracting me.

He gritted out, "A fight." He seemed embarrassed by it. I bowed my head, acknowledging his discomfort, and leaned in to kiss it, trying to communicate that it didn't matter. It didn't look like any kind of fight scar I'd ever seen. There were too many jagged lines. But it wasn't like I hung out with dangerous men either.

"Perfect." The word escaped my lips, and I blushed when Thomas's eyebrow lifted, first in confusion, then amusement. I walked around him, keeping my fingertips in constant contact with his toned skin, and explained, "You've been bulkier. In the past."

"True." He sounded surprised by my comment. "Had more free time a while back and competed occasionally. How'd you know?"

"You remind me of a professional athlete in the off-season."

"Sounds bad," he nervously murmured.

"Not at all." I brushed my hands across his back muscles as I spoke. "You're fit. Strong. Beautiful. It's a warrior's build. It's beautiful, if you don't mind the descriptive."

He chuckled. "From you? It's giving me a big head."

"Stop. Never." I laughed at him and placed my hands on his

pecs, brushing his nipples with my thumbs. Then I leaned in and flicked them with my tongue, receiving a deep sigh in response. "You're going to be fun to play with too."

"Dammit." He swooped me up into his arms and carried me down the hall into his bedroom, then let me shut the door with my feet while I giggled. The Virginia boy in him read loud and clear in his sanctum. A handmade early-American—not the cheap, seventies chain-store kind—four-poster bed with a navy quilt anchored the center of the wall to the left of the door. Farther down, in front of a window, he had a seating area. I made out the small paintings of what looked like an eighteenth-century boy and girl sitting on the side table. A huge, braided rug covered the hardwood floors and framed the bed. I didn't remember it being there in October and wondered if he bought it to keep the bed from skipping across the room again.

He placed me on my feet and aggressively kissed me, sweeping his tongue into my mouth as I fumbled with the top button on his jeans. He took over, and since they were button-fly jeans, opened the two sides with a well-practiced flick of his wrist. They dropped to the floor, and he smoothly stepped out of them. *Jaysus.* The man had been deliciously commando this whole time. I ran my tongue over my bottom lip at the sight of his stunning, erect penis.

Our gazes met and held. Over the past weeks, moments from my drugged stupor had been trickling back to me. The biggest chunk of returned memory revolved around what happened in the garage. I figured it had to do with my feeling safe in Thomas's care. Now he stood before me and looked ready to give me all the things I had demanded of him then. Like he wanted extraordinary too.

While my heart rejoiced, my head jumped in the way with words like *This shouldn't be.* I couldn't pretend casual would ever be enough. I wanted more. I wanted all the tomorrows. With him. But how many more did he have compared to me? This beautiful man finally stood before me without walls, perfectly comfortable in his own skin in a way I only dreamed of. His deep stare took me in and made my heart sink. He deserved better. The most handsome smile spread across his face. I turned toward the door. And ran.

30

Arms of a Woman

Thomas

SEEING KICK STANDING IN HIS BEDROOM, READY TO BE HIS, overwhelmed Thomas as a gasp escaped his throat. Yeah, he'd made the right decision. She was worth the extra whatever it took to protect her. He would hide her to keep her safe if he had to.

Any amount of time with her would be precious. His body vibrated at the thought of spending more time together, so much so his cock danced on its own. More than anything, he wanted to jump off the cliff with her, like she'd spoken of in the parking garage. He smiled in anticipation as Kick's eyelids descended, perusing his body with lust. Thomas straightened to his full height, fists on his hips, and gave her a show. He couldn't help it.

In a blink, she turned and bolted. Her spunk thrilled him, and it excited him even more to learn she liked a little naughty in her play. Thomas laughed as he chased her. His hands wrapped around her waist in three steps.

"Nothing like a good game of chase." He set Kick down and spun her around, but the newfound terror in her eyes told him she wasn't playing. Her visage shocked him out of his glee-filled stupor.

Fortunately, they were close to the bed, and it caught him behind the knees before he fell on his ass. Thomas kept his hands around Kick so she wouldn't get away as he realized she was desperate to do so. She had the wild look of a prey animal about to be killed when he had been expecting a sultry seductress. Then her tears welled up, breaking his heart. He reached for a curl to tuck behind her ear and pulled her between his knees.

"Please. What could possibly be wrong? Is the guilt back? There's no—"

"I-I… I'm no match. Shit." She exhaled hard and met his eyes. "I want to be what I was the last time I stood in front of a man for the first time. I didn't know how perfect I was then."

"Some things don't change." He sighed, gently brushing away the tear with his thumb.

Her shoulders fell. "I'm serious. Everything's changed. It's one thing to go through it with someone who remembers the days before, but you only get the after. My body's been through hell since then."

Thomas couldn't believe his ears. He stared at her, shocked, trying hard to school his features.

"Come on," she pleaded. "I'm sure none of the women you've been with were as scarred and sagging as I am." Kick put her hands on his shoulders. "You're in your prime and deserve a woman who's in the same place. I might look younger than my age now, but it's a race against time. From here on, the best I can hope for is a compliment ending with the words *for your age*."

Thomas's whole body acknowledged the mood change as he sighed. He brought his other hand to Kick's cheek. He wanted to be offended by her lack of faith in him but thought better of it when he realized she shared her feelings about *her* perceived inadequacies, not his.

"Kick…" Thomas set his hands at her waist but didn't let himself caress her or move at all. He simply craved the contact. "You're the blessing I didn't dare ask for. No other woman has been that for me. I want you for you, not for anything you can do for me.

And I don't see flaws. I only see a tempting wonderland I want to explore."

At his words, Kick shook her head sadly. "The thing is, I adore you. I could love you. Hell, I probably love you already. Sorry for throwing it out there, but it's my truth and you probably should know it." She sighed. "To me, it means your happiness is more important than the love I feel. You may not think you want a family now, but what about a month from now? A year? You could still be reeling from the death of your wife."

Thomas let his head drop while he figured out his answer. "How can I explain this?" He lifted his chin and allowed himself to stroke her forearms lightly. It let him find the honesty he'd held inside for as long as he could remember but never confessed. "Your infertility was one of the things that attracted me to you in the beginning." Kick opened her mouth, and he raised a finger. "Hear me out. Alicia died having our daughter. After the funeral, I made a vow never to impregnate another woman. Ever. My head knows I didn't kill her, but my heart still struggles with acceptance."

She nearly collapsed into him. "Jaysus, Thomas. I'm such an idiot. And the child?"

He swallowed and sat back. "She's dead too."

Kick's groan sounded like a lament, so he changed the topic immediately. Nothing was going to ruin this day, his day, *their* day. Especially not his past heartaches.

"After how hard we fought to get here, tell me why you still thought I wouldn't want you?"

"I don't know." Kick kept her head down.

"Can I tell you another secret?" Thomas asked, then settled her into his lap. His cock twitched, begging for attention, but it could wait. It knew how to wait.

"You can tell me anything."

He let out a cleansing breath and mentally jumped. "About the other thing you said—I'm relieved you might have fallen for me."

"Why?"

Thomas studied Kick as he caressed her cheek. Her stunning

green eyes still held a shimmer like diamonds. How could she doubt herself? "The truth is, I already know I love you."

Her hands rose to her mouth and shook. Thomas gently massaged the back of her neck. "*Je t'adore aussi.*"

She clicked her tongue. "Sure but—"

"I. Love. You. I have since the first night, when I drove you home. Hell, you grabbed my heart by the way you walked across the parking lot in your cowboy boots and short shorts."

Thomas's fingers slid down Kick's arms as he let his words sink in. He gently brushed the curls off her shoulder and kissed her there. "I have an idea." He gestured for her to stand facing him. "Present yourself like the gift you are." He pointed at her, adding in his professor's face. "Mean it too. Be the woman I love, Kathleen Allen McKenna."

She answered with a tight nod and a lift to the corner of her mouth. Then she uncrossed her arms, revealing her beautiful body. She let her shoulders fall back and held her head high. Kick did him in. How could she ever doubt herself?

"Believe in this confident, enchanting woman. It's how I've always seen you anyway." He reached out and let his fingertips travel over Kick's body again, this time for her benefit.

She swallowed hard as her eyes tracked his movements. "Everyone says I'm a badass, but at my core, I'm afraid I'll end up disappointing you."

Thomas wanted to kick his own ass. This had to be about their breakup. "I'm such a fool. Don't ever listen to a negative word I say, especially if it's regarding you."

"But—"

Thomas palmed her breasts, her belly, her mound, anywhere his reach would allow. "I know who you are and what you are, baby. Possibly more than you do. You'll let me love you now for it."

Thomas pulled her mouth to his, licking at her lips, asking her permission to let him in. Kick settled into him as her mouth opened and her tongue danced with his.

Thomas lay back on his bed, stretching Kick out on top of him. He breathed deeply, enjoying the vanilla-and-lavender scent surrounding her, grateful he had her back so quickly. With him, where she belonged. His hands floated along her sides, then back up and under the swell of her breasts. Kick's body responded in kind as she slowly writhed against him. He shifted to the center of the bed and turned to his side.

"I want to savor you this time. We can do quickies later. A lot of quickies." He tilted his head to the side to catch her eyes. "Do you trust me?"

Kick gave him the confident, radiant smile he lived for. "Definitely."

"Let me take my time and take care of you."

"Please."

Thomas stretched her right arm over her head and placed it under the bottom of the headboard. "Don't let go until I say so."

"Again?" She teased as she laughed. "This is your thing, eh?"

"You're my thing." Thomas shifted and removed a feather from his nightstand. He quickly opened his playlist on the Angel system. He would've changed tack if Kick hadn't had a sweet smile on her face.

Her breathy voice went straight to his cock. "I'm starting to believe you."

He paused, keeping the feather behind his back. "Starting to? Then you'll stay right here until you absolutely believe me. Now hush." He shifted alongside Kick. "I have a surprise."

"Thomas…," she drew out in a warning tone.

"Time to feel, Kick. Let my actions tell you how much you mean to me." His gaze traveled along her stretched-out body as he took in the visual feast that was her curves. Having her like this with only occasional flashes of lightning before hadn't done her body justice. Turned out, she wasn't an elf queen after all. From here on out, Thomas would think of her as his goddess. He planned to worship her, didn't he? He decided they would stay naked all weekend. A devilish grin spread across his face as he prepared to make her come until she cried for mercy. "Eyes open or closed. It doesn't matter. Just tell me what you like."

31

It Had to Be You

Kick

I LET MY LIDS FALL, SHUTTING DOWN ONE OF MY SENSES TO heighten the others. My heart jumped when "It Had to Be You" started playing. Thomas had remembered my love for Cole Porter. Who doesn't fall for a guy who listens?

He placed a soft kiss on the spot behind my ear, like it was an On button to my pussy, revving my motor and making me hum. I thought he'd pick up where we left off downstairs, but a tickling sensation moved over the spots he kissed, and a smile spread across my face.

"A feather? The light touch."

"Like it?"

I muttered incoherently, caught in a blissful haze, before managing a raspy, "Very much, thank you."

He chuckled in his deep, dreamy baritone, now heavier with lust. "So polite. What will it take to make you feisty again?"

I sighed at the reminder of my pent-up need. "Teasing. Get to business, buster." I bit my lip as the feather found a ticklish spot.

"There she is. How's this?" After spending some time running it underneath my breasts, he let the feather circle my nipples. Goose bumps traveled over my skin, and I forgot all about my foolish insecurities.

"It's incredible." I opened my eyes and caught his playful wink as he decided where to go next. The headiness of watching him did more to turn me on than a lack of sight had. Wetness gathered between my legs as I scissored my feet and the pressure began to build.

He dropped his lips to my breast again and flicked his tongue over the tip of my nipple. Is it possible to become audibly insane? I knew I made no sense. I almost came from that alone.

"You have gorgeous tits, baby."

In my brain-shorting euphoria, I blurted out, "I wished they were functional again. For you."

"What?" Thomas stilled, looking at me with a questioning curiosity.

"I wish I could give you the… taste of them."

Thomas tipped his head back. "You're trying to slay me." He stretched over me and slid his fingers between my folds, then dipped them into me, rotating two fingers to make sure I was ready. His eyes moved down to look at his hand, then back to my face. "How wet you are for me. I'm stunned."

His fingertip grazed the scars occupying the area formerly known as my G-spot, and I bucked into him, panting and gripping his fingers as they slid out. The area had changed, but it wasn't dead. When body parts rearrange and mishaps settle in for the long-term, nerves have a way of finding new life in different places.

The feather took a path down my sides, which were only mildly ticklish, and circled my belly. Thomas paused and peppered light, reverent kisses over my scars. He nuzzled below my navel, saying, "This is sacred and beautiful." Then he kissed and nipped at my stomach, claiming me as his woman. And he was my man. It reminded me I was more than a mother of three. His tongue circled my navel, and I swear my body jolted from an electrical hum.

"How the hell do you do that?"

Thomas responded with a happy, teasing chuckle from his throat. He shifted to his knees between my legs and ran his hands along my thighs. The feather strokes were quick here and kept true to his other light touches. Each upstroke went higher until it danced over my core, his fingers following, grazing the already sensitive folds eager for him.

He paused, and I peered down the length of my body at him to see what caused him to stop. The sight of him between my legs, his head bent, caused me to roll my hips, edging again. He blew on my clit and murmured, "Like one of my orchids."

"Please——" My pants increased when he flicked his tongue over my clit. I vaguely recalled the music changing to one of my favorite Norah Jones songs as I let my mind float away. I was swept up in the sensations, the romantic melody, and his earthy scent on the sheets. The singer was right about how all along I'd been waiting for this man to turn me on. When his fingers twisted and massaged my already sensitive inner walls, I began the climb to release.

"So damn responsive," Thomas praised, rubbing his stubbly chin along the sensitive flesh of my inner thighs. "Such a vixen." He returned his mouth to my clit and continued sucking and twisting his fingers, hitting all the nerves in my pussy he could find.

My back arched as my walls clenched and released around his fingers until there was a sensation of riding on the top of a tsunami of pleasure, waiting for the wave to crash over and through me, praying I had the strength to ride it out. It started in my toes and made its way up my legs until it shattered my core.

A lifetime existed in this moment, hoping it never ended. I growled as I twisted with delight—the tsunami taking my whole body along for the ride. I grew louder with each crest and briefly wondered if the French were right about death by orgasm. At least it'd be glorious. And there was no end to this pleasure. "Okay… okay," I pleaded.

"More," Thomas insisted, lightening his touch on now too-sensitive tissue.

As if truly electrified, several more rippled through me while triumph filled his features. As his fingers danced across my skin, I surrendered and moaned with each new touch.

He bent over me, kissed the tip of my ear, and said, "Now we can go together."

Out of breath, I gasped, "More?"

He chuckled. "With you? Always."

I continued to pant. "I don't know yet."

"Let's try something." Thomas turned me to my side and curled behind me. He lifted my top leg and pulled me onto him with a victorious purr of his own. I pushed back and felt his chest rumble in pleasure. "Nice and easy," he encouraged, rocking slowly into me.

He reached around me. One hand went underneath, squeezing my breast while the other crossed my hip and vibrated my clit. To my surprise, it worked. My body reawakened, and I craved more, hoping it would never stop. He pulled out as I squeezed, then slammed in hard. The friction from the angle set me off again as I cried out his name.

"Yes, baby. With me." He slammed up another time and pinched my nipple and that was it. I threw my head back, overwhelmed by the fervor of climaxing again. This one felt different from the first. It washed over and in me, filling my soul the way Thomas filled my body.

He nosed my hair away from my neck and placed deep kisses on my shoulder. He grunted, "This is me loving you. This. Is. Love." Then he lost himself to his own orgasm.

Somehow we did it. We'd jumped. He wouldn't be my friend and sometime lover, but my new love. Right then the music changed to Tony Bennett's version of "Fly Me to the Moon," such a perfect description of what we'd done and of what I hoped we could be.

Breathless, Thomas stilled and squeezed me, humming into my neck. We extended our orgasmic fog with quick pulses for as long as possible. I sang quietly to the song as I reached behind me and caressed his strong jaw. I turned to face him and swore his blissedout face made him glow like an angel. My fingers tingled with a pleasant, warm buzz as they continued tracing his cheeks. Touching him did that for me. I thought he was falling asleep, but his mouth lifted into a wide grin as I sang the last words of the song, "I... love... you."

When he opened his eyes, dark with lust, I saw the love Thomas had professed in them. His breathing slowed while small beads of sweat escaped from his hairline. He looked exactly like my future.

32

Praise You

Thomas

DESPITE THEIR DELIBERATELY SLOW LOVEMAKING, HE WAS SPENT, physically and emotionally. This had been what he'd missed for as long as he could remember. In his dreams, he'd hoped their chemistry equated with magic, but the reality shot it to the moon. In his contented state, with a remarkable woman wrapped around him, Thomas dozed.

He jolted awake during one of those falling dreams. Kick still lay alongside him, resting her head in her hand, stroking the feather up and down his stomach.

"How long was I out?"

"Only ten minutes." She bent and kissed his chest, then his jaw. He turned his head to meet her lips. It wouldn't take long for him to go again, but knowing how long it had been for Kick, Thomas didn't want to hurt her. Besides, he still had to feed her. But first he had questions.

"That was amazing. Primal." Kick turned her beautiful hazel eyes to him. "I swear, I thought the earth quaked." She giggled and absently ran her fingernails over his pecs. "Did you know you look angelic when you come?"

"Ah, no?"

She looked back up and gave him a shy smile. "I believe you now, Thomas."

"Thank God. If that was your version of a fuck-buddy romp, I don't think I'd survive more."

She swatted Thomas on the shoulder as he laughed hard, then watched her face growing serious.

In a quiet voice, she said, "I thought I could be fuck buddies with you, but I never could."

He lifted her free hand and kissed it. "We're not." He sat upright and said, "Before we move on to the next thing, tell me about your freak-out. Let's put it permanently behind us."

"Oh." A deep blush spread across Kick's chest as her shoulders fell. She stretched her hands in Thomas's direction. "Well… look at you."

"Alright." He hopped out of bed and stood before her. Planting his hands on his hips, he looked down at himself and shrugged.

"Thomas… you're perfect."

"Thank you. Still don't see a problem." Kick's frustrated growl delighted him, though he knew it shouldn't.

She rose to her knees and faced off with him. Thomas's cock woke back up at the sight. "Not only am I *not* perfect, I'm a physical mess."

His brow drew up in honest confusion. "Where?"

She held her breasts, and he almost groaned. "My boobs are asymmetrical."

Thomas grabbed his balls. "So is my nut sac." He tilted his head to the side. "Are you going to leave me now?"

"Of course not." Kick's words encouraged him, but her frown didn't.

Thomas held up a finger, then bolted for the closet. This conversation—and what he had planned next—called for robes. He grabbed his summer and winter ones, ran back to the bed, and placed the thick one around Kick's shoulders. He slipped into the lightweight robe and sat on the bed next to her. His gaze tipped to his semihard cock.

"Isn't the evidence of what you do to me enough to prove there's nothing to worry about?"

She leaned into his shoulder as she stared out the window and answered, "The way you turned cold when you broke up with me… Are you sure it had nothing to do with disappointment in me?"

Thomas raked his hands through his hair. "I'm an asshole." He reached around Kick and pulled her tight to him. "It was all about this thing I've been struggling with. You've only ever been a miracle."

"The thing with your research and Bordeaux?"

"Yes." After the weekend, he would definitely call Alaric. He didn't agree with everything Banger and Tess had directed. Once he informed *Grand-père* of his plans—not ask—he would come clean with Kick. He kissed her temple and said, "No more fears about me leaving, alright?"

"I'm still getting used to this, but okay." She tipped her head back and smiled. "You make me feel good enough. I can go from there."

Thomas smacked her thigh. "Damn. I'm aiming for perfect." He jumped up and lifted a finger. "Hold on a sec." He disappeared back into his closet to the wrapped boxes he'd left there. He grabbed a big one and left another small one.

He pulled one chair close to the bed and sat across from Kick. "When I knew I needed you back, I called Deana to see if I still had a shot." Thomas hung his head and chuckled. "She told me she knew exactly what you wanted." He presented the large box to her and sheepishly grinned. "This."

She carefully undid the bow and ran her finger through the taped seams, trying not to rip the pretty paper. She opened the box and laughed as she lifted a Lord University letterman-style jacket. Kick turned it around and saw the "Harrison" across the back. "Aww." She held it to her chest. "I told Dee I missed the days when a boy would give a girl his varsity jacket to ask her to go steady."

He nodded. "She told me about your talk. Took a bit of work to pull it off so quickly. Fortunately, I did a favor for a coach last year. He hooked me up." He rubbed his chin. "Would you really wear it?"

Kick tipped her head back in an angelic laugh. "You bet your ass."

Thomas felt his smile stretch across his face. *Christ*, he was a goner. Soon he'd get to the tricky part when he gave Kick the small package. But it had to wait. Thomas had a special moment in mind to give it to her. "Happy New Year's Eve-Eve." He kissed her deeply and declared, "We need to eat."

"Yes, we do. After I clean up." Kick stood, smiled when she caught Thomas staring at her fabulous ass, and sashayed into the bathroom. The confident vixen had returned. His first goal had been accomplished.

After they filled up on food, Kick reached into one of the shopping bags she had brought and pulled out a present for Thomas. She removed his place setting and set the box on the island.

"Happy New Year's Eve-Eve, sweetheart. This is your first present."

He lifted an eyebrow and smirked. "The first?"

"The other one was too heavy. I barely heaved it into my trunk and couldn't get the right leverage on it to take it out."

Kick fidgeted from foot to foot, piquing Thomas's curiosity. He ripped into the paper with gusto. On the counter sat a polished hickory box, a work of art on its own. He lifted the lid and found a Shinola Runwell Chronograph watch with a blue face and a dark brown band.

"It's gorgeous, baby." He held it up and examined it from every angle.

"It reminded me of your eyes," she said shyly. "I also wanted to give you something from Detroit—my original hometown."

"I remember," he whispered as he smiled down at her.

Sometime soon he'd plan a trip there so Kick could show him all her favorite places.

These moments of proof of Kick's feelings before this weekend let Thomas know he'd done the right thing in fighting for her. Making her a priority the first time had been an emotional decision done out of fear. This time he let himself jump with the clearest of intentions and would do whatever it took to keep Kick happy as well as safe. He couldn't wait to give her the last present.

He kissed her on the cheek and clipped the watch around his wrist. "It'll track our time together." Funny, Thomas had been planning to buy a watch to wean himself off his phone.

She answered with a slight nod. "So, how are we supposed to get your other present? The wind is still strong, and the temperature is dropping."

"I'll bring it in after we dress. I still have two surprises to show you while there's daylight, and we'll have to leave the house for them."

They dressed quickly, as Thomas's interest in his other present grew.

Once outside, she popped the lid to reveal another, much larger, box from Shinola. He carried it into the house.

"Before you set it down," she said, "let's take it into your music room. That's a hint, by the way."

"Music, huh?" Thomas raised his eyebrows out of curiosity and took it into the downstairs office. The room was large enough to have one wall devoted to his instruments. An adjacent cabinet was command central for the Angel network, along with various components for amateur recording and mixing. He gingerly set the box down, snapped apart the tape from Kick's repacking job, and stared at what sat before him.

"Well, pull it out," she coaxed, antsy like a child.

He carefully extracted a Runwell turntable, speechless. Thomas wasn't a sucker for toys. In fact, he was picky about which new gadgets he indulged in. This piece was a work of art. When he looked at Kick, her tongue worried the inside of her cheek and her brow furrowed.

"Is it stupid?"

He whispered in awe, "It's amazing." Thomas cleared his throat. "Banger's going to be jealous as hell. He has the toy addiction."

"I liked the retro feel of the wood trim." She chuckled and said, "Liam saw it and thought he'd stumbled upon one of his presents. The poor boy almost had a coronary, which rebounded when I told him it was for you."

Thomas rested it on the coffee table since it would need to wait until he could clear a spot for it. It would make a fabulous focal point in the room. He stood and held his arms out. When Kick stepped into them, he engulfed her in a bear hug, lifting her off her toes, then set her down and nuzzled her neck.

"Your thoughtfulness and desire to see me happy humbles me, but having you here is the best present. It's what I've wanted most."

She stretched her chin and kissed a spot underneath his jaw. "I agree."

Thomas became distracted and held her for a few minutes until the clock over the door caught his attention. "Shit. It's getting late. He's going to be mad." He pulled Kick into the mudroom.

"Who's going to be mad?"

"One of your surprises."

"My surprise is a *he*?"

"Come on." Thomas held Kick's new coat out, then zipped her in it. "You'll see. Wear your hood up."

He wore an oilskin duster and matching hat.

"A drover coat?" she laughed. "Are we exploring the outback?"

"Sort of. It comes in handy on days like this."

"Do you have chaps to go with it?"

"Actually, yes." He ushered her out to the kitchen garden and down the back path.

"Hold on… Are you saying you've been to the Outback?"

Thomas shrugged. "Maybe."

She raised her hands. "How the hell many things have you done?"

He arched an eyebrow, mocking her, and answered in a falsetto, "A few."

Then he wrapped an arm around her as they walked the trail past the barn and around the west side of the pond. Grateful it was wide enough for them to travel side by side, he savored this new reality, aware it could end too soon.

"How long do you think an orgasm can last?" Kick's question saved him from falling into a thought funk. Her giggle piqued his curiosity. Her curls' attempts to burst from her hood were also a welcomed distraction.

"Want to run some experiments?"

She bumped Thomas's shoulder. "No, Professor. It feels…" She sighed and said in a rush, "It feels like aftershocks keep running through me. I don't remember this happening before. Then again, I can't remember the last time I had sex in the daytime either."

"No kidding?"

She twisted her lips in thought. "Yup, can't remember. The loud thing was pretty amazing too. I mean, with no one around it just… seemed to explode, but still."

Thomas crooked his elbow and pulled her into his chest with a resonant growl. "You have no idea." A few silent minutes later after he replayed their romp on a loop in his mind, he said, "What was it you said to me the morning we met? You purr… you growl… but you don't prowl. Baby, you should've mentioned the roaring. I would have dropped to my knees on the spot." He thoroughly enjoyed watching Kick turn a delightful shade of pink.

She slugged him on the shoulder. "Don't remind me. It's embarrassing."

"No, darlin'. It's hot as hell. You should roar for me every day."

"I would love to." She sighed.

"Why do I hear a *but* in there?"

"Not a *but*." She slowed and shrugged. "We haven't talked about what happens after this. Will we still struggle to schedule our time together?"

"Come over here." This would be the perfect time to give Kick her last gift. He walked her to an old, southern live oak tree sitting about fifty yards from the path. The trunk was wide enough to provide full shade and shelter. This was the center of the original plantation. Now, it marked the four corners of the divided land. The view from here was incredible. Situated on a small clearing on top of a hill, they had sight lines to Thomas's house in one direction and the farms in the other three.

Thomas was certain this tree was an offspring of the grand live oak in the center of town. At this point, it was an elderly "lady" in its own right. *She* had obviously been around when the original settlers broke ground. Based on the number of initials carved into the tree, this had been a favorite spot for many lovers. Some carvings looked to be over a hundred years old.

"How do I picture us from now on?" He entwined their fingers, Kick's sweet face consumed his thoughts, and the words came from the place in his soul she'd unlocked.

"Let me be your Atlas, darlin'. Let me hold you up as you direct your world. I'd say loved ones, but it's obvious how you adopt strangers who walk into your life and make them your own." Thomas laughed and shook his head, having a hard time believing this could be true. "Counting myself grateful to be a stray."

Tears welled up in her eyes as they laughed together.

"Let me support you so all those who rely on you can continue their orbit around you."

Kick sighed and looked around. She tucked some errant hairs into her hood.

Thomas jostled her hands. "What?"

"I love this."

"I still hear a *but*."

She shook her head. "As much as I love warm and attentive Thomas, I still have burns from your hot-and-cold routine. How do I know it's really gone so quickly?"

"Ah." She gutted him. Thomas pulled Kick close and leaned his forehead against hers. "It hasn't been fast for me, though you're right about the back and forth. It's a battle I've been waging inside myself since we met. I'm used to being alone, Kick. The icy part of me is a protective measure. I can't promise I'll never revert to it since this is new for me too. I can promise I've thought hard about what I want, and you're it. Can you call me on my bullshit if I do shut down? Can you see my request as proof I've changed?"

"I can do that." Kick wrapped her arms around his waist and tipped her head back to speak. "And what do you want from me?"

"From you?" He reached into his coat pocket and pulled out the last present. "How about this for a start?"

Kick carefully unwrapped the box like she'd done with the first one. She opened the lid and lifted the bracelet within. "Oh, Thomas," she gasped. "It's stunning. Truly. Are these… This is your birthstone, isn't it?"

He nodded. "With yours." Her reaction thrilled him, but he wondered how she would take the meaning of it.

"Wow." She clicked her cheek and observed, "You know, this roping design between the gems reminds me of the old handfasting traditions. It's beautiful."

Thomas laughed at his short-sightedness and should've known she'd see it. "It is." The jeweler had created a braided effect from rose gold, wrapping around fire opals and moonstones. "When Deana told me you needed a commitment, I knew I did too."

He clasped the ropelike bracelet around her wrist. "I'm a modern scientist, but the old ways have always held a special appeal." *My ways*, he meant.

Kick cocked her head to the side. "What exactly are you saying?"

Here was his chance. Either way, Thomas knew he would jump off one hell of a cliff when he eventually let the cat out of the bag. If he *knew* she loved him deeply already, it would make the leap easier. "Deana mentioned a class ring, but I don't have anything like that to give you." Thomas fingered the bracelet. "Can you consider this an ask for tomorrow—like a mature version of a class ring?"

"Are you asking me to go steady, Thomas?"

"Grown-up going steady? Sure." He grinned before bringing Kick's fingers to his lips and kissing them. "I wanted to give you something so you knew I'd changed. I want more than a casual arrangement with you." Kick beamed and Thomas kissed her nose. "We suck at casual."

"Word." Kick's shoulders bounced as she laughed.

As a rule, Thomas never ruminated on what he wanted. He had goals. He helped others. That was it. After speaking with Deana, one word announced itself like a speaker blasting in his head, telling him to grab ahold before it slipped away—*home*. "Without my noticing—or it could've been by design, I don't know—life had become a dark and cold, postfamilial existence." He pushed Kick's hood back and slid his hands to the back of her neck, running his thumbs along her jawline. "Would you be my home for now? Wherever you are, I want to be with y'all. With you and your amazing kids. One day at a time? We can figure out the details as we go."

"You know, you're more than an adopted stranger." Kick placed her hand on Thomas's chest. "If you're saying what I think you are, you've become my heart too." Her fingers traced up to his shoulders. "It's funny how you mentioned Atlas. I've noticed a melancholy about you, like you carry a great weight around. But every so often, I see your weight lift. Sweetheart, if I can ease those burdens at all, I promise I'll do what I can. If it's an opinion, my talents, or my body you need, I would be honored to be the soft place where you rest." She lifted her wrist. "I'll gladly wear this as long as you're through with thinking temporarily. I don't need big promises, but I don't want to make this jump with you if you already plan to leave."

Thomas remembered how angry Kick had become with the things he'd said after the gala. He stroked her cheek and tucked a curl behind her ear. "There's no expiration date for me. It's just… I thought this might seem fast. It was inappropriate to ask for a commitment when I don't even know if you want one. One day at a time seems fair though. Don't you think?"

She unbuttoned his big coat and snuggled inside as the wind practically whipped the flaps back together. "Silly man. So we're going steady grown-up style?"

"Exactly." Since they were making vows of a sort, he asked, "What do you want from me?" He listened to Kick breathe while he waited on her answer. Thomas marveled at how quickly their heartbeats synced.

"I've had champions before—men who emotionally tucked me behind their bodies and kept me out of the line of fire psychologically. It was necessary then, but not anymore. I want you to walk with me. When needed, you can stand against my back as we fight like hell together." A fierce, challenging gaze gave way to the familiar signs of insecurity as she worried her cheek.

"My butterfly." He brushed back the curls on her face.

"You do get it." She stretched up and kissed Thomas under what would henceforth be their oak tree. "Thank you for this."

"Anything for you." Feelings this deep had eluded him for so long Thomas couldn't remember the last time his heart had been filled with such gratitude. He knew Kick had come to his house with casual intentions. He had hoped he could convince her of more, even the smallest of commitments before their weekend ended. To find out they were of the same mind so quickly was a gift. He led her back to the path with their hands linked and checked the time on his new watch. "Good, I can still get his exercise time in."

"Whose?"

"Patience, baby. We're almost there."

33

I'm Feeling Good

Kick

WE EMERGED FROM THE WOODS FACING A LARGE WORKING STABLE. "We're not on your property anymore."

"No, but all this was a plantation back in the day. My place was what some would call the second house while this would be the big house."

As Thomas finished speaking, a large Georgian-style home came into view down a lane to my left. "And your brother lives here now?"

"Wh-why would you… No. Joe won't leave Virginia." He lifted his chin and pointed at the stable. "I want you to meet Ed. In the stable."

We turned a corner and faced the center aisle of an upscale barn. The heavy wooden support beams and design let me know it was old but had been recently renovated. It had what looked like all the modern trappings of an equestrian complex. Box stalls lined both sides. Thomas strode ahead as if pulled by a magnet. After hearing the same whinny for the third time, I realized the horse called out to him.

"Coming, buddy. Keep your shoes on." He stopped in front of a box, and a gorgeous black horse stuck his head out and knocked Thomas hard on the shoulder. "Sorry about being late. I was distracted." He rubbed the horse's muzzle and chin like he was on autopilot, then his hand moved up to scratch his ears. "There's someone here to meet you, Ed."

I sidled next to him and waved at the horse like an idiot.

"Kick, meet Eddie. My horse. He's the reason I had to wait to come back. The stable wasn't ready for him until this morning."

I stepped closer to Eddie and let him smell me, making our introductions. He quickly couldn't get enough of my hair and nipped at the curls. "He doesn't seem skittish at all."

"Nah." Thomas pet him some more. "He's a brave fellow, but I'll warn you, he's a lot like his namesake."

I lifted my eyebrows in inquiry, "Which would be…"

"His full name is Edward Teach… Harrison."

"You named your horse after the pirate Black Beard?" I burst into a laugh, then reined it in, in case loud noises startled the animal or one of the others.

Thomas lifted an eyebrow and flashed me a rakish grin. "For a good reason."

Ed began to bump my hand, so I pet his chin, noting the wisps of longish black hair hanging from it and smiled. His coat was inky black with a small, thin star on his forehead. Eddie's mane and chin "beard" were tipped with auburn, creating an ombre effect. I knew women who paid good money for hair with the same look. Add in his dark chocolate eyes and long lashes, and Eddie was one hell of a handsome guy. "He has the beard, but he's way too pretty for a pirate." Then the horse bit my hair and pulled. "Ow!" I immediately grabbed my head. Maybe looks were deceiving.

"Enough. That's hair, not hay." He turned to me with an apologetic pout. "Sorry, baby. He proved my point though. This fella takes what he wants." Thomas slipped Eddie's bridle off its hook, unlatched the door, and stepped inside. "Time to stretch those legs, big guy."

He leaned over the door and said, "Don't worry, we're not

riding today. He's still antsy from the drive and new digs. We're just going to burn off his piss and vinegar in the ring."

"Okay. Are there treats for him somewhere? What if I brought him one?"

"Good idea. Ed's into carrots." Thomas tipped his head. "The office is behind us on the left. Look for a woman with long silver hair, named Betsy. She can find one. Or one of the stable hands."

I never ran into anyone, but I found a tray of carrots and took a large one. Seeing the obvious affection between the horse and his human, I knew Eddie and I needed to become good friends. Bribing him was completely within my moral parameters.

When I turned back to the center aisle, I heard a clip-clopping and saw Thomas and Eddie already at the far end of the barn. They veered left once outside, the late afternoon sun shone golden upon them both, making them look like they were about to star in a Western. The coat made sense now.

I hustled out of the barn and joined them before they disappeared into a building I didn't know. The wind whipped as I crossed the threshold, stealing my breath.

"Isn't there a manège around here?" I called out over the howling sound.

"Yes, but he prefers the outdoors. Ed grew up wild."

Thomas exercised his horse while I leaned on the fence and watched. A petite but solid woman with a swagger as big as John Wayne's and a silver ponytail waving behind her approached me. "Are you a friend of the professor's?"

"I am." I held out my hand. "Kick McKenna. Are you Betsy?" The wrinkles around her eyes and her hair gave the initial impression of being much older than me. On closer inspection, I guessed her age at no more than five years my senior. Her whiskey-colored irises sparkled with the joy of someone who had spent their life doing what they loved.

"I am. Did he mention me?" She seemed a tad smitten, and I couldn't blame her.

"Only your name, but you have the look of someone who runs the place."

Betsy's laugh was loud, rough, and warm. "I like you. My husband says he pays the bills and I do everything else." She dipped her head toward the center of the arena. "Our new boarder is quite the looker." At first I thought she referred to Thomas and considered her brazen for mentioning her husband, then immediately ogling my man. *Mine. Shit.* A pleasant shiver traveled up my spine as I realized I could make the claim now.

"Oh, you mean Eddie? He is gorgeous. I just met him."

We watched them work for several minutes. The deep, gold light kissed Thomas's skin and added to his cowboy effect. The light bounced off Eddie's shiny coat as he circled Thomas, and I pulled out my phone to take pictures. Seeing Thomas work comfortably with his horse and Eddie's trust in him stirred my libido. Theirs was a rugged, primal connection to the past, more real than any of the folksy traditions I grew up practicing. I wanted him. Again.

Jaysus, when did I become wanton? I stopped clicking and checked the time. About four hours ago, I guessed. I crossed my arms on the rail and set my chin on them, watching their magic unfold.

The duster shifted around Thomas's body, egged on by a petulant wind, making him look like a wizard performing magic tricks. Eddie's attention focused solely on his human stunned me. I knew from experience the horse was right—Thomas inspired trust from those who held his loyalty and his love. It was an honor to possess it. My desire to please the man matched the animal's.

I murmured, "The way his mane and tail flow in the wind, he reminds me of the Corolla horses." Perhaps it was the influence of Thomas's earlier comment about Ed being a little wild. I thought it meant his initial owners didn't take good care of him.

Bonnie turned her face to me, puzzled. "Well, he is. The professor adopted him from the Wild Horse Fund. Didn't you know?"

I shook my head, amazed at yet another golden nugget of insight into this amazing man. *My* amazing man. "It's been a fun surprise." Who was this man who I suspected had been a soldier, considering his knowledge of weaponry and the way he carried himself. I decided to ask him about it soon. Along the way, he'd had and lost a family, became a scientist, an expert dancer, a renovator, played guitar, and now was an equestrian? The last part might have to do with his family's business, but when did he have time for the Wild Horse Fund? At the gala, he'd mentioned real estate people who worked for him. Again, it could relate to something he'd inherited. As I did the math though, the answers didn't compute. It buzzed in the back of my mind for the rest of the day. I needed to ask Thomas about it but was afraid he'd change the subject, like he did any time I asked him about what was in Bordeaux.

As my Gran used to say, "Careful what you wish for, Katie darling."

"Best... view... ever... Don't... want it... to end."

We had put on a movie after a simple dinner. However, Thomas's naked weekend plans made it impossible to hang out together and watch *New Year's Eve* to the end. It didn't take long before we were thoroughly aroused again. Thomas planted himself squarely on the center cushion of his sofa and pulled me onto his lap. From just a straddle, he moved my hips up and down, my sensitive clit once again ignited by the velvety friction of his cock. My head fell back as I gave in to the sensation, and he entered me. This wasn't like the slow and delicious time we'd spent in the afternoon. This was a no-holds-barred, libidinous screw from the bottom. My job was to hold on and enjoy the ride.

"This... right here... It's heaven." Thomas purred as my breasts bounced against his face, my core ready to explode.

"Same," I gasped.

He lifted my breasts closer to his face, fingers massaging, kisses hectic. "I love your tits."

My head buzzed from the fluidity of our movements, his tongue on my skin, the scent of Thomas's woody aftershave, the sheen of perspiration developing across his forehead, and the intensity of his piercing stare. I didn't dare to look away from the unsaid words he communicated.

"Please, Thomas." The pressure became too much.

With an obliging hum, he lowered his hands, one circling my clit, the other clamped to my hip as he drove us home with more force than I thought possible. The waves came fast and took me over the edge. I screamed my ecstasy and brought him along with a "shit, yes" of his own.

When we fell back to earth, I collapsed into his neck, nipping at my favorite spot under his jaw. My vocabulary had taken a hiatus. As it eventually returned, the only sentence I managed burst out of me as a gasp.

"I really, really love your penis."

A delicious rumble came from Thomas's chest, reaching to the depths of my core. "You want to high-five, or something?"

"Maybe." I laughed and let my forehead fall to his. "You're very good at this."

"Baby, you've got me. You don't have to stroke my ego."

"Well… I might be orgasm drunk."

"Mmm. Good. Let's keep you this way." He brushed his fingers across my back as our breathing matched and slowed. This was more than satisfaction, more than love. We were worshipping each other. I hoped he felt the same. Our coming together honored our past lives along with our present and future. Whether on a bed, a sofa, or the grass, I believed whenever we made love, that place would be an altar of thanksgiving.

Something had shifted earlier when we made a commitment under the tree. If we had been casually dating, my heart would've remained shielded to a degree. I knew I wouldn't have entered this space so freely. Our commitment changed us fundamentally, making our expression of love visceral and celebratory.

"What are you thinking?" he murmured into my ear. "Your smile's infectious."

"This isn't what I expected. I didn't allow myself to hope for so much, Thomas."

"Feel the same, baby." He shifted us back down to the blanket on the cushions and covered us with a second one. Thomas brushed a curl off my face and studied me intently as he listened.

"I love your home too."

"You make it a home." He held my braceleted wrist and kissed it. "Let me show you the estate as soon as we can get away."

"Ooh. Can't wait." My eyes were half-lidded, enjoying the sensations of his light kisses and touches along my skin. I didn't know what I craved more, the physical sensations or listening to Thomas finally open up. It seemed like he might be on the verge of telling me everything, but I didn't dare push. I kept up the easier questions, the ones still letting me see inside his heart. "You like old houses?"

"I do. This one's about the same age as the one in Virginia but only because our original house burned in the mid-eighteen hundreds. The estate itself goes back to the seventeenth century."

"All this time in your family?" When he nodded, I added, "So, you're a Son of the American Revolution. How cool is that?"

Thomas dropped my wrist and shrugged as the darkness I thought he'd vanquished from his face reappeared. When it cleared, he seemed distant. It unsettled me. Hell, had I pushed too far? If so, I wasn't sure what I'd said.

"It's all ridiculous."

"Don't you keep the heritage designation though? You mentioned how part of the house is a museum."

"Sure, for educational purposes. It's mostly for locals and school-children."

I reached up to caress his cheek. Even if Thomas thought little of himself and his family, they fascinated me. "My heritage feels like it's someplace else." I thought about it for a minute and giggled. "Though you know what the family in Ireland calls us?"

"Uh-uh. What?"

"The Americans. For the longest time, it made me mad. Then I realized they were right. You feel more authentic, I guess."

"You were born here. Raised here. Y'all are as American as me." Thomas kissed my temple and stood, leaving me chilly despite the plush. "Getting water. Want one?"

"Yes, please." He'd given me one helluva ride.

I rolled onto my stomach, propped on my forearms, and

watched him retreat to the kitchen. The light from the refrigerator put his perfect ass in silhouette. Movement as his muscles did the simplest task, hypnotized me. When he bumped the door closed and returned, strong thighs walked with purpose as he carried our glasses. Shredded abs and shoulders remained tall and set back and held an air of pride I hadn't seen in him before. Thomas padded into the den like a lover providing for his beloved. The knowledge empowered me.

He sat on the edge of the cushion and handed me a glass. I took a sip and moved to sit up. "Wait, baby. Stay there." He set our waters on the coffee table, next to my glasses. Then he glided his hands along my back. The chill from his fingers set gentle goose bumps loose, but the slight temperature drop felt great. Thomas leaned over me and purred into my ear. "Your back is exquisite." My mind jumped to a sarcastic snip about back fat, and I shook my head, rebuking the stubborn, self-deprecating thoughts.

His hands moved to my ass with light sweeps, barely touching my skin. "How's this?"

A warmth formed in my core, but it wasn't from another orgasm build. This type of change had been forming recently, along with a pleasant buzz, right before my skin glowed. I dropped my head into my hands and willed it to stay away. Until I met with an aura reader, I couldn't let anyone know about this. What would Thomas think of it? He was a scientist, for feck's sake. There was no way he'd accept my woo-woo aura even if it did make me feel better. I guess I still had a secret too.

"Get out of your head, baby. I feel you going far away."

"Don't worry, sweets. It's all good." Thomas tickled my sides and broke the hum. I wiggled away before giving him a playful stink eye even though I wanted to thank him. "You…"

A cheesy grin flashed across his face. "Me?"

"Yes, you." I waved my hands in front of his body. "You hypnotize me from behind with your ass divots, then you do the same on the way back with your V-shaped muscle things. Do you know they make me forget my name?" I arched my brow. "You've made me wanton."

He pulled me against him as he barked a quick laugh. "Sounds good to me, as long as you keep making those sexy-as-hell noises. My plan is working."

The movie ended and Thomas's music came on. We finished our waters and snuggled back into the blankets while listening to Nina Simone's "I'm Feeling Good."

Another deep sound of approval came from Thomas. "No better song for right now." We stayed in this lovers'-pillow-talk haze until the song ended.

Then he jostled my shoulders and asked, "I have ass divots?"

"You know you do." I sighed. "We used to call them dancer's dents, and yours are spectacular."

All silliness left his face as he pulled me into him. "Remember the first time you came here, when you made the smoothies?"

"Sure."

"You hypnotized me then, you minx. I heard you singing as I came down the stairs with my suitcase. Then I saw you dancing in your yoga pants and was gobsmacked. I stood there, staring like a creeper. Talk about forgetting my name. I almost forgot about my commitments and begged you to let me fuck you for days. Weeks."

"No kidding?" My jaw dropped at his confession. I bit my lip, recalling how he came up behind me and led us around the kitchen in a dance. I was too afraid to do more than enjoy the surprise. Too guilt-ridden over falling for someone new. "Neither of us were ready then."

"True. You had me mesmerized all the way to the airport though."

I tipped my head back and laughed. "Aww. I love this side of you. You know, your sweetness is as hot as your body."

"No, darlin'. Yours is."

I drifted off in Thomas's arms, listening to the rest of his playlist. The sound of his own melodic heartbeat and his masculine scent were the last things I noted, along with the feeling of rightness in my world.

. . .

A MEEK DAWN HAD BROKEN AS GRAY LIGHT CLUNG TO THE REMNANTS of nighttime, reluctant to leave its dark embrace. My gaze lifted to Thomas on a horse, in an old-fashioned coat, with tall riding boots and what I could swear were authentic breeches—not modern equestrian gear either. His jaw set and his brow narrowed as his eyes continuously scanned the scene. He looked younger, barely a man.

He seemed to be heading to a Revolutionary War reenactment, and I wondered if this was another of his many hobbies. How many hobbies could a man in his midthirties balance?

I didn't understand why Thomas wore his inky black hair long and queued.

A chilly mist surrounded us and my arms. Higher areas of the landscape twinkled from beams of young sunlight touching the frost, morphing the dark foliage into a bright silver. Thomas's breath puffed steam on his exhales.

His horse huffed steam puffs too, antsy to be on the move, and I wondered where they were going. I turned as a muffled sound startled me. A company of men appeared out of nowhere. Most of them were behind Thomas, waiting on a muddy road. They were close enough to smell the wet dirt and sweat, but I couldn't hear any words aside from grunts or murmurs.

The keen sense of an emotionally charged atmosphere overwhelmed my reason. Thomas and the men exuded an anxious anticipation. Some vibrated with fear. The worst, to me, were the few who seemed genuinely happy, almost aroused. A shiver slithered over my skin.

Recognizing a lucid dream, I tried futilely to wake myself up. I couldn't move beyond twisting my torso as my feet stayed glued to the ground. I couldn't speak to anyone either. Panicked butterflies took flight in my stomach. Two more men on horses pulled up to Thomas and stopped short in front of me. My hands flew up to my face out of fear the animals would trample or bite me. This was too real. Again, I tried to call out, but no words left my throat.

The three riders led a march, their horses trotting in unison. Men in single file passed on both sides of me within a hairbreadth.

Heavens, they smelled. I didn't think any of them had brushed their teeth ever. Their puff-of-steam breaths were deadly.

Before I knew what was happening or what I should do about it, shots filled my ears. It sounded different from anything I'd heard before, but I knew it was a type of gunfire. My ears wanted to burst from the reverb, and I slapped my hands over them to muffle the noise. The movement caused a soldier to knock into my elbow, twisting me to the right. On the other side, another man bumped me again and twisted me to the left. It continued with each passing man, turning me into a human pendulum. The perception of falling overtook me, and I begged to be set free from the horrible sense of fear.

It was common for me to have a terrible time waking from lucid dreaming. My head was partially relieved as I woke but also confused about my location. I was in a big, comfy bed, and someone shook me gently.

It was Thomas. My Thomas.

We were in his bed, in his bedroom. Rays of new sunlight mixed with the gray, predawn light in his room, like it had in the dreamscape. I grabbed my head and bolted to sitting.

"You're not a Son of the American Revolution," I declared, half-awake and raking my fingers through my hair. "You're a *veteran.*"

Considering the light in the bedroom matched the light in my dream, my head stayed trapped in the fog between both, but the oddest thing came to me as clear as the sun. Thomas hadn't dismissed me for saying something so preposterous. He hadn't reassured me or lifted his eyebrow in his mischievous way to tease me. His face filled with terror, like he'd been caught. He sighed and closed his eyes in resignation as he bowed his head.

From under the covers, I jumped to the corner of the bed, despite my lack of clothes. I scrambled to my knees, crouching in a protective ball. I wasn't steady enough to run away, but I needed distance. From him and the clear look of guilt on his face. A chill ran through me, the shiver rattling my bones. It wasn't from the cool morning air against my naked skin. It was the recognition of truth I saw all over him.

What did Liam say I had? A secret radar? The murky soup of dreamland wore off, and I knew, somehow, I'd discovered Thomas's deepest, darkest secret. Here was the shadow behind his eyes. Here was his fear. The math of his life hadn't added up because the sum was unthinkable for a normal person. Take away what everyone thought was impossible, and it made sense.

"JaysusMaryandJoseph! Am I right?"

Thomas dropped his head as if the vertebrae in his neck had disappeared.

He had to be hundreds of years old.

How does something like that happen?

To be continued...

Thank you for taking this wild ride with Kick and Thomas. To read the blockbuster finale of their journey, *Kick Home*, scan the QR code below for ordering information.

Follow Kallyn

You can find Kallyn here:
    Website: kallynjones.com
    Facebook: KallynJonesAuthor
    Instagram: KallynJonesWriteNow

If you have a minute to review *Kick Back* at your retailer and/or favorite review site, it would make my day. Book reviews (even short ones) are the best way to spread the word about Kick and Thomas to other readers like you.

Listen to the *Kick Back Tunes* playlist on Spotify! The link to it is on my website, or search for it in the app.

Acknowledgments

- To my fabulous editors Jenny, Lisa, and D.A. There is nothing better than making you laugh and giving you a real word that's new to you. I can't think about what a mess my story was before your amazing minds touched it.
- To the vibrant writing community in the Triangle. Thank you for your inspiration and support. Hugs and squeezes to Laura, Annie, Jennifer, Renae, Sheon, Jamie, Patti, Beth, Jeanne, Stuart, Crista, Jake, Nancy, and Barbara. Writer friends are the best.
- To my friends and family who have been so supportive during this new venture of mine. Special kisses go to Mom, Linda, Joye, and Shannon. Thank you for trying to hawk my grown-up fairytale wherever you go!
- Finally, to my beloved men, W, C, N, and J. Y'all may be messy as hell, but I can't imagine life without you. I'm forever grateful for you love and support.

Kick Home: Book Three

A LATER IN LIFE ROMANTIC MYSTERY

For WEJ. My best friend. My boo. With a heart so big it inspired two heroes. Thank you for your unlimited belief in me, for humoring my "what if…" questions, and the tech support.

1

The Longest Time

Thomas

"Damn."

Damn. It. All.

I stared at the terrified, naked woman shivering at the opposite corner of my bed. Her eyes wildly darted around the room, avoiding mine, tearing me apart.

My shame and lifelong confusion. *Lifelong*, there's a laugh.

My fear. That was the problem. I couldn't love Kick and hold on to my fear at the same time. I'd laid my cards down, making it too late to fold. Not that I would. Not on her.

Kick's untamed morning curls mimicked the shock in her feral gaze when she braved a glance at me. How I wanted to comfort her but knew better. I let myself get caught up in the rage of a panicked female once—the mama bear who'd thought me a risk to her cubs. Kept the scars on my arm as a reminder to never do it again.

I'd planned to ease Kick into my unique reality. Instead, my secret escaped like a wild horse jumping a low fence.

Finally she slowed her heaving breaths enough to speak. "This is a nightmare, right? I'm still dreaming?" Kick lifted her head. "Please wake me up."

A tear threatened to slide down my cheek. My heart splintered as I looked at her beautiful body huddled in a protective ball. I cleared my throat. "Sorry, darlin'. Don't know how you did it, but you figured out my secret before I could prepare you for it." I chuckled—no, sneered—at my idiocy. "You warned me though. Didn't you?"

Why couldn't I just play it off? Let her think it was a damn dream? Because keeping the truth from Kick had been torture. I longed to share everything with her, even this. To be honest, in the hazy minute after she'd declared that I'd been a veteran of the Revolutionary War, my heart soared. Before I remembered that Kick wasn't ready to hear the truth.

"Jesus fecking Christ!" She leaped from her perch on the bed and paced the floor, fingers dragging through her hair. "This can't be happening. This doesn't happen." Kick let out a spine-chilling cackle. "Of course it happens to me. Why wouldn't it? Is there no end to the weirdness in my life?"

I sighed and shifted her way. "I'm so, so sorry. It is the truth. My truth."

"Stay away from me!" Kick's plea came out as a squeak, but the fury and hysteria in her eyes registered as an all-out scream.

When I'd met Banger and he explained our lives as he understood them, the news came as a welcome relief. Of course, by then I had already passed my two-hundredth birthday. After endless decades of solitude, with only my uncle and grandson for comfort, I embraced every aspect of Banger's life as a breath of fresh air and security. Like I'd been found.

Kick's reaction was everything I feared, what every Felidae member feared.

"When were you born? The real date?"

I pinched the bridge of my nose. "June. Seventeen-fifty."

"JaysusMaryandJoseph." Kick fell into a reading chair and let her head drop into her hands.

I carried a quilt over to her and placed it around her shoulders.

When the material touched her skin, she jumped, making me wince too. I cautiously eased into the other chair, picked up the portrait miniatures sitting on the table between the wingbacks, and handed her the first.

"This is me. My mother commissioned it before I went off to fight. I was supposed to be a career soldier, but my older brother enlisted too. Then he died." I held out the other, angled it toward her and cleared my throat. "This is Alicia after our betrothal… uh, engagement. Her mother gave it to me since I traveled a lot."

Staring at the painting in her hand, Kick shook her head like it was full of cobwebs. "This is impossible." Her hands trembled as she traced my features in my portrait. "Who are you?"

After sheltering my heart for centuries, it was suddenly in danger of shattering into a million bits. "I'm the man who loves you," I said, hoping my words sank in. "I've been and done many things, but nothing has meant more than the possibility of loving you. We're just beginning." I cleared my throat to hide a sob. "Please don't take it away."

She placed the portrait back on the table and turned away from me.

Dammit.

"Were you ever going to tell me?" she asked, a harsh bite in her words.

"Yes." I leaned toward her. "I promise. Once I knew for certain we were solid. You must see this isn't something I just tell casual friends. These aren't only my secrets you now possess. I had to be sure of us."

"Hang on." Kick sat up, her posture tight. "Are you saying I can't walk away? That I'm trapped?"

"No, baby. I won't force you to stay. Ever. It would tear me in two if you left, but knowing this won't trap you with me. I trust you'll keep these secrets."

Kick jumped up, swiped her glasses from the nightstand, and stormed into the closet. When she returned, she wore my winter robe. She stood over me, skin flushed, breathing hard like she'd run a marathon.

"Why didn't you trust me before? Hell, I told you things my kids don't know. You were completely in my world and you…" Kick gestured toward the paintings. "You held the biggest part of you back." She jutted out a hip and glowered. "I know about being special, Thomas. About people not understanding, even resenting my reality. How could you trick me—"

"You were in danger!"

Kick jerked as if my bellow had knocked her back, and she fell into the chair. I continued more quietly. "I'm not the only one with this… curse… gift… *affliction*. My existence was lonely, confusing, and filled with constant fear until I found people like me. They call themselves the Felidae Society."

"Liam used to be obsessed with zoology. Isn't Felidae Latin for cats?" Kick scoffed.

"It's said cats have nine lives—"

"Nine?" Her breath caught on the word. She dropped her head, curls flying in all directions as she shook it violently. "This isn't funny. I'm often called dramatic for the odd way I live, but this is downright mean. Cruel. You're not like this. I can't—"

I reached across the chasm between us and turned her chin toward me. "I am *profoundly* sorry that you found out this way. Wish I could have eased you into the truth. But I'm not sorry you know."

Kick's chin quivered. "You're not joking?"

How I wished it was a prank. I closed my eyes and sighed. "No, darlin'."

She blew out a long, wavering breath that I felt on my face and in my soul. "How old are your 'cat people'?"

I paced the room now, unable to keep my panicked energy controlled. My life had been laid bare in a matter of minutes. I couldn't stay still in a damn chair. I stormed into my closet and jammed my legs into a pair of sweatpants, finding a modicum of protection, like Kick had. This cliff dive of an introduction demanded full disclosure.

"Some are over a thousand years old, but it's hard to pinpoint exact dates."

Her jaw fell open.

I dropped to my knees in front of her chair and looked up into her perfect forest eyes clouded with despair and fear. Desperate for her to understand, I said, "Until recently—a few decades, really—someone like a Felidae was eventually murdered. People fear what they can't understand, so we hid in plain sight and moved often."

"Okay." Kick's fingertips blanched as she grasped the armrests. "How does knowing this put me in danger?"

I moved back onto my heels and tried to catch her gaze, silently begging her to see me, to believe me. "When I joined the Felidae, I'd already been with a woman for years." Kick's back stiffened, and I continued quickly. "We weren't close like you and I. Don't know how to explain it, but no one's ever reached me the way you have. Anyway, Vivienne and I lived our lives apart, but also together. Back then, I settled for someone like an anchor, and she needed protection. When she had to flee Paris, I set her up with a boutique in New York."

As if propelled by an invisible force, Kick padded out into the hallway to the gallery of old photographs. I followed, finding her in front of the picture of Viv's grand opening. Kick had noticed it the morning after our first night together.

"Your 'family friend'," she said sarcastically, touching my image in the frame. "I thought this was your grandfather or something."

I scoffed. "Or something. We were close, like I said."

Kick kept staring at the photo. "Not a *bic* then."

I flinched at her words as they hit their target. "No." I had never felt comfortable with Banger's term for his disposable women. Now I despised it, hating that I used to use it too.

She turned toward me and folded her arms. "But you do know how to be casual."

I nodded and shrugged at the same time. "With anyone but you."

"Thomas…" Kick exhaled a frustrated sigh. "You still haven't explained how this puts me in danger."

"I'm trying to." I heaved a breath. "The night before the gala, I found out that the Felidae had Vivienne under surveillance back then. The men watching her were supposed to kill her if they gathered evidence she knew about the Society."

Kick stepped away from the wall. Away from me. She tilted her head as she scrutinized me. "You think they'll kill me now that I know about them?"

"I did in December. It rattled me something fierce. That's why I walked out that night. Hell, baby, here I'd been racking my brain, working with Banger to figure out who wanted to hurt you and your café. Then I find out you were in more danger from me?" I groaned as I shook my head.

"Okay. Then what's changed?"

I stepped up to Kick and took her hands, smiling on the inside when she let me. "Two things changed. First off, Banger reassured me he would do everything in his power to protect us when I saw him in France. Tess was there too, and she declared herself on our side. So you'll have more than me fighting for us." I brought our hands to my heart. "I promise to protect you with my body and anything else in my power. Do you believe me?"

Kick narrowed her gaze, studying me, making seconds seem like hours. Finally, in a quiet, rough voice, she answered, "Shit... I think I do believe you."

"Do you understand why I had to keep my secret now? I swear I—"

"No, I don't." She stepped away again and tracked a circle around me in the hallway. "Even though no one will ever hear about this from me, it feels like you tricked me. You... you drew me in. Made me love you. Why, Thomas? Why?"

"Because I've never loved anyone like I do you. Still, I had to be sure."

"Sure of what?" She threw her arms up. "Do you think this is the first time my weltanschauung flipped on its head in a nanosecond? There have been days where it seemed like my whole life was a matter of learning that left is right and up is down. Aw hell, the genetics research..." Kick grabbed her head, and the robe fell open. She quickly retied it. "You're studying yourself, aren't you?"

"Sort of. My two-times granddaughter is my main subject."

"Your *two*…"

"Toni."

"Her husband has Alzheimer's?"

"That's her."

"Jaysus fecking Christ!" Kick tipped her head back, her lips moving like she was counting her breaths to calm herself. "It's all half-truths, isn't it? I thought you were her younger brother, Thomas. How is this—"

"My neighbors tried to *kill* me!" My bellow echoed through the house and practically blew us apart.

Her accusations had to stop. I ended up sitting on the floor across from the line of old photos, not sure how I got there. "I protect my family, Kick. When we met, you were beautiful… infuriating… intriguing. That said, you weren't family." I looked over at her and spread my hands apart. "You are my family now, and that's why we're here. I'll protect you with everything I have, but I'll be damned if Toni, or anyone else I love, will have to face what I did back then."

"What do you mean, your neighbors tried to kill you?" She settled against the wall across from me.

The memories from that time had faded to the point they were almost gone emotionally. Or I thought they had. Everything flooded back as I spoke. "Ridiculous rumors floated around the village. Some called me a wizard. Others accused me of making a pact with the devil because I didn't appear to age. What hurt the most was… my sons. They grew impatient with me. Their peers inherited lands from their dead fathers, while I showed no signs of slowing down. One night, a group of men made their way to my plantation to put an end to me."

"I thought your family bred horses."

"Kick…" I clipped, too emotional to handle the change in focus. "We did and still do. It was also the eighteen hundreds in Virginia."

She wrapped a hand around her hair and brought it over her shoulder. "Well, shit."

"Yeah." I scrubbed my scruffy face with my hands. "So I visited my daughters, ending up at Alice's—my youngest—in Kentucky. Joe is her son, George Jr."

"Joe is George?"

"Rotating names is part of how we survive… as is the fierce protection of our privacy."

"Jaysus." Kick stood and approached the gallery wall again. She stopped in front of each photo, often touching my image in it. "So it skips a generation? This… thing you have?"

"Depends. Some families skip several generations. Some don't." I wrapped my arms around my knees and let my head settle on them, thoroughly worn out. "Are y'alright?" With each step came a hitch of her breath, so I aurally followed her path to every photo without having to watch her.

"I don't know."

"That's me and my Uncle Theo when we founded a bank in San Francisco. For the longest time, it was just us. There were rumors about his grandfather, but nothing for certain. Disappearing was easier back then."

Step. A low keening sound floated around the hall.

"Uncle Theo, me, and Joe just before boarding the train to join World War I." I scoffed at the thought of those years. "We bought into the idea of ending all wars."

A shuffle. Another hitching breath.

"Joe and me, Paris in the twenties," I murmured. "He had switched back to George then, and I was going by Michael."

"Mic—" Two swishes of the robe and a gasp.

"Banger and me in the fifties. In Australia." I lifted my eyes when I didn't hear any more movement.

Kick tilted her head from side to side as she studied the photos. "I haven't kept up my retouching skills, but back in the day, I could've done a decent job with these." She reached back to the nearest black-and-white picture. "Maybe not the colored ones, but I used to switch heads on images like this. Kids today can do this with color photos. It's a basic skill now."

What I would give for them to be faked. I pinched the bridge of my nose, feeling the start of a headache. Or was it heartache? I couldn't shake the ominous feeling I was about to watch her walk out the door.

Over before we'd begun.

Despair rushed through me as I cleared my throat. "They're not Photoshopped. They're not my ancestors. They're me. My life. Hung there to keep me from losing… myself."

Kick moved to the top of the stairwell. She stood stock-still, buzzing with energy. I braced for her to run. Instead, she placed one hand on the banister and the other on the railing defining the balcony to the guest wing. Then Kick burst out a full-on scream at the top of her lungs. "Fuuuck!"

When she ran out of breath, she dropped down on the steps, her gaze trained on the open space below and nothing at all.

Again, seconds turned into hours. I wanted to turn back the clock to the night before, when she rode my cock and we just had beauty and freedom between us. I hung my head in shame, convinced she'd abandon the promises we'd made to each other yesterday. At the same time, I felt an inexplicable relief from bringing her fully into my world. The struggle to maintain my sanity through the loneliness hit me full force, knowing that I was about to lose it.

"Do you want to leave me now?" That waiting tear let loose and dropped onto my knee, sinking into my sweatpants material.

Despite a rasp, Kick's voice sounded angelic to my ears.

"No, Thomas. Heaven help me, but I don't." Her breath hitched again, and I lifted my head when I realized she was crying too. "I don't know why, but I can't walk away." Kick looked over her shoulder at me, her eyes searching. I hoped like hell she still saw me there. "I'm scared."

Each shuddering breath I took felt like a fight for life. "You may not believe this, but I'm more frightened than you."

Kick spun around to face me. She was bright red from screaming. "Are you s-sure you're not a vampire?" she asked through another hitch.

I laughed once, needing the joke, even though it had been a sincere question. "You and your damn fantasy books."

"Paranormal."

"Fine." I flicked a wrist. "Promise… I'm a human man. Just have variances in my DNA."

"What variances?"

"That's what my research is about." Another damn tear slid down my cheek.

Kick covered her mouth. She scooted across the floor and pulled me into a tight embrace.

I lifted her hand and brought her flat palm to my heart, holding it there. "This had been locked up tight for centuries. Do you have any idea what that feels like? I'd grown so used to the cold and loneliness… thought it would always be this way. Damned if you didn't have the key. This"—I tapped her hand over my heart—"is what you need to know about me. You're my locksmith."

I fingered the strung-out curls hanging in her face and tucked them behind her ear. "No matter what happens after today, I'll watch over you—even if it must be from afar. Your safety is more important than mine."

Kick sat back on her heels, let her hands fall into her lap, and stared at me.

Please make the vulnerability worth it. Please don't make me regret my honesty.

She sighed a ragged breath, her beautiful hazel eyes darkened with sorrow. "It would be easy to make you love me from a distance. Life would be much easier. But who says love is easy? If this is what makes you the man I love, then I must accept it, right? You accept my health issues. What's an impossible birthday added to the mix?"

"Come here." I grabbed Kick's wrist with one hand and opened her robe with the other so I could hold her skin to skin. It had been an exhausting morning, and it wasn't even eight o'clock. The way a life could turn on a dime, but Kick had plenty of experience with such things, didn't she? This was what people meant when they said home wasn't a piece of land. It was a woman who could lighten the load and give life meaning with her smile.

Kick shifted to straddle my lap and settled into me, occasionally kissing my jaw. I felt a warm, low hum stir in my limbs—the telltale sign of my aura appearing after a highly emotional experience.

Kick murmured, "Why though?"

I kissed her temple and held my lips there, breathing in the scent of her hair. While tracing light kisses down to her cheek and across to her mouth, something incredible happened as she responded. A literal warmth emanated from us, starting with our hands. I laced our fingers. "Wish I knew. Have to figure out *what* first." She shifted, and I closed my eyes, taking in the feel of her embrace. Hope warred with my hard-earned cynicism.

"I'll grow old and decrepit while you stay young and perfect."

"Don't think you'll have to worry about that."

"Why not?" Kick sounded tired, like the morning had worn her out as much as it had me.

I nudged her, making her sit back. "The second reason I decided it was safe to ask you to come back to me in December…"

"Oh, right." She pushed her hair off her face. "What's that?"

I raised a hand, letting the blue aura I thought I'd lost float above my skin. I flexed my fingers as waves of light rippled around them.

Kick gasped and brought her hands to her face. "You do it too?"

"It disappeared a long time ago. Until you."

With a kind of awe, she whispered, "It started recently for me. I thought it had to do with meditation."

"I know." I grinned and lifted Kick's hand.

The same light washed over and around her, only it was a pastel violet color. Her eyes flashed wide.

Then she fainted.

Never Tear Us Apart

Kick

"I'M SORRY I YELLED."

It was the first thing out of my mouth after I came to. I didn't scream again after fainting, but the feral bellow played in the back of my mind when I woke. It took a minute to remember everything that came after, including…

"My promise stands. You don't have to stay."

Shit. Thomas's confident, chiseled face had melted into something reflecting heartbreak. I touched his cheek, hoping I could coax the cocky back out of him. "That's not why I screeched like a banshee. It's what I do whenever life goes sideways. Who knew I'd end up with a routine for such things?" My brow furled as I thought about the ridiculousness of it.

Thomas rubbed my arm. We were lying on his bed, his arms around me like a child would hold a teddy bear. He must have picked me up and settled us here, yet this didn't feel like cuddling. His movements were slow, jerky—like he had shut down.

"You don't want this life, do you?" he whispered.

I thought I understood what he wasn't saying, and it scared the hell out of me. "Before I passed out, you and I—"

He raised our hands. What remained of the light still pulsed around our fingers. I couldn't tell if I heard the pleasant hum or felt it in my body. In places, the colors swirled around each other. In others, they blended together, forming a pretty lavender. I stared at the light, stupefied. "What does it mean?"

Thomas sighed, like his thoughts stayed stuck on his last question. Then again, I hadn't eased his worries. "I think you have the variances I have," he said slowly. "Whether it's all of them or some of them, I don't know. I would like to do some tests."

I scratched at my nose. It tingled the way it often did before a cry came on. I sensed Thomas couldn't handle any more freakouts, so I had to keep my shit together. Fortunately, I had a lot of practice there too. "Do you think I'll live as long as you have? You said something about a second reason to get back together. Is that what you meant?"

"That's my hypothesis. Obviously, we need proof."

"Wow. Well, shit." I ducked my head into Thomas's chest, trying to absorb this news with grace, fighting like hell to squash the urge to scream at the top of the stairs again. "If you're right," I said, tipping my head back to meet his gaze. "Your life has me whether I want it. It's best if I get used to it. Like with the autoimmunity—there's no wishing it away."

He squeezed my shoulder. "You don't have to join up with the Felidae. Or me. You can live your life on your own."

"Without you? Sounds like a nightmare." I bit my cheek when Thomas flinched. I'd basically disregarded everything he'd done so far. "I'm sorry. I didn't mean—"

He lifted my hand and kissed my knuckles. "It's alright. At times, it has been a nightmare."

"It's just…" I fussed with my hair, trying to tame the rat's nest as I moved to sit. "My head won't stop spinning. And the questions… Jaysus, they're innumerable."

Oh hell, what about my kids? If I have this, would they grow old without me, like Thomas's children had? It was unthinkable.

"Knowing you? I bet." He jostled me, some mischief returning to his face as he chuckled.

I wanted to laugh but couldn't. While it made me happy to see a shy little grin replace the despair on Thomas's face, I was drowning in my overwhelm.

The realization of how alone Thomas had been for so, so, long had hit me like a Mack truck when I stood in his photo gallery. I ached for all he'd been through. "Anyway… despite the mess in here…" I tapped my temple. "Love is the strongest feeling in here." I rubbed over my heart. "Having you to guide me through this tells me it'll be okay."

"At least one of us is sure."

"I have to be."

People often told me I looked young for my age. Did that mean Thomas was right? Or did some people just age better?

One thing at a time.

It had become one of my mantras through other life upheavals, and it applied here. I couldn't jump ahead months or years to know if Thomas was right, but he'd go into scientist mode soon enough. Hell, his work always simmered on the back burner in his mind. So I knew we could progress one step at a time and not worry about the unknowns. I'd learned to handle all the what-ifs the hard way too. It took a strong focus on what I knew for certain. Ultimately, my heart trusted the gift that was Thomas.

"If you hadn't survived this long, you'd only be a gorgeous man in some old photographs. I wouldn't know you. As delicious as your orgasms are, I can't stand to think about going through my life without my friend. Without you. If what you say is true about me— and that's the biggest head-scratcher of all as far as I'm concerned —I'll need you with me."

Thomas pulled me back against his body and kissed my temple.

I wiggled my arms around his waist, and we snuggled for real for a long while. Eventually I laughed. "A thousand years of your orgasms is quite the bonus." Thomas's startled laugh filled the room as he held me tighter.

· · ·

After our emotional restart, we needed space. Thomas used his horse as an excuse to leave the house. His attachment to his adopted, formerly wild horse made more sense to me now. I saw it as a way to connect him to the man he used to be. Thomas claimed he and Eddie were getting back into their old routine with him boarded at the neighboring stables. I predicted their ride would end up longer than planned. Much longer.

I didn't mind. It gave me the opportunity to go into the bathroom, shove a small towel in my mouth, and scream again until my vocal cords crapped out. What can I say? It helped. It also left me with a slight sore throat and a grumbling stomach.

Before my hunger could be sated, I had to find a peaceful way to move forward. After I showered and dressed, I sat on the edge of Thomas's bed, staring at his miniature. "What the hell?" I reached for it and looked closer. As if there hadn't been enough revelations already, I would swear this was the face of the man in my dreams for all these years and not just the one from the night before. He was young in this rendering, but there was enough diffusion of his features from the brushstrokes to get the same impression of who'd been in my dreams. Could Thomas have been the one haunting me all this time? I would need to ask him more about his time as a soldier. I thought he'd been a horse breeder in middle-age—or the equivalent if he'd lived a normal life. As the visions in my dreams formed more clearly, the man starring in them had been mature, not a teen.

My hands shook with more possibilities, so I set the miniature back down and went in search of a meditation spot before I broke down for real. This was small compared to everything we'd already been through, but it also felt like it could be the last straw if I didn't settle my mind.

I found the perfect place on a small balcony off a guest bedroom. I grabbed a few pillows and a heavy blanket from the bed and embraced the chilly air. Cool inhales and steamy exhales brought me back to center as I let the morning sun warm my face. I soon walked down the staircase in my mind, then sat on the porch there. I found peace as the smell of the gardenias in my meditation spot blended with the crisp air in the real world. No one visited me in the meditation, but I required solitude. No aura showed up either. I suppose I was too tired. I sat in this reality mash-up and focused on these new possibilities.

What did I really think?

It was banana bonkers. But it also weirdly made sense. More accurately, Thomas made more sense from this perspective. Me though? I couldn't believe I would end up like him. Maybe if I hadn't been a mom. Each time my thoughts turned to them, to the possibility of outliving them, I swore a volt of electricity sliced through me. My brain refused to wrap around a world with me in it but not them. Where they aged and I didn't.

"Fuck it." I threw the blanket on the bed as I ran through the room and into Thomas's. I'd pack my bag and go home to think. Not necessarily leave him outright, but take some time. Hell, we'd just met. Maybe I'd have him run the tests, then decide about us.

As I carried my bag out into the hallway, the gallery of photos caught my eye, making me freeze. Something in the photos had seemed off. I stepped away from the bag and studied his pictures again. There was no denying they were of Thomas, but he looked different in them. It hit me hard enough to take my breath away. There was no spark in his brilliant silver eyes.

I raced through my memories of us—Thomas laughing at me the night we'd met. I'd had the feeling he didn't do it much back then. Dancing in his arms. His enthusiastic interest in my gluten-free and dairy free cooking. His smile when we accidentally admitted we loved each other. The angelic look on his face when he came, and it wasn't his aura. It was him letting go. Deana practically told me from day one that the man lit up when I was around.

The gallery showed me inside Thomas's life without me in it. It broke my heart to think of him so alone, alive but not really living. Whether for one year or a thousand, it didn't matter. Something about me, about us, had given him that spark.

I grasped my arms, wrapping them around my torso to control the shaking that swept over me. My gaze shot between the photos and the stairs. Wondering what to do. Both choices were hard as hell, but which was right? And why did I think loving Thomas would be easy? Oh, it was easy as breathing to fall for him, but the doing of it was the feat of a lifetime with anyone. My ridiculous naivete had me surprised.

I'd known he held a secret this whole time. Instincts had told me it was a doozy too. An impossibility? No, but deep down I knew it would rock me. And still, I trusted Thomas more.

Then the tears flowed.

As I rolled my overnight bag back into his closet and unpacked it a second time, the tears kept coming. Grateful ones and fearful ones alike flowed as they cleansed my soul and steeled my spine. After losing one great love, I knew what a gift it was to find another.

It was a shit choice. At the same time, there wasn't a choice between him and my kids at all. If I had similar DNA variances, then I'd be a fool not to stick close to Thomas, lean on him for support. If I didn't have them? I hoped like hell he'd want to stick by me for the years I would have.

On the way to the shower, his T-shirt caught my eye, laying on top of a dresser in the closet. I picked it up, inhaling his woodsy scent still in the soft cotton, feeling it quiet the roar thundering through me. Still holding the shirt, I grabbed my toiletry bag and padded into the bathroom to wash the morning off.

"THAT SMELLS FANTASTIC."

Thomas cautiously approached me at the stove as I cooked up a pack of Paleo bacon for us. It was noon, but it had taken all morning for me to finally think about food.

"I know, right?" I answered, breathing in the heavy smokiness mixed with salt. "It's not at all like the common brands." Sticking with foods that were organic, grass-fed… yada-yada… was a requirement for remaining in my doctor's practice. At first, the cost difference in the grocery bill had intimidated the hell out of me, especially with growing boys in the house. The improvement in taste ended up being a pleasant surprise. I could get past the sticker shock for amazing flavor.

"Joe makes this with the smoker at home. Nothing has ever smelled as good as his until now."

"Funny. When I first tasted this, it seemed like a new food." And so went another reminder that Thomas was from a different era. Something as simple as bacon probably reminded him of the past.

He touched my shoulder. "I bet."

I snorted softly before jumping away from a spot of airborne grease, sliding a few feet in my thick socks. I also knew that bacon wasn't what was really on his mind. Since he'd showered and we'd avoided each other long enough, I didn't want him treading lightly around me anymore.

"Feel better?" I asked.

He stepped closer. "Do you?"

I bit back the growl threatening to escape my throat. I was in a stages-of-acceptance kind of situation. Caught between my desire to pelt Thomas with questions and wanting to eat our meal in peace. A tentative spark had returned to his blue-gray eyes, and I was afraid of saying something to make it disappear again. I shrugged. "I'm hungry."

He stepped up behind me. "You're wearing my T-shirt. Take this as a good sign?"

"You could say that."

He leaned against the island as I placed cooked strips on a plate lined with a paper towel before adding the last of the package to the pan. The tension between us crackled on my arms. After becoming so close yesterday, I wanted to snap my fingers and make us go right back there. Would all this craziness be worth it to have that connection again? I had to find out. I flipped the bacon and said, "Told you I'd figure it out."

Thomas barked a quick laugh, and the knot in my stomach loosened as his eyes brightened a little more. "Yes, you did. Can you understand my need for secrecy?"

My tongue circled in my cheek while I thought about it. I hated how he kept asking, like his insecurities wouldn't let him move on until we were on the same page. I doubted if he'd ever been so vulnerable with someone before. It helped my answer. "I think so. You have to protect your friends."

"And you."

I looked over my shoulder. "Who protects you?"

"Felidae vows go both ways."

I pressed a freshly formed curl behind my ear as I shook my head. "Do they really? According to you, these people threatened Vivienne and me. How is that protection if you can't be loved? Are they supposed to choose your partner?"

Thomas loosely wrapped his arms around my waist. "People used to pair off more, but it's been a while." I felt his shoulder rise. "It never appealed to me. And I'm still a kid in their eyes. Women are also rare in the Felidae. It's why there's so much buzz about my work with Toni."

"Okay, fine." I turned the meat strips one last time. After a sharp crackle and snap, a speck of hot grease splashed my skin. I jumped, shaking my hand in annoyance. For my skin or for Thomas, I couldn't say. "You were just supposed to, what? Live like a monk? Be a player like Banger? Either way, it sounds miserable." My mind flashed to the photos upstairs. Proof of that life.

"It didn't matter. I'm used to being alone. This is what's frightening."

"Me? I frighten you?"

Instead of answering directly, he asked, "Are you staying?"

And it hit me. Had anyone ever loved Thomas for himself? I believed Banger did in a brotherly way. I hoped his wife had, but couldn't be certain. I turned off the burner and spun around so I could put my arms around his neck. "I don't know what the future will bring. Autoimmunity broke me of that kind of thinking. But today and tomorrow? You've got me."

Thomas closed his eyes and sighed in relief. "You do get it."

"Not planning ahead because life is too weird and potentially isolating? You bet I get *that*. My best life has to be today no matter how it looks."

Thomas lowered his forehead to mine and clung to me. He whispered, "No one's ever chosen me before."

I chuckled at the absurdity. "Need I remind you that you've been married? Plus there was Vivienne."

He shook his head, letting it rub against mine, then placed a reverent kiss to my temple. "Alicia could have called off the arrangement, but she never would have out of fear of her father's scorn."

"He needed you to take care of his land," I said, understanding.

"Precisely. And Viv? I offered her a way out of a difficult life, along with protection." He swallowed stepping back. "Don't get me wrong, I wasn't miserable. Hell, my peers considered me a lucky son of a bitch. But—"

"But I want you as much as I need you."

Thomas pinched the bridge of his nose before nodding.

I sifted my fingers through his hair, then let my hand settle at his firm jaw. What a gift his vulnerability was. I wondered if the other women had ever seen it. I also didn't care. If they couldn't bring it out of him, that was their loss.

Thomas picked me up and set me on the counter. His body pressed into mine, our embrace physically saying more than words could. Next came the kiss, his tongue sharing his gratitude for the ways we complemented each other.

"Mmm." He growled into my neck. "I do need you. So much."

I hadn't felt Thomas's hands travel up my thighs, though my legs were bare—my compromise, not knowing if we were still doing naked weekend. His needs were obvious as he pulled me forward and rubbed me against his hot arousal. I froze, blinked, and placed my hands over his.

"There's still something wrong." The self-rebuke in his silver-blue stare broke my heart as he stepped back.

"I… yeah, suppose there is." I grabbed his wrist to keep him from leaving the room or worse. "Don't get me wrong, I wouldn't want to go through this with anyone but you. I'm grateful you promise to be there to guide me. It's everything else."

"You can't take it one day at a time after all."

"I've learned to take things one hour at a time, if necessary. It's just"—I pressed my hands into the edge of the counter—"ever since my diagnosis, I've worked my ass off to make my life mean something. I figured that was the reason I ended up with these autoimmune diseases. Then the kids became my sole responsibility, and I had to be there for them."

"None of that has changed, darlin'."

I wished I could believe Thomas, wished he would surround me in his woodsy scent and make my fears go away. "How do I make a difference for others when my life's shrouded in secrets now? Helping people requires openness, putting yourself out there. You're telling me I have to lie to everyone I love now." I fought a tear threatening to drop and could tell Thomas noticed it. "More than that, how do I plan a future where my kids will grow old and I won't, if it skips a generation like your family? What about my babies? How am I supposed to be okay with burying them?"

3

(I Got a Woman Crazy for Me) She's Funny That Way

Thomas

I PULLED KICK INTO MY CHEST. "I'M SUCH A DUMBASS."

She tipped her head back, her brow furrowed. "That's not what I meant."

"But I should've factored your kids into this. Of course you're afraid for them and what it means for y'all's relationship." One of the blessings of walking into my life blind had been not knowing I'd bury my children *and* their descendants. Technically, I didn't, but I watched for news of them, and it tore at my heart each time it trickled in.

Kick pulled her hair to one shoulder, twisting the bottom curls around her finger. "We have to lie to them, right?"

We. I closed my eyes at the sound of the word. As hard as this was for Kick, she wanted me to be a part of the solution. I pulled the hand fidgeting with her hair into mine. "Nothing has to change right now. All couples keep things from their kids. This won't affect how we live for a time. Hell, you're still working on your remission. The best thing for the both of us is to do what you said earlier—live in the moment."

She pulled her hand away and touched her heart. "But I'll know in here. What do you say to that? Give me some kind of hope. Please."

"Alright." I took her hand in mine and tentatively squeezed it. "Let's take Banger. He's an example of the variance moving from the parents to their child. In his case, both his parents were already Felidae. I don't know how it works if the parents haven't transitioned yet. Or if it's more important to have the variance from both parents. About the only thing we've figured out before our modern research was the fertility aspect. It lasts longer but eventually wanes. That's why the world isn't full of Felidae children."

"Are you saying there's no way to know about my kids?" Kick bit her lip, the worry written all over her face. I fed her a strawberry from a bowl on the counter, hoping the simple pleasure of the taste would ease her mind.

"You had a DNA test done, right?"

"About a year ago, yes."

I gave her hand a light shake. "We start there. I'll run blood work. Check my hypothesis about you. Then we'll focus on the kids. Test them against you and my database." Excitement filled my voice, the scientist in me coming alive with the prospect of tracking the McKennas, adding more data to my research. *Dammit.* I saw the thought-wrestling match in her worried hazel eyes and cringed at my callousness.

"What does all this mean though? What about my autoimmune diseases? Or aging?"

I tilted my head, searching for the words. "It means evolution's alive and well. Despite our progress, we understand just a small part of how it all works." I scratched at my chin. "The discipline you've practiced putting yourself back into remission could be your catalyst. You've come a long way already. Didn't you also say your aura recently showed up?"

"When I started taking meditation seriously. Yes." Kick bit into another strawberry, licking the dark pink of the berry juice from her bottom lip.

Christ, I wanted to give her a normal life. To tell her I was kidding, then lick the juice off her myself. Get back our naked weekend and worship her the way she deserved. The reality was, that had never been my life and now I'd dragged her into my chaos. Instead, I smiled at the reminder of how she had to be nagged into trying meditation. "Alright. Mine also came back recently while meditating. As to your autoimmunity, it should reverse itself over time. And aging? You already look younger than your years."

Kick huffed. "I feel... stuck." Her hands floated around her head, physically expressing her frustration.

"Do you believe me so far?"

"Honestly? Part of me thinks it's bonkers. That you won't find these variances in me. Another part says why the hell not? We already know I hit the genetic jackpot with not one but two autoimmune diseases. Why shouldn't I go full mutant?"

Even though she was being her snarky self, Kick sparked an idea in me. I clicked my tongue and touched the tip of her nose. "Good point. I should see if your autoimmunity factors in. Might help my overall research."

She sighed and hopped off the counter, moving toward the refrigerator. "You're talking about epigenetics, right? Will you study my telomeres? Ever since I read about them, I wanted to get it done." She grabbed a tomato and sliced it on a cutting board sitting next to the stove. The earthy flavor of the heirloom variety filled my nose. I guessed we were having BLTs for lunch.

I chuckled at her words. I'd forgotten she was a magazine article researcher. "It's part of it." I inhaled deeply, remembering my endless years of confusion. "For the longest time, the only possible explanation I could lean on came from a piece written by Aeschylus. In it, he talked about learning via suffering, but what sustained me most came at the end: '...against our will, comes wisdom to us by the awful grace of God.' It's been equal parts a curse and blessing to live this life, particularly because of the secrecy." My hand reached for hers, my thumb rubbing the top of her knuckles. The quote intensified at the moment. "I find myself more awed by grace now that you're here. I am deeply sorry about burdening you with the secrets."

Kick impressed me further as she accepted my words with no attempt at deflection or her often-used self-deprecation. She just nodded her head and added, "I'd love to see your lab if that's possible. It'll help to see your work, give me some reassurances."

A wide grin spread across my face. "Absolutely."

"YOU THINK THERE'LL COME A DAY WHEN I'VE HEARD ALL YOUR stories?"

Christ, I hope so.

I shrugged and grunted a response as I checked in with the lab on my phone. Kick currently tried to commit homicide-by-overquestioning. Two more and I swore I'd die. *Finally.*

After clearing the lunch plates, she changed into a purple satin robe and snuggled into me on the sofa in my sunroom—the toastiest room in the house thanks to the greenhouse wall and ceiling. Surrounded by my small orchid collection and the afternoon sun, she did her best impression of a hardline journalist, pelting me with questions about eighteenth-century life.

One of my deepest fears involved being imprisoned in a government facility if my secret escaped. I'd never contemplated the possibility of a hellish version of a Barbara Walters interview.

I ran my hand through my hair and pressed on tension points at the base of my skull. My foot kept jumping, so I took it as a sign and paced the room.

"Understand something. I hide in plain sight, but so does everyone—Felidae or not." I pulled at the invisible collar at my bare neck, feeling like it wanted to choke me. Kick's questions brought back memories of things I never understood myself. At least I had some answers now.

I should have been preoccupied with the goddess sitting on my sofa—mine. We should've finally been ready for another round of hot-and-heavy heaven, one where we would never sit in this room again without thinking of it and smiling. Instead, I was out of breath from revisiting things best left alone.

But Kick needed this even if we walked through my graveyard

of remembrances so painful I avoided them at all costs. It all started with, "How many outfits did you have?" Like I'd ever worn an "outfit" in my entire life.

"This eases out of a man in small bites under normal circumstances, darlin'."

The truth is, neither of us could have prepared for this situation. Kick was the first regular person I'd ever talked to about my life. Joe had first approached Toni about who she was, so I hadn't had to explain anything when we met. I had no manual on how to explain *me*.

"I'm sorry." Kick scrunched her nose as disappointment wrote itself on her face as clearly as the freckles on her nose. Her chin did a little wobble thing, and I sank back down on the cushion next to her.

"Baby." I sighed, feeling like a shit for losing my patience. "I haven't time-traveled. I'm not *Dr. Who*. I've lived every second of my years. Not all of them to the fullest but with all I've been capable of at the time. In my book, that makes me a twenty-first-century man." I dropped my head and kissed her knuckles, silently asking for it to be enough. "I-I'd appreciate it if you'd quit treating me like an alien discovery."

I chortled and finished, "Honestly, it was easier when you thought you'd robbed the cradle." Expecting to see her smile at my joke, I looked up. Instead, her eyes glistened. My shoulders slumped in disappointment. Her jabbering was a defense against her own heady fears. *I'm an idiot.*

I reached for Kick and pulled her into my lap. "Where are you right now?"

She took one long inhale and quietly answered, "This… this has been a lot. I know I've said it before, but that's all I've got."

"Agreed." I rubbed her back with my free hand. "Too much?"

She scoffed and answered, "Does it matter?"

"*You* matter."

"Perhaps." Kick blew a curl off her cheek and smiled, though it didn't reach her eyes. "I'll deal with it." She squeezed my hand. "I already live a strange life by most people's standards. Hell, a lot of folks don't believe I'm sick. My health insurance won't acknowledge my condition, which is why most of my treatments are out of pocket. Plus I keep most of my life under wraps because those who need to know do. The rest can kiss my ass. There's a similarity between us already."

I laughed at her comparison. Plus she was right.

We sat in silence for several minutes, watching some deer pick at the vegetation through my garden fence, then walk away.

"Can I ask one more question?" Kick kept her focus on the backyard. "I promise it'll be the last. For now."

I pulled her hair away from her neck, pressed my lips to the back of her jaw, and growled to make a point. She already had from me everything that mattered. Of course she'd get all the questions. "Hit me."

"When did you figure it out? About yourself, I mean."

I snuck another kiss while considering my answer. Then I lifted our joined hands that were again humming with my blue aura. Kick's slowly buzzed to life, startling her. I pressed her back into me with my other hand so I could answer.

"This happened first. Like you, my instincts led me to keep it to myself."

Kick gasped, her eyes wide in shock. I raised my brows and winked, reminding her that she hadn't hidden it from me. "When Alicia died, I lost myself for a while. I kept seeing her around every corner, you know?"

"I do."

Right. She'd also been a young widow. I continued, "My mother-in-law kept the kids and hired a wet nurse for the baby. I traveled a lot for business, so it wasn't odd to go away. I left to spend a night or two on my favorite peak. Ended up sitting on the damn mountain for a week. Not sure if I even ate anything up there. I was angry with myself for not being home when Alicia passed. For not saying goodbye. Angry with her for leaving us. I yelled until I lost my voice. Then the aura happened."

"Oh cowboy." Kick moved her free hand to my chest and rubbed over my heart.

"The aura was darker back then. No idea why." I lowered our hands and caressed her arm, needing more contact. "When I returned home, I convinced myself it had been a dream and resumed my life. The first real clue came when I stopped getting sick. Smallpox swept through the valley, and many neighbors were lost. We almost lost my oldest daughter, but I didn't get more than a runny nose. Later, people would comment on my lack of wrinkles, gray hair, and such. When my first son and I looked like twins, I had to admit something was different."

"You stopped aging?"

"Yeah. At first, people complimented me. Women tried to match me with their daughters, even women my age wanted me to marry their daughters. Friends of my girls." I shuddered at the memory.

Kick lifted her head off my chest and caught my gaze. "You were never tempted?"

I shook my head vigorously. "They would expect babies from me. As I said before, I refused to risk killing another woman with my seed."

"But Thomas—"

"That was how I thought. No correcting it now. Then the accusations started, followed by rumors and threats. So I left. To save my family and my legacy, I left them." My voice quieted at the memory. "I packed up my horse and headed for my youngest daughter's homestead. It was past the time for my sons to inherit anyway. Most of their peers had been running their estates and businesses for decades. Alice had married and settled in Kentucky. Joseph is her son. Stayed about a year. Then I kept going. I had Alice write to her brothers and tell them I died, to make everything tidy."

"All that time and you never knew why?"

"No." My voice sounded sharp, though I'd forgiven my former friends long ago. This was the first time I truly told my story. Everyone else who knew my truth had been through similar situations. They never needed the details or the emotional consequences. "I knew all the things I wasn't. I just never knew what I was. Not until 1957."

Her head popped up in surprise. "No shit?"

"Not a bit. That's when I met Banger and the rest of the Felidae Society."

"Oh sweets." Kick wrapped her arms around my waist and held tight. I soaked in every ounce of support she offered, realizing for the first time how much I had needed someone to listen to me.

I lifted my foot out from under her and set it along the length of the couch, placing her between my legs. "Can we be done with questions for now?"

"You're drained."

"Completely."

"Me too." As if on cue, Kick yawned, popping her jaw.

I yanked on the blanket that lay over the sofa and draped it over us as we shifted down. Kick fell asleep instantly while I slowly drifted off with my lips pressed to her temple, relaxing in her vanilla scent mixed with the sweetness of the orchids. Did she have any clue how much her presence meant to me? Changed me? I hoped we could find a normal life soon. Our normal. Without having to hurt anyone to do it. Especially someone in the Felidae. I had to make sure Alaric believed my thoughts about Kick and accepted her.

Then I'd figure out how to incorporate her into my research. I couldn't add it to my grant, so I'd have to find a way to work around my contract.

After our nap, we'd wandered outside to watch the sunset while dinner baked in the oven. We currently snuggled back together in the den, changing channels between the New Year's Eve concerts. The weight of the day had lifted when we agreed to focus on us, on the day-to-day of knowing each other and our inconvenient truths. Nothing pleased me more than returning to the Kick and Thomas we were the day before—just a man and a woman in desperate need to begin again, and grateful for the chance.

Kick's eyes cut to the television screen in the den and lit up. "Ooh, I love this singer."

I tilted my hand back and laughed. "You've loved all of tonight's performers."

"True." Kick bit her lip, then chuckled too. Her pert nose scrunching, urging me to lick it, so I did.

The slightly grumpy normal me would have cringed at each of the pop bands. This new, crazy-gone-for-the-goddess-next-to-me guy that I'd become loved them for the way they lit her up.

I turned up the volume and stood, holding out my hand. "Dance with me."

"Naked?"

This woman. As if we hadn't been running around like Adam and Eve since we returned to the house. "What better way is there?" I moved my hands up and down in her direction. "Why cover up your magnificence?" I spread my arms and shook my hips to some Latin beat. "Let me see it move, baby."

"You're so goofy."

My soul found new freedom as I watched Kick's luscious, swaying body. In a few beats, our hands explored each other, feeling the notes on our skin. Everything disappeared in the moment—the walls I'd built, the loneliness, the push to succeed in my research, worry for Toni, and the underlying hum of fear continuously running through me regarding Kick's safety. She lit the way out of it.

At the commercial break, I dashed to the kitchen for water while she headed for the bathroom. I returned to the den and collapsed into the sectional after slaking my thirst.

Kick appeared in the archway, leaning against the wood trim and staring at me, her eyes hooded with desire.

"What's going on in your head?"

The curve of her hip outlined by the glow from the bathroom light was a sight my cock enjoyed. A lot. My breathing deepened as lust filled my chest and reawakened my cock. I caught the moment Kick noticed. A sly grin spread across her face. My goddess became a predator. *This naked weekend thing was a genius idea.*

Kick dropped to her hands and knees and eased toward me, like a slinky feline. My chin lowered as I watched her cross the room.

"What are you doing?" I rasped out. Despite the long drink from a minute ago, my throat turned to cotton as soon as she began her prowl. Her shoulders, breasts, and hips swayed rhythmically, like she was stalking me.

"When we first met," she answered, reaching forward with a hand like it was a forepaw, "I told you I roar and purr. I also snipped at you and said I wasn't in the habit of prowling like a cougar." Kick paused halfway to me. Her gaze lifted from my dick to my eyes. My hand instinctively followed her cue. I started stroking myself, squeezing, beckoning her closer. She licked her upper lip. "But you… sprawled on the couch like a king. So strong, so serene, so delicious. Then your cock came to life… for me. This prowling business suddenly makes sense." Kick finished her trek across the room, her swaying breasts the sweetest sight. My dick bobbed as if it were begging for her.

She reached for my ankle, ran her nails up my calf, then caressed my leg with her cheek the way a cat would. Her tongue followed, and I swear I heard a purr.

"Kick," I groaned, drawing out her name. I couldn't finish my thought once she began carefully kissing her way up my leg. The pain of reliving my memories peacefully retreated to a new shelter in my soul. No need to lock them up anymore. With Kick for a balm, I wouldn't fear my past again.

She nuzzled… *nuzzled* my damn cock. Her tongue, traveling across my ridged bands, nearly did me in as she lightly pumped the foreskin over my shaft. Her other hand scooted under me to access my balls, and I bit my lip. A moan escaped so loud that I knew I wouldn't last if I let her continue.

Then she looked up and caught my eyes as she descended. Her lips stretched around me did me in. I needed her mouth on mine, or I would bite my bottom lip until it drew blood. She mewled when I lifted her up.

"I'm coming in you," I declared in a rough voice I barely recognized.

"It's okay. I wanted to——"

"Another time. Let me come in you."

"That works too."

I centered her hips over my cock, eager to make her come apart.

In my excitement, I grunted and lifted up as I settled her on me, so ready for a rough ride like the night before. That's when I caught her slight wince. I quickly settled her back on my thighs. "You're sore."

"Out of practice," she countered.

I wanted to kick my own ass. "Shit. I'm sorry."

She placed two fingers over my mouth. "Shush." She ran her fingers through my hair and laced them at the back of my neck, encouraging me to continue, but I refused. She needed me to take care of her in every way. I was a damn dog.

"You're taking a break." I stood and paced the room, unsure of what to do next. I considered drawing a bath for her, but my tub was small. On my second trip around the den, I saw a huge grin on her face.

"I could watch you walk all night. You're turning me into a lust-filled harlot."

I took a drink from the glass I'd left on the coffee table. "What're you saying?"

"I could be pissed at you for slowing our roll, but it's supersweet. I'm also a grown woman who can make my own decisions." She waggled her eyebrows. "Pretty hot though."

Kick might have the variances I did, but she also had an autoimmune condition that demanded respect. Thinking of her genetics gave me an idea. Grasping her hands, I had her pivot and lie down on the sofa so I could begin a light massage. As we both relaxed into the rhythmic movements, our auras released, mixed. As if it sought mine, Kick's violet light reached up to meet my blue when my hands moved over her.

I reached the apex of her thighs and gently worked her folds, creating a warming in her sweet pussy. I shifted and placed my free hand on her abdomen while my fingers moved inside her. The light and warmth intensified as I sat in awe of what my instincts led.

"Mmm," she drawled, her eyes half-mast. "This feels amazing."

"Hell yeah," I answered roughly, just as turned on. "I meant to do a little massage. But this—"

"It's like you're filling me everywhere."

"Me as well." I focused my attention on letting our energy mix and run wild. Seeing what it could do.

I moved up her body, working the light—for lack of a better term—over her breasts. When I eased a nipple into my mouth, the warmth flowed through me, down to my balls. We both moaned low and long, drawing out our pleasure at the new sensation.

"I need you, Thomas. Please fill me." She gasped. "Now."

Our energy alone had worked me up enough to almost come on myself. I carefully slipped inside her, and the vitality consumed me. We set a leisurely pace. Each fraction of an inch was a caress like I'd never known, all the way to my toes.

It didn't take long until her moans shifted into the keening I already knew. "So close."

"Same, baby. Let it go."

The light pulsed in time with our movements. The waves created a tiny wind that blew over us, shuffling Kick's curls as she writhed under me. The way the light mixed around us made her appear more like the goddess I adored.

As her orgasm continued, it grew in intensity and set mine loose. Right there, in my den, as the clock plodded toward midnight, we knitted ourselves back together after having nearly come apart. If this was what we had to look forward to, I would never fear my past or my future again.

"Where did you learn to do *THAT*?" Kick asked. She brushed some hairs off my forehead, a smile and an expression of wonder on her face. I felt the same, to be honest. "Or do I not want to know?"

I kissed her nose, not wanting to move any other part of my body. I could've stayed buried in her, surrounded by her, through the night. "From you, I guess. It's all new."

Her brows shot up like she doubted my words, so I elaborated. "Remember this morning... I told you how my aura had disappeared until recently?"

"Oh, right."

"Plus I hid it, like you did." I winked at her and watched Kick's skin flush a deeper shade of pink as she bit her lip.

Her scent filled my nose differently. I inhaled the vanilla and tropical floral fragrance that I associated with my woman. This was more intense. What we'd done had amplified it. "You smell like a holiday cookie. Love it." I nipped her shoulder playfully.

Kick laughed and said, "I was thinking how your scent reminds me of standing in the middle of the woods. I mean, you always do, but this is… more."

"Is it a good thing?"

"The best."

I peppered small kisses along her jaw, then finally shifted us so she could lie on top of me, afraid I'd crush her. "Let's practice using our energy together, now that we have each other."

Kick showed her approval by giving me the sweetest smile. Then she kissed my chest.

I pulled the quilt over us as the people on the television shouted, "Happy new year!" A new beginning, indeed. One of our phones dinged with a text. Kick didn't jump for it, so I let it go too. Whatever it was, it could wait.

4

I Melt with You

Kick

THOMAS PLAYED WITH MY "PINEAPPLE" OF CURLS SCATTERED ACROSS the pillow as I lay in his bed. I turned toward him standing at my side of the bed. He kissed my temple. "Be back soon, baby. Snuggle in as long as you need."

Then it hit me. "Your nickname for me... baby. You... It's literal. *You're* the cradle robber."

Thomas froze with his leg bent over his jeans in the middle of stepping into a leg. He had the nerve to smirk.

"Was it a joke?" I fought the temptation to take offense. I dreaded starting another day with drama, and I wanted to give him the benefit of the doubt. Still, I had to ask.

He pulled up his pants and sat next to me while I pulled up to sitting. "You're never a joke." He fingered the tips of my ears, his eyes doing that sparkle thing I was noticing more. The gesture helped me finally make peace with one of my many flaws. Thanks to him, I might grow to actually like them. "To be clear, a grown-up is a grown-up. If I wanted to spend all my time with people my age,

I'd live at the vineyard. Now, a woman the age of my students? There's a big no." He leaned over and gave me another kiss. "Not you."

"Okay. It makes sense, I guess." I pulled the scrunchie out of my hair and shook it out. "Sorry. I'm so used to being made fun of—especially for things beyond my control. I had to ask so I wouldn't assume."

"No apology necessary."

I reached for Thomas's hand and squeezed it. "Then it's a vineyard? In Bordeaux?"

"Yep."

"I'd love to see it."

He scratched his nose. "I'll speak to Alaric soon. He owns the estate and oversees the American team of the Felidae." Thomas's strong posture slumped a bit. "That was my last reason for waiting to tell you about everything. Alaric deserved to know my plans. I owe him the courtesy. Also, I had to be certain he didn't hold any negative thoughts toward you."

Jaysus. The reminder of another potential danger to me didn't sit well. Not like it ever would. "And now?" I struggled to understand why Thomas would stay with them after what he'd discovered, but again… I'd learned how the benefit of the doubt, and patience, went a long way.

"Let's talk with Banger. Make us official. Last I spoke to him, we were broken up. We'll go from there." He tapped my knee. "Oh, you should know I told him about seeing your aura too."

I worried my tongue in my cheek, not sure if Thomas was ready for my next request.

"Don't worry about it upsetting him. It had the opposite effect."

Well, that was weird, but I'd think about it later. I bit my lip and rumpled my nose.

His eyebrow lifted. "Spit it out."

"Well… I hoped we could spend tonight at my place. You know, get you used to it without the kids around. Liam and Macushla won't be back until tomorrow afternoon. It'll give us time to settle things between you and Shane's ghost." I squinted at the startled expression on his face. "Let me rephrase that… You know I've moved on, obviously. I feel there's a need to assure you the house has as well."

Thomas let his head drop. "Damn."

I swiped his hair off his forehead, trying to get him to look at me. We had to get it all out and sorted quickly. "It was hard to miss, but I understand. No judgment from me."

"I'm sorry. Consider it the misplaced emotions of a confused man." He squeezed my hand. "I meant it when I told you it made me happy to know you were loved."

My hand moved to his jaw, and he settled his cheek in my palm. I loved the notion that Thomas needed me as much as I did him. "It makes it easier to recognize this time."

"It does, doesn't it?" Thomas reached across the bed and picked up his phone. "I'll have Banger meet us at your house this afternoon."

"Perfect. Maybe we can watch the Rose Bowl at Finnegan's Wake? It'll make coming back to the empty house all the better when we can celebrate Michigan State's victory."

Thomas pulled his shirt over his head. "Why do I think that means more to you than it does to me?"

I laughed, gesturing around the room. "This is an extremely rare treat, Professor. I hate the idea of bursting our love bubble, but the world—especially my children—won't stay away."

"True. You McKennas are a package deal." Thomas kissed my temple again and grabbed his cowboy boots. "Since you're up, check your texts. Think one of your packages texted last night."

"I saw it when I got up to take my thyroid medicine. Dylan has an issue, but he stressed that they're physically okay and I'm to—and I quote—chill. I'll call him later."

"Good to hear." He stomped into his second boot. "I won't be long. Enjoy your quiet time."

After this glimpse of life with an empty nest, I couldn't wait for the real thing. "Oh I will, believe me. Tell Eddie-the-horse good morning for me, and have a nice ride."

"Won't be as long as yesterday's." Thomas waggled his brows and left.

After washing up, I enjoyed a long meditation session, followed by yoga in his workout room. Thomas's house turned out to be a dream home for me. I loved every room, nook, and cranny. I also noticed the miniatures of him and his late wife had disappeared. While I never would have asked him to remove them, the fact he'd done it meant the world. I figured, like with Shane's photos at my house, they had found a new home in a more neutral place. I just hadn't seen them yet, but I also didn't venture to the third floor. For some reason, it felt off-limits, and I'd ask about it later. My surprise quota still overflowed.

I massaged my muscles after my workout, noting how different they felt. The yoga session had been different too. I went through my standard sequence, but the poses were more comfortable and went farther than normal. My mind still struggled to settle without focusing on my meditation porch, but it felt clear and raring to go once I was done. Was this a sign of the variances Thomas would search for? Who knew?

As I bent forward to stretch my hamstrings, I caught Thomas's reflection in the studio mirror.

"Didn't mean to bother you," he said.

"Please bother me." I jumped to standing. "I've been at this forever. Just when I think all is right with the world, my mind takes off at the speed of light in four directions all over again."

"Don't worry, darlin'. Everything will settle." He wrapped his arms around me and inhaled. "Mmm, you smell like dessert. How can I ever go back to my lab when my body cries out for you after a mere hour apart?"

We ate our breakfast in the nude while watching the Rose Parade. Laziness was becoming a new luxury. Days stuck in bed were a regular part of the autoimmune life, but they were about recovering. This decadence without guilt was a new concept. Not to mention the crazy whirlwind of belonging to someone again. I couldn't help giggling.

Thomas stopped stroking my thigh and raised an eyebrow.

I pressed my lips together to make it stop. "It's like we're elite Romans or something." When had I ever had the freedom simply to be with the man I loved? It made any worries about our future dissipate.

5

It's the End of the World as We Know It (and I Feel Fine)

Kick

WE DROVE SEPARATELY TO MY HOUSE BECAUSE WE EACH HAD WORK the following day. Tension grew during the drive, winding me up tight as a drum by the time I pulled into my garage. My mind kept running scenarios about how Banger would react to my knowing everything Thomas had told me. The man and I had started off terribly back in September. I worried we'd lose the progress we'd made. Since he was Thomas's best friend, I hated the idea of Banger's disapproval.

I missed the extra car in the driveway, not to mention Liam's on the street. It was such a common scenario, the wrongness of it this day slipped by my happy heart. I exited my Camaro and met Thomas in the driveway, my arms filled with grocery bags for dinner. It would take a few trips to bring in everything.

Having missed clue number one when I parked, clue number two danced in circles in front of me. Then she licked my leggings-covered ankle. Macushla met us at the door, her fierce tail-wagging and spinning a canine command for "Rub my butt." Since this was our usual greeting whenever I returned home, it still took a minute to catch on.

"Hi, Kooshie. Did you miss me?" I set my bags down and squatted to her level as she leaned into my knee for a head rub, taking stock of my travels as she thoroughly sniffed me. When my fingers stayed on her ears, she froze, her soulful brown eyes rolling back as she went into "eargasm" mode, complete with drool from the side of her mouth.

A mental light bulb finally clicked on. "Hang on, what're you doing here?"

I glanced past the mudroom into the kitchen. Dishes were piled high in the sink. If I took a guess, I'd say all my dishes were dirty. Paper plates were stacked on the island because the garbage overflowed too. Used pots filled the stovetop.

My eyes widened as I scanned the rest of the first floor. It looked like Monday morning at a frat house. Chips were scattered across the dining room table and the floor—a generous helping of both the poker and tortilla variety. The anger that comes from total disappointment woke in my belly and rose until the accompanying temper practically shot out my ears.

My first thought turned to harassment at my café. Maybe someone had tossed my sanctuary. But that didn't fit this visual. "What the ever-living hell happened here?"

Macushla dipped her head and sent me a mental message. She moved toward the island with her tail wagging low like she was trying to explain.

"Oh, hey fam." Liam sauntered down the steps and had the nerve to sound chipper.

Hey fam? Was he kidding? Still in pajama pants, his curls stuck out in all directions, like they'd been electrified. "What happened here, Lee? My delightful home looks like you lost a game of Jumanji!" Seriously, artwork hung precariously askew on the walls, and a plant lay overturned in a corner. Then I saw a massive stain on the area rug. My heart fluttered like I was running a race. I pressed my chilled fingers to my face to cool it down. To keep from punching something. Not that the house would've been worse if I had.

Liam laughed nervously at my colorful description while Thomas opened cupboards in the kitchen, searching for heaven-knew-what with diligence.

"Sorry about the little mess. We didn't think you'd be back till tomorrow."

"Little mess?" I asked with incredulity. I spun to Thomas and said, "He thinks this is a *little* mess." A goofy grin spread on my face. I'm sure I appeared half-gone. "Son, this is a desecration. You've defiled my piece of the planet." I pointed a finger at the living room and growled. "Mine. Not yours! You will respect our home, not to mention how hard I've worked to keep it over your head."

Liam swiped a hand in my direction. "It'll be fine. We'll take care of it. Besides, Carmen can fix what we don't get to."

Where to begin with that one? Thomas found the garbage bags, pulled out a few, and flicked one open.

"Please don't," I told him. This was not the way I'd envisioned his day going. Guilt mingled with anger now. I wanted Thomas eased into a new arrangement, not thrown into the fire known as my family. "This is Liam's mess, sweetheart, not ours." I pinned my son with my fiercest glare. "He'll clean it up."

Liam shrugged. "It's not like I'm alone here. So—"

"Why aren't you at Dylan's?" I said over him, the puzzle pieces coming together in my mind. "You and Koosh are supposed to be at your brother's for another day."

Dylan's roommate—who went by Dummy despite my pleas to change his mind—trotted down the steps, yawning, his floppy hair still wet from a shower. "Afternoon, Mrs. Mack. I thought I heard your lovely voice."

"Don't even with me, Henry." I held a hand up to him. "With all due respect, why are you two here? Where's Dylan?" My questions ended in a screech.

"We're out of coffee," Liam said, as if that answered anything.

I rolled my hand for him to continue, then pressed my fingernails into my palms. The number of hours it would take to set everything right added up in my head. We didn't have time for this. Sure, Carmen was in charge of keeping the house, but that was regular maintenance. We set a schedule for the deep stuff so she could bring in more help.

Thomas opened the door to Macushla's cupboard, who contributed a vigorous bark to the familial cacophony. He found a treat and gave it to Koosh after making her sit. He did seem to fit right in. Then he disappeared into the garage. I assumed to retrieve the rest of our stuff.

"Since we're out of coffee," Liam continued, "Dylan went to the new Starbucks to get us lattes."

My hand flew to my chest as if I was having a heart attack. "What? This house disaster isn't bad enough. You have to secretly plot against my business too? Why?"

My son frowned at me like a disappointed father, like *I* was the source of our current drama and not my offspring. "The Perked Cup is closed today, remember?"

I stomped my foot to get his attention. Okay, maybe I was a tad dramatic. He was on my last nerve, and something needed to get through to the boy. At that moment, I longed for the empty nest everyone had been warning me about. *Syndrome* my ass. I'd call it peace. "You have keys to the coffeehouse." Then I remembered the critical issue and shook my hands in frustration. "Nevermind. My question was why aren't you at Dylan's?"

Henry—aka Dummy—spoke up. "There's a… situation with our condo, so we couldn't stay there."

The partly shy, partly discouraged look on his normally sunny face caught my attention. "What situation?"

Liam jumped in. "Let's say Suzy didn't move out well."

"Go on." *Shit.* I should've frog-marched her by her silky hair right out of Dylan's life.

"Well… she vandalized it before leaving." Henry opened the fridge and removed an empty jug of juice. It was a good thing I'd brought groceries, though there wasn't nearly enough for five.

I sighed and placed my hands on my lower back to massage the tension. "How badly?"

Henry leaned against the counter. "Didn't you get Dylan's text?"

Thomas passed by with our suitcases, heading toward my bedroom. He gave me a small, sympathetic smile but kept on moving. Smart man. *Stay away, Professor. Stay far away.* They were my spawn after all.

"The message said he wanted to talk to me. There was nothing about an emergency, let alone vandalism."

"We hated to disturb you," Liam explained. "Didn't want to worry you either."

My son walked by me to push some of the paper plates off the counter and into a garbage bag. He reeked of alcohol. "Were you drinking? You're underage."

Liam sent me another frustrated glare. *That's my role here, pal.* "I had two and they were an hour apart. *You* let me do that on holidays."

"Two what? Gallons of beer? Vats? You smell like you swam in it."

"You're not far off. A lot landed on me when Dylan flipped over the table." He giggled, like he was contemplating a pleasant memory. "It was big."

I leaned into the counter, dropping my face into my hands. I didn't want to think about which table he meant. Hell, it was probably the source of the rug stain.

"I haven't showered yet." Liam brought his shirt to his nose and flinched. *No shit.* "Being the excellent host you taught me to be, I let Dum have the bathroom first."

"Lee—" I planned to tell him there were two other showers in the house, but Henry brought us back to the topic of the condo. "Speaking of bathrooms… the bulk of our condo damage is in Dylan's suite, although my toilet was stuffed with something that made it overflow into the hallway and down the stairs. Dyl and I turned off the water main because his fixtures were smashed. He called your friend Charley, who sent over a guy. The repairs start tomorrow. So we came here."

I jammed my fingers into my hair, messing up my ponytail as I slowly spun around. "I still can't believe the three of you did this."

"There were other guys here for poker." Henry pressed his lips together a minute then added, "We're sorry."

What could I do? They didn't want to ruin my time with Thomas. Plus calling Charley would've been my advice. "No, no. You boys did good with the condo."

"Louie—that's Charley's guy—said everything's stable. It shouldn't take much to fix since we caught the damage pretty fast. Can you believe Suzy took all the towels? Half of them were mine." Henry shook his head angrily. "Anyway, we had to go out and buy a bunch to soak up the water."

My anger subsided toward the boys and moved toward Dylan's ex-girlfriend. "I'm sorry you had to deal with her rage."

"Yeah, well"—Henry threw his thumb over his shoulder toward the bedrooms—"Dyl drank a lot of beer. I tried to cheer him up, but... you can see things got out of hand. He's struggling, Mrs. Mack."

When I looked around, my anger stirred again, as did my embarrassment. On the one hand, I couldn't believe my boys would treat our home this way. I also knew all about my son's temper when he was hurting. He came by it honestly. I pointed, moving my hand around the entire living space. "You will clean this up. All three of you. It's not my job." I shot a glare at Liam. "And this is *not* what Carmen's hired to do."

"She's our maid. Cleaning our house is her *job*."

"Son..." I swallowed my first thought, then held up a finger. "This kind of mess has always been outside of Carmen's contract. Also, you will not disrespect her again. She's a loyal family friend *first* and an employee second. And third, she doesn't get home from San Juan until tomorrow afternoon. I'm not dropping this on her out of nowhere. There's no way I'm living in this crime scene for another hour, let alone for days."

"Fine, fine," Liam grumbled.

I snapped my fingers in his face. "I'm serious, Liam. Remember this: the blue you were born with lives long in your collar, not in your blood. We will *not* be those kinds of people no matter how you're raised."

He lifted his hands in surrender. "Sorry. I'll get cleaning."

I reached into my purse and pulled out the keys to the Perked Cup. "Go to the coffeehouse first and pick up five pounds of the Breakfast Blend for you fellas and a pound of decaf for me." I swatted his shoulder. "I still can't believe you traitorous boys planned to bring the competition into my home."

"It'd take too long," he whined. "Plus we need *food* food."

"Oi!" I rolled my eyes to the ceiling. I thought I'd taught these boys to think. "That's what the walk-in cooler is for. In fact, bring back lunch and snacks for everyone. Banger will be here in an hour, and you've torn through all my food." After another motherly eye roll, I huffed. What did I expect? Just because I suddenly was involved with a spectacularly secret and exceptional group of people —and I might be one of them—that I would stop being a mother? Leave it to my kids to throw a heavy dose of real world my way. I padded into my bedroom for some peace. Who knew what would happen when Banger arrived?

6

Love Struck Baby

Thomas

THE DOORBELL RANG WHILE KICK AND I WERE HOLED UP IN HER office. I studied staff notes from my time off while she finished the scheduling and fussing about still needing another employee. We didn't really need to work. I was sequestering us away from the 'cleaning crew', knowing she'd jump in the minute she stepped out of her office.

"Saved by the bell." I sighed, closed my laptop, and greeted Banger in the entry. "Hey man, we're in here." I smiled when his eyes landed on Kick. They softened ever so slightly—a clear sign of acceptance where my best friend was concerned. It had taken a while for them to warm to each other, but she had his heart now, especially after our talks about her in Bordeaux. It helped to know he had my back with the Felidae. I needed it sooner than planned.

"Look at you two," he practically purred.

"Happy New Year, Banger." Kick gave him a hesitant hug.

I moved to the desk chair, pulled my lady into my lap, then indicated a wingback chair with my hand. "Have a seat."

He plopped down and stretched out his legs. A mischievous grin spread across his face. "So we're lovebirds again? Not so broody today, brother." He crossed his legs at the ankle and folded his arms behind his head, letting the grin grow smug.

"*We* are," I answered. "Not so much you."

Banger chuckled from deep in his belly. It was something he only did around close friends and family, telling me everything I needed to know about his regard for Kick.

She laid her head against mine. "Long time no see. Where'd you disappear to?"

Banger twitched his nose. "You remember my assignment. It's why your daughter watched my fish for me."

"You're a spy, aren't you? Fess up."

He answered her with a lift of his eyebrow.

Kick responded by placing her finger along the side of her nose and winking.

I burst out laughing while Banger shook his head.

"This isn't *The Sting*, darlin'."

"I know." She grinned. "Banger's bona fide. I'm simply letting him know I know without *saying* I know. You know?"

Banger chuckled. "Speaking of my detecting skills…"

I held Kick tighter. I wasn't ready for her to learn about what had gone down in Bordeaux with Taylor Johnson, the guy who had tried to kidnap Kick from Ducky's nightclub in November.

"I have updates. We also need to talk about your protection," Banger continued.

"That's not cryptic at all," she murmured in her native sarcasm. Kick looked at me, and I gave her a reassuring wink. I considered Jonn Graham, his father, and anyone else in the community the least of our worries.

"Before you delve in"—I swallowed and pointed at the door—"there's something more pressing we need to tell you. Can you close that? Lock it too."

Banger slowly rose and did as requested. "What's more urgent than the goings on in your woman's life?"

I turned Kick's jaw, lining up her mouth to mine, then gave her a slow, deep kiss. I used my other hand to rub circles over her hip.

"Um, thanks for the show? But—"

"Will you stop and look?" I lifted our entwined hands. A tiny light flowed around our fingers, working its way up our arms. It wasn't the full-blown aura show we'd experienced at my house, but it did the job.

"Ho…ly shit." Banger nearly jumped out of the chair. His gaze raced from our hands to our faces and back again. "You were right."

A stupid grin filled my face, as if I were responsible for what was happening to Kick.

"You think she's—"

"Like us? Yeah."

Kick raised her free hand. "Hang on, fellas. I thought we were taking this one step at a time."

"That's the plan." I couldn't hold in my excitement, though, and gave her a squeeze.

"This is a hell of a stroke of luck. What is your next step?" Banger shifted in the chair and leaned forward, elbows on his knees.

"One, I have a new test subject. I'll run her DNA against our samples and go from there." I kissed Kick's cheek. "She's a miracle in multiple ways."

Kick stood and leaned against the windowsill. "Thomas told me both your parents were Felidae too—I hope you don't mind. It's been a lot to take in, and I've had many questions."

I chuckled at her statement, getting a glare in return.

"I bet." Banger laughed too.

"Anyway… Thomas implied there's some tough history there, but what about your sister? I'm asking because I'm concerned about my kids. Is Tess Felidae too? Did it skip anyone?"

Banger coughed as if he'd choked on a drink.

She whispered to me, "Am I not supposed to know about Tess?" Then she turned to Banger. "I swear this stays between us. I get how dangerous it is to know about you. Except… I'm also a mother." Her eyes were shadowed with worry, like she carried a too-heavy weight.

Banger rubbed his jaw. "I believe you." Then he looked at me. "Appreciate you leaving some surprises for me."

"All Kick knows is what she just said. Your story's yours to tell."

Kick's gaze shifted between me and Banger as she studied what he and I silently communicated.

"Tess isn't like you? Does she know? What about your parents?"

I shrugged at him. *May as well tell her.*

Banger held up his hand. "Tess *is* my *maman*, Kick."

Kick's jaw dropped, then closed. Up and down that way a few times. Fearing she'd hit her limit on life-altering surprises, I reached for her hand and brought her back to my lap. Not that this knowledge did a damn thing to Kick's life, but she'd taken in her share of shocks in two days' time.

"Mama? As in Tess is your mother?"

"We say *maman*," Banger clarified as he slumped back. "But that's exactly what I mean."

"JaysusMaryandJoseph." I gave Kick's leg a squeeze as she quietly added, "Tess doesn't just appear young, she acts it too."

"Tell me about it." A distant expression crossed Banger's face. His mouth ticked up at the corner. "She was a fine *maman* when it counted. When my arsehole sire let her be." Then his eyes cleared, and he continued, "She feels most like herself when she projects a young image, so to speak. I believe her happiest memories are from back then."

Kick took a moment and closed her eyes. "Wow." She shook her head. "I can't imagine wanting to be twenty again, let alone for forever. I get it too."

"Get what?" I asked.

"You do?" Banger asked at the same time.

Kick bit her lip. "I was in my late thirties when I was finally diagnosed. I'd dealt with gaslighting for years while knowing in my heart something was wrong. Anyway, once I had the information, I looked back and could see the signs of the autoimmune disease as a teen. So I understand filling in the pieces after the fact."

Banger's head tilted as he studied Kick like he saw something new.

I kissed her cheek, feeling compelled to offer comfort. Hearing about how much she'd already been through and the injustices she'd had to fight against left me uneasy.

Banger shifted, settling back on the chair with an ankle over his knee. "You're handling this better than I would've predicted."

"No way, pal," Kick scoffed. "I'm not handling *anything*. I blew up at my boys earlier when I should've recognized the signs of my oldest son's struggle. Connecting what you have already experienced to what I know gets me to the next minute. That's as far as I can let my mind go for now."

Her eyes settled on me. Kick gave me her smallest smile, the one that didn't reach her eyes but let me know she planned to hang in there. *Damn.* I wished we could send Banger home and let her rest. Only my friend's bouncing foot told me he had more news.

Banger stared at us while rubbing his thumb over his bottom lip, except his eyes weren't focused. Then he burst into a laugh. "Hell, brother, you might be a genius."

I raised my brows to encourage him to get to the point. Like Kick, I also grew weary, wondering when either of us might hit a wall.

"You might be the ace up our sleeve, Kick. What you just said shows you're able to walk in others' shoes. Maybe you can help solve your own mystery."

"My mystery?" Kick turned to me. "I have a mystery? I'm not keeping secrets."

Banger held up his hand. "All I'm saying is Thomas has me working two problems for him. One is who ordered your attempted kidnapping and why. The other involves the death of his lab assistant."

"Presley? I thought she was hit by a car—an accident."

"Banger suspects it wasn't accidental," I answered, then rolled my neck. Kick stood again and shifted from foot to foot.

Banger filled her in on what he'd told me in Bordeaux about the Ducky's bartender making a call to a number in Oxford. I'd been so caught up in his interrogation of Taylor Johnson that I'd forgotten this detail. It was a mistake I couldn't afford to make anymore. As Banger went on, neither Kick nor I could connect the events.

"Coincidences don't happen in my line of work."

"And you don't trust Nigel," I insisted.

"That too."

"Which reminds me… Any chance you can get Kick's DNA results for me?"

Banger waved his hand, letting me know it wouldn't be a problem.

Kick folded her arms. "You really are a superspy, aren't you?"

Banger cleared his throat. "If the events are connected, we can benefit from Kick's instincts. That means, Kick, you see something or sense something? Let me or Siobhan know. Speaking of, Von told me you won't agree to having a bodyguard. Given all this"—Banger spread his hands apart before pointing them in Kick's direction—"I insist on it. In fact, he's meeting us in—"

Kick vigorously shook her head. "No. Why do I need a body-guard?" She held up our hands. The surrounding light lingered some. "Because of this? I've been experiencing this for weeks, and Thomas is the only person who noticed. I'll keep it under control." She made fists as her emotions made the energy pulse again. "The kids and I were fine over the holiday, and that would've been a perfect time for an unknown bad guy to pounce."

I scratched my neck. "Ah, darlin'—"

"One of my men shadowed your family," Banger interjected.

I braced for the blow. We had to wrap up this meeting. Kick truly was about at her wits' end. She opened her mouth, but Banger spoke first.

"Kick, do you ever check your security footage?"

"Isn't that your job? Or your team's job?"

"That's what I thought."

She turned to me. "I won't live in fear."

I reached for Kick's hand and rubbed my thumb over her knuckles. "I don't want you to either. In fact, that's the point. Hear us out." I pegged Banger with a pointed glare. "Anything else he has to say can wait a day."

Banger closed his eyes and nodded.

"You know how I feel about the damsel in distress business. It's not a good state of existence."

"You also can't reshuffle the cards in the middle of play, baby." I squeezed her hand. "You go with the hand you're dealt."

"A bodyguard in this situation will be an advantage," Banger said. "People will think you're taking charge of your situation because all anyone will know is you hired him."

I hated seeing Kick's shoulders slump as she mulled it over. "Okay, fine. But I still don't see the connection."

"Thomas won't say it, but I will—"

"Banger… it can wait," I protested.

"No, it can't. She needs to know all of it." Banger stood, offering Kick the wingback chair, then leaned against the windowsill. "Has Thomas told you that Bordeaux isn't the only place where there are people like us?" She nodded. "Within the Felidae Society, there are some that don't like the work Thomas is doing. There are even people who want to see an end to certain family lines."

That last was shocking news to me. I looked up at him. "How do you know this shit?"

Banger rubbed his neck. "Tess. Remember when she warned us to watch our backs? She and I agree that Edmund's death wasn't right. She's heard rumors from the staff. Add in everything these past few months—including Kick." He wiggled his fingers. "I've got the tingles. Don't like tingles."

A loud crash came from the other side of the office door, making the dog bark. *Christ.* There were so many new lives on the line now. I leaned onto the desk and held my head. "Banger…"

"I'll let the rest wait since Kick agreed to the bodyguard."

"Thank you."

Kick frowned as she checked the wall clock by the door. "We should get over to Finnegan's Wake. The Rose Bowl kickoff is soon, and tables fill up fast. It also sounds like the fellas could use a break as much as us."

Banger pulled out his phone and sent a text. A minute later he said, "Mateo can meet us at the bar."

"Who's Mateo?"

"Your new bodyguard. He served with Jake in the military and does security work now." As we filed out of the office, Banger patted my shoulder. "He passed my background check with flying colors, brother."

"WE'LL MEET WITH YOUR MOTHER'S NEW BODYGUARD SOON." All three sets of eyebrows raised as Kick's sons and Dummy registered what I'd told them. They were at a high-top in the bar waiting for the Rose Bowl game to start.

"When did it get bad enough for a bodyguard?" Dylan asked.

"When a mob tried to run y'all out of the store," Liam answered for me.

"No, it was the drugging." Dummy added his two cents.

"That was Aunt Cyndi," Liam argued. "But things are escalating." He ran his hand through his hair. "I haven't told fam about the rumors at school. Figured she was upset enough."

"Rumors about Kick?" I asked him.

Liam peeked over his shoulder at his mother and nodded. "Her. The café. Snow too. It's like one dies and another replaces it. It's tragic. Frustrating."

Now I had to find out what else I didn't know. I pulled up the to-do list on my phone and typed in *have Banger investigate rumors at high school.*

Dylan exhaled hard. "I should put off my thesis."

"No," I nearly shouted, then reined in my tone. This kid took on too much when his father died. It was time for him to learn to live for himself. Kick had told me that's where his temper came from, which made sense. "No need for that. I promise." I'd spent the least amount of time with Dylan and made a note to get to know him better. "We'll fill y'all in soon. For now, know that this is a good thing. It shows everyone Kick's taking charge of the situation."

Liam snorted. "I bet. My dude, we know fam. She agreed to this after much kicking and screaming. Pun intended."

I bit my lip to keep from laughing. "Anyway... order whatever y'all want. As soon as we're ready, I'll bring Mateo over for introductions. Sound good?" I tapped the table, and Dylan grabbed my wrist.

"One thing…" I leaned toward him to hear over the crowd, and he said, "Hey man, I'm sorry about you having to come to the house like it was. I didn't… I didn't know Mom had invited you over."

Oh, the things to unpack there, especially given Dylan's frown.

"First off, you apologized to your mother, so I'm good." I caught Dylan's eyes so he could see that I was sincere. "Truly. I'm sorry for what you're going through. I can relate some, and… well, I don't want to tell you how to move past it. The days do get better." I had been angry on Kick's behalf initially and did everything in my power to keep from butting in with them. However, Dylan had carefully cleaned up his mess. He even scrubbed the carpet stain on his hands and knees. Apparently, after drinking twice his weight in beer, he got into a fight with another guest over a poker hand.

"Second, I thought you were good with your mother dating me. You accepted my apology in the café after Kick and I made up. If you need to talk through anything more in private, say the word." I lifted my head and saw that the patio was empty. "We could go outside now if you want."

"No man, it's my bad. I didn't know Mom was ready for… you know… more." Dylan actually blushed. "Anyway, we're good. Except you have to deal with a house full of McKennas."

What a different day it was shaping into compared to what Kick and I had planned. I chuckled, realizing Dylan was right. "Enjoy the game. We'll talk about our arrangements after. Sound good to y'all?"

All three boys—well, young men—shrugged. It hit me how Kick's dating was as new for her children as it was for her, especially her fully grown son. I asked for Dylan's phone and typed in my number. "Call or text me anytime with any concerns. Got it?"

He nodded slowly and cleared his throat. "Thanks."

When I returned to our table, both Banger and Kick were on their phones. "Everything alright?"

Banger put his down. "Following up with Siobhan."

Kick bit her lip as her brows drew together. "It's my brother Bert." She set her phone down. "Bobby's been *Bobby*, of course. This time it means she's coming home later than planned. She made Bert change the ticket."

"That's good. The woman is responsible for more than half your stress."

Kick scoffed at my words. "When I made the work schedule this morning, it was specifically around her arrival plans. You saw me send it off to my employees." Her phone pinged. "Annnd she's picked a time when I'm scheduled to work. Feckity feck. That b—" Kick bit her lip, shaking her head. Hell, her whole body shuddered. "It's not like she saw the schedule or knows I'm putting in extra hours to make up for time off. Bobby simply never looks beyond her own belly button or thinks to seek advice on anything. I'm just supposed to be eager to serve her above anyone else."

Kick texted back as she said, "She can finally get an introduction to ride-sharing then."

"Kick…" I stretched my arm across the back of our booth, scooching closer. "Let me see the ticket information."

"Why?" She texted another thing with several exclamation points. "Jaysus, she went off on Bert's boys and made his youngest cry. He's precocious, but he's not a wicked child. I mean, his parents recently divorced. What does she expect?"

I tapped on her shoulder to pull her attention from the rant. "I can get your mother. Classes at the university don't start until the third week in January."

Kick's gaze swung toward me, her brows making a little crease that told me I was crazy. Banger snorted. He took a drink of his Scotch to keep from laughing, silently letting me know he found it funny how Kick's family troubles rubbed off on me now that I chose what he called *life in the real world*.

I glared at him. *Zip it. We're fine.*

Then he *did* chuckle.

Kick set down her phone. "Sorry, gentlemen."

"I'll pick up your mother," I said, squeezing her shoulder.

"Thank you, but no." She gave me a small, placating smile. "I won't allow her to torture you."

I tilted my head and stared back. "She doesn't scare me." I peeked at her text thread. "Yeah, see? I'm working overnight in the lab the day before this. I can get her on my way home."

She set the phone down and harrumphed. "Are you sure? According to Bert, our mother's in a rare mood. Since she spoils him, that's saying something."

"Send me the flight information." She kissed me solidly on the lips. I waggled my brows. "If it gets me more of this, it'll be worth it."

"Not if she kills you on the ride home. Or you get wise and decide to move away." Kick bit her lip as Banger burst out laughing. He dipped his head to say *Told you.*

I ignored him and wiggled my finger over Kick's phone. "Tell your brother I've got it. Then send me the flight plan."

Her phone pinged right away and Kick snickered. She spoke as she typed. "Trial by fire, I guess." She added some more words, then set the phone down for good and sighed. "I can't even with her."

"I'm not hiding us, darlin'. We might as well figure out where your mother fits in too." At least Kick's kids were delightful. Even Dylan's grumpiness didn't bother me. At his core, I sensed a tender heart and a young man doing his best for his family.

"You're a glutton for punishment."

Banger smashed his lips between his teeth, but I already knew I'd slay any dragon for this family. *Even a beast in her sixties.*

Maybe I'm Amazed

Thomas

After filling up on wings, meeting with Mateo, and introducing him to Kick's sons, we were ready to leave, but I could tell Banger had more to say.

He kept rubbing his jaw and sipping his drink, each swallow smaller than the last.

I rolled my wrist. "Spit it out, man."

He set his glass down. "For the love of anything holy, don't let people see your auras. I can't stop thinking about it. For Christ's sake, I've never been able to do that."

Kick had been half listening as she followed the football game. She did a double take and pulled a cute face. "You mean it's not a normal thing with you people?"

The corner of my mouth lifted in a smirk. "No darlin'. It's a sign of a deep bond." I leaned in and whispered, "I sure as hell didn't know about… last night."

Kick's blush sprinted up her chest to her hairline, her pointy ears turning a deep cherry color. Banger frowned and rolled his eyes.

He pointed at me. "Anyway... I didn't know this one could flame on until I saw him last."

"Remember how I thought it had gone? I didn't tell anyone about it because I didn't think it mattered."

Kick's eyes widened. "Wow." She leaned in. "So... you have different *abilities*?" She made air quotes with her fingers.

Banger nodded. "It's something we've known for a long time. A matter of trial and error to survive."

She tilted her head. "What can you do?"

"A dot-connector, this one." He grinned before swallowing the last of the amber liquid in his glass. "I blend in."

Kick scoffed. "You? No offense, Mr. McHenry, but you stand out. Between the buzzed blond hair, the nearly white eyes with the" —she circled her eyes with her finger—"navy rim. Hell, you're practically a doppelgänger for Rutger Hauer."

"Standing out at home helps me blend in when I'm on the job. No?" Banger lifted an eyebrow.

Kick sat in stunned silence, her mouth saying "wow" without making a sound.

I fought with myself to keep from calling bullshit. Banger spoke the truth to a degree, but he also enjoyed playing up the drama when the mood struck.

He finally broke and grinned. "This is fun. Coming clean to a civilian has its merits." Banger tossed me a little salute. "Gave you a hard time about pursuing this, but your instincts were spot-on. Once again."

"Ooh, what else has Thomas done? I feel like I know everything and nothing all at the same time."

I turned to her. "Aren't you upset about what he said about us?"

Kick waved her hand. "I could tell he didn't want us together."

Banger shrugged and chuckled again. I'd never heard the amused sound come out of him so many times in one day. He tipped his head my way. "There are other research facilities besides our Thomas's, but he has the best approach. You prove it."

"Really? Go on," Kick urged. She crossed her arms over the cleared table and leaned forward, settling in for a good story.

"Well." I rubbed my neck and began. "In general, I play a long game with the research, hoping it leads to helping all people, not just the Felidae. The pressure for results that I'm under now is new and damn well better be temporary."

Banger added, "We believe there are many people who have the variances but die before gene expression."

Kick pointed at me. "Epigenetics."

A wide grin spread across my face. "Precisely. If you didn't have the café, I would hire you in the lab." I gave her a squeeze. "So we have to figure out this piece first. Then—"

Banger cut in. "Then he wants to see if our blood can improve the quality of life for everyone. Or some such."

Kick smiled at me with stars in her eyes. "You are a hero."

I dipped my head. "The thing is, other members are dead set against it. They've lived a traumatic life, which makes them generally hate mankind. They want to keep any new knowledge within the Felidae." I tipped my head toward my friend. "He hasn't said it outright, but I think Banger suspects some would love to be the ultimate dictators." I chose to believe he was wrong. Very wrong. "He's watched too many supervillain movies."

Banger spread his hands as if to say *we'll see*.

"What does Tess think?" Kick asked.

"Right." The question perked up Banger, and he cleared his throat. "Speaking of, she'll be here next month. I blame you, brother."

"What'd I do?"

"You showed her your lab. Tess won't stop with your damn mice. Like I pay attention to them."

"I'll send her an update."

"Appreciate it."

Kick's tongue moved around in her cheek. Knowing she was about to ask about the mice, I shook my head, encouraging her to let it rest for now. We'd gone over enough.

She gave me a shy smile while nodding her agreement. Then she shifted her attention back to Banger. "I, for one, can't wait to see Tess. It would be nice to start again with her. I have so many questions." Both my friend and I shook our heads. Kick elbowed my abs. "I want to know what she's good at, what she enjoys."

"Yoga and collecting." Banger lifted a finger. "I'll have her bring some of her jewelry. It's older than dirt. A few pieces were made for the Medici family."

I didn't think Kick's eyes could go wider. Her mouth parted slightly as she stared across the table.

"Oh, she's a brilliant painter too. You'd like that."

"Yup, probably."

The look on Kick's face reminded me of when she'd been drugged—part numb, part ecstasy, completely checked out. I figured her new weltanschauung had reached its limit.

KICK, LIAM, AND I MADE A COFFEE ASSEMBLY LINE IN THE KITCHEN back at her house. The fellas were wired from the Michigan State win, though not as fired up as Kick. Meeting Mateo had also ticked up everyone's emotions. I wanted a moment to process this new reality together. Everyone but Kick received their espressos, and she shooed us toward the dining table.

"What about you?" I protested.

"I'm making a decaf pour-over," she explained as she dumped the used grounds in the trash. "It'll just take a minute. I can hear you from here."

"Alright." I kissed Kick's cheek and pivoted toward the dining area. Three sets of eyes stared at us like they were watching a zoo display.

Kick pulsed her brows and smiled. "Do I have to give you boys another talk on what people do when they date?"

Dylan and Liam shuddered. "God, no."

"Uh-huh. Thought so," she said as she watched her coffee flow through the cone filter. She added almond milk to her mug, then came and sat next to me. "I figured one birds-and-the-bees talk with your mother is about all the torture a boy can take," she said while blowing over the top of her cup, a cheeky grin on her face. She took a sip, then grabbed my hand, placing it on top of the table for the boys to see. I appreciated the power of a simple display of affection.

"What did y'all think of Mateo?" I asked the group.

"Isn't it up to fam?" Liam asked.

Kick spoke up. "No, Lee. You'll be working with him at the coffeehouse too. I want all of you to have his number"—she dipped her head toward Dummy—"even you, Henry. If you see or hear anything that's relevant to the harassment or the attack on me and Cyndi, you can update Mateo. He'll pass the information on to the team at Angel Security."

"Well, I mean Banger and Jake trust him, so...," Dylan said while shrugging.

"So you won't mind him being around us... a lot?" Kick asked.

"I won't be here with my project ramping up." Dylan ran his hand through his hair. "Guess I like you having some extra muscle. You know if you need it. Unless you need me to postpone my thesis and help out more."

Kick tilted her head as she swallowed her drink. "Why would I want you to do that?" She reached across the table and patted his hand. "I hate that you grew up way too fast. This is your time now. Do what you need to finish your degree and prepare for the investor meetings."

Good to see we were on the same page when it came to Dylan. I rubbed the top of her hand with my thumb. "As many times as you need me to say it, your mom's my priority. In fact, we're putting her self-defense lessons back on the schedule. We took a break for her recovery, but it's needed." I turned to Kick to make sure she saw I meant my words.

Dylan dropped his head into his hands. "Ugh, I need to get out to your range."

"It's there whenever you have time." I took a sip of my espresso. "Send me a text when you're free."

Kick tapped the table. "As for tonight... I think Thomas and I will go back to his house."

Dylan and Dummy shifted in their seats.

"We can get a hotel for the night, Mom."

"Or stay at the condo." Dummy went over to Kick's carafe of decaf coffee and poured a cup.

"Not when the water's shut off," Kick said. "No, boys, this is your home too. But by the way you reacted to a peck on the cheek, I think you need a little time to get used to Thomas spending the night." She leaned toward me, and I placed my arm around her shoulder. She looked up at me and smiled, then set her eyes back on the fellas. "Get used to him fast. I want Thomas here as much as he wants me at his home. Besides, this may be your home, but my name's on the mortgage."

Dylan raised his hand slightly off the table. "But... what are your long-term plans? I mean, is this a real thing between you two?"

Kick and I nodded as we looked at each other. "As real as it gets," she said.

His eyes narrowed on me. "So you're going to live together? Get married?"

I almost choked on the last of my espresso.

Kick answered for us. "We may live together at some point. It's early, lad."

"You mean fast," he said.

"No," she insisted. "When you know what love looks like, it doesn't take long to recognize it when it shows up again. You know?"

She tilted her head back to meet my gaze and smiled. Then she turned back to her sons. "But I don't think marriage is for me anymore."

My back stiffened at her words. So caught up in the Felidae revelation I'd never considered the idea. How did I feel about it? I rubbed my chin, thinking.

"Why the hell not?" Dylan asked.

Yeah, why not? Leave it to the kids to boil everything down to the equal sign in life's equations.

"Dylan," Kick soothed. "It's not like it was when I met your dad. I have money now. Thomas has his own. So no one needs financial protection." She lifted a shoulder. "We're good like this."

"There's more to it, Mom. There's—"

"Enough," Kick said, gentle yet stern. She patted his hand again. "We're good. I have no desire for a fancy ceremony with a gazillion people in a church again. The relationship is important to me. Be happy for me. For us."

"Dyl, ease off, bro," Dummy cut in.

A loud exhale whooshed from Kick's oldest. "Okay." He held up his hands. "I give. I get you're grown. You know what you want."

"Thank you, lad. You'll have the same support from me when you're ready again. Okay?"

"It's not happening from where I stand," he answered with a heavy sigh.

"Give it time and space. You're too good of a man for it not to."

Dylan's face brightened at her words, I think more from his mother acknowledging his adulthood than his goodness. Pride filled my chest for both of them.

"What about you, Wee Man? Do you have anything to add?"

Liam spread his hands without lifting them off the table. "I'm vibin'."

"What about next of kin?" Dylan asked over his brother.

We shifted back toward him. "You kids will still split what's mine. The will's tight," Kick said.

"Sure." Dylan ran his hand through his hair. "But what about an emergency?"

Kick waved her hand. *"Pffft."*

"But the drugging… What if it had gone south? You designated me to make your hospital decisions when I came of age because you don't trust Grandma. If I'm not around, will Thomas get a say?"

Fuck me, the kid had a point. I wouldn't trust Kick's mother with the life of a toad, let alone any of the McKennas.

"It's one thing to recognize we're already in love. It's another to jump into marriage status after a couple of months," Kick said.

I swallowed, blinked. Both of them were right. A sense of urgency loomed over me, an impression that we didn't have time to develop like a normal relationship. Whatever that was. I spoke to Dylan. "Lack of a government paper will *never* mean your mother isn't protected. You do bring up a good point though. I'll have my lawyer research it."

Back at my house, Kick settled her overnight bag on the empty bathroom vanity. I hoped she thought of it as hers. Then she sat on the edge of our bed holding her head in her hands.

I settled beside her and rubbed her back. "It was a big weekend."

She turned to me, a feisty smirk on her face. "Liam big?"

I laughed. "You take out all the huge revelations, research, and bodyguard shit. Boil it down to you and me? It was also wonderful in a 'Liam big' way."

She leaned into me but let her gaze drop back to the floor. The tension rolled off her like her tight muscles were trying to grab it and throw it.

I hugged her tight. "This is why I wanted to ease you into my world." I brushed a curl off her forehead and kissed her temple. "Too much happened all at once."

Kick sighed and shrugged. Her reluctance to share every feeling she carried surprised me. Scared me if I was honest. I couldn't remember her ever being this closed off. It's not like I ever cared about dragging things out of someone. Kick was the mentor in that department.

"You want to go downstairs and watch a movie? I don't have a television in the bedroom like you do."

She shook her head. "It's only there for the days I'm stuck there."

I opened my mouth to repeat the question when she asked one of her own.

"Is your guitar nearby? Could you play for me?"

My lips curved. "My guitar's always nearby. Do you want to go down to the music room, or should I bring it here?" Hell, I'd have driven to the music store and demanded they open if I didn't have something handy.

"In here please." She lifted her face and gave me a small smile. I gladly took it.

When I returned with my favorite Gibson guitar, I sat in the wingback chair next to her. As I settled the strap around my neck, she pointed to the space on the table between us.

"You moved the miniatures."

I closed my eyes and strummed the strings to make sure they were tuned. "They're not right for here anymore." I plucked my tricky string and adjusted the tuning peg. "They're in a better spot."

Kick bit her lip as I moved to the last string. "Because of me? Thomas I don't want to impede your memories. I'm okay with—"

I stopped tuning and turned to her. "Did you move Shane's photos because of me?"

"No," she said. "It was for me. Moving them to a neutral space helped me move on."

"Neutral. Exactly. They're in my third-floor office if you're wondering." I brought her hand to my lips and kissed her fingers. "Is that what's bothering you? I want you to think of this space as yours as much as it's mine. In fact, I'd love it if you brought bathroom supplies and clothes so you don't have to live out of a suitcase when you're here."

Kick closed her eyes and sighed. "Sounds great, sweetheart. I'll work on it this week. Thank you."

"No, thank *you*. Ready for your song?"

With her eyes still closed, Kick nodded as she settled back into the chair. I played the opening bars to the acoustic version of "Maybe I'm Amazed." She swayed her body to the song as if she were hypnotized by the notes. Though her eyelids stayed down, Kick smiled, her breaths lengthening as she relaxed.

I paused after the second verse. "Good choice?"

Kick shifted forward. "This is the version Jem sings. It's one of my favorites. Did you know?"

I lifted an eyebrow, and she guessed it with a sly smile on her face.

"The playlist?"

I nodded and laughed, falling more for her as the tension she'd been projecting transformed into something like excitement.

"I'd forgotten about the thrill of being thoroughly pursued. Thank you, cowboy."

I cleared my throat. Kick was my woman. I'd do anything to put a smile on her face. "Feel like singing along?" My singing voice would have ruined the mood, for sure.

She leaned in. "I'd love to sing with you."

I restarted the song, and Kick sang it with the word *girl* instead of the original *man*. We sounded amazing. My fears about whether I could help her dissipated with each note.

When I finished playing, Kick walked to me, cradled my jaw with both her hands, and kissed me. "Thank you for making old thought patterns fade."

"Old thought patterns? Are you upset about Bobby?" To me, the text exchange with Kick's brother had been a minor bump compared to everything else this weekend. "Put those negative feelings away."

Kick sat across from me on the foot of the bed. "I'm trying to, but it's kind of an addiction." She tapped the side of her head. "They won't move out of here."

"Acknowledging it is progress. Judging the thought keeps it tied to you. Did recognizing it let you step away?"

"I suppose. Singing with you—remembering who you really are to me—helped more."

"Who I really am? What does that mean?"

Kick shrugged. "She'll rub your supposed age—what everyone thinks is our age difference—in my face." Her body shook as she exhaled slowly. "You reminded me that it doesn't matter."

"Damn right it doesn't matter." I leaned the guitar against the chair and pulled Kick up for a hug. Embracing her full body, I said, "No way in hell am I letting your mother or anyone else come between us."

8

I Love You Always Forever

Kick

I WENT INTO THOMAS'S BATHROOM—I COULDN'T THINK OF IT AS mine yet—naked and wondering where my nightshirt had landed. The navy walls made it difficult to find anything without turning on the lights, and I wasn't ready for the brightness.

Fortunately, Thomas had raised the heat for me when he left to visit with his horse, Eddie. I stretched, testing my body to see if anything was sore or different. The notion of having a life like Thomas and his family, let alone Banger and the others—*Jaysus*, how old was Tess? Would it be rude to ask her?

Memories of specialists gaslighting me—telling me I'd been too young to have the symptoms I did—rushed through my mind. *No shit. That's why I made an appointment.* My spirit might have been resilient, but my body never had been. I walked a tightrope where it was concerned. Clearly I couldn't wrap my head around Thomas's belief that I was graced with a special genetic profile.

I bent forward and touched my toes. Did I just imagine better flexibility? I tried it again, and my nose touched my knees. That never happened before. Could it be attributed to more recent exercise or was it another sign of Thomas's suspicions being right?

After he had played his guitar for me, we'd snuggled in bed and talked until we didn't. Afraid of pushing my body more than it could take, he'd gone slow and easy. I didn't know which side of Thomas the lover I liked more. Hell, I had to admit, when it came to sex with the man, I wanted a Thomas smorgasbord.

It wasn't a shower day plus I ran a little late. So I washed from head to toe at the sink, humming "Something Stupid"—the jazz song from our date to the Italian restaurant back in October. It felt like a lifetime ago. I propped my foot on the side of his bathtub as I dragged the washcloth up my leg.

"What are you doing?" Thomas's rough voice made him sound like he had laryngitis, but he'd already told me he didn't get sick. He stood gloriously naked behind me, his stare unwavering as he held his shirt in midair.

"Morning, cowboy. I'm almost done." I glanced over my shoulder. Wow, he was beautiful. Dust particles floated around me from the morning sun's rays, making it difficult to see him clearly. Still, I bit my lip to keep from drooling. We didn't have time for pleasure. "Would you like me to pour you a coffee to go?"

No response came from his mouth, only a swallow and a stare. He stepped into the sunbeams, letting them caress his skin.

"No hurry." He really sounded like he struggled to speak. "Please don't stop."

"Okay… just doing a quick birdbath." I straightened, my head tilting, eyes sweeping him from top to toe and back. Something was off. Could he have been on the verge of crying? "You okay, sweetheart?"

"I…" He finally dropped the shirt and scrubbed his face with both hands. "Everyone I know takes daily showers…"

"Not everyone, obviously." I took a step toward him and touched my hair. It was still in the pineapple style I wore at night. "My hair gets weird from too much washing."

"No. I… Christ, I'd forgotten how"—Thomas made a groan that

convinced me tears were eminent—"sexy it is to watch." As much as his words lit my fire, his body language puzzled me. He tensed, muscles locked as if ready for a fight. His face paled, like he'd seen a ghost, like he couldn't decide between fight or flight. From me.

I took another step and reached for him. Thomas began babbling things I didn't understand, and his accent thickened. Whatever was happening, I instinctively knew he needed me. Not just my support or my opinion. Something told me he required my body. *Now*.

To hell with schedules and responsibilities. Thomas said I was his priority now, well, he'd become mine too. I turned toward Thomas fully, my arms extended, offering myself.

As if fired from a gun, he put me on the counter, entered me, and began kissing my neck in desperation. With each thrust, his lips traveled farther down, settling on my breasts, worshipping and punishing each one. Sudden as it was, I was wet and ready and it didn't take long for me to let go. For him. For us.

Thomas groaned like he was falling apart emotionally. Our auras flared into a flame of brilliant color.

"Ohmygod... ohmygod...," I chanted as he set a brutal pace. What had come over me, and when had I become so wanton? Life had flipped in more ways than one.

On the verge of climax, tears gliding down Thomas's cheeks, my head smacked the mirror frame, causing it to crash behind me onto the counter. We froze from shock, then I laughed. I felt nothing but surprise. Thomas jumped back, pulling me into him, lifting me away from any glass. He felt around my head for any sign of a bump. I winced at a tiny, tender spot. "Dammit. Sorry, Kick. I'm a selfish asshole."

I touched his face. "Stop. If you can be my refuge, I can be yours. I barely noticed."

He clung to me, burying his head in my neck, and squeezed me like his life depended on it. "Been alone so long. It's hard to believe we're real. Forgive my irrational nonsense."

"Shh...," I soothed. "You're not alone anymore. I'm happy to fuck your ghosts away for you. Anytime you need it."

He pulled back, peering into my eyes. "How'd you know?"

"The emotions on your face felt familiar, I guess." I ran my fingers through Thomas's hair, brushing it off his forehead. "Want to talk about it?"

We clung to each other after we ended up on the edge of the tub. In the bright light, Thomas blushed. "I've been haunted by a woman for years. She's in my dreams—or she has been. They started as nightmares about the war when my uncle died. Then this angel would show up." He leaned back and stared like he saw me for the first time.

That's what had been familiar about him earlier—he looked like how I'd felt when I saw his miniature.

"Just now I realized…" Thomas's voice caught. "It's been you this whole time."

I pulled him against me as a sorrowful groan escaped him. It only took a moment for me to fall apart with him. Unlike my fear of falling apart in the past, I knew we would knit each other back together. Apparently we had been doing that already. For years, it seemed. I encouraged Thomas to tell me about this angel from his dreams. He let everything out as I held on. The parallels were ridiculously similar to mine—especially the emotions we'd been left with afterward.

When Thomas quieted, I leaned back and played with the hair at his temples. "Have you ever had gray hair here?"

A wrinkle formed between his brows, then he nodded. "I usually do. I feel the most myself that way, but I use meditation to keep it at bay for now. To stay on the younger side for the professorship." Right. He couldn't just show up with credentials and teach, he had to go through the steps to get where he was. That meant appearing a certain age—midthirties at the moment. "Why do you ask?"

"I recognized something in your miniature." I filled him in on the details of my dream man. The gray temples had been the last mystery, and Thomas explained it easily. He'd fought in the War of 1812. When he described his uniform from back then, I knew it had been him all along.

We had haunted and encouraged each other for years without knowing it.

I wiped the tears from my eyes as we settled down from our revelations. "You know, most of my male friends saw their temples turn gray in their thirties. Some even earlier."

He laughed against me, and I sighed in relief. My Thomas was back. He even leaned back and flashed me his cocky smirk. "You like it."

I grabbed his chin as I studied his face despite knowing it by heart already. "You'd wear the hell out of the silver fox look." Then I jabbed him in the abs with my elbow. "You shit."

He chuckled as he stood. "What'd I do now?"

"You tortured me."

The laugh deepened into his diaphragm. "You damn well tortured me too."

THE PERKED CUP'S BELL CHIME TATTLED ON ME AS I FLEW THROUGH the door thirty minutes late. Cyndi stuck her hand out palm up and wiggled her fingers to Deana. Dee clicked her tongue and handed my closest friend some money. A ten, I thought.

I stopped behind Cyndi's stool. "What's going on?"

"I bet Deana here you'd be thirty minutes late this morning."

I looked at Dee. "What'd you bet?"

She folded her arms and tipped her head up to the ceiling. "I said an hour." She pointed at me and raised her brows. "You've been an hour late the past three days."

My face heated. "I'm sorry, Dee. Thomas and I are trying to figure out a schedule."

"Don't apologize. I know exactly what you're figuring." Dee shrugged. "Sounds like you wasted thirty possible minutes of man meat to me."

I lowered my head as the corner of my mouth lifted. "Wasted nothing."

They "oohed" and stared me down as I strutted to my office to settle my bag. Their eyes continued to follow me when I glided behind the counter. Freshly brewed coffee lingered in the air, and I moved some used cups to the washer.

"There's a lull, so spill, Kicky," Cyndi demanded.

I wiped the counter, glancing around at the mostly empty café, thanks to snow in the forecast. The mother and baby story time had been canceled. Of course, the way North Carolina snow-forecasting juju went, it was currently sunny and dry outside. Midmorning sun streamed through the windows, bouncing off the warm wood tabletops. They reminded me of my morning.

"You're bossy for someone who waited days to ask me about my new beau. Where have you been?" I asked Cyndi.

She waved. "Hellooo? Tax season. My early clients are already booking. It's been busy. Besides, I left messages. Why didn't you return any?" Cyndi's "disappointed mama" face rivaled Deana's.

I gave her a salute and shrugged to say *back at you.* Then I played coy with my bestie as I wiped down the bar. "But do *I* come to *your* business and bother you?"

"If I made the best coffee in town and had recently landed the hottest professor? You bet your ass you would." She waved Deana over for support. "Don't be so tight-lipped."

I hadn't planned to, but messing with Cyndi lightened my mood, not that it was bad. There'd just been so much going on. I kept finding myself fighting for every ounce of energy and relying on meditation like it was a double shot of espresso.

I turned to Deana. "Will you give Cyn one of your mama stares and keep her in line like you do the kids?"

"Naw," Dee answered with a snicker. "I've been trying to get you to talk since you came back, but you keep deflecting." She looked at Cyndi. "Kick's only bored me with the basics."

"I don't kiss and tell." I fussed back while pouring myself a decaf coffee. I couldn't wait for my appointment with Dr. Chaddha next week. Hopefully, I would have my beloved Americano in my hands in a few short days. It was another reason I relied heavily on my "Om time." I didn't want anything to ruin the appointment.

"Yes, you do. You just won't make the opportunity."

"You better." Dee pressed in unison with Cyn.

Cyndi plopped her chin onto upturned hands. "Was it still magical? Or is the tin roof rusted already?" She waggled her eyebrows at the B-52's reference.

I blushed. *Fecking hell.* "No rust chica." I tried to keep a straight face, but it wouldn't behave. "You could say the roof sparkles—it's even shiny." They made gasping and squealing sounds as I raised my wrist and showed Cyndi the bracelet Thomas gave me.

Deana jumped in and played Vanna White, glorifying her role in Thomas's purchase of it.

I told them it represented our promise to give each other the next day. We didn't need to define ourselves beyond that.

Cyndi swooned but Deana gave me her best side-eye and shook her head. What did she want? A proposal already? Like Dylan? Was a line forming somewhere? The thought made me squirm. Then it warmed me somewhat. Maybe marriage could be an option eventually. Definitely not now.

According to Thomas, his mentor Alaric and a woman named Ellie had been together in different capacities for centuries, though they'd never married. I could never imagine diluting our relationship into a business partnership. That much was certain.

"Does it feel weird to be with someone else?" Cyndi asked out of the blue. She took a sip of her latte.

I thought about her question while absent-mindedly wiping the counter down. "It did at first. By the time I'd made it to Thomas's house last week, I'd missed him so much. The first time had been amazing, but this... with the commitment part settled..." I shook my head, searching my brain for words to explain and settled on, "It's spectacular." Images flashed through my mind—Thomas kissing me on the kitchen counter, the afternoon in his bedroom, meeting Eddie, the fun parts of our naked weekend. The frenzy over finding out Thomas's age and how I might be like him had overshadowed those fantastic memories. It was nice to have amazing ones balancing out the shock of everything else.

Cyndi's eyes shimmered with tears before her expression changed. Her face filled with mischief as she asked, "Are you sore?"

I barked a laugh, causing my lone customer to start. I flashed him an all's well smile, then leaned down toward her. "You're such a teenage boy. You only care about the sex."

"Stop stalling."

"Fine." I flicked my wrist. "At first, sure. The man can give a *massage* though." I thought about the way our combined energy healed my muscle pains and nearly swooned. "I feel great now."

She reached for my hand and smiled. "I'm thrilled for you, chica. Somewhat jealous too, but it's all good."

"Jealous? Didn't you and Manu go away to an exotic island or something over the holidays?" I gestured toward her. "I'd kill for your tan, not that I'd ever have your warm glow. I just get weird, red patches everywhere."

Cyndi sighed. "He's great, but I don't know."

"One of these days you're going to have to trust a man again." This time I held her hand. "If Manu's a good one—and it sounds like he is—then it's not fair to expect him to do what Joel did."

"Maybe that's the problem," she muttered, looking away.

I tried to catch her gaze but let it go when she persisted in staring the other way. Did she still pine for her ex?

"How is it you struck gold twice, and I haven't hit it once?" Cyndi asked sadly.

Deana caught my eye and winked. I squeezed Cyndi's hand tighter. "You *had* gold with Joel, but the dumbass pawned it. He's never going to find something as precious as you. It's his loss." I gave her a moment to consider that, then continued, "Sounds like you're afraid this time." Did she not see her worth? "Thanks to Shane, I know all about that gold. I also know love and fear can't exist in the same place. Your heart can only live by one or the other."

I glanced up and saw Deana's satisfied smile. "It wasn't easy for me to jump again," I said.

"You can say that three times." Dee chuckled her deep, bubbly, I-told-you-so-you-dummy laugh. "You and I saw it before Kick did." Closing the space between the three of us, she added, "You gave her solid advice, shug. Take some of it for yourself and let the baggage go."

The phone rang and Deana danced over to it, swaying her hips to the beat of Donna Lewis's "I love you always forever."

"You should listen to her," I quietly told Cyn, moved by how much our roles had flipped. In the past, it had always been my bestie gauging whether I was ready to find another love. My answer always was *not yet*. "I bet you'll find a true love when you least expect it, like I did."

"I suppose. Can I have a refill?" Cyndi handed off her cup as I blew her a kiss. She took her life advice in small doses, especially during tax season.

Deana returned with a frown on her face.

"Who was on the phone?" I asked.

"The bank that holds the line of credit."

Shit. My blood went cold. "What'd they say?"

With a straight face, she said, "Nothing. Just one of those bugle things playing taps." Then her face broke into a grin.

"Seriously? You stinker." I shook my head as she belly-laughed at my expense. Like I needed more to deal with, but Dee couldn't ever know the total story. I ended up laughing too. "So who actually called?"

She gestured behind her with her thumb. "Hugh from across the way. He has a letter from the tobacco board about complaints from the citizenry."

Double shit. A wheezing sound like a balloon deflating whizzed between my lips. "Of course he does."

"What's going on with the tobacco board?" Cyndi asked.

A familiar-looking woman entered the coffeehouse, her demeanor shouting "nervous to be here." At the moment, I agreed. I'd forgotten the harassment hadn't been resolved. It had simply stalled out for the holidays, like a temporary cease-fire.

I answered Cyndi while the woman scanned the menu board. "It has to be over the hullabaloo from last month. The paper's coverage of it was so one-sided my lawyer's talking about suing them. The governing body may claim it's for the common good, but it's all really an old boys club. I hate that Hugh's caught up in it though. If my dad were still alive, they'd have no problem securing a cannabis license."

"Nonsense." Cyndi tapped the counter. "That whack-job crowd would've still gone after you and thrown Mr. Mickey into it for good measure." She winked at me. "You have a secret weapon though."

"I do?" I glanced around. *Mateo?* Probably not. "Who? Banger?" The man scared me sometimes. He seemed like the kind of person who had no problems going to the dark side to protect his own.

"Me, silly." She pointed at herself with both index fingers. "Most of the board is local. It's a pain in the ass to drive across the state for the meetings, and these guys are shit with videoconferencing."

I rolled my hand. "So…"

"Over half of them are my clients." Cyndi's face filled with a wide grin as she spread her arms wide. "You triple a man's tax return, word spreads among his buddies. Like you said, it's a club."

"You can put in a good word." My fingers tapped an excited rhythm along my chin. "Oh. You. Are. Brilliant, Ms. Sendaydiego."

She shimmied on her stool. "That's what I keep telling you."

Deana filled the order for the familiar auburn-haired woman. A vision flashed through my memory as she handed off the cup.

I leaned toward the counter when she neared me. "Batman's mama."

The gaunt young woman jolted and dropped her cup. Her shoulders drooped like that had been her last straw.

I raised my hands to keep her from crying. "No worries, sweetheart. I'll fix a new one. What was it?"

Her chin wobbled as she stepped back to the counter. "It's just… your coffee doesn't upset my stomach."

I tilted my head. "I hear you." Deana mopped up the spill while I tossed the used cup in the trash. "You were here on Halloween." Jade green eyes risked a glance my way then turned back down as she nodded.

"I'm so sorry you went through that nightmare." I tentatively touched her hand, and she met my eyes again.

She quietly answered, "I was mad at you. The paper said

horrible things." She ran her hand over her ponytail. "But… I don't know anymore."

I huffed. "Most times, I don't either lately." I remade her drink and handed it over. "I'm Kick, by the way."

She took her latte, in both hands this time. "Faye. Nice to meet you."

I pointed to the new surveillance screens. "If it helps, we updated the security system." I gestured toward Mateo. "I hired security too. Until everything is settled."

Faye nodded and gave me a small smile.

I tucked a curl behind my ear and leaned in. "You know, I've been having dreams about that day."

She blew into the cup. "So has Nox. My son."

"I'm truly sorry, Faye." My shoulders dropped along with my head. "Tell him the police are working on getting justice. I have a private firm on it too. Okay?"

"I will. Thank you."

She smiled, and I gave her one back. "Come by anytime. Please. Nox can get a new snack, on the house, okay?"

"Thanks, Kick."

Faye walked out with a lighter gait, making my day brighter too. Conversation quickly turned back to me. I told the girls about meeting Eddie the horse and Thomas exercising him in the corral as the sun set. They both swooned, sighing in sync as their eyes glazed over.

Deana said, "Thomas reminds me of my favorite musical."

I paused midwipe in my counter-restoration ritual. "Oklahoma?" It was the first one I could think of with a cowboy.

"No." She sighed again. "Thomas is 'practically perfect in every way'."

I puffed a little laugh at Dee's reference to "Mary Poppins."

"Ooh." Cyndi clapped. "Let's call him Marty Poppins from now on."

My eyebrows raised. "At your own risk."

The door chime rang again. It made a crisp sound, more like a warning than its usual warm welcome. *It knew.*

My mother had crossed over the threshold.

9

Tainted Love

Kick

IF IT WERE POSSIBLE FOR SMOKE TO SPEW FROM BOBBY'S EARS, SHE would have been covered in soot. The glare from her narrowed eyes set off warning bells, telling me to throw the shields up. At least Thomas didn't look physically harmed. That wasn't nothing.

Well, screw it. I couldn't help the smile spreading on my face when my gaze met my man's as he entered behind the dragon lady.

Bobby settled onto a stool two down from Cyndi and nodded to her, a phony smile in place. She tossed me a disapproving eye roll.

"Good morning, Mother." I greeted her with a tight kiss to the cheek. "Your flight good? Want some coffee?" I bit my lip. Why did my heart race? *Was my face warm?* Clearly the shield wasn't secured as tightly as I'd hoped.

Thomas gave me a quick squeeze, pressing a warm kiss on my temple. Bobby clucked her tongue disapprovingly. Her gold drop earrings swayed as she snapped her fingers for Deana's attention.

"Morning, Kick." It was clear Thomas had stayed calm and clearheaded on the drive from the airport. I wondered if that was another one of his magical skills.

"Thank you," I said under my breath.

"Anytime."

"You don't want to mean that." I chuckled.

"But I do." He turned to Cyndi and Deana. "Morning, ladies."

"Hey, Dr. Harrison. You're looking fine as always," Cyn drawled.

"Thank you, Cyndi. Please call me Thomas. We're friends after all, right?"

"I don't know." She smirked, her eyes darting between us. I flinched, preparing for however Cyndi planned to embarrass me. "According to Kicky, we should call you Dr. Feelgood."

I rolled my eyes while Thomas and Deana laughed. "That so?" He looked to me for an answer.

I played it off with a shrug. "It is appropriate."

"Good to know." He leaned in for another quick peck. "Mind if I work in your office?" Then he yawned. "Plan to ride Eddie soon and don't want to risk falling asleep at the house."

Deana and Cyndi sighed again as I said, "Help yourself."

Dee handed Thomas his usual, and he headed into the back with purpose and ease. I noticed her watching his retreat as intently as I did. "Hey!"

"What can I say? He's fiiine." She drawled the word out before giving me her warm chuckle.

"Mm-hmm," Cyndi agreed.

"You too?" We all laughed then.

Bobby snapped me out of my cozy spell when she spat out, "It's disgusting." Her face pinched like she smelled a fart. I scanned the dining room. The one customer with the laptop stayed focused on his work. My bodyguard, Mateo, sat in another corner. I supposed I could take her bait. Thomas and my friends had given me a shot of strength.

"Okay, Mother, I'll bite. What's got your underwear in a bundle? According to Bert, you were miserable at his house. I figured you'd be happy to be back."

Something about my words acted like lighter fluid for her heated mood. "Well, I need a coffee for one. Really, Kathleen, how long can you keep running this place with such lousy service?"

When I set Bobby's latte down, Cyndi gulped the last of her refill and stood. "I'd best be getting to the office. Those taxes don't file themselves."

I leaned over and hugged my bestie. Who could blame her? Not me.

"I'm truly happy for you," she whispered in my ear.

"Thanks, chica."

As Cyndi left, my mother jumped back in. "A lady doesn't show affection in public. It's indecent."

"We weren't sucking tongues, Bobby." It pissed her off when I used her given name, and I used the little dig to tell her I wouldn't be controlled. Not anymore.

"Don't be crass." She began a slow cackle, one that sounded like it had been fermenting for days. "You turned out just like me after all. What would Mick say?" She popped her eyebrows for effect.

I sighed and jammed a hand onto my hip. "Never." I was the anti-Bobby to a fault.

"*Pffft.*" She flicked her wrist, bracelets jangling along her arm. "Can't hide from it, girly. I caught a younger man. So did you." She leaned on her elbow like she truly cared about her next words. "I thought you might end up a dried-up old maid like your mother-in-law Anna. Except she's not your mother-in-law anymore, is she? Has that Tom introduced you to his parents yet? Or are you just *temporary?*"

"His—" *What the hell happened in Michigan?*

"I'm back with Juan," Bobby blurted out, a grin reaching her still-high cheekbones. "I ran into him at Royal Oak Market while shopping for Christmas dinner." She sighed like a Disney princess.

I stared back, blank-faced, like a helpless prey watching a pounce play out in slow-mo because of my denial.

"Anyway, as I waited for Gino to wrap my lamb—the same Gino by the way." *Yes, that's how owning a business works, Mother.* I tapped my nails on the countertop, wishing she'd just get this over with. "Juan bumped my shoulder with his." *Annd pounce.*

She placed her hand on said shoulder, a dreamy visage in place. "He said I look more beautiful now than I had when we were—you know." Bobby scrunched her nose to look cute. "Together."

"It's called an *affair*." I hissed.

She spoke over me, a sick light twinkling in her eye. "We had lunch the day after Christmas. Dinner too… Breakfast the next morning." Her head bobbed on her shoulder as if she were dancing to her own song.

"Jaysus—" I ran my hands through my hair.

"Juan asked about you. How you were. We talked about what a beautiful dancer you were."

"Don't." My spine froze, stock-still as I silently willed her to stop talking.

"He asked if you had found someone new," she sang, a malicious grin spreading her lips thin.

My hand slammed on the cold, smooth counter. "I. Said. Don't."

"I told him you had, and a dancer at that." Bobby ignored me, delighting in my discomfort. "I also told him how your husband made you stop. I mean, money can't buy *everything*, can it? But now…" She lifted her eyebrows, as if it were a big secret that Thomas and I liked to dance. Rachel had probably brought it up in passing. Leave it to Bobby to use it against me. She could turn anything into a weapon.

"Stop!" My hands shook. Hell, she'd blasted through my shield with awful reminders of Juan. My embarrassment. My insides thrashed around under my skin, like a helpless animal fighting for its last breath.

Bobby stared out the window behind me as she gloated. My angst fed her, letting her know she'd won this round. So this was why she'd had Thomas bring her here instead of going to the condo. "Juan still has amazing moves. In many ways." She gave a lusty sigh so there was no doubt what she meant. "It was the best trip."

The woman must have been shaking with anticipation the whole ride home. She couldn't wait to brag. No one would have cared as much about her hookup as me because no one else knew the whole truth. Years of putting up with this shit, stuffing it down and packing it tight. It all burst. "Seriously? Then why didn't you stay up there?"

Bobby leaned in, a Cheshire grin in place, like she one-upped me. "Juan had to leave town. He judges ballroom competitions now." She repeated, "He said it was such a shame you quit."

"Enough!" My hand trembled as it flew to my mouth. My customer glanced up from his work and frowned. I gave him an apology and offered a refill for disturbing him.

When I returned to the counter, Bobby jumped back in, her words like blades slicing me open. "You spoiled brat." She seethed through her teeth. "Everyone takes care of their *precious Katie*." She pointed at her chest. "While *I* gave up *everything*. And you… you always get *your* fairy tale. You always ends up smelling like a rose, don't you? But what do I get for my sacrifice? When do I get to be happy? Huh? I wasted my best years on *you*." Bobby's light blue eyes narrowed to dark slits as she quietly added, "You little *bitch*."

It wasn't a tiny word in my book, especially coming from her. In this context, I considered it violent.

Turning on my heel, I pulled a to-go cup from the dispenser, taking care to fill it exactly the way she liked it. Handing it to her, I answered coldly, "I told you long ago to never bring up that man's name. But you couldn't wait to rub my nose in it. Tell you what, you withering ball of bitterness, you think you have a major scoop on Thomas and me? What we have is nothing like you and that deceitful asshole you cheated on my father with. Now take your cup and get the hell out of my coffeehouse."

"Your boy toy gave me a ride here, remember?" Bobby rolled her eyes, certain she had me beat.

I threw my hands in the air. "For fuck's sake. You're a grown-ass woman. Figure it out yourself."

"Don't you swear at me." Bobby's voice climbed into a higher register with her anger. Her eyes darted to each person in the coffee-house, like she was making sure they were paying attention to her.

"You rub my nose all up in your *pussy exploits*, think you can call me anything you want to my face, *then* have a problem with me saying *fuck* to the universe? Get over it," I scoffed, laying on the sarcasm as thick as I could muster.

"You really are a *bitch*."

Thank God Deana jumped in because my arm was cocking back. Mateo scrambled over too. Bobby and I had our fists clenched tight, ready for action. Dee stopped me with a hand on my shoulder, a calming voice in my ear. "How about I take her home?"

"Oh, the help can drive me, but my family won't give me a minute?"

"Not even a second," I snapped back, then held my hand out to Dee to keep her from going for her purse. "Make sure you thank *my friend* for offering. As far as I'm concerned, you can walk home now."

Bobby gasped, her eyes wide with fake hurt as she reached down her leg. "But my knee."

"You don't disrespect the people I care about and expect me to keep catering to your whims. You've been—"

Deana placed her free hand on my jaw and turned my head. Her empathetic eyes defused my fury. "Go to the back. I'll handle this."

"No," I insisted, not wanting anyone else to be dragged into our mess. *Maybe I should just take her.*

"I can't leave the café, but I can sit with her and call a cab. Will that do?" Mateo quietly asked.

Deana nodded, deciding for me since all I could hear was the buzzing of emotions in my head. "I'll call for the ride," she said.

"I won't sit in some immigrant's car," Bobby snapped.

Deana folded her arms. "Would you rather hobble home on that knee?"

"A taxi was good enough when I auditioned for the Rockettes in New York. I guess it'll have to do now," Bobby snipped with an exasperated sigh.

Dee shook her head as she worked her phone, then looked up at Mateo. "The woman's yours. You're earning your money today, son."

Mateo pointed at his table. "Can you tell me about your trip over here, ma'am?"

"I don't need a babysitter—"

"The hell you don't—"

Deana touched my arm, then tipped her head toward the back. Great, we required two referees. What the hell had happened? I walked away in a daze, fighting for breath and filled with shame over taking her bait. Bobby had dug her claws into a scar and ripped it open where the original wound had formed a hardened seam, toughened by years of purposeful forgetting. A tear rolled down my cheek when I entered the back hallway.

The tears were flowing fast as I turned in to my office. I halted at the sight of Thomas behind my desk. I'd forgotten about him working there. My only plan had been to make it to the office before falling apart in peace.

Now I needed to keep it together. If anyone saw me fall apart, she'd know. That couldn't happen. I spun in circles, searching for somewhere to escape. Nothing came to mind even though there were other rooms in the back. Strong, loving arms circled me, spinning me into Thomas's solid chest as I cried.

"Easy," he soothed.

I shook my head. "No. I'm weak and stupid… should've known better."

Thomas's hands moved up my arms in a gentle caress. "You're the strongest woman I know. Come on, tell me. I saw the camera feed. Only your mother can get you this worked up."

I stepped away from the safety of his body. I didn't deserve it. "We have enough on our plates. I won't put this on you too."

"You'll never be a burden." He jammed his hands on his hips and looked up, muttering, "Dammit. Should've taken her straight home." He sat in a club chair and pulled the other close so our knees touched when he had me sit in it. "Is this why you were upset on New Year's night?"

I filled in the details of the fight for Thomas, including how my mother had apparently rekindled her affair with the man who broke my father. Correction, *his wife* did that—I couldn't think of her as my anything at the moment. I also filled Thomas in on the key aspect, mainly, Bobby's pity punch about having to marry my father because she was pregnant and how that ruined her life. Oh, the many times I had heard from her, and all the other Sullivans, how much Bobby wanted to be a Rockette and would have been one if it wasn't for me.

Well, I'd had plenty of dreams change over the years. Hell, by my estimate, I was working on plan G at the moment. That's why I "smelled like a rose," as she liked to put it. Dreams shift. You adjust or you crumble to pieces.

Thomas rubbed his jaw after I finished spewing my word volcano at him. "You told me about the affair before, but I don't understand what has you so far gone today. After everything we've been through in the past week, why is this triggering you?"

I sat back and adjusted my glasses. "You want to know about Juan and *me?*"

"Think so, yeah." Thomas leaned forward and took my hands.

I blew the curls off my face, an attempt at drying my wet cheeks, as I decided on where to begin.

"When I was in high school, interest in Irish dance was waning in our area, so Bobby added ballroom to her school's schedule. Juan taught the Latin classes while Bobby was in charge of the rest. I took to Latin immediately. It came to me easier than what I'd been doing since toddlerhood."

I let my head fall to gather the words and give myself a moment to deal with the embarrassment of what came next. "The summer before my senior year, Juan asked me to be his assistant instructor. He called me his 'special instructor.' I spent the afternoons teaching beginners step and the evenings teaching Salsa. I was in heaven."

"Let me guess… you developed a crush." Thomas fingered a stray curl before placing it behind my ear, his voice full of under-standing.

"Juan was a huge flirt, and I didn't know anything about romance. So I fell hard." I blushed from the shame and residual anger. "Hell, I didn't know what love looked like thanks to living with my parents. I convinced myself there were deep feelings between us." I blew out a long cleansing breath. "My girlfriends helped me plan a full-scale seduction—teen style—including giving him my virginity." I let out a shuddery little laugh.

"That came to a screeching halt when I walked in on them."

"Oh, baby." Thomas pulled my hands to his lips, kissing them, letting me know he was on my side. It gave me the courage and energy to stay with one of my worst memories.

I rubbed my nose and sniffed. I had to be a puffy mess. "What's almost laughable is that at first I thought Bobby was hurt—like there was an emergency hurt. I dropped my stuff by the door and bolted up the stairs, following the shrieks and moans. They were so into the act I could've been an elephant and they wouldn't have noticed." A terse laugh exploded from my lips. "So there they were, on the piano bench in Juan's room." A tear dropped again. Thomas reached up to wipe them, but I shook my head. I craved the cleansing. I tilted my head. "Know what hurt most?"

"Did they play it off, like a misunderstanding?"

I shook my head. "No. I stood in the shadows, stunned and slightly fascinated, if I'm honest. I mean..." I tipped my gaze up to the ceiling and snickered. "Now that I know what I do... Bobby put a porn star to shame that afternoon."

I pulled Thomas's hand to my heart, seeking strength from his touch. "What hurt most was Dad's reaction. It broke him, Thomas. If I'd just kept my mouth shut—"

"Kick... no."

I shook my head. "How did it help Dad to know?" I told Thomas about the fallout. I raised my hand toward the dining room. "Now she gets her wish. In Bobby's world, you and I together justify her actions, past and present."

Thomas shook his head. "How?"

I shrugged. "I'm with a younger man now. It doesn't matter that Juan was closer to my sixteen than he was to Bobby's thirty-six."

Thomas wrapped his hand behind his neck. "For fuck's sake." His eyes glistened in sympathy, which made my tears fall in earnest. Thomas pulled me off the chair and into his lap. The love and safety there let me finish the last bit.

"Dad looked like you just did… his eyes shimmering. Not for me, for him. See, I had no idea how sex worked, so when he pulled it out of me, I told him everything. The vocalization, the carrying on. I certainly didn't know about orgasms. Thinking on it… remembering my father's reaction… I'd bet he hadn't seen that from her in ages, if ever." I tucked my head into Thomas's neck. "Bobby broke me but she shattered Dad, then blamed him for it."

"Christ."

"When will the drama end?" I hiccupped my question.

"It will, baby. Promise." Thomas swiped a hand over his face. "Remember what I said about your mother's gaslighting?"

I growled down to my toes. There's *being* gaslit. There's *knowing* you're gaslit. Then there's *immunity* to it. Like an autoimmune disease of the mind. "I remember."

"Your father was wrong to drop the burden of her happiness on you. It wasn't his responsibility, and it's not yours."

The accuracy of his words surprised me. "Dad told me the same thing last month."

"He…" Thomas's eyes flashed with surprise. "What?"

I clarified. "He came to me in a dream."

He chuckled into his belly. "Of course he did." Thomas's face steeled with seriousness as he inhaled. "Let me fix this."

I rolled my eyes at him, but Thomas raised his hand. "If you don't want to see your mother again, I can make her go away."

This time my brows climbed into my hairline in surprise. I opened my mouth to protest anything close to murder, but Thomas placed his finger across my lips.

"It's nothing nefarious." He nodded his head along with each point he made. "I'll set her up wherever she wants to be. Give her staff to take care of any need. She won't go without, Kick. Except for going without *you*. If your brother wants to visit, that's up to him. Same with the kids, but you won't be responsible for her ever again. I have the means to make it happen. If you want me to."

I jumped up and walked over to the clerestory windows in my office. The glass figurines Thomas had given me when he asked for my forgiveness refracted tiny rainbows of light. Could it be that easy?

"She'll have the best care."

I giggled at the prospect. Hell, I'd mourned the lack of a real mother for as long as I could remember. What would life be like without Bobby in it? Despite her complaints, the woman was healthy. I imagined myself saddled with her for decades more. My giggle grew into a laugh. "You'd do it, wouldn't you?"

"In a heartbeat."

I paced the space behind my chair, starting sentences only to have them stop after a simple squeak. Finally I stretched my back, easing the tension I'd been holding for over an hour. "I asked you to stand by my side as I fight my battles though, not to battle them for me."

Thomas came to me, placing his hands on my shoulders. "Kick darlin'"—he bent his knees to level his gaze with mine—"I'll be whatever you need. Your best friend." He kissed my forehead. "Your mentor. Your student." He kissed my nose. "Your lover." He cocked an eyebrow, making me laugh, releasing more emotional tension. "Baby, you've fought this dragon your whole life." Thomas tilted his head as the corner of his mouth lifted. "Perhaps this challenge requires a champion."

10

Our House

Kick

"Please tell me you're on your way here. The roads are getting worse. We just heard an accident in the shopping center driveway. It's fishtail city out there. So Dee and I are closing up."

"Almost reached the parking deck. Don't worry, darlin'." Thomas's calm voice soothed me through the phone.

The first snow forecast had been a dud, but January decided to leave behind a direct-hitting bomb cyclone. Department of Transportation trucks had brined the roads for days in preparation, then the initial wave of sleet washed most of it away. To make matters worse, the storm had sped up overnight. Schools and businesses that had planned to release early were scrambling to get everyone home even earlier. By noon, we had the gridlock usually found in a hurricane evacuation. The news called it a "Snowmageddon" even though there seemed to be one a year lately.

"Deana's husband's been on the road for an hour, and he's still not here. It could take you all day in the Camaro, not to mention sliding from the rear-wheel drive."

"That's why I switched to my Range Rover after checking on Eddie yesterday."

I froze midwipe on the back counter. "You have an SUV?"

"Yes, baby. Comes in handy on occasion. It's been in the little barn while I fixed the brakes."

"Your brakes are bad?" The question came out more like a panicked screech, and I envisioned Thomas holding the phone away from his head.

"No. They're perfect now." I held my racing heart, like that would force the beats to slow. Apparently, I had PTSD when it came to the men I loved and their vehicles. Thomas's tone lowered into soothing-the-horse mode as he continued. Funny how it worked on me too. "Should I remind you of my vast snow-driving experience? I'll be fine, Kick. Promise."

I blinked several times as I stared out the window, watching the snow pile up. Right. Vast experience and Thomas covered many things. I blew out a steadying breath. "Okay, cowboy, I'll calm down. Just get here as soon as you can. Without rushing, of course."

Thomas chuckled into his phone, further settling my nerves. They wouldn't truly stop until I knew every one of my people were safely secured. It didn't help that I hadn't heard from Dylan or Rachel yet. They were terrible about returning messages—voice mail or text. "More speed, less hurry. Got it."

"Thank you," I whispered back.

As if he could read my mind, Thomas closed our call with, "We'll all be fine."

Our last customer walked out as Liam walked in from school. "You-ready-to-leave?" He asked at his typical 10x speaking speed.

Pointing to the customer climbing into her car while dodging sleet, I said, "She was the last one. Help me transfer as many of the perishables as we can from the cooler to our cars in case the power goes. Then we're free to go." Our neighborhood utilities ran underground, so we never lost electricity at the house. As I was about to insert the key to lock the front and turn off the OPEN sign, Deana ran back inside.

"Of all the times to go diva on me. My car won't start."

"Gave up on Gordon picking you up?"

"Had to." She sighed. "Several lights went out on G's route. The police are directing traffic where they can, but it's a mess."

"I'll drive you," Liam offered.

"That would be sweet, sugar," Deana answered. "Thank you."

I pegged him with my laser-eyed mom stare, silently asking *are you sure about this?* Liam was a novice on snowy roads, but he also had four-wheel drive. "We could swap cars and I could drive Dee in the Jeep."

"Naw, fam. We got it," he said with his top-of-the-world confidence.

I blew a curl out of my eyes. "Okay. Just remember a Jeep has its limitations, ice being a major one."

He flashed me the dimples. "I'll be a good boy with my special cargo." He wrapped an arm around Deana.

"Even after you've dropped her off and are by yourself."

"Yes, fam. Then too," he drawled. I sent some good juju their way as they rolled out of the parking lot, the back filled with food for Dee to take home and a bag of salt to weigh it down. I had no idea if it would keep my boy from a vicious slide, but my dad had always put a few in my trunk when I started driving.

Dylan's BMW greeted me when I pulled into my driveway. His roommate's presence in front of the flat-screen television, even more so. There was one text I didn't have to send again.

"What are you two doing here?" I called out. "Don't you know there's a storm outside? How're you planning to get home?"

"Not too bright there, Ma," Dylan answered, taking the bags from my hands. "You've got us for the storm."

"Why?" I asked, my brow furling as I calculated the state of our groceries. Store shelves emptied days ago.

"We're out of food." He raised a shoulder. "The grocery stores near the warehouse district are bone dry."

"Yeah, emp-tee," Henry-slash-Dummy added. Maybe this was the time to finally speak with him about his name.

"Well shit." I ran my hand over my damp curls from the snow, starting to plan. "Let's get cooking, boys. Our numbers may add up to five, but y'all eat like ten people."

"Aw, Mrs. Mack," Dylan's roommate swooned. "I love it when you talk Southern."

"Is that so?" I laughed, relieving my stress. I smiled at the thought of my adopted hometown rubbing off on me.

"Wait, are you still Mrs. Mack?" he asked.

I paused in my unpacking of supplies. "It's been my name most of my life."

Dylan took the bag of beans from his roommate. "I'll make the espresso, Dumb. Yours is awful."

"You complete me, bro." Henry leaned in and stage-whispered near my ear, "I knew if I picked up the bag of good beans, he'd freak and make some."

"You are a genius, Henry," I said. "A devilish one, but a genius nonetheless."

He rocked his head. "Please, Mrs. Mack, not Henry. Dummy. Or Dumb."

I thought about it and shook mine vigorously back at him. "Sorry. No can do, sweetheart." Maybe the time was now. "What about Harry?"

"That was my name until middle school. Then I became"—he switched to a bad British accent—"'Arry Potta."

"Aside from glasses, you two look nothing alike."

Dummy pouted like he might cry. "Tell that to the masses."

I handed him clamshells of premade sandwich wraps, wondering how long they'd last now. "Load these into the fridge for me."

As we worked, I suggested, "What about Hal? You don't hear that much in the States."

"Hal was my great-grandfather. He went to jail for having two families. It's… a taboo name in the fam you might say."

Jaysus. This was harder than I thought. Too bad he wasn't a William. We currently had a dozen variations on the name in our family. "Well, what's wrong with Henry? It's a wonderful name. Regal, even."

"God no." He sighed, then explained, "Henry is my old man. I have to stand on my own, you know?"

Right. His parents had been awful to him for the years I'd known him. I snapped my fingers. "What about Hank?" I handed over the salads. "It's a good romance hero name," I encouraged. The boy was a hopeless skirt-chaser.

Henry shook his mop of dirty-blond curls and blushed. He reminded me of Liam in that regard, only light hair instead of dark. "Cute, Mrs. Mack." He rubbed his chin, a sweet, slightly sad smirk on his face. "My grandfather went by Hank."

"Then it's perfect." The boy obviously loved his grandfather. "It would be a beautiful tribute to him."

Henry's face grew wistful. He moved to the sink, so I handed him a bag of potatoes and slid the peeler over too. Without a word, he began washing and peeling, the skins piling up in the sink. "It would be a hell of a lot to live up to."

"Were you close?"

"Yeah." A sad smile stretched across his lips. "Gramps understood."

"I'd bet he'd love it." I tilted my head at him. "It fits you. Can I be your beta-tester, perhaps? You can see how it feels."

He nodded shyly.

"Think about it… Hank." I smiled, nudging his shoulder.

"I don't know. He was so… good." He sniffled, his nose twitching. "It's easier to surpass expectations when they're nothing."

I wished I could punch his parents. "You underestimate yourself, sweetheart."

"Who's your sweetheart?" The front door burst open letting in a whistle of wind.

"Thomas!" I strode over and kissed him as he removed his soaking-wet jacket. "Thank God."

He flashed me a brilliant smile, his cheeks and nose rosy. "Took longer than expected, but at least I'm not still stuck on I-540. There are cars in the ditch left and right out there."

I grabbed a freshly dried towel from the laundry room and

handed it to him. "Did you see the car fires on Glenwood from the freeway? We heard about it on the news."

Thomas nodded and shivered. "Mostly the smoke and a ridiculous backup."

I gave him a hug, grateful he missed the danger. "Go change into dry clothes. Dylan's making espresso, and there's enough for you."

"Perfect." He dipped his head toward my ear. "There a reason the boys are here? Something happen to the condo again?"

I tucked my hair back and whispered, "They surprised me when I arrived home. Apparently, they're riding out the storm where the food is."

"And it's alright for me to be here?"

I shrugged. "It better be by now." Thomas had spent several nights at my house already, but he and Lee had already spent the most time together. Being a teenage boy, my son basically ignored me anyway. Not only did Thomas have a second set of essentials at my house and me at his, Liam had taken extra clothes and spent a night in the farmhouse's guest room the previous weekend.

Thomas nodded and padded down the hall toward the bedroom.

I had just set up the slow cooker when the garage door opener went off. Liam had finally made it. I breathed a tremendous sigh of relief. *One more baby bird to check on.* I'd text Rachel again in a minute.

Liam shook out his jacket and called out, "I've been good, I swear. It took forever because of an accident on Roland Dairy Road."

"Jaysus." I gave him a quick hug. "Glad you're safe. Go change. You can help me with lunch as soon as I get the stew going."

He started when he saw our guests. "What are Dylan and Dummy doing here?"

"Seeking appropriate shelter, pretty boy," Dylan answered over his shoulder.

Liam nodded slowly. "Big. Did you get the sleds down?"

"Not yet." Dylan turned back to the espresso machine and made another.

"Hel…lo fa…mi…ly." The singsong soprano of my daughter's voice surprised me. I almost bumped my head on the refrigerator as I pulled out an appropriate number of wrap sandwiches. Rachel carried three massive travel bags too. I was about to scold her for leaving the front door open when her roommate, Isabella, entered with her own weekender case. The girl promptly closed the door. She even noticed the draft dodger on the floor and shuffled it into place with her foot. I made a note to make sure she had extra blankets at bedtime. *What the hell is happening to my space?* I pivoted back to the fridge and grabbed more sandwiches.

The girls didn't appear overly soaked. In fact, their jackets looked dry and toasty.

"How were the roads?"

Bella sighed dramatically and answered, "Took almost two hours. Capital Boulevard is a mess."

"Yeah," Rachel cut in. "It was so icy my back end fished three times."

Bella flicked her wrist. "Don't listen to Rach. She drives like a stuntwoman."

My heart raced and palms sweat as I pictured the girls nearly dying in Rachel's Honda, cold and scared. Did these children have any regard for my car-crash triggers?

"Who's a stuntwoman?" Dylan asked, jogging down the stairs. "Ah, Snow. Thought I heard your screeching."

"Yo, butthead." Rachel glared at her brother. "What the hell are you doing here?"

"Same as you, apparently."

Then it hit me. This was New Year's weekend on steroids. When I twisted around to check on Thomas, I was dumbstruck by his shit-eating grin. We were invaded by overgrown teenagers, for who knew how long, but it didn't appear to faze him. I guess he'd taken my encouragement from earlier and ran with it. Me, on the other hand… a twinge of fatigue made me pause, roll my neck.

After Rachel and Bella went upstairs to settle in, I walked back to Thomas and whispered in his ear, "Is it too late to escape to the farmhouse?"

He pulled me into a hug, rubbing my back. "This is about me, because like you said—"

"It's the crowd," I answered, a bit curt. "I mean, no one called. I texted them several times to see if they were set up for the storm. Why didn't they send one back?"

"I shouldn't be the one to talk to them about it." Thomas took a step back and scratched his head.

"No, no. I didn't mean for you to fix it, just to listen to me vent."

"Ah. Gotcha." He turned me toward our bedroom. "Why don't you escape to the suite and recharge? Now that everyone's safe, take a minute for you. I can monitor supper, and the others can fend for themselves until then."

"If you insist." Easing up onto my tiptoes, I kissed him gently and left him in the kitchen, lifting the slow cooker lid to sniff the stew.

The front door opened, which meant Liam and the dog had returned from a quick walk, only my son's face appeared pinched and strained. He nearly stumbled into the mudroom, wincing as he kicked off wet shoes and socks—Lee's clues for a migraine. My heart sank.

"How bad is it?" I asked. Seemingly unable to remove the rest of his stuff, I unzipped Liam's jacket like I did when he was little and carefully pulled it off.

"Bad and quick."

The storm made the barometric pressure drop fast. Liam had an app to alert him of barometer drops. Then he was supposed to take his medicine and make use of special earplugs. It had been an issue for him for a few years. He let out a shaky breath and closed his eyes.

"Pain level?" I asked.

"Nine going on a hundred," he said, his lids still down. I sifted through his coat pockets for sunglasses and settled them on Lee's face.

Sighing as I gently pushed his curls out of his eyes, I murmured, "Mister learn-the-hard-way." I waved to Thomas for help. "Let's get you to the sofa, Wee Man. I'll grab your medicine and the ice hat."

"Thanks, Mama."

Thomas placed Liam's arm around his shoulder and walked with both their weight.

"My leg's not broken, fam," he said to Thomas. "I'm only a bit woozy."

I gasped at the use of "fam" for Thomas—the goofy endearment he said to all his relations—and smiled slightly. Thomas backed off on the support, still making sure that Liam arrived at the sectional couch safe and sound.

I brought over the migraine medicine, a glass of water, and a cold wrap we called his ice hat. "Do you want me to make the migraine tea?"

Liam's face soured even more. "That stuff's so nasty. The pain goes away out of spite so I don't have to drink anymore."

"Bone broth?"

Liam shook his head. "Mmm." He shuddered from the pain. "Not now. Too nauseated."

I popped up from my squatting position in front of him. "I'll get a bucket, just in case."

"Thanks."

Rachel yelled at Dylan about something nonsensical in the kitchen, and Liam's hands flew over his ears as his whole body jerked.

I ran to the kitchen, grabbed a towel, and snapped at them both. "If you can't be respectful of your brother's pain, get the hell upstairs." My stress over seeing my kid's pain and annoyance at their assumption to just come by converged.

"Sorry," they mumbled.

Rachel added, "But—"

"No." I cut her off. "You don't get to show up unannounced and act like you're both preteens anymore. Liam's got a migraine, and you two will grow the hell up for once."

"Fine," she snipped.

"I'll see if Dum wants to play Smash," Dylan said. He glanced at his brother and turned back. "We'll mute it."

"Oh sure, leave the cooking to the womenfolk—" Rachel turned to me and jumped at my glare.

"Whiny womenfolk aren't needed here. Seriously, Snow. If you can't control your mouth, go upstairs too."

"Why don't you send Liam upstairs where it's quiet? Public areas are supposed to be noisier."

"I want to keep an eye on him." I gritted through my teeth. "Anything else you can criticize regarding the way I run this house?"

"No." She dropped her head and resumed slicing mushrooms.

"Where's Bella? She could help you make quick work of this."

"She's not much of a chef."

"I'll help," Thomas said. He reached out and squeezed my shoulder. "How about you stretch out on the other side of the sectional? Pull up a book on your e-reader."

"Thank you." I kissed him lightly on the cheek. "Can you make rice too, to stretch the stew now that we are seven?"

"Sure, baby."

I walked away with a big pot and placed it on the floor by Liam.

"Baby?" I heard Rachel ask. "That's your thing? Baby?"

"It is," Thomas said with confidence. I turned toward him and saw a corner of his mouth lift as he winked at me.

"Ironic, isn't it?" she prodded.

"You have no idea."

I snickered quietly and lifted Lee's head and pillow so I could rest his head in my lap to massage his temples. Removing the ice hat, I rolled it and placed it under his neck. I lightly rubbed his head until the deep crease between his brows eased.

Macushla—an expert at sensing when we needed her—appeared at the side of the sofa, nudging his hand with her nose. "Thanks, girl," Liam said.

She carefully jumped up on the couch, stretched out her body like a Slinky, and belly-scooted alongside him, ending with her head resting on his stomach. Liam's breathing quickly deepened and slowed as I continued to massage his head and neck. He fell asleep soon after.

For all the years that I dealt with my often debilitating health issues, watching my baby struggle with his pain was worse by far even if he was technically larger than me. I mumbled over his head, "We need to get you back to the doctor. It's time for you to seriously consider a Celiac diagnosis." He didn't hear me though. I allowed my head to rest against the back of the sofa and fell asleep too.

By the time the evening news aired with footage of a thirty-car pileup and two on fire, my attitude about the day had changed. With my family safe around me, I sent out thankful thoughts to the universe.

I padded into my bedroom to change out of my jeans and into sweats. The soft gray joggers were on my right leg, and I bent over with my left leg ready, when I glanced out my window—movement had caught my eye. A man stood on the frozen sidewalk. Despite the maelstrom swirling around him, I could tell he was staring through the open blinds. At me.

I dropped to the floor, my heart pounding against my ribs.

"Thomas..." Fear mixed with anger made my voice choke in my throat.

11

My Babe

Thomas

"KICK... EVERYTHING ALRIGHT IN HERE?" I KNOCKED LIGHTLY ON the bedroom door while entering the darkened bedroom. She'd taken longer than expected to change her work clothes. Usually those things flew off as fast as her fingers could fly—especially the bra—when Kick had declared her day's end.

"Shh..." She waved at me as she leaned around the drapes at one window from a kneeling position. She was filming something with her phone. "Get down. And shut the door."

The door closed with a soft snick. "Are you recording the snow?"

"No. A person," Kick murmured while studying the fuzzy image. "A peeper, really."

I quickly crept over to her position and squatted behind her. "What the fuck?" I said, peering over her shoulder. A young man paced the sidewalk across from her side yard. Every minute or so, he'd stop and glare. I ducked, though I figured couldn't see us in the dark. "The son of a bitch is staring this way."

"I know," Kick answered. "The little shit watched me undress."

An icy chill tap-danced up my spine. "What? Why didn't you say something?"

She cleared her throat. Come to think of it, her voice sounded wrong. Scratched. "I tried, but nothing came out. My vocal cords locked up, probably from shock. Anyway, when my heartbeat settled down, I figured I'd spy back on him." She adjusted the image. "He can't keep at it much longer. If it hadn't been for the storm, a neighbor would've noticed him by now."

The peeper stopped pacing and stared up at the second floor. Kick gasped. "Do you think he can see into Rachel's room?"

"Maybe." It was a good guess, actually, but I didn't want to stir her more. I started hashing out a plan in my head.

Kick adjusted her glasses and squinted. "It can't be Cody wanting her back. He's too lazy to go out in this weather. You think it's whoever's been harassing Snow?"

Anger spiked over these two women I cared about being violated this way. I pulled my phone out of my pocket and brought up the Angel Security app. I told it to play the video feed at the house for the past thirty minutes. The system Banger had installed operated like any voice-assistant service, except it ran on a private network. Kick let me monitor her properties along with mine and vice versa.

"Why didn't I think of that?" she said as she shook her head.

"I've had Angel for years," I said absently as I studied the footage. "It's new to you." I saw the figure—dressed head to toe in black winter gear—move past the front of the house, then disappear as if he were a regular neighbor passing by.

Shit. "Bet he knows how to spot the cameras. He found a hole in the coverage." The question was how?

Kick glanced at me over her shoulder. "I thought he ran away after I caught him, but something told me to wait a bit in case he came back. When he showed up across the street and just stood there, my alarm bells really rang. I mean, if he was a regular peeper, wouldn't he just move on to another house? Or maybe I'm still on edge after Halloween and everything. Anyway, that's why I started filming. I should've texted you though. Sorry, cowboy. My brain kind of shorted."

I kissed her head and stood while texting Banger. Maybe he could see something in the footage.

"You think it's Jonn?" Kick asked as she fussed with her glasses again.

"Isn't he on an ankle monitor?" I tried to get a better view over her. From this distance, with the snow falling, it could have been any young man.

"Right. Plus he was mad about the business. It was the café he tried to hurt."

That's what I had thought until the kidnapping attempt, but again, I didn't want to stress her further. I simply had to get to the bottom of this. I shifted back to stand. "I'll gather Dylan and Dummy and see if we can flank this guy—"

"Hank," Kick said.

I pointed out the window. "Do you recognize him?"

She shook her head. "Not the peeping twerp. We're calling Dummy Hank now. Well, I talked him into beta testing it with me, but you should be on the team too. You know, so he can see how it sounds from a masculine voice."

Not for the first time, I wondered how the hell Kick kept all her thoughts spinning simultaneously without driving herself mad. "Will you focus on yourself and the kids for a damn minute?"

"I can walk and chew gum. Or in this case, film and think about the family. Besides, Hank needs someone to protect his future. He's been so beat up by his family; he won't do it."

I gripped the back of my neck, taking in everything as I crossed the room. "Fine... Hank." With that settled, my mind ran through potential scenarios to handle the guy outside. I called over my shoulder, "Oh, and keep the dog in the house." Couldn't have any barks give us away and spoil my plans. *Plans that might involve fists and threats.* My patience had run out with this shit.

Kick stood and followed me. "No problem. I'll quickly close her dog door before I grab my coat."

"Your coat?" *Oh shit.* I didn't like where this was headed. No way would I let her near this guy. My shoulders moved back as if with their own resoluteness as my arms folded across my chest.

"You need to gather the girls and the dog. Stay in the loft out of sight."

Kick approached and placed her hand over my heart. "Remember our promises to each other at the oak tree?"

"No." Of course I did, but this was different. My promises to keep Kick and her family safe came first.

"Yes, you do." She went up on her tiptoes and kissed the underside of my jaw. It was this weird yet cute thing she'd started doing. Probably had to do with the way my jaw flexed when I stressed about something. Like most things Kick did, I liked it. It settled me.

"I know you can fight this battle for me, but what if we did it together? Back-to-back, like we talked about when you gave me the bracelet."

I closed my eyes and silently counted.

"Have you reached ten yet?" she asked.

I opened an eyelid and saw her brow raised.

"Nine… ten."

"Good." She squeezed each of my shoulders. "You can still wear your shining armor. Just let me wear my own." The corner of her mouth ticked up. "Think of it as the kind the female characters wear in video games."

Then my brow lifted, envisioning Kick as an elvish wet dream.

She didn't give me a chance to respond. "I want to ask my own questions, get answers firsthand. With you at my side, I'll feel safe enough to do it. Please don't turn it into a fight between us."

"Aw hell." I pinched the bridge of my nose and growled. What did she plan to do after this? Walk into a tiger's den and make it purr?

"I'll take that as a yes. It's not like he's going to hurt me with you three there."

I exhaled a weary breath. "Meet me in the garage. I'll send Dylan and Hank-or-whomever out the screen porch. We'll take the side door. But stay behind me and promise you'll do everything I tell you to."

"Got it, cowboy."

"I mean it. You're. My. Shadow."

She made a crisscross over her heart with her pinkie finger. "Promise. Besides, it's not like we're going to hurt him. We need answers. Right?"

I growled again as I held the bedroom door open for her.

The operation started out as planned, but our timing was off. When Kick and I emerged from the hedges at the side of her house, the peeper had disappeared from his spot across the street. We moved into the front yard and saw him several houses down, jumping into the passenger side of a bright red BMW. It fishtailed several times as the driver sped out of the neighborhood. The boys took off after it, but it was futile on foot.

"Damn it all."

Fluffy snowflakes still fell the following morning. I watched them through a crack in the drapes at the window. Kick turned and snuggled into me as I listened for any indications of life outside our sanctuary.

"Good morning, handsome," she said, her eyes still closed as she clung to me. She yawned and rubbed her eyes. "Did you sleep?"

"Not much."

Banger beat the police to the house, thanks to multiple accidents tying up the Oakville PD. We found plenty of tracks in the snow near Kick's bedroom window. A few of them were good enough to tell they came from a high-end men's basketball shoe. Not that it meant much in suburbia. Banger did his Banger thing, though, and sent the information off to his right hand, Siobhan. It was a good thing he had. By the time the police were free enough to send an officer over, the footprints were almost covered in new snow. The whole thing left me with a headache. Nothing like Liam's, but it was a rare occurrence for me. Made me grumpy.

Watching an action movie had helped ease the group tension last night. The boys were as ready to pound flesh as I had been. None of us could figure out what the hell the peeper wanted. What it meant. What he—or they—had planned. One thing was certain —that kid didn't come out in a veritable blizzard for shits and giggles. Was it because everyone had gathered together? Or was that what kept him from doing more?

The questions spinning through my head kept me up most of the night.

Kick stretched and flexed her legs like a cat before draping one over my thigh. "I didn't sleep much either."

I pushed a loose curl behind her ear and rubbed the cartilage at the tip. "I noticed." Her sleep had been fitful at best.

"If it wasn't Jonn Graham out there, do you think it was someone related to the kidnapping attempt?" she asked, picking up where last night's conversation had left off.

That had been the thought playing on a loop in my head, keeping me up. "Doubt they're separate things. We know the guy who tried to take you was a part of the attack on your squawk box. We just don't know who ordered it."

"Well, it couldn't have been Jonn doing *that*. Attacking my business is one thing. Why try to take me? And for what? He worries me more when it comes to Rachel." She fluffed out her hair. "Honestly, I'm afraid he's obsessed with her." Kick shook her head, making the loose morning curls stand out in all directions, like they were waking up along with her. "I can't make the dots connect."

Hell, I couldn't either. I slid my free hand into her tumble of soft brown curls and massaged the back of her head. I loved watching them fluff out, then settle before she went through her morning routine refreshing them. "Most criminals don't make sense, baby." Taylor Johnson had vehemently stuck to his story about not knowing who had hired him. The arrangements had been made through texts via the bartender. I thought he'd been too spooked to speculate but had my suspicions.

"Argh." Kick grumbled despite the massage that should have settled her. My sentiments exactly.

I pulled her closer. "What can I do in the meantime?"

"Just a minute." Kick sighed as she moved the covers back to leave the bed. Then she shivered. "Jaysus it's freezing." She returned to my side and pulled the quilt higher than it had been. "You know, every winter I swear to myself that I'll upgrade the insulation come spring. Then the weather warms, I get busy, and I forget all about it."

I waggled my eyebrows. "How about I warm you from the inside?" A little nookie could take both our minds off the night before.

A slow, sexy smirk spread across Kick's face. "Yes please." As I slid under the covers, kissing my way down her neck to her belly, she added, "Just… no screaming Os, okay?"

"I'll bite my lip." I teased her with a smirk and demonstration for effect.

Kick rewarded me with her sultry, exasperated schoolteacher glare. "I know you love to hear me holler and all, but the boys are early risers. That little hobby of yours is fine when we're alone—"

I inhaled the vanilla scent from her lotion before looking up and teasing her with a pout. "But it's always been just us when you get your freak on."

"All I'm saying is"—Kick's head fell back on the pillow—"there's value in a quiet freak too."

I focused more on the value in seeing that crease between her brows relax. Or watching her hazel eyes sparkle again, but I could abide. I already knew how to make her orgasms detonate. I liked the idea of experimenting with making them creep up and linger.

"However you want it, baby. I'm your man. Get ready for a low and slow moan." *Christ*, I couldn't wait. I ducked my head back under the quilt, moving down her body with open-mouth kisses, touching her skin with the tip of my tongue until finally tasting the fruity sweetness of her magic spot. Low and slow. Hot as hell. My new favorite way to wake up.

After several minutes of postcoital cuddling, Kick darted into the bathroom like a water sprite running from Jack Frost. I typed a note on my phone to consult with the insulation guy who'd done my house, then leaned back against the pillows, ruminating on the odd direction my life had taken. The privilege of making love in a house filled with children—even grown ones—was a cherry on my ice cream dish called contentment and newfound purpose. It was both new and pleasantly familiar at the same time—waking up memories that had long passed.

Dylan meandered down the stairs as I helped Kick with breakfast. He spotted us and scowled, taking me by surprise. I distinctly remembered him saying he was fine with my staying over. He'd also mentioned being relieved I could take charge of last night's incident.

"I get you're the queen of the house and all, Mom, but it was pretty rude to keep me up most of the night with your"—his face scrunched up as if he'd taken a body blow—"noises and shit."

Damn. I was certain we'd kept our recent playtime quiet.

Dylan's eyes narrowed at Kick. "Aren't you a little old to go all night? I mean three in the morning. Come on." He made the same disappointed face his mother was so good at. "I need a triple shot in my latte."

Kick blushed red, then her brow pinched together as confusion replaced embarrassment. "Son, in the immortal words of Shaggy… It wasn't me. Last night's excitement wiped me out. I slept fitfully, but uh… my mind was on other things…" She glanced at me and bit her lip. My eyebrow raised in anticipation of what would stream next from her lovely lips. "Last night."

"Then who the hell was squealing with"—Dylan swallowed hard—"*ecstasy* in the middle of the night? I swear I didn't imagine it since it continued after I woke up." Dylan yawned, his jaw popping, then he took a long pull from his mug, made a face, and emptied the rest of the contents down the sink. "Don't you have real milk?"

Kick folded her arms. "No. We're out. I wasn't expecting to be snowed in with a crowd." She stepped toward the sink and picked up the cup. "Want me to make you a bulletproof one?"

Dylan thought for a moment and nodded. "Sure. Thanks."

"Pay attention so you can do it yourself next time." As she demonstrated the process, I turned the oven on and placed a dozen gluten-free scones on a cookie sheet to warm.

Rachel and Bella bounced down the stairs in matching Pierce

University T-shirts and joggers. Bella stopped at the large window in the living area and squealed. "Look at all that snow! Can we go sledding soon?"

"After breakfast," Rachel grumped. Her hair and face were perfectly coiffed and composed, but her demeanor said she wanted to be back in her bed.

Dylan winced at Bella's high-pitched noise. Both his eyebrows and Kick's rose in unison, equal parts recognition and disbelief. After glancing from her son to me and back, she mouthed a silent *You think?* I shrugged and laughed. My sense of humor was easier to find given my relative distance to the kids. Rachel had been dating a boy when we first met, but it ended with a load of drama. Maybe she decided to try something new.

"Morning all," Liam chimed as he sauntered in. He grabbed a mug from the cabinet and prepped his own pour-over. "What'd I miss?"

Kick, Dylan, and I exchanged glances before laughing.

"What?"

The three of us took turns getting Liam up to speed on the peeping incident.

Liam propped his elbow on the counter and dropped his head in his hand. "Can't believe I was out for all that."

"At least you look well rested," Dylan said.

Liam sighed. "I'm spicy, bro." He pointed to his ears. "Used my earplugs and fam refroze my ice hat. Your snoring couldn't even keep me up."

"I don't snore," Dylan grumbled.

Kick held out Dylan's mug, then pulled it back. "Maybe you should go back upstairs and try to sleep some more. We can always make another one of these later."

"Dum and I plan to snowboard after breakfast."

A flash of a memory raced through my mind. The face of my eldest son when he had been equally exhausted. I hadn't thought of Young Tom in a long time. Those memories were more like a hot coal to my heart—touch them and get burned by grief. This time the sorrow didn't come. I tested it again, allowing myself to remember something else about him. The day Tom married came to mind for a second, not long. I turned toward the window over the sink and let a smile spread across my face, delighted to remember my children with happiness again. It had been so long since I had let myself go back there.

Kick interrupted my thoughts. "The snow's not going anywhere today. An extra hour or two of sleep will probably keep you from hurting yourself out there."

The moment was over, but it stayed with me the rest of the day. I decided to explore more areas of my closed-off heart when I managed some alone time. As it was, I felt lighter and taller all at once. I had planned to work in Kick's office for the day but figured I'd use the bonus holiday and go snowboarding with the boys instead.

"Fine then. I'll go. Thanks, Mom." Dylan bowed his head slightly to both of us and asked, "Can you say something to them?"

Kick patted his shoulder and murmured, "I'll take care of it."

The girls had perched on stools by then while Liam filled a large thermos with coffee and ground more beans.

"Should you be drinking that after yesterday?" I inquired. "Not to lecture but—"

"Naw. We good," he said. "Caffeine's not a trigger."

"It's nice to see the migraines are getting shorter," Kick added, then handed Dylan's abandoned cup of bulletproof coffee to Rachel.

"Ew no." She waved it off. "My body is a temple. I don't drink that swill anymore."

Kick jumped like she'd been slapped. I pitied anyone who insulted her coffee. "They're locally roasted, organic, fair trade beans. Even tested for mold. What more could you want?"

"An herbal blend with chicory," Rachel answered smugly. "No coffee beans at all."

"You're shitting me? That stuff tastes like bark and dirt if you're lucky."

"Not this one. I found an amazing blend online." Rachel added water to the kettle and set it to a low boil. "It gives me energy without any nasty toxicity. Then my body performs the way it should."

"So I've heard," Kick quipped under her breath.

Isabella reached across the counter and drew in the orphaned mug, taking a sip. "Tastes great, Mrs. Mack."

"Thank you, sweets." Kick turned to me and sighed. She shot me a *what do I do now?* look.

Maybe they needed me after all. I leaned down and whispered in her ear, "Talk to them. Ask questions. Do you want me to go to another room? Give you privacy?"

She grabbed my arm. "Would it be wrong for you to stay? I'm so tired of doing these things on my own."

I patted her hand and tipped my head toward her second son.

Fortunately, Kick caught on to my signal. "Hey, Lee… take your coffee into the living room and check on the forecast, will you?"

Liam frowned, his eyes darting around the four of us. When they landed on me, I tipped my head toward the television and mouthed, *please.* "Okaay." He cautiously made his way across the area and settled on the sofa.

"So… girls." Kick squeezed my hand as she swallowed hard. "Is there something you need to tell me? Or us? You know… any big news?"

Rachel said a quick no through a yawn, but Isabella froze with her cup in the air.

"Nothing's different between you two?" Kick leaned forward. "You can tell us."

"Rach…," Isabella started.

Rachel picked up her cup of chicory and blew on it. "What?"

"I think they know."

Rachel scoffed and took a sip while I sent the girls my best supportive look. Hell, I rocked that thing around the entire room. Had I really signed up for this? Yeah, I had. Honestly, this was the aspect of teaching that I liked best too. Not just the passing of information but helping kids with life.

"Well shit." Rachel set her cup down and folded her arms. "How? We were planning to talk to you later."

Kick worried her tongue in her cheek. "So you're… like together?"

Isabella beamed as Rachel sighed. "Yeah, we're trying it out."

Rachel smiled at her roommate, but it didn't make it all the way to her eyes. She patted Isabella's hand as the girl preened.

Kick sent me another questioning look, which had me returning an encouraging nod and smile. Again. My way of telling her, *you're doing fine, keep going.*

She moved between the girls and hugged each one. "Okay then."

And really, that was all there was to say except for the part about Dylan.

"How the hell did you find out?" Isabella asked.

"Told you she figures shit out," Rachel answered. "Mama has superpowers."

"Not quite," Kick said while chuckling. Considering what had happened on New Year's Eve, I sided with Rachel.

Kick put on a stern face and said, "You practically announced it to the house when you kept Dylan up last night with your"—she waved her hands while turning beet red—"noises and such. That's why I told your brother to get more sleep. Snow, that was fecking rude. Especially after what you went through with Cody. You should know better than to come back here and carry on."

Isabella turned a deep shade of pink while Rachel kept a stone face. My instincts told me something wasn't right with Kick's daughter, but this wasn't the time to pull it out of her. Her roommate, or new girlfriend, seemed to be on cloud nine, however.

"Way to embarrass my new girlfriend, Mama," Rachel grumbled.

"You did it yourselves last night." Kick came over to me and squeezed my side. "Believe me, I'm glad you're moving on, but your brother's pretty sensitive right now." She looked up at me and smiled. "New love is amazing. I'll vouch for that. All I'm saying is, it doesn't give you license to throw consideration for others out the door."

Rachel's shoulders dropped at the word *love*. Maybe that was the issue. Were the feelings lopsided? The girls would have to work that out for themselves. For the time being, I let my pride for Kick and happiness that Rachel could at least move on show on my face. I turned around and pulled the scones out of the oven.

"Fine. Sorry, Mama." Rachel kissed Kick on the cheek. "I didn't think you'd freak out, but thank you anyway." She turned to Isabella. "Come on, Bella, let's shower and get ready for sledding."

Isabella gazed longing at the tray, so I wrapped a scone in a paper towel and held it out to her. She smiled, took it, and followed Rachel up the stairs.

Kick called after them. "Alone. Shower alone."

Liam slinked back to the kitchen and picked up a scone for himself. He grinned at me. "Did I hear that right? They..." He waved his finger between the two girls and waggled his eyebrows as they padded up the steps.

Kick blew on her own pastry. "You were supposed to be minding your own business, Mr. Big Ears."

I answered him with a quick nod. The boy whistled, his eyes as wide as an owl's.

"So Snow White wasn't waiting for Prince Charming after all." A quiet chuckle emitted from him, the kind that I already knew meant Liam thought more of his joke than the rest of us would. "Turns out she wanted *Cinder* Bella."

Kick shoved his arm. "Don't tease."

He took a bite and swallowed slowly. "All night?"

"They woke your brother up at three. Beyond that?" She lifted a shoulder.

Liam's whole body shuddered. "Glad I had my earplugs in." His face morphed again with realization. "That's the reason for all the grumpy faces when I came down."

Kick touched the tip of her nose as if they were playing charades.

12

Under Pressure

Kick

THE SNOW STOPPED FALLING AFTER BREAKFAST TO BE REPLACED WITH the bright blue, cloudless sky that followed every major storm in North Carolina. It was the kind of sky that put a smile on my face. After the drama of the past twenty-four hours, we were ready to play.

We found enough snow toys in the garage for each person to take something to the neighborhood hill. One side of it was perfect for sledding. The other, a tad steeper, attracted kids with snowboards. Everyone took turns doing both except for me. I stuck with sledding since I never could get the hang of a snowboard and didn't want to risk an injury. Technically, I was still recovering from my flare and the drugging in November.

It lifted my spirit further to play with the kids. They were still young enough to consider themselves invincible and attempt stupid stunts. I marveled at how easily they shook off their crashes and walked back up the hill to do it again. One incident in particular, Hank—the name fit him perfectly—and Rachel collided midhill and rolled the rest of the way down. They ended up in a heap, laughing so hard it took several minutes for them to stand again.

In the midst of all of it was Thomas. His eyes lit as bright as the sky each time he met me at the bottom of the hill. He would pick me up, dust me off, and then throw snowballs at each of us as we trekked back up. He became the same, easy Thomas I saw when he was with his horse or when making love. That, added to his willingness to let me join the reconnaissance party last night, made me love him more. Even when a snowball splatted on my back.

In time, the crew became too soggy and too hungry for another round. We headed back home to enjoy the rest of our bonus holiday inside. Macushla and I led the pack back to my house as I mentally inventoried the groceries. A chorus of masculine whooping behind me stopped my trek. I turned around and saw all four fellas lined up on the snowboards in the middle of our frozen street. They stood in the crossroad, which plateaued the hill my neighborhood had been built upon. The last section, which went past my house, made the steepest part of the incline. It prevented any flooding during hurricanes but made the road downright deadly after an ice storm. Especially when adventurous SUV owners ended up carving tracks into the road ice. Liam had learned that the hard way a few years ago when his sled caught in a rut that dumped him into the storm drain at the bottom of the street.

"Countdown from three," Liam called out.

"Guys, hold up. Stop!" I yelled. When they ignored me, I added, "Come on, you know better!"

Thomas, of all people, egged the boys on. "Hear that? She said go…"

It happened all at once. A second of hesitation from either party and no one would have been wiser.

I waved my hands in a futile attempt to make the man-children kill their bad idea before it killed them. At the same time, Macushla spotted a rabbit with a death wish of its own. She bolted and the leash loop slid off my splayed thumb. Once the chase began, no one involved heard or saw anything other than their prize. The adrenaline-junkie hare shot across the street halfway down the block.

"Ma-cush-la!" I bellowed to no effect.

Dylan caught a superslick rut and pulled in front of the group, his competitive focus homed on the finish line. Koosh had the same focus on the rabbit as she darted in front of all the racers except for Dylan. She took him out at the knees with the same tackling skill she displayed when I went down at her expense last fall. Both of them rolled and hollered. After a few flips, Koosh found her legs on the neighbor's lawn and limped home.

My mountain of a son fell on his back like a mythical giant crashing to the ground. Still in the frozen rut, Dylan flew down the road thanks to his slick snow gear. We all winced when he crashed into the same storm drain Liam had hit those few years prior.

"How's your back, Lad?"

Dylan stood in the living room, rubbing his sacrum, looking too skittish to navigate the long drop to a sofa cushion. "It'll be fine," he gritted out through his teeth.

Thomas helped situate him, and I settled ice packs on my son's back and shoulder. "You take the painkillers I gave you?"

He nodded, his eyes glazing over, and he turned his gaze down toward the floor. I recognized it as him retreating inside to deal, breathe through the pain.

"Ice now. Soak in my tub after lunch," I ordered.

"I remember the drill from football days. Thanks, Mom."

I ruffled his recently cut hair, turned on cable news, and handed him the remote, adding, "I bestow the power upon thee."

I walked to the kitchen window to check on the rest of the crew, who were shoveling the drive and sidewalk. I turned to Thomas. "With seven in the house, we did well with one casualty." Macushla had stopped limping as soon as she saw her brother walking so gingerly. Her Nurse Nightingale instincts kicked in. She currently lay on the sofa near Dylan's hand.

Then I swatted his shoulder. "What was the big deal egging them on?"

"What can I say?" Thomas ducked his chin. "The promise of victory and male posturing lured me in."

"I told you guys to keep the boards off the road for a reason."

Thomas shrugged and gave me his middle school half smile.

When I glared back, he kissed my forehead and sheepishly said, "Sorry about breaking your boy. *And* for not noticing the dog on the loose."

What could I say to that? Dylan was grown now after all. I sighed hard, admitting the obvious. "Nobody talks the lad into doing anything he doesn't want to do." I went up on my toes and added, "I'll gladly forgive you for a massage later."

"I'd love a massage. Thanks, baby." Thomas winked as I slapped his ass.

We heard a scraping noise in the garage, and I checked the front again. "The crew's finished. Can you oversee the requisite cocoa-making while I figure out lunch?"

"My pleasure."

Hank came in, removed his gear, and checked on Dylan. Isabella was second, beelining for the kitchen and helping Thomas set up the mugs while he heated the cocoa. Rachel and Liam finally entered together. He bolted for the stairs, and she joined us in the kitchen, a mischievous grin on her face.

I watched Liam with interest, then turned a narrow glare on my daughter. "What did you do?"

Rachel kept her grin. "I don't know what you're talking about."

"Sure you don't. Come cut these quesadillas."

She scrunched her face and shuddered at my food. Again. I pulled in a deep inhale. Again. Whatever was going on in my daughter's head, I didn't like it.

Rachel pulled items from the fridge, the freezer, and even stepped into the pantry. Eventually she had a decent pile of ingredients on the counter, along with the food processor.

I surveyed the haul. "You're making a hash? Chopped almonds will go nicely with that." I didn't like deferring my plans to hers, but my daughter gave off an air that I wasn't of a mind to mess with. My spine prickled with the telltale sign of my temper beginning to climb. I struggled for deep, even breaths, had to purposely tell myself to take them. *When this was over, the older two and I needed to talk.*

"No, thanks," she answered.

I checked on the progress with the hot chocolate and turned back to Rachel. "Do you want ice in your cocoa?"

"Nope. None for me."

Oh, hell no. I leaned into her space and planted my hand on the counter. "No coffee, no grains, no nuts… Rachel, are you doing the AIP?" The autoimmune protocol was a diet most newly diagnosed patients went through to check for food issues. Some stayed on it longer than others. While it was a lifesaver for most patients, *autoimmune* was the operative word in the plan. Like going gluten-free, it wasn't meant to be a fad diet.

With a set jaw and practically gunning for a fight, she answered. "As a matter-of-fact, I am."

I scanned her from head to toe, wondering what I'd missed. Had falling in love narrowed my vision so much? "What's wrong? What are your symptoms? Do you want to see someone at the clinic?"

"Nothing's wrong." She shrugged me off and turned back to the food processor. "I told you, my body is a temple."

"That's not what AIP's for, Snow. Food restriction isn't something you do for the hell of it."

"What are you getting your underwear twisted for, Mother? I thought you, of all people, would support me."

"Fresh, quality food? Absolutely. But this is the kind of behavior that gives elimination protocols a bad rap. People who turned gluten-free eating into a fad, or worse, a nutrient-vacant cash cow, have also turned it into a punch line."

"This isn't a whim," Rachel bit out through gritted teeth, her eyes narrowed, reminding me too much of the Sullivan side of my family.

"If it's not needed, it's a whim," I retorted. "Unless you have autoimmune issues, you're not worshipping your system, you're depriving it."

"Annd once again… I'm not supported." She had some kind of

silent conversation with Isabella. Then she blurted, "I do have symptoms."

"Oh." I looked at Thomas, who was watching me with silent support as I inhaled and exhaled slowly, counting to ten. Heaven help me calm my last nerve. "That's what I asked. What are they, sweetheart?"

She murmured, "I'm fat."

"Where? In your big toe?"

"Mother!"

Our volume had ratcheted up with each exchange to the point where Dylan lifted onto an elbow and bellowed, "Hey!"

Was this fear for my daughter's health, my default jump to defensiveness in matters of all things autoimmunity, or leftover tension from last night? I didn't know. But I didn't like it one bit. My head spun with it all.

Thomas stepped between us, picked up the platter of finished quesadillas with one hand and backed me out of the kitchen with the other. "Your lunch looks delicious, Rachel. If you have any leftovers, I'd love a taste."

Tension eased off her shoulders. "Thanks, Thomas. I'll be sure to save you some."

He leaned toward my ear and whispered, "This is getting nowhere. Let her be for now."

"But—"

"Sit. Relax."

My shoulders threw back like I was a soldier. "Are you handling me?"

Thomas's hands went to my back. His thumb immediately found a giant knot. "Consider it pressing the pause button and trust me." He stood back and called out, "Lunch is ready, everyone."

Isabella set a salad on the table but went straight back to the kitchen, fussing with the mugs of cocoa. I had the feeling she didn't want to leave Rachel.

Thomas walked over to her and whispered something. Bella nodded, answering in a muffled voice. I heard the word "Cody" and made a rumble low in my throat. They spoke some more until Thomas finally said, "Come on then."

He and Bella carried the mugs to the table, distributing them to the six of us. By the time Rachel sat down, we'd both cooled enough to eat a quick but pleasant meal. She'd made enough sweet potato hash for everyone too.

When I finished, I was so tired my head wanted to drop right onto the table. A loud yawn made my jaw pop. Maybe that's where my ire had come from. I carried a load of dishes to the dishwasher and caught sight of the rest of the gang sitting around the table doing much of nothing. The ridiculousness of it impressed upon me.

I adjusted my glasses before stretching. "Hey gang, it appears I'm plumb out of spoons. Y'all are definitely big enough to clean up. Can one of you roast a few dozen chicken thighs for later too?" Roasting chicken thighs in large quantities saved my hide when I opened the coffeehouse and the kids each had their own after-school activities. They were easy, tasty, and convenient. They also fit the Paleo protocol.

"There you go again, Ms. M—"

I raised my hand as I crossed the space, heading toward my room. "Not now, Hank. My tank's on fumes."

Rachel scratched her head as she rose from the table. "Who the hell's Hank?"

"Your mom's beta testing a new name for me," Dylan's roommate answered her.

My daughter shook her head. "Because why wouldn't she?"

I stopped to explain but couldn't. I remembered the food though. "Oh, can someone be in charge of saffron rice?"

"Show me where the spices are and I'm in, Ms. M," Hank said.

"We've got it," Dylan added.

"And steam up something green."

"Dum and I have that too."

"Thanks guys. Really. I-I need a bath and… something. I don't know." Brain fog and guilt overtook my senses. It shouldn't have been a surprise.

"We're good. Go ahead," Liam said.

Thomas opened the silverware drawer. "What do you mean, you're out of spoons? There are plenty in here."

I turned around to clarify, but the connection between my brain and my mouth still short-circuited. Rachel waved me on. "I'll explain spoon theory to him."

Despite the sudden onslaught of soul-deep fatigue, I padded the rest of the way to my bath with gratitude in my heart. Our conflict hadn't gone off the rails the way everything between Bobby and me always did. Thankfully, the power had held at her condo. I didn't know what I would've done if we had to bring my mother over too.

I stood in my room, eyeing my bed, the meditation area, and my bathtub. Even though speech eluded me, my head spun with images. Flashes of the events of the past two days bombarded my brain and prevented it from shutting down.

A bath it is.

I settled into the balmy water, salts efficiently dissolved, the oils effectively scenting the air and coating my skin. I turned on the jets and the chroma-therapy lights, then reached for my e-reader. Then I noticed I'd left my glasses on the counter. Well, shit. I stood and stepped over the tub, carefully crossing the tile floor to retrieve them. I was certain one chapter of my book would quiet my brain and allow it to rest. Grabbing them, I turned back, took a step, and went down with a crash.

13

Oh Girl

Thomas

RACHEL BROUGHT HER LAPTOP TO THE COUNTER AND PULLED UP A website called ButYouDontLookSick. An article there told the story of a woman who used spoons as a metaphor to describe life with a chronic illness. She also clicked traditional medical websites that embraced the concept as a tool for patients and their loved ones. With what I'd learned from Kick, it all made sense. In the middle of reading the article, an echoing thump coming from the primary bedroom made my heart stop.

Thankfully, the bathroom door hadn't been locked when I burst through it. After hearing the loud bang that sounded like a death tumble, panic ensued. We were lucky I turned the handle instead of crashing through the door.

"Are y'alright? What happened?" I grabbed the back of my neck as I assessed the bathroom. Too much water on the floor. Some jars overturned. Kick winced and blew out a long breath through tight lips as she eased herself into the water.

"I'll have a nice hip bruise." She looked down and raised her arm. "One here from smacking it on the counter too. Otherwise,

I'm hunky-dory." Kick settled into the water and closed her eyes. "It's what I get for forgetting my glasses."

I eased over to the side of the tub and sat on the edge. "You didn't hit your head?"

"Naw." She kept her lids shut as she smiled. "Any future stupidity is just the brain fog waiting to clear."

My shoulders dropped in relief. "Christ, darlin'. You scared the shit out of me. The street's not fit for an ambulance yet."

Kick opened an eye. "It wasn't fit for your snowboards either, but it didn't stop you lot."

I took her hand and checked the darkening red mark. "Are you mad about that?"

"No." She adjusted her scrunchie, making a top knot. "It comes with the boy-mom territory. I'm simply pointing out I'm not the only one prone to accidents."

That was a relief. I pulled a towel off the warming bar, spread it over the wet floor, and wiped up the puddles with my feet. Then I began to strip.

Kick pushed her glasses up her button nose. "What are you doing?"

"Relaxing with you." I breathed in the floral scent hanging in the humid air. "It's already working."

I took a step forward and held out my hands. "Stand please. Reassurance me your bruises are as minor as you claim."

Kick pushed a button on the light panel. The cycling colors became a solid warm white. "The colors will make it appear worse than it is." She took my hands and stood. As I carefully turned her, checking for signs of something needing a doctor, Kick's hooded gaze told me she was checking me back. Water droplets meandered down her skin, making my mouth water.

The corner of my mouth ticked up. "Like what you see?"

"Always. Can't get enough."

The possessive, heady looks passing between us proved our like-mindedness. I stepped in opposite Kick and lowered us into the steaming water. I lifted one of her feet and ran my thumb along the sole. I felt her muscles relax and heard her breaths lengthen.

I'd always been a shower guy, or variations of it. Between the scented oils, the relaxing water, and the woman I loved, I could get used to this. The extralong tub helped.

Kick settled her head against the bath pillow. "I'm a terrible mother."

Well, that took a turn. "The stuff with Rachel bothering you?"

"Yes, but there's more."

My ministrations moved up her calf, rewarding me with a moan. "Tell me."

"My body hates the cold. And any other year, I would've taken it easy outside. Gone home earlier. I guess I thought this talk of me being like you… you know, the Felidae stuff. Well, I thought it meant I could have all the energy again."

"I see." I took my time on Kick's calf, digging into the muscle there. "I need to be more sensitive to your limits. It's not like flipping a switch, you know. The first time I noticed something was different was ten years after Alicia died. Remember how my aura appeared when I spent a week on the mountain? It didn't come out again until much later. During the time between, I wrote it off as grief."

Kick turned the chroma lights back on, and it amused me how they created an effect similar to our own energies.

"What happened ten years later?"

"Aside from my peers going gray or dying early, a terrible virus spread across the valley. It almost killed my son and my mother-in-law. Many families were devastated, but all were touched by it to a degree. Everyone but me. I didn't catch a sniffle."

Kick flexed her now-relaxed foot as I switched to the other one. "So it could take a while until I see a total remission, or will it always be an issue, you think?"

I focused on a tight knot below the ball of her foot. "Keep up with your doctor's advice. But there's old folklore specific to the Felidae, or those like us. The elders have been around long enough to make long-term observations." My thumbs dug into the length of her sole. "They say healing works in reverse for us. In other words, a recent issue resolves first. Older ones take longer." I lifted a shoulder. "Of course, when you have all the time in the world, it's still a short time. What's interesting to me is I've observed similar things on a cellular level in the lab. Guess they have a point."

"You're saying be patient and watch."

I chuckled at her summation. "Spoken like a scientist."

"Hopefully it won't take so long to help my temper. Thank you, cowboy." Kick sighed and settled into the massage as my hands moved up her second leg.

"You've called me cowboy on and off since New Year's. Is this a thing now?"

Kick smiled like she was visiting a memory. "There was something about the time you took me to meet Eddie."

"It's the damn coat, isn't it?"

She laughed and brushed the damp hairs off her face. "The coat leaves a fantastic image in the mind, for sure. It was also like you were telling me something without words. Considering everything I know now, you probably were. It suits your soul, I guess."

"It would be nice if cowboying could combine with healing mankind."

"You really want to end diseases like Banger suggested?"

"I want answers to my existence first." I stretched my neck, letting the water loosen my own tension. "Why not take it as far as it'll go? I have all the time in the world." We sat with the words, and I listened to the tub motor hum as the tub jets pushed against my back.

Kick's free foot eased up my thigh. I closed my eyes for a moment, absorbing the contact. Thoughts circled back to her reason for my new nickname. "I like the way you look when you call me cowboy. It's possessive. Zings straight to my cock." I sank down in the water, let my legs fall some so her foot could travel. We still had things to talk about. Items on my agenda. We had to get through hers first. Back to her lack of patience and time to test mine.

"Do you want me to talk to Dylan and Rachel about their rudeness by not calling first?"

"It's okay." She sighed. "They didn't mean it."

"They're old enough to infer it, darlin'. They have their own households and understand the amount of work to keep one. Or they should." I squeezed her calf to get her full attention and winked. "As much as I love your elven ears, you're not magical. Evidenced by how run-down you are now. That's also why your temper appeared."

"I suppose. If you think it'll help." Kick propped her elbow on the edge of the tub and held her head like her tiredness wore out her neck muscles. The kids and I were definitely having words. "I think I'm actually ready for the nest to be empty. Their bickering gets to me, along with the constant need to think several steps ahead of them. I love them to the moon and back, but they can drain me."

I kissed the top of Kick's foot, then took her hand and spun her around, sliding her back against my front, and scooped water up over her body.

"What are you doing now?"

"Drain in to me. I'll talk to them." I kissed her temple. Now for my agenda. "Speaking of talking to people, you never gave me an answer about your mother." Kick's back tightened, and I coaxed her back. "Why is this so hard for you? Since you're working on self-care, this would be a giant step toward it. After all she's done. Help me understand."

Kick turned and wrapped her arms around my waist while I continued lapping water over her. "It's stupid... I keep hoping she'll apologize. That one day we'll have one of those big reconciliation moments like in the movies and books and such."

"She'll never do that."

"I know. She can't."

"Exactly."

"I'm not sure I can take another stressor right now either. What with the investigations, the kids' problems, the peeper last night. Blending you into everything. My stomach does this coiling thing when I get anxious, which often leads to a panic attack. I'm working hard with meditation to change it, but I swear it's creeping up on me again. Another person to battle is too much."

"That's the point of the offer—to relieve your stress." Damn her stubbornness. "Let me take care of it."

"And what? Ghost her without an explanation? Any other tack invites World War Three. No, Bobby talks to Juan every day, according to her text messages. Heaven help me, but they may have something real. If I can keep her at arm's length, she'll probably move away on her own."

"Alright." I tipped her chin up and kissed her soft lips until they swelled with proof of my love for her. "Let me know if you change your mind." I set my head on top of hers. "You're not alone anymore."

"I know." She squeezed me and added, "Even though it's fast, and we've made a big deal about going slow more than once, what would you say to officially sharing our places?"

I shifted to catch her gaze. "You mean moving in together for real?"

"I do. I also want to work my schedule around yours to free up more time together. My doctor's appointments are winding down. I could work longer hours when you're at the university, less when you're here. You know, use our time strategically. What do you think?"

"I think you're brilliant. Since you're reworking your schedule, let's be serious about your self-defense training."

She tipped her head back and pulled her brows together. "Why'd you go and ruin the smarmy mood?"

My head dropped as I sighed through the frustration, determined to stay firm without starting a fight. Kick made a joke, but this was important to me and should have been to her. "After last night, *you* should be asking me to make time. The faster you can add to your skill set, the better I'll feel. Oh, and Mateo is with you anytime I'm not, Kick. Any. Time."

She surprised me by tightening her hold around my waist instead of storming out of the tub. I feared my bossy lecture would amp up her stress, but it had to be said. I shook her shoulder. "Are you listening?"

"I am," she whispered. "Thanks for having my back."

. . .

I tucked Kick into bed for a nap after promising to wake her for supper. Then I put on fresh sweats and a Lord U T-shirt. I headed to the living room in search of my e-reader. Liam, Rachel, and Isabella were in the kitchen finishing the trays of chicken.

"Are y'all opening a restaurant?" I asked, stepping around the island.

Rachel brushed her hair back in a way that reminded me of her mother. "The boys could each eat a tray full. Mama used to say she felt like she was cooking for a fraternity."

"She still says that," Liam said as he washed his hands.

"When do these go in?"

Rachel checked the clock on the microwave. "About an hour and a half. We're going upstairs to do homework. I'll come back down when it's time to turn the oven on."

Bella stacked the trays in the fridge, then washed her hands while Liam put the spices away. It was nice to see the kids working together. Gave me confidence that I could talk to them about being more respectful of Kick.

"Write down what's left to do—what temperature and when? I'll finish up. That'll give y'all more time to work, as long as we can have a chat before I wake your mom."

"Thanks, fam."

Not going to lie, hearing that from Liam helped my mood as much as, if not more than, horsing around outside earlier had. The whole day assured me I was on the right path. It was time to make that call to *Grand-père*. Tomorrow. I needed to do it from my secure line at home. It gave me a hell of a boost to know I'd done the right thing by bringing Kick into my world even if she'd been the one to barge her way through.

I checked each window for signs of another intruder before settling down in a lounger and reading a science article. According to Rachel's notes, Dylan and Hank would work on their dishes once the chicken went in the oven. So, after sliding the trays into the heat, I jogged upstairs and gathered the kids in the loft.

"We need to talk about showing up here unannounced. As much as your mom loves you, it's taken a lot out of her to host four extra people during a snowstorm. Especially with everything else going on."

"We didn't know there would be four," Rachel said.

"Yeah, and we don't exactly know what's *going on* either." Dylan used finger quotes for emphasis.

Alright, man, take care of this right or Kick won't let you intervene again. I focused on Dylan first. "Y'all know what we know. Banger talked with the suspect who tried to take Kick from the club. He was moderately helpful. The one who knows the most—the bartender—is in the wind. Jonn Graham is supposed to be on an ankle monitor, but after last night, I'm not sure. Banger talked about keeping a better eye on the Graham house.

"We have a good print of a men's size 11 basketball shoe from near Kick's bedroom window. The fact he got so close pisses me off. I'm sure she's trying to play off how upset she is about it. When the weather gets back to normal, you can bet the Angel Security team will come in and adjust the system. Also, Kick asked me to move in officially. I hope you don't mind me saying it and not her. She just… she needs a break, y'all."

Dylan nodded along with each point I made.

"Rachel… if you had called or texted before coming up… any of you, there could have been coordination. Hell, at this stage in your life, it wouldn't hurt to ask Kick for permission to spend the night, any time. You never know how she's feeling."

Rachel shrugged. "It's fine. We're used to her disappearing to lie down or fending for ourselves."

Liam cleared his throat, catching our attention. "The prof's trying to say y'all were damn rude assuming we could handle it. Have you seen the refrigerator, Snow? It's wiped. Fam had planned to use the potatoes you cooked earlier for tomorrow's dinner."

"Oh." Rachel hung her head. "But we were out of food."

Liam scoffed. "There's a pizza place and a grocery store around the corner from your apartment. Ours is a mile walk. Sure it's out of bread and milk, but you don't eat that stuff anyway."

"I hadn't realized you'd cottoned on to her stress," I said to Liam. Guess it was hard not to when you were raised in it.

He lifted a shoulder like it was no big deal. "Since it's just been us, we kind of made our own language about how we're doing. I can tell if she's off by looking at her. Mom's the same with me."

Ah, these kids. I saw the reason for Liam's reluctance to pick a college in that moment. The fear of leaving in the way his cocky grin disappeared. The way he nervously fingered imaginary chords against his thigh. I'd do something about it later.

I clapped my hands and rubbed them together to get back on track. "Do y'all understand where I'm coming from? No hard feelings for being here on my part, or on Kick's. You should know that. I'm impressed with you. All of you. Just… understand your mom means a lot to me. You might think it's fast, but we're in it nonetheless. And I admit to being overprotective right now. It still pisses me off that she could've been seriously hurt right under my nose. Twice." My fists flexed with unspent anger. I craved a sparring session at the gym as much as I did answers from any damn person in the investigation.

Dylan rubbed his new beard during my speech. He cleared his throat. "I hear you." His eyes moved over his brother and sister. "We all do. Thank you for what you're doing for our mom. Snow and I will apologize for not calling her. I knew better but was in a hurry to get ahead of traffic."

We all bumped fists before heading down to the kitchen to finish prepping dinner. I considered it a mission accomplished and hoped it would sell Kick on letting me handle Bobby even if she were the human equivalent of rescuing a village from a dragon.

A fter dinner and apologies, the older kids agreed to head back to their respective apartments the following afternoon. Icy morning roads kept the schools closed for at least another day, but Kick was set on opening the Perked Cup.

The best part of what Kick kept calling our "bonus holiday" came in the evening. We gathered around the big television for a movie, but nothing caught our attention.

"I know." Liam jumped up off the sofa. "We'll have a jam sesh."

In a matter of minutes, we were gathered back together. Lee and I had practiced together in the past, so one of my guitars was already at the house. Dylan kept a bass guitar in Liam's room since his old sanctuary was now a workout room. Kick rigged up drums for Hank from cookware, a cookie tin, and wooden spoons. The girls dug out kiddie tambourines from Rachel's room.

After tuning our instruments, I turned toward Liam. "Want to work on the song?" His eyes darted to Kick as a sheepish look crossed his face.

"What's wrong, Wee Man?" In typical Kick fashion, she caught it straightaway.

He studied his fingers and strummed a chord. "It's one of Dad's songs. You probably don't want to hear it."

He hadn't told me that when he asked about it. Hell, it was a song that often hit too close to home for me, not something I imagined touching Shane.

Kick moved to the sofa, next to where Liam and I perched on the fireplace hearth. "Journey? As long as it's not—"

"No. You know… 'Desperado' by the Eagles."

Kick leaned forward and chuckled. "I love it. The song was special to Dad because Granddad sang it all the time. Hell, he could whistle it like a bird." She reached out and shuffled the flop of curls off his forehead. "Dad would be thrilled to hear you play it. He's so proud of you. All of you."

Is? The use of present tense startled me, but I didn't have time to dig into it. Liam grabbed my attention when he played a chord. "G, right?"

I nodded, and we began.

Kick harmonized easily with her son, reminding me of her stories of singing with him in the car, Liam strapped into a car seat as they ran errands. Pride and peace shone in her eyes as everyone else joined in where they felt appropriate.

As for me, the song that haunted me in the past—an indictment of the prison of my lonely existence—now cleansed my soul. The queen of my heart found me, forced her way into my prison, and gave me all this. Damned if I'd take it for granted.

We progressed through several more classic songs with Liam and Rachel taking turns singing lead. Kick and Bella sang backup and shook their moneymakers with the tambourines. We turned it into an old-fashioned hootenanny, playing and dancing the night away.

When Kick drifted off to sleep later, I slipped out of bed to check the perimeter of the house, trusting my eyes more than what the camera feeds showed. I owed it to them to protect Kick and her family with everything I had.

14

Just Can't Get Enough

Kick

CYNDI TOOK A LARGE PULL FROM HER LATTE AND SIGHED. I COULD practically see the stress float off her. She'd entered the coffeehouse thoroughly wound up, but who could blame her? I saw footage of the multicar pileup she'd been in on the news.

"Thank you for the use of your man, chica. He saved my hiney."

"Anytime. You helped him scratch his itchy hero complex." I held my glasses up to the light and rubbed the lenses. They'd been blurry all morning, but the lenses looked clean. "Guess the helping thing went both ways."

"Where is Dr. Feelgood anyway?" Cyndi's nickname for Thomas had occasionally popped up during the past month. It always made Thomas shake his head, but I thought it beat Marty Poppins and left it alone. She craned her neck to case the café's dining room. "I want to thank him with a coffee and muffin."

I stopped filling the napkin dispenser in front of me and clicked my tongue. "You know he eats for free, like you."

"Exactly."

Cyndi's Cheshire cat grin made me shake my head. Then I tipped it toward the back. "He's tinkering with the HVAC system. The offices are ice cold, and the maintenance company said it wasn't an emergency."

"Is there anything your man doesn't do?" If I could live as long as Thomas, I supposed I would be a Jack—Jacqueline?—of all trades too. Not like I could tell Cyndi though. I lifted a shoulder. "He grew up on a farm. They're a resourceful bunch." I hoped my explanation would suffice. I patted her hand. "Can't believe you were caught in the middle of our Snowmageddon."

She shuddered at the memory. "I'm at the top left of the photo from the News website." Her mouth lifted into another grin. "The officer who rescued me gave me his number. A young buck at that. I'm taking a play from your book, Kicky."

I put the lid back on the dispenser and reached for the next one while biting my tongue. I didn't want to ask what happened with Manu. Silly me thought he might finally be the one to repair the heart her ex-husband had shattered.

"An…y…waay…" She nervously tapped on her cheek.

Oh hell. We'd fought over her playing the field in the past. She must have interpreted my silence as a judgment. My guilt over having to keep this huge secret from her probably looked the same. I gave her my best smile. Now I just wanted to see her happy, however it looked.

"The roads were fine once Thomas made my little car drivable again, which is a good thing since I have a tax appointment in an hour."

"Cyn, I—"

"Speaking of, when will you have your shit together?"

I laughed, breaking the tension, knowing she meant my paperwork to do my taxes and not my life. "My shit's all good. I'll send it over tonight. Oh snap." I stopped my chores and actually snapped my fingers. "I better check in with Uncle Hugh. This is his first year doing taxes on his own."

"Tell him to call me if he needs anything. He won't have to wait for an appointment."

"I will. Thanks, chica."

The bell chimed and Jake walked in, two hours early for his shift. "Well, hey, mister. Did I call a meeting and forget about it?" I reached for my phone in my back pocket to check the calendar.

"No, Mrs. Mack." He grabbed a pastry and took a bite. His eyes shifted around the dining room, then he pointed toward the back. "I'm uh… catching up on my paperwork."

Jake's steps slowed when Banger's second-in-command turned the corner from the back hallway. "Hey Siobhan," he said, dipping his chin to the side.

The spiky-haired redhead gave him a coy smile. "Hey yourself."

My eyebrows rose up my forehead, and I turned to Cyndi. "Paperwork my ass. Someone has a crush."

The attraction made sense. I never saw Jake with a "little woman" type. Siobhan gave off serious Lara Croft-meets-Tolkien vibes. And people said *I* looked like an elf.

Jake pointed over his shoulder with his thumb. "Can I talk to you when you're done out here? In my office?"

Cyndi and I made faces at each other while Siobhan smiled back. "Sure. Give me a minute."

We still snickered like proud aunties when Siobhan approached us. "Your update's all set. Again, my deepest apologies for the gap in your coverage. Let me know if you need anything else."

"Thank you, Von. I appreciate your hard work. If you have any insight into how this guy found the hole, can you speak with Thomas? He's not sleeping well over it." Cyndi opened her mouth, but I raised a finger to ask her to wait. I hadn't mentioned the peeping incident yet. I wanted to forget about it and let Angel Security handle it all.

Siobhan grimaced at my words, then bit her lip. "I'll be sure to do that." She turned and disappeared into the back offices.

"What's wrong with your security system, Kick?"

Before I could answer Cyndi, Deana, and Thomas emerged from the hallway, both moving in our direction. Dee vigorously rubbed her arms and poured herself a cup of coffee. "Not used to it being so cold." She took a quick sip and sighed. "I sorted the new shipment and couldn't tell the difference between the walk-in, the hallway, or the outside."

"Won't be long." Thomas stepped near me and moved my ponytail aside to kiss my neck. He pulled harder than I expected and made me shiver. I wasn't sure if it was from surprise or something else.

"Interesting." His quiet rumble reached only my ear.

I smiled at him over my shoulder. "What?"

He winked. "Making a mental note for later."

I raised an eyebrow, but Thomas moved away before I could say anything. "Getting my other toolbox from the SUV."

I watched him walk out, admiring the way his worn jeans fit his ass. He wore a sweatshirt without a coat and walked with sure-footed confidence as he navigated the icy patches in the parking lot. When he rounded the Land Rover, I turned around to find both of my friends ogling him too. "Ladies?"

Deana graced me with her warm chuckle. "You can't blame me for admiring God's handiwork, can you?"

My lips pressed into a smile as I looked at Cyndi expectantly.

"What she said." Cyn tipped her head like she was studying something—the something being me. "That little hair-pull business tells me you like a little 'funky bump bump'." She shimmied her shoulders with the words. "I learned something new today." Both women fell apart, giggling.

I folded my arms, struggling to keep from laughing too. I opened my mouth to say something sarcastic, but Cyndi put her hand up to stop me.

"It's all good, Kicky. You're just fun to tease." She sighed, the action leaving an introspective expression on her face. Or was it sadness?

"Want to do a girls' night tomorrow?" I asked. "Not like last time with the dance club. We can stay in, drink wine, eat cashew cream. There's a new rom-com I want to stream." I turned to Deana. "You too, Dee. Please."

Cyndi tapped her lower lip. "Let me guess, the professor's out all night and you don't know how to be alone anymore."

"Well—"

"What's Lee up to?"

I shrugged. "Band stuff. Friend stuff. He's hardly home anymore."

"You're afraid you'll sit around all horny and moping for your man." She pretended to pout and Deana belly-laughed. Apparently, I was an absolute hoot to tease.

I dipped my chin and glared. "I thought we could use some catch-up time together. All of us. There's also a new shipment of gummies coming in for Hugh's place. We could test them out. Take notes."

Cyndi finished her latte and slid the cup to me. "Sorry, chica. I have a date with Officer Hotpants. But let's sync our calendars and find something." We hugged and said goodbyes before Cyn left for her appointment.

I placed her mug on the dish tray, then asked Deana, "What about you? No obligations on the gummies." Deana hadn't come around to the possibilities of cannabis. To her, it remained an evil drug. "Hanging is plenty. In fact, Carmen brought over more of the empanadas you love this morning."

"It sounds exactly like what I need, but I can't either," Deana said while flushing and wiping down the dispersion screen on the espresso machine. "I'm babysitting Dex's boy. We hope they can smooth out this rough patch." She began scrubbing the rest of the machine, getting heavier handed than usual. She quietly added, "Something has to help."

I felt the pang of her worry deep in my gut. It still grumbled over the near fight with Rachel, wondering if she'd be okay. Deana's son's marriage had been rocky from the get-go. Watching her struggles over it had been part of the reason for my relief at Dylan's breakup. It could have been so much worse. "It's wonderful how you and Gordon support him."

Deana sighed. "Sometimes we're not sure Charice's firecracker ways are worth the trouble, but Dex loves her." She wrung out the dishcloth an extra time. "For the sake of that angel boy, I hope they figure it out."

. . .

Dee emerged from the restroom area, drying her hands and mumbling about the convoluted things people did to public bathrooms. The word *wrapper* caught my attention. I looked up from my work.

"What's wrong?" she asked.

It was then I recognized how much I'd missed her. Between time off for my health and Thomas, our interactions had become sparse. I sat on a barstool, working on my laptop, since my office was still too cold for more than a couple of minutes. I was setting up new ads to counteract the harassment efforts. Business had improved but was pitiful compared to the previous year.

"What makes you think anything's wrong?"

"Puh-lease." Dee stood in her trademarked fist-on-her-hip stance, not taking guff from anyone, including me. "You showed up this morning like you were walking on air. Now I find you staring at the coffee grinder like you're about to burst into tears. Is it your mother? Usually you get this way when you regret calling her."

I let my vision soften as I stood in front of the window, thoughts tossing in my head like decision salad. "Huh…? Oh. It's not her, thankfully. By some miracle, she started texting me instead of chewing me out when I can't answer her calls immediately. She still implies that she and Juan had crazy monkey sex, but it's easier to read than listen to. At least she sounds happy *and* she's leaving soon." Juan needed hip surgery, so my mother planned to fly up to his bedside.

"So—"

"I don't think I can partner with Hugh in this cannabis venture, and I don't know what to do," I blurted.

"What the—?" She shook her head. "Why?"

While running a hand over my curls, I blew out a shuddering breath. "Business may be on the mend here, but the campaign to ruin my character has worked with the tobacco board. The good old boys' club."

"You're saying all this…" She circled her hand in the air, what she did when desperately trying not to swear. "All this *crap* has been over Mick & Hugh's?"

"No, but it overlaps. Cyndi talked to some board members for me, and even she can't convince them I'm a good bet. The smear campaign has quieted, but it was successful." I rubbed my cheeks and forced my hands to stay out of my hair. Nothing said *out-of-control Kick* like sudden disco hair. It was the last thing my precarious reputation needed. "I've enjoyed learning about a new product and business model, but after everything else… I'm tired, Dee. Cyndi and I dodged a huge fecking bullet at the nightclub. I don't want to let Hugh down, but I can only fight on so many fronts, you know?"

Deana reached across the counter and had me in a hug before I registered the movement. Her breath at my neck, the beat of her heart against my ear, and shea butter lotion in my nose allowed me to take my first deep breath in what felt like hours. Her beautiful, sincere face that refused to show her age had grounded me long before Thomas came along. She was there for me first, and I would never forget it.

"So you want to what? Give up?"

I grinned into her shoulder. *Here comes her tough love.* I leaned back to answer. "I'm trying to figure out if it's worth the fight." My fingers pressed into the base of my neck, seeking relief from the tension knotting my muscles. "Now that I have Thomas, I want years with him. If someone's trying to hurt me or one of mine… It doesn't do Hugh any favors to pretend he has my focus. Or am I simply a stubborn fool who can't say no?"

"Of course." Dee smiled. "But it's also who you are. It's why you've come so far."

I knocked her arm lightly and chuckled. Leave it to Deana—the consummate optimist—to turn a character flaw into a strength. She helped though, except… "What about the near misses? Here. You and the rest of the staff. Customers—*children*—who hang out after school. I mean, there's bravery and female empowerment, and then there's stupidity."

She nearly snapped her own neck, recoiling in shock. "Female empower— Are you saying someone's after you because you're a woman in business?"

"The board members believed those articles about my 'moral failings.' One of them brought up Thomas to Cyndi, as if being with a younger man makes me a harlot."

"Didn't Hugh ask you in order to diversify the next set of licenses?"

"That's right. Hugh wants me to consult too from a health angle. That's why I've been researching pain relief and cancer patients."

"Then go behind the scenes and put someone else up front." I half expected her to finish the order with a *duh*.

"It's not a bad idea. But who? Jake? Play the veteran card?" My shoulders dropped. "He and I are working on a way for him to open another Perked Cup location when he graduates. The coffee business suits him."

"It does." Deana leaned down, placing her elbows on the counter. "Will this cannabis thing be profitable?"

I barked a laugh. "Ridiculously so."

Deana straightened her tiny spine with the majesty of a queen. She almost appeared taller than me when she declared, "We've come too far, earned too much with our blood, sweat, and tears to be chased away from what we've worked so hard for. Remember what I told you last fall—we don't let our ancestors down."

"There's an Oprah speech if I ever heard one."

This time she swatted me. "You can't let these people run you off, a'ight? Promise me. I have an idea too."

"What's that?"

"Well, would Hugh work with Dexter? He's perfect for it."

A smile bloomed across my face. I couldn't love the idea more. Deana's son was a hard worker, so charismatic. He held a degree in entrepreneurial business or some such. Hugh would adore him. I tapped my bottom lip. "I could stay involved as a consultant. Does Dex need a job?"

"It's a big part of this round of problems with Charice."

My heart broke for Dee and her son but lifted at the possibilities for all of us. "You might be a genius, my friend."

She pierced me with her fiercest gaze. "Now go surround yourself with your army of fine men and run your damn empire like the queen bitch you are."

My brows spiked in amusement, my smile even bigger. "Deana Douglas, did you swear? Twice?"

She pursed her lips and dipped her chin hard. "Sure did." Following her naughty words with her bright smile set my mood to rights again. The ton of weight that had pressed my shoulders down lifted off like it was a feather.

I called Mateo over, then touched Dee's shoulder. "I'll go talk to Hugh."

15

Milestones

Thomas

Morning arrived too fast. Kick and I had accidentally slept in, creating a frenzied rush to meet the day. Blending our lives together was another level of joy that also came with its own road bumps.

I slid into the bathroom in my socks, my eyes darting around the space in annoyance. I stopped for a moment to watch Kick shake out her curls as she readied herself. It was the only thing that could make me pause. She caught my reflection in the mirror.

"What's wrong?"

"Can't find my watch and keys." At the farmhouse, everything went in a bowl near the coffee station on the way to the mudroom. The layout here was different, and I hadn't figured out my routine.

She paused with the stuff she called a finishing serum. "Are you serious? You're a grown man."

Instead of arguing, I kept staring. I didn't have time to debate. Shit happened, and we'd been distracted last night. Hence, our lateness.

"For Pete's sake." Kick lifted her eyes to the ceiling. I couldn't tell if she was thinking or praying. "Are they all the same? This one's almost three hundred years old and still can't keep track of his shit." She looked over her shoulder at me. "They're in the kitchen by the coffee station."

Well, damn. I kissed her check. "Thanks, baby. Love you." Then I shot out of the bathroom.

As I wrapped the watch around my wrist, Kick called out as she entered the living room, clipping her earrings in, "You know… you should research the finding-things gene on the Y chromosome. You'd transform humanity. Or at least improve life for my side of the gender pool."

I laughed and slid my feet into my shoes. How she handled this new reality of hers with such grace and now humor, I couldn't figure out. It did lift my mood. But the keys hadn't been what flustered me. A looming phone call did. "I'll put it on my to-do list. For you."

She stopped in front of me and nodded at a corner of the mudroom. "What if we put a small catch area there?"

I slipped my jacket on and pulled her in for a proper kiss. "I have a small table that'll work. I'll bring it after I see Eddie. Thank you, darlin'. You blow my mind."

She stroked the dent in my chin with her finger. "There's something else, isn't there?"

"Today's the day to call *Grand-père*," I confessed. I had hoped to give him solid proof that Kick was in transition but hadn't found it yet. We were coming up on a month since our commitment to each other. It felt disrespectful to both Kick and Alaric to keep our relationship quiet.

"He'll listen to you. From what you've told me, I can tell he loves you."

I squeezed her again, felt her heart beating against my chest, absorbed her optimism. "Hope so."

Kick turned me and gave me a gentle push toward the door. "You've got this. Are you still working with Liam this evening?"

He had scheduled one last SAT test and asked me for help with his weak spots. "Wouldn't miss it."

"Thanks, cowboy."

It had been easy enough to make the plans with Liam. I cared about the boy and loved teaching. Seeing Kick's eyes shine like I was her hero was another reminder of how much she'd been carrying. I cleared my throat. "He'll do great this time. Don't worry."

I left her with a sweet smile on her face, one that didn't come from an orgasm, yet I still felt like a king. Yeah, I could make this call.

I PACED THE SPACE IN FRONT OF MY OFFICE WINDOW, WATCHING students rush across the quad on paved walkways crisscrossing campus. Coeds had worn the grass down first before the university made the paths permanent, safer. Wasn't that what I was about to do? Break the rules and carve a fresh path out of necessity. I dialed *Grand-père*.

"*Allo.*" The unexpected feminine voice of Ellie came through the line.

"Um… hello *Grand-mère*. My apologies. Did I dial the wrong number?" I checked my phone screen.

"Thomas? No, my dear. You reached Alaric's office. You called him, yes?"

"I did. Good to know nothing's wrong with my phone." I hoped she didn't catch my nervous chuckle, except the woman missed nothing. "It's nice to hear your voice. I just don't understand. You've never answered this line before."

She made an annoyed, growly "*rohhh*" sound. "Something broke at his distillery while we were looking at the finances. I stayed to finish them."

"Well, uh…" Damn all the cross-continent tension making me tongue-tied. "*Grand-père* is proud of his brandy. More so than the wine. Hope it's fixed soon."

"*Bof.* Can I help?"

I'd never known Ellie to be annoyed by anything. She'd always been the epitome of dignity and poise. The definition of ladylike.

Between her responses and my anxiety before the call, I was in a veritable tailspin. "I'll call his cell phone."

"He left it here so he wouldn't be disturbed."

"Can you tell him I need to talk? It's urgent."

Had they been fighting? Alaric and Ellie hadn't been involved for a long time. They were more like business partners now. These hints of tension, mixed with Banger's concerns, suggested bigger problems than I thought at the top of the Society. It didn't bode well for what I needed to add.

"Let me guess, you're not allowed to speak business with me."

Hell. I pinched the bridge of my nose. "It's not business, I mean my research." It would be doubly rude if Alaric felt like the last to know. I'd already be on thin ice with him as it was with this news. "I should speak with him first."

She sighed an exasperated "*oui*" down the line. "I will leave a note. He should be available after dinner. If you don't hear soon, call him then."

"I will. Thank you, *Grand-mère.*"

"A pleasure, my dear."

Despite Ellie's plausible explanation, I spent the rest of the morning with the same question rolling around in my head. "Why the hell was she in Alaric's office?"

16

The Good Life

Thomas

KICK STEPPED UP TO ME AND PULLED MY RIGHT HAND TO HER LIPS. It had a significant cut from fixing the Perked Cup's HVAC system.

"Ugh, God," Dylan complained.

I smiled at the idea of an eight-year-old's reaction coming from the mouth of a twenty-four-year-old. *Might as well get used to it.*

"Come here, lad," Kick ordered. Dylan took a step toward us.

She planted a sweet kiss on my lips. "Get used to it, because I'm keeping him."

"Thomas isn't a new puppy." Dylan rolled his eyes as I laughed.

She tapped my cheek. "No kidding. He's housebroken." I raised my eyebrow at her tease. "Definitely a plus."

From the corner of my eye, I caught Dylan shaking his head at us and wondered if the hesitancy I felt from him came from our perceived age difference. I was aware of the various "oohs and aahs," as well as blatant snickering around the coffeehouse over her dating a younger man. Hell, it had been part of why Kick kept me at arm's length in the beginning. Now we loved our inside joke regarding the truth.

Did these murmurings bother Dylan? At least I had an opportunity to find out later. We were about to play poker at Mick and Hugh's. This game was set up by Dylan himself and featured his friends instead of Hugh's senior crowd.

Speaking of Dylan's friends, his roommate had entered the smoke shop during our exchange. "You go, Ms. Mack."

"Not helping, Dum." Dylan groaned.

Hank lifted his shoulder. "I'm happy for her." He knocked my shoulder with his fist. "You found a treasure, Professor."

"Don't I know it," I said.

Kick swooned. "You're very kind, Hank, sweetie."

The young man blushed. He leaned toward us and whispered, "It's not you. Suzy called earlier."

"Should I…" Kick pivoted toward the office, where her son had just gone.

"Let me," Hank said. "I swear, he's happy for you. Given everything else, it might be hard for Dyl to let go of his protectiveness."

Kick worried the inside of her cheek with her tongue. "He better learn fast. I never wanted him to be anything other than my son anyway."

"What can I say?" Hank raised his hands. "He's a reluctant alpha."

What the hell did that mean? Kick laughed at his words.

"Are you sticking around? I heard you host these things," he asked her.

"No," Kick answered. "I just do that for Hugh. I came by to sign out a product to test and say hello. I'll head back to the coffeehouse now."

"I'll pop over after I go out. I always lose my shirt at these things." Hank nodded slowly, like he was thinking and speaking at the same time. "Imma head back to the office and make the roomie laugh before we get started." He waved at Kick. "See you later, Mrs. Mack."

I worked hard to keep from frowning. The term *Mrs. Mack* rankled my possessiveness despite Kick having been a McKenna most of her life. It made no sense for her to go back to her maiden name. I liked where we were at, what we had. Blending our schedules had helped us become more comfortable as a couple. Why blow that up by pushing to take our relationship to another level? Nevertheless, the desire to be more had sparked in me.

I threaded my fingers with Kick's. As she tipped her head back, I saw the shadows under her eyes. "You're tired."

She gave me a small smile. "I'm fine."

"If we're still here when you close, don't come over. Go home and sleep."

Kick wrinkled her nose. "What about Mateo? Is he supposed to watch television while I snooze, like a babysitter?"

As much as Kick liked her bodyguard, she still wasn't comfortable with the day-to-day reality of him. "Tell you what… Have him do a thorough sweep and text me. Or I could just come get you when you're ready to close."

"And make you leave early?"

"I'll be fine. Your safety is more important." I touched my forehead to Kick's as she grumbled. "I could give you a massage… help you relax before you sleep."

The corner of her mouth ticked up. "That sounds like you're offering me some vitamin O, Professor."

"Yeah? You want another piece of me?"

She kissed my chin. "Always." She stepped around me and slapped my ass. "See what you've done to me?"

I waggled my brows. "Love what I see."

Kick opened the door and waited for Mateo to lead. Her bright grin threatened to stop my heart. "Go fill up on cigars, lewd jokes, farting, and chips. I'll call you when I'm ready… Oh, hey Banger."

I was laughing at her words when my friend walked in. As if the description of our poker night motivated me to stay away from her.

Banger and I grabbed arms in greeting. He tilted his head as he studied me. "Yep. Still googly-eyed and shit."

"What can I say? When you find your goddess, you hold tight and worship her."

Banger spread his hands out to his side. "All I know is… 'no woman, no cry.'"

I shook my head, knowing where the sentiment came from. I wasn't around to see his heartbreak but had known all about the tragic story.

He patted my back before I thought of a defense. "Seriously, brother. I'm happy for you. It looks good on you."

I grinned like a kid on Christmas morning on the inside, but kept my visage tight on the outside. Banger would've just given me more shit.

We wandered into the game room where Dylan sorted poker chips.

"How's your project coming?" Banger asked him.

"The pretend one or the surprise for Mom?"

Banger turned to me with an expectant eyebrow raised. I lifted a shoulder and lightly shook my head. "Maybe you should start from the beginning."

"Oh. Sure. See, Mom thinks my final project is a game because my team has focused on that until now. In fact, we plan to keep the game development side going since it's lucrative. It'll help with research and development for what else we want to do. Anyway, my final project is inspired by her."

"Go on," Banger encouraged as he took a seat next to him.

Dylan finished the last stack of chips and stretched his back. "You're familiar with the functional medicine clinic we help support?"

"Yes."

"I'm working with Dr. Drummond at the clinic to create an app doctors and patients can use together. It'll let them keep in touch between appointments. It's basically a symptom journal, a food and medicine diary, and workout tracker, all in one. It'll analyze what's input, detect any trends, and send reports to both the office and the patient. In addition, certain things will flag and send alerts to the doctor, who can then post a prescriptive message right away."

"Sounds brilliant."

"Yeah," Dylan sighed. "The functionality developed as expected. The problem came when we took it to the clinic for beta testing. We tightened up HIPAA compliance but hit a roadblock with hacker-proofing it in the cloud. You see, insurance companies can be hostile toward this type of patient. I've heard many stories from Mom—hers included—about how hard it was to get a diagnosis because the insurance wouldn't cover the tests." Dylan shook his head in disgust. "It's why a lot of these treatments end up out of pocket. That's why my dad started the foundation. It's one thing to know criminals are poking at apps to steal from regular people, but the board members are more afraid of big, domestic entities who'd want access to highly personal information. If you know what I mean."

"Whoa," Banger said. I could see the wheels turning in his mind.

I rubbed my chin. "Thought insurance companies couldn't deny coverage anymore."

Dylan's eyes darkened. Made me wonder how much he'd watched of Kick's experience. Did she even know? There were deep waters in this young man. "Plenty of politicians openly admit they want to revoke that part of the law. So many families would end up screwed. Doctor-patient confidentiality is a joke from what I've heard. I don't want to put in all this work and have it blow up the career of a good doctor, or the life of the patient."

"Well?" Banger turned, his attention on Dylan. "Did you figure it out?"

A wide grin spread across Dylan's face. "I did. I've developed a new security login system. The clinic received it at the beginning of the month. Initial feedback is encouraging."

Banger leaned in and quietly asked, "Can your security system be used in other applications? On other platforms?" He bubbled with an enthusiasm I hadn't seen in a while, like Dylan had just given my friend proof of Santa's existence.

Dylan's grin stayed put while he made a deliberate nod.

"Hot damn." Banger gasped. "My team's been working on something like this for six months for the Angel System. Could you adapt it for me?"

Dylan steepled his fingers and tapped them with a cockiness that made me laugh. "I think so. Sure."

"If it can, kid, it could mean millions."

The hands stilled. "Come again?"

Banger laughed, letting his head fall back. "You do not know. I have high-value clients who'd give a firstborn for better security." His gaze lifted. "What are you planning on doing with it after this?"

"As long as it stays on course, the gang and I have two venture funding meetings set up this spring. We're working on two more."

"Cancel them." Banger knocked his knuckles on the table.

"Really? Why? I haven't told you who they are."

Banger waved a hand. "Then don't cancel, but give us first crack at it. I think you have something we need. I want to help you finish it and grow it right here. In Raleigh."

"Who's us?" I asked.

Banger sat back and glared at me. "You and me, numpty."

"Why do I need—"

"Your research. We've danced around the idea of taking it into the private sector. Thanks to the developments with Ki—ah… your new subject—security will be your first concern."

I ran my hand through my hair, catching up to his train of thought. "Christ, you're right."

"You two have the capital my team needs?" Dylan asked, his tone doubtful. He looked at us like we were investment amateurs. The kid knew nothing.

Banger clapped his hand on my shoulder. "Son, your mama's new beau is a gazillionaire. And I'm a bigger one. Trust me, we have your capital."

"True?" Dylan's eyes shifted to me, studying me like he was searching for typical signs of wealth.

My brows narrowed in a tight grimace. I kept a lock on my funds and an even bigger lock on who knew about them. It wasn't that I didn't trust Dylan, but I'd learned the hard way to trust no one.

Keeping this project in the family, so to speak, had its appeal. Kick would be thrilled if her son could stay close. Raleigh would be the perfect place to launch both aspects of Dylan's future enterprise. "Banger's right. We could be equally beneficial."

"Wow," Dylan whispered.

"Moreover, your mom's going to be thrilled you did this."

He answered quietly, "Her first remission took forever. If this can shorten the time it takes to sift through tests and symptoms… do you know how many supplements made her worse before they figured out the right combination? It could save so much heartache and money."

I patted him on the back. "Let me know how I can help."

The rest of the guys walked into the game room with Hank making introductions. Banger stretched his arms and cracked his knuckles. "Let's whoop these punk kids and take their candy."

At the break, Banger and Hank were in the lead. The game had grown so intense that we needed a release valve. While everyone else filled up on junk food, I pulled Dylan into the humidor. "Are we alright?" The tension I'd felt when I arrived hadn't lightened despite the easy conversation at the table. "Hank mentioned you had a rough day, but I want to make sure it's not something else. For Kick's sake as much as mine."

Dylan scrubbed a hand over his cheek. The few day's growth he had during the storm was turning into an actual beard. "You're going with the Hank thing too?"

"Your mother has a point." I lifted a shoulder. "Can't put *Dummy* on a résumé."

"He won't have to. Dum will head up my marketing team."

I'd already heard about Hank's branding talents, which made me question his choice of nickname all the more. "You want a C-level executive with the name *Dummy*?"

Dylan folded his arms across his chest and set his feet like he'd become a wall. Something did bother him. Instead, he deflected. "You know he has a crush on your girlfriend, right?" He grimaced at his own words.

"Why don't we go with my 'partner?' Kick doesn't like the 'girl' reference anyway."

"Partner, huh?" Dylan's face scrunched before he nodded. "That works."

"Regardless, she told me enough that I know Hank's parents don't support him. I think he's smitten with her as a mother figure. Seeks her approval."

"She mothers everyone my age."

"Exactly. Like I said, is there something else?"

"You didn't know about Spoon Theory," Dylan blurted.

"Pardon?" *This conversation just took a turn.*

"Yeah. Rachel had to explain it to you." He ran a hand through his hair. "Guess it worries me."

At least he was talking, though I had nothing but questions swirling around in my brain. "I don't understand why that of all things—"

"All three of us… hell, Gran knows about the spoons. She sneers at it, but she knows the concept."

"Go on."

Dylan's fingers laced at the back of his head as he pivoted away from me. "Mom will go to the very last drop of her energy. She'll be like a car sputtering on fumes. We never paid attention when Dad was alive because he'd step in. When it was just us, running out of spoons meant we had the house to ourselves until she was back on her feet. I-I didn't mind doing it, except it scared the shit out of me. It always came with this…" He made a fist in front of his waist.

"Anxiety?" I guessed.

His eyes pressed shut as he sighed. "Yeah. I hate when it happens. Feels like I fucked up, made her push too hard."

"Are you afraid I'll push Kick?"

Dylan paced away from me and spoke while staring at the back wall. "I need to know you protect her. Not just this bullshit with the investigation, but her health too." He turned around but spoke to the cigar boxes on the shelves. "This is new to me, man."

I stepped closer but studied the boxes too. I doubted Dylan had ever shared anything like this before. The weight of it hit me hard. "From what Kick's told me, she didn't want you to step in as the man of the house. She'd rather you stayed her kid."

Dylan dropped his head as his shoulders fell. I watched the facade crack. How much had the responsibility crushed him all these years?

"I've got her. You too if you need it." I reached out and touched his shoulder. "Focus on finishing school. On your future. On *you*, Dylan."

"Thanks." When he lifted his head, Dylan gave me a tight grin, but it was enough. His demeanor brightened with my promise. We could build on that.

I picked a cigar from the shelf. "I don't know about you, but I could use another beer."

He chuckled as he opened the door to the muggy room. "Same."

"Too rich for my blood. I fold." Dylan was the last man to toss his cards to the dealer, leaving the pot to me.

Damnit. I'd bluffed—went all in on a pair of threes because I wanted to go to the Perked Cup before it closed. What Dylan had said about protecting Kick's health—her energy—had stuck with me all evening. And damn if she hadn't looked spent when she left here. Except the kid had chicken-shitted on me. I'd been certain he had a pair of Jacks, thanks to the river.

Our night dragged on, with the table evenly matched. It had been entertaining too. Dylan's friends were mature for men with whole lives ahead of them. By the end of the evening, Banger and I concluded that Hank's "Dummy" schtick was just that.

Between the cigars, the drinks, and decent winnings, I was in the middle of a successful guy's night—an important thing when the host is your new love's son. Then I received a text from her bodyguard.

MATEO

Someone on your "no fly" list walked in.

I checked my watch as more text bubbles bounced. Ten minutes to closing.

MATEO
That Jonn Graham guy.

Damn.

ME
The kid??

MATEO
The dad.

Fuck.

It's My Life

Kick

A FAMILIAR WOMAN WITH A BOY STEPPED UP TO THE COUNTER. Well, she did. He sat on the floor, kicking his feet. I wasn't a newbie to sleepy-time fits though. I snapped my fingers when her name matched up to her face in my mind's contact list. "Faye, right?"

"Hi, Mrs. Mack."

"Call me Kick please."

She dipped her chin. "Hi." The little boy howled.

I bent over the counter. "I remember you. You're Batman."

He tipped his head back and scowled at me. Faye grabbed his fist and shook it. "Nox, stop. We won't be long."

"Wanna. Go. Home." His lip stuck out in a pout that reminded me of little Liam.

I bit my lip to keep from laughing. "It's Nox, huh? What a cool name." He growled, and I bent farther over the counter. "Am I not supposed to say anything? You know because Batman's name is a secret."

Nox rolled his eyes at me. "That's Bawoos Wayne. I was pwee-tending."

"I see. Thank you for clearing that up." I smiled at his mom before glancing back down. As she swayed on her feet, I swear I felt her fatigue more than mine. It had been a while since I'd worked so late.

Jake walked over to us, and Faye's face lit up like a romance cover model had walked in. Then she turned bright red. He had that effect on a lot of our female customers.

Nox kicked the floor again, and Faye appeared ready to cry. She bit her lip, I presumed to keep from doing just that.

This time Jake peeked over the counter at him. "Hey, buddy. Can I get you something?"

"Not talking to strangers," Nox said to the floor tiles.

"That's enough, Mr. Man," Faye scolded. "When you're with me, it's okay to answer a question. No matter how tired we are, we can be polite. Besides, I'm almost done. Fall asleep in the car after this for all I care."

"What are you getting at this hour?" I asked Faye, afraid she needed dinner for them. We didn't have much left, but there might be something in the cooler for the next day. I raised my hand to clarify. "I didn't mean to sound judgy. Just being nosy. It's unusual to be graced with a mom and her handsome son at this hour. Do you work nights?" *Jayz*, I hoped she didn't have to. Faye appeared ready to drop.

Her hands fluttered around, like she'd forgotten why they'd entered. "Right. I'm out of beans for tomorrow morning and… it's a big day. I can't risk an upset stomach."

"I hear you," Jake said. "What size bag?"

"A pound. Ground please." She blushed again.

"On it."

I rang up her order and quietly asked, "You think Nox might like a chamomile tea with a touch of honey? It used to help my youngest when he was overtired."

His grumpy, high voice floated up from the floor. "No hot stuff."

I leaned over again. This kid's surliness cracked me up. "What if it came with milk in it?"

He blew a raspberry. "Boo cow milk."

"Allergy?" I asked Faye. She blew out a long breath and nodded. "You like almond milk?" I asked.

I waited for the answer and heard nothing.

Faye looked down. "She can't hear your head bobbing, son. Please stand up and use your words. One more time."

He slowly obeyed. "Yes, pweese."

I winked at him. "Coming right up, Mr. Man."

His mouth dropped open. "How did you know?"

This time I did laugh—a big, energy-building belly laugh. It was what I needed. "A birdie told me."

Faye smiled too.

"How about one for you? It helps after a long day."

"Sure. Thanks."

"My pleasure."

Nox crossed his arms on the counter and laid his head on them. As I worked on their to-go cups, I couldn't help noticing what a tight unit they were. Faye obviously made sure her son had as much as she could give him. Nothing expensive or flashy. But they were both dressed cute and trendy. Her floral puffer vest over a soft pink sweater was just the kind of funky and artsy that I liked. A part of me was proud of her for doing as well as she was.

However, the tiredness in Faye's eyes wouldn't let me go. Or maybe the memory of my years like that was too familiar.

I handed her the teas. "They're on the house."

"Again? Mrs.—Kick… you can't keep giving me drinks."

"I can, and I will. Have you called the functional medicine practice I told you about last time? It could really help."

Faye lifted her cup and stared at it a minute before blowing on the lid. "No. I'm sorry. I can barely afford an in-network doctor, not to mention a sitter for Nox."

I kept a stash of McKenna Family Foundation cards in a corner by the window for when I ran across customers like her. I quickly passed one over. "Call this place. They'll take care of the bills. You can even get a voucher for the drop-in daycare around the corner from the clinic. Please check it out. I swear, I know how you feel."

"McKenna Family Foundation? Aren't you a McKenna?"

"My late husband started the endowment after I met a woman with my same illness, only she couldn't afford the out-of-pocket treatments. She was a single mom, like you." I patted Faye's hand. "They'll take care of you."

She shrugged but pocketed the card. "The doctor said I'm just stressed."

"Of course you are. You don't feel well." I tapped the counter indignantly. Whether you called it a brush-off or gaslighting, it pissed me off. Jake passed her the bag of ground coffee. "Think about it. If you have questions, you know where I am. Or call the foundation. The staff is eager to help."

She gave Nox his tea, who took a sip through the straw. His eyes flashed wide with enthusiasm as he gave me a thumbs-up. The three of us laughed in relief at pleasing our tiny dictator.

"Thank you, Kick. I'll… be back if nothing else."

Jake waved at them. "Bye Nox and his pretty mama."

Faye blushed as they waved back at us.

"Look at you dancing and stuff at this late hour," Jake said.

I checked the clock over the door. It was late. I'd found a second wind from serving Faye. And from working with Jake. I'd forgotten how his enthusiasm to learn from me boosted my energy.

The door chime announced a new customer, and I adjusted my glasses. What the hell was wrong with them? They had helped my fuzzy vision for a month or two, but I kept getting days where nothing seemed to work.

As the man approached the counter, my brows climbed onto my forehead. I took a step toward the emergency button as I tried to keep my poor poker face. "Hello, Big Jonn. Wh-what brings you in tonight?"

I glanced at Mateo. As usual, he tracked the three of us, me especially. It made me feel safe enough to hear the man out.

Jake moved to step between us even though a hefty counter already did the job. Mateo must have read Jake right because he moved from his perch in the corner of the dining room too.

"Hello, Mrs. McKenna." Big Jonn checked over his shoulder. "What's with the muscle?"

I wrinkled my nose. *Be honest, Kick. Be brave. No fear.* I nodded toward Mateo. "Thanks to men in your employ, I have a bodyguard." I pointed to Jake. "My assistant here apprehended your son when he terrorized us. You'll have to forgive the fellas for being protective."

"Men in my employ? I don't understand." Big Jonn's hand moved over his bald head.

"Your nephew and one of your crewmen plotted to kidnap me two months ago." He had to know about this considering his nephew had lawyered-up with the Graham family's personal firm. My palms began to sweat even though they were suddenly ice cold.

He dropped his gaze contritely and slid a newspaper across the counter. "A peace offering."

The three of us examined the headline for tomorrow's edition of the *Oakville Weekly*. It read, LOCAL BUSINESSWOMAN REDEEMED. I scanned the article and looked up at him. "You vouched for me?"

"In the beginning, I thought the articles were filler for a slow news time." Big Jonn shoved his hands in the pockets of a company jacket. He gave off the impression of being just like any one of his guys until your eyes traveled down to the Ferragamo shoes. "That scene in December went way out of hand. So I asked around."

I tucked a curl behind my ear. My overwhelming need for answers made me take the bait. "What did you find out?"

He raised his shoulders without moving his hands. "Nothing. Whoever's behind it is good." He dipped his chin toward the paper. "This is my backup plan. Like I said before, we single-parent entrepreneurs should help each other out."

"Thank you, Big Jonn." I followed the caption to a photo with my finger. It was from the near riot at my café and Hugh's. It got me thinking. "Aren't you friends with tobacco board members?"

The corner of his mouth quirked. I wondered if he'd already caught on to my meaning. "Two members are my oldest friends, actually. I heard about your venture with Hugh Reynolds."

I closed my eyes and inhaled slowly. Hugh hadn't told me if he'd passed on the revised application yet. "Can you let them know they won? I pulled out as Hugh's partner."

"But Kick… I thought you were in the deal to fulfill a diversity request." He acted like I'd disappointed him.

"Hugh's new partner still meets their goal. Plus he's lined up a proper budtender once the license is approved. She'll oversee product acquisition and education while Hugh's new partner will run the business." Summer, the budtender, came courtesy of Thomas's vast connections. Both Hugh and I had conferenced with her. She'd spent years in the industry on the West Coast and was searching for more responsibility.

"I see." Big Jonn nodded as he scoffed. "And you're just, what… stepping out of it?"

"I am." For now. Big Jonn didn't need to know everything. "As long as Hugh gets to see his vision come to light, I don't mind that your misogynist friends won."

Big Jonn faked a head snap, as if my words had hit him. "That's harsh for a simple business policy."

I scoffed. "Is it *not* a boy's club over there?"

"The whole government complex is a boy's club, Mrs. McKenna. That's my point," he said with a sly smile.

I raised an eyebrow in question, and Big Jonn tapped the newspaper. "If you need a bailout from a small group of loudmouths, how will you run with the big boys?"

I adjusted my glasses, wondering if my temper was fogging them. Then again, Big Jonn had a point. "Anybody can be targeted and accused of things they didn't do. If any board member had come to me, I would've eagerly cleared up their questions." I waved my hand to keep him from saying something worse. "No matter. It's done, and Hugh has a fine arrangement. That's what matters."

"You're truly altruistic," Big Jonn said, but he made it sound like a character flaw instead of a compliment.

"Thank you," I answered with a grin.

Jake sighed loudly. "Alright, Mr. Graham. You've made your hero play."

"Jake…" I elbowed him. To me Graham was neither fully dirty

nor fully pure. But Oakville was my home. If his help made it possible to regain my status in the community, I'd take it. With a tight smile.

Big Jonn leaned toward me, and both my guards stepped closer. "The loyalty you inspire is admirable." He tapped the counter and turned to go.

Then I remembered the peeper again. "One more thing—"

Thomas burst through the door with Banger and Dylan on his heels.

Big Jonn stumbled backward like he'd been pushed. "What are y'all doing? Running in here like there's a fire."

Thomas glared as he answered. "I'm Kick's." Steam practically rushed out his nose. The protectiveness in his dark expression turned me on. Made my grin wider.

Big Jonn pointed two fingers at Thomas. "The cigar-smoking ex."

"Yes. And not anymore," Thomas answered with a steely coldness. He'd been serious when he said he'd "had enough of this shit."

"I see." Big Jonn's eyes traveled up and down Thomas, assessing. Then they shifted to me. "Interesting." He raised a hand and waved. "Nice talking to you, *Mrs. McKenna*." He stared straight at Thomas as he drew out my name, making my man's head snap back. Then they both glared. I wondered if they would grow horns and headbutt each other. Or maybe just piss on each other's nice shoes.

To break the tension and get an answer to my current burning question, I blurted out, "Is Young Jonn on his ankle monitor?"

Big Jonn's head whipped around to me, his brows cutting into a deep crease. "It's a condition of his parole."

The nonanswer didn't help, but something told me it was futile to press. "Your kind gesture regarding the article is much appreciated. One last thing… will you get your son some therapy?"

Instead of answering my plea, he rubbed his head and said, "You should mind your daughter. Teach her not to mess with a young boy's mind."

"That's it." Banger stepped forward, but Big Jonn sauntered around him.

He opened the door and said, "My kindness only goes so far, y'all." Then he winked at me and left.

"Why the hell didn't you throw him out? What were you thinking?" Dylan yelled, pitching a fit in my direction.

Since he came by his temper honestly, I didn't take it personally. What did surprise me was he'd turned to both Mateo and Jake, expecting answers from them too.

We'd closed up the coffeehouse, but all five men stood guard over the dining room as I quickly cleaned. Thomas stayed near me, helping with the machinery. He cleared his throat and did his jaw flexing thing, but I placed my hand on his chest to hold him back.

"Mateo and Jake did their jobs exactly as we required. You could tell Big Jonn knew better than to pull anything in their presence." I nodded toward Mateo. "Hell, he was the one packing."

Banger grunted. "Guys like him… it's not their character to get their hands dirty anyway."

"See?" I pointed at Banger with both my hands. "I still want those questions I have for his family answered. I had the advantage. So you bet your ass I took it."

Dylan stared at me, both his fists planted on his hips. Thomas cleared his throat again, this time annoying me.

I turned toward him. "I know how this goes. I've got it."

Thomas leaned down and whispered, "You don't know as much as you think. Give him a break."

My eyes swept back over my son. I saw his worried stress—from the planted feet to his quick breaths. *Shit.* Thomas understood my kid better than me. What the hell was that about? "Dylan…," I started. "The plan worked." I turned to my employees. "I assume one of you texted these guys."

Mateo nodded.

"See, lad? I was fine the whole time. In fact, it's been a good night overall." I showed him the newspaper. "Whatever his reasons for helping, Big Jonn seems confident his 'magic mojo' made the deranged articles and rumors go away. I call it a win."

Dylan ran his hand through his hair as his posture relaxed. "You're sure?"

"Some help here, someone?"

Mateo spoke up. "She wasn't in any danger. I bet he won't be back again."

I moved around the counter and stood in front of my son, looking up at his stubborn face. Jayz, I missed the days when I could pick him up and reassure him. "See? All this will end."

"Fuck all, Mom." He bent over me as I hugged my ornery son. He sniffed and said, "I can't be an orphan, okay?"

I answered, "Everyone is eventually."

At the same time, Thomas said, "You won't be."

His tone—and the jaw flex when his head turned my way—told me I'd be in more trouble when we were alone.

18

Need You Tonight

Kick

I PADDED OUT OF MY BATHROOM, WEARING ONLY MY ROBE AS IT floated around my legs. Thomas had already been in bed working on his laptop when I entered, heading straight to the bathroom. Already the key differences in our houses were making themselves clear. The biggest one being a need for him to have his own office space.

Our drive home had been tense. Being in no mood to fight, I walked straight to my office and finished the paperwork I'd planned to do at the coffeehouse after closing. Between Dylan and Thomas, I'd been eager to get out of there once we cleaned up.

I sat on the edge of my side of the bed, finally calm enough to listen. "Okay, let me have it."

Thomas shook his head without looking up, but he wasn't on his laptop anymore. Instead, he read a book, his hair falling enough to shade his eyes. I did a double take at the cover. He was reading a romance novel Cyndi had recently returned. I had left it on my nightstand instead of reshelving it in the bookcase.

I froze as a broad grin painted Thomas's face. It put me off since I expected a grumpy look. This was his middle school mischievous smirk.

"You think a man should act like this?" he asked.

My spine straightened in defense, knowing what he insinuated. "He's what some call an alpha male," I answered, biting my lip. Did he think I wanted him to behave like that character? *Jaysus*, I hoped not.

Thomas held up the book with his finger in his stopping spot. His eyes shone with incredulity. "You call *me* a man-child? This punk's temper is off the charts. He refuses to listen and… Christ, he takes her any and everywhere and lets his spunk just… what? Run down her leg in the middle of a cocktail party?" He pulled a face of disgust.

My head tipped back, laughing, as I thanked the universe we were, once again, on the same page. "Caught that, did you?"

"How could I not?"

"That's the fantasy part of the story."

He "pfffted" at my answer as I slid under the covers, chuckling.

Thomas rubbed his chin a moment. "Would you want me to handcuff you to the bed like he did? Because there are moments…"

Since my new bed was a sleigh bed style, the current chances were slim to none. I gave him my best innocent look, hoping to take his mind off our not-finished argument. "Silk ties sound comfier—"

He lifted a hand. "No, no. Handcuff you and leave you there while I run out to catch a bad guy."

I remembered the scene he referred to and raised an eyebrow. "I wasn't in danger tonight. If Jake and Mateo hadn't been there, I would've pressed the emergency button. Even though Big Jonn doesn't have a restraining order against him, I know he's on your 'bad man' list."

Thomas narrowed his eyes and flexed his jaw, letting me know he doubted my logic. To be honest, he was right, but I wouldn't admit it. Big Jonn ended up doing me a favor. Two, actually. Whatever his reason, I'd take them.

"Need I remind you that the heroine was thoroughly pissed, *and* the hero promised not to do it again."

Thomas folded his arms across his chest. "Still reads like he's measuring his dick to prove his manhood. That's a little-boy ego there."

"Alpha's not a real thing anyway." I leaned into him and brushed his hair off his forehead, treasuring the silky feel as it sifted through my fingers. "You missed the most important part of the story."

"What's that?"

"Our heroine owns her sexuality without apologies. You know, the earliest romances were influenced by society's rule that good girls don't and bad girls do. In the books, if a woman had sex outside of marriage, she was essentially date-raped and shocked when she discovered she liked it."

"You're kidding?"

"I wish. For way too many, it's true."

Thomas's eyes squeezed shut. "I hate that I ever bought into the patriarchy."

He'd never acted that way with me. Then again... Oh. "Did you?" I couldn't imagine him being violent with a woman.

His face crumpled like he might cry, but that wasn't Thomas's way. He owned all the parts of himself, even what he regretted. "I coerced Alicia after we were engaged." He sighed deep and sad. "She asked me not to, but the men in my life had told me the refusal was part of the game. They gave me ideas on what to say to convince her to give in."

I adjusted my glasses. "How long have you felt this way?"

He blushed like he was reliving intimate memories he didn't want to share. "There were clues while Alicia lived, but I didn't truly understand until I befriended a sex worker years later. In my second life."

I raised an eyebrow, intrigued. Thomas laughed at the face I made. He brought my hand to his lips and kissed my knuckles. "You know I said I'd never risk another woman's life." He shrugged, as if the gesture explained everything while it created a dozen more questions from me.

"Thomas..." I laced my fingers with his. "Alicia had to operate under the same idiocy as you, except in the opposite way. For all you know, she wanted to be with you but was brainwashed into thinking it would make her dishonorable. Lord knows I lived under a similar cloud, and it was the twentieth century."

His moue stayed grim, so I leaned over and kissed him. "I forgive you on Alicia's behalf." As weird as it sounded, it also felt like we were talking about a different person. Now I understood why Thomas and the Felidae people referred to having different life-times. He had been another kind of man back then.

Thomas pulled me into a hug and held on tight. "Thank you."

When we finally let go, I sighed and pointed to the book. "Anyhoo, this one is signed. It is nice to see the heroine's growth across the series. If you want to read about my favorite hero, I can lend you that one."

Thomas returned the paperback to the nightstand, slid down to rest his elbow on his pillow, and propped his head in his hand. I grabbed my e-reader, brought up the regency story, and slid it in front of him. Then I joined him, matching Thomas's position and tracing circles on his broad shoulders with my free hand.

"Tell me about it," he said, his voice like smooth whiskey to my ears.

"It flips tropes. The heroine's father beat her and the hero had to sell his body when he was young. Of course, they start their journey with a misunderstanding or two, but how else would they grow? Anyway, it was a beautiful navigation of the period, as far as I can guess. Not like I was there."

"What period is this?"

"It's regency, so… Georgian." I started, then it dawned on me. Thomas lived this time. I blushed as my fingers went to my mouth. "Whoa, shit."

His smile morphed from cocky to sadness. He cleared his throat. "Let me guess… the hero was the youngest son."

My eyebrow raised. "Yes. How did you know?"

Thomas shrugged. "As the third son, I was meant for the military from the time I was little. My second brother was supposed to inherit Mother's land. Then the war happened and my brother enlisted too. He was killed instead of me." He shook his head. "Since I became the second son, the land went to me after the war."

"I'd read that story," I said in awe. I could listen to him talk about his life for hours.

He absently stroked the tip of my ear as he pressed his lips together. "It didn't end well, Kick. The heroine died and left the hero bitter for a long damn time. Until you."

"Well, shit."

Thomas chuckled as he connected the dots running through my mind. This was worse than his masked iciness from our early days. I'd do anything for this Thomas, who was brave enough now to be vulnerable.

"My blood pressure spikes every time something happens to you. I'm terrified I can't protect you. That it's all wishful thinking."

I closed my eyes and let my forehead fall against his. "I should've texted you as soon as Graham arrived, especially since you were only across the parking lot. We could've worked through his 'peace offering' together. It was probably scarier coming from Mateo."

"Probably." He kissed my temple, letting me know we were good. "There's more to it than tonight. As we do this day-to-day thing, I see farther down the road. I want you there with me."

"Me too," I breathed through a smile.

His expression turned to business, like it did each time we met with Banger to go over the investigation. "Something about the laws here have been niggling in the back of my mind since I had to take you to the emergency department. The hurdles I had to jump through then were hard enough, but what if you'd needed surgery?"

I opened my mouth to speak, but Thomas's warm hand settled on my shoulder to stop me.

"I want my attorney to draw up papers of Healthcare Power of Attorney for each of us."

I winced at the formality and shook my head.

"Without a marriage contract, if something happens, I have no say in your care and vice versa."

"Dylan has that now, to keep Bobby and her moods away from anything regarding my healthcare."

"Should he though?" Thomas asked. "I won't breach his confidence, but he needs this to help him let go too. You're mine, Kick. And I'm yours. What if it's me? Do you want to wait for Joe to drive down from Virginia?"

"It doesn't work that way… does it?" Did it? Hell, I didn't know. All I knew was how nice it had been to take each day as it came. I hoped we could do that… well, forever. "I'm in no hurry for any of this."

"Under normal circumstances, I'd say we have time." Thomas winked as his fingers wrapped around a curl. "Literally. But every time I get a text about you, my heart drops into my stomach. I can't keep my head when it happens."

I cupped his jaw with my hand and slid my thumb over the stubble. "Okay, I give." As hard as it had been for me to lose Shane, when the time came for us to part, I hoped Thomas would go first. I never wanted him to be left alone again.

19

Forever Man

Thomas

THE FOLLOWING AFTERNOON, I FINALLY REACHED ALARIC.

"*Allo*, Thomas. Everything alright with you?" The hesitancy in his voice told me Ellie had passed on my message, yet I wondered why he hadn't called back.

"*Oui, Grand-père.*" To keep my wits, I switched to English. "I'm fine. But there's important news."

"Oh? Have you found your mystery genes?"

I laughed at his simplification of my work since Alaric understood the intricacies of what I did. "It's coming along. No, I have a new test subject. She's younger than Toni, and the work pairs well. I only wish I could match this person's ancestry against the Felidae records. I haven't found anything in my files."

"Another woman?" he asked excitedly. "She's not from your family?"

It had been the first test I'd run. We all ended up cousins if we went back far enough. Kick's family history had been different from mine, but it would've been irresponsible to not verify it. "No, although her ancestry's European. You still don't want me to consult with Nigel right? It's also why I didn't speak about it to Ellie first."

He gave me a firm French, "*Non.*"

"Alright. Banger's running her background for me. It will take more time, but it's doable."

Grand-père chuckled. "You two picked well with your friendship. Like brothers."

I took a deep breath. "*Grand-père—*"

"Who is she?"

"Her name's Kick—"

"*Keek?*"

"Well, Kathleen McKenna. Kick is a nickname everyone uses. It fits her."

"I see."

"We're together. I couldn't be casual with her. You should know… we're living together. Blending our lives."

"You didn't think to say something?" I could picture the offended curiosity on *Grand-père's* face.

"She can manifest her aura. In fact, we can blend ours together, do… remarkable things with them."

There was a significant pause before he quietly said, "Edmund could do that."

Edmund had been Alaric's best friend, although the term didn't do their relationship justice. They'd been partners, brothers—even more—for centuries. Ellie had spent time as a wife to both men. Edmund had mysteriously died right after I joined the Felidae, so I hadn't known him well.

I swallowed hard, wondering if I'd just found Kick's connection. "I'll let Banger know." Edmund came from a Saxon kingdom, so I saw the possibilities.

"Sorry, my boy, Edmund's line died with him."

Damn. I still planned to tell Banger about it. Maybe it would give him ideas of where to look. My big fear had been finding out Kick was descended from Nigel. Since Banger had mentioned a connection to the bartender and a phone number in Oxford, I'd wondered if Nigel had wanted to end his line. He wanted Felidae abilities kept to as few people as possible.

"To be clear, she knows about the Felidae. Banger and I have promised to protect her, including from any of us." I closed my eyes and braced.

"Why would you do this without consulting me first? I told you to find a companion. Have a good time. Not to tell a girl our secrets! What about your vows?" His words tumbled over each other angrily. A series of French curses followed, some of them old ones.

"My deepest apologies." What else could I say? There was a reason Kick and I had found each other. There had to be. The line went quiet, as if Alaric waited on my explanation.

"Like attracts like," I said. It was the most succinct explanation I knew.

He scoffed at my description, but I pushed on. "I didn't betray the Felidae, *Grand-père*. I wanted to tell you about her and seek your permission, but here we are. See, Kick's had abilities for years— sight is one of them, from what I can tell. Also… she figured it out. It took me by surprise."

Alaric grumbled over the line.

I changed tack. "What do you think will happen when my research produces real-world results? Unless you are like the others, the day is coming when we won't be able to keep our people a secret. Banger's work gets harder every year."

"So better to beg forgiveness than seek my permission. Is that it?" His petulant tone ground at my nerves.

"I told you I'd planned to tell you about Kick." Damn him. Was he even listening? Hell, it had taken several days to reach him.

"You were here last month. You could have said something then."

"She and I had problems then. We…" I sighed, remembering why I'd broken it off with Kick, more like what had scared me enough to do so. "Before I left North Carolina, Joe finally told me why he left the Felidae. You hired him to assassinate Vivienne. That scared me shitless. How could you? I broke it off with Kick to protect her. She and I were over when I arrived last month." I absently rubbed my chest to calm my racing heart, lost in my thoughts, wondering how he could justify his past actions.

"I'll do anything to guard our secrets. Without each other, we'd be extinct. Don't you see that?" Alaric tried for a mollifying tone, but his anger seeped through.

"Don't you see how the world has changed?" I shot back. "What about the fact that Kick is probably one of us? Would you rather she walk around for years questioning her own existence like we did? Terrified of her life? Her friends and family?"

"The Felidae take priority over potential family, even blood," Alaric steadfastly insisted. "That's why we wait before considering someone new."

"We don't need to anymore. You're excited about my work with Toni, and she's not a hundred years old. If I can interpret her physiology, I can track Kick's. If we don't evolve our attitudes, we'll drive ourselves to extinction."

How I wished to be in his office. Having this conversation over the phone added another layer of frustration. "She won't betray us, Alaric. Are you so removed from your first life that you've lost hope? Because if you don't have hope, why am I doing this research? I reinvented my life for this, not only to answer all our whys but to make a difference for every person." I drew in a long breath to slow my heartbeat.

Alaric groaned in his own way. His voice dropped like he was also forcing himself to calm down. "Perhaps it's time to get away from the vineyard," he murmured.

"What do you mean?"

"Oh my boy." I heard squeaking and shuffling, like he was walking around his large office now. "Ellie and her people hold the opposite opinion. It's why I want you to send updates to me alone, instead of conferring with Nigel's team."

I ran a hand over my chin, watched a cardinal settle on a branch outside my window. "Then what's the point of Nigel's work? I don't understand this thinking."

He clicked his tongue and made a gallic grunt. "You're young in our world, but I didn't think you were naive. Knowledge is power. Eleanor has always been made to rule. She'd like to do it again."

"You know how futile that sounds, right?"

"Not to her and Nigel. You're a son of revolution, a man of the Enlightenment. In Ellie's first life? Science was *alchemy*."

The phone calls to Oxford poked at another question. "Did you know about Kick? Is someone tracking her? There's been—"

"You just mentioned her." Alaric scoffed. "I work fast but not *that* fast."

I told him of Banger's suspicions, just enough to feel out the situation for myself, but he insisted Kick's identity was new to him. "What about Nigel? Could he have someone on her? Like you did with Vivienne."

"I told you—"

"I know. You protect the family. Understand that my family has expanded. I'll protect them with everything *I* have."

The old man growled—a warning for me to remember my place.

The cardinal sang to its mate, sitting a few branches lower. I thought about the indigenous legend of the cardinals and the maiden and wondered what force on earth had brought me to my lonely woman. If only handsome birds had led me to her. *Like attracts like.* Could it be that simple?

I didn't want to trade thinly veiled threats and barbs with Alaric. I still loved and respected him even if I didn't approve of all his ways. He'd been family when I was lost. I'd never forget that.

He finally spoke. "My world was a dark and dangerous place. Life crushed the weak for the good of the village, whether it be a runt or a wayward son."

"My world was like that too, *Grand-père*. It's why I lost the mother of my children."

"Ach. *Oui.*" Emotion filled Alaric's acknowledgment.

"We don't have to be so brutal anymore. We can be patient. Give a little extra to the weak until they stand on their own. You'd be shocked by how much they'll contribute. Especially when it comes to compassion."

"I hope you're right, Thomas."

20

Just Like Heaven

Kick

"This last test isn't just improved, it's in ideal range. Excellent work." Dr. Chaddha shuffled her set of my lab work papers. "Congratulations, Kick. You're officially back in remission. Keep it up."

Thank the heavens. My last IV appointment had been four weeks prior. The food reintroduction was chugging along too. I still had problems with raw vegetables, so I took that category slowly.

I smiled at my video camera. "Thank you." My smile faded when she had no answers for why my glasses didn't want to work anymore. She told me to go back to the optometrist, but I doubted the prescription was the problem.

"Anything else?" she asked. Her eyes darted to the lower right-hand corner of her screen—the clock. We had ten minutes left, which included speaking with the lifestyle coach and ordering my supplements.

"As a matter of fact…" Thinking about supplements reminded me of a question I'd forgotten to write down. "Can you recommend a sleeping remedy… for nightmares? My dreams have become quite violent lately. Is there a mineral, herbal combination, or cannabis strain that helps with it?"

Dreams about my mystery man used to be my nighttime concern. Now that I knew I'd been channeling Thomas somehow, I thought the overnight upsets would go away. They had only morphed into another thing.

Dr. Chaddha recommended a mineral and an herbal remedy, but her philosophy had always been to take as little as possible. I appreciated that, given how much I still took to make it through a day.

"Meditation should have helped this too." She paged through her notes. "In our last appointment, you mentioned meditating daily. Are you still doing this?"

I sighed. "I am." And I was, though I had needed to shorten some sessions to keep up with my schedule. Self-care sometimes ran short to make time for Thomas, but that was self-care too.

"Try lengthening your sessions. Or try a different focus. I'll have Audra go over the clinic's recommendations."

It was like she read my mind and gently chastised me. "Okay. Thank you."

As I finished the tele-session and filed my papers, Thomas walked into my home office. I had taken the call at home to keep from causing a fuss about turning off the surveillance in my space at the Perked Cup. Some days it seemed like everyone I knew was waiting around for me to get shot. Hmm. Maybe their stress showed up in my dreams?

"You're having nightmares," he stated.

Well, hell. I bit my lip. "I am."

"You have Friday clear?"

This time his tone lifted like it was a question. "I do. To match your day off, in fact."

Thomas shoved his hands in his pockets. "We'll spend the weekend at the farm. The fence should be finished for Macushla. Liam can drive over after school."

"Okay, but—"

"We're having a training session." He cut me off in a voice that brooked no argument. "See if Dylan's free too, though he mentioned working with a trainer at school."

Dylan had been. Working out helped him release pent-up emotions from his breakup. It also counteracted those long hours in front of his computer.

I blew out a breath and made a rumbling sound of frustration.

Thomas chuckled as he rounded my desk. "So stubborn." He bent down and kissed my temple. "Self-defense skills will clear your mind. That'll help your dreams more than any supplement."

I turned my head and glared, making that chuckle drop farther down into his belly. "You going to pout now?"

If that was all I had to do to feel that resonance, I'd glare at the man all day long. As it was, I'd probably end up frowning at him all weekend. At least his rumblings did fun things to my lady parts.

He took my hands and pulled me into a full-body embrace, making me relax faster than anything I'd learned on my call. "Congratulations on your remission. Let's celebrate tonight." He tilted his head and sighed. "Christ, woman, don't look at me like that right now."

I didn't realize I wore any particular expression. I blamed the chuckling and the thought of celebrating. I felt his reaction against my waist.

"Not until we have time to do something about it. We both have places to be," he murmured in my ear. "Dinner first. An actual date. Where do you want to go?"

How wonderful to focus on normal things.

THOMAS WHISTLED AT ME, THE SAME WAY HE HAD WHEN HE accompanied me to the holiday gala for Lord University. I entered the living room from my bedroom, wearing a dusty rose-colored velvet wrap dress that fell just below my knees. It paired perfectly with block-heeled Mary-Jane's in cognac. I hoped the color complemented the maroon lowlights my hair still rocked from the holidays. I had also found an online tutorial and learned how to put my hair in an easy, twisty updo. According to his face, I'd done well.

Thomas though… as much as I still loved his old-school suits, he rocked the hell out of the sexy professor image. He wore black flat-front trousers, a gray grandfather shirt, a black vest, and a gray tweed sport coat. We were doing a fancy date—for a provincial town anyway.

Thomas took my hand and had me do a spot turn. Then he dipped me and kissed the open space on my chest created by the V from the wrap.

"Damn, it's pinned," he whined.

I righted myself and laughed. "You're lucky I didn't tape it. No unwrapping until we get home. No flashing the restaurant staff either."

"Keep it up and there'll be no waiting till we get home," Thomas said in his delicious baritone, as we entered the restaurant and he removed my cape, his eyelids heavy with lust.

I didn't realize I had hummed when we entered the elegantly restored nineteenth-century mansion. It had been so long since I'd done something like this—usually for one of the kids' accomplishments—I'd forgotten how much fun each moment of the experience would be. The staff was especially good at creating a luxurious yet attentive atmosphere. I took mental notes on how we could adopt something similar at the Perked Cup.

When the host found our reservation, he gave me a soft smile. "I see madam has food allergies."

"That's right." I bit my lip and looked at Thomas.

"They asked when I made the reservation." He shrugged. "Figured you knew about the chef since you seem to know all the others."

"Uh—"

"No worries tonight, Mrs. Harrison," the host interjected. "Chef transformed the kitchen after his Celiac diagnosis. We've got you."

No shit? I let out the breath I didn't know I'd been holding. Could I actually relax in a high-end setting? Eat something more than a salad?

At the same time, I smirked at the name the host used and caught Thomas's stuttered step from the corner of my eye. I could swear he walked taller the rest of the way to our table.

"You haven't stopped smiling since we walked in," Thomas said as I bit into a delectable almond and date bread-ish appetizer that I'd received instead of the homemade country breads the other patrons received.

"It's nice to be seen instead of feeling like a pain in the ass." Seriously. Our server took the initiative and asked about my diet. After taking notes, he spoke to the chef and came back with a marked-up menu. The kitchen even offered to make a butter sauce to substitute for the spicy one they served with the filet. It sounded so amazing I went for it.

I closed my eyes as I swallowed the last bite of almond bread. "I feel like I'm floating." Why did so many other places make it so hard? *Because they were more interested in their recognition for unique recipes than service.* I answered my own question and vowed to do better with the coffeehouse.

Thomas pushed the basket holding his rolls aside. "You sure you're ready for a cocktail?"

"I am." I wiped a bit of honey butter off my fingers. "You're also usually better at the covert eye-dart-around-the-room thing."

He gave me a guilty smirk.

"What's riled you up?"

"New questions keep piling on before the old ones have answers." He brought my fingers to his lips and pressed a kiss to them. "I'm impatient."

I thought about his description of the hypothetical romance and understood. I also didn't have the heart to remind him my drugged drink had been nonalcoholic, and we were already drinking water. "As far as the cocktail goes, I'm sticking to one, and you're with me." I leaned in and said, "You can go upstairs with me to the bathroom when the time comes. If it'll make you feel better."

"Can I unpin your dress?"

I rolled my eyes. "Are you telling me all I need to do is flash my boobs at you and you'll relax?"

Thomas shot me his middle school smile.

I was still laughing when our drinks arrived.

A talented mixologist is a god in the hospitality industry. I stuck to one drink but was determined to make it count. I saw absinthe listed in the Elixir Alpestre on the cocktail menu and knew it was for me, although I requested a swap of one ingredient for a local gin that I knew for certain was gluten-free.

I took a sip of the delightfully tart art in liquid form and sighed. Thomas raised an eyebrow, making me laugh again. "Isn't it wonderful to feel normal?"

I held my glass to his for a toast, surprised when he said "*sláinte*" along with me—the Irish toast my family used. I tipped my head toward his drink. "Nice to see you keeping with your brand." Thomas chuckled from deep in his belly as he sipped his Old Fashioned. Anything to keep him at ease. Hell, I purposefully leaned toward him several times just to give him an eyeful. Anything for this man.

We were coming to the end of one of the best meals I'd ever enjoyed when both our phones pinged with a text. Then Thomas's rang.

"It's Banger." He put the phone to his ear. "What's happening?"

I swiped my phone and read the text. Someone had tried to break into Rachel and Isabella's apartment.

Have a Little Faith in Me

Thomas

"Kick with you?" Banger asked.

My gaze swept over her as she read her text. "Yep."

"Need you two to get to my condo ASAP. I'm driving Rachel and her roommate there now." His voice rasped like he was out of breath. "We're shutting this shit down."

I pictured spit flying out of Banger's mouth as he bit out his words. The unexplained tingle that kept dancing along my spine all evening now made sense, except the wrong McKenna had been in danger.

"On our way."

When Kick stepped out of my Camaro, Rachel bolted straight into her arms. "I've got you. Mama's here," Kick murmured softly as she rubbed her daughter's back like she was an infant. Isabella stood to the side until Kick opened an arm and drew her in too.

Banger stalked over to me, reminding me of a blond version of the Hulk. If the women in front of us didn't motivate him, nothing would. I was ready to spit nails and struggling to keep my breathing smooth.

"I want you to tell me this was a college apartment prank, but you wouldn't have brought the girls here over a coincidence."

Banger pointed with his thumb toward his condo. "Inside."

Kick walked the girls into the house after kissing each one on top of her head—a feat for Rachel, given their height differences. That was the thing with my lady. The more the weight of the world pressed on her, the higher she rose to the occasion.

We hadn't even finished celebrating her new remission. Seeing her ease those girls simply by being there pissed me off to no end. Beneath her steely grace, Kick wasn't giving a thought to her own needs.

Banger addressed us as he walked toward his bar. "First off, it could've been worse. The girls handled the situation exactly as they should've. Be proud of them." He raised a glass. "I was pouring us each a tipple when you arrived. Should I add two more?"

Kick did a double take at Banger's use of Scot's slang. Tess was French, but Banger's father had been a notorious Scottish laird of old. After his father's death, my friend traveled the world for a century—a surefire way to stifle someone's original dialect. Like me, he held on to a precious few words connecting him to his roots. He only let them out in safe company.

She shook her head at the offer. "Water would be great though. Thank you."

I squeezed her knee, encouraged to hear her recovery had stayed on her mind. "I'll take whatever you're pouring. Thanks, man."

Everyone stayed quiet until Banger finished playing host. He sat on the end of a large, circular leather sofa filling most of his den. Rachel and Isabella were together in the middle, blindly staring at a muted Seinfeld rerun while Kick and I sat opposite Banger. I stretched my arm across the low back and tried to gather her into me to no avail. She gave me a small smile over her shoulder and shook her head. As cool as she played it, Kick's stiff posture told me she wanted to hurt someone too. I acquiesced by lightly rubbing her back, finding some way to remind her that she wasn't alone in this anymore.

Banger turned off the television and zeroed in on the girls. "Who wants to begin?" Both shook their heads. He sighed. "Fine. Jump in if you need to correct anything." They nodded. "Around eight o'clock this evening, Rachel and Bella were disturbed by a loud pounding on their door."

Kick opened her mouth, but Isabella spoke first. "A neighbor had let them in when he went out."

"Right," Banger continued. "My team found that point on our camera." He took a sip of Scotch. "We're looking for three young men."

"Jonn's friends," Rachel said, her voice hitching on an inhale. She took a long pull of her wine.

"Those geniuses did nothing to hide their identities." Banger pointed in Rachel's direction. "So Rachel gave a solid statement to the police."

"I didn't open the door," she clarified. "I saw them through the peephole, then called Angel Security and the police."

"They kept screaming at us, demanding we open the door… said horrible things to Rachel… threatened to take her to Jonn… other things too," Isabella told us in a faraway voice, her eyes focused on the television like she still watched the comedy in her mind.

"Bottom line… they took off when the sirens grew loud. Rachel and Bella are shaken but physically fine." He leveled the girls with a stern look. "They're staying here for the time being." Banger raised his hand as they both shifted from their trancelike states. "No isn't an acceptable answer."

"You should move back home," Kick said. "Bella can come too."

"Mama—"

Banger smirked at me. It was small, so the women didn't catch it. It took me back to our predawn breakfast a few weeks ago when he told me to cut ties with Kick. I patted her shoulder. If it kept everyone safe to bring all the McKennas under one roof, I'd do it. But I'd take them to the farmhouse. My friend briefly rolled his gaze up to the ceiling.

I shrugged. *Yeah, I'm a goner. So what?* My eyes challenged back.

Banger's plans ended up making more sense. "Ladies… You still have school, and my condo is much closer. Why interrupt your routine more than necessary?" He addressed Kick. "We're just making them more secure. Besides, we don't want Rachel any closer to Jonn Graham."

Kick scrunched her nose. "Hmm. Good point." She finished her water, set the glass on a coaster, and finally settled into me.

"On that note," Banger added, "I'm also putting guards on Rachel and Bella."

Kick and I nodded as the girls exploded from their seats. They spoke over each other, complaining about privacy and inconvenience. Isabella, especially, didn't understand why she needed one.

"*Enough.* Sit down, girls." I jerked when Kick brought out her mom voice. "You know how I fought working with a bodyguard." She looked at me. "Having Mateo around has eased everyone's tension. The mood in the coffeehouse is even more relaxed. Plus there was an incident the other night that I *know* went in my favor because Mateo and Jake were there to back me up."

"But—"

Banger went over to Rachel, crouched in front of her, and grabbed her hands. "Hear me on this… you've done nothing wrong."

"But—"

"Why won't the police do anything?" Isabella burst out. "One of those assholes waved a gun in front of the peephole and threatened to use it!"

The answer pained and frustrated me. I gnashed my teeth at the helpless feeling. It's why I was determined to make sure Kick could hold her own long enough to get away if she was ever attacked again.

Banger's eyes swept from me back to the girls. "Laws suck, little one." He squeezed Rachel's hands. "You've been doxxed." He turned his head toward us and said, "Jonn Graham's behind the online bullying. The proof's in my office."

Kick's body stiffened as she growled low in her throat. "Son of a bitch."

"Agreed." Banger continued speaking to Rachel. "You did everything right, but *no* isn't a word in that little fucker's vocabulary."

Rachel tucked her hair behind her ear, reminding me of her mother. "Maybe I should call him. Talk some sense into him."

"Absolutely not," both Kick and Banger said with equal authority.

My friend softened his voice and added, "Don't let him mess with your head. My people will keep you safe so you can finish the year. We'll snare the bastard before then."

Isabella crossed her arms, making white marks where her fingers clutched her biceps. "I don't know if you're the nicest, most protective guy on earth. Or the most terrifying."

"Good." Banger let the word hang in the air without explanation. His posture tightened as his gaze shifted between the girls.

Isabella flipped her bangs off her forehead. "I still don't understand why *I* need a guard."

"Once the bastards realize Rachel's untouchable, you'd be the easiest way to get to her."

Rachel smiled at the word *untouchable*, and Banger gave her the sweetest grin back. It took me by surprise. Guess he had a weakness in the McKenna family too.

"We don't want to intrude on your privacy though, Rafa." She patted his clasped hands, then laced her fingers in her lap.

I stared at Banger, trying not to show my surprise. Rachel knew about his real name? Tess probably told her about it when she'd visited, considering how quickly the two women had hit it off. *Except Banger didn't flinch or growl when she said it.* Then again, she hadn't called him Rafael.

"No worries." Banger moved to sit at Rachel's free side. "I'm leaving tomorrow, so you ladies won't invade anything."

"And you'll be gone until May? Come on." She rolled her eyes at him.

He rubbed his stubble as he laughed. "I have other places to stay when I'm in town." He spoke to me. "I'll be in Orlando for a few days first."

"Again?"

He went down there about once a quarter, but he'd already been last month. Banger nodded his head stoically, and I knew. I pressed my lips together and tried to express my sympathy without giving anything away.

Banger turned back to Rachel. "The guards assigned to you are good men. You'll have Siobhan at your beck and call as well. You won't miss me."

"Oh…" Rachel finished her wine and stared into the glass.

"I can still check on you when I'm in town, yeah?"

She nodded, then blushed as Banger laughed. "Come on, Bella. Let's get settled." Rachel stood, lacing her finger with Isabella's. "Mama, can you come up before you leave?"

"Sure, sweetheart," Kick said while texting someone.

"Who are you messaging?" I asked.

"Cyndi. I need her to set aside funds for the guards." She turned her head toward Banger. "You're billing the business, right?"

He and I both shook our heads in objection. Then a three-way stare-down ensued, each of us angling to foot the added expenses. I didn't know why Banger wanted to comp it. I was currently covering everything. Or I thought I had been.

He leaned toward us. "Need I remind you? Compounded interest. In case you didn't catch it the first time, it means more money than I can spend."

"We," I pressed.

Kick tapped her chest. "My. Daughter."

Banger made mistake number one and spoke to Kick as softly as he'd just been speaking to Rachel. "You have money, but you don't have our bank accounts. I know things have been tight."

She moved to stand, but I held her to me. "Come on, man." He was right but didn't understand her pride. It wasn't that bad either. Kick did fabulously with her finances, considering.

He raised his hand in surrender. "We'll do a three-way split."

When Kick went upstairs to help the girls settle in, Banger pulled me into his office. The dark, woody space reminded me of the one on the third floor of my house. The air was thick with the scent of old books, thanks to two walls of floor-to-ceiling shelves filled with first editions—and lightly of cigars. I did a double take at the bookcases. They were newly crammed full with volumes from his collection in France. *He'd moved everything out of the vineyard then.* This was the only room in Banger's home that didn't smell like the lemon cleaner his service used. We didn't allow just anybody into our sanctums, which said a lot about him having the girls use the condo as a safe house.

"Did you get through to him yet?"

There was no other him he could mean besides Alaric. "Yep. He gave me a lead for you." My gaze traveled the room as I listened for the sound of feet prematurely padding down the stairs though this wouldn't take long. "The old man's alright. He was pissed but intrigued by Kick." I sighed heavily before dropping my notes onto his desk.

"We need to get to the bottom of this shit."

"Here's his take on both the Oxford team and Edmund's abilities." I pointed to the last bullet point. "Tell me you can get his DNA." The dark Chesterfield behind me beckoned, but I wouldn't get back up if I did. My head was tired of spinning so many damn plates.

Grand-père had said Edmund's descendants were gone, yet Banger had his own special detective skills. He tucked the folder into his bag on the floor. "I have an idea but need to speak with Tess first."

My shoulders dropped as I exhaled a tight breath. I jammed my fingers into my hips. "Can't tell you how much it'll help."

"No need. I see it." Banger handed me a folder in return. I

didn't see him pull it out of the bag. "Kick's good for you, but worry isn't."

"Tell me about it." I perused the papers in my hands—bios of the new bodyguards for Rachel and Isabella.

"These fellas know the girls are together? They won't give them a hard time? It already happened to them on campus and just walking to a damn coffeehouse." I couldn't believe how horrible men had been to them when Kick relayed the events. Then I remembered some of the men I'd known over the years and wasn't surprised in the least.

"They're professionals." Banger folded his arms over his chest and leaned back in his chair, glaring up at me. "Don't act like I started this work yesterday."

"Shit." I hung my head and closed the folder. Part of me worried these men were like that alpha bastard from Kick's book. But this guy was also a security expert. "Can't help being protective." I held out my hand and squeezed it shut. "I hate the worried V Kick gets between her eyebrows. Had her relaxed and laughing all evening at the restaurant. It showed up again as soon as she received that text. She's more scared for Rachel than herself."

"Look at you in daddy mode." Banger teased me, though he kept his wry face.

"Whatever."

"Naw, brother." Banger waved his finger up and down in my direction. "This is a new visual. Told you they were sticky."

"Let it go, man..." My brows lowered. "Or we'll pivot to Rachel calling you Rafa."

22

Everywhere

Thomas

"You have an excellent memory, Professor. Thanks to the state's Marriage Amendment, the rights for unmarried couples do 'suck,' as you say. For hetero couples too."

Dammit. I sat in my office at the farmhouse, speaking with my lawyer. "What should I do, Penn?"

His chuckle mocked me as it came through the line. "Either move or put a ring on it."

"What about the Healthcare Power of Attorney?"

"It'll help, but your lady, in particular, is vulnerable in other ways. A significant number of politicians in our general assembly don't like their neighbors living in sin, sir. I read the articles you mentioned too."

"Can't they just… mind their own business?"

The laugh grew louder. "Not when they have the power. You know how it is."

Unfortunately, I did.

"You've given me a lot to think about. Put a rush on those papers please. Thanks, Penn."

"My pleasure, Professor."

I ended the call and rubbed the back of my neck, trying to loosen it. *What did I want?*

I wanted—no needed—Kick by my side, whether I was right about her genes.

Was it too soon to ask her for more? We had been together officially for a little more than a month. I thought back to the morning. I had stayed up late working with Liam and turned off my alarm while still asleep. Then I found myself buried inside Kick before either of us had fully awakened.

"You sure you don't mind?" I'd asked her.

"Mm-hmm," Kick said in a sexy, sleepy tone. "I don't know why, but when you want, I want. There's no question, only instinct. And trust. It's never been this intense before. Of course, I've been alone a long fecking time."

Her words made me gasp. I'd known exactly what she'd meant. We'd been alone for so long, and yet we'd bonded very fast. After she'd been worried about whether I'd judge her body for what Kick viewed as flaws... I hadn't seen her doubt herself, or me, since. Getting to be the recipient of her ownership of her sexuality was a privilege that left me speechless. In awe. Kick told me she admired the one heroine for the character's growth, but I'd witnessed no one taking their life by the reins like Kick. The defamation campaign against her had always been personal, still she stood up to the ridiculousness, especially with our relationship.

How I desired to be a better man. It was a gift to unwrap her every night and make her smile. Watch her come undone for me alone. I adjusted my pants as I thought back to her giggle afterward and how she sang to me, changing the words to the Beatles' "Norwegian Wood" into "Mmm, morning wood."

I knew what I needed to do.

Before I could take the first step, Banger's voice boomed through my house. "Hey brother! You home?"

"Third floor," I yelled back. "You're back fast."

He sauntered up the last few stairs. "Private jet," he answered, beelining for the bar on the far wall. He surprised me by bending down to the little fridge and grabbing a water instead of pouring himself a whiskey.

He plopped into the corner chair, his face drawn, contemplative.

"The other night…," I started, "sounded like you're losing another girl."

Banger twisted the top off and chugged half the bottle. "She was in hospice."

"Weren't you there last month? Seems quick."

He set his ankle on his knee, like the relaxed posture meant he wasn't hurting. "It was nice to comfort her through it, yeah? Everyone she's ever had passed first. Was an honor to be there for her."

"Wow."

Even a man like Banger, who put solitude before emotions, needed connection every so often. He made peace with the fact he would always outlive his special companions centuries ago, like all the Felidae did. Usually he gave them a few months, occasionally a year, then he'd disappear.

Lately, he'd find one here or there, in her old age, thanks to the population living longer and better. The way memory played with their advanced minds, the former girlfriends often recognized him since Banger's features stayed the same as when they'd been together. He found a certain peace in being able to say goodbye in his own way. My hard-as-nails best friend had a soft center, though I'd never tell.

"I'm sorry, man."

Banger swiped his hand across his body. "Don't care if I sound like a heartless bastard in this. She had a beautiful life, brother. A lot of love and living. In my book, that's cause for gratitude, not sorrow. I just brought her some comfort at the end."

While stewing in the meaning of his words, Banger stood and handed me a folder. "Tess turned out to be a gold mine for Edmund's DNA samples."

I slid out the paperwork detailing his profile. I couldn't wait to run it against Kick's after hours. Gautam would have no problem putting in the extra time. He loved this stuff too. Plus he'd signed a nondisclosure agreement. After the near debacle with Presley, we had them all updated. Gautam would swoon over these profiles. In fact, it wouldn't hurt to also run it against my cache of current Felidae members to study how much had changed since Edmund's time. I jotted down a quick note to the effect.

"How'd Tess manage it?"

Banger pulled a chair closer to me and sat. He ran a hand over his cropped hair. "He'd been like a father to her, yeah? A thousand times better than the trash who raised her."

I nodded along since I knew this.

"Plus she loves her memories. Tess had hats, gloves, a hairbrush, even a razor of Edmund's, for Pete's sake. She kept envelopes from letters he'd written to her." He groaned and slumped in the chair. "She loved playing spy for me. Even paid off the lab like I told her to. Now I think she misses us again. Thanks for that."

"Stop it. It was your suggestion. You know she's searching for a purpose. Maybe she's trying to fit into your life. Better late than never."

Banger clicked his tongue. "For how long?"

"As long as she can handle it, I guess," I answered with a shrug. It was harsh but true. No sense sprinkling sugar on it when Banger would've called me on the bullshit.

"Precisely." Banger hated how Tess had been an inconsistent presence. In fact, this was one of the rare times she'd come through for her son when he'd asked for a favor. It usually went the other way around.

I leveled him with a sly smirk. "You know, she could stay with the girls."

He pointed at me, grinning. "Now there's some good news."

23

Dreams

Kick

FEBRUARY FLEW BY. THERE'S NO OTHER WAY TO PUT IT, OTHER THAN life became sort of normal. Big Jonn Graham came through with his article in the town paper. The opinion pieces and social media slander stopped. Business picked up. More high school kids studied at the Perked Cup in the afternoons.

More importantly, putting guards on Rachel and Isabella relieved the pressure on them and me. I felt terrible for Bella taking on more than most would for a budding relationship, but she handled it like a champ. The girls also loved playing house in Banger's condo. It might have been the consummate bachelor pad, but it also oozed luxury and came with a cleaning service.

I hadn't seen or heard from Banger since the night he'd installed my daughter in his home, but I could tell Thomas spoke with him regularly. However, my man had been spending many late nights working in his lab. When we did find precious time together, we didn't talk about his friend or whether he'd made progress. I figured if Banger wanted me to know something, he'd make sure Thomas passed it on.

As March approached, I planned a romantic surprise for Thomas. We'd made our commitment to each other two months ago, but it seemed like much longer. I blamed some of that on how crazy life had been. Mostly, I think it came down to how well we clicked once we let ourselves get over our baggage.

The open-mic night would be the perfect time to do something romantic for Thomas. Liam's band planned a short set at the end. The kids were graciously going to let me jump on stage and sing one of my favorite songs to Thomas.

A smile burst across my face as I double-checked every corner of the coffeehouse. It looked perfect. Setup had been a breeze. The crew all showed and pitched in. In fact, I'd been waiting for the other shoe to drop, as it usually did. I guessed life could go your way sometimes.

There was one small snafu. Jacklyn, one of Liam's best friends and a bandmate, arrived late, making it hard for Metaphorical Chemistry to get in a warm-up. Her deep frown and the way she kept biting her lip were familiar for the girl I'd known since she'd been four. For most of their lives, Lee and Jax had been each other's person. After Shane died, I learned her father had allowed their mixed-gender friendship because of my late husband. Alton Moore enjoyed being able to rub elbows with a football Hall of Fame player. Ever the patient celebrity, Shane accommodated the man as much as he could. Plus our whole family adored Jax.

In Alton's eyes, Liam became a bad influence overnight when Shane died and our family was a single-parent household. Over the years, I'd bent over backward to appease the Moores, but nothing helped. Then my father opened a smoke shop with Hugh. I supposed rumors about my family's morals were floating around all the way back then.

"What's the matter, sweetie?" My instincts had me moving out from behind the counter to fix what I presumed had been another fight with her parents over the band.

Liam intercepted her before I could round the snack display, and I made myself stop. Jacklyn would turn eighteen in the spring, and Lee already was. They needed room to sort this out on their own.

After five minutes of animated conversation near the walk-in cooler, he stormed over to me anyway, his face beet red.

"What happened?" I asked.

Liam did his best to keep his voice down and ended up growling in my ear. "Mrs. Moore saw the sheet music for our opening song. She forbids Jax from singing it."

I ran through the song list in my head. "She has a problem with 'Keep on Loving You'?" If anyone should appreciate that song, it was her, considering how many times she took back her philandering husband.

Liam scoffed. "It's because we're doing the arrangement by Cigarettes After Sex. Their name was at the top of the note sheet."

"JaysusMaryandJoseph." I lifted my eyes up to the ceiling. "When will that woman learn there's never been a way to make someone sin-proof?"

"Sounded like she's afraid of Mr. Moore finding out." He threw his hands in the air. Liam knew better than to run them through his hair. It turned into a wild, fuzzy mop when he did, thanks to inheriting my curls. "At first we planned to do 'Apologize.' You remember the arrangement you showed me by Kacey Musgraves?"

I nodded. "And…"

"Mr. Moore said it's never too late to apologize. Our harmony was big too."

"Why am I not surprised?" I muttered. I'd tried my best not to speak badly of the Moores. The couple seemed perfectly qualified to dig their own graves where the kids were concerned. This night, I neared my breaking point with their ways.

"I don't know what to do now. Jax is depressed, and we don't have an extensive list for her."

I adjusted my glasses and leaned closer. "Actually depressed? Or is this another of your Liam-isms? Because if she needs to talk with someone—"

Liam made to stick his hands in his hair, but I tapped them away. The kid was truly upset. "She's fine, fam."

To be extra certain, I said, "Like *big* fine?"

He rolled his eyes. "Sure." Then he cracked a smile while shaking his head.

I snapped my fingers. "I know, why don't you do 'Maybe I'm Amazed'? She sounded just like Jem when I heard you practice. It was beautiful."

"Well… I don't know." He bobbed his head once in decision and pecked my cheek before I could argue my case. "Thanks. We got it."

"Oh, okay." I forced a quick hug on him. I couldn't help it. It was one of those moments of parental pride where you pause and notice your kid's growing up. "When you get home, print out the REO Speedwagon arrangement—or at least cut and paste it. They're just notes for Pete's sake."

He laughed back. "No kidding. You still have the third song?"

"Yup. Can't wait."

"Me either." He gave me a cheesy grin, an echo of his little-boy self, then bounded off to confer with the band.

As I prepped a tray of drinks for Thomas to take to the band, my friend—and go-to for any construction needs—Charley Rodriguez stepped up to the counter. "You made it." This would be her first time hearing Metaphorical Chemistry. "Give me a minute to finish, and I'll hug you."

"I've got this," Thomas said in his sexy baritone, taking the last cup from my hand. "Go catch up. Good to see you, Charley." He slapped me on my ass, and I gave him some side-eye, along with a smirk. Then I reached across the bar to hug Charley.

"Glad you could get away. I've missed you."

"Yeah," she sighed. "Work's been centered on Durham, thanks to the growth in restaurants. Two extensive projects out this way will start in the spring. Hopefully I'll be able to stop by more often."

"Your usual?"

Her head shook a crisp no. "Decaf, hon. I'm still wired from the day."

"Sure thing." I made her drink and set it on the counter. "I can tell your team's been jumping. Three different groups have come by since the New Year to see your handiwork in person."

Charley scrunched her face. "I hope you don't mind."

"Not at all. They obviously like seeing two different projects in the same shopping center." After she'd done a fantastic job on the Perked Cup, my dad and Hugh had hired Charley to remodel the smoke shop.

She let out an exhale of relief. "Probably. Thanks anyway."

"Anytime. Are you staying long?"

"Not sure. Like I said, it was a long day."

Deana cut off our conversation when she stepped on stage and introduced the first act. I don't know why she'd insisted on coming back for this open-mic night, but she had. Then she wanted to emcee the thing and reminded me how I promised to delegate responsibilities. Her version of an "offer I couldn't refuse," I suppose.

The night's sign-up sheet was short, so it didn't take long before it was time for Metaphorical Chemistry to play. Their first two songs were fantastic. They improved every time they played. Jax was featured in the first song. Then she and Liam performed an original duet for the second. My heart pounded when Lee called me up for the third song.

"You're singing?" Thomas asked. He stood with me at the counter, talking to Charley and listening to Liam's band.

"Surprise! It's kind of a present to mark two months together."

"Lucky me." He kissed me hard for luck and patted my ass again. "Break a leg, baby."

I sang "Dreams" by the Cranberries. The only one surprised was Thomas. I'd been listening to the song at least once a day since we'd decided to be more. It even became an earworm for Liam, who practiced it to appease me. To me, it summed up how my heart had changed since meeting Thomas.

After the song, I gave hugs around the band for letting me crash their gig. The kids were improving so quickly my heart swelled with pride for each of them. Thomas greeted me at the bottom of the stage step. He kissed me on the cheek, then hopped up on the platform himself.

"Where are you going?" I'd expected more emotion after pouring my heart out in a song.

The jerk winked at me. "I have a surprise back."

"You're not… Oh good Lord." It took restraint not to make the sign of the cross. Thomas was amazing at many, many things, but his beautiful speaking voice disappeared when he tried to sing. The man couldn't carry a tune in a basket. Shaking my head as I backed up, I quipped, "Please tell me you're using Autotune."

"Faith, lady." Thomas put his hands to his heart, feigning offense. Then he high-fived the band while Liam introduced their new guest. My eyes watered when Lee introduced him as his new fam.

Jacklyn opened the song with a perfect Jamaican accent. Though she'd occasionally say things with her grandmother's inflections, it took me by surprise. It was good to see her enjoy herself after starting the night frustrated. I should've recognized the song immediately. We played it in the café enough. Shock was my only defense.

Then Thomas broke out in a spirited—if not-quite-on-key—rendition of "Say Hey (I Love You)." The music flowed through me more than it had when I sang my song. I stayed up front, dancing for my man as he spoke-sang about his love for me. His handsome face kept blurring, and it had nothing to do with my glasses. It was a fearless declaration of his love for me and the life we were making. He knew exactly what would get me.

His hand suddenly took up my field of vision. I put mine into it, and Thomas pulled me up on stage with him. I let loose and shook my arse for him like a go-go dancer. A few taps on my shoulder and his eyebrow lifted as he sang. I remembered the song was essentially a duet. The stinker wanted me to join in. Jax fed me the first couple of words, clearing my head. Then she shoved her phone in my hand, open to an app with the words and music. My part was a mix of call and echo. We shared the mic, dancing and pseudo-singing like a funky reggae version of Sonny and Cher but with height and curls.

Under the lights, the audience fell away, and we were just jamming with the band. Thomas spun me into a dip and planted a deep kiss on my mouth. A dull roar filled my ears, but the audience didn't become a reality until I heard, "Eww gross! Kissing is yucky!" I knew that voice anywhere, except the last time he'd said those words it was several octaves higher.

Thomas stood me up, and my eyes found Dylan. He'd brought his poker crowd with him. In fact, the place was now packed to standing-room only. My first thought went to fire codes, but it was a moment to celebrate love. Thomas and I had given each other the same surprise. How cool was that? Most of the audience would probably grab a drink and take off in a few minutes anyway.

I turned around and found that the band had rearranged itself around two chairs in the middle of the stage. Each chair had a low mic stand. Thomas took one and waved me over to sit in the other. He grabbed his guitar, and I couldn't believe he'd snuck that in too. Seriously. I was supposed to be the woman who noticed everything.

I sat as Thomas strummed the opening chords to the song he played for me over New Year's and many times since. It was the acoustic version of "Maybe I'm Amazed." So this was why Liam looked at me funny when I suggested it. I waited for him and Jax to start after Thomas's intro, but no one did. After swiveling my head around, I saw the whole band had left the stage. It was just Thomas, me, and his guitar. He stopped and gave me one of his smoldering eyebrow raises.

I pointed to my chest. "Me?"

He nodded.

"Like Jem?" I mouthed.

He nodded again, with a little, impatient smirk. He dramatically restarted the song. His face told the audience I needed to get with the program. The guests up front laughed.

I heard an encouraging, feminine "You've got this, Mama" from the back.

Was Rachel here?

I searched for her but couldn't see past the first tables with the lights fixed on us. This time I caught my cue and started the song. It meant a lot when we'd discovered we both loved this version over that weekend. Since then so much had happened, it was easy to forget how romantic it all had been.

Like before, I sang the song as if it was written for a female. So, when I got the part where I would replace *man* with *girl*, Thomas stopped and shook his head. It was my turn for the eyebrow raise, trying to communicate my question telepathically. He huffed and pointed to himself. *Oh.* He didn't want his voice to flatten the song, but he wanted me to understand the song was coming from him. I nodded my understanding, and he resumed.

A single tear teetered on the edge of my lower lid as the words filled me like they truly were the words of his heart, telling me how much it meant for him to find me after being alone for so long. I knew what he meant.

The interruption.

The angst.

The fear.

The awe.

Joy.

As soon as he finished, Thomas quickly returned the guitar to its stand and dropped to one knee in front of me. The gasp from the crowd filled my ears before I registered what he was doing. Deana let out a shriek, but I couldn't see her. It was like a weird dream where I could hear my loved ones but I could only see Thomas.

He took my hand to bring my focus back to him. Thomas had a velvet box in his free hand.

I leaned into him, out of range of the mic I'd sung into, my performance smile plastered on my face. "What the hell are you doing?"

"What the hell does it look like I'm doing?" he answered, his wide grin a challenge to my dumb question.

"Something I thought you didn't want," I snipped back through a frozen smile, my eyes wide. The last thing I wanted to do was to embarrass him before the crowd.

"Do you trust me?"

"What?"

"Answer the question. Do you trust me?"

"With every fiber of me."

"Then trust me now."

"Louder!" A discombobulated voice cried out.

"Yeah, we can't hear!"

"The crowd's getting restless," I said while doing my best impersonation of a ventriloquist.

"Then dial back the sarcasm and listen."

I shimmied my shoulders and settled into the chair to give Thomas my attention. The struggle was real. A proposal was the last thing I expected from him, given we'd already said we'd take things one day at a time. How could I not give him my full attention, though, when his navy eyes filled with emotion? His cheek twitched slightly from nerves.

This man, in a fitted, overdyed navy button-down and ass-hugging black denim jeans. This man with his statuesque face and body. This man who could do anything with competence—he'd even won over the crowd with his awful singing voice because it was all heart. This man had become my world. Thomas made it okay for me to let go of my baby birds.

And he loved me.

"Kathleen McKenna, in the briefest of time, you've become my heart and soul."

A collective "Awe" filled the room.

"The afternoon at the oak tree, I vowed to be your Atlas, and you promised to be my home."

I opened my mouth to tell Thomas I remembered it all, which was why this seemed so redundant. His mastery of a professor-ly glare reared its head. I clamped my jaw shut, put the smile back on and waited for him to continue.

"You're already my wife in my heart. You've done that for me and much more these past weeks. Nothing about our pledge has lessened. It's only grown." He looked up at the ceiling, a shaky breath filling his lungs. "You told me once you needed an extraordinary, transforming love. My lady, you have transformed me. You're *my* extraordinary. Trust me, Kick, and take this last leap with me. Let's make our day-to-day official. Let's take it all the way."

"You really want this?" I asked, bending to his ear again.

"I do."

What do you say when the man of your dreams just told you he remembers the deepest desires of your soul, and he treasures them? You give him whatever he wants. A peace swept through me, and I knew if Thomas thought it was best, I could trust it.

"Can we keep it a small ceremony?"

"Anything for you."

My frozen grin became real and spread across my face. "Yes, Thomas. I've pledged myself to you already, why not make it official? Now show me this ring."

The crowd roared, and Thomas flipped the top on the ring box. He'd been so nervous he'd forgotten to open it.

"Ho…ly shit!" I bellowed at first sight of the work of art. The cheers turned to laughter. Thomas placed the most beautiful symbol of our commitment on my finger. The word *ring* didn't do it justice.

A rose-gold setting was sculpted into tiny vines circling my finger. At the top, a purple stone sat in what looked like a bed of leaves. Smaller leaves peaked around the vines at the sides, without poking into my skin. Sapphires were set in the center vine, in varying shades of blue. I stared at it as Thomas gently took my hand and slid the ring on my finger. The huge gem shifted color as I moved my hand. Something about it seemed familiar, like it was me in ring form or his vision of me. Then it hit me… it was us.

I gasped. "It's our—"

He leaned toward my ear and said "Energy. Yes, baby. It's my forever attraction to you, wrapping myself around you as you glow."

At a loss for words, I cradled his jaw in my hands. I pulled him in for a kiss. He tasted faintly of cigar, making me wonder if he'd needed it earlier to settle his nerves. This had been a ballsy risk, considering I'd said I was done with the marriage label.

Our kiss deepened into one so big, so hard it was a miracle our auras didn't release. Boy, did it try. It prickled until we pulled away before we had serious explaining to do. Thomas's hands fell to the seat on either side of my thighs, his forehead landing on mine, as he laughed. Take that back, he roared with joy. Then came more cheers, whistles, and catcalls from the crowd, our extended family. Then he stood and lifted me up and off my feet in a bear hug.

"Office. Now," Thomas growled. He grabbed my hand and dashed us off the stage.

24

The Nearness of You

Thomas

I'D DONE THE RIGHT THING. A PRESSURE VALVE THAT HAD BEGUN building in me over Kick's safety was released when she accepted my proposal. It turned out I wasn't the modern man I thought I was. I needed Kick to be my legal kin, and it had to happen before I found the results of her DNA analysis. For my sake more than hers. If I had to take care of her fragile, aging body the way Banger occasionally did for his former girlfriends, I'd do it with joy. It would be an honor.

We were swarmed by the crowd in the Perked Cup, small as it was. It took ten minutes to make our way from the stage to the counter to get drinks. Loved ones and strangers alike—who came for the Open Mic Night—stood in a reception line to give us hugs and congratulations.

When an opening to the back hall was made, I took advantage, pulling my new fiancée with me. Banger's profile caught my eye as he spoke to Deana and her husband. Damn him for arriving so late he almost missed it. Despite his recent travels, he'd promised to be here for the proposal. Securing his support in all of this had meant more than I could express.

The part I hadn't considered? The downside to a public proposal? The part that was drastically different from the first time we promised to be together?

I didn't factor in how horny I'd be.

We were real, not a fling or a hidden affair.

Real.

Kick.

My woman.

She wore my fucking ring. I needed to celebrate inside her. I had to unwrap her, tear away her pretty, satin-and-lace bra—knowing she'd fuss at the waste—and make her orgasm all night. I hoped the office cameras were off. I opened the door, spun us around, and lifted her up against the wall. The slit to her skirt fell away for me, rising to her waist, letting me rub against the satin of her underwear. My hand holding her steady touched the wetness in the material, causing a growl of desire from us both.

Kick batted at my hands, but her eyes held no anger, only teasing. "I should stop you. Make you suffer." She panted.

"Me? For what? Outside of blowing your mind with a fabulous proposal?" I asked between kisses I peppered down her neck.

"You stole my thunder. I poured my heart out in song, and you upstaged me." Her writhing in my hands told me I wasn't in trouble. Yet I felt bad. *A little.*

I smiled against her neck. "The ring makes up for it, doesn't it?"

She gasped as my fingers found her sweet spot, letting me know I was right.

My free hand sought the bow of her sweater. I needed more arms, dammit. With my present unwrapped, I kissed Kick down her chest. My free hand reached around to her bra hooks. There were too many. Damn, these long-line things.

"I loved your song," I said as I worked the tormenting clasps. "Especially the banshee notes in the middle. Sounded beautiful. You should do it again, in fact. Encourage my efforts."

She let go of my shoulder to slap it, both mischief and lust filling her woodland eyes. "Nitwit."

Giving up on the hooks, I lifted a breast from its cup. My lips ached to suckle it, but I paused and teased. "Are you saying you didn't like my surprise? Do we need to talk more?"

Kick nearly wiggled out of my hands from her writhing. I pressed my hips and thighs into her, making sure she didn't slip. Her groan grew louder with the friction. "You know you won the night. Shut up and kiss me."

My primal brain became a caveman who needed to conquer. "Where?"

"Ahem-mm." The clearing of Banger's throat jolted me back to reality. I righted Kick and shielded her body from our intruder.

"What the hell, man?" I growled. "You almost caught us *in flagrante*."

"You were *in flagrante*, my dear," a familiar feminine voice said from behind Banger. I caught the smile in her inflection. "Fortunately, you were not *delicto*. Not yet." Tess stepped out from around her son, her arms wide. "Congratulations, kids."

"We knocked." Banger had the decency to appear repentant as he rubbed his jaw. "Guess you didn't hear it."

"Tess," I said, more in shock than greeting. Kick's frantic movements to turn and fix herself while squeaking at being caught snapped me out of my stupor. I stepped toward our visitors and hugged Tess, keeping my body between our company and my fiancée. "Heard you were thinking about visiting again."

"Surprise." Banger spread his hands wide like it answered everything. Considering he had Tess with him, it did.

"Tess texted me just before she boarded the plane. We came straight from the airport."

"Hel-lo-o." Tess flicked her hand. "Stop talking about me as if I'm not in the room. You boys know it's a pet peeve." Her French accent on that last word made it sound like *piv*. Like a pin bursting my pent-up energy, I snickered. Then I bent over and dissolved into an uncontrollable fit as my emotions crashed in the ridiculousness of the moment.

Banger and Tess stared at me like I was an unruly child. Kick's hand ran down my back, soothing the last of my nerves as the laughter settled down. I threw my arm around her, pulled her in, and kissed her temple.

She looked up at me, blinking. "Did you get it all out, cowboy?"

I nodded, not trusting myself to speak yet.

"Cowboy?" Tess asked. A gleam in her eye said *aren't you two cute* as she studied us.

I grunted as Kick scoffed and stepped toward them. She gave Tess a warm hug, saying, "A lot's happened since we met."

"So I've heard." Tess kissed Kick's cheeks in greeting, then held her at arm's length, her eyes traveling over every inch like a new mother making sure their newborn was healthy. "Rafa tells me you're one of us."

"The fuck, Tess?" Banger rubbed the top of his head. "I told you—"

"Thomas is running tests. I know." She tilted her head and smiled. "He's right."

Tess hugged Kick again and whispered something in her ear that elicited a smile.

Since the celebration time with my lady had been crashed, I turned on the desk lamp. We needed more light than the streetlight shining in through the windows could supply.

"So everyone is telling everyone everything." Tess glanced over her shoulder at her son. "How efficient," she added with a devious smile in place.

"The secrets need to stop," Banger said, his words tinged with a defensive tone.

I moved to shut the door and almost bumped into Charley.

"Sorry, guys. I've been waiting out front with Deana, but she thought it would be alright since you weren't alone." Charley turned to Kick, who had crossed the space to greet her. "I have to leave. Early morning and all."

"Absolutely. Thanks so much for coming," Kick said while giving Charley a hug. She laughed and pulled back. "Who knew it would be so exciting?"

As Charley laughed in agreement, Tess stepped from Banger's shadow and made one of her distinctive French sounds.

"Teresa?" Charley's face twisted with confusion. "Is that you?"

Tess paled as she breathed, "Carlotta?" Her eyes widened like she'd seen a ghost.

These women knew each other? The tension in Kick's office thickened like an epoxy had filled the space. Tess and Charley practically vibrated with emotion.

"It's Charley now." Kick's friend's demeanor shifted before our eyes. The warm smile she'd given us transformed into the cold steel of the construction worker I'd first met. Now I wondered if there were other reasons she possessed this ability.

Tess's delicate, charming manner crumbled before my eyes. "But of course," she stammered. "I-I didn't know…" Her gaze darted around the room as if trying to figure out where Charley fit in.

We all ended up staring at Banger.

I cleared my throat. "You mentioned investigating…" I tipped my head toward Charley.

He moved to Tess and put his arm around her shoulders, causing me to do a double take. "Yeah. I uh… wanted to speak with Tess first."

Shit. My eyes couldn't stop shifting between the two women. They were in pain. Old pain… which would mean Charley…

"You know each other?" Kick put her arm around her friend.

"We *used* to," Charley said. An awkward hush fell across the room. The two women shifted like they wanted to bolt.

Kick being Kick went into fix-it mode. Her face brightened with the smile she gave a customer on a bad day. "That's wonderful!"

Charley must have noticed it. She spoke to Tess. "I didn't mean to intrude. I-I just wanted to give my congratulations. I-it was a… lovely night."

Kick gave her a tight embrace. "It means the world you were here for us." She glanced over her shoulder and frowned at the room before turning back. "Let's talk soon, okay?"

Charley nodded. "Alright, my friend." She waved at me and dipped her chin to Banger. "Gentlemen. Teresa. Good night."

She left the office, then we heard the thump of the back door closing.

"Whoa." Kick's eyes moved from Banger to me like she didn't know where to begin. Not sure about him, but I couldn't take my thoughts from the implications for Charley.

I kept going back to our conversation over Thanksgiving dinner. She and her brother had been born in New Mexico. When though? Her gray eyes… just like… I shook my head, forcing the thought away. I'd think about it another time. Soon.

Kick crouched in front of Tess, who had dropped into a club chair. "Are you okay?"

Tess's hand shook as her fingers covered her mouth. "Fine, my dear. Just give me a minute, yes." She giggled in a way that reminded me of my earlier hysterics. "There goes the reason I'm an official yogini."

The pain in her voice sparked me out of my selfish state. Tess needed us. I squatted down by Kick while Banger took the other chair.

His fingers dug into his forehead. "Sorry, Tess. If I'd known she'd be here, I'd have told you Charley lives here now."

"Carlotta," Tess snapped back.

Banger nodded once, showing an unusual patience for Tess. "I thought you deserved to hear it in person, but…" He grunted with derision. "We've been busy."

Tess waved him off, her brows pinched like she was in physical pain.

"She looked familiar," Banger muttered. He rubbed his knee as it bounced. *The son who felt he had once again let down his fragile mother.* "Her background search didn't add up. Dug into it personally. Then I saw the photo of her in your room when you were out of town."

"Well, you don't forget a face, Rafael. Do you? You also won't let a puzzle go until you solve it." Tess scoffed. "You never asked about that photo either."

Banger flinched like he'd been punched. I didn't know whether to defend him or let him take it. Moments like this reminded me how new I still was to the family.

"Maybe Kick and I should go," I offered, attempting to defuse the tension.

Tess put her hand on my shoulder. "Stay please." She stared straight at Banger. "I feel the need to speak now."

"Of course." I moved to lean against the desk and pulled Kick in front of me, wanting to support and be supported by her. This felt like some deep shit, but maybe it was what Banger and Tess needed to break through the walls they'd erected.

"Rafael and I were in one of our distant times when I was with Carlotta… pardon, Charley." She growled, her eyes spiked with anger as she stared at her son. "You were off earning your *disgusting* name."

The misunderstanding between them didn't need rehashing on top of all this. "You two were… friends?" I jumped in to keep the conversation from rocketing down its usual dark tunnel.

Tess tipped her head back at me, her brow drawn in disappointment. "Foolishness doesn't become you, Thomas. Would I react thus if we were just acquaintances? It's been decades since I've seen Charley. Still, no one compares." A tear slid down her cheek as she added softly, "She was the love of my life, and the Felidae put a stop to us." Her hands shook more violently. "I chose their security over her."

So that's why she'd been adamant about me pursuing Kick. I grabbed Tess's hand and squeezed. "I'm so sorry."

"Hang on," Kick interjected. "Does that mean Charley is—"

"A lesbian? *Oui*—"

Kick waved off Tess's words. "That I knew. I mean she's—"

"Like us?" Tess answered again. "Also yes. Carlotta's younger than the boys here, but much older than she appears."

"You were together in Spain, weren't you?" Banger asked.

"Very good, Rafa. Yes. She and her brother… we fought against Franco. We thought we'd get a chance to do something big with our useless lives." Tess released a sarcastic laugh full of self-disdain and regret.

I turned to Kick. "Did Charley mention her brother's name at Thanksgiving?"

Tess answered instead, a faraway expression on her face. "Teodoro. Theo."

Fuck. I looked to the heavens and muttered, "You old bastard." Then I squeezed the back of my neck to relieve the pain. What my uncle had said to me in my dream… *Your work… your cousins can help.*

"What's wrong, cowboy?" Kick ran her hand up and down my arm, melding herself closer to me.

I swallowed, blinked, tamped down my temper before I spoke. "I think they're my uncle's children."

25

Nuttin' But Love

Kick

I slid onto a stool next to Cyndi. "Hey chica. What brings you in at this hour?" Afternoon visits from her were highly unusual during tax time.

Cyndi tossed me some side-eye. "Are you some kind of Vegas boss now, monitoring your empire from the back?"

"Jake said you'd come in." Then I checked the monitors in my office. Her slumped posture worried me. From the tone of Cyndi's voice, I had reason to worry. I wrapped an arm around her shoulders. "Something wrong?"

"Aside from exhaustion and needing a pick-me-up?" She took a drink of her latte. "I'd bug you about being the caffeine police, but we just know each other too well, don't we?"

"We do. You go for cola in the afternoon, which means you came by for a dose of 'Kicky,' so spill."

"Fine." Cyndi put her drink down, her shoulders drooping. "The cop didn't work out."

"Oh, honey, I'm sorry." I gave her a squeeze. "I thought you wanted him to be a quick fling anyway. I didn't know you'd hoped for more."

She shrugged. "Maybe it's you too." Cyndi pointed at my engagement ring. "I'm still wandering around in the dating thrift store, and you hit pay dirt the first time you go shopping."

"Thrift store?" I raised an eyebrow. *Cyndi abhorred thrifting.* Jake caught my attention and pointed at the tea carafe, silently asking me if I wanted some. Thankfully, he knew I took it iced and unsweet with lemon. I nodded, thanking him when he brought it over.

He slid the iced goodness to me. "No problem."

"Dating over forty is like trying to find the least damaged merchandise at a thrift store." Cyndi sighed.

"Oh." *Oh.* During all the times Cyndi had bugged me about getting back into the dating game, her analogy had been my biggest fear. I had been terrified of digging through the options, trying to find someone normal without any more baggage than I had myself. I hated finding out that was her reality. I gently turned her chin to me. "Yet you came here anyway. You want me to tell you how badass you are? Because it's true."

Cyndi lifted a shoulder and smirked. "Maybe I just wanted to stare at Jake's butt for a while."

There's my bestie. Not that I always appreciated her antics. In this case, it beat seeing her so down.

Jake glanced our way and shook his head.

I grimaced. Jake received a fair share of comments on his looks at the café, just like the girls and I did. I'd never be comfortable with it though. "Don't ogle my staff, Cyn. You know they're family."

She cocked a brow at me. "There's *no* scenario where that man will be like a godson to me."

"Fine." I rolled my eyes. "Just do it in silence." I could tell she was deflecting anyway. "Want to tell me what happened with the cop? I didn't even get to meet him."

Cyndi waved off my words. "Consider yourself lucky." She drummed her fingernails on her coffee cup, considering. "Ever meet someone who's built like a god, then you have time alone and find out that when he's turned on he kind of brays like a donkey?"

"So you didn't make it past dinner?" I gave her a sympathy pout and patted her arm.

"Oh no." Cyndi took another sip. "I wasn't wasting *that* body. It's just… I ended up semipolitely asking him to shut the hell up in the middle of sexytime."

I had taken a sip from my iced tea, laughed at her words, and began choking. It was worth it to see her amusement. "That would" —I tapped on my chest a few more times—"suck." I hoped a subject change would settle my lungs. "How's work going?" She always had terrific stories.

"Busy." She dropped her head in her hand.

While pointing at her, I circled my finger. "I figured, given your roots situation. I can't remember the last time they were this deep." She hadn't used hair makeup either. Man, the dating situation really had her bummed. "Wait… is your stylist sick again?" I rubbed her arm. "Shoot, Cyn."

She shook her head. "It's nothing like that, thank gawd." She sat a little taller and shimmied. "I'm growing them out on purpose. A couple more months and I'll get a major transformation."

I fought like hell to keep from choking at another surprise and slid the glass of tea away. "What do you mean? You're like… going silver? Before fifty? *You?*"

She slapped the counter. "Damn straight, chica. I've had it with the patriarchy." She played with her front part a bit, moving pieces to the side. "See how white the front is? I think I'll like the contrast with the dark in the back." She dipped her head so I could see the roots on top. "It goes all the way down."

I rolled my eyes again. "Do you know how much shorter you are than me? I always see the top of your head."

"True." She sat up straight and shrugged.

"Doesn't it take years to grow?" My bestie wasn't the patient type. Not anymore.

Cyndi brought her hands together and tapped her fingers like she had a diabolical plan. "That's the best part. My stylist has trained under this master stylist who taught her how to use the new growth to blend it into the old color. The samples are gorgeous." She pulled up photos from her phone and slid it over to me.

"Wow." I scrolled through a half dozen pictures. None of the women seemed dowdy. Or old. "It's like the opposite of covering your roots. They're a feature."

"I know. Can't wait."

As I kept scrolling, I gasped at how much the women sparkled. One photo had LIFE GOALS written across the bottom of it. The silver-haired model stood in a spring forest, dressed like a goddess, her still-toned arms firmly planted on her hips.

I pulled my hair over my shoulder. "Life goals for sure."

"No kidding. Why can't we be silver foxes too?" Cyndi asked. She had a point. I loved the idea of aging like this... proudly.

Plus Cyndi's mood had lifted, so I asked, "What does this have to do with the patriarchy?"

"Have you ever noticed how men our age and older get rude when you have an inch or more of roots showing?"

I scratched at my head, probably from all this talk of root growth. "You know, my curls kind of hide them. I'd have to wait as long as you have for them to show." I lifted the front of my hair. "It's just a little right in front." Come to think of it, I should have had my touch-up appointment already. *Maybe the remission brought some color back.*

"Trust me." Cyndi finished her latte and slid the cup to back of the counter. "It's all about fuckability. For so many of these overaged boys, as soon as they see your sparkle hairs, their faces shift from flirty to asshole mode. As if I'd been trying to trick them into thinking I was as fresh as Rachel." She shuddered, then tucked part of her still-gorgeously-sleek bob behind her ear. As if *I'd* ever fuck *them*." Even with the long, silver roots, I considered her exotic and stunning. I could see her vision in my mind. She would look like that model in the forest.

"Anyway," Cyn continued, "those misogynists can suck it with their rudeness. Of course, it helps that I work for myself. No boss can tell me what to do. And if a client doesn't like it, they can find someone else."

I scrunched my face. "Are you saying—"

She nodded, "I have a friend who was given an ultimatum—dye her hair again or quit. Her much older boss didn't want to have to endure an 'old bitty' all day."

"Isn't that illegal?"

Cyndi shrugged. "Does it matter? She didn't have the money for a lawsuit. Besides, this was a few years back, and her boss was from the *Mad Men* generation. Hell, it took her six months of threats to get the man to stop slapping her ass. They got away with that shit when they were young, and the women bought into it because... bills."

I slid my tea toward me and took a long pull through the straw. It seemed safe to do so again. "They were gaslit."

"Whatever." She waved me off again. "Just saying we don't have to take that shit anymore. Especially not from some wrinkled-in-his-own-right stranger at the hardware store. If I can go there for parts to fix my own sink, I can wear my hair however I freaking choose."

I smiled at her righteousness. "You can hire a plumber and still decide how you want to appear before the world."

She nodded her head briskly. "Damn straight."

Oh, how I wished Deana were here. She'd get a laugh out of all this. I didn't know how she felt about color, but Dee supported the natural hair movement when it came to curls and texture. I bet she'd enthusiastically back Cyndi.

Cyn leaned in for a hug. "Thanks for the ear, chica."

We kissed each other's cheek. "Anytime. You want something to go?"

She slid off her stool. "No, thanks. I had my pick-me-up." Cyndi waved at Jake and bounced to the beat of the music as she made her way to the door.

As the afternoon moved into evening, my thoughts kept going back to the visit with Cyndi. I imagined letting my little streak of white grow out. Would it stand out? Or would it just disappear inside the coils around it? What would Thomas say?

When I was little, Grannie Allen had told me folktales about women growing into their power as their hair grew whiter. At the time, I thought she'd been trying to convince me of her awesomeness, as if she needed the help. The stories were about healers who grew more connected to the earth as they aged. What would that be like? It sounded incredibly powerful.

Then my speculations landed on what Bobby's reaction might be if I did what Cyndi was planning. I was sitting in my office when I thought about it, and my desk rumbled from the violent shudder that rolled through me. She'd probably try to pull out my hair.

"Here you are. What are you doing?" About an hour after dinner that evening, Thomas found me in our closet at my place, surrounded by multiple boxes of clothes. Skirts, pants, and jeans, in particular, had been spewed all over the space. He was in his boxer briefs, ready for bed or some reading before turning in. I didn't take the time to admire his fine form standing there. Not that I took it for granted. His ass was always a topic of appreciation to me, but I was too upset to focus.

"Thought you were in the bedroom relaxing," Thomas said. The crease in his chin deepened as he grimaced at the mess.

"I can't relax when my pants keep sliding down." As I fussed with my ponytail, I barely glanced his way. "I'm searching for my smallest-sized things." I pointed at one stack of boxes. "Those are the big sizes, from the early days of the flare. Then I dropped into my regular size." I shifted my hand to two boxes behind me. "But they're…" I held on to the waist of my jeans and pulled my pants up and down without unbuttoning. "So I'm taking an inventory of what's buried in these boxes." I gestured to those in front of me. "If I lose any more weight, I'll have to go shopping again."

Thomas's head tilted from side to side, like my dog did when she looked at me like I was a bit kooky. "Thought women enjoyed shopping."

I bit my tongue to keep from complaining. Ultimately, this was a good problem. Many would consider it a blessing. My BMI had dropped from too high to acceptable, and now it was optimal. But I'd been burned by my metabolism before.

I sighed. "I don't trust it." I carefully tried to un-pretzel myself and stand within the tiny space of floor I'd left for myself. Thomas reached across the boxes and helped me up. I pointed to the entire collection of plastic tubs. "I could open a boutique with all this, but I don't dare send anything away. What if my weight swings back again? It would be a waste to buy an entire wardrobe every time my size changed."

Thomas rubbed his chin. "You know, between the two of us, there's enough money to keep you clothed no matter your situation."

"Sure, but our money's better spent on other things."

"True." His hands landed on his hips as his gaze swept over me. "It's not a temporary swing. But if you want to hold on to these boxes to be sure, works for me. If you don't have room here, I can take them to the farmhouse."

The thing was, I didn't want logical Thomas in fix-it mode. I was in a bad mood about several things. I wanted him to grump with me. I didn't have the heart to tell him though. When I'd grabbed at my hair, I'd committed frizzy hair crime number one. So I gathered it into a scrunchie I kept on my wrist.

Thomas folded his arms over his chest. "Alright, what's really going on?"

I gestured toward the bathroom and stepped around the boxes. Thomas followed me and stopped behind me as I leaned into the mirror. "My roots don't show."

He pinched the bridge of his nose. "Darlin'…"

I started separating little sections in the front, the way I had when I'd washed my face about forty-five minutes earlier. "I'd forgotten my hair appointment is next week." He sighed, but I pressed on. "Before you get sarcastic, let me finish. I should have to touch up this area with hair makeup by now. But it's as brown as the rest of the new growth. In fact, I could reschedule the whole appointment."

"Still not comprehending."

I gave him points for risking my sarcasm at this point. "Something's happening to me that's not normal. There should be a bright patch of white right here." I touched the front of my hairline.

He rubbed his jaw. "So… you're prickly because your clothes are too big and your silver hairs have disappeared. Am I following?"

"Prickly?" He had best watch it, or I'd give him prickly. "As a matter-of-fact… My glasses have been acting up for weeks as well. They're blurry no matter what I do to fix them. For the hell of it, I took them off this afternoon and looks like I have my distance sight again. I went back to using the old readers for small print stuff." I turned around and folded my arms. "Is this some kind of remission side effect? Because no one ever mentioned it to me."

Thomas drew close and spun me back around. He pulled my T-shirt over my head and slid my jeans down without unbuttoning or unzipping them. It left me in my underwear. His hands moved up and down my arms. "Remember me telling you about the body healing itself in reverse order? How the last symptoms to occur heal first and so on?"

"Um, maybe," I said as I watched him assess me in the mirror. "Do… do you think this is hap… happening to me?" I closed my eyes and focused on his soft touch.

His fingers traveled up my neck. Then he rubbed the tips of my ears and smiled. "I do." He kissed my jaw and nearly short-circuited my brain. It certainly stopped the spiral of upset I'd been in. "I remember the first time I finally had gray hairs. After so long, I was thrilled. Disappointed when I had to make them go away to get my degree."

"Wh-when did it happen?" My words grew breathy as Thomas's fingers brushed over my stomach. I sank into the front of him.

"Around the time I found the Felidae."

I gasped at his answer.

"The point is… you can have whatever hair you want. Hell, dye it white if you want."

"You wouldn't mind?"

Thomas chuckled in my ear, and it rolled through me. "I just told you how much I liked it when I had them."

I found his eyes in the mirror. "Why don't we both work on it then? Thirty-six isn't too young to go gray. That's the age your license reads, right?"

He cupped my ass and gently squeezed. "Good plan."

I shut my eyes and let myself feel, then opened them when his hands came back around. "Never will forget the first time I saw you naked. Such a gift." He stilled his hands over my navel. "From the beginning, every inch of your body has been a feast for my eyes." His hands moved to my hips. "Some parts are smaller, tighter. I adore it now and did then because it's you."

Had he noticed my changes before me? I paid more attention to how my clothes fit than what I looked like. No one enjoys staring at themselves in a mirror.

Thomas growled near my ear. "Don't ever think your body doesn't do it for me. I have a theory based on my observations."

"What's that?" I gasped as his fingers undid my bra, exposing my breasts until his hands covered them, massaging.

"Most Felidae members learn to control their energy little by little, over decades and by accident. But you've already been practicing intention, thanks to your autoimmune issues. I think your body's already responding to what you want it to do." One of Thomas's hands drifted back down until it glided into my underwear. "I wonder how much you'll be able to influence since you're getting a head start."

My knees buckled some when his fingers slipped inside me. "Focus on what you really want, not how you think it *should* be." He peppered kisses along my jaw, then tugged lightly on my ear lobe. "Silence that critical voice in your head—the one that made you run away from me. A certain someone planted it in there when you were a little girl. I could hurt her for that, Kick."

My hips found a rhythm of pleasure, instinctively helping his fingers spark our flame.

"For your sake, I'll leave her be until you tell me otherwise. But you have to kill the critical discord living in your mind."

"I will." I hummed. "Promise."

"This is changing too, you know."

My brows pulled together as I watched Thomas pull my bikini

pants down my legs until I stepped out of them. "What do you mean?"

He spread my lips apart in front of the mirror—a shocking move, but I trusted him. "Look at it. Feel it."

My breath caught at the first light brushes of my fingertips. I didn't like touching that specific area. It made me feel damaged. Wrong. The scars were still there, but he was right. The jagged edges had smoothed. Would it change any more?

"Such a pretty orchid." He growled against my neck. "Don't ever think you have to change for me." His hands disappeared from where I needed them, and he placed them on my shoulders, spinning me around. "Set your intentions for you. Got it?"

I didn't care about any fecking intentions or energy or healing. I wanted Thomas's hands back on me. I frowned and almost pouted.

He kissed my mouth. "I've got nothing but love for you baby. Never forget."

I pulled back from his lips and raised an eyebrow. "Did you just quote Heavy D and the Boyz?"

"Sort of." He had the nerve to grin and boop my nose with his finger. The one I wanted back on my body, along with the other nine.

I pointed at him. "You've been listening to my '90s playlist."

"How do you think I found the song for your surprise?"

The mood in the room shifted from lust-filled to looney. Thomas's grin turned into his middle school smirk as he jumped his feet apart and started singing Heavy D's "Nuttin' But Love," his hands on his knees as he twerked. In his black Calvin skivvies.

I couldn't believe him. My eyes narrowed, but my smile betrayed me. "Stop listening to my music."

Thomas just sang louder, grinding harder as he jumped around the bathroom, gyrating to one of my favorite hip-hop songs. He bumped my hip, making me stutter-step to keep standing. "Come on, sing and dance with me."

"You're only saying the hook. Over and over." That egged him on. I gestured to where we'd been standing. "Seriously? You're shutting us down like that?"

He grabbed my hand and rubbed it up and down his erection as he shifted into *Dirty Dancing* mode. Thomas bit his lip like he was enjoying a moment of bliss. Is that what this was? "It's not going anywhere. Now…" He spun me around and shook his hips against my back. "Let loose and dance with me."

I had to admit, I loved it and couldn't help but laugh. He'd pulled me out of my grump.

I shimmied against Thomas and added in the female backup lines to the song as he kept repeating the hook.

"Dancing is like making love standing up," he said with a lusty lick of his upper lip. The ham.

If we had unlimited time together, like he claimed, at least I'd laugh my ass off.

He stopped when a giggling fit overtook me. He stepped around me, pulling me in for an embrace. "Did it work?"

"I suppose." I pretended to push him away but actually took a moment to breathe him in. "Except for the part where you worked me up and left me horny."

Thomas stood tall and drew a finger down my face as he backed me into the counter, pressing into me. "Just know how much you love edging."

"Jaysus." I chuckled and gestured to where we'd just been dancing. "Whatever that was, it had nothing to do with edging."

"Mmm." Thomas waggled his brows and pressed his erection into my belly. "Beg to differ."

I swallowed hard. The temperature in the bathroom suddenly went tropical again. I gave him a small push. "You think you can, what? Snap your fingers and turn me on?"

"What was it you told me?" *Curse that smirk of his.* Thomas put it to full effect as his fingers rubbed the tip of my ear. He had me. "That's right…" His voice rose in an imitation of mine. "Oh, Thomas… 'when you want, I want… It's never been this intense before'."

I pressed my lips together as I folded my arms. "Touché."

"I know." He leaned in and lightly licked along the edge of my ear. "Also know precisely what I'd find if I dipped my fingers into those satiny folds of yours."

The frustrations from the day that had built until I was in a closet surrounded by plastic boxes fell away. It's what Thomas did. He made the nonsense disappear and showed me what was possible. I dropped my forehead onto his shoulder and whispered, "Thank you."

He pulled me close until I felt our heartbeats sync. We did that for each other. "I didn't mind, baby. For you, I'll never mind." He lifted a shoulder. "Delayed gratification, makes the finish line that much sweeter." He pulled me toward the door to the bedroom, and I swung my ass as I passed him, getting me a crisp slap there. I winked at him, egging him on.

"Just want to cross the line in the sheets"—he bit his lip—"with you making those banshee noises again."

26

Something to Believe In

Thomas

I cracked Kick's office door while knocking and heard Charley on the phone. She waved us in, then raised a finger to let us know she was almost finished. When done, Charley walked out from behind the desk and sat in a club chair. I took the other and Kick settled in behind her desk. "Thank you for taking some time to come in," Kick began.

"Is this about Tess, because—"

"No." I waved my hands. "That's y'all's business—"

"If you want to talk to me though," Kick said. "I'm here."

Charley tipped her head up to the ceiling. "I really don't." She turned to me. "What's going on?"

Now for the hard part. If there were ever an etiquette for this kind of thing, I'd yet to figure it out. "Charley, have you… do you know—?"

"You know Tess's secrets, don't you?" she asked.

I clamped my hands on my knees, wishing Kick was sitting in my lap so I could draw strength from her. It's not that I wasn't excited to give Charley this information, but I feared that she wouldn't receive it well. "I do. I'm a member of the Felidae Society too. That's how I know her."

Charley sat stick-straight in her chair, but she gave me the feeling she wanted to bolt. Not that I could blame her. "So you've made the vows of secrecy."

"Yes."

Charley's hand moved in Kick's direction. "Then why is she in this meeting?"

"She's one too. Unofficially."

Charley's head swiveled like a flash between Kick and me. "How? She's not old enough."

That vow of secrecy still had its hold on me. I gave Charley the bare facts. "She's transitioning."

Her brows lifted to her forehead. "You're kidding?"

Kick shrugged. "Thomas's tests kind of confirm his suspicions."

"Wow." Charley popped forward and pointed at me. "First off, I won't be one of you people, so don't even try to recruit me. I don't trust those sons of bitches."

I raised my hands. "Promise, it's not why I asked you here." I tried a different tack. "Let me start by telling you about my Uncle Theo." She lifted an eyebrow. If I was right, her brother was named after him.

"Uncle Theo and I founded a bank in San Francisco in the late nineteenth century. First we'd found an abundant line of gold in a creek feeding the American River in California. As rich as we became, he hated the business. Adventure was his first love. Even overseeing our mining efforts in the mountains and traveling the barely-there trails to the city didn't satisfy him."

"Why are you telling me this?" Charley asked. Her hands shook as her knees bounced a staccato.

"Bear with me." I rubbed my jaw and prepared for the worst. "He took off for several years. When a letter reached me, Theo was helping a rancher in New Mexico, named Carlos."

Charley's head snapped up. One knee practically bounced a foot off the floor.

"Carlos had a widowed daughter."

Distraught, her eyes shimmered. "Stop."

I rubbed my temples. "Most of us can control our bodies, especially in areas of fertility."

"Stop please," she squeaked.

"Uncle Theo didn't believe in it. He—"

"No," she whispered.

My shoulders collapsed. This should be happy news, but I knew my uncle never went back to them. He broke their hearts. He did that to anyone foolish enough to love him. Even me.

I lifted my head and just spilled the rest. "I think you and your brother are my cousins. I promise not to press you about the Felidae Society if you don't want it. That's not why I bring it up. But I'd like to run a few tests in my lab to confirm my suspicions. I won't share the results with anyone outside this room, not even Tess. However, she knows about my theory. I figured it out the other night when we were all together. In my shock, I let it slip."

"Well, shit." Charley dropped her head in her hand.

"She and Banger already knew the important stuff, and they support your decision to live apart from the Felidae and the other groups," I said.

"Other groups?" Kick asked with alarm.

"We focus on Europe and the Americas. Others like us gravitated to each other elsewhere." I didn't have time to go into detail. My focus stayed on convincing Charley that I wouldn't hurt her. With that in mind, I told her, "I have a grandson who took the vows, then revoked them a decade later. He's now helping his granddaughter through her transition. They live in Virginia. Haven't told them about this, but I think they'd like to know about you."

Kick came out from behind her desk and sat on the arm of Charley's chair. She hugged her friend and said to me, "You're dumping a lot on her today, sweetheart."

"Right. I'm sorry." I made a fist, letting the edges of my nails dig into my palms. New bloodlines meant a lot to the research, but it represented more to me as the head of my family. I'd been piecing together the tracks of my broken lineage for over a hundred years. At first I wanted to know they were alright, to help them out secretly if needed. In the end, they were my motivation for taking on this work. What if one of them were on the verge of transitioning and it never happened? They should be able to have the choice.

In a soft voice, Charley said, "It's alright. I think I understand."

"Tell me one more thing. Was your mother's name Magdalena?"

Kick hugged her tighter as another tear fell. "The bastard told you about us?"

"Well…" I didn't have the heart to say he only mentioned Magdalena. If I'd known about the children, I would've made him go back for them. "He spoke about… her. Did he know about you two? Knowing Theo, he ran when his feelings became too much."

"We were six when he left us."

My eyes squeezed shut as if from pain. Then again, my heart ached for her. I couldn't explain Theo's behavior to myself, let alone his own child.

I leaned on my knees and nudged once more. "Don't you want to know where you came from? Let me at least find some way to make this right. The test is simple. You'll be in and out quicker than a lunch break. I'll do the analysis myself."

Charley moved her gaze to Kick, who gave her a sweet, sympathetic smile.

"You have the same eyes as him," I said. "That bright silver. Some memories have faded since he died in World War I, but his eyes were burnished in my mind."

Her hand dropped to her heart. "He's dead?"

My shoulders fell again. "He took a direct hit, right in front of me. There was no healing that kind of destruction. It threw me for a loop for a long time."

She sank into the chair. "Yeah."

"Theo was a strange paradox, Charley. He hoped he could be something like a genetic Johnny Appleseed, but he refused to watch another loved one die. He was a coward who only spoke about his love for Magdalena when he drank enough to let his defenses down." I scoffed at the memory flashing through my mind. "That required a lot of booze."

"Dios mio." Charley covered her eyes with her hand, and I knew she believed me. "I'll do it."

"Thank you." I reached across the gap between us and grabbed her hand. "If I'm wrong, we're still friends. I can study your ancestry line if you'll let me, but no matter what, you have my confidence. I'll do everything to keep it."

Kick took Charley's free hand, then reached for mine. She winked at me before turning back to her friend. "I wouldn't love him if he wasn't an honorable man."

She gave us a small smile. We stayed like that, holding hands. Lost family found.

27

The Way I Am

Kick

"Nice. Remember... toes face me. Pivot... good. Now your combo... Shit." I'd nicked Thomas's nose with my jab. He grinned at me. "Well done. Keep your back heel up."

It was our day off, and Thomas had me spar with him in the back by the firing range at the farmhouse. I'd taken defense classes before, so I already knew some of the concepts he taught me. Still, I struggled to keep my shoulder hidden as I struck him, which was why he insisted I use my full force. He wanted my muscle memory to be as real as possible.

Normally, we trained in Thomas's workout room. Today he said he wanted to add more reality to our efforts. He briskly rubbed his hands, then pointed at the table set up. "Now to the guns."

I was puffing steam out my nose, trying to catch my breath on this chilly March day. "You've got to be kidding." I took a pull from my favorite water bottle—pink with a pen drawing of Tinker Bell. It was the only one Liam didn't steal, then lose.

"No baby." Thomas tapped the table with his hand. "This is self-defense. Brawling, shooting, quickly finding another weapon.

Fighting to live another day. It happens all at once." He waved me over. "Come on. Give yourself one deep breath to center and go."

I reached for the Sig—the one I felt most comfortable with—stood in mountain pose, and sighted the target. *Breath in for four, hold for four.* I squeezed on the exhale.

Thomas's head tilted to the side. "Not bad. Do it again and empty it this time. Focus on where you need those shots to land to keep yourself alive."

My curls had gone crazy in our workout, coming out of my ponytail. Thomas made me keep it loose, since there was no way of predicting my hairdo in an actual fight. I tucked what I could behind my ear. "Okay, boss."

"Hey." He rubbed my ear to get my attention. "You still struggling with imagining a person?"

"Honestly?" I swiped some hair behind my other ear. "Knowing what I do about Jonn Graham, it would probably be easier if his face was on the target."

Thomas laughed as he checked his Glock. "Except it's not a given that it'll come up in the moment. Getting away and surviving will matter most. If you have to kill to do it, you go for it. Then deal with the aftereffects."

"But… in the scenario you see in your head… isn't the weapon used to manipulate? You know, make me obey or whatever?"

"Never assume that." With a deep frown on his face, Thomas lifted his piece and emptied the weapon like the expert he was. Talk about muscle memory. He'd been around countless types of arms and munitions since he was a boy. I bet he could target and fire in his sleep. Or at least half-asleep. "Always… always assume a weapon pointed at you is intended for use. If you raise a weapon… Don't care if it's the wasp spray you keep by your bed. Use it, dammit."

"Gotcha." From my perspective, the best part about this scenario was me no longer flinching when I fired or any of the times Thomas had. As much as I still hated this talk—barely believed any of it, to be honest—I was becoming accustomed to it. I took it as a win. Then I sighted the Sig Sauer again and made a better pattern on my target. The small victories. Did I wish this came more naturally to me? For Thomas's sake, hell yes. Maybe it would in time.

I actually liked the physicality of fighting. There was a connection to the past, not just to making my body move better but to the history of how people have been defending and protecting their own… since the cave times, I guessed.

As for our daily life, except for lectures and exercises like this, it was downright peaceful. Most weeknights it was Thomas, Liam, and me. Lee had received his latest SAT score. He'd come downstairs with a smile on his face, so Thomas and I were happy. The boy had been so excited that I let him take my Camaro to band practice.

Last Sunday, we finally arranged a family dinner at Thomas's. Nailing down Rachel in her tight schedule had been the victory, and she only stayed for the meal. It did my heart good to have the kids together. Hosting it at Thomas's farmhouse made our situation that much more real. Lee already had some things in the main guest room. He'd made it clear, though, that he didn't want to move in officially, like I had with a duplicate of anything I'd need. Still, we called the room Liam's now.

"How's it going at Banger's condo with Tess there?" I'd asked Rachel as she plated sweet potatoes and I carved the roasted chickens. From the way they'd hit it off the first time they'd met, I hoped their friendship had grown. I couldn't tell her the truth about Tess's age and all, but I thought they could help each other through their current hurts and stresses.

"Good. We know about Charley," Rachel said.

My eyebrows instantly rose to hairline heights. "Really?" How much could she disclose? Tess was as secretive as the rest of the mysterious Felidae. "What'd she say?"

"That they're exes." Rachel stopped mashing as she sighed. "Isn't it romantic?"

I put my knife down and turned around. "Snow, they'd seen neither hide nor hair of each other for… a while. What I saw looked tragically painful, not romantic. Trust me, no one smiled in the moment." *My daughter and her desire to tell a story.*

"Exactly, Mama. They still love each other."

I laughed through my incredulity. "How the hell did you conclude that? From the little I know, they came to a massive impasse and called it quits. I think for the better."

She resumed mashing. "Still, Charley's the love of Tess's life."

Jaysus, she told the girls that? With my knife, I dug into the stubborn hip joint. I'd never liked this part of cooking chicken, but the memory of Charley's despairing visage gave me the mojo to push through. "I don't think Charley feels the same."

Rachel rinsed the masher in the sink and placed it in the dishwasher. "Bella and I plan to get them talking again."

Oh hell. "Snow, let them be. Please. They're not like you and Bella."

Rachel started to pick up the bowl but folded her arms instead. "What's that mean?"

"Uh…" How do I explain the Felidae without explaining it? "You and Isabella are in a rush. To finish school. To start your life. To live. Remember when you cried last fall about not yet being engaged to Cody?"

She clicked her tongue. "Of course. Thank God though."

"I know, right?" Macushla had been waiting at my feet, so I dropped a small piece of meat to my sweet pup. "You've been in a hurry to grow up pretty much since the day you were born. I'm telling you, some people aren't like that. Give Tess and Charley time. Their own time."

Rachel picked up the bowl and hip-checked me. "Sometimes people need a gentle push."

I shook my head as I watched her leave the kitchen, the dog tight to her heels. *Heaven help those two women.*

Thinking back to that conversation with Rachel reminded me of something Thomas had needed for his research. As we carried our gear back to the house, I cleared my throat. "Hey cowboy…"

He turned to me and smiled.

"I can't believe I forgot to tell you… my brother, Bert, agreed to do the DNA tests for us. Well, for me. I told him it'll help with my diagnosis, like you suggested. He's all set at your friend's lab at Wayne State tomorrow."

Thomas blew out a long breath. "Excellent news."

I moved the bag I carried to my other shoulder. "Will you check him for variances?"

"Absolutely. We've moved into the phase where Gautam's algorithm is pulling most of the workload, looking for patterns and anomalies. So, yeah… the more information we get, the better."

We moved past the narrow trail through the woods and into Thomas's backyard. He opened his arm and pulled me in. "You think you could get Bobby to test? She could use the same lab in Detroit. They're sending it straight to me without registering it."

I lifted my gaze, my brows raised. "This might come as a shock, but my mother's a bit of a conspiracy theorist. She thinks DNA tests are for suckers."

Thomas tipped his head back and laughed.

My fingers moved to adjust my glasses, but they weren't there anymore. Funny how quickly the gesture had become an unconscious thing. I ended up rubbing my eye. Considering pollen had irritated it a little, it helped. "I could pop over to her townhouse if you tell me what to look for. Or you can come with me."

"Well…" Thomas rubbed the cleft in his chin. "I've never run a panel without consent before. It's technically illegal. Immoral. Would you have a problem with that?"

If it helped me or, more importantly, my kids? Nope. When it came to her, something about the wrongness of it added to the appeal. Immature, I know, but I didn't care. "You promise it's staying in your database and no one else will have the information?"

Thomas crossed his heart with his pinkie finger.

I shrugged. "I'm good."

He squeezed me into his side. "Now you're thinking like a Felidae member."

"Naw…" I gave up the hair fight and pulled my scrunchie out of it with my free hand, letting the curls fly free. "I'm thinking like Banger."

28

Love Me Tender

Thomas

HUGH JOINED ME IN THE HUMIDOR IN HIS SHOP. I'D DISTRACTED myself with cigar shopping while he finished a call.

"Thanks for coming in."

I held up four perfectos. "Not a problem."

Hugh took them and led the way to his office.

I cleared my throat. "You're not ringing me up?"

"Hell no. You saved my keister."

Aside from the day we'd met, Kick hadn't let me pay for anything at her coffeehouse. Not that it mattered. Deana would have snuck stuff to me, regardless. This was different. "So a guy can't spend his money anymore?"

Hugh chuckled. "Don't act like you're not about to drop a cool chunk of change on my desk, Professor." He gestured to the chair beside him. "Sit please."

Before doing so, I reached across the other desk—the one that had been Mickey Allen's now faced Hugh's. According to Kick, this was the setup the men used while her father had been Hugh's partner. I shook hands with the man sitting there—the new manager, who would oversee the cannabis expansion. "Dexter Douglas, I presume?"

He gave my hand a solid, confident shake. "That's right. Call me Dex though." The handshake fit him. Dex took after his father in size, though not as broad. His facial features reminded me of an edgier version of his mother. Or he'd just inherited Deana's cordial smile.

"Thomas Harrison. Feels like I already know you."

"Same, man. I've heard all about the 'mighty fine professor'." The corner of his mouth lifted. "My moms has a crush on you."

Hugh and I laughed. "Spent enough time with your parents to know your father has nothing to worry about. What's that my students say?" I snapped my fingers. "Right. Hashtag, life goals."

Dex blew out a hard breath. It puffed out his cheeks, but he didn't say anything.

"I didn't realize you two hadn't met," Hugh said.

"Not officially." I shrugged. "Between Kick and Deana, it just seems that way."

"Exactly," Dex said with a nod.

Hugh's mouth twisted as his brow furrowed. "Why would you go to bat for an unvetted stranger?"

"Wouldn't call Dex, here, unvetted." I brought my ankle over my knee and settled in the chair. "Kick went to bat for him first. I trust my fiancée's judgment." I looked straight at Dex. "My team did do a background check. You found a good one, Hugh."

"I agree," he said. "Can't thank you enough for also recommending your lawyer. You were right about the one who'd been working on our license. The man turned out to be a big conflict of interest." He leaned back in his chair and folded his hands behind his head. "You wouldn't believe the flak I received from the board for replacing Katie with Dex on the licensing petition."

Oh, I'm sure I would. "Let me guess… the racism is as strong as their misogyny."

Dex pressed his lips together as he rolled his eyes.

"That first lawyer would've let them veto us without a fight. Roly-poly bastard. Then my contact calls… tells me they just wanted Katie to sweat a little… make her more *grateful* for her opportunity. Pliable is what he meant. They didn't want her showing up with any feminist ideas."

I scoffed at the comment. If you claimed to want progress, then do it, dammit. It didn't matter if it was a local government or the Felidae Society.

Hugh misunderstood my outburst and said, "Your guy made the difference, Professor—"

"Thomas please. Since we're partners now."

"Yes, well. The new lawyer reminded them of the suits in other states where black entrepreneurs weren't given equal access to the licensing process. He convinced them we had the bankroll to take them on."

There was an understatement. Whether it was Kick or Dex being hassled, I'd go all in. I would shake up the whole system if needed.

I turned to Dex. "You good with this?"

"It's nothing new." He slid his tortoise-framed glasses up his nose. "Fuck 'em. Let's do this."

I shifted my gaze back to Hugh. "Dex has full powers as manager? He has oversight of the remodel and set up of the new store?"

"Katie wasn't lying about your protective side." Hugh raised his hands. "Our new partner has an MBA. He's more than capable, and I can't wait to step back some." I knew this, but I liked hearing the praise in Hugh's tone. The man sounded equal parts grateful and relieved.

"Damn straight." I rubbed my hands together. "What do y'all have for me?"

Hugh slid some papers my way, and I leaned forward to read them. "Walt left these for you to sign."

"Yeah." I uncapped my Mont Blanc. "His partner, Penn, mentioned the family emergency. I hope everything's alright."

"Me too. Hang on a moment…" Hugh pressed the intercom. "Liz… can you come on back now?"

"Sure, Mr. Reynolds."

Hugh explained, "Liz is a notary."

When we took care of Hugh's stack of papers, making me their silent partner, Dex cleared his throat. "Hang on, Liz." He placed a smaller set on the edge of his desk.

I lifted an eyebrow as I read the first lines. "Right. The loan." Dex nodded. "You know this is just a formality?" I reminded him.

With Dex's finances tied up because of his pending divorce, he needed a quick loan in order to buy into the partnership. "Would've cut you a check from my personal account."

He shook his head. "I wouldn't have taken it. This protects us both."

"True." I signed and initialed the highlighted areas. Then Liz made everything official.

I reached into my briefcase and produced two new Mont Blanc pens. I handed them to Dex and Hugh. "Will these buy your silence, gentlemen?" The silent part of our deal included Kick and Deana. I didn't want to risk anyone thinking I was throwing money around for the hell of it. Or worse… to prove something. As Banger liked to say, compounded interest ensured that I had enough to help when I saw an opportunity. But I didn't want to have to explain it to Deana or put Kick in the situation of hiding more from the people she loved. She knew I had enough to live on. She didn't know exactly how much. Not yet.

Dex whistled at his gift. "You never have to worry about me. The silence is written into our deal though I appreciate this kind of bribery." The men laughed.

"What Dex said," Hugh added.

"I started the deal to see Kick smile." Her smile motivated so much lately. I also believed these were men who wouldn't ask many questions. I liked that about them, especially Dex. If he did as well as I thought we would, I had plans for him.

"Oh." Hugh raised the new pen like he was pointing with a finger. "Thought you should know… Kick told me about asking Big

Jonn to pull whatever strings he thought he could with the tobacco fellas. From what I can tell, he followed through." He dropped my cigars into a bag and handed them over. "One of the board members was furious over some conversation his wife had with Kick."

I slid the bag into my case. "Do I want to know?"

Hugh grinned. "This woman treated herself to a weekly outing at the Perked Cup when she was going through chemotherapy. Katie noticed her, as she does. They talked. The treatments caused some kind of… you know… vaginal dryness or some such. Katie recommended some kind of cannabis remedy to fix it, and it worked."

"Christ." I tapped my pen on the desk, not liking where this story might be heading. "This was a problem because…?"

Hugh swallowed hard before turning a bright red. "According to Big Jonn, it put her… uh… in the mood."

What was wrong with men? I wrapped my hand around my neck. Could've howled at the stupidity, but Dexter barked a laugh instead.

Hugh giggled as he added, "The guy claimed it drugged her or something."

I moved toward the door, but his words struck a chord as I reached for it. I turned around. "Are you saying this is the reason for the whole 'immoral whore campaign' against my fiancée? Some idiot's wife got her mojo back because a caring barista gave her *advice*?" My nostrils flared from the effort to contain a roar. My new partners didn't deserve it.

If only Hugh had seen the pain and confusion on Kick's face when she saw the graffiti on her café wall. I don't think he would have stayed so calm. Not to mention how tortured she'd been over what Big Jonn's son did on Halloween. I'd still throw the kid out of either store if I saw him again. Hell, I'd never trust either of the Grahams.

Hugh sighed, adjusted his cap. "I don't know. Just wanted to tell you about Big Jonn, is all. I know there's bad blood between you. He's always been supportive of me. Plus he helped with the board."

"I hear you. I do. I also believe Kick and Rachel. Then there's what I've personally witnessed." Thanks to the men connected to Big Jonn, I could've lost Kick before I had her officially. I'd never forget it. I gave Hugh and Dex a chin tip and opened the door. "Gentlemen… pleasure doing business with y'all. Let me or my team know what else we can do to help."

WITH OUR FINGERS LACED TOGETHER, I PULLED KICK THROUGH THE door to my lab. My heart raced faster than when I showed Tess around. To be swift and efficient, I'd drawn Kick's blood at home, so this was her first time in my lab. My space. As I tried to see it through Kick's eyes, a vision formed in my head regarding what changes could improve workflow in the new lab.

It hit me for the first time how, in my heart, I'd already left the university. *Damn*. I'd miss the lectures. When I pursued this new life, I never expected to fall in love with it or with teaching the next generation. But it was best for the work, and I'd bring over my post-grad students in partnership with the university. It was the compromise I made to get out of my contract, though I'd planned to take them anyway.

For added moral support for Kick, Tess came with us. The information I was sitting on might thrill her the most. Besides, she'd been asking about the mice. I had a feeling they'd have names by the end of this. Either way, both women were about to be floored.

Kick's bright face fell when I had her sit around Gautam's computer setup—what he called "the *Enterprise*"—because we were going "where no one else had gone before."

Tess had talked up the mice on the drive over, and Kick was more eager to see them than she was to learn about her results. It's possible my face already gave it away. I had lost my practiced poker face in matters related to her.

I made the introductions between Gautam and the women. Tess stayed true to form and remembered him. She asked about his classes with the interest of a mother.

"Tess please." I gestured for Gautam to bring up the report. It contained numerical data, along with graphs and pie charts for readability. We'd based the output on reports that other DNA services provided. "Give us about twenty minutes," I told him once everything was ready. Nondisclosure agreement or not, it had been hard enough to explain this new project to my assistant. He already knew the details but not the personal significance of it.

"No problem, Professor H. Anyone want a coffee?"

Kick smiled at him, then said, "No, thank you." I'd only known her to drink coffee from another café once.

"I'm fine too. Thank you, dear," Tess said.

He gave her a double take before heading for the door.

I moved into Gautam's chair, feeling the grin form on my face as I turned to Kick. "According to this, you're officially related to a Felidae member."

"Thank God we didn't have to search outside the Society," Tess said while squeezing my fiancée's shoulders.

No kidding. Kick's extraordinary amount of European ancestry had been a big clue. The frown on her face surprised me.

"Are you not happy about this?" I thought for sure she would be.

She rubbed her palms on her thighs. "Is it you?"

I grimaced at the thought. It melted fast as I logged myself onto the computer. I couldn't wait to show her the good news. Then I pointed to the smile on my face. "Would this be here if we were related?"

"I don't know. Your uncle was apparently prolific." She shoved her hands between her knees. "We could be cousins."

"True." I ran my hand through my hair. "Go back far enough and we're all cousins eventually. But not in this case. You're from another bloodline. We'll have to take it all the way back to find our genetic crossing." I kissed her temple and felt her tension fade.

"Anyway…" I clicked on the screen, and Tess's hand shot to her mouth. Kick's gaze darted between us. "Meet Edmund Stanton. Well, it's the name he used last."

Kick stared, speechless, at the screen, like she was looking in a mirror for the first time.

"Don't search for a resemblance, darlin'. You're too distant to worry about such things."

She turned to Tess, who shrugged. "I only gave birth to Rafael. What do I know?"

"Here." I clicked on a chart. "We connected you through your brother's Y-DNA, so Edmund's line runs through your father."

That put a smile on my lady's face. *Just wait, my love.* Before I moved on, I thought she deserved to know about her ancestor. It's why I'd asked Tess to join us.

"So… Edmund was a founding member of the Felidae Society. He oversaw the European operation before Ellie. It focused on protection and politics back then. He was also Alaric's closest friend and spent many years as Ellie's partner, which is why she took over Europe when he died."

Kick's head tilted to the side. "He's dead? I thought you didn't die."

"We age extremely slow, and we are hard to kill. But we are not immortal," Tess said.

"Remember, my uncle died in World War I."

"Right." She tapped her chin. "Alaric is the one you call *Grand-père,* correct?"

Tess scoffed, but I smiled at her. "He is. I can't wait to tell him about this." I frowned at Tess. We didn't need her old wounds influencing Kick. I wanted her to make up her own mind about the Felidae and its issues. I told Tess, "Alaric knows about Kick. He promised to leave us alone. He'll be thrilled with this news."

Tess leaned toward Kick and placed a hand on her knee. "We thought Edmund's line had died out, yeah?"

"It happens easier than you'd think. Through the ages, it's been harder to keep health and wealth than it's been to lose it," I explained.

Kick blinked at me, like she was struggling to keep up. I clicked on more photos that Tess had sent of Edmund. In one, he and Ellie stood together in the manicured garden at the chateau. They made a regal image, even centuries after their first lives. It was the characteristic I saw echoing the most in my lady.

Tess squeezed Kick's hand and smiled as her eyes moved over the photos. "Ask me any questions you have. There's so much to share, and everyone I know already has the same stories." She seemed downright giddy to pass on the information.

Kick opened her mouth, but I raised a hand to keep her from asking. They had all the time for sharing memories. I was still on the clock and only half-done. "Before you go off on a tangent, there's more."

I closed the files on Edmund and opened another set. "You have another Felidae ancestor from your mother's side." I clicked on the link and pulled up Ellie's information. The irony of a match to these two had struck me right away. By the way Tess's features twisted, she shared a similar opinion. "Your *mtDNA* is traced through mothers and evolves the slowest of any DNA."

"Is this woman as bitchy as Bobby?" Kick asked.

Tess broke into a hard cackle as I shook my head at her. "We're not researching those traits."

"I must disagree with you." Tess wiped away her tears from laughing.

"More stories?" Kick asked.

"It seems," I answered. "Again, you two will have to catch up another time." I clicked on my photos of Ellie. I was in many of them, as well as Alaric. Banger was even in a recent one. Since he'd been able to develop a secure system for the Society, we'd loosened our rules on the sharing of videos and photos for documentation.

"As you can see, these are fairly recent. Since I've mentioned her before, you also know that Ellie's alive and well. She's another Felidae elder."

Tess's eyes narrowed as I spoke until I added, "You two aren't ready for introductions."

"Why not?" Kick asked.

"Let me tell you what I know," I started. "Ellie is short for Eleanor. She was a queen in her first life. She was denounced for having her own mind in a time when royal women were no more than brood mares and prizes to form alliances."

"Then she was ahead of her time?"

"You can say that. This blending of two powerful lines, so to speak, points to why you've already shown abilities."

Tess scoffed and stood, moving to the work area where the mice lived.

"She and this Ellie have issues, don't they?"

I pulled Kick closer and kissed her temple, pausing for a moment to appreciate this news. I understood Kick's reluctance to believe my theories about her, but I buzzed with the implications of this news. I'd found a true life partner.

"The vibe in Bordeaux has been changing for months. I didn't know it had spread to Tess until recently, but yes, there's a particular iciness between the women. You can trust Tess's instincts."

Kick folded her hands in her lap. "Okay."

"There's a discord between the American and European teams that's new. That said, Ellie's always been supportive of my work. So I don't have all the answers. We just need to keep this information quiet for now." To lighten the mood, I added, "We also brought in a genealogy specialist with a team of her own. She also found your connection to Ellie. They're working on an ancestry tree for you."

"Okay." The little V formed between Kick's brow as she studied the photos. She had so much catching up to do. And I couldn't stop my smile. *Like attracts like.*

"What about my kids?"

I sighed deep. "This tangent has taken me away from Toni, my grant work. Since there are only two months left in the semester and four for the academic year, I need to pivot back to her. I can't take on anymore diversions until I'm out on my own. I'm sorry, darlin'." I raised her hand to my mouth and kissed her knuckles, wishing for all the world I could work faster. "As soon as I can, I'll study them. We'll watch them the way I keep tabs on my descendants."

"Except they're direct from me, and I have two lines of influence."

I grinned at her. "True."

.   .   .

Later that night, as I sat in my office on the third floor of my house, I dialed Alaric. It was just past breakfast time in Bordeaux. This time he stayed true to his routine and was in his office. Something told me Ellie wouldn't like hearing about Kick. At least Alaric could decide how to broach it to her.

He picked up on the first ring.

"Allo, Grand-père. Are you sitting down?"

29

More Than This

Kick

"Is it safe?" Charley asked while conspicuously scoping out the Perked Cup's dining area.

"If you mean is Tess here? She's at a yoga studio. You should know she plans to teach there soon."

"Then she is sticking around." In the years I'd known Charley, she'd been certain of her path, even cocky about it as she bulldozed her way through a man's industry. It unnerved me to see her deep brown eyes so lost and confused. "What about your daughter? I-is she here?"

I dropped my rag onto the counter. "Well, hell. You're getting it from all sides, aren't you? No, she's not in yet." I expected Rachel soon. She always worked on Saint Patrick's Day, though I used the term *work* loosely for her once the partying started. I gestured toward a stool, and Charley sat. "Your usual is on the house."

She patted the counter. "No, Kick. We pay each other."

I called over my shoulder as I made her latte. "Humor me today." I set the mug in front of her grimacing face. "I feel partially responsible for your troubles. For what it's worth, I tried to call off

Snow and Bella. But they're rooming with Tess. I believe they're using her happiness as a diversion from their own stresses."

Charley stared into her drink, blinked, and sighed. "When I left Spain, I told Teresa I didn't want to ever see her again. That hasn't changed. *Those people* don't change."

I knew she referred to the Felidae, except... "I don't want to meddle, but Tess has been great to me. It doesn't make me love you less..." I smiled at her, but Charley stubbornly held on to her frown. "Listen... she's helping me through some hard information—"

She threw out a hand. "Yada, yada... you can't talk about it. Believe me. I know. Teresa always chooses them. Now you're doing it too."

Right. For a minute, I'd forgotten Charley knew about the Felidae. For all intents and purposes, she was the one without the protection they offered. What the hell. I leaned in. "It turns out I'm descended from someone who had been like a father to Tess. She's been sharing memories of him with me. I think it helps her to have someone to pass the information along to, you know?" I chose my next words carefully, wanting her to really listen. "From what I've heard, she's been a fan of Thomas and me since the beginning. He risked his status with those Felidae people to be with me. In a huge part, it was because of a push from Tess. She and Banger both had his back." I lifted a shoulder. "Can't help wondering if that isn't because of you."

"No shit?" Charley said. She picked up her cup but set it back down without drinking. She dropped her head into her hand.

"Total honesty, my friend, I haven't asked her or anything." I didn't want to interfere beyond this little pep talk. "The impression I get from hanging around Tess suggests she's not the blindly obedient woman you used to know." I wiped the counter as I sorted through my thoughts. "They are a ridiculously secretive bunch. You're right about that. And I don't think it's easy to let it go."

"They have reason to be. My brother and I have barely escaped death multiple times, and it wasn't because of anything we'd done. It was over who we are."

I froze in the middle of my chores. "That sounds a lot like an incident Thomas shared with me."

"If he only had one, he's damn lucky."

"Careful…" I adjusted my ponytail. "Sounds like you're defending your ex now."

She finished her latte and stretched her back. "I understand the appeal of safety. It's the way they protect it I can't abide."

Did these women have any clue how closely they aligned? "I swore I heard Tess say pretty much the same thing the other day."

Charley scoffed at my words, but her shoulders relaxed some.

"Are you sticking around for the bands?" I changed the subject to give her room to think.

"Maybe one. I have a meeting nearby this afternoon."

"Refill?"

She nodded. "If you charge me for it. Along with a chicken wrap." Charley's phone rang, and she grimaced again. "This can't be good. It's my new site supervisor."

I tipped my head toward the back. "Take it in my office. I'll bring your stuff back."

"Thanks, my friend." Right before turning down the back hall, Charley called out, "If she comes in, don't tell her I'm here."

I brushed my pinky finger over my heart. "Promise." I didn't know if she referred to Tess or Rachel. I bit my tongue and reminded myself to let it go. As tempting as it was to want to spread the relationship bliss around, not everyone was ready for it. Heaven knew I hadn't been for a long time. Meeting Thomas didn't equal readiness either. It forced me to face what held me back, but I had to knock down the walls I'd built up on my own. Maybe it was the same for my two friends.

"YO MAMA!" THE BELL ANNOUNCED RACHEL BEFORE SHE CALLED out. Seeing her brightened my mostly happy day even more. Our Saint Patrick's Day party was always a highlight of the year.

"Are you ready to dance, sweetheart?"

"Fired up for it. Do you want help setting up or serving right now?"

"Serving would be fantastic. Your brothers will be here soon with the equipment."

Growing up, we celebrated Saint Patrick's Day as a holy day. My dad hated the revelry associated with it. I still cringed at memories of dancing on the sticky bar stages. The coffeehouse provided the perfect compromise. All the culture without the hangover. It was our tagline for the party ads too.

This year, four bands were lined up to play from lunch to closing. Popular bands used the café as a warm-up, then moved to one of the Irish pubs in the area during prime party hours. We ended our celebration with older folk groups who didn't like the rowdy scene either.

The bell chimed and in walked Big Jonn Graham. It was nice to see him enter without the vision blurriness I'd experienced in the autumn. That didn't stop my spine from tightening as he approached. My gaze swept toward Mateo. Like the good guard he was, he caught it and nodded. His head shifted to the other two guards stationed in their corners of the dining room. I watched their silent exchanges. Except for the Open Mic Night, when Thomas proposed, this would be the biggest party the Perked Cup would throw since the Halloween fiasco.

I had to admit, Big Jonn's gesture of good faith helped us. I was back in good standing with the community, and Hugh was moving forward with Dex Douglas. Still, I didn't like the possible omen that the presence of a Graham might mean.

A cold chill whispered along my neck. I plastered on my service smile anyway. "Hello, Big Jonn. What can I make for you today?"

He sent me a seriously flirty grin. I'd watched it fall upon so many women in the community that I knew it meant nothing. He showed me his phone. It displayed an ad for the festivities, along with our tagline for the day: ALL THE CULTURE. NO HANGOVER. "I took the day off since it's raining cats and dogs outside. Got to say, your ad intrigued me. Can't tell you how many of my boys will show up at a jobsite still drunk tomorrow morning."

"I bet." I cringed at the thought of someone operating heavy machinery under those conditions.

"Exactly." He shifted the display to a barcode. "How does this thing work?"

"I'll scan it. It gives you half off a latte or cappuccino with a four-leaf clover in the foam."

"Well, isn't that cute?" Big Jonn ran a hand over his chin. "I'll take a cappuccino if you don't mind. When does the music start?"

"Soon." I gestured toward the stage. "The fellas are almost ready. The kids from the dance school will perform for an hour first."

"How sweet. Everyone loves a neighborhood pub, but I hate how it can get debaucherous on this day."

After scanning the barcode, I lifted my shoulder. "I've never known Finnegan's Wake to get too bad. It probably depends on the management." He ordered a pastry to go with the drink. "If you want a seat, maybe grab one now? The full crew of dancers and their families will be here any minute. We fill up fast."

"I think I will. Thank you, Mrs. McKenna."

I rolled my eyes at his use of my married name, wondering if it was some kind of dig at Thomas. Surely he'd noticed the engagement ring. I'd shifted the three-stone mother's ring I wore for years to my right hand. The center diamond on that one—for Rachel's April birthday—had often fooled customers into thinking I was married. It had even confused Thomas the day we met.

Despite the harassment campaign dissipating, rumors occasionally floated to me and the staff about Thomas living at the house without us being married. Some people just refused to let go of the immoral mother box they'd tried to cage me in. I wondered if Big Jonn followed that same train of thought or if he just pretended to. Pretending could take someone a long way in our area. I thought many of the disturbances against me related back to my refusal to play along.

I wouldn't engage this time either. "And thank you again for putting in a good word for Hugh. It's made a big difference. I think his expansion will be good for the community."

Graham's face twisted before he found his smile again. "It was my pleasure. Reynolds is a good man."

"That he is."

Rachel walked past us, moving from the stage to Deana in the drive-through. He leaned toward me. "You should know… Young Jonn is in therapy like you suggested."

My brows shot up to my forehead. "Really? How's he doing?"

"Good, I think." Big Jonn tapped the counter. "I'll go find a seat. Can't wait to see those little ones with the big, bouncy curls."

"They are super cute." My phone vibrated in my pocket with a text from Thomas.

THOMAS

Hey, my Irish Eyes. Meeting went well.
OMW. No dancing without me. XO

Per his new custom, Thomas attached a song to the message. This one was Van Morrison's "Have I Told You Lately?" I sighed deeply as Deana approached. "Thomas is running late."

"Thomas is here," he declared behind me.

I turned around, my phone still up high. "That's weird. I just received this."

He shook his head and shrugged. "Remind me to put you on my plan. Your network stinks."

"It's—"

Deana's whistle cut me off. "Looking mighty fine, Professor." At her pause, I realized the whistle had been a full-blown catcall. "Is that a custom sports jacket?"

Thomas's gaze dropped from me to his front, then back up. He lifted a shoulder. "Good tailor's hard to find."

"What has you so fancy this morning? Most people wear jeans and T-shirts to this shindig."

"Early meeting with the boss's boss. They tried to re-woo me into staying at the university. I showed him around the lab and briefed him on our progress."

"Did it work?" I asked.

He gave a crooked grin. "I have to let him think there's hope.

We're still finalizing the affiliation. Banger and I thought of a way to keep them as a partner."

"Your message said it went well."

"Very. They're coming around to my way of thinking." He leaned in to kiss my temple. It was like a brief meditation, letting my soul pause for a breath. "Let me change into my party clothes."

"Sure. Just change in Dee's office. Mine's already occupied. Oh, you should know…" I tipped my head toward the bistro table with Big Jonn.

"Fuck me." Thomas groaned. "Here I had a great day going too."

I tapped his arms. "The guards are watching him closely. Our interaction went well… enough. He's put his son in therapy."

Thomas lifted an eyebrow. "There's a wonder." He pinned Mateo with a look, and they did that silent macho talk thing. Then Thomas squeezed my ass out of sight of the patrons and headed to the back, a duffel bag in his other hand.

"Remember to turn off the camera," I said, hoping I wasn't too loud.

"Shh." Deana scolded. "Don't take away my fun."

I clicked my tongue back at her. "Behave."

Her warm chuckle filled my ears. "Never and always."

30

Star of the County Down

Kick

"THE ONE OUT FRONT REMINDS ME OF RACHEL," MY MOTHER SAID to me from her perch at the bar. She'd come home in part to see the dancers. It always cheered her up to watch the kids go through their routines. I still didn't know why she didn't teach part-time. She obviously missed it. Then again, Bobby would despise not being the boss. I laughed at the thought, and Bobby's brows squished together, like she couldn't make sense of me. It was also her default face where I was concerned.

"She certainly can't dance like Rachel though. The child has no rhythm."

"Jaysus, Mother, can you be a little louder?" I whisper-yelled at her. "The baby's what… six?"

"Rachel knew her steps and felt the music at that age."

"Not every child will be a professional, but they can have fun."

"I think she's adorable." Rachel interrupted us. My peacemaker.

"You've always been too generous." Somewhere in there, I believed Bobby said it as a declaration of love for her granddaughter. Judging from the smile on her face, Rachel took it as one, so that's all that mattered.

"Where's Juan again?" I'd been determined to not mention his name, but Bobby's harsh criticisms could get out of hand. I took one for the sake of the tiny hearts on stage.

She smirked like she'd won something. "He's judging a competition in Ohio."

"How come you didn't go with him? You must enjoy watching the formal events too."

"I need to figure out what to do with my town house."

Rachel and I both stopped working and looked at her. "Are you selling it?" I asked.

She took a sip of her latte. "Probably. Juan lives in a high-rise, and I like being on one floor. I might rent my place or buy a beach property. I don't like the idea of having nothing of my own."

Bobby turned back around on the stool and watched the end of their current routine while rubbing her knee. I wondered if she'd ever noticed how mentioning anything that could aggravate her knee made her massage it for several minutes. That's what she implied with the one-floor comment—she'd complained for years about having a two-story condo. So much of her life seemed to be driven subliminally. It was a huge part of why I tried to do things with intention.

The music ended, and Bobby turned back to her latte while the dance teams transitioned.

"It's smart to have your own place," I said.

"Well, thanks for your permission," she snipped.

I raised my hands. "Just trying to say I think it's a good idea. The renting thing is too." I watched my reflection in the wood as I wiped the counter. "I appreciate you for taking a rideshare from the airport. We've been swamped around here."

"You're always swamped," she responded.

I sighed, about to give up. I kept thinking about Thomas's offer to cut her loose. Constantly dodging the lines she relentlessly tried to hook me with was exhausting.

Bobby added, "Juan showed me how the ride thing works. He

couldn't drop me off, so he set it all up on my phone. It's easy. A nice Italian boy picked me up. Not too sure about the one who brought me home here." She leaned in and said, "I held on to my purse the whole time."

Jaysus. I rolled my eyes. How many times had the kids and I offered to set her up with the app? We thought it would be safer than her driving anywhere beyond Oakville, especially since her doctors were on the other side of the county. Why would her lack of independence be used as a means of love and attention from the family, but she made no demands on Juan? Was their relationship okay? Could it be that she wasn't compelled to manipulate him? Did it matter?

The only thing I really knew was how nice it had been with Bobby out of town. Thomas and the kids and me. I rolled my head, stretched my neck, and tried again. "Sounds like you're happier up there. Maybe you should buy a place when you go back. In his building, possibly."

Bobby held out her cup for me to refill it—another sign of my failings. This time it was for my lack of customer service. *Whatever.* There was something about Thomas's out that made these attempts to hook me fail. It empowered me. Stay or go… it was my choice now.

Bobby twisted her face again, like I was too stupid to be her blood. "I'm moving in with Juan when my house is settled. If it's good enough for you, it's good enough for me."

Wow. So if it goes South, I'm to blame? I let that one roll off my back and handed her the new latte. Decaf this time. "If it's what you want, sounds great. You don't have to answer to anyone anymore."

My words were the complete truth from where I stood. Thanks to Thomas and this Felidae business, I'd become more intentional with what I wanted.

Bobby squinted and studied me for a moment. I raised my hands. "I'm serious. You worked hard. You didn't choose many of your life… situations." I shrugged. "You can now. Go for it."

Bobby nodded. "I'll look at beach property. We can winter there and live at Juan's in the warmer months."

I laughed, hoping this was the beginning of something good. "Living the American dream."

The music started again, offering a chance to decompress as Bobby turned around to critique the next set of littles. She'd been a miserable witch my whole life. If Juan floated her boat, it would be easier on my psyche all around.

"Please tell me the band is on schedule," Thomas whined, and Rachel laughed.

"The showcases do drag on."

"All the babies get a chance to shine," I defended. Thomas checked the watch I'd given him for Christmas.

Rachel tapped his shoulder. "It's almost over. Then Liam and I are dancing with the first band."

My youngest was changing in my office. Charley had watched the first showcase, then skedaddled to her meeting. Big Jonn also left without incident. I'd take the wins where I could get them.

Deana held her head in her hand, standing at the pastry display. Service always ground to a halt when the kids danced. "We could use some real tap dancing."

"Don't worry. You'll get that from Liam," Rachel said, loosely holding in a grin.

"You turned him into a monster with that old *Lord of the Dance* video." I scolded her. They watched it over and over when they were little, the way most children rewatch Disney movies.

"At least you're both dancing. I didn't come all this way to see other people's grandchildren on stage," Bobby said.

"That reminds me." Rachel snapped her fingers and pulled an innocent face that immediately made me suspicious. "Fi can't come. She's miserable with allergies. Also, Arianne is spending the day at the pub, for her first Saint Patrick's Day since turning twenty-one." She batted her lashes at me. "Can you help a girl out?"

"Your step-dancing buddies ditched us?"

"They couldn't help it." She pouted. I knew the pout was for fun, but her eyes showed total disappointment. I was about to turn her down and tell her to bow out as well, but my mother rolled her eyes like it was a cure for her aging sight. I turned the other way and noted Thomas's lust-filled face. Did he want to see me make a fool of myself, dancing? It had been so long.

"I'd need shoes."

Rachel shuffled her feet like she was already on stage. "I stopped by the house and picked them up. They're in my car."

Like a Corleone lackey, I couldn't refuse. "I'd be glad to do it then, sweetheart."

Her eyes lit up, and she did a vertical leap. "Thanks, Mama. It'll be fun."

The more I thought about it, the more I warmed to the idea. I hadn't danced in front of Bobby since I'd quit. I taught my kids their basic steps before they'd taken a class, but we lived across the country from my parents back then. Like I'd just advised Bobby, this was my time to do what I wanted too.

A wide, kind of vicious grin spread across my face. "It will be fun." I ignored the gasp of disgust from my mother. My days of trying to please her were done.

"NO, NO, NO… DON'T YOU DARE GO ALL *LORD OF THE DANCE*, Lee," I scolded under my breath, trying in some way to will him into submission with "the Force." Instead, Liam tucked his chin like a toddler and let his dimples loose. Then out went the arms as if he was Jaysus Himself, pointing at the musicians, pointing to the lights. Not to mention, he wheeled his arms and pointed to his sister. I hung my head in embarrassment. This was why we pulled him from a formal program way back when. He never could contain himself in class. He was better suited to making music and performing with his guitar.

To my chagrin, he received enthusiastic applause when the band stopped playing. One song was left for the first band. Liam chatted with the lead singer, and before I knew it, they brought Thomas up on stage with his fiddle. Rachel jumped on the mic and pretended to coerce Bobby into dancing.

"Keep in mind my knees aren't what they used to be since my surgery," she told the audience. Her Irish lilt, which could turn on and off like a light switch, was at full strength. For some reason, it made me chuckle. The party put me in a celebratory mood, and her attention-seeking antics came across as quirky rather than weaponized.

"Ah Gran, you're the one who taught us," Rachel bantered with her on the second mic as the musicians checked in with Thomas and each other. "How about we stick with the basic eight?" She turned to the crowd to explain, "Those are the steps that are taught in a beginner class." My daughter pivoted to Bobby again. "Lee and I can take on the advanced moves."

I leaned into the first mic. "I'd appreciate that." The audience chortled at us.

Bobby raised her hands, soaking in the attention. She morphed into her version of an Irish lilt. "*Foine, foine.* Get on wi' it then."

The band began a lively, albeit slow version of "Star of the County Down," changing the name from Colleen to Kathleen in my honor. Refraining from the usual speed of the song allowed Bobby to keep up, and she came alive, leading the rest of us.

The song ended with a roar as Rachel called out, "A big hand for my Gran, Bobby Allen."

Thank heaven for my daughter. She allowed us all to have a much-needed family bonding moment. Something in me had shifted. My mother's antics rolled off my back, and I was proud of myself. *This* was what I wanted.

"He plays like an Irishman," Bobby observed of Thomas's musicianship as we made our way back to the serving station.

Smiling at her, I said, "Why, Mother, are you complimenting my fiancé?"

"*Pffft.*" She waved a hand. Whether it was at my tease or my reference to Thomas's change in status, I didn't care. "I thought you said he plays the guitar, is all."

"He plays both, plus…" I caught myself and swallowed hard. "He learned the fiddle first." I bit my tongue and nearly drew blood. I'd almost told her that Thomas learned the old folk songs from his Irish miner friends—the ones from the California Gold Rush. My first near slip made my heart race. How the hell did he keep these secrets every day? I ambled behind the counter to take a minute.

With Jake as an apprentice to Liam and Thomas, they broke down the first band and quickly brought in the second one. Those of us behind the counter took care of the rush to order and resettle with equal efficiency. Before I knew it, I was back up on stage with both my kids, dancing to "Galway Girl" and wearing myself out. My face ached from smiling.

The fiddle player graciously gave Thomas time to feature, and an old, familiar feeling rushed through me—celebrating culture and ancestry as a family. I loved how well he fit in.

A flush of melancholy swept through me as we were supporting the band by clapping to "Whisky in the Jar." I wished my dad could have joined the party. He would have adored everything about this day. *Craic* like this, as he called it. He would have been down in front, doing a jig and bellowing every word of the traditional songs. I also wished he had met Thomas.

Deana came up to me and gave me a hug, pulling me out of myself. "That's the first time I've seen all y'all up there."

"And?"

The mirth in her eyes told me a joke was imminent. "Give me tap dancing any day."

"You mean like this?" I gave her a few skips and jump-overs while my arms did their best exaggeration of Savion Glover, side-eye added for effect. Then I finished with a time step and arms at my thighs, mixing both dance forms. "Neither sits right if you ask me."

Her warm chuckle rose through the area. "I guess not."

"Thanks for making me laugh though."

"You looked like you needed a distraction."

"I love the idea of featuring other dancing traditions. Let's talk to Jake about it. Maybe we can host more showcases."

At the end of their set, the lead singer brought the kids back up to accompany them on their version of "I'm Shipping Up to Boston." It was a guaranteed crowd-pleaser.

Somewhere in the middle of "whoa…," I spotted Mateo out of

the corner of my eye as he exploded from his position, one of the other guards and Thomas fast on his heels. I couldn't tell what startled them, if someone had come in for them or if there was a text. They ran down the back hall as my heart pounded.

I was about to push through the crowd after them when Thomas appeared. He read the panic in my eyes and held his hands up to keep me behind the counter. They must have handled whatever happened in the back, but I was dying to find out what lit them up. Then I remembered the panicked stampede from Halloween. Desperate to communicate everything running through my head, I peered into his eyes. He mouthed, *it's handled* and gave me a discreet thumbs-up.

Thomas stood guard in the hallway, apparently taking Mateo's place as security until he received an all clear. *I should've known something would happen today.*

31

Into the Mystic

Thomas

"Dammit, brother! You've lost your edge. Hell, you've chucked it off a cliff!" Banger slammed his hand on Kick's desk. He and I were conferencing in her office the evening after the Saint Patrick's Day party. "I don't blame Kick for this one. I blame your dick." He ran his hand over his buzz cut. "Swear to God… if you *ever* turn off the cameras in here again…" His beet-red face told me all about what he'd do.

"The security team worked." We'd tripled it to accommodate the crowd.

Banger's nostrils flared. "Mateo and his guys are good, but they're not you. I can't spare my top-tier associates for the daily shit. They're working behind the scenes. If the cameras had been on, we'd have this guy." He paced to the back door and returned, wringing his hands as he murmured to himself.

At least we were alone. Kick wouldn't handle the rebuke. My best friend laid it on thick like I was a juvenile delinquent, and I let him. I took every harsh, right word he spat out. Even the dick thing. The night before the party, I let myself get caught up in emotion. I'd spent several days at the lab and missed Kick. Finding her in her office afterhours, growling with frustration over the shitty service from the stage rental company, I distracted her with some desktop play. Convinced her it would ease our tensions.

"You're right, man. No more." Not until life's back to normal—whatever that looked like. I pinched the bridge of my nose. "The thing I don't get… it's like this kid knew the cameras were off."

"Yeah." Banger crossed his arms and ground his teeth. "This two-steps behind shit is…" He stopped and stared out the window, his jaw flexing. "I keep coming to one conclusion. It's unthinkable."

He didn't say anything else, just stewed as he gnawed on his lip. I could practically taste the anger emanating from him.

"What's going on?"

He spun around. "What if I have a mole?"

My eyes flashed wide. "Fuck."

Except it made sense. The working cameras picked up a male in a winter-weight hoodie who slipped into the hallway and disappeared into Kick's office. When he left through the back door, he tripped the silent alarm, which set off Mateo and me. "Kick's furious with herself for telling me to turn off the camera in Dee's office, but this guy didn't even touch the doorknob there. He came straight here." I slapped the desktop.

"He knew how to keep his face out of the cameras," Banger said. "Not to mention the size of the crowd." He settled into a club chair, though his posture stayed stiff. Now I knew the anger wasn't only about me. He vibrated with fury at himself too. "Listen, rein in your woman with these big nights. Not until I'm done. I don't know if she's planning an Easter bash. But it's off if she is."

"Don't worry. Remember Liam's senior trip? Angel's been vetting it for us. It's over Easter—Spring Break." I sighed and stretched in her chair.

Banger's shoulders relaxed. "Thank fuck."

"The proposal party had gone so well we thought the system worked."

"Part of why I think there's a mole. But who? And why? It's just…" He rubbed his face.

"I don't understand why nothing's missing." Desk drawers were left half-open, and Kick's bags were dumped on the floor, but everything was accounted for. Kick, Deana, Jake, and I went through the contents with the police, and after they'd gone, Banger also swept for listening devices. Nothing. "What the fuck was he looking for?"

Banger's foot bounced along with his jaw. Hell, we had a jaw flex-off going on as we both seethed in our thoughts.

I drummed my fingers on the desk. "Let me guess… you're going out of town."

"More like underground. You don't understand."

Except I did. Angel Security wasn't just Banger's company, it was *him*. I'd been there when he fought with Alaric and Ellie over his vision and plans to protect the Society while also taking it into the twenty-first century. It required working with regular humans, but he developed a system that rewarded loyalty. The higher up and closer to Banger's inner circle someone went, the greater their reward. Like the rest of the Felidae, loyalty was personal. He couldn't abide a traitor.

His foot resumed bouncing. "Need you to hold down some shit for me now that Tess is dug in here."

"Damn." My hands raked through my hair. "What do you need?"

"First, Siobhan's taking over our real estate hunt. The woman I'm working with usually reports to her anyway." He lifted a shoulder and grinned. "There's only so much of me to go around. It's narrowed to four sites. You'll have to give final approval when they're ready to bring you in. Are you still on schedule with your end of things?"

"Yep. My lawyers should have the proposal for the university by the end of the week."

"And what's your timeline to start?"

"If we secure a building soon and get a clean construction crew on board… beginning of August. The dean will warm up to a partnership if I show them we'll be ready when the students are back."

"Siobhan's prioritizing facilities with minor modification needs," Banger assured me.

"Excellent."

"Also, Tess knows to call me if she needs anything, but she won't. Can you keep a close eye on her? She won't talk about it, but the Charley business rocked her."

"That's easy. Yeah, man. We've got her."

Banger almost grinned. "Kick's girl and her roommate are determined. They give Tess a taste of her own meddling medicine."

I lifted a shoulder. "Kick said something about spreading the love around. Anyway…" I stood and stretched my legs, letting the tension go. "Tess can stay at the farmhouse if she needs a break from the girls. I'll tell her."

"I don't know." Banger stood too. "We're testing the next upgrade at my place. I'd rather she stay where I can keep an eye on her from afar."

"Then I'll… schedule time with her."

We clasped forearms and said goodbye. "Thanks, brother."

"One last thing…" I rubbed my chin, hoping I wasn't about to overstep. "We've set a wedding date for Memorial Day weekend. Will this be over by then?"

"Fuck." Banger dropped his forehead against the door. "I hope so. Why can't you wait until we're sure?"

I forced air through my cheeks as I grabbed the back of my neck. "Something's niggling at me. Telling me we should've done it yesterday. Can't explain it, but the sooner the better."

Banger tapped the doorframe. "Fine. I'll do my best. If you catch wind of anything, holler."

"Of course." Unfortunately, I was swamped at the lab. Many items on my to-do list had to be pushed until after the new lab was finished. I hated the idea of pushing Banger, especially now. He'd always been intense, but he balanced it with a play-hard attitude. I worried about what would happen if he didn't get to release it soon.

"I can hear you thinking," he said. "Don't worry about me. This became more than you and Kick today. I'm sure it all ties together. Whoever's behind it is taking advantage of our closeness. Since my eyes are open now, they're going to pay. Just hold tight. Yeah?"

I nodded. "Sure."

"Be in touch." He opened the door and turned back. "I have the last point now… When you speak with Siobhan, have her find you a damn event planner. You and Kick have too much to do to add in the running around for that. Don't make those guards taste cake samples, and don't play it shoddy. I'll only play this best man role once."

I laughed as I let my head hang. "Sure thing. And Rafa…" He lifted an eyebrow. I never called him by his given name, but this was vital. I walked over to him, looked in his eyes. "Stay smart. You're needed here. You listening?"

He grasped my shoulder. "Keep the faith."

"In you? Always." If I found out who'd betrayed Banger, I'd kill them myself. Still, I worried about how he'd take the information once he had it sorted. How bad would the fallout be?

Banger jerked his chin up and stalked out to his waiting Harley. I heard it rumble as he thundered out of the parking lot. A modern-day knight on a quest to protect his family and avenge his honor.

I sank down in a club chair and brooded over the day's events. As usual, my thoughts moved to Kick.

"It's too much, Thomas," she'd said when I explained about the silent alarm tripping. This time had been different. She'd spat the words through her teeth and added, "I want to wring his fecking neck."

"Let Banger and the team handle it. We're your secret weapon. It's the benefit of living life in the shadows. Graham thinks he's the one with the connections. He has no clue who Banger and I really are." At the time, I was convinced that Big Jonn was involved with what was essentially a break-in. My gut still believed it, but we needed proof.

"I appreciate it, cowboy. Honestly, I do. It's just… the damsel-in-distress thing? It's… I don't know." She shook her arms like something was crawling on her.

"Come here." I pulled her in for an embrace. "Much better." My hands ran up her sides, pushing her special edition Saint Patrick's Day T-shirt up to her breasts. It was a knee-jerk response to help us settle. Her eyes closed for a moment, lost in the feeling before Kick regained her senses and pulled the shirt down.

"You can't fix this with sex."

"Wasn't planning to. I'm sorry, baby. Touching you calms me. For the record, you're not a damsel in distress, unless I am too."

Kick's hands jerked up between us, making me step back. "The hell I'm not. I've been one before. I know how it feels."

"This is different," I insisted. I lifted my eyes to the ceiling, searching for the right words. "You've spent your life battling your family and your body. There are similarities here. Consider yourself like a warrior in training. Your instincts are fine."

She sighed a long breath and scoffed. "A warrior who can't focus with a weapon?"

"You're getting there." I bent my knees to make sure I had her attention. "I was supposed to be a career soldier, remember? My father made me train long before I enlisted. Hell, I understood a battlefield before I even knew how to use my cock properly."

Kick lifted an eyebrow, a glint of humor in her eyes. "I'm pissed."

"Good. So am I. And that's not the response of a damsel in distress. It's how a fighter feels when their ass is handed to them."

"If you say so."

"We'll figure out why we're always a step behind."

"Thanks, cowboy. I know what I need to do." Kick's face was resolute.

"What's that?"

"I need to figure this self-defense out the same way I did those others."

"Yeah?" I tilted my head, wondering what she'd decided.

Her eyes narrowed, like she could see through me. Then she tapped her heart. "It's in here. I need to hunker down and find it." Kick went up on her tiptoes and kissed my jaw. "I'll be at the range."

"Hang on, I can't go with you." I'd been neglecting my horse thanks to so many hours at the lab. Sure, he was an animal, but our rides cleared my head. It's where I did my best thinking, and my mind was swirling with too much shit. But first I needed to go over the papers my lawyers had drawn up for my proposal to Lord University. It was a healthy stack that I couldn't take for granted.

"I know," Kick said. "Mateo will come with me. I need to do this myself anyhow. I also know you need your trail time. Please don't make me wait till you get back."

I didn't protest. In fact, I was proud of her. She'd crashed through this mental block. As I walked through the empty coffeehouse an hour later, my mind struggled to think of anything but Kick's progress. I pulled my phone out of my pocket and sent her a text.

> Done here. On to Eddie. How're you doing?

Kick didn't answer, but after watching Mateo work these past weeks, I trusted them to have each other's backs. She had to be still on the range. I did, however, receive a text from the lab.

> BETHANY
>
> Call me ASAP.

32

Closer to Fine

Kick

"Do you need anything else, Ms. Kick?" Mateo had helped me collect the weapons and set up the range on Thomas's property. The hardest part was bringing the bag down from Thomas's main office since no one else had access to it. Mateo scouted the property and made sure we were alone.

"Why don't you keep watch by the path on the high point? I know you like those. Maybe we can take turns, but no coaching, okay?"

Mateo chuckled as he held up his hands. "I heard you the first time and promise to zip it."

My first three tries were mediocre at best. One shot even ended up in a tree trunk again. I made a mental note to bring a tree surgeon out to the property. I didn't want to be the reason any of these beauties became sick.

I waved at Mateo. "Come at me."

He turned his head and chortled. "Pardon?"

"I need to loosen up. You know..." I waved at him again. "Pretend to attack me."

His brows rose. "Ah. Alrighty."

My muscle memory surprised me. It clicked in fast, letting me parry Mateo's first moves. He'd worked out with Thomas and me twice, so he knew where and how to push me.

"Let's try something different." Mateo taught me new moves from a slightly different discipline. Within a few minutes, my hands and knees were useless. He put me in a hold I didn't know how to escape. I kept testing joints to see if they had enough give to wiggle away. "Good," he said in my ear. "Remember this... your goal isn't winning a match. You want to live."

He squeezed me so tight it quickly became difficult to draw a breath. My heart rate soared through the roof as panic set in. I knew he wouldn't hurt me, truly, but the adrenaline spike almost made me pass out.

"Living to see another day might mean complying for a time. It's more important to stay calm. Keep your head."

"Can't... breathe."

"You can. Shallow breaths, Ms. Kick."

They were still coming too fast as my lungs longed to take a full inhale.

"Come on...," he ordered. "Mind over matter. Get your bearings. Look in each direction. See the path?"

I barely managed a head twitch, let alone nod, but he felt it.

"Good. Eyes on the pond. Now straight ahead."

It worked. My heart rate wasn't normal yet, but it stopped racing.

"Nice," Mateo said in my ear. "Stillness can be self-defense too."

He let me go, and I gasped the longest inhale in my memory. I felt like I'd been kicked in the stomach. I was furious with myself for falling for it, but Mateo smiled at me like a proud parent.

"Good work, Ms. Kick."

I chuckled as I held my head. The world still tilted a little. "What are you talking about? You made me into a chump."

"Self-defense starts here." He tapped his head. "There's always the possibility an opponent will be bigger, stronger, or hell, they might sneak up behind you. Panic kills. You stay alive with your mind first." He pointed at the range. "That's also what I see when you hold a weapon. Odds are, if you need a gun, you'll use it in close range. It's not the aim you have to perfect, it's having the balls to pull the trigger." He tapped his head again for emphasis.

I hated that this had become my life and wanted the madness to end. My tongue rolled around in my cheek as I thought through everything he'd said.

We'd talked the adrenaline down. Mateo had shown me a quick move to keep my bearings. Maybe I could do something similar with the Sig Sauer.

Multiple coils of curls had fallen out of my ponytail. Instead of fixing it, I tucked them behind my ears and picked up the weapon. I thought about finding my bearings. Looking around wouldn't help, since shooting required a focus on the target. What else had grounded me over the years?

As if summoned from deep inside me, the song "Closer to Fine" bubbled up. I began singing it from that place in my soul. I stopped relying on the gun to save my life. Like Mateo and Thomas had been telling me this whole time, the answers came from within. So did self-defense.

"Focus," Mateo called out.

He didn't understand, the song was my focus. I belted the hook as loud as my voice allowed and emptied the clip.

"Holy shit." I whispered hoarsely. It wasn't perfect, but it was pretty freaking close.

I changed out the magazines and sighted the second target as I sang the song again.

No more time spent as a victim.

No more time as the family scapegoat.

And no one knew my body better than me. It was up to me to protect it in all ways. Self-defense started in my mind. I took a deep breath and fired as I kept singing the song.

Mateo's whistle out-shrieked the weapon's reverb echoing off the pond. "Nice!"

The shot pattern rivaled Thomas's and Mateo's. My grin stayed plastered on my face as we switched out the targets. "Want to shoot side by side?" I asked him.

"Are you gonna keep singing?"

I shrugged. "Maybe."

"Good thing I have these." Mateo set his ear protection in place. Then he yelled, "Even if you do sing nice."

I bit my lip to keep from laughing and readied my weapon. I inhaled and found that deep place inside again. This time I sang the song inside. It wasn't the words that mattered. The magic came from revealing what had been waiting for release. After a nod at each other, we each emptied our magazines. My streak continued through two more rounds.

"Now you're just showing off," Mateo said, a smirk on his face.

"You're right." I didn't want to stop but hated the idea of wasting bullets.

"I was kidding, Ms. Kick. If you need more time, we can keep going."

"No, no. My goal's accomplished. Let's clean up." I picked up the rake we kept nearby and cleaned up the mess on the ground.

"Do you remember how to break these down?" Mateo asked.

"Good point." I thought so, but Thomas often did that work for me to make it go faster. "Let me take a picture of this last target, then you can quiz me."

After we cleaned the guns and secured them, I sent the photo of the target to Thomas. He had texted me about ten minutes earlier, but I hadn't noticed it until now.

ME

Going very well. Are you finished yet?

THOMAS

Knew you could do it.

The message included a kissy-face emoji. I smiled at it, thinking of how far Thomas had come from the serious man I'd met in September. Then came the second part.

THOMAS

Actually, had to head to the lab. Might take a
while. Can you apologize to Eddie for me?

I laughed.

ME

Of course.

Thomas hated going more than a day without seeing his horse, and it had been a few already. He claimed Eddie pouted if Thomas became too busy to ride. I couldn't blame the horse. I felt the same. Still, I thought Thomas used the time the way I used my meditation pillow in my room.

"Hey Mateo…"

My bodyguard swung the bag of weapons over his shoulder and spun toward me.

"Want to go meet a horse?"

THE REST OF MARCH FLEW BY IN A BLUR EVEN IF IT WAS A QUIET one. No more weird break-ins happened at the coffeehouse or at home. The only thing I couldn't find was my lip balm, but I blamed Liam for its disappearance.

Banger had gone underground and, according to my fiancé, was hot on the heels of whoever wanted to harm me. All I knew was he'd gone to England. I couldn't keep the cities straight, but Thomas had the details. The hush-hush-ness of it all made me antsy even if I trusted the men. They handled our current circumstances like danger was an everyday occurrence. Then again, it was sort of old hat for them.

Even the bodyguards stayed need-to-know. Thomas only allowed Tess and me into the inner circle that included Banger's right hand, Siobhan. The first time I met her, when she led the security installation at the Perked Cup, I saw her spiked, fire-engine-red hair and knew I liked her.

Since Thomas insisted on getting married on the Saturday of

Memorial Day weekend, Siobhan hooked us up with a top-notch wedding planner. I knew what a crazy zoo planning a wedding could be, especially a fast one. I'd done it myself my last semester of college. Even though we wanted a family affair, getting someone else to do the heavy lifting was an immeasurable help.

Then the day before Liam's spring break arrived. The three of us were to join a group of families from Liam's high school on a cruise to the Bahamas. Thomas walked into the bedroom while I packed my suitcase.

He sat on the edge of the bed but wouldn't look me in the eye. "I have news."

I stopped rolling a T-shirt. "What's wrong?"

He cleared his throat. "*Grand-père* wants—"

"No." I dropped the shirt on the floor. "Don't tell me you can't go on our trip."

My chest tightened at the thought of breaking this to Liam. I couldn't see how we could go without Thomas. We'd have to bring a bodyguard or two. "We can't get another room. The ship is booked." Ironically, I knew someone in the group chat was on a waitlist for two rooms like ours. They'd been quite vocal in their disappointment over missing the booking window.

"Can't Alaric wait?"

His shoulders slumped. "It doesn't work that way, darlin'. The team and I caught a big break with Toni's project. That's why I've been at the lab so much. Plus he wants updates on you. Alaric doesn't want me sending updates online anymore even though it's encrypted." Thomas grabbed the back of his neck and stretched it. I bet mine was tighter. "The last time I updated Alaric, he guessed Banger's mole situation before I brought it up. Besides, I've stretched his patience as much as he'll take with our... circumstances. It'll go a long way to stay the good soldier this time."

"Our circumstances?" I squeaked. "You mean where we're engaged or where I'm one of you?"

Thomas's Adam's apple bobbed. "Both."

I picked up a pair of already packed shorts and threw them on the floor. "Here, I thought our engagement meant *I* was your priority."

He grabbed my wrist as I reached for a sandal. "You are. Look, I know the timing is bad, but finals are also fast approaching. I can't miss them. This is the only nonessential time on my calendar."

"Shit." I stared up at the ceiling while I bristled at his rightness. Liam's delivery had been induced during Shane's team's bi-week so that he could be there for it. My son's first five birthdays though? It had been me and the kids by ourselves. My eyes widened. This trip had been just as important to me as it was to Liam. The last senior trip. How would I fix this?

Thomas pulled me between his legs and wrapped his arms around my waist. "I'm sorry. I'll make it up to both of you."

I'd heard that before too. But Shane tried his best to come through. Why shouldn't Thomas be as beholden to the Felidae as my late husband had been to his team? Both entities basically owned the men.

I laid my head on top of his and hugged him back. "I'm still taking Lee somewhere. He'll probably pick a place with topless beaches to get back at me."

Thomas groaned and squeezed, pressing himself into me. I stepped outside my hurt heart long enough to note his messy hair. He hadn't showered yet either. He needed time to relax as much as I did. "Mmm. You at a topless beach. You're killing me."

"Good." I kissed his head. "You get 'topless beach' me every night. What's the difference?"

"The sun. The sand. The water—"

"The burned skin. Besides, no nude beaches will be allowed."

"Your presence alone will keep your boy in line."

"Exactly." I moved back and stood with my hands on my hips, wondering where to begin first. "How many guards will we need?"

Thomas rubbed the bridge of his nose, considering. "Two should be fine, as long as it's a resort I know and you take a chartered plane."

"You know resorts?" I folded my arms and stared down at him.

This was yet another of those moments where the reality of Thomas blindsided me. Somehow it still made sense.

He lifted a shoulder. "Some of my connections own resorts."

Of course they did.

And that's how Liam, Mateo, Wes, and I ended up spending five balmy days on a sunny beach in Barbados. It didn't diminish how hard it had been to break the news to my son. All his close friends went on that cruise, including Jax and her parents. The poor kid almost cried over it.

As a consolation, I arranged to fly in the Irish cousins for Liam's graduation, under the supervision of Shane's mother, Anna, and Uncle Billy, and I agreed to let Lee fly back with them for the summer. It turned out my nest would empty earlier than planned.

Then? I did cry.

33

All the Small Things

Kick

"Will it be too much trouble to stop by a jewelry store on the way home?" I asked Mateo. We were standing in a parking lot in front of the restaurant I'd taken Rachel to for a birthday dinner. We'd had painfully little time alone and decided on a quiet evening without the boys. Dylan was buried by his school project. Liam's band had booked a paying gig. Rachel asked for a family dinner the following weekend too, when all three men could come. Thomas was due home later this evening and would join us for the second dinner. I loved how she included him in the ask.

The end of an era loomed heavy on my heart. Rachel had landed a role in a summer theater production in the Outer Banks. This was the first summer Rachel wouldn't work at the coffeehouse. I'd have to consider myself lucky to see her for the wedding and Liam's graduation. It took a lot of effort to keep my shit together during dinner. I spent the evening focusing on celebrating my girl and all she was about to become. It helped a little.

Despite how much my body had been physically changing—reversing, according to Thomas—these upcoming changes made me feel old. Even if I'd begged for the empty nest when the kids frustrated me. Even if I liked Thomas's promise of naked weekend every night. So I took advantage of the opportunity to celebrate Rachel one-on-one, afraid those times would become few and far between. Except with guards eating across the room from us, of course.

They were wonderful about it. Mateo and Wes—Rachel's detail today—gave us plenty of room for privacy and agreed to let me drive my Camaro while they tailed us in the Escalade Wes used to chauffeur Rachel. All of that was on the condition that I agree to stick to a preplanned route.

Fortunately, the Graham's were busy with Young Jonn's trial. It was set to start soon. According to the tail Banger had on him, the boy was faithful to his therapy appointments. I hoped we were nearing the end of this weird-ass year.

"You pay the bill, Ms. Kick. I go where you tell me," Mateo answered with his sheepish grin.

"Right. Let's head to this artisan market then. The jeweler promised to stay open for me. Mums the word to Thomas too. I'm picking up his ring." I shared the location of the store with Mateo.

"Promise." He held his fingers up, Boy Scout style. "The GPS report still goes to the office."

I waved him off. "Feel free to explain the stop to Siobhan. Just keep the stop from my guy."

"Of course. Everyone's expecting some of that, given the quickness of your wedding."

I shook my head. "Don't know why he's in such a hurry to make it official, but thanks."

A half hour later, I buckled back into the Camaro, giddy with excitement. The ring turned out better than I'd hoped. Southern oak set in tungsten. It was masculine and earthy.

The wood came from live oak in the park at the Center of Oakville. It inspired our town's name. The tree was thought to be around a thousand years old. When we first moved there, I often took the kids on picnics under its shade. The heavy branches bent to the ground, seeming to invite the kids to climb them. After Shane's funeral, I often escaped to those sturdy branches to clear my head. It became a sanctuary, a way to escape the pain, where I could just be.

As soon as the ring landed in my palm, it occurred to me I'd chosen the wood because Thomas was my sanctuary now. Plus that tree was one of the few things I knew of older than him. We speculated it was an ancestor of the tree at the edge of Thomas's property where we committed ourselves to each other. I couldn't wait to see this visual representation of that commitment on his finger.

"You had it inscribed?" Rachel asked, holding the ring up to the interior light. She turned on her flashlight app and read the Gaelic out loud. "*Mo chuisle, mo chroi.*"

Her face twisted into a frown. It wasn't the reaction I'd expected.

I placed the ring safely in my purse, then hit the road, checking the rearview mirror for our bodyguards. "Something wrong?"

Her chin quivered. "My heart's pulse, right?"

I spared her a glance as I watched the vehicles around us. "Pretty much."

Turning in her seat, she faced me and said, "But Daddy's ring had the Gaelic for *soul mate.*"

"It did." My chin dipped in agreement, not liking where this was heading.

She huffed at me, her hands reaching as high as the interior allowed. "How can someone have two soul mates, *Mother?*"

Mother? When did I land in the doghouse? "Thomas has always liked the meaning behind Macushla's name. It'll make him happy." I thought about her question and the answer hit me hard. "Besides, it's true. I have had two soul mates."

A quick head turn her way showed me no sign of a smile. She pressed her lips together as she stared out the window. Glared was more like it.

I took a deep breath and pressed the pedal to the floor, both literally—to enter the freeway—and figuratively—to make Rachel understand something I wasn't sure I did. "What if my soul is completely changed from when I married Daddy?"

Again with the scornful face. She looked like a raven-haired version of my mother. "That's impossible."

"I disagree. Your dad's death changed us all. I can't speak for you precisely, but I believe it transformed me in my deepest parts—you could call it my soul."

"So you think you're a fundamentally different person now than you were before his accident?"

A light bulb went off in my mind. "Do you think Thomas is my second choice? That's not fair either, Snow."

"Can you honestly tell me that if Daddy were alive, you'd marry Thomas?"

"You know we'd be together." I shrugged. "My point is… I'd also be different from who I am now." Her chin quivered harder. I had to think fast. "Do you think I'd have the Perked Cup if your father still lived? Do you think I'd have learned to stand up to your grandmother the way I do?"

Her mouth twisted as she thought. "You could."

I shook my head. "I'm certain I wouldn't. Back then, I just wanted to paint in peace and feel better. I never wanted to be an entrepreneur with the responsibilities that come with it. I wouldn't have needed to either. Nope." I shook my head with vigor. "I know I'd be different if he were here."

"So that's bad?"

"It's life." I reached for Rachel's hand. "It's neither good nor bad." From the corner of my eye, I saw her head stay down, eyeing my engagement ring. "What I mean is, Thomas fits exactly who I am now. He's not a consolation prize. He simply… fits." She lifted her head and stared out the windshield. "Tell me you understand," I pleaded.

"Can I think about it?"

I patted her hand. "Absolutely."

Music from Blink-182 filled our silence as we made our way down I-540. The skies opened up yet again and began a steady sprinkle. April had been one of those months with all the weather, especially rain. At least it wasn't pouring, and it washed the pollen away. As much as my eyes had improved, I still hated driving in the rain after dark. The days might be getting longer, but it wasn't summer yet. Not sure why, but squinting helped me keep my focus on the road.

I went over the schedule in my head to keep from being irritated by the road. Next we'd pick up food for Rachel, Isabella, and Tess. Then Wes would drive her home. Only a few more exits until the grocery store.

I shifted our conversation from me to my daughter. "So are you and Bella still doing well?"

A sarcastic smile returned to her face. At least she hadn't forgotten our native language. "Are you asking me if *I'm* getting any? Do you ask the boys if they are?"

"Dylan acts like I do. But noooo." I drew out the last word. "I'm asking how your household is faring in general. You were with Cody a long time, and the change to Bella seemed quick. You can't blame me for wanting to make sure my girl's happy. Then you two jumped into repairing Tess and Charley. Thank you for letting up on that, by the way."

Rachel flicked her wrist. "Absolutely. They're destined. They'll speak soon enough. I guarantee it." She tucked her foot under her thigh and turned toward me. "As far as Cody goes…" She sighed heavily, her posture easing in my periphery. "It's a relief to be free of him."

I quickly turned my head and smiled at her. Rachel was the most relaxed I'd seen her in a while.

Rachel lifted a shoulder. "Anyway, Bella's great. We're having a great time. It's all… great."

I reached over and squeezed her hand. "That's all I care about. How are you planning to handle summer theater and a new relationship?"

She perked up. "Oh, it couldn't have worked out better. Bella has an internship in Virginia Bea—"

Something pelted against the passenger-side window, spider-webbing it. A second burst made a hole, sending small shards across the front seat and who knew where else. Sharp drops of water hit my arm. Rachel's scream pierced my ears before it registered that we'd been shot at.

A few more bullets thudded into the rear quarter panel. My heart pounded as my head swung to the right. Mateo's words came to me—*get your bearings.*

I saw the spoiled rotten son of a bitch, gun still drawn, trying to steady his filthy hand. Jonn Graham. The piece of shit was in the back seat of a red BMW, just like the one from the snowstorm. The window was down, a buddy drove, one more cheered from the front passenger seat like he was at a Hurricanes game. For a split second, I watched the bastard gleefully bounce in the back.

Forget the shine on the road from the rain, I saw red. How the hell was this asshole out of his house? My chest pounded, but not from fear. I was enraged.

"Get down!" I grabbed Rachel's arm and practically threw her under the dash, causing the Camaro to swerve toward the Beemer.

I straightened the wheel as another bullet shattered the small back window. "Fucking hell!"

We had to get away. *Self-defense starts with your mind.*

I'd forgotten about the Escalade until I heard more shots, ducked, and swerved, but no bullets hit the car. Wes was firing at the BMW.

I chanced a glance to the right. Graham's deadly stare stayed pegged on us, glimmering as much as the water droplets clinging to the bits of glass on the edges of my windows. He gnashed his teeth at us like a mistreated, starving beast. Another quick look and he aimed at the door where my daughter was curled up on the floor. I had to get her away from this monster.

An exit I knew like the back of my hand was fast approaching, so I slid my car from the left lane all the way to the right. The tires squealed from the maneuver as we cut off the Beemer and accidentally also lost Mateo and Wes.

A call came in over Bluetooth. I hit the button on my steering wheel.

"Kick! Where the hell did you go?"

"Shit. Sorry, Mateo. I had to get Rachel out of there. He was aiming for her. For my daughter!" I shrieked. Flying down the road, I nearly rear-ended a car stopping for a yellow light. My tires squealed again as we swerved around it and flew through the intersection.

"Where. Are. You?" Mateo repeated.

For an instant, I forgot, though instinct told me safety was close. Why were we here? Six Forks! "We're on Six Forks. There's a police station coming up." I had to think. "You still have eyes on Graham?"

"Yep. Call 911. Let them know what happened and you're coming."

"Gotcha."

"Fuck. Remember… keep your head. I'm gonna stay on these guys until we stop them. This ends tonight."

"Thanks, Mateo. Be safe." I hung up and watched the business parks and shopping centers roll by as I searched my memory for the location of the substation. "Rach…" My voice was shaky as hell, but I made it as commanding as I could. "You have your phone down there?"

"Yes," she whimpered.

"Call 911. Tell the operator about them shooting. Tell them we're going to the substation. We'll need cover when we pull in. Hell, ask them if one's handy for an escort." I watched my rearview mirror more than the front while I spoke. I couldn't help thinking they'd given the Escalade the slip. Every car I saw looked red to me.

"K-kay," Rachel said, dialing.

She handled the call well enough to tell her story. Unfortunately, the intersection where we were supposed to turn left had a red light. The logical part of my brain knew Mateo and Wes kept Graham and his buddies occupied, but the primitive side of it stayed in flight mode. I'd keep Rachel safe no matter what. I treated the intersection as a four-way stop, or really, as a yield, turning the wheel as I slammed on the brakes. An icy mist hit my face and fought with my lashes, blinking rapidly as I made the turn. The car's momentum pulled it into the new street more than the wheel did.

Thank goodness it was a Sunday evening, the road virtually

empty. Another quick left and we were in the police parking lot, flying way too fast. We skidded to a stop, the rear end fishing, making one hell of a squeal on the wet pavement. It saved our asses when we stopped inches from smashing into two cruisers with the side of my Camaro. We were too close to open my door.

I took a moment to gasp for breath as I reached for Rachel. She whimpered in terror yet again as four officers cautiously approached us with their guns drawn.

"We need to see your hands. Are you the one who called in a drive-by?" A surprisingly kind face bent toward the open area of the passenger window. Rachel screamed anyway.

"Shh, Snowy… mama's here." I instinctively reverted to soothing her the way I had when she was little. As far as the police were concerned, obedience was no problem. I raised my hands up as far as they'd go. "Okay, okay," I called out. "We were shot at. C-can I pull forward a bit? I can't open my door."

The first officer shook his head. "You'll have to crawl out this side."

Over the glass? Maybe if I yanked off my jacket. It could be a buffer between my hands and the glass. "My daughter needs help getting out. Please."

"Sure, ma'am." He opened the door to lift Rachel out when I truly saw her. She reached for him, her right arm covered in blood. She was bleeding so much from her head I couldn't see her right eye.

To hell with keeping my mind clear. This mama turned into a full-on banshee.

34

The Sky is Crying

Thomas

I LANDED AT THE AIRPORT TWENTY MINUTES BEHIND SCHEDULE AND powered up my phone while waiting to deplane. My heart started pounding as I read a series of texts from Banger.

BANGER

Heard from Kick? No one's responding. Not her. Not the guards. Not Princess.

I was doing the penguin walk down the airplane aisle when another came through.

BANGER

Graham's on the loose. His tail never checked in. Sent a man to investigate. The tail's dead.

My pulse immediately pounded so hard I couldn't hear the woman behind me speaking.

When another came through saying, *Where the fuck are you????* I knew Banger had lost his cool.

The second I stepped onto the jetway, I bolted. Tried my best not to knock anyone over, but I couldn't be certain and apologized while passing each person. Finally able to run through the open airport, I turned on my Bluetooth and called Kick, hoping my shoes didn't slip on the slick floor as I kept up the sprint. The call went to voice mail. I needed to keep her away from the house, figuring that's where Graham would head. Unless he went after Rachel. Then I remembered Kick had taken Rachel out for her birthday. *Fuck!*

I thumbed my contacts for Mateo, but he called me first. My heart dropped into my stomach as I answered. "Tell me they're alright."

He sounded out of breath like he was running. "Have you landed?"

"Just." Thank Christ I'd parked in the airport deck and didn't have to wait for a shuttle to long-term parking. "Throwing my gear into the trunk now. Did Banger reach you?" I heard three sharp bangs—like gunshots—over the phone, then tires squealing. My heart simultaneously stopped and jumped out of my chest. *Not again.*

"Talk to me," I ordered. My Camaro roared to life, the growl mimicking my anger at feeling helpless.

"The fucker took a shot at Kick's ride. He unloaded on her passenger side."

Fuck! Kick.

She sat in the passenger seat when Mateo was on duty. Hell, she hadn't driven herself in weeks. "Where are you?" More squealing tires. "Why isn't everyone in the Escalade?"

At this point, I was maneuvering around the parking deck's circular exit tower way too fast to be safe, even for a Sunday evening.

"Um… Kick and Rachel took her Camaro and Wes and I followed behind. It should've—" Another gunshot shut him up.

I slowed enough to go through the gate, then I bolted the hell out of there. "Where are my girls? Talk to me!"

"Sorry, sir. We're uh… following Graham and… Kick got out of dodge like a pro, sir. She should be at the police station by now."

"You *lost* them?" My temper grew murderous in an instant.

"Technically… she lost us. We're keeping Graham's car occupied… till the cops intercept us. Wes is on the phone with RPD now. We're trying to lure them off the freeway and away from innocents."

Fuck. Find Kick or help the guards? I could help Wes and Mateo if the Escalade was nearby. That is, if the women were away from danger. Frankly, I was long past wanting to kill Jonn Graham. I needed it like I needed air. If either of my women had been hurt… I couldn't think about it.

"Which freeway?" As I approached the eastbound ramp that would take me home, two cars flew past the airport exit. "Was that you? Did you just pass the airport?" I pressed the brake and switched lanes to take the ramp going west, the decision made for me.

"Huh? Yeah! Guess we did."

"Don't exit yet. I'm coming up behind you. Keep them occupied. Be right there." I opened up my muscle car up on the entrance ramp. The wipers were on high to keep up with my speed. I'd never known a car that could beat mine in a flat quarter mile. I saw the two cars in no time. Made out one gunman sitting in the back seat. Saw the shadow of a head in the front passenger seat. I had to assume he was armed, but only the one shithead fired at Mateo and Wes. Thank Christ the Escalade had been bulletproofed.

"You driving, Mateo?"

"Yes, sir."

Another shot fired. Kid must've reloaded. Bastard must've snapped.

"I'm here. Inside lane." I patted the dashboard. My secret weapon. "Sorry for the next few minutes, Ginger." My Camaro wouldn't mind. If my plan worked, I'd still drive her home. I spoke to the guys again. "Listen. Keep them occupied till the straightaway. On my signal, slam on the brakes. I'll put the Beemer into a skid. Then I'll back off. You guys get back in and ram them. Understand?"

"Got it. Signal. Brake. Smash. We end it."

"Right." We took a curve to the right. The BMW either didn't notice me matching their speed or was too hyped to care. With their attention on the Escalade, I stayed two lanes over on purpose. I moved my car into the middle lane as we came out of the curve. Even with the SUV now, I called out, "Brake."

Mateo backed off as I cut the wheel and hit the gas. My faithful muscle car bolted for the rear bumper of the BMW and sent it into a sideways skid, like it was angry too. Then I pulled away and ordered, "Go, go, go!"

The Escalade rammed the passenger side of the BMW. Mateo pushed it into the grassy median. A loud "Take that, asshole!" echoed over my Bluetooth.

As well as the BMW was made, the car couldn't hold up against the heavy SUV. It was through. However, the driver's side stayed unscathed. We all stopped on the shoulder. No one was firing, but being behind Mateo and Wes blinded me to the action in the BMW. The rain at night didn't help either.

I'd had enough. I wanted that nightmare finished yesterday. Kick and Rachel flashed through my mind. They hadn't called yet, not that I could've answered. *Christ*, I hoped they were alright.

As I reached for the gun under my seat, the red and blue lights of multiple police cruisers flashed in my rearview mirror. "Mateo... still with me? What's happening?"

"So far... nothing, sir. We might've knocked them out."

Fuck! I wanted my piece of them. But fighting in three wars and then some had taught me the most important part of war—living to see another day. My leg bounced as I talked down my rage. "See the cops?" I asked Mateo.

"I do. About time."

"Let the police handle them now." I gnashed my teeth, wishing I could take back my words. Getting to my women came first.

"Roger that."

I beat on the steering wheel. What good would it do for Kick to get away from those idiots and lose me to the police? I didn't worry about being shot by the likes of Jonn Graham, though anyone can be lucky. The weather conditions and our circumstances primed the situation for confusion.

The flashing lights turned into no less than five cruisers. I rolled my window down as they skidded to a stop around us and exited their vehicles with guns drawn. I raised my hands as raindrops pelted my face, hoping my hands could be seen in their headlights. My heart pounded again, praying like hell that they figured out who was whom in this fucked-up scenario.

"Out of the car!" The gun pointed at me seemed to speak since the cop was shadowed by the night.

I kept my hands visible as I opened my door in obedience. Before I even took a step outside, gunshots opened up, sounding like a damn firing squad. On instinct, I yelled for Mateo since the earpiece was still on. "What's happening?" I couldn't see a fucking thing back behind the Escalade.

A hand came from nowhere and shoved me down. "Get on the fucking ground!" As gravel bit into my cheek, the gun that had been pointed at me fired.

"Not the Escalade! They're good guys. They're my security team." It was a stupid thing to say, but I wasn't thinking straight. For a minute, I was back in a war trench in France, laying helpless as my uncle bled out. What would I tell Kick if her guards died trying to end this madness?

Not daring to move my hands, I coughed away the wet dirt sticking to my mouth. I figured the heat of the moment was the only reason I hadn't been cuffed. Better to make my hands as frozen as possible. The hard part was keeping them from shaking with the cold. I coughed as exhaust from the Escalade filled my nose.

In seconds, the shooting stopped. Police called for ambulances. The acrid scent of gunpowder replaced the exhaust. Risking turning my head toward the bottom of my car didn't diffuse the smell or the PTSD that sometimes followed. The muscles in my arms spasmed as I forced myself to stay calm. I despised the helplessness of the moment. Then more cruisers arrived and shut down the expressway.

Wes had been on the phone with a 911 operator during the start of the chase, so the police knew the situation of the BMW and the Escalade when they arrived. They didn't know what to make of me and the Camaro, but the bodyguards straightened it out once the scene abated.

I ended up with a bump on the head and small scrapes from the shove to the ground. It was a move to keep me out of the line of fire as much as it was to subdue me.

Mateo and Wes were fine, thank Christ. They'd been kneeling on the ground, their shields in their hands when Jonn Graham and the driver of the BMW tried to make a run for it. As soon as they realized they were surrounded, they fired on the police. The firing squad sound of the moment ended up being real. Those sick boys died anyway—suicide by cop.

Whatever. As long as my men were alright. My ladies too.

Then the real challenge started. While I sat on the side of the freeway in the pouring rain, with what seemed like all the police in the county milling around, I plotted how to get the hell out of there and find Kick.

I FOUGHT MY NERVES ALL THE WAY TO KICK AND RACHEL. IT WAS A new form of torture to keep my speed respectable while I kept dialing her phone. Since my Camaro was drivable, law enforcement let me follow a cruiser back to the station to give my statement. They knew about my women but wouldn't divulge any details.

She never picked up, which amped up my worry. I was going out of my mind. I heard an ambulance siren while exiting the freeway. My heart did a somersault. Had one of them been hit? Mateo never answered that question.

Every.

Damn.

Light.

Was.

Red.

Sweat poured down my temples and my back. I'd grabbed my drover coat from my car and slid it on to cut the chill once the police were satisfied I wasn't a threat. The horse smell on the coat, the wind whistling through the crumple in my front bumper. Everything grabbed my attention. The wipers still smacked at full speed from the earlier chase. I turned them down to appropriately handle a misty night at street speeds. At least I could fix something.

If anything was wrong with them—

Two more left turns and I was in the parking lot. Every available officer was in the damn parking lot. Most of them stood around Kick's car. A flashlight fixed on a bullet hole and my blood boiled.

I nodded to the officer who parked ahead of me, letting him know I was right behind him. As soon as I found my woman. Entering the vortex of activity, my eyes landed on her. Hard not to. She was yelling at an EMT attempting to wrap her hand in a bandage.

"It's fine… Why won't you tell me what's going on with my daughter?"

I wiped at my face to get any leftover dirt off. I hadn't checked myself in the mirror. Didn't want to scare her.

"Ma'am, I promise, your daughter's—"

"Kick!" I bellowed, relief rushing through me as she turned. Except for the bandage on her hand and shallow cuts across her cheeks, she looked alright.

The wind blew the sides of my coat apart as I stalked toward her. Kick flew at me full speed, slamming into my body, making me step back to recover. I wrapped her in my arms, the coat engulfing her, swallowing us both. I breathed in the lavender scent of her hair. Her heartbeat pounded against my chest like it sought mine. Proof I hadn't lost her. Then we both started shaking violently.

"Sir." A cautious officer approached. "Need to see your hands."

He held his gun on me, and I reluctantly lifted my hands as Kick yelled, "He's my fiancé!" She stuck her left hand straight up out of my coat. Her voice was hoarse, almost laryngitis bad. What the hell had she been through?

"This true?" the cop asked me.

"Yes." I nodded. "May I?" Pointing with my hands, I asked permission to place them back around Kick.

The officer who'd escorted me here told the one speaking, "He was at the shoot-out on the 540."

Kick's eyes flashed wide. "A shoot-out?"

The first officer lowered his weapon.

I squeezed Kick and drank in her life… her living, breathing, wellness. My worst fear hadn't come true. If I could have, I would've floated, but my lady wasn't ready to celebrate. To answer her, I gave her the important facts. "It's over, darlin'. Bodyguards are fine. Jonn Graham and his driver are dead. Third guy's on his way to the hospital. In custody."

Kick let her head fall into my chest and whimpered. I repeated "it's over" countless times as I rubbed her back.

Another officer came up to us. "Ms. McKenna? You can see your daughter now. The EMTs are finished. Good thing it was just a graze, huh?"

Kick started shaking like a chihuahua in an ice storm.

"Come on, baby. I've got you."

"Ms. McKenna?" the same officer called out as we walked to the rig. We turned toward him as one. No way was I letting her go. "We'll have to keep your car for the investigation. We want to make sure the bullet holes match the gun from the scene. It should be easy, honestly."

I caught Kick as her knees buckled. "My car." She buried her face in my chest. "I'm not sure I can drive it again, Thomas."

"Shh. We'll figure it out… I'm sorry, darlin'. So sorry." I kissed her temple over and over. There was no way I'd let her out of my sight again.

"I loved that shirt, Mama." Rachel's sad voice sounded miles away as we walked into the house in the middle of the night. We had more questions to answer, and it felt like we'd been at the station for a week. Kick's arms held her daughter and mine held them both.

She kissed Rachel's cheek. Despite the height difference, she kept her daughter close, expertly steering her through the first floor and up the stairs. Of the three of us, Rachel looked the worst. Her arm had been grazed, and a shard of glass had hit just above her hairline. She had multiple stitches from both injuries and an assortment of smaller cuts all over. A large bruise bloomed on her cheek from hitting the dash when Kick shoved her down.

I felt every one of those injuries, and I wasn't her father. Standing in the kitchen, I glared out the window into the dark until the reflection let me know they were upstairs and out of sight.

"I'll get you a shirt just like it, sweetheart. Are you sure you have to go to school tomorrow?" Kick's voice filtered down to me, answered softly by Rachel, poor kid sounded ready to drop.

"For my afternoon class… yes. I'm doing a scene with three others. If I don't go, I'll mess it up for everybody."

"Learning early that the show must go on, eh?"

"You've taught me that since I was two." Rachel laughed, but the tone wasn't right. The distance in her voice concerned me. They disappeared into the loft, and I made a fist, slamming it on the cold, hard granite counter.

Fuck me. Fuck Banger too. I was certain he was reeling from the loss of his man, but what the hell happened to the surveillance? How did an idiot like Graham slip through? The answer shouted loud in my head, and I hit the counter again.

Traitor.

I raked my hands through my hair, then turned to the kettle. I could make tea in case Kick or Rachel needed some. As the water heated, I turned on my laptop and checked on the university's policy regarding therapy. Rachel would get trauma counseling as soon as I could arrange it.

Whether out of practice or simply a macho clod, I should've also considered Kick. Her instincts, like most parents, went first to her daughter. She took care of Rachel with nerves of steel—settling her into bed. Brought her chamomile tea. Called Isabella and Tess.

I admired her pluck. Stood in awe of it. I was a fool.

35

Somewhere Only We Know

Kick

"There you are." The words bounced off my ears in slow motion, sounding like they were underwater. Or maybe it was me.

Thomas's gentle tone irritated me as he maneuvered to my side of the bed. He'd found me too soon. I'd planned to hold on to my secret for a while. For the first time, I welcomed the darkness that used to periodically envelop me. Instead of the scary monster who would frighten me with whispers of self-loathing, it nestled deep inside me like a warm retreat. It transformed into a friend offering escape from the discord all around me. Intrigued by its promise, I played with it, swam in it. I relished in the numbness—health and gene expressions be damned. I wanted more time with it.

"Wes texted. Rachel's safe at class. He's sitting in the back of the theater." Thomas's strong hand caressing my back scratched like sandpaper. "I also found a counselor for her. Appointment's tomorrow morning. Tess and Isabella promised to make sure she goes. Tess will tag along in case she needs someone to talk to afterward."

"Great." The dull, uninterested echo in my tone reached my

ears. The irony of my not caring if Tess mothered my daughter through her trauma didn't escape me. Maybe that had been the takeaway message when Tess comforted Rachel after her breakup. I'd been doing this on my own for too long. Even when Shane lived. Too late, I added, "Thank you."

"Not feeling well?" Thomas pressed his lips to my forehead in that parental way that told me he checked for a fever as much as he expressed affection. My eyes squeezed shut, a long sigh stalling for time. How could I explain just enough to make him go away and leave me to linger in my black peace? All the versions I knew of "Somewhere Only We Know" played on a loop in my head, and it was the only thing I wanted to think about.

"My immune system's fine." A pretend smile. That quick lift to the corner of my mouth was all I could muster. "I'm taking a little nap after the long night." *Now go away!*

He brushed curls off my face, exposing me to the world. *Shit.* Then he ran his hand across my shoulders. "No... something's wrong."

My eyes opened just enough to see through my lashes. Thomas scrutinized my face, his eyes way too warm, way too caring. "You've unraveled." His shoulders fell as he exhaled. Then he moved around the bed and snuggled in behind me, pulling me into his chest. He murmured into my hair, "I'm so sorry, baby."

"You don't control the world, Thomas," I clipped. "Maybe this isn't about you." I felt the wince against my back and didn't care. I'd do anything to be alone. Blissfully alone.

"We should've figured out the mole. Doubled security. Those boys had to know you weren't in the Escalade. Someone told them you'd changed your routine."

I appreciated how he didn't blame Mateo and Wes for what had happened or me for thinking it was safe to spend alone time with my daughter. It didn't mean I wanted Thomas blaming himself either. "It's not that at all. Please... just go." I risked glancing over my shoulder. "I don't want to pull you into this. I promise... I'll be back soon." Where my body called out for the security of the darkness, his touch hurt.

"No." He shifted to look me in the eye. "Your messes are mine, and mine are yours. That's how we work. Tell me why you're sad. Please."

The word *sad* lit a fire in me. This wasn't about an unfair grade or a bully's tease. It wasn't PMS either. It made me want to scream, but the motivation had vanished. The peaceful darkness consumed my focus and dampened any fire that would have stoked my temper. I settled on leveling him with a glare.

"Don't patronize me and don't excuse my weakness. *I* fucked up last night. I'll pay the price. You shouldn't have to." Then I rolled away.

I didn't blame myself for the shooting, but I sure as hell despised falling apart. I was supposed to be the poster child for meditation, supposed to be beyond this by now.

Thomas took a deep, ragged breath. His patience had found its last leg. This was why I wanted to be alone. He didn't know how warm and soothing the liquid depths of the darkness were. Well, I could swim in here for a good long time. He might as well baptize himself in my world.

Welcome to the real me, cowboy. Maybe this was the beginning of the end? I was too far under to care. I deserved it.

"Sorry for patronizing," he responded softly, ignoring my efforts to push away. "Please talk to me." I chanced a quick glance at him without moving. Thomas stared at the ceiling and spoke to the room. "Forgot how much we steel ourselves for the sake of the children. Should've noticed you doing that." His lips brushed my neck. "Your demons don't frighten me, by the way. Mine are close friends."

I looked over my shoulder and was shocked by the compassion in his eyes. No one had ever offered to trudge through the trenches with me. Even Shane had his limits. He'd never left me over it, obviously, but he'd emotionally distance himself until I found my way back. At least he had never yelled at me to snap out of it, like other family members.

Since Shane's accident, I'd perfected "fake it till you make it" in public and sinking in the pool in private. Still, maybe Thomas told the truth. Maybe he was brave enough to offer a hand.

I sighed and confessed. "I had a panic attack in the bathroom after Rachel left." The sound of my voice made me recoil. "It kind of… came out of the blue. Only it didn't, you know? The sh-shooting wasn't the catalyst, I don't think. It was more of a last straw. Like a switch flipped, then I turned around and here I am. Again. I should've expected it. It's not so scary this time, so there's a plus."

I felt Thomas nod. He was such a good listener, but I wasn't ready for it. "Doesn't surprise me. You've been through a ton of shit recently. Hell, I'm an upheaval to your life. Just hope it's a positive one."

I couldn't laugh at his self-deprecation. I closed my eyes and imagined the deep waters caressing my skin.

"What do you mean, it's different this time?" he asked.

I attempted an explanation after taking forever to collect my thoughts. "The darkness used to terrify me. Like another kind of narcissist in my life, it chased me… clung to my skin… a cross between toxic sludge that wouldn't wash off and a seducer offering relief. The taunting and provoking scared the shit out of me because it came from within." It seemed to be proof that the doctors were right about everything being in my head. Until someone finally listened and diagnosed me. It turned out mental health symptoms were a part of my physical diseases.

"Anyway, this time feels different. I saw little clues here and there, but there's been so much to juggle." I rolled to my other side, placed my hand on Thomas's cheek and breathed him in—his sandalwood scent. "You've been an amazing surprise. Don't blame yourself."

The tenderness he expressed as he closed his eyes. *Jaysus*, he calmed me. Why didn't I want it? I continued, "The blackness doesn't frighten me now." I shrugged. "It's not healthy, I know. I just don't care right now."

A tear slowly slid down my cheek. In a dare to make Thomas flee, I didn't wipe it away. Not even when a few more followed.

"Please," I begged. "Leave me alone. I'll be back to Miss Sassy Sunshine tomorrow."

He didn't go, and I remembered how he hadn't left any other time I'd pushed at his boundaries. Instead, Thomas kissed my forehead again. "No."

Irritation filled my voice. "Why the hell not?" I'd be damned if I would snap out of it like everyone always wanted me to do.

Thomas tilted his head. "Like attracts like, remember? My world's also been rocked. I need this *darkness*, as you call it, as much as you do."

"Really?"

"Damn straight. I won't be your fair-weather friend. Ever. I love all of you... even the demons." He squeezed me gently.

A shiver ran up my spine. "My shell might be cracking... a little." Thomas smiled as I touched his face, recognizing his melancholy. "I'm sorry I can't help you back."

He rolled me around until we were spooned again, and I gripped his arm with both hands as he asked, "Tell me, if you could go anywhere physically to escape, where would you go?"

"Muir Woods," I answered immediately. The national park north of San Francisco had been one of my favorite places during those early years in California.

"Tell me about it."

I turned toward Thomas, confused. "Haven't you been there before?"

He smiled and cocked an eyebrow. "Yes. Tell me your version."

My smile surprised me. "So you know where I'm talking about, right?"

"Of course."

My breath hitched. "I've been in countless churches, but Muir Woods was the first place that inspired my heart to worship. The light... was more reverent than stained glass windows. The smells... clean and spicy. If heaven has a smell, that's it."

Thomas nodded like he could smell it too. "Tell me more about the scents."

"The bay laurel and evergreen oils..." I closed my eyes and

remembered sitting on a park bench. "Sunrays sliced through the layers of vegetation, but the area gets so much fog it was always damp at ground level. It made the essential oils spring from the plant life. You could breathe better just sitting there."

"Oh yeah." Thomas inhaled, like my memory had been a suggestion. "Mountain air's the best."

"I loved how the forest floor had trillium, rhododendron, and azalea, like we do here. But the little redwood sorrels were my favorite. The first time I noticed it, a small grouping opened after a light beam shifted away from it. They don't like direct sunlight, see." I almost giggled as a memory surfaced. "I once convinced toddler Dylan that his baby sister was a sorceress. I stood her in front of me as we shaded a patch of sorrel. He bent over them in awe as they opened and showed us their pretty color. Then I picked her up and stepped away, letting the sun shine back on them. And they closed. Dylan stopped complaining about Rachel's crying for a week. She was teething, so everyone in the house suffered along with her."

Thomas chuckled softly, like that, too, touched another old memory. Despite my heavy heart, the pleasure of reuniting Thomas with long-forgotten memories found me.

"Did you go there often?" he asked.

"As often as we could. Little Dylan pretended he was a dinosaur on our early walks. Then it morphed into acting out *Star Wars* scenes as he grew. It helped me relax during a time when that eluded me the most."

The clock caught my eye, and I gasped. "Your lunch with Charley—"

"Already canceled." Thomas squeezed me.

"Don't let me keep you from your cousin. You say like attracts like and all that, but it's a miracle you found her."

He kissed my neck and spoke into my shoulder. "Could've lost you yesterday. As I said, my soul's shaken."

We lay in silence, absorbing and reassuring each other. "You appeared from nowhere in the parking lot, like an avenging angel," I whispered. Is this what I needed—to decompress and process with him?

Thomas's deep chuckle rolled through me. "Rafa's the angel, darlin'. I'm the terrified man who probably knocked over a senior citizen, sprinting through the airport. Nearly ran innumerable cars off the road."

"I'm certain I won the crazed-driver award," I answered with a sigh. "There's a vague memory of running two red lights."

I shuddered at the thought and sent a word of thanks that no one had been hurt. I also remembered how Mateo's words stayed at the front of my mind. My reflexes and focus had felt like they'd heightened. Maybe that's why I had handled the car okay.

Somewhere deep inside, my soul lifted off the bottom of the black lake. It didn't equal surfacing, but I wasn't stuck in the depths.

"Liam will be back by two thirty," I said, afraid I wouldn't be ready by then.

Thomas rolled away and typed on his phone. "Liam has an AP study group after school. We have until five. Said he'd pick up dinner, but we can eat in here if we need." He rolled back, returning his hands to their former places on my body. "In the future, let's promise to take a retreat if either of us feels over-whelmed. We'll hole up here or get away to the woods. Something like that."

I pressed a kiss to Thomas's lips and felt the edges of my real smile. "I do love you to the moon and back."

"Same, baby." He raised a questioning eyebrow. "Think you could do a comedy?"

I bit my lip. "Maybe."

He patted my behind and added, "See if there's something you'll like. I'll get us food."

Twenty minutes later, Thomas carried in a tray of lettuce wraps with avocado and smoked salmon, plus tea. It still surprised me that my inner mess hadn't scared him away. He embraced it, nonplussed.

We ate in the window seat, then Thomas stripped to his boxers and crawled into bed behind me as I queued up *So I married an Axe Murderer*. My shell continued to crack each time his soft laugh rumbled against my back as I recited the lines.

"Funny you'd pick a film set in Northern California," he said as his fingers ran a gentle glide continuously along my side.

I squirmed away, taking it as a sign of friskiness. "Don't."

"I wasn't," he responded. "Promise."

"You're frustrated with me." I sighed with worry.

"Not at all." Thomas rolled me, forcing me to face him. "It works both ways." My brow pinched as I tried to catch his meaning. "What you said before about wanting… when you don't want, I don't want either. Just touching you reminds me you're alive." He lowered his forehead to mine and shuddered. "It was obvious something was wrong when I went looking for you."

"How?"

He touched my nose with his finger. "I usually feel you when you're nearby. Like your energy finds me." Thomas raised our entwined hands. "Our auras have started intermingling after this much time together, but they're not. Not worried though. They'll be back."

For emphasis, he repeated, "It kills me you've been there for everyone else but had to fight your demons by yourself. Thanks for opening up. Your demons are also mine now."

"Everyone has their own shit, Thomas. Why should I pile on my family and friends?" I huffed and sarcastically added, "It's not a polite way to friend."

"That's your mother talking." Thomas growled, like he rebuked her. "Remember… it takes strength to let someone in. You showed courage when you let me in." He brushed a curl out of my face and lifted the corner of his mouth. "Now you're stuck with me."

Overwhelmed, I returned to watching the movie. He'd touched a nerve with the reference to Bobby. Before I had a dark lake to sink into, I'd hide in my closet and work out my issues. The thing with years of gaslighting was, moving on didn't automatically make it easy to accept the "happy, happy" talk. Even from Thomas. It was easier to let hope build in small doses.

His laugh made the bed jump. We were at the wedding reception part of the film. "Can't wait to see you in your wedding dress," he whispered into my skin. Shivers tingled down my back. "Bet you'll look like an elf queen."

"Shut up." I smacked his hand, laughing, pleased to know I could handle goofy Thomas again. Seriously, though, how the hell did he know about my dress?

In a moment of pure serendipity, Rachel had hooked me up with a friend majoring in fashion. The centerpiece of her senior project had been accidentally ruined, putting her degree in jeopardy. The young lady jumped at the chance to make my wedding dress and have it double as the finale of her show. Her other dresses featured light silks and chiffons. The pieces reminded me of woodland royalty. It ended up being a win-win for both of us.

A memory from my first fitting made me smile, and I held on to it. Not everything had gone haywire this year. I finally breached the surface of my moody lake. I was still far from shore, but I could see a clear blue sky.

I rolled into Thomas. "Hey, thank you for accepting me." My chin quivered and my voice caught. "I promise to walk in the darkness with you when it's your turn."

36

Lovesong

Thomas

"Ready, fam? I don't want to be late," Liam called out while bounding down the stairs, Dylan on his heels. "Do we have to do pictures in the park?"

Liam possessed steely nerves on a stage and now looked pasty enough to throw up. His hand tapped out a fast rhythm on his thigh as sweat dusted his freshly shaved upper lip.

"You mean miss the last prom photos under the big oak tree? Are you nuts? I'd crawl there if I had to." Kick adjusted the lapels on Liam's black tuxedo. Her chin subtly quivered as she adjusted the ends of curls around his ears. "You're so handsome and grown."

Liam's Adam's apple bobbed as he swallowed.

It occurred to me that Kick would need a distraction after the photos, or I'd have an overemotional fiancée on my hands.

"Load up, y'all." Liam twirled the keys to my '69 Camaro around his finger. Thanks to its unibody, the damage to Ginger—my car's name—had been minimal. The shop had it back to mint in a week. Kick's car wasn't so lucky. Insurance totaled it, to our relief.

Was it a big deal to let an eighteen-year-old boy take the car that

I'd driven off the lot decades earlier? Not when the boy was Liam. I already loved him like he was mine. Damn, my world had changed fast. I enjoyed seeing the grin on his face when I asked if he wanted to take it. Compared to the shit Kick and I had dealt with, it was an easy decision.

"Are you coming, Dyl?" Liam asked.

"Sorry, pretty boy. I'm still working here." Dylan pretended to wipe tears from his eyes. "You're so handsome, pretty boy. Now don't do anything I wouldn't do."

Liam punched his brother. "You did all the things."

Dylan waggled his brows. "Exactly."

"Dylan…," Kick began.

I cut her off with a hand to her back and a kiss to her temple. Dylan still had no sense of when to ease up on his family members, particularly with Kick.

"Let's go, clan," I said, checking to make sure I had the keys to my Land Rover. "Your mom and I will follow you to Oakville Square."

B ANGER CALLED WHILE K ICK PUT THE DINNER DISHES AWAY. WE'D taken Macushla along to the park and walked the trails after the kids left for prom. For a moment, it had taken Kick's mind off this next item in a lengthy list of parental lasts. We'd made it back to the parking lot as a quick spring storm popped up. Then we ate a quiet dinner with Dylan.

I hoped Banger had good news I could share with her. "What's new, man?" I moved into the office and shut the door in case he had bad news.

Banger breathed a long-suffering sigh through the phone. "I'm back and staying at the corporate apartment for now."

I sat behind Kick's desk. "Did you find the mole?"

"Several leads have converged. Just haven't found the linchpin, but I have an idea."

"Hit me."

"Let's shrink our circle of trust. You, me, Siobhan, the guards, and Kick. I want the guards to report directly to you. They're new, but they've proved themselves. The guy I had on Graham had pressed Siobhan for more responsibilities, so she gave him that assignment as a test."

"Who got to him?"

"I'm this close to nailing it down. That's why I need to tighten the trust."

"I'm not sure how Kick will take keeping the guards. She's eager for it to be over."

"Won't be long. Remember when I told you the bartender at Ducky's took a call from Oxford?"

"I do. Are you still looking at Nigel?"

Another sigh filled my ear. "I almost had the bartender. He slipped by me like he'd been tipped off."

"The mole."

"Right. Nigel has to be part of this. The problem is, he's known me my whole life. He knows my moves." I heard a thump, like a fist pounding. "The guy's a veritable Machiavelli."

I always pictured Ellie in that role, but I saw the comparison. "You need new moves."

"No kidding. Speak to no one about this except for the circle of trust. Understand?"

I drummed my fingers on the desk, ready to do anything. "What about the old man?"

"Bare minimum for now. What have you told him lately?"

"He knows about the shoot-out. I'd missed a check-in the day after. Alaric also knows between finals and the wedding, I don't have time for a summons no matter how important he deems it."

"Good. Keep conversations to nothing more than lab facts for now. I'm serious, brother. My plan depends on keeping the circle airtight."

I pinched the bridge of my nose, thinking of Kick. Hell, her entire clan had come to her side in the two weeks since the shooting. I'd almost overrode Kick's wishes and cut off Bobby on the spot over the way she had ripped into her daughter regarding Rachel's injuries. As if Kick didn't blame herself. As if she didn't have cuts and bruises too. Bobby then changed tack and blamed me for all the bad in Kick's life now. I wished it were that easy.

"I'll tell her," I said.

"Hit it hard, brother. I don't care about what's already happened. She stays tight with her movements. Force her to listen to you and Mateo. Rachel's situation is harder, but the end of a semester always shakes up a schedule. That works in our favor."

"It'll happen. You can count on it."

"Talk more tomorrow."

We finished the call, and I filled Kick in on the situation while helping her clean the kitchen. True to her nature, she saw the wisdom in Banger's plan. She'd come a long way since her first impressions of him.

"Jacklyn's dress was gorgeous, don't you think?" Kick and I had parked ourselves in the corner of the sectional sofa in her living room, me with my feet up, stretched down one side. She lay in the other direction, her head in my lap. A movie played, but I couldn't say which one, because my fiancée kept talking about the kids at the park as she thumbed through the photos on her phone. "I love this group shot. They've been an adorable bunch since they first met in kindergarten. Dylan's grade always had several assholes, but not Liam's."

A dried-off dog lay on my legs, snoring in between squirrel-chasing dreams. At the park, Macushla had bolted for a puddle as soon as the clouds opened up. The dog turned mischief into an artform.

"I'm so glad Jax's parents let her go with Lee."

"Did they buck on that too?"

Kick's nodding head rocked in my lap. "She already had a church prom with some boy from Raleigh. Jax really wanted to go to the school one, and fortunately for Liam, Regina Moore still trusts him."

"She should."

"Yeah, well, it's her father who looks at Lee and can't see anything but a penis."

"Typical." I'd forgotten many aspects of parenthood, but that stuck in my memory. Then again, my girls were married by eighteen, and modern society was night-and-day different. Not so much for Alton Moore. I also remembered how impossible it was to say no to my daughters' heart's desires.

A scene or two went by on the television.

"I'm going to miss them," Kick said softly.

There it was. I gently stroked her hair, making sure to not rake my fingers through it. "What's with the photo shoot though? You'd think the kids were in a fashion layout. I don't know how they put up with it." From my experience, parents had always fussed over the next generation, but the extent of this attention was new.

She sighed. "It's the end of an era."

"All finished, peeps." Dylan entered our space, two beers in his hands. He gave me one, lifted his mother's feet, and sat. "Can I pause this and show you how to connect the house computer to the outside world?"

"Absolutely."

Dylan gave us the gist of his upgrade. Since Banger was using his place to test Angel's latest tweak, Kick's house and mine were the betas for Dylan's project. The Felidae-related system always ran on a separate network. The upgrades allowed our computer to do the things smart homes did but with extra layers of security and no third-party data mining. No risk of a hacker taking over a camera and the like. Since Banger hadn't flushed out the mole, I welcomed the additional protection.

If the algorithm worked, it would be the launching point for Dylan's future business. This was his audition for Banger, so to speak. Everything with the medical clinic had progressed smoothly, so he planned to launch it on Mother's Day weekend as a surprise for Kick.

"Is this part of your thesis project?" Kick asked Dylan.

"Yeah. The initial use is almost ready to launch. This is a secondary system that my team's testing."

"I heard Banger's interested in implementing it too. Siobhan said you might work together after graduation."

"Banger wants to make Dylan a millionaire in his own right," I told her. Why not brag up her son's accomplishment? Kick might as well clue into the hell of a big deal he'd become.

"What?" She bolted upright.

"Yeah." Dylan blushed. He took a long drink from his beer, like he tried to hide behind the can. "We get to stay in the Triangle if we go with Banger's mentoring plan."

"Will you be the… what? CEO? How have I missed this?" She moved her head back and forth between us, murmuring as her brow furrowed. "My son's going to be a CEO."

"It's not that big of a deal." Dylan deflected. He pulled at his T-shirt and I almost laughed. Kick had the right reaction. He continued, "This has to work first. We haven't finalized anything yet. The only actual decision we've made so far is to partner with Banger and not the Silicon Valley companies."

"It's a *fecking huge* deal, lad. I'll make sure it works too." Kick's mouth parted a moment before she softly said, "You envisioned this and built it. I'm so…" Her voice caught. "Your father…" She reached out, grabbed his hand. "This beats any NFL gig to him. You know that, right? Never doubt your decision to leave the game."

Dylan nodded several times, keeping his head low. Kick's use of the present tense caught my attention. I wondered what she meant by it.

Dylan patted his stomach. "Might regret the growing belly not playing has created. A few hours on the field helped to counter the effects of sitting at a desk."

"I can help you with that," I told him. "Spending too much time in the lab makes me sluggish."

"Yeah? You have a gym?"

"Yep. I'll send you my schedule. We can meet there, and I'll show you around."

"That would be fabulous. Thanks, my dude."

Kick's eyes shone with tears as she grinned at us. I didn't need to ask her what moved her. These small steps with Dylan did my heart good. Now that he planned to stay local, we had years to develop our rapport. She brushed at her eyes as she padded into the kitchen.

"Where're you heading, Mom?"

"This calls for a toast. I'm getting a Bull City Cider from the fridge. Either of you want another?"

"I'm good." I checked Dylan's bottle. "Your boy could use a second."

"Great. Hey lad, since Thomas and I are restarting the movie, would you want to watch it with us?"

Dylan checked the time on his phone. "Can do."

With Kick out of earshot, I took a pull from my IPA and said, "I'm glad you told your mother. She needed happy news, and the main surprise hasn't been spoiled."

Dylan finished his bottle. "Yeah, that's what I figured too."

"Any chance you can show me how to change the system's name?"

Dylan laughed. "You have a problem with Angel?"

"You know it's a reference to Banger's given name, right? I'd rather be like *Star Trek* and call it Computer than have to keep calling it Angel."

"Ooh, if you can make it have a Spanish accent, we could call it Alejandro." Kick handed her son his beer while I shook with laughter.

"You want to lust after the house computer?" I asked.

"No, but it'd be fun. Besides, Carmen would love it." She snuggled into my side. "Except let's not talk about lusting in front of the lad, okay?"

Dylan barked a laugh and almost choked on his drink. "Appreciate that, guys."

"How late do you think he'll stay out?" Dylan asked.

"Liam will have Jacklyn home by whatever time her father wants. He knows the merits of abiding by Alton's rules by now."

"I don't know." Dylan lifted an eyebrow my way. "I expect he'll be home earlier than requested."

"Why is that?" Kick sat up, refilling her small popcorn bowl from the big one on the coffee table.

I suspected the same as Dylan. Saw it coming. You couldn't miss the attraction between the kids when they sang together. Kick would've noticed it, too, but for everything else on her mind.

"While I helped him get ready, Lee told me he planned to declare his love to little Jaxie."

"What? No!" She stood up and planted her hands on her hips. "They're just supposed to go as friends." She turned and paused in each direction, then flopped back down. "Oh hell."

"Don't blame yourself." I pulled her to my side and rubbed her arm. "Sometimes the heart needs to leap, or it'll break from the want."

"Fecking hell."

"Watch the movie, darlin'. Either way, it's a learning experience for him."

Kick turned to Dylan. "Not a word when he comes in, hear? When you broke up with Suzy, no one rubbed it in."

"I knew you never liked her."

"For Pete's sake, lad. It was never about her. The two of you simply didn't fit, but you had to learn for yourself." She adjusted her ponytail. "Jaysus, I hate this. For any of my kids."

I kissed her temple, wishing I could do more to help. "They'll be fine. Dylan has his software. Rachel's in counseling. Plus the summer theater gig will get her out of town. We'll visit her as much as you want." Taking her chin in hand, I tilted it toward me. "It'll be alright. Now let's finish this awful blockbuster."

THE FRONT DOOR SLAMMED, ROCKING THE HOUSE. KICK, ASLEEP IN my lap, jumped—catching air—and almost rolled off the sofa. Dylan had left an hour earlier when the movie ended.

"Liam," Kick called out from her groggy state. "How'd it go?" I could've laughed at her effort to sound nonchalant. Liam's anger vibrated through the room. Didn't take an empath to see his misery.

While the stairs boomed from his stomping, Liam growled, "Don't want to talk about it."

I bent my head and caught Kick's gaze. She looked like she was bracing for a crash. She pressed her lips together. "Shh." I wrapped my arms around her, whispering, "He's loved. He'll be alright. Not tonight. Not tomorrow. But we'll get him through it. For now... let it go."

"I won't sink away again, Thomas," she snapped.

"Maybe. Maybe not. If you did, I'd be there." I kissed her forehead. It was imperative she heard me. "Take care of you first. That's my priority from now on."

"He won't open his door." Kick slipped off her yoga pants and climbed into bed.

Raising my arm, I pulled her to me. "Hate to say told you so—"

"So don't."

I obeyed and squeezed her. "Let the boy process it his way. His ego needs time. Hell, the kid can have his pick of girls."

"Just not the one he wants." Since Liam refused to share, we were stuck speculating. Her breath made a hitching sound. "I'm angry with myself."

"Let it go for now." Out of ideas for what to do, I unbuttoned Kick's nightshirt.

"What are you doing?"

Like she needed to ask. I slipped it off and motioned with my hand. "Roll over."

She complied but added, "Why?"

"Hey Angel, shuffle and play the 'Well You Know' playlist at volume level three," I called out.

"Thomas—"

"Shh." I yanked on the warm quilt, pulling it high over my shoulders until it cocooned us.

Now playing.

The opening bars of "Lovesong" filled the room. *Perfect.* Kick had told me the song made her toes curl, whatever that meant. I liked the look it put on her face—like we'd become home for each other.

Reaching for the nightstand, I grabbed some oil and lubed my hands, then leaned down, my lips against her ear, her luscious backside stretched out under me. "I'm taking your mind off the children."

After enough time devoted to light-touch massage, with the appropriate amount of moans and sighs for my benefit, Kick smiled into her pillow and asked, "What children?"

37

Thin Line Between Love and Hate

Kick

"Hey, cowboy. Mateo's mother had an emergency early this morning." I called Thomas with my cell phone while in my bathroom. He had spent the night in the lab, so my trusty bodyguard stayed over in the loft—part of Banger's plan to tighten security, except everything had gone dead quiet since the shooting.

"On Mother's Day morning? How awful."

"It's horrible any day, but yeah. I'm sending him home."

"No, Kick. I'll leave soon. He can wait."

This was why I'd taken the phone into the en suite. I knew Thomas would balk, but I could push back too. "I can handle an hour. Hell, Dylan's expected any minute."

I looked out the window over my tub at the beautiful May morning. A mockingbird trilled from its perch on the shrub outside. The little bugger had been waking me up before my alarm for a month. I longed to open the window and take in the fresh air, but it was against security protocol.

"Exactly. Mateo can wait."

Shit. "Come on, Thomas. His mother's in the emergency department right now. Mateo's father needs him."

My guard was his parents' firstborn. They depended on him for more than language translation. He was the family's rock.

A rustling of papers came through the line. "Dammit. I'm shutting down now. But check in with Siobhan. Wes too. Perhaps he and Rachel can leave now."

My daughter make herself ready before noon on a weekend? Hardly. But I'd take the win. "Will do. Then I'll send Mateo off with our best wishes."

"Sure."

"Thank you, cowboy."

I left the requisite messages and sent Mateo on his way with a thermos of coffee. He was too upset to eat but took a container of scones for his family. I was beginning our brunch preparations when Siobhan called.

"Hey Kick. I received your message. You good?"

"I'm peachy. Thank you." I wore my Bluetooth set so I could chop fennel and celery for a frittata. "Wes said he'd try to light a fire under my daughter. My oldest will be here soon too."

"Oh? When's that?"

He had texted about running late. "Probably an hour or so."

"You're sure you're fine?"

I looked out the kitchen window and waved at my neighbor. They were loading their kids into the van. "The quiet's actually nice for a change."

Siobhan chuckled into the phone. "I bet. Call me if you need anything. Any sign of trouble, hit the bat signal."

I laughed at her joke. My world felt a bit superhero adjacent, to be honest. "Will do."

"And Kick… Happy Mother's Day. I hope it's… relaxing."

"Thank you, Von. Now that you mention it, I think I'll hit my meditation spot as soon as I'm done cutting these veggies."

. . .

"Yo, Mom. Got your ginger beer and cupcakes." Dylan placed his contribution to our brunch on the island and kissed the cheek I offered. "Happy Mother's Day."

"Thanks, lad. I thought you were running late. Now you're early."

He lifted an eyebrow. "Are you complaining?"

"Of course not. Simply wondering what changed?"

"Oh." He gestured toward his shirt. "As you can see, I didn't take a shower after my good-boy workout at the gym. There was no way to shower and make it to the bakery before the gluten-free ones sold out. I figured the shower upstairs is worlds better than the locker room ones anyway. I practically threw my credit card at the cashier in the bakery."

I waved in front of my nose. "Whew! No kidding. Stand on the other side of the island, lad. You stink."

Dylan folded his arms… after he complied. "Why not just wait until after I shower?"

"I might forget what I want to say by then. So… well, I don't know. You're just… cheery this morning. Does this mean you had a date last night?"

Dylan leveled me with his devilish grin. He'd mastered it by age two, and I fell for it every time. "Does my mother want to know if her little boy got laid?"

I should've kept my mouth shut. Except he'd been understandably miserable these past months. "No. I just want—"

"One plus one equals—"

"None of my business. I just want—"

"Bingo." Dylan pointed at me.

I pointed back. "I can inquire about the state of my son's happiness without knowing about his"—I waved my hands in the air, butcher's knife still in one—"exploits."

He poured himself a cup of coffee. "My heart's good. Thanks for asking." A huge smile graced his handsome face, saying he was proud of himself for getting a rise from me. Then he hid it inside the mug.

I turned back to the counter. "Pest." Then set down the knife while Dylan laughed at me. "Use the guest shower down here. Something's wrong with the one upstairs."

"Pretty boy and those curls again?"

"Hey." I hated when the kids razed at each other. The world was hard enough to deal with. "We have to wait until Banger says we're clear to let unvetted people back in the house. Then I'll call the plumber."

Please let that be soon. This way of living had worn out its welcome, not that I ever really welcomed it.

I picked up an avocado. "Please go wash the stink off, then help me chop this stuff."

"Right-o, Mama." Dylan laughed and headed toward the guest bath while I sliced into the avocado. My counter was filling up fast with bowls of cut veggies, which would make the cooking part go faster.

A split second later, he reentered the kitchen. "You're out of towels in the little bath. Mind if I use yours?"

"Huh? Shit." My head stayed occupied with my to-do list. I'd just remembered the steaks that were supposed to be placed in the refrigerator to thaw overnight last night. How the hell would I get them defrosted in time now? "Sure. Can you fix the towel situation in the guest bath when you finish? Help me keep my focus on brunch."

"Gotcha."

The steaks were in the chest freezer in the garage. I crossed the threshold and saw that Dylan had left the door up. He was always a stinker for that. It used to drive me nuts when he lived at home. The number of times I woke in the morning to find out he'd left it up all night… it would make me fume. Now it was a breach of security.

A hand clamped across my mouth as I reached for the garage door's button. An arm squeezed around my chest while a familiar, gruff voice spat in my ear. "Not a word, *Mrs.* McKenna. You bitch."

My first thought was that we'd left a stone unturned—Jonathon Graham, Senior. My second thought went to Dylan.

Now what.

38

Two Tribes

Thomas

I ACCEPTED THE INCOMING CALL WITH A LAUGH. IN OUR SHORT TIME together, I'd found Kick to be a perfectionist with her family gatherings. I chalked it up to what she called her "impending empty nest."

"Dylan. Let me guess… your mom forgot—"

"I think someone has a gun on Mom," he whispered, cutting me off. "Here. At the house."

An icy shiver ran up my spine. *What the hell?* "You know who?" If the mole was showing their face now, I wouldn't step off for the police this time.

"Mr. Graham, I think. Sh-she screamed. He yelled at her to shut up. S-sounded like him."

My heart beat a tattoo in my chest. *Ten minutes.* I was ten fucking minutes from her. I punched the pedal to the floor. "Where are you?"

"Your bathroom since our shower's broken. I heard boots pound up the stairs. Don't know how long it'll be till someone checks here. Where's your gun?"

"My safe's under the extra pillows in our closet."

"Gotcha." I heard a quiet shuffling and gave him the combination. Dylan seemed to keep his head about him. Despite his terror, his voice stayed determined. "Oh, good. I know these," he added. Dylan had worked with Banger at my range. Banger had declared the kid a natural. I hoped he was right.

"Keep one by your side and hide the other in your waistband. Under your shirt," I advised. Then I heard a banging sound. "What was that?"

His voice choked. "I think he hit her. Sounds like someone else is out there. Should I just run out firing with both guns?"

"No, boy. You could hit her. Keep yourself as calm as you can. How many are there?"

"Can't tell. I saw a guy outside your window for a second, so… maybe three."

"Is Kick the lone woman?" It was an impossible hunch, but the icy shiver turned to artic steel as the thought washed over me. *Christ*, I hoped I was wrong about the mole, but it was the only thing that made sense after this. "Dylan…"

"Um… I-I think so… Not positive."

"Alright. Stay quiet. Assess the scene. You hear me? Kick's smart. She's come a long way with her training." *Fuck.* She'd stand in front of every weapon to keep it from her kid. Horns blared around me and tires screeched as I executed a fast right turn against the light at Main Street. I swerved to beat the left-turning cars with the right-of-way. "Almost home. Stay low and find out how many are with Graham. Then call the cops. I'm almost there. If you can, find a way to stall them."

Kick's house was second from the corner, and the neighbor's drive faced the side street. I parked near their mailbox and ran through their backyard, scanning for anyone who might work for Graham. From what I could tell, everyone was in the house.

The garage door was up, so I peeked around the corner and saw the shadow of a large man in the mudroom. If he'd been a few feet back or to the right, I could sneak up on him. He chose his position for its sight lines. He could see perfectly and be seen. If he checked back on the garage, I'd have to fire on him. Using the shadow of equipment attached to the walls, to sneak close, I turned the corner with my weapon on him and whispered, "Don't move, asshole."

The scene before me broke my heart. Kick was in Graham's hold in the kitchen, a gun to her temple. Her lip and cheek bled. A shiner bloomed around her left eye. Tears slid down her face, but her sneer told me she was more pissed than afraid. Or in pain. *Fuck.* Or both.

Dylan stood in the dining room with a gun in each hand, one pointed at Graham and the other at a second accomplice holding the kitchen island. Thanks to the many times I'd watched the footage of Kick's attempted kidnapping, I recognized this asshole as the bartender who'd spiked her drink—Graham's nephew. I held my guy's full attention while my focus stayed on Big Jonn. No idea what he'd told these idiots about the job, but none of them would be walking out of here. Like an old friend who'd been waiting on me, I flipped the switch. I wasn't Good Thomas anymore.

I reached around the wall behind me without taking eyes off the scene and pressed the button closing the garage door in case I was wrong about extras outside.

That's when Kick noticed me and started. Her eyes flashed with fear instead of relief and damn if I knew she was thinking of my safety over hers, ranking who took priority, as I had. I silently shushed her with pursed lips as another tear trailed down her cheek.

"Did you reach the cops, Dylan?" I asked, my eyes glued to my lady and Graham.

"Not before this one found me," he answered, referring to the guy I kept in my periphery. Dylan had a black eye of his own and cuts on his knuckles. He growled at the bartender.

"Doesn't matter. They're coming." It was half true. At the last minute, I sent a panic text to Banger. It should've been enough for him to alert everyone, including the authorities. Hell, he was the cavalry all by himself. Still, for all intents and purposes, we were on our own for a bit.

"Hang in there, baby." I tried to send Kick strength. I'd be damned if she lost any more loved ones, and I sure as hell wouldn't lose her.

Graham's sinister laugh betrayed his break from reality. His darting eyes shone with the maniacal lunacy of a man with nothing to lose. "Three guns are on you, young man. One wrong move and this goes off. Right... through... your Yankee *cunt's* temple." He pressed the muzzle into her skin. "A couple of bitches sleep their way to the top of a Fortune 500 company, and now they all think they can shake their asses and get whatever they demand. Isn't that right, whore?" He shook Kick's shoulder hard. She bit her lower lip and closed her eyes. I silently begged her to keep quiet. *Let him pontificate until backup arrived.*

"Need to learn your place." Big Jonn jolted Kick sharply with each word, and her eyes flew open, sparked with rage, on his last word.

No, no, no, baby. Keep your cool...

Dammit, why hadn't I developed telepathic powers? I'd heard rumors about them around the vineyard.

"What happens when you let bitches run amuck?" Graham yelled. "Why, they raise little bitches that bewitch fine young men."

"You've got to be—" Kick's face scrunched with indignation.

I cleared my throat to get her attention and shifted my chin to the side to keep her quiet. Needed to think of a way out.

"Haven't I been charming, attentive, polite... *whore?*" Graham kept shaking her violently. She pressed her lips together so hard they blanched. "Answer me! I gave you attention after your famous husband died. I welcomed you to the business community because I knew what you were going through. And what did you do? You ignored me! Then you hooked up with a... *boy toy.*"

"Are you jealous?" She blinked, then flared her nose, her chin set in defiance.

"Kick...," I warned.

"No, Thomas. He doesn't get to throw threats around... tell me the reason he terrorized us is payback for not returning affection." Her eyes shifted up, like she tried to see Big Jonn. He kept too tight of a hold on her. "I'm sick of arrogant assholes thinking women owe them adoration only because they deem us worthy of their attention."

Graham's hand moved from a death grip on her arm to a clamp across her throat. The gag as she tried to breathe called my bluff and shortened my temper.

"Let her go, old man. Face it… you can't match me. Y'all are already dead men walking."

"Why the hell would I let her go? Damn straight, she owes me. The question is… who gets to pay? Should it be the son?" He quickly pointed his gun at Dylan. "Or you… boy toy?" Kick squealed in terror and flailed violently. Graham skillfully evaded a stomp to his foot. He moved his hand back to gripping her arm to regain control. At least she could breathe again.

He leaned to her ear and said, "She promised me endless years… like you and him." Graham tipped his head toward me. "Yeah… I know your secrets, asshole."

Kick gasped, then her gaze moved regimentally around the room. It helped to calm her. *Good.* Her eyes stopped on Dylan. His brows pinched with confusion. Not that I blamed him.

"What do you mean?" Kick asked innocently.

"Don't play dumb, you cunt." Graham cackled. The spit from it hit Kick's cheek. "I'm a descendant of the Marquis."

The Marquis?

Fuck.

My.

Life.

I swallowed audibly. "Do you mean the Marquis—"

Graham beamed like a son for a treasured father. "De Lafayette? Yep. That's what she said." He laughed and almost gave Kick an out. Then he caught himself and tightened his grip. "I made a joke."

"Big Jonn—"

"It's Mr. Graham to you, *boy*. Or should it be Mr. Lafayette? Or Mr. de Lafayette? I'll have to ask them. See… he had a son… when he served with Washington. He arranged for the mother to marry a man named Graham—thought he'd been my great-whatever grand-pappy. A good soldier. Gave them land right here."

Graham spoke to Kick again. "Why couldn't you be a good

soldier? Just cooperated a little. Hell, I wanted to give you more... once I found out you have it too. See... I'm like you... or will be. Once the serum is perfected." He tapped the gun on her shoulder. "All they needed was your DNA. Had a hell of a time getting it. Thanks to your stupid muscle."

He stretched his chin toward me and stage-whispered, "That's you... boy."

"If you know my secret, you know I'm no boy. If you really knew me, you'd release my fiancée. You'd get down on your knees. You'd beg me for mercy." I tilted my head to the side, letting my eyes settle on each man. "Clearly you're misinformed."

"Naw," Big Jonn said. "I just have no desire for mercy. With no heir to pass a legacy on to, what's the point of money or immortality? Revenge is all that's left." His gaze shifted to Dylan, then back to Kick. "Too bad little whore junior isn't here. Your heir-apparent will do as a trade for mine, but I'd love to take them both out."

"What about me?" the bartender asked. "I'm your heir now, Uncle Jonn. You said so."

"Shut up, Jared! The offer was for me. Young Jonn and me." He tsked and shook his head. "If *you* knew what I did, you'd respect me."

Kick kept moving her eyes and taking regular breaths. I wanted her away from Graham, but for now she stayed calm. Banger should be here soon, and I wanted answers. Namely, who this woman was. I had a sinking feeling that I knew.

"What'd you do, Big Jonn? Impress me," I challenged.

"Call me Mr. Graham! You say you respect me... prove it. Don't think I don't know you're the one who threw my son out of Reynolds's shop."

Fuck. I closed my eyes and nodded. He could win this one. As much as Graham soaked up the attention, his nephew and muscle grew twitchy. The one on me sighed hard.

My small head bob was enough. Graham leaned down and spoke near Kick's ear. "It was me... the rumors. The newspaper articles. The crowd storming the stores. *I* stirred everyone into a tizzy." Kick closed her eyes and inhaled. I knew her enough to know she was counting through her breaths. "You know why?" She shook her head and Graham rattled her again. "Use words… *whore*. Or is your mouth good for just one thing?"

Kick took another long breath and set her chin. "No, Mr. Graham. I don't know why you sabotaged my reputation."

Graham's lips stretched in a cocky smile. "Because I *could*. See… when y'all were on the ropes, I planned to save the day. Get in y'all's good graces. Then I'd take you to her. That was the first plan, but you're too stubborn, aren't you? You wouldn't take advantage of my offers of affection. Then you wouldn't drink a damn drink with me. You stupid, stupid bitch. This could've been easy. No one would've been hurt. Not really. Now it's ruined."

Kick's eyes flashed wide as she turned her head in horror. My breath caught in my throat, afraid she'd lay into Graham. But she recovered, her face schooled again. "If I may… Mr. Graham… wh-what about the graffiti? The way Rachel was tormented? Your son—"

"Kick…," I warned. It worked in our favor to keep Big Jonn going, sharing his "accomplishments" with us. Her submissive act also kept him calm.

Graham sighed. "Young Jonn always loved your *cunt* daughter. I tried to set him straight. Honestly, I did. Everyone saw she wasn't worth it. Flaunting her body… her uppity-ness… in his face." His nostrils flared as he looked my way. "I blame my late wife for spoiling him. He… he could make it hard for me. Sometimes. But your people interrupted my plans too. Took it from every side, didn't I?" Big Jonn whined the last bit, his damn chin quivering with self-pity.

I couldn't have the guy falling to pieces and escalating the scene before Banger arrived. The goons grew antsy, but they still paid attention. Dylan also did. It wasn't go-time yet. As far as I was concerned, there was one more thing to pry out of him.

"Tell me about the woman, Mr. Graham? Do I know her?"

39

Alive and Kicking

Kick

A LAUGH STIRRED DEEP INSIDE ME AS BIG JONN'S GREW FRENETIC. I winced, blinking from him spitting in my eye again. *"Does he know the woman?"* he asked me and no one.

"Well, Professor… I spoke to an uppity Englishman and your devious Siobhan. They actually work for… my *grand-mère*."

Well, there's the mole, or moles, I suppose. Shit. Banger.

For a split second, Thomas's posture fell, like he'd been punched in the stomach. He'd called Ellie—my ancestor—*grand-mère*. That made Big Jonn and I weird-ass cousins? My laugh grew. It wasn't a giggle or a chuckle. It was a cynical, barking, cackle starting in my toes and surging its way up, bursting out my throat. I surprised everyone in the room—Big Jonn the most.

My shoulders shook, and the gun pressed harder into my temple. It did nothing to stop me. I was pissed and terrified but couldn't get the picture of four teens and Great Dane out of my head. Or maybe I needed to fill my head with anything other than the madness of the Felidae and the past five months.

"Rut-roh," I said through the fits.

"Shut up, *whore!*" He jerked his arm so hard it stole my breath. As if nasty names would upset me when the asshole had already mangled my face and knocked the wind from me. Not to mention the guns pointed at my family. I'd been doing my utmost to follow my training.

Self-defense starts in the mind.

The strain of keeping it together, trying to stay three steps ahead, then hearing Big Jonn's defense for all this—some kind of promise from the Felidae Society—one I wasn't sure I wanted. It was too much. I switched to a mocking voice. "If it hadn't been for you meddling kids, my son and I would be mutant superhumans by now."

"Easy…," Thomas warned. Behind the macho gruff, I heard the fear. My entire house vibrated with it.

"If you'd taught your woman in her place, this could've been avoided, Professor."

"You've got to be… motherfucker." I lost the little cool I still held on to.

Anger flared in Big Jonn's eyes to the point they looked black. I didn't care. My temper woke, shaking me. "Everything about this catastrophe is on *you*. Not me or my kids. I was literally minding. My. Own. Businesses… When you and your half-witted son sighted my family in your crosshairs."

Graham growled, but Thomas cut him off. "Don't let the fact that I teach science fool you, old man. I can drop you right here. Right now."

"You'd chance my piece going off? On her?" Big Jonn took the gun he'd mostly kept pointed in my shoulder and shoved it into my jaw, making me choke. His laugh sounded demonic. "Didn't think so."

I forced myself to breathe, relying on the training to regain my calm and stay in the moment to think. *Keep my family alive.*

A cold determination passed over Thomas's face. We'd been monitoring each other's cues this whole time. Reading each shift and twitch. Keeping each other calm. He kept Big Jonn talking as a stall tactic, I could tell. But the stalling was over.

With what appeared to be the flick of a wrist, Thomas shot the gunman closest to him and produced a second weapon from the back of his shirt. My sightline didn't allow me to see what warranted the response. All I could think was, where the hell did he get two guns?

When Thomas fired his shot, Big Jonn's gun hand jerked and I pushed as hard as I could. Before he regained control, I donkey kicked him in the balls. The gun tumbled to the floor without going off. We scrambled, and I grabbed hold first.

Thomas had a clear shot on Graham but didn't see that the nephew, Jared—the bartender who'd drugged me—had aimed at him. The lackey with the bullet wound recovered his weapon and trained it on Dylan.

Who to take out?

Who to save?

Don't leave me alone again.

Self-defense starts in the mind.

Noise faded away until I only heard my breaths. My heartbeat. The song "Closer to Fine" quietly surfaced in the back of my mind.

This was it.

My senses heightened. The smell of nervous sweat filled the air. The gun was warm in my hand, thanks to Big Jonn gripping it. It was usually cold when I'd pick one up. I never liked that. I liked them better warm. Funny, he carried a Sig. The gun I preferred.

I breathed in… out. In… out.

The answers are in me.

In… aim. Out… squeeze.

Seven shots fired in precision, as if we'd choreographed them. The bartender took a bullet in his firing shoulder.

I had to trust in my choice. "Drop!"

Dylan dove for the floor and shot the big guy shadowing Thomas. My fiancé fell backward, out of my periphery.

What had I done?

Don't leave me alone again.

In… aim. Out… squeeze.

The bartender took a second hit between the eyes and crumpled. The floor boomed an echo as he bounced on it. My first thought was *bull's-eye*.

A gurgling noise caught my attention. Big Jonn Graham, gasping his last breaths, lay at my feet. He'd taken Thomas's bullet in the heart.

Nice one, cowboy. I might have lost it.

"Fuck!" My head snapped at Thomas's exclamation. Blood soaked his shirt.

What did you do?

Wetness seeped into my underwear. No way. I seriously did not just… I looked down. Blood spread across the lower part of my shirt and out the leg of my shorts.

Fear blanched Thomas's face, but not for himself. I was covered in red warmth.

I'm sorry, cowboy.

40

She's Leaving Home

Banger (Thirty Minutes Earlier)

BANGER MCHENRY—HIS LATEST NAME AND FAVORITE ONE SO FAR—growled at the perfect May morning sky. It beckoned him to enjoy a lazy morning on his back deck, sipping a black coffee while listening to the birds. His mood called for the thick fog of a highland afternoon. Dark and dreary.

He trudged through the entrance of his featureless corporate headquarters in North Raleigh, North Carolina, with one thought on his mind… *bitch better prove me wrong.*

He'd spent weeks traveling the globe, shoring up his offices and outposts. If he was right, he'd have to do it again. The phone calls from the bartender to an address in Oxford, UK, never sat right. Nigel worked at the university and considered it his hometown. But Banger knew all of the bastard's estates, safe houses, and hidey-holes, not that he couldn't add another. This flat was new and out of character.

Tess pressed her theory that Eleanor was the brains behind everything going wrong with the Felidae, but Banger pegged Nigel for it. All the clues pointed to his weasel face. Through too many lives, the man played the role of kingmaker, the one with actual power. Since the time Nigel stood at Banger's monster father's side, acting as his right hand, they'd been rivals. Banger's sire saw to it.

At a certain point, men like Nigel grew tired of their invisibility... craved admiration... acknowledgment of their brilliant maneuvers... glory. Banger had watched it happen countless times in countless cultures. Humans were humans no matter where they lived. He figured the time was now for his old adversary.

However, Nigel never connected to the flat. Then, when he'd been about to call off the quest, in nearby Raleigh Park—he took the irony of the name as a big "fuck you" to the city he based out of—he met up with a witness who'd watched someone leave the flat on multiple occasions. It wasn't Ol' Nigel either, unless the man added cross-dressing to his list of talents. Banger wouldn't put it past him. The witness described a tall, nondescript woman, about thirty, dressed in black—sunglasses too despite the heavy clouds. Nothing to go on, except... her boots.

"The ones with those red bottoms," the fellow had said.

Banger had wanted to die.

He relocked his main office door and marched straight to Siobhan's room. It was in the corner opposite his, equal in space and importance. That's what she was to Angel Security. Banger was the head, Von the heart. This was the last step to proving his right hand had betrayed him. Idiot that he was, he held on to the thread of hope he was wrong.

Banger heard fingers typing on a keyboard in Siobhan's office at the same time his phone buzzed with a text. Probably Tess to pester him about their schedule—brunch at Kick's. Like he was in a mood to celebrate anything. Definitely *not* family.

Pulling the phone out of his pocket, Banger planned to blow off his needy *maman*. He'd update Thomas with his suspicions too in case things went south in the next few minutes. But the message wasn't from Tess.

THOMAS

SOS. Graham and men @ Kick's. Guns on
her and Dylan. Called cops. Siobhan or
Wes? Only options for tip-off.

Banger swore under his breath.

Siobhan practically jumped four feet off the ground when he crashed through her door. He almost did the same.

"What are you doing here?" she asked.

"What the fuck have you done?" he said at the same time.

They shared a ten-second stare-down, Banger glaring at his protégé, arms folded, feet planted shoulder's-width apart. Even like this, he seethed with energy, ready to strike. The years with Siobhan flashed through his mind. When had she changed? Why wasn't he enough? She'd been like a sister—a daughter, really.

As the vignettes of their relationship played on, Banger's most trusted soldier transformed. He saw the moment she realized he'd discovered the betrayal. The familial affection usually showing in her eyes became cold, resolved. Siobhan flexed her hands at her hips.

Was he too late? As they faced off in her office, what had she set in motion at Kick's? He'd made vows to the McKenna's and his closest friend. Banger might be the sole man who considered that sacrosanct, but a vow meant something, dammit.

"No fucking around, Von. Answer me."

"Why should I? I'm not leaving here. Am I?"

True. "Do I mean nothing to you anymore?"

Von stared past Banger's shoulder, like a smart perp in an interrogation room.

He pressed. "Will you at least tell me when Nigel hired you?"

Siobhan pressed her lips together before chuckling like he was a dumb shit. She let a long whistle blow past her lips. "How old is your resentment of him?" She relaxed her stance and added, "Fine, I'll help. There's nothing you can do anyway. The shit-show's doing what it's going to do. I'm guessing you know that." She ran her hand through her spiked red hair, breaking up some of the perfectly placed gel. Like him, Siobhan made herself stand out when she was at home in Raleigh, to keep the disguises effective when underground.

She put her hands in front of her. "It was supposed to be a simple side gig. Help some guy Nigel paid to nab a woman Eleanor had a beef with. You know the guy is Big Jonn Graham and Kick's the woman, obviously." She sighed heavily, like the thing had been an ordeal for her. "I rented a small warehouse and was supposed to sneak Nigel into the city under your nose once Graham set up the dinner date. Those assholes way overestimated Graham's wooing skills, but you ancient-ass men still think modern women will do anything for security and a few bucks, don't you?"

Banger took a step back, like he'd been shoved. Ellie was at the root of this? He didn't risk taking his eyes off Von as he processed the connections. The stories of Ellie's first life were as notorious as those of his own, but Banger had never known her that way. Ruthless and formal, sure. But… Eleanor. Edmund. Alaric. Kick. Power. *The woman behind the throne.* The queen.

"Have you finished your calculations?" Siobhan needled, folding her arms to match his stance.

Banger's jaw flexed as he ground his teeth, thinking.

"Careful…" She wiggled a finger at him. "If you people break a tooth… will another grow back? Or are they superstrong? Lord knows you should've pulverized your molars by now, the way you do that."

There it was. "You're fucking kidding me." She knew. Banger let his head drop, shaking it as he accepted the truth. He figured she hadn't taken the job for money; he paid Von enough to keep a vast collection of her precious Louboutin's for fuck's sake. Immortality though? *There* was a payoff. Made sense for Graham, too, however it was Nigel found the fucker.

"Do you have the variances?" he asked. Thomas had tested her. He would've said something. Anyone with variances was on a watch list.

"Still catching up, Boss?" She clicked her tongue several times.

Banger ran a hand over his bald head. He'd shaved it for his travels. "Nigel's project alters DNA, not enhances it."

Siobhan waggled her brows. "Still a risk, but… YOLO." She shrugged. "It's not like you offered."

YOLO… Not if you're Felidae. He threw his arms out and yelled, "What the bloody hell about my existence attracts you?"

Siobhan took a step toward her desk, her face twisted with rage. "You do, asshole!"

His jaw dropped. "After everything you know, you… want me?"

"Like the disposable girls do anything for you anymore. They haven't for years. Like my boy toys. Boring as fuck." She pointed at him. "I see your face after spending time with Kick and Thomas. You're either grouchy as hell or gloomy. You're lonely, Rafa."

"I'm skeptical." Thomas and Kick *thought* they were happy. For now. Banger knew better. He had watched. Hell, he'd begged the universe to show him a relationship that worked. If Banger was gloomy, he was preparing for Thomas's heartbreak, knowing it would fall to him to pick up the pieces.

Siobhan's arm dropped as she pushed a button on the desk. "We match in every way. I never could figure out why you held back when we'd be amazing together. Hell, I know more about you than Thomas does, considering you keep the really dark shit from him."

She reached inside the top drawer. "Last summer, Nigel sent me a secured message on behalf of Ellie. There's a visionary leader. She's gathering a new group—with a matriarchal line. Fuck the patriarchy shit." Von grabbed her gun, pointed it at Banger. "I planned to play along with that part. Figured they could do their thing in Europe. It wouldn't take much to convince them to let you and I be partners, here in the States. As equals."

"Von…" The word was a lament. If Siobhan had ever paid attention, she'd know the one thing Banger never tolerated was manipulation. He'd been raised in the thick of it, fought against it. Then again, she was right about keeping some things from Thomas.

He noted the gun but didn't care. Staring down the business end of a Glock was part of the work. "If you'd just come to me." They'd have taken out that fuck-face and wannabe-queen together. Murder between the Felidae was unheard of. Loyalty to each other above all else was central to their vows. But everyone knew it happened occasionally. Politics found its way into everything.

"You'd what? Make Thomas change me?"

"If it's possible. Sure. We'd have talked about it. Now?" He backed up to the door, needing the support. "Christ, lass… You were a young coed when I found you fighting off the attack behind your apartment."

"Draw your weapon, Boss. I've answered enough." Her face twisted, Banger hoped the memory pulled at her the way it did him. Siobhan had no skills back then, but she'd been fierce, as ruthless as… fuck.

He narrowed his eyes. "Taught you everything you know."

"That's why you should've figured me out as soon as that grad student turned up dead."

Thomas's lab assistant. That's why his internal alarm went off when he saw the police report. If he'd taken the job, it would've looked the same.

Banger shut down his emotions, used the cold from the solid wood door holding him up to cauterize his heart. "What's going down at Kick's?" As much as he wanted to play cavalry, he trusted Thomas, Dylan, and Kick to handle it. Graham and his associates were idiots.

"Nothing surprising. Kick's guard had a 'family emergency,' so she relieved him early. I dropped the house surveillance. Was supposed to unlock the door, but someone left the garage door up." She inhaled deeply and exhaled arrogance. "There's nothing like the melding of stubbornness and a soft heart."

Dammit, Kick. Von was behind Mateo's emergency too. "Ellie and Nigel?"

"Show your gun, Rafa."

Right. They were in the wind. Those two invented the long game. Their best talent was survival. It's why they worked so well together. Banger reached behind his waist and paused. Siobhan set her feet, gave her shoulders a quick shift. Perfect.

Siobhan's favorite movies were Westerns. She loved a good

gunfight but considered the standoffs before them even better. The drama of the pause between moments. She lived for them. They suited her natural sharp-shooting skills. Too bad for her.

With a fluidity coming from hundreds of years of practice, Banger pulled his *sgian dubh*—his trusty, old Scottish knife—from its waiting spot and threw. End over end, in an instant frozen in time, the little knife flew, landing square in the heart of its target with a crisp thud. Siobhan still managed two shots, as expected. She'd earned her spot at his side after all. Her movements shifted the knife more, tearing enough of the organ to ensure a quick death.

Von's first love had always been guns. She'd taken to them like a kid to sweets. Banger, though, had been throwing knives since he was a toddler. He'd grown up in a violent time, and the Felidae made his childhood more like a training camp, even when he was under Tess and Edmund's tutelage. As soon as the knife left his fingers, Banger dove to the right—he always went to his left. The bullets buzzed past, less than an inch from him, as they tore through the solid door behind him.

Despite his heavy heart, the first thought he had when he landed on his side was, *Not bad, lass.* Banger had taught Siobhan everything she knew, but not everything *he* knew.

41

My Hero

Thomas

"IT'S A SCRATCH, DAMMIT. LET ME SEE MY FIANCÉE!" THE POOR emergency department intern working on my arm fetched the attending physician because I'd turned into the human equivalent of a rabid animal, seething and gnashing my teeth.

The woman with salt-and-pepper hair chided me like I was a petulant child. "Sir, there's a big enough tear in your deltoid muscle to justify stitches. We'll fix it and get you out of here as soon as we can. Just be patient. We're understaffed thanks to the holiday." She checked my bandage and tsked at me. "You're a lucky man, but it won't help your fiancée if you bleed all over my department. Now please… sit still. Let the medicine work, and we'll get those stitches in when the patients ahead of you are finished."

They didn't know my shoulder would be fine. Hell, the scar would fade in a few months, a year tops. If Kick hadn't been somewhere upstairs, having who-knows-whose hands inside her belly, I wouldn't have come in. With a skill borne of long years of practice, I played the good boy. I even let the nurse put unnecessary prophylactic antibiotics in my equally unnecessary IV. What I needed was an update on Kick, and the staff was too busy to check. A family in a boating accident on Falls Lake had come in minutes before our posse rolled up.

Finally my turn, I forced myself to relax and tipped my head back on the pillow, releasing my tension via a rumble in my throat. The intern did all the useless things to my shoulder. Each item checked off their list brought me closer to Kick. That's all that mattered. The door to my unit whooshed open. I figured the attending was coming back to check on my doctor's progress.

"You're a right noisy bastard today." Banger pulled up a squeaky chair, sitting by my head. "They're not supposed to let me back here, but I promised to make you shut your gob." He tossed the young doctor a flirty wink. "Hello there. Nasty-looking burn he's got."

"He's lucky," she answered back without lifting her eyes from her work.

"Kick's the reason it's a little graze."

"Finally hit her bull's-eye, did she?"

I laughed at the thought. She'd done well after her breakthrough but hadn't practiced since the freeway incident.

"Stunt driving and sharp-shooting. Your woman's solid under pressure."

"I'll take her fumbling with no pressure from now on, to be honest."

"Bet."

"As long as everything's over. And I keep my lady." I pinched the bridge of my nose with my good hand. Absolutely could not think of losing her. "Any updates?"

"That's why I came down. She's out of CT and was taken into surgery."

"Just now? What the hell? Why the wait? Why wasn't I told?" The paperwork had recently been filed, but I didn't know how long it took to go into effect. "Where the fuck is Dylan?"

Banger rubbed his head. "He's upstairs. Almost took a swipe at his grandmother. That woman's a piece of work. Got a bee up her arse about transferring Kick to the hospital at Lord University."

"An hour away? We're already at a Level 1 hospital, for fuck's sake." I shook my head and received a dirty look from the intern.

"Please stay still, sir."

"Sorry. I'll behave."

Banger motioned with his hands for me to relax. As if that was happening anytime soon. "Dylan tracked down their lawyer. He located the old legal next-of-kin documents. Smart lass, your Kick. According to Dylan, she'd done that as soon as her daddy died. When the old lady heard about it, she hit the ceiling and caused another delay until security escorted her out. Everything's good now. He also told the staff you're Kick's fiancé and will take responsibility from here. You should know, there hasn't been much communication between departments. He didn't know if you were conscious. That's why I came down."

"We're swamped right now." The young doctor defended her coworkers without looking up from her sutures.

Banger raised his hands again. "Didn't mean to offend."

"Everyone in the hospital is stressed. Goes with the territory," the young doctor said, still never stopping her task. She finished and pushed the instrument stand aside, assessing her results. "All done, Mr. Harrison. My attending will check in once more, and your nurse will be back to give you your shots. Shouldn't be long."

"Thank you, Doctor. My apologies for being an ass."

"I understand. I'll say a prayer for your fiancée. And rest assured, Dr. Jacobs is one of the best trauma surgeons in the Triangle."

Tried my best to give a smile but couldn't get my lips to behave. Probably looked like a psycho. "Appreciate it."

Once we were alone, the shakes started, but not from shock. I needed to get to Kick. The image of her in my lap, blood spilling out on the kitchen floor... so brave, so pale. I raked my hair with my good hand. "She did everything we asked of her, Banger. Everything. Now she's paying for it."

Banger bent down, his forearms on his knees. His head dropped.

"Hey man, I didn't mean you..."

"You should have."

"Siobhan?" I quietly asked, though I knew.

He stared at the floor. "Fuck."

"How'd you—"

"That's why it took me so long to get to you," he started. "I surprised her at the office." Banger stood, a restless ball of energy. He turned in circles on the tiny floor before dropping back into the chair. "Wes had already told me about Mateo's emergency while I was en route." He stretched, like the chair itself pained him, and kicked his feet out in front of him. His hands folded behind his head. Banger's face twisted, looking more vulnerable than I'd ever seen. "Von was there when I walked in, acting squirrely as fuck. Hadn't expected me, obviously. But I was playing a hunch. When your text came, I knew." He shot up and walked to the glass wall. "Fuuuck!"

"I'm sorry, man."

Banger didn't look at me. He practically vibrated as his clenched fist froze in the air with nowhere to land. "Worry about your woman. I'll deal with the fallout."

"Trying to think of anything besides her since I'm stuck down here."

Banger came back and sat. "Stay here as long as you can. Kick will be in surgery for a while. It's a madhouse in the waiting room."

"Who's here?" I exhaled, flopping my head back on the pillow. I didn't want to have to take care of anyone when my heart was on an operating table with an abdominal wound.

"There's been a steady migration since we arrived."

"Deana? She needs a call, but she doesn't have to—"

"She's here. Tess too. She rode with Rachel and Wes."

I imagined Deana, Gordon, and Tess taking care of the kids. Being with them would help me feel close to Kick.

I stared through the glass to make sure the staff stayed busy with other patients. There was more we needed to say in private. "Dylan say anything to you?"

The question granted me a knowing grin. "He gave me the basics before the police took him for questioning. He's the sole witness not needing medical care, so he's theirs for a while." Banger rubbed his head. "I told him to leave out the things that sounded weird and emphasize Graham's madness over losing his criminal son."

"Then he told you."

"He did." He huffed a quiet laugh. "Hold him off, yeah? Kick should be there if we have to let him in."

"Christ." What had Nigel and Ellie done? The Felidae secrets were on the verge of getting out. They were the team that protected us above all else—or so I thought. "What the hell was Ellie thinking? I can't…"

"Before I killed her, Siobhan filled in the details. It seems Nigel discovered the Edmund connection last summer. The convoluted plans revolved around getting samples from Kick, which they finally scored on Saint Patrick's Day." He shrugged. "I guess Ol' Ni-ni wanted to experiment on her at first, but he reluctantly settled for a lip balm and hair samples from her office."

"That son of a bitch. But… what about Kick's brother?"

Banger sighed. His eyelids were heavy with exhaustion. I could relate. "They broke into his house first. Without a surveillance system, he never realized it. You know since they don't take anything obvious. There was also something about Ellie targeting women— making matriarchal lines, specifically. The bastard and Ellie are both in the wind now. If I ever get a team I can believe in again, they're my first priority."

Shit. What a clusterfuck. "Did Siobhan say why? I mean… I have a theory. Why did Kick matter so much? Hell, I thought Ellie would be thrilled." Alaric sure as hell was, and I knew it wasn't an act.

Banger pressed his lips together as he shook his head. "Long story, brother. Fuck all, everything with the old ones is. Edmund's death never sat right with me. Tess is convinced Ellie arranged his accident. That woman plays a mean long game." Banger scooted his chair closer to the bed and grabbed my forearm. "I promise you… my house will be purified. Wes is already going through the rest of my personnel… finding out if Siobhan had turned anyone else, like she did the tail on Young Jonn." Banger shook his head, his nostrils flaring. "I might fly out and see the old man if… if you don't need me."

If Kick survives, he meant. I swallowed hard, wanting to curl in on myself, but she didn't deserve my fear. The memory of the morning she'd discovered my secret flashed through my mind. I had prepared myself to let Kick walk away, and my heart felt like it was imploding—as it currently did. She fought her way through every unbelievable explanation I threw at her then. Damn if she didn't up and choose me regardless. "She has to come through."

"Listen… the trauma team wouldn't tell us anything specific about Kick's condition, but you and I know how abdominal shit goes. A shot to the gut can fly right through and hit nothing, or it could be the worst way to… yeah." He scrubbed his hands over his face, swallowed hard. "She'll fight, brother. She wouldn't want to let us all down. Count on her fighting for you."

If Kick survived this—when… dammit—Banger would end up the one who'd lost. He'd need us whether he'd want it or not. I grabbed his arm. "You're not alone either. Whatever we need to do."

We sat in an awkward silence, both of us reeling.

"Where the hell is the attending?"

42

Zombie

Kick

NOISE.

So many sounds.

Please… make it stop. Holes pounded in my head and colors filled my vision. Too colorful. My eyes refused to open.

Turn the lights off. They hurt.

"She's tacky…"

The hell? That was mean.

And the pain—like fire all over.

The noise again. Thumping, pounding in my head.

Stop it please. It hurts. *JaysusMaryandJoseph*, I hurt.

"…still Kick… you better… Go, go, go!"

Yesss, *at last*. The pain stopped.

WARM BREEZES TICKLED THE TENDRILS FALLING FROM MY PONYTAIL. My gaze fell to recycled wooden floorboards under my feet. Salt permeated the air. The ocean. A deep breath was a welcomed relief from the pain of a tight chest. Gratitude filled me for the absence of that pain. Atlantic waves crashed on the beach in front of the house. I was on Emerald Isle.

We'd done it. Shane and I had built the beach house—our dream home.

Filled with glee, I spun and hopped, eager to explore the inside.

Pain sliced from my knee to my hip, chinking my step before I reached the screen door.

Where the hell had that come from?

A cane leaned against the clapboards. I grabbed it to stay upright.

How odd. I hadn't used a cane since the worst days of my diagnosis.

The interior of the house was exactly as I remembered, but how could it? I hadn't been here before. Not only did I know where we'd placed everything, I held hazy memories of purchases, decorating, even small tiffs about what would come with us and what went to charity.

A thick, driftwood mantel ran the length of the wall facing the door. The fireplace below was stunning, but photos on the dark-stained wood beckoned. I limped over to them, wondering why the hell my leg refused to cooperate.

Fatigue lived in my bones the way it had in the old days. It made no sense. I lifted weights, did yoga, occasionally ran. Didn't I?

Frustration grew. A voice in the back of my head told me it was naptime, like I was a damn baby.

Damn… Damn it all.

I knew someone who said that word. Often. Someone I loved. He called me "baby"—our private joke. The word rumbled at my ear in his velvety baritone turning my insides to liquid. That honeyed Southern accent. Gray-blue eyes that sparkled with his smile. I wanted desperately to see *him*, except he was gone.

Dylan's bright silver eyes looked at me from a hand-cut frame, and I picked it up. Why was he wearing a Michigan State University football uniform? He turned down the offer to play and stayed close to home for some reason. Hadn't he? Despite the grin, my son's eyes were sad. My brow furrowed, wondering what happened. Several images of him with concussions flashed through my mind. Doctors' offices and tests. *Were these memories?*

A picture of Rachel as Elphaba Thropp from the musical *Wicked* brightened my spirit, as did one of her holding a toddler. Her smile didn't reach her eyes either. Her face held that hidden concern that mothers carry for a sick child. Something was wrong with the baby. More vague memories of worrying about him flooded me. For both of them, really.

I turned and found his *Fisher Price* toys in the corner. We often kept him.

The football-themed office in the Northwest corner irritated me. I'd wanted Shane to put his office upstairs and let me set up my studio down here. But his knee replacement made stairs difficult, and I'd become too sick to paint.

Too sick to paint? What the hell?

Memories of coffee filled my mind so crisp I could almost smell it. And cigars.

And guns.

No!

Where was everybody? I ached to see the gray-blue eyes. But… Shane's eyes were the color of the sky on a Carolina morning.

No… they were silver when *he* smiled. And navy when aroused.

My heart raced. Breath caught in my throat. *Where was he?*

Something didn't sit right about the house.

I didn't belong there. The light was wrong.

Light?

We had a light… blue and purple. If I could find it, I'd feel better.

I bolted for the door and tripped when my joints wouldn't behave. I slid through the threshold, scraping my side. *Is that why it hurts?* "Hurt" didn't begin to describe the furious pain. I crawled to the porch railing and pulled myself up as I called for *him*. Words wouldn't come. Air moved through my throat, but no sound projected from it. Dread made me shake.

I hated the house. I hated the pain, the fatigue. I'd lost something.

Me.

All that work on my health.

I'd lost someone.

Him.

I wanted him back.

A song reached my ears… "Maybe I'm Amazed." We danced to it. I sang it when he… proposed?

But Shane didn't dance.

Tears spilled down my face.

Down.

My gaze dropped to my stomach. Pain, fire… a hole.

I needed *him.* Where are you?

43

Ain't No Sunshine

Thomas

"She's taking too long to wake up."

The nurse, Joy, patted my shoulder. She'd come in to check Kick's fluid output and lines. Until she woke, there wasn't much else to do.

She patiently reiterated the facts I already knew, like I was a child. "Her surgery was long. Most of the damage was in her liver. Her son told me she's sensitive to medicines too?" I nodded and triple-checked that they had the list of antibiotics she couldn't take. "Put those things together, and it means it'll take a while for the drugs to clear her system." She checked the IV bag. "The pain medicine Ms. McKenna's on keeps her sedated. It shouldn't be much longer. Just... don't expect much when she wakes, okay, sugar?"

"Kick."

Joy blinked at me. "Pardon?"

"Please call her Kick. It'll help. Right?" Again, I didn't resent her last name, but I ached for her to have mine. I hated that I hadn't been able to talk her into eloping. As if I wasn't equally busy. I didn't care. Fear made me irrational. Not to mention irritable.

"Of course. Kick." The nurse nodded and turned to leave.

"Thank you, Joy."

"That's what I'm here for."

When she left, Banger slipped into the room. "How's our girl?"

I sighed. "See for yourself."

I needed her to dance with me, tell me to shut up, or ask me if I'd checked on the hospital cafeteria's cross-contamination precautions. Her tight, curly coils had even loosened, thanks to shuffling between beds. Rachel pulled most of them into a high bun, but the stragglers hardly bent anymore. They lacked energy too, I guessed.

The bright overhead lights made the purple bruises on her face look nothing like the pretty color of her aura. These contrasted with her paler-than-normal complexion, turning her into something like an extra in a zombie movie. My beautiful lady, my strong fairy queen, my heart... blown apart and stitched back together into colors she was never meant to show. For the thousandth time, I reminded myself they were signs of her healing, just like her unconscious state. Kick was gone.

Her chest rose and fell like a metronome. At least she was off the machinery. As I breathed along with her, my fists clenched in the blanket covering her. I should've taken comfort in her audible heartbeats, but I needed her voice, not her vitals. The antiseptic bite in the air held my nose hostage. The stale air blowing on us didn't help. It all disrupted any peace I could draw upon.

"She saved me and Dylan. And I can't do anything for her." I laid my cheek on her thigh and said, "If I could kill Jonathon Graham a thousand times over, I'd do it for her."

"It's not your job to help her yet. She's still in the hospital staff's hands. Your turn will come." Banger sat on Kick's other side and squeezed her hand. "Isn't that right, purple lady?"

I wished I could laugh with him. Each blooming bruise made me want to punch the wall. I'd been born into a world of bruises and scars. No one felt sorry for them. They were a testament to the life you'd lived. My Kick came from a different time. The stitches and colors screamed at me about how much I'd let her down.

"I keep playing her songs, hoping they'll wake her up. Except, will she be alright when she does? The doctors say one step at a time. They won't predict anything. I don't know how to handle the wait. It's so… new. Feels like the worst of my memories wrapping the past and the present together. What have I done?"

Banger ran his hands over the back of his neck. "Based on what I witnessed last fall, you had no choice with Kick. Now? I'll tell you this… your woman is no fragile flower. Her body gives her hell, but her will is made of iron. She'll wake. She'll recover. She loves you something fierce."

I dipped my chin in acknowledgment.

"Use your energy when she wakes. A birdie told me it helps."

My head knew Banger was right, but my heart still beat with fear.

"Are you family?" Joy, the nurse, poked her head in and stared straight at Banger.

"Sorry, ma'am. I brought Thomas here a coffee. I'll be going."

"Her daughter's waiting in the hall."

My abused bladder, the one I'd been ignoring most of the night, screamed loud enough to catch my attention. With Rachel here, I could step out for a minute. Reluctantly, I said, "I'll come with you."

I kissed Kick's head. "Love you, baby. I'll only be a minute."

Beeps mocked our one-sided conversation.

Banger held the door open for Rachel, who hugged me like a koala. "Hey, pretty lady." I lifted her chin with my finger. "The nurse said she could wake any minute."

Her voice cracked. "I-is it over? Are we safe now?" Tears sat at the ready on her lower lids. They'd been that way ever since she arrived at the hospital yesterday. We'd had this same conversation a handful of times already. If she needed it one more time to believe, so be it.

"Yeah, darlin'. All the bad guys are in jail or dead." I couldn't tell her about the Felidae part, but they'd never been after her. Her terror was all Young Jonn's obsession. "You're safe, Rachel."

"I'm sorry. It's… still hard to accept."

I gave her shoulders a gentle squeeze. "You three kids went through hell this year. I'll answer every question whenever you need, got it?" *The ones I could.*

"Sure." She cracked a small, sweet smile. "Thanks."

"Go sing to your mama. Bet it'll wake her." I winked at her and gave a small wave.

Banger grabbed my arm and pulled me away from Kick's room. "You want a reason to be strong? It's those kids. They're one loud beep machine going awry from being orphans, and their next closest relative is a looney bird."

"Fuck you, man. I'm doing the best I can."

"You can do better. For Kick's sake, her kids accepted you into their hearts. They need you now. I walked in on you on the verge of giving up. Then Rachel came in and you gave her hope. Stop blaming yourself and go be with them."

Banger tipped his head toward the waiting room. "Liam's climbing the walls back there, but he's too scared to go into her room. You can talk him back to earth. For some reason, the boy's almost as fond of you as Kick is."

The picture he painted in my mind did its job. He was right. Kick would want me to step up. I grabbed my neck and stretched it, preparing myself for Liam. "Thanks for scolding me, man."

"Anytime. Listen… if the nurse doesn't mind, I'll stay with Rachel until you get back. She shouldn't be alone."

"Right again." We grabbed forearms as I nodded. "Thanks." After my pit stop, I entered the waiting room. "How long have you been here?"

Liam sat with his head in his hands, looking like a giant little boy. "Colin dropped me off last night."

I sat beside him and stretched my arm around his shoulders. "Why didn't you come back? I know your mom wants to see you."

"I peeked in." When Liam sat up, the dark shadows under his

eyes were almost the same color as Kick's bruises. My anger flared for his sake this time. "She can't see us right now. You know that."

"Ahh, Lee." I pinched the bridge of my nose. Was I really up for this? "The nurse believes she hears us." I stood and took him with me. "First let's freshen up and get a bite to eat. We can't help your mom if we're on the ragged edge, can we?"

He let out a shaky laugh. "Guess not."

MY PHONE BUZZED WITH A TEXT FROM THE ICU AND MY HEART leaped. "Finish fast, gang. She's awake!"

Dylan and Banger had joined Liam and me in the cafeteria while Rachel and Bobby sat with Kick. Dylan was still incensed with his grandmother and couldn't stay in the same room as her. I hated how Rachel played peacemaker between them. From what Kick had told me, she'd been the self-appointed go-between for her mother and grandmother since she was little. Now she stepped in for her brother—the golden boy.

A cheer rose from the table, and we dumped our trays. I stayed twitchy during the ride up to Kick's floor. What—or who—would we find in her room? I'd been so excited by the summons I hadn't asked the staff anything. What did "awake" mean? *Christ, I hope she tells me to shut up. Or strokes my chin.* Last night, I had held Kick's thumb and made her do it, hoping it would stir something in her. Without her intention, the desperate, empty gesture brought me to tears.

"THERE'S MY LADY." I SAT IN THE SEAT RACHEL HAD OCCUPIED. SHE hovered in the corner while the boys shuffled an obstinate Bobby out of the room. The kids honored and humbled me by insisting I was immediate family.

Kick's hazel eyes turned at my words. Her head slowly followed the movement. I attributed the fuzziness in the green of her irises to the drugs. The brown barely showed. I watched her fog turn to recognition as she perused my face. Her chin quivered.

"Hey," I soothed, caressing her cheek with my hand. Tears streamed from the corner of her eyes. "Please don't cry." I smiled at her and cried too.

"I l-lost… you. Looked for… you… didn't like it there. Not without you."

I stretched across the space between us and kissed her temple, her nose, her quivering bottom lip. "I've been here… waiting for you to come back. So were the kids."

Kick squinted to focus and found the trio on the opposite side of the bed. "My babies." A sweet smile stretched across her face in recognition. Her voice sounded distant and scratchy. Her vulnerability sent my protective mode into overdrive. I'd make sure she received the best of everything while she was here.

Kick's eyes landed on Dylan, and I watched her eyes clear. I guessed memories returned from the shooting. Graham had threatened to kill Dylan with his warped life-for-a-life sense of justice. Her head moved up and down, checking every inch of him the way a parent does when they meet their newborn.

"Dylan? You doubled over." A new tear trailed down her cheek.

He stepped forward, taking her other hand. "Something about Thomas's face told me to duck. Then you yelled 'drop'." He gave her a coy smile and squeezed her hand. "You should follow your own advice."

"Really, Dyl?" Liam snapped.

"Not funny, twat waffle," Rachel said as she smacked her brother in the abs.

Their frail jokes and tenuous laughter broke the tension. It also gave away how much stress the kids carried. It filled the room every time they crossed the threshold, because children shouldn't be made to watch their parents suffer like this. Kick once told me that after Shane's accident, the kids would freak out whenever she had a bad day. Like they were waiting to lose her. Now she was in a hospital recovering from a gunshot wound. *Recover* being the takeaway.

Kick brought her gaze back to me and saw my sling. "He aimed at your heart."

"It's a small graze. Your bullet hit the bastard aiming at me, and he hit my shoulder instead." I ran my hand over her hair. "You saved my life."

"You thought I was dying." My throat dried up at her words. I couldn't respond, just kept swallowing. "S-sorry I scared you," she said.

"Christ, Kick." I'd been furious at her heroics at first. The truth was each of us would've gone down for the other. I brought her hand to my lips and kissed it.

"I'm tired." She yawned and winced from the pain it caused. She did her best to not moan from it but failed.

The kids gasped, like they'd been waiting for signs of Kick's fragility. Dylan ran his hand through his hair. "I'll go get the nurse."

Liam slipped into the chair opposite mine. He leaned toward his mom. "Sh-should we go?"

Kick squeezed his hand and gave him a pained smile. I answered for her. "Give her a minute. You're more of a balm than you think."

Joy arrived and added medicine to the IV. "Why don't y'all give mama an hour? Patients only have about ten minutes of energy at the beginning. Don't worry, it grows. Before you know it, all y'all will be out of our hair."

I walked toward the door with the kids. Joy followed, leaving us with hope. "It doesn't look like it to you, but she's doing great."

Kick quietly called after us, "Can Thomas lie with me? I'm a-afraid to sleep without him."

Joy turned around, her hand on her hip. "We need to order bigger beds around here. Everybody wants to crawl in with the patient." She walked back to the IV stand. "Let's see if we can scoot you over without pinching the lines. You've got two hours until the shift changes. I can give you that much."

"Thank you." I hugged each kid and told them I'd text when Kick woke again. I promised this was a nap and nothing to be frightened of. Climbing into the bed alongside her, I encouraged her to rest while I watched over her. My eyes continuously scanned her monitors and her body for signs of change. I held her free hand under the blanket, willing my energy to come out and help her heal.

It was a shock when Joy shook my knee to get me to leave the bed at the end of her shift. I'd been up almost two days and had fallen into a deep sleep with Kick safe in my arms.

1031

They

Kick

"Ow! Don't make me laugh, Liam. Especially when my belly pillow's missing. One of you bozos stole it, and I want it back."

"*Must you* with the Oscar-worthy performance? You don't hear me griping about my knee." Bobby indignantly folded her arms and turned away, smiling at the room, like she was scanning it for allies. Even now, the competition she'd built between us from the day I was born continued. The one-way one-upping would never quit with her.

"I was *shot*, Mother. A chunk of my fucking shitty-to-begin-with liver is gone. Besides, you gripe about your knee every chance you get. You're the one who turned pain into an Olympic competition I never signed on to." I sighed and closed my eyes to her performance. "I can't care anymore."

Bobby clicked her tongue. I couldn't see her eyes rolling, but I practically heard them rattle around in her head. I supposed the chance to recruit more fans to her side of our mother-daughter war had energized her. The hospital staff was fresh meat where she was concerned.

"You've always been a hypochondriac and never took care of me. You hate when the spotlight's off you."

Funny how my memories were the exact opposite. Thomas's offer from back in January roared in my head every single minute of Bobby's visits this past week.

"There's my cue to leave," Liam said.

Of my three, he'd been the hardest on himself for being out of town while everything went down. How did he not see my immense gratitude for the band's gig? But he'd always been sensitive to my ups and downs. As a toddler, before the diagnosis, he'd go out of his way to snuggle close or entertain me on bad days.

"Okay, Wee Man. Promise me you'll go to practice. The café's doing fine." When he leaned down for a hug, I whispered in his ear, "Keep the gig in Chapel Hill this weekend. Last-minute bookings like this don't come around often."

His shoulders dropped as he sighed. "Yeah, gotcha. We've got a new girl to get up to speed anyway."

"So Jax won't sing with you at all?"

Liam's brows pinched as his fingers beat a rhythm on his thigh. "Chill, fam. We need…" He lifted a shoulder. "Space." Dark shadows still sat under his eyes, where everyone else's had faded since I was officially recovering. My poor baby had lost his best friend, and we'd never talked about it. He still refused to open up.

"Sure, sweetheart. What's your new singer's name? Do I get to meet her soon?"

"Her name's Mary Lawrence. You can meet her the next time you come to practice."

"Mary Lawrence? Is she studying to become a nun? Does anyone call her Mary Larry?" Bobby chuckled, but Liam looked embarrassed by my flippant remark. *Shit.* I'd let Bobby's critical nature rub off on me again. "I'm sorry. That was rude."

"It's the South, fam. Girls get men's names all the time down here."

"True. I forgot. Name them after Grandpa, but don't let them have their own opinions."

He laughed at my joke and said, "Like we're better." I childishly smirked at the dig at Bobby, who'd named both her daughter and son after her, in her never-ending need for validation.

Liam turned and waved. "Bye, Gran."

"Yeah, yeah." Bobby flicked a hand in his direction.

I called after him, "Tell Macushla I miss her."

"Gotcha." He blew me a kiss and left the door ajar as he disappeared down the hall.

Once he was out of sight, I glared at Bobby for a long time. If this Felidae business could develop the power to shoot lasers from my eyes, I would have gleefully toasted her.

She shuffled in her chair, as if she'd been on a radiator instead. She knew I judged her for the way she treated Liam. This ancient fight between us had become so predictable.

Bobby was spot-on too. I judged her for a hell of a lot. She was lucky we were in a hospital. Biting my tongue kept me from screaming at her. I'd spent my life biting my tongue around her. It's a wonder it wasn't pierced.

"Are you ever going to forgive and forget?" Bobby demanded. She reminded me of an adulterer who blamed their spouse for their destructive behavior. *Then again, she'd done that too.*

The truth was, I'd forgiven her years ago. It didn't mean we were resolved, though, or ever would be. Resolution required penance from the offending party. Or at least acknowledgment and honest reflection. Bobby was so busy hiding from herself I suspected true contemplation would cause a breakdown.

I needed that resolution.

Bobby wanted permission to fly her mean flag as high as she wanted whenever she wanted. Especially at my expense. If I continued to allow it, I would end up unable to look at myself in the mirror. Time for this to come to a head.

"Forgive what exactly, Bobby?" My words spilled out more clipped than planned. "You've never apologized for anything. How am I supposed to forgive someone who—according to you—has done nothing wrong?" My voice rose with bitter sarcasm, and Joy stuck her head in my room. "Sorry," I said, though I didn't mean it. Our timing stunk. What was new? Joy nodded and ducked back out.

"I apologized for the sweater I shrank."

From high school. *Seriously?* "No you didn't. You put me in charge of everyone's laundry as punishment for being upset with you." I gritted through my teeth. "All you do is make excuses for your mean streak."

"You know how my family treated me," she shot back. Her chin quivered as bitterness instantly dissolved into self-pity.

"Intimately. Instead of taking responsibility for yourself, you responded in kind. You could've done better, but you turned love into a weapon. That's on you, not your parents. For my self-preservation, I can't care anymore with you." Sighing, I turned my head away, refusing to see her someone-just-made-a-rank-fart face anymore. An icy shiver skated up my spine, doing a quadruple something-or-the-other jump, landing hard on my heart. Numbness replaced all the years of hurt and bitterness. Numbness was all I could hope for with Bobby.

"I built my school from the ground up. Who helped me? No one." Bobby fretted, refusing to let go of the pity party she was hosting.

True. She worked her arse off to run the best school in the metro area. But, uh… Daddy worked his ass off between shifts playing single parent.

I said nothing, so she continued, "You and your father made me give it all up!"

You sold it for a fecking mint after the orthopedist told you to retire. Then Daddy did his money magic and set you up for life.

"It's called retirement." I hissed. "The doctor warned you that your knee couldn't take the daily punishment. Daddy had to get away from the cold, and Raleigh reminded him of home. You've never given life here a chance."

"You took me away from Robert."

I'd heard this at least a million times. My field of fucks was harvested. There weren't even any left for gleaning. Numbness was a welcome relief to the pain of her accusations. I made my decision. If only Thomas had been here to witness it.

"We're done." I exhaled a long, quiet breath. The peace that I usually required meditation to achieve washed over me. "I'll have

Thomas's assistant arrange a mover for you. You'll have a nurse to oversee your health issues if you need it. Hell, anything you want, you can call her. But never call me again." I swiped away a tear. "Move in with Juan. Do the things you've always wanted to do, whatever lights your fire. I don't care. From here on, we're dead to each other."

Bobby's voice rose above acceptable hospital volume. "I never know how to act or what to say around you. My words get twisted." She fussed with an invisible piece of lint on her shirt before spitting, "I'm damned if I do and damned if I don't."

No surprise she didn't know what to make of my decision. Except this fish was done swinging from her hook. I cut the fecking line. "Right back at you, Mother." I tucked a wavy tendril behind my ear. "Now neither of us needs to worry about it… anymore."

Bobby clenched her fists as if she were restraining herself from hitting me. In my hospital bed. I lifted my eyes to the ceiling tiles, wishing I could walk away from her. I contemplated pressing the nurse's button and having her thrown out.

I swallowed and said the words I'd known my whole life but never admitted. "Listen, I know if given a choice, you would have never picked me to be your kid."

"I wouldn't go—"

"It's the same for me." I interrupted, and hearing the words shut her mouth tight. "We're never going to be one of those mother-daughter bestie duos. It was never in our cards."

Her brow pinched in anger. The truth hurt, I guess. It didn't matter anymore.

Bobby loudly exhaled several times, sounding like a horse after a long carriage ride. "I wish… well, I wish…" She never finished her sentiment. Instead, she sat in her chair, staring out the window, her cowardice shouting louder than her temper ever could.

"Yeah. Me too." And that was the closest to an apology I'd ever receive from her.

"I'll be going then." She stood, smoothing her clothes, checking her purse, anything to avoid eye contact.

I channeled the speech Thomas had given me in the bathtub as

I called after Bobby. "You'll want for nothing. Money, medical care, a shopper, a companion. You can have it. You just won't have me."

After she slammed the door, the tears let loose. Overwhelming relief and crushing pain mingled together. The judgment of friends who'd lost good mothers raced to the front of my mind. *You'll regret it when she's gone,* they always said. The thing was, I'd been mourning the mother I'd never had since I was a girl.

I pulled the blanket to my mouth as a sob escaped. The pain wracking through my chest didn't register. I didn't even press the button on the medicine dispenser. Emotions took front and center, and no button existed for them. I felt good and bad, guilt and relief all rolled into one. Moreover, I was proud of myself for finally sticking up for the little girl who'd been treated like shit for so long.

Sowing the Seeds of Love

Kick

"YOU CUT YOUR HAIR." I INHALED DEANA'S SHEA BUTTER AND vanilla scent as she leaned down to hug me. "It's so Anita Baker."

She laughed, her deep rumble, taking my mind off the post-op pain. After my cry over everything with Bobby, the physical pain came back with a vengeance.

She touched her short, wispy hairdo. "Gordon calls me Halle Berry."

"Your cheekbones stand out like hers for sure. It's beautiful, Dee. Not that you weren't before." Exhausted from talk of recovery and therapy and my family drama, I took full advantage of mindless beauty experiments.

She laughed and patted my shin. "No worries. I know what you're saying. Thank you. Now tell me… y'ight?"

My shoulders shrugged with ease, thanks to the meds. "Distract me please. What's new at the Perked Cup?"

Thomas had told me about the vigil she'd kept during my surgery. This was our first time alone, and we both buzzed with pent-up energy. I wanted to thank her for holding the kids together.

She wanted to chew my ass out. I didn't need to read her mind to know that.

"Jake bumped up his hours. You'll be proud of him." She slid the visitor's chair closer to me and fell into it.

One more restless day in this bed and I could go home. Thomas, the kids, and Cyndi helped me make slow laps around the unit each morning and night. The infection was minimal, and a new antibiotic didn't cause any reactions. The nurses regularly commented on my quick recovery. Little did they know. Every night Thomas spent with me, he ran his energy over my skin until mine woke up to it. He promised to study what it was all about when he took his work over to the private sector.

"How's Dex doing with Hugh? Have they started the expansion into the space next door?"

Deana swiped her thumb over my palm several times and wouldn't lift her gaze. "They have."

"I can't wait to peek at what Charley's crew came up with." I grabbed her hand and squeezed it. "There's something you're not saying. Are the men getting along?" I didn't know what I'd do if there was a problem. Despite my resolve to say goodbye to Bobby, I was still drained. Constantly fighting pain made it harder for me to give the way I was used to.

"They get on great, shug. I didn't know Hugh made him a partner though," she said.

Thomas had mentioned it in passing, but I had other things on my mind. I shrugged. "It's a great idea." I tilted my head. "What am I missing?"

"You were supposed to be Hugh's partner. I feel like we've taken something away from you. Your future security. Your kids…"

"Are you talking about money?"

Deana's normally spot-on posture fell as she looked away.

"Hey…" I shook her hand to get her attention back. "The kids and I are fine. We'll stay fine. My involvement had been a favor to Hugh—to honor my dad. The kids plan to do their own things. So why shouldn't the Douglases have a stake in the success of this venture? It makes more sense anyhow."

"We're employees."

Talk about pain. Her words felt like a slap. To my heart. Then again, Gordon and Deana had been burned by promises from employers before. In our part of the country, it was difficult for true friendship to cross racial lines. Rudely and brutally so. Like me with my mother's side, there was always a part of them that expected the worst so they wouldn't be disappointed.

"Tell me you know you're more than my morning manager."

When Deana said nothing, I swore to keep from crying.

"Thomas likes to say you're part of my clan. Dee, you're more my family than my mother's people have ever been. Who's managed her all these years for me? My dad?" I waved my hand. "*Pffft.* We both know it's been you… propping me up when she hit me with a zinger. You were the first one I could count on after Shane… You're family."

Deana's face dissolved into a visage of tears and fury. "What the *fuck* were you thinking… shooting a gun like a *damn* cowgirl? Getting shot." She jumped out of her chair and paced the little space in my room, lecturing. "You expect me to pick up these kids' pieces because you went off half-cocked? Like Superwoman?"

Her emotions opened my floodgates. My hands shook as the memories rushed back. "I was so terrified. He said he'd kill Dylan. Then Thomas." I don't remember Deana moving, but we ended up holding each other for a long time.

"You're the one we almost lost," she muttered into my neck. "Stupid girl. G agrees with me."

"Does he now?" I pushed her back and wiped away her tears with my thumbs. "I thought Gordon always agreed with *me.*"

She sniffled and reached for a tissue. "I tell you that to make you feel better."

"Appreciate it," I said, laughing as I dabbed my eyes with the blanket.

Deana picked up a scrunchie that Rachel had left on the windowsill. She finger-combed my hair, creating elaborate twists with an eased skillfulness that awed me. She fashioned everything into a high ponytail.

I began to giggle as she worked. It had been the first real laughing fit since the attack. It felt so good to release this way that I didn't mind the pain. I welcomed it.

"Hold still, you mess," she commanded through the bobby pins she seemed to have magically conjured and held in her teeth. "What's so funny?"

"I made you swear, Deana Douglas."

"Shut up." She pulled a little tighter on my hair because she could. "You'd make my *Grandmama* swear."

"THERE'S MY BEAUTIFUL LADY." THOMAS HAD SPENT A NIGHT AWAY from the hospital because Banger required his help with something. It had to do with the betrayal and putting Angel Security back together, but I didn't have the mental bandwidth to get into the details with them. My heart ached for Banger though, and I encouraged Thomas to help his friend however he could. I wouldn't hog all his energy when Banger was wounded too.

"You should consider glasses, cowboy. My face is doing an impression of a failed stained glass project."

He leaned over and kissed me in greeting. "Your eyes are bright today. The doctor must be tapering off your pain meds." His fingers lightly swept over my cheeks. "Swelling's going down. Your hair's damp from a shower. All clues that you'll be out of here soon."

Thomas swiveled his hips on the side of the bed, making room for him to lie next to me. He pulled me against him, wrapped his arms around me, and buried his nose in my hair.

"Did you sniff me?" I smiled at the memory of him asking me that same question after I sprained my ankle and he had to carry me home. It felt so long ago.

"Damn straight." He continued inhaling as he paved a trail of kisses along my jaw, down my neck. "I missed you last night. It's too cold in our bed without you."

My favorite nurse opened the door, a clipboard in her hand. "It's official. Since you pooped this morning, you get to go home today. You can start on these papers while I do my magic at the desk."

Thomas turned to me with a wide grin. "You did?" He laughed into my shoulder, bouncing me up against him, getting more than a twinge from me.

"Um, careful. One BM doesn't equal an all clear." My skin heated with its red flush of embarrassment. Then again, Thomas had helped change many bandages and one nurse showed him how to give me a sponge bath on a night when the staff was short a nurse. We had no mysteries between us anymore. Though I'd still insist on doing my business in private when we went home. Some things are sacrosanct.

"Wish I could've been here to celebrate."

I clicked my tongue. "I'm not potty-training, you knothead. If I were, Joy would've given me ice cream for breakfast. Well, dairy-free ice cream."

"You gave your kids ice cream for breakfast for pooping in the potty?" Joy asked. "That's genius. We can't motivate my three-year-old to stay on it long enough to do anything, but that might work."

"Instant rewards get the best returns. Oh, right…" I tapped my thigh. "A successful week earned the boys a Thomas the Tank Engine." I turned to Thomas and held my hand flat. "I'll take Lady, thank you very much. She's my favorite engine."

"*You're* my lady." He kissed my palm. "This Lady character must be amazing if you remember her."

"She shoots magic gold dust out her stack, or something like that. And she gets kids to believe in themselves."

"Sounds just like you."

I laughed and winced. "I wish you guys would stop doing that. How can I heal if you keep making me hurt?"

"Hate to tell you, honey, but you have many more weeks of hurting until everything's considered healed," Joy said. "Which reminds me… I can tell you two will need to see this in writing." She flipped the pages on the clipboard to the fourth in her stack of what looked like twenty papers. "No orgasms until you can walk a mile or three flights of stairs."

"You're making this up, right?" I asked, annoyance saturating my voice while my cheeks flared with heat.

"The doctor will explain everything when he visits. Just keep in mind, you were basically fileted. Those muscles need time, and orgasms are intense contractions."

No shit. Lovely, mind-blowing, intense contractions. Now I wanted one… no, many. It had been too long.

Joy must've read the discouragement on my face. "No need to pout." She folded her arms over her chest. "Keep up with your walks and follow your discharge orders to a T. You'll be up to speed before you know it. Just remember… if something hurts, stop it immediately. Okay?"

Thomas scoffed at her orders. "Better keep her here."

"Hey!"

Joy tapped my compression-hose-covered calf. The cankles were going down. "I have all my faith in a full recovery. Shoot, I thought they wrote the wrong number when your chart said you're forty-seven. Then I saw those two huge boys of yours and couldn't believe you didn't have a surrogate. You'll be fine." She gave me a wink and left us to do the paperwork.

"Thomas?" I held the clipboard up, bringing my hand toward my face, then pulling it away. "Speaking of glasses, I can read this without specs."

"It's all part of the reverse order of healing."

"But I thought getting shot would override any reversing."

He twisted his lips as he pondered my question. "My scientific guess is, you're in mega-healing mode. It could be a bonus side effect."

"Mega-healing mode? This a scientific term?"

He smirked. "I never dealt with aging eyes, but I had a stubborn ankle wound from the war. Also, I'd occasionally deal with muscle pain after contracting a bad illness as a kid. Both mysteriously improved in the first few years after my aura manifested. I guessed at a correlation but wasn't certain until I found the Felidae."

"Well, shit. Is there a hand mirror around here? I want to see if

I can apply mascara without my x10 magnification mirror. Now *that* would be something."

Reach Out, I'll Be There

Thomas

NOT TEACHING A SPRING SEMESTER CLASS ALLOWED ME TO HELP WITH Kick's recovery. My team also hit a roadblock in the lab, so a step back benefited everyone. We held off on the next push until after moving into the new facility in Research Triangle Park.

A couple of weeks later I came home early, expecting Kick to be at the desk in her office. She'd taken on work she could do from home while the rest of the staff had her hours. Plus Liam was graduating in a few days. His party was pushed back to allow for more recovery time, but she still went all in with the planning.

We'd also pushed the wedding out. In fact, Liam's party would be the last weekend in June, then the guests would drive to the mountains for our wedding. It allowed the family members from Ireland to attend both events. After hearing about the shooting, Kick promised to check in with her former in-laws regularly. It helped ease the pain of breaking ties with her mother. It stung her deeply to make the hard call, but I couldn't have been prouder of her. Her near-death experience gave Kick a clarity that Bobby would never comprehend.

I looked forward to meeting her former mother-in-law and uncle. We spoke on the phone, and their support meant a lot.

Joe and Toni planned to attend the wedding. They spent very little time off our estate in Virginia, so I hoped they'd like the surprise I planned for everyone, especially my fiancée.

I'd bought a mountain retreat between Asheville and Lake Lure in western North Carolina. Since it was a vacation spot, most of the houses on the mountain were rentals. I secured them all for our guests to stay in. Kick did her damnedest to pry the details from me, but my lips stayed sealed. The surprise would be worth it.

Unfortunately, my lips felt stifled in other ways. Not so much my lips, but my cock sure missed her. Kick acted crankier than me. She'd picked a fight that morning over her cereal. When the dust had settled, I knew she was bored with her rehabilitation. And horny.

There was no sign of the dog as I entered the house. A sense of dread spread over me because of the quiet. Then I figured Kick was napping. The low hum of the dishwasher suggested Carmen was around. Probably had taken the dog for a walk on the greenway.

I peeked in the bedroom, surprised to find it empty, except for Macushla. Upon seeing me, she wrapped herself around my leg and sat at my feet, asking for a head pat. Once satisfied, she woofed low and bounced from me to the door, doing a perfect Lassie impersonation to make me go upstairs.

The whooshing hum of the treadmill gave away her human's location. It sounded too fast, and my brow furrowed with irritation.

"What are you doing?" I growled at the sight of her red, sweaty face.

Her smile beamed back at me. "Koosh and I did three flights of stairs, took a break, and now I'm at three-quarters of a mile." She could speak. Breathing steady, not too hard. "What're you doing home?"

"Gave my team the afternoon off. Picked up burgers for lunch."

Her eyes lit up. "With the good fries?"

To Kick, that meant a dedicated fryer, making them gluten-free. "Of course." The glee on her face was comical. Ever since we'd been involved and I drove near the joint on my way home, they'd become her guilty pleasure. Mine was watching her moan as she ate them. "The curry Dijon dipping sauce included."

Her squeal zinged straight to my neglected cock, but it didn't derail my annoyance with her so-called workout. It was too early for her to push like this. What if it messed up the wedding plans again? "Step on the side rails."

"But—"

"Do it," I ordered. She rolled her eyes and complied, making the machine cut off.

Before I could chastise her, Kick whined her defense. "I'm bored. Carmen won't let me clean because I can't bend over yet."

"She's a good woman."

"Thomas." She swatted my hand resting on the handrail. "I'm listening to a book and going at a slow pace." Her eyes saddened. "I wanted to walk the dog, but it'll hurt if she pulls on her leash."

"Macushla isn't neglected. She has Liam and me. Carmen also takes her on a short loop around the neighborhood when she's here." I bobbed my hands in front of her. "Pull up your shirt please."

"Seriously?"

I folded my arms, spread my feet in a commanding stance, and waited.

"Fine." She removed her tank, showing me a clean bandage.

"May I?"

"Do I have a choice?"

"Nope." I chuckled and eased the tape away from her stomach. No seepage. "Looks good. Did you change this before coming up here?"

"Yes, doctor."

"Don't forget it." I gently smacked her ass. I swear the contact made us both gasp.

"A *fud* doesn't count."

"Fud?"

She folded her arms, but the zipper on her workout bra had slid down. "PhD."

The move put her perfect breasts on display for me. I nearly swallowed my tongue. *Right.*

I remembered what I'd been trying to do and made a circle with my index finger. "Turn around. I'll check the exit." It was the harder site for Kick to clean, and she usually waited for me to do it. I pulled this bandage away. "Have to admit… you're healing like a champ."

"Told you."

"Sorry for snapping."

"You're forgiven for worrying. But I'm bored, cowboy. I can't work at the Perked Cup. I'm all caught up on paperwork. I've always done laundry, and Carmen's taken that too. She said I couldn't carry the baskets."

"She's right."

"I know!" She sighed and slapped her hands on the rests. "We have a gazillion relatives coming here in three weeks for three important events. And everyone tells me I can't do anything for them. Cyndi even banned me from making centerpieces. She said I needed to stick with fine art and leave the crafting to her. But I think she's upset about being out of town visiting her mom when shit went down. She feels like she has to do all this herself."

"I was here when shit went down. I'm still helping. Make a list of what's left, and we'll divvy it up." I took her hand, helped her off the treadmill, and pulled her into my arms. I did this every chance I had now. Each time, gratitude over what I still had versus what I almost lost swept through me. "Your clan wants to help, darlin'. Let us." I gave her my best seductive smile and kissed her neck.

"Stop with the smirk. Plus they already have enough to do. Deana and Jake are working around the clock."

"I'll hire an assistant, and you can promote Tina for the summer."

"Thomas…"

My lips stifled her complaint. "I almost lost you. Hell, we all almost lost you. We were in a tailspin over the what-ifs, even after you made it through surgery. Helping you helps us heal."

Her chin quivered a moment before she set her shoulders back.

Then her hitching tells started. "His gun was on you... you didn't see it. I could've been alone again instead."

My forehead dropped to hers. "I saw it. I know. Believe me... I know. When I wake from nightmares, I hear you in the middle of yours."

"Then let's celebrate being alive." Kick ran her hand up my biceps to my neck and pulled my lips to hers. "Focus on the good."

Her rusty attempt at seduction made me smile against her lips. "All this fussing is about your empty 'O' tank."

She breathed in my ear. "My sugar bowl's empty, cowboy."

I pulled her body tight to mine, letting her feel we were on the same page. Except for one thing.

"Your pain concerns me. What if one of your incisions opens when you come?"

"Jaysus." She laughed. "You make me sound like a wild animal." Her brows raised.

"If you'd ever watched yourself orgasm, you'd understand. It's erotic as hell. Makes me feel like a king when you come multiple times. And now? With you asking like this... knowing you need me? I want to lock the door, take you right here. Against the wall, on the mat, on the ball. Anywhere. I want to slam into you, hear you cry out for me."

"The ball?" Her tongue worried her cheek as a grin grew. "I did promise you a backbend on it, didn't I? Once the wounds heal. But you know, good sex is more than the freaky-deaky, right? It's always eating steak."

She laughed at what I assumed looked like a confused expression on my face, then tapped my chest. I had a feeling of what it was like to be mansplained. "I love a juicy filet as much as anybody. But sometimes I'd kill for an authentic, grass-fed burger with hand-cut fries. The bottom line?" She went up on her tiptoes, kissed my lips.

"It's..." Kiss.

"About..." Kiss.

"Having a happy fiancée."

She spun around and wiggled her lush ass against my cock,

getting the groan she sought. For Kick, I was a sure thing. Couldn't say no. She took advantage.

My head tipped back as I barked a laugh. "Mission accomplished, you minx. On these conditions—toys in your sweet pussy. We'll take it slow." I unzipped her workout bra and cupped her tits in each hand, teasing her nipples with my thumbs. "My mouth works these lush nipples till you come." Her sharp intake of breath hit my heart and turned my cock into a rod.

She tilted her head and traced a finger from my pecs to my cock. "What if I want to play with you?" She popped her lips for emphasis and went down in a Twist dance move as if she were Chubby Checker's backup dancer.

"Ow." Kick thumped on her ass when it became clear she couldn't twist her way back to standing.

"Yep." I crouched down to her level and stroked her ear. "A for effort, but I'm in charge now." Before her fluttering eyes could change my mind, I had an idea. "You'll stretch out on the bed on your back, your head will hang off the side—just a touch—and I'll take your mouth. If you can handle the stretch, you can reach around and hang on to my ass. But only if it doesn't hurt."

"You'd let me do that?"

My shoulders shook as I laughed. She killed me more with love than with her reckless behavior. I ran my thumb over her bottom lip. "How can I refuse your mouth when it's offered so sweetly? Know this though… if you're in pain and say nothing, I'll figure it out. And I'll be pissed. Feel something, you say something. If we need to change up, we do it. If we have to stop, we stop."

"I love you." She sighed, her eyelashes fluttering at half-mast.

I stood and swept her up in my arms, carrying her downstairs to our room and locking the door behind us. To hell with the burger and fries for the moment. I was her pleasure. Without the guilt.

Road to Nowhere

Kick

THE SOUND OF SIXTIES MOD MUSIC REACHED MY EARS AS SOON AS I closed the front door. After a few hours back at the Perked Cup, I channeled a cast member from a zombie film, mindlessly kicking my shoes in their cubby. My first shift back hit me like a Mack truck in the past hour. By the time I'd dropped my gear off in the office, the music perked me up. I'd even done a couple of easy steps of the Pony along with the soundtrack.

"Wee hoo! Wee hoo! Woo pah!"

A pair of baritone voices complemented each other as they floated down from the loft.

"My dude. That was big."

"Good one, pal."

Ah, the telltale sounds of male bonding over the crazy adventures of Mario and his brother.

"Oh Lucy… I'm home," I called up.

"We're upstairs," two deep voices yelled back.

"I heard."

After crouching low to let Macushla sniff my new smells, followed by a vigorous butt rub, the two of us padded up the steps. She kept turning her head as she led me toward the action.

"I know, Koosh. I heard them." The sound lifted my heart. Thomas had held the kids together when I was in the hospital, and it further bonded him and Liam. I'd be forever grateful.

"Hey, guys." I sat and watched them collect coins for a few minutes before saying to Thomas, "Thought you were working late."

A huge grin turned my way. "My dishes are marinating. So I came home."

In my mind, we had two homes, and I loved that he thought the same. My attention turned to Liam. His eyes were bright and posture engaged, like he was moving on from heartbreak. "You look better, Wee Man."

He lifted a shoulder. "Meh. I'm vibin'."

Thomas and I exchanged a secret smile. "Good to hear, sweetheart."

"Anyway..." He paused the game and set his controller down. "Thomas has something to show you."

I turned to my fiancé. "Really?"

Thomas dropped his controller and stood. "Indeed."

"What's this mystery?" I asked as we descended the stairs.

"Patience, darlin'." Whatever it was, it couldn't top seeing Liam's buzz of excitement.

The two of them hit the wood floor and went straight to the mudroom. "Where is the magical joy-giving entity? I didn't see anything when I came in." I'd parked Thomas's Land Rover outside on the driveway. It was a tight squeeze to park it in the garage next to Liam's Jeep. After the police finished with it, my car ended up going to Camaro heaven. Besides the insurance company declaring it totaled, I knew I couldn't drive it without seeing Rachel's terrified face every time I slid in it.

Thomas stopped in front of the garage door. "Open it."

I hadn't opened the door to the garage since Big Jonn surprised me. Most of my nightmares involved me standing in this very spot, my hand hovering above the knob. I swallowed hard. "Thomas, I don't…"

He reached around me and opened the door. The shadowed shape I was accustomed to filled my parking space, only the gray shape the red car made was lighter. The motion detector switched on the light when I hit the first step. I turned back, my brows drawn together in question. Thomas shooed me forward with his hands.

I stated the obvious. "This is new. And a Z." It was fresh off the line, had a leather interior, a sunroof, and was white with orange stripes. My favorite design.

"When a rider gets back on the horse, it doesn't have to be the same horse. It helps if it's a better horse," Thomas said lightly.

I ran my hand along the plate at the back, touched the rally stripes on the spoiler, and giggled. "It's the opposite of yours." Thomas's was orange with white striping—the reason he'd named it Ginger.

"When we met, you said this was your favorite design. It took longer to arrive than I planned, but…" The silly man looked apologetic.

With my hands on my head, I stared at the car, uncertain what to think or how to feel, a bit like deciding to adopt a puppy right after losing the best dog ever. Was I ready to do this again?

Thomas came up behind me and leaned his head down to my ear. "Is it alright?"

His hesitancy made up my mind. I spun and circled my arms around him. "It's fantastic. Thank you." I lifted on my toes and kissed him. "I was waiting for the insurance to finalize before deciding what to do."

Thomas closed his eyes and inhaled, as if he was taking a moment to let the little kiss sink in. He'd been doing that a lot since the shooting. "It's an early wedding present. I was concerned you'd end up in an übersafe SUV." He tipped back his head and sighed. "These aren't made with a unibody anymore. Hell, I almost gave you Ginger for that reason, but you'd said this had been the one you always wanted. Hope it's different enough and familiar at the same time. Besides, now that we know about your stunt-driving skills, you'll be fine."

I buried my forehead in his shoulder. "What exactly have you heard?"

He murmured, "There's camera footage." Then he barked a laugh when I whined. I hadn't thought about that. "If Hollywood calls, I'll be your agent."

My hand sounded like it played on a bongo drum as I tapped his tight abs. "Shut up."

Liam pressed the garage door opener. "Does anyone plan to get in?"

"Yeah, darlin'," Thomas encouraged. "Slide in. Give her a test drive."

"Um… my car is a him. He has a Spanish accent." I patted Thomas's jaw. "You still have the best accent, but that'd be weird if my muscle car sounded like you."

"Christ." His eyes lifted to the ceiling, the muscles in his face fighting a smile. "Get in." Thomas opened the door and gave me a nudge into the driver's seat. Then he let Liam in the back on the passenger side before settling next to me.

The engine purred to life without bringing back memories of my nightmare drive. It made my stomach flutter… deliciously. Perhaps my new car did have Thomas's accent. It growled in a way that reminded me of him. I felt it flow through my core. A grin of delight spread across my face. I tilted my head toward my fiancé.

Thomas looked back at me with the smug expression of a guy who knew he would get lucky later. I bit my lip, and he barked another laugh. We needed this minute of pure happiness.

I checked over my shoulder at Liam. His hands explored the soft suede inserts of the gray seats. My hands did the same on the steering wheel. The lack of worn spots on the soft surface called for future adventures together. Good ones, where no one chased us or shot up the body.

I raised my eyebrows, grinned at Thomas, and said, "Where should we go?"

He opened his hands out wide. "Anywhere you want, darlin'. How do you want to celebrate?"

"Liam?" I called out to the back, though I already knew his answer.

"Food, of course. I'm a growing boy."

Thomas and I laughed. He turned around and said, "You mean you're a bottomless pit."

"Same thing, fam."

I shook my head at my son as I made the final adjustments to the seat and mirrors. "Ready?"

"Impress me, Mama." Liam stretched his arms across the top of the rear seats.

I put the car in drive and eased out of the driveway. "I thought the current year didn't feature rally stripes," I said.

Thomas squeezed my hand as I navigated the neighborhood. "That's why it took longer to deliver than I'd planned."

As suspected, he'd commissioned them for me. To give me the vehicle of my dreams. Except I'd already had my dreams come true in the form of him.

Going against traffic on the expressway allowed me to open up this new car, and "he" didn't disappoint. The new coupe leaped to speed on the ramp.

My son yelled, "Woo-hoo!" from the back, competing with the ten-speed engine for volume.

"We need to take our two cars out to a test track," I told Thomas as we raced to our favorite sushi place in Brier Creek. It wasn't the closest, but I wanted time to enjoy the ride, revel in this new feeling of freedom. Not only from the joy of new transportation but from the lift of the ominous weight of danger that hung over us for months.

"Don't get cocky," Thomas warned. "No one beats Ginger in a quarter-mile. Ever."

I breathed deep the new car smell—more of a new life smell—and shrugged. "You do you. I'll do me."

. . .

"WILL YOU PARK MY CAR ON THE STREET BEFORE YOU LEAVE tomorrow morning?"

I was safely tucked under Thomas's arm, snuggling under the covers and catching up on local news. We could watch it again now that the station stopped using us as their lead story.

He pulled back, staring down at me with a furrowed brow. "Whatever for?"

I scrunched my nose. Wasn't it obvious? "Did you see me shaking when we entered the garage this afternoon? The second the white shape of the freezer landed in my periphery, I jumped. And you were there. What will happen when I'm alone? I'm not ready."

"When will you be ready?"

I made a frustrated growl sound. I hadn't considered the ask a big deal and wondered why Thomas couldn't just say *no problem.* "I don't know. One day at a time, right?"

"Not always." Thomas climbed out of bed and slid his arms through his robe. He reached for me. "Come on."

I sat up and wrapped my arms around my legs. "Not the back on the horse thing. Isn't it enough that I drove the new car?"

"This is different. Trust me." He grabbed his tumbler of whiskey from the nightstand.

Like I wouldn't trust him. Thomas had asked me that since the beginning of our relationship. Whether it was remembering dance steps, learning to shoot, or giving my heart away again, he never let me down. I slipped out of bed and put my robe on. Tying it shut as I walked to him. "Are we going to dance in the garage?" I didn't want to be loud, if for no other reason than Liam's mental health. He and the dog were sleeping safely up in his room, but I wasn't the only family member with nightmares.

"Something like that." Thomas tapped my ass before giving me a little push.

I made sure to end up behind him by the time we entered the mudroom. He opened the door, activated the motion-detection light, and my heart started racing. I might have to sell this place now. Ironic since we stayed after Shane's accident. But every corner of the first floor held fresh nightmares threatening the good memories.

Quick flashbacks stopped me in my tracks several times a day. If it weren't for meditation and deep breathing—not to mention my promise to Liam to stay through graduation—I'd have moved to the farmhouse already. Maybe that was it. Maybe Thomas wanted to meditate out here.

I crossed over the threshold, and a frigid chill slithered up my spine. My eyes landed on the chest freezer, and it held me prisoner.

Thomas's voice sounded like it was a block away. "Are you back there? Mother's Day morning?"

I whipped my head around. "You know I am. It's all bad memories around here." The warm light in the center of the garage prevented the space from looking garish, but it also deepened the shadows. At least the fumes from a fixative spray lingered faintly. Weird as it sounded, and as health conscious as I was, the artist in me loved the smell. I had used it on an art project the day before the attack.

"What if I gave you happy memories to override what happened?" The sudden closeness of his voice next to my ear made me jump. Thomas's arms wrapped around me from behind. "Hey now… Easy."

I hated how Big Jonn had done that—taken away the comfort of the velvety voice I loved.

Thomas spun me around. "Eyes on me." He lifted me and set me on top of the freezer. He cradled my face in his hands and kissed me thoroughly, banishing all other thoughts. His tongue swept into my mouth, dancing with mine in the way I craved. Slow and tender. Worshipful.

He pulled away and grinned as his thumb rubbed my lower lip. I bet it was as swollen as his. "Better, but not quite there."

I shook my head, laughing. "Is your plan to kiss away the old memories or something?"

"Or something… First…" His eyes sparked as he looked up. A hank of nylon rope hung from a hook above the chest freezer. My brows rose to my hairline when he removed it and snapped it, testing its strength.

"What are you—?" We'd played this way at the farmhouse but with silks. I loved it. This though…

Thomas winked at me before writing a quick note with the pad and pen in his pocket—he kept them everywhere for when research ideas popped into his head. He took a piece of packing tape from the next hook and stuck the note to the mudroom side of the door. Then he looped the rope around the handle and secured it back on the first hook, testing the door to see if it would open. He nodded approvingly at his work and said, "In case the boy hears something and gets concerned."

I tilted my head. Guess I'd been half right. I didn't know what turned me on more, Thomas's obvious plans for me or how he thought of my kid's feelings. My voice caught. "Here?"

He opened my robe and started unbuttoning my nightshirt.

His eyes darkened with each inch of skin he exposed. "My nightmares are in here." He stepped between my legs and palmed my thighs, his gaze following the path they took as he stroked up toward my core. The hum started under my skin.

"First time I saw his arm wrapped around you, I stood in the shadows back here. Felt your terror and pain." He turned and picked up the tumbler of whiskey from the top step. I hadn't noticed that he put it down.

"Then I saw the gun pressed into your shoulder." Thomas took a long pull of the whiskey, closed his eyes as the liquid went down. I didn't need my own glass to know that feeling, the burning away of the visual. "I need this too. New memories. Victories."

He returned to his place in front of me. Thomas kissed me again and pushed me back with his free hand. I hummed at the taste of his lips, licking the smooth, spicy flavor of Defiant whiskey off my own as he proceeded to kiss his way down my stomach. The local single malt was serendipitous. We were defying the ghosts living in the shadows of the house and our hearts.

Thomas paused, assessing me. Then he dribbled the remaining liquor over my breasts and stomach. My breath caught as the chilly spirit fired up a round of goose bumps, making my nipples stand on end. The corner of his mouth ticked up in approval.

Just then, the light went out, throwing us into darkness. Thomas hummed, I think to keep my focus on him. My eyes quickly adjusted to the moonlight pouring in through the narrow window on the opposite wall. All the distracting, unromantic household items in the space disappeared, but I wasn't afraid. It reminded me of our first night together during the storm. Like then, the world melted away to only Thomas and me.

He pulled a vibrator out of his other pocket and shoved it into my hand before placing another slow kiss on my lips. "Take your pleasure back. In here and everywhere. You decide."

A quiet moan escaped my throat as the tip of his tongue traveled around my nipple before flicking it. "What else is in this robe of yours?" I giggled and teased. "Got a steak in there too?"

Thomas grabbed his cock, pressing it into my thigh. "There's a juicy T-bone right here. Whenever you're ready." He lapped the whiskey from my stomach. "Mmm. My two favorite flavors."

Well, shit, let's do this. I pressed the button, bringing the vibrator to life.

"That's it," Thomas encouraged, grinning as he descended on me, licking up the rest of the Defiant with long strokes, still humming his pleasure. This turned into quick flicks and hard pulls on my other nipple. That was all I needed to put the toy at my pussy, letting it tickle the edges of my lips until I shivered with need. The connection between my breasts and my clit grew into a fevered pitch. Still, the climax evaded me. My mind clung to thoughts instead of feeling.

"Thomas…"

"I got you." He reached down, adding his fingers to the vibration, letting one of them breach the tight rosette of nerves at my ass.

It was everything. I gave in to the sensations and let everything go. At the last minute, I remembered we weren't technically alone in the house and closed my mouth, biting my lip to keep from crying out. The sensations flowing through me ran in Thomas too. He struggled to keep his volume down as we growled through our bliss.

The moment when time stood still, like I could come forever. He continued sucking on me and twisting his fingers until the waves subsided. Then he stretched over me and dropped his forehead to mine.

"The bastards couldn't take our lives or our love. We won't let them live in our heads."

"Thomas…" I gasped, writhing on the fecking freezer. It wasn't enough.

He raised up on his elbows. "What do you need?"

"Your T-bone. Now. The car." I pulled at the tie on his waistband.

"You have the best ideas." Thomas scooped me up. His pajamas inched down as we moved into my new Camaro, but he didn't miss a step.

The overhead light flashed back on from our movements, letting just enough atmosphere through the tinted windows for me to see the soft sheen of sweat on his chiseled face. Panting and dizzy with need, I clung to him as we settled in the driver's seat with me straddling his lap. I caught my breath as he palmed my breasts. "Up for more?"

"Don't you dare stop."

He'd never forgotten what I'd told him about missing this and always took his time with my breasts. I stroked my pussy against Thomas's hard cock as he worked my nipples. The buzzing quickly returned. The victory of leaving our trauma behind hummed through us until we giggled with joy.

By the time I reared up and settled down on Thomas's thick length, we glowed. Our energy healed our physical bodies and our hearts as I eased onto him.

His eyes virtually sparkled with awe. "Damn, I love you."

Within minutes, my hands were gripping the headrest as Thomas buried his face in my cleavage—his preferred spot. We grunted and moaned as our strokes built to a frenzy until the waves went off again. I slid my body along his, pushing down with each ripple as Thomas pushed up. He pulled me down and captured my cries of ecstasy with his mouth as I rode him pedal to the metal like we were crossing the finish line—breaking in my new car in our own way.

All fears of this space, this house, disappeared as our heartbeats slowed, in sync. Thomas stroked my back as I collapsed against him, still attached. Always one.

"Wherever you are, wherever you go… remember this. Remember I love you." He pushed me back to meet my gaze. "I'll take it with me too."

48

Wonderwall

Kick

"Whatcha reading, chica?" Cyndi asked, sliding onto her preferred barstool at the counter. She lifted the front of my book before I could answer. "A car manual? Only you would read an owner's manual."

"Hey." I grabbed it back. "It's good to know what's different in my new—"

"Wait a minute. Is that smoking new supercar out there yours?" I nodded as she whistled. "I was ready to make you introduce me to the hot customer it belongs to." Her mouth turned into a pout. "But it's just you. How's it drive?"

"Like a dream," I said with a sigh.

"You're good with the same model car, huh? I figured you drove your man's Land Rover now."

I tucked away the manual on the shelf under the counter since I wouldn't be reading it anytime soon. I didn't need to think about my answer. A true peace had settled over me. "Thomas suggested I get back on the horse and he was right." In all the ways. "It also helps knowing the bad guys are dealt with."

Cyndi's brows drew together, and I braced myself against the counter. We'd done the hug-and-cry thing as soon as she returned from her Mother's Day visit to Michigan. Then we jumped straight into wedding prep mode. We hadn't talked about the details of that day, not that I could say much.

I made her preferred drink as she talked over the espresso machine.

"I read the write-up in the paper, but I still don't understand."

My elation over surviving felt stunted since I couldn't tell my closest friend the whole truth. Like it or not, the Felidae Society had sucked me in even though I wasn't an official member. I struggled to look Cyndi in the eye. With my trusty rag in hand, I wiped down the counter as I relayed the acceptable explanation Thomas, Banger, and I had pieced together.

I called over my shoulder. "Big Jonn's obsession with me went as deep as his son's for Rachel. He'd been willing to wait for me to notice him, but I committed the cardinal sin of falling for another man." I'd shared this version enough times now I almost believed it. "Their delusions fed off each other until both men were crazed with jealousy." I handed her a flat white with a heart on top.

"I'm sorry, Kicky." Cyndi reached across the counter and stilled my busy hand. "I can't imagine. Those two turned your life upside down over their delusions."

"Not to mention because they could." The power-crazed never considered the consequences of their actions. I squeezed her hand back. "They didn't count on my friends and family. In fact, if they hadn't paid off Siobhan, I'm sure everything would've resolved sooner… before the bodyguards and such."

Banger's right-hand's role was another aspect of the story we had to manipulate. We told the authorities that she'd been working for Big Jonn and not the other way around. True to form, Banger had planted information to that effect.

Cyndi rested her chin on her hand. "The guards made fabulous eye candy though. What's Mateo up to anyway?" She sighed. "I miss that sweet dish of flan."

I chuckled at her version of looking on the bright side. "He's helping Banger put Angel Security back together. It was a stroke of luck that Jake hooked us up. Mateo and Wes weren't corrupted by Siobhan."

Enough with the reminiscing. I'd come a long way since Thomas fucked the fear out of me the previous night. I didn't want to risk it coming back and threatening my recovery. I thought about my orgasm in the car and sighed. Then, naturally, I changed the subject.

I touched the ends of her silky hair. "Can't believe you come in here, talking smack about cars and boys, and nothing about your sparkling hair. You did it."

"I did." Cyndi gave me an uncharacteristically shy smile. "What do you think?"

"Are you kidding? It's stunning." The way the glowing front contrasted with the dark back reminded me of the model Caroline Labouchere. After Cyndi mentioned her plan to transition to her natural hair color, I started following a few silver models on social media. I wondered if I'd get the chance to look like them. Still hadn't gone in for my color service and still didn't need it.

"Thanks, Kicky. I didn't expect so many people to act weird about it."

"Like how?"

She took a sip of her drink. "One client told me it's ridiculous."

"To your face or in an email?"

"Oh, to my face." She spread her hands wide. "Does something about me compel people to just… blurt their opinions?"

My brow furrowed in fury for her. "Fuck him."

"Her."

"That explains it." I reached for my ice tea and took a pull. "Seriously though… your hair complements your gray eyes. It's even more exotic than you were before. Screw anyone who gives you shit." I patted her hand. "Did you come in for a pep talk? I kind of like talking about other people again." Every fecking hour, someone walked in and expected me to recount the events of the past year.

"Ha, ha. I wanted my flat. Plus…" She slid a card across the counter. "Debra's desperate to finish the bridesmaid dresses. I made a long appointment and hoped we could make a girls' afternoon of it? Unless there's too much on your plate."

"Are you kidding? I'd love to help with something. All I hear is 'everything's taken care of, darlin'.'" I did a shitty imitation of Thomas's baritone and made Cyn smirk. We could use girl time, except… "What about Snow?" Rachel had been performing in the summer theater in the Outer Banks since the beginning of June. She wanted to pull out of her contract, but the shadows under her eyes had never lifted. Not even when I came home from the hospital. I insisted she go, knowing my girl needed a change of scenery. What better way to move on with her life than doing what she loved?

"I'll speak with Deb at the shop, see if she can fit us in on the morning of Liam's party. I can take her since you'll be swamped. Unless Isabella will be with her. I wouldn't want to be a third wheel."

I shook my head. "Bella's busy with her internship. Rachel will love to get time with her Aunt Cyn."

Cyndi tapped her chin. "Are you sure that's all?"

"It's what Snow told me, but I've been a bit distracted." I tucked a curl behind my ear. "Why do you ask?"

"It's a feeling I had after a hospital visit." Cyndi waved her hand like she was erasing the question. "Don't mind me."

I shrugged. "Ask her about it during the fitting."

She gave me a sympathetic, twisted-lip smile. "You can count on me. Snowy and I can commiserate over asshole men. I'll pass on my 'sing-gal' wisdom."

I laughed as she waggled her brows. "Considering I took two seconds to renege on my vow to never marry again, you mean?"

She winked at me and smirked. "Something like that." As much as Cyndi championed my relationship with Thomas, she still took advantage of any opportunity to give me shit over the impending nuptials I'd sworn to never take again.

"I still can't believe Thomas is getting married," Tess said as she approached us. She took the stool next to Cyndi and greeted us with hugs and cheek kisses.

I chuckled. "I bet." *Talk about swearing to never marry.*

Tess didn't just shake her head, her whole body joined in. "You two do not know how much he's changed this year."

"Pretty sure I do." I scrunched my nose, a bit insecure considering they'd known each other twice as long as I'd been alive. "I take it you consider this a good thing?"

"The best, my dear. Don't worry. I didn't mean to sound negative."

My oldest and newest friends chatted together while I made their lunches, then fixed a third one for myself. It was time for me to clock out anyway. I wouldn't be back to a full schedule until after the wedding.

"See you before the wedding," Tess said to Cyndi.

"What's this?" I placed the dishes and cups in front of each woman. I collected my meal and sat on the other side of Tess, keeping an eye on the door. Apparently, I lived a new normal now.

"I told Cyndi that Rafa and I are leaving for France tomorrow."

"Thomas said something about that. He didn't mention you're going," I responded after taking a drink of tea. I'd become an afternoon, unsweet ice tea woman, thanks to my doctor's dietary changes. "I'm sure Rafa appreciates your support." I almost said "your son," and bit my tongue to remind myself to keep the brother-sister ruse. How did these people do it?

When the girls left for their summer jobs, Banger moved back home with Tess. From what I could tell, he leaned on her now. I took her traveling with him to the vineyard to mean she was finally stepping up.

Tess gave me a small smile and nervously brushed wisps of hair off her forehead. Her clothes often said "going to the yoga studio," but the slightly disheveled braid and dampness around her hairline told me she'd been teaching a class. In the colder months, a sweater had hid her activities, but June temperatures made it too warm to cover up. "I hope you're right."

"You're coming back, aren't you?" Cyndi asked.

"Of course." She took a moment to chew her bite of the veggie wrap, then set it down like a dining ritual. "Rafa must meet with someone important. Like Kick said, he can use some… what's the word?" She tapped the counter. "Oh, yes… Backup."

Cyndi smiled approvingly. "Will you tell him I hope it all works out?"

I loved how my new friends were blending in with my old ones —as much as they could anyway.

"I will. Thank you." Tess reached an arm around Cyndi and hugged her. "This is why I'll come back with Rafa. His friends are so sweet it makes my heart happy too."

I played with the lettuce in my salad, but my appetite wasn't there. My bed called out to me. Despite the fatigue, my heart was happy too. Small steps in the right direction still equaled progress. "Speaking of a happy heart…"

Tess uncharacteristically froze with her sandwich in midair. "Please, Kick."

I shrugged in my defense, my hands raised in submission. "I only wanted to know if you and Charley have talked."

"We have." Tess sighed as she stared out the window across from us. "That's all I will say."

Cyndi touched Tess's shoulder. "Don't mind Kicky. She wants to match-make everyone now that she's found her person."

Tess scoffed.

"I'm sorry. I didn't mean to make you uncomfortable."

"It's nothing." Tess waved off my apology, adding in a little French. Still, I felt horrible. Rachel and Bella made it sound like there was hope between the women, but maybe not. Cyndi was right about me too. I wanted Tess's smile to reach her eyes.

49

Waterfalls

Kick

"'Waterfalls,' Mama? Must you? You're so embarrassing."
Rachel set her hand on the back of my chair, glaring. She didn't
bother to acknowledge Shane's mother or anyone else sitting at the
"old people's table" for Liam's graduation party. The Perked Cup
was closed for the family party but also shut down for the week for
vacation. Most of my staff were coming out to the wedding after
this anyway.

I tried hard to stay positive through Rachel's obviously bad
mood. *My* mother aired her dirty laundry at my graduation party to
guarantee herself the center of the day's attention. There was a
chasm between getting silly while celebrating your last child's graduation and making a fool of yourself because of unyielding jealousy.

"You know… Lee offered to accompany me on 'Sweet Child O'
Mine' but…" I sarcastically raised a glass of sipping rum. "Thomas,
here, pointed out it might look odd."

Thomas tipped his head, acknowledging his role in the
exchange. Shane's Uncle Billy wrapped the table in his hearty
chuckle.

"At least someone has a sense of dignity." Rachel folded her arms on a long-suffering sigh.

What more could I expect? Bobby had called Rachel on the way home from our last interchange at the hospital, to put it lightly. She hadn't heard my side of the rift because I couldn't handle involving my children in our shit show. My daughter was grown and should've asked me for clarification, but she'd been through hell too. I couldn't pile on that. It felt like it would be cruel and manipulative on my part. Bobby, on the other hand, started collecting allies against me as soon as she'd left my hospital room.

"Liam never noticed my singing." I gestured to my son across the dining room. "He's in his own world with his friends." Minus his best friend, Jax, but Lee had assured me he'd made peace with it. I picked up my napkin and dabbed a stray tear.

"'Forever Young' and 'I Hope You Dance' were bad enough at my graduation. You made a trifecta of drunk-mom-sappy karaoke with the TLC song."

A warm, rough hand engulfed mine and squeezed. "You sounded lovely, Katie. I thought it was grand." I'd forgotten how much I'd missed that hand.

"Thank you, Uncle Billy." I held up my glass to his, letting them clink.

My late husband's mother, Anna, and Uncle Billy had arrived safely from Ireland the previous afternoon. They came with two of Billy's grandsons in tow to celebrate the youngest McKenna's entry into the big world.

Billy clinked his glass edge to mine. *"Sláinte."* I returned the sentiment and sipped my drink. "How about taking a turn at 'Danny Boy' next?" he asked.

"Uncle Billy…" Rachel stomped her foot as jammed her hands onto her hips. "Help me make her stop. Mama and drunk karaoke at our parties shouldn't be allowed." A definitely drunk neighbor currently sang his rendition of "Born to Run." I didn't see where I'd made it worse.

"I'm tipsy, not drunk." I shifted my gaze back to Uncle Billy. "I'll give the song a whirl when the crowd thins." I knew that song in my sleep, thanks to my father, but I didn't trust myself to not cry and actually make a spectacle of myself, considering.

I raised my glass again and flashed a cheesy grin at my daughter. At her scowl, my brows mirrored her pinched stare. "Oh hell, Snow… Ease up. I'm an empty nester now. I'm entitled to celebrate in style."

"Whose party is this again?" She wouldn't quit. Bobby blamed both shootings on Thomas since we met the same night everything with the Grahams had started. Except now we knew it hadn't. They'd been pulling shit without us realizing it for a while before that night. Not to mention they would've succeeded if it hadn't been for Thomas and Banger.

I also knew my daughter suffered from PTSD. I suspected the crowd triggered her, but bringing it up would set her off more. That's what had happened the night before.

Rachel had a therapist where she stayed in Manteo for the summer, but I didn't know if she went to the appointments. You mix privacy laws with how long it took for the insurance company to pay anything, and I guessed I'd find out by the end of the year. For now, the cues pointed to my daughter having taken Bobby's bait about her version of the truth. She'd been on my case since arriving with Cyndi.

I tapped my chin. There was an idea. Maybe Rachel could drive with Aunt Cyn to the mountains tomorrow. As much as my bestie loved being Liam's godmother, she had a special bond with my daughter. If anyone could unhook Rachel from Bobby's line, my money was on my bestie.

I pointed at Liam's table. "They don't care. Think of it as cohabitating parties, sweetheart."

Rachel shook her head and fled back to her table with Jake and the Perked Cup part-timers.

"You have a brilliant idea there—the cohabitating parties," Uncle Billy said, bumping my shoulder. From the moment I'd met Shane, the McKennas were my examples of a family's happy insanity compared to my spitefully dysfunctional one.

"I bet you like it." I waggled my eyebrows at him. It was a well-known secret he and Anna—Billy's widowed sister-in-law and his first love—had started shacking up a year or so back. We even gave them the use of Thomas's farmhouse until it was time to leave for the mountains.

"Easy now. Perhaps you've had more than a nip." He reached for my tumbler. "Better take this before you end up pissed, darlin' niece." He toasted me and swallowed the last of my Raleigh Rum. Billy's face scrunched in a way that reminded me of my mother, albeit comical. "Ugh. How do you drink this swill?"

"Hey!" I'd planned to keep it to two drinks, spaced hours apart. "The doctor says whiskey has too many parts per million to be Celiac safe, so I abide." I pretended to elbow Uncle Billy. "Besides, a birdie told me you were supposed to cut back." I wiggled a finger at his tumbler. "I don't see it."

Billy sighed and narrowed his eyes at Anna. "Listen… I'm a good patient."

Anna clicked her tongue and shook her head.

"I am." He tilted his head toward me like he was sharing a secret. "First I had a wee cry. Then I switched from Jamison's to Redbreast. In fact, I'll go get another one to wash down the burned piss you poured in your glass." Billy scooched his chair back and went to the bar we'd set up next to the stage.

"Not fair—"

"Now who sounds like one of the children?" Anna gently chided. "You're not on any of those opioids, are you, dear?"

"Heavens no." I counted off three fingers. "Herbal anti-inflammatories, Aleve if it's bad, cannabis if it's superbad. Today's good so far." I held up my empty glass. "One more and I'm done."

"Or… tea." Thomas's buttery voice melted the prickliness left over from Rachel. I instinctively leaned back in my chair to connect with him, inhaling his calm. He reached over me and placed the cup on our table. Then he kissed my temple.

Uncle Billy returned and smiled approvingly at us.

"Is she behaving, Billy?" Thomas asked.

"God, I hope not." Billy howled, his bright blue eyes twinkling and his belly shaking like Santa's.

"Sounds like my kind of uncle," Cyndi drawled while the rest of us females rolled our eyes. Uncle Billy turned a beet red and danced his eyebrows in her direction.

He leaned toward her and stage-whispered, "I'm secretly taken, love."

She stretched her arm across his wide shoulders and stage-whispered back, "It's not a secret, Uncle B, but my lips are sealed." She mimed locking them with her fingers as I shook my head.

Voices rose from the table where Rachel sat, and she stormed off to the restroom area.

Cyndi leaned around Billy and whispered, "Our girl's in a mood."

No shit. "Any idea why?" I had mine but wondered if they had spoken during the fitting.

Cyn's mouth twisted. "The dress needed the tiniest taking out in a couple of places. A cloud descended over her afterward." Her eyes lit up, and she tapped the table. "I'll get her to do some karaoke. Does she know '50 Ways to Leave Your Lover'? When I saw it on the song list, I thought of our talk in the car. Why didn't we think of it earlier?"

"She was too busy criticizing me... but you're right. Rachel knows it."

I moved to stand, but Cyndi patted my hand. "Let me." I blew out a loud sigh and agreed, too tired to risk going another round with my daughter.

This had been my first bone-tiring day since the shooting. However, exhaustion couldn't defeat me when I was surrounded by people I loved. Family was as much who you picked as who the universe saddled you with. The only faces I missed were those of my brother and nephews. He couldn't score enough time off for both events, so Bert and the boys were meeting us in the mountains. It meant the world since Bobby had tried her best to sabotage that too.

Tears threatened to fall as I took a long pull from the ice tea.

No more meets, games, or matches... Ever. My baby graduated from high school.

No more getting up to make sure he caught the bus. Had all his supplies. No more stopping by the ATM to give him lunch money. No more... mommy. Not that any of my kids had called me that recently.

I'd cried for hours on Liam's last day of school. I'd been in too much pain to make his breakfast and Thomas had to cover for me. He even took the last-day-of-school picture for me as Lee stood by his Jeep. It hadn't come close to what I'd imagined. I lamented what else the Graham's had taken from me. Though small, it was significant to me.

Today I vowed to keep my shit together for the party. Despite Rachel's disapproval over my song choices, I'd smiled at the back of Liam's head as I sang the songs about him. I wouldn't make the day about me.

"Be right back, darlin'." When Thomas walked away, Anna leaned in and said, "I love his accent." The irony of her declaration made me bark with laughter.

"It's as smooth as a fine Bourbon, isn't it?"

"I was thinking a whiskey, but good enough."

"Come now, Mama A, Uncle Billy's accent has the soft whiskey tones."

"Sin an fhírinne."

It took me a minute to remember she'd said something akin to "True, that." Since my dad died, no one spoke Irish around me anymore. I missed it. I kissed her on the cheek, grateful to know some things never changed—and it was a good thing.

She squeezed my hand. "Sorry your mother couldn't be here."

"No, you're not." I snort-laughed. My mother had always been jealous of Anna's amiable nature, no surprise there. "Seriously, it's all good. If she's happy with her one true love, I'm thrilled for her. I would love to see her happy, but I guess love isn't always enough."

Anna tsked and shook her head. "I'll never understand her. Her only daughter and youngest grandchild. It's not right."

Billy leaned across me and added, "I agree with Katie. Good riddance to the hag." He pressed a whiskey kiss to my cheek in support. It meant everything to have Shane's family with us, not to mention supporting my new relationship.

"Don't worry, you two. I've learned there's a difference between a mama and a relative. A 'cessation of hostilities' is the best we'll ever have." They stared at me with sympathetic eyes full of disbelief. I'd already dealt with pity looks like this from Cyndi and Deana. Both women had the kind of mothers girls like me used to dream about. They wouldn't understand the peace that had settled on me when I admitted the truth and let her go.

I tried one more time. "I promise I'm good. You're here when it counts. Bert and the boys will be at the wedding. My kids are great. My friends are better than I deserve. And then there's Thomas…"

"I like him." Billy's voice cracked. He reached across my shoulder and shook it. "You did well, Katie."

I laid my head on his shoulder. "Thanks, Uncle Billy."

Life *was* good. Finally.

My fingers tingled under the table.

50

Giving You the Best That I've Got

Kick

"Hey sleepyhead." Thomas pulled my hand across the center console and kissed my palm.

I stretched into the ceiling of the Land Rover, all the way to my toes under the dash. After blinking several times, the scenery took me by surprise. We were climbing a narrow asphalt road at a steep incline. I did a double take at Thomas. "You drove the whole time? You were supposed to wake me at the halfway point."

He reached over and chucked my chin. "But you looked so cute I couldn't bring myself to wake you. Figured the extra rest to be necessary after your long week."

We took a hairpin turn, and the ascent grew steeper. "Should we be in five-point harnesses?"

"We're fine. Almost there."

"Oh, this is *the* mountain?" I watched the rhododendron blooms fill out the undergrowth as far up as I could see from my window. "How high are we going?"

Thomas navigated an interior curve. "To the top."

I hated taking these roads in the passenger seat. In fact, it surprised me to know I'd slept the whole way. I never slept in a moving car. Something wet annoyed my shoulder. I pulled my shirt away to investigate. "Oh hell, did I drool?"

Thomas flashed me his middle school grin. "Like I said… adorable."

"Ugh."

We crossed under a stone archway and ended up in a courtyard of a modern palace. Really, it was a five-thousand-square-foot stone-and-log lodge sitting on a plateau just below the mountain peak. A manicured cottage garden occupied the side of the entrance, adding to the atmosphere. I imagined taking our vows in the center of it.

Thomas drove through a portico and parked in back by a four-bay garage.

"Only four bays?" I muttered sarcastically.

"We can add more."

On a rental? Huh?

He killed the engine and pressed the button for the tailgate.

A young man appeared out of thin air and opened my door. "Good afternoon, Ms. Kick. I hope your drive was pleasant."

"Apparently it was amusing," I answered, thinking of Thomas laughing at me sleeping with my mouth open. Shit, had I snored? *From now on, I drive.*

Thomas gave the key fob to another young man and chatted him up a bit as I gathered my bearings.

Past the covered area, a walled veranda edged the back of the property until it met more rhododendrons traveling up. The property appeared to fall away beyond that.

My fiancé wrapped his arms around me from behind, making me jump. I'd become jumpy again after the attack. I hated that. For the thousandth time, I reminded myself of little steps. "What do you think?" he asked me.

"It's…" I tugged at the curls whipping around my head and into my eyes. The winds were brisk this high up. "I'm speechless." The view was breathtaking. I wanted to hurry and settle in so I could sit on the veranda and stare out at the neighboring peaks.

"Happy wedding surprise."

I patted his arms around my waist. "You did good with the rental. If I owned it, I wouldn't rent it to just anyone."

"I'll keep that in mind, since you do own it." Thomas jerked back—that grin back on his face—as I spun around.

"You own… this? Since when?"

"I said *you* own it. I bought it while you were in the hospital. My lawyer's working to transfer the title to you as we speak. We'll sign the papers when we go back." He held out his hand like it was no big deal. "Let's check the place out."

I stayed in my spot. "Who the hell are you?"

"Your fiancé, remember?" Thomas glanced over his shoulder and back to me. "Don't you like it? Was the surprise a bad idea? Tess warned me—"

"It's not the lodge, per se." I shook my head. "Sometimes you still surprise me."

He walked back to me, pulled my hand to his lips, and kissed them. "Keep these two words in your memory bank whenever you wonder how I do these things… compounded interest."

An inelegant snort escaped my nose as I remembered Banger's explanation for the questions I'd thrown at him.

I SAT ON OUR NEW LOUNGE CHAIR IN FRONT OF OUR NEW FIRE PIT IN the middle of our new, spacious patio, attached to our new mountain home. Like everything else Thomas did, the man had gone all out. At forty-seven-hundred feet of elevation in the Blue Ridge range, the house didn't have a typical view of the mountains. It *was* the mountain view. The ground-floor veranda in the back looked over the tops of the closest trees except for the ones to the front of the house.

From the second and third levels, the view lasted for miles. I swore I could see all the major peaks in the range. Thomas said he'd bought it so we could do naked weekends out here without worrying about another human seeing us. He was right there. The only hint of neighbors came from that cottage garden in the front. From there, you could see down the mountain road and catch sight of our three closest neighbors. Well, I saw the mailboxes. The houses were mostly in the trees.

Since the Blue Ridge Mountains were a major vacation area, most of those houses around us were also second homes. Thomas had rented as many as he could for our guests. This would leave us alone at night despite the lodge's ability to sleep sixteen. We could've easily housed most of the guests. Maybe another time when we weren't about to celebrate our wedding night.

Thomas walked out to join me, two glasses of water in his hands. He gave one to me, then settled in the next lounge. "It's amazing out here." He stretched his legs, crossing them at the ankles. For as packed a schedule as we had, I couldn't remember the last time he relaxed like this. Not since before Mother's Day. "An associate of mine owned the house and needed quick cash. The sale had been serendipitous, to be honest. I told him about my amazing, brave fiancée and how I wanted to give her a majestic present, not that it could equal her grace and majesty." He squeezed my hand. "You're my lucky charm."

Considering how quickly he'd set up Liam and me in the lap of luxury for spring break, courtesy of "an acquaintance," this shouldn't have surprised me. He could have bought an island. I scoffed at the label *lucky charm* though. "Doesn't Banger call me a menace?"

Thomas shook his head. "He's a grumpy old man. Don't listen to what he says."

"Speak for your damn self," Banger called out. He spread his hands as he approached, Tess and another man following behind. "Nicely done, brother." He bent over and gave me a hug. "Good to see you doing well… Menace." He sat on the end of Thomas's chair. "It's not my castle in the highlands, but…"

Thomas tipped his head back and laughed. I'd never seen him more in his element. He did a double take as his eyes caught our new visitors. Then he shot off the lounge chair. "*Grand-père?* Holy shit. What are you doing off the vineyard?"

Banger quietly said, "Surprise," as Thomas dashed off. While the men greeted each other with hugs and cheek kisses, Banger leaned toward me. "This is a big fucking deal. The old man hasn't left his chateau grounds since the late forties." He tipped his head in their direction. "Go say hello."

I slowly stood, suddenly scared to death of what this man would think of me. This man—who had been built up in my mind as the most important man on the planet—left the security of his estate to see me? What if I disappointed him?

Thomas turned Alaric around, their arms around each other's shoulders as they spotted me. The deceptively older gentlemen stepped away from my fiancé and toward me. Tess stood back, her arms folded, as she observed the scene. How I'd thought she was Rachel's age, I'd never know now. Tess relied on her outward presentation to fool most, but the wisdom in her eyes couldn't be missed. I smiled at her and received back a motherly twinkle. Maybe it was a sign she and Banger had resolved their differences.

Thomas moved to me, his arms stretched between me and Alaric, like a bridge. "Alaric, meet my fiancée, Kathleen Allen McKenna. Kick, this is Alaric Kraus, the man I call *Grand-père*. Patriarch of the Felidae Society."

"My dear." Alaric took my hands in his and brought them to his heart, like meeting me was an honor. He tipped his head from side to side as he studied me. I suppose I did the same.

Thomas had cut off our budding romance because he believed this man had posed a threat to me. Banger and Tess clearly held grudges against him, yet here we all stood. They'd brought him with them. Thomas's face lit up when he saw the man. Those two things convinced me all would be okay. What family didn't have its issues? Look at mine.

Banger and Tess joined our trio, standing a step back. Banger set his feet wide and folded his arms, like a bouncer protecting... me?

"Don't worry yourself, Rafael," Alaric said without taking his eyes off me. "Thomas is right about her." He kissed me on both cheeks, European style, smelling of fresh air and old spices—not the grandfather's aftershave, actual ancient spices. Though salt-and-pepper, Alaric's hair was darker than I expected for a man of his... experience. He wasn't particularly tall, but he stood straight, shoulders back, like he knew exactly who he was. And accepted everything.

THE FIVE OF US ATE LUNCH AND SETTLED IN BEFORE THE REST OF the guests arrived. In that time, I found out my man had pulled off this surprise because he was a real estate mogul long before he'd become a scientist. That's what happened when you lived an abnormally long time. He had holdings across the East Coast and Europe. The assets Thomas had fully liquidated upon leaving them had been the ones in San Francisco when he left to serve in World War I.

Soon our table grew as Thomas's blood family arrived. It was easier to think of them this way than as grandchildren, considering they appeared older than him. My brother and nephews arrived twenty minutes later, allowing me a reprieve from the tension between Joe and the other Felidae members. He didn't believe things would change. Not yet.

I gladly showed my family around the lodge, discovering the lower-level rooms for the first time with them. Thomas told me the house came furnished and only needed minor remodeling for now, though he had revamped the owner's suite on the top floor. It boasted a new, two-person jetted tub with a view, and a shower that could have been its own room. One side had a love seat sized bench installed underneath a waterfall shower. Thomas called it a "make love" seat.

Three other bedroom suites were on the main level, so the kids each had their space when they visited. He claimed the house would rent better with multiple masters. I'd met the realtor and the couple who handled the property management while exploring the first-floor gaming room and bunk area. My nephews wanted to spend their entire time down there, of course. I couldn't get over the idea of having a game room and theater.

Presently, I found myself in time-out, wrapped in a blanket, in front of the fire after the rehearsal. Stupid, wobbly knees. I shouldn't have worn platform sandals out in the garden. Good thing my wedding shoes were hand-painted sandals with a tiny wedge heel.

I itched to stand in the kitted-out kitchen and run my hand over the solid oak, live-edged bar. It was one hell of a focal piece, indicative of the regal yet comfortable decor in the lodge. But the catering company had charge of the space for the next two days. I didn't mind my lounging spot too much either.

A stage area was already set up under the main-level balcony. Everybody took turns playing. Liam surprised me by singing Anita Baker's "Giving You the Best That I've Got" with his cousins accompanying. He continued his quest to put his spin on my favorite songs. Lee used his raspy baritone to full effect, creating a haunting, soulful version of some of my all-time favorite lyrics. Then my other two kids joined in. Dylan never caught the performing bug like his siblings. But he played the bass, claiming it helped him think through mental blocks in his work.

Rachel's practice performance of Kelly Sweet's "We Are One" brought me to tears. It was the song I'd asked her to sing for the reception, and she learned it on the drive up with Cyndi.

When Thomas plugged in his guitar and performed Stevie Ray Vaughan's "Pride and Joy," my ovaries flipped. I physically couldn't stay in the chair any longer, knowing my man played and sang his heart out for me. Grabbing Cyndi, Deana, and Tess, we shook our tail feathers on the veranda in front of the fire. Thomas's relative, Toni, joined in too. He had explained to me how her transition, as he called it, was the official focus of his research. Her life had been challenging for the past two years. I couldn't imagine being in Toni's shoes, her body stopping aging while losing family and friends at the same time. It could happen to me eventually, but Thomas promised to help me prepare for it.

As the evening wore on, Toni engaged in a long chat with Alaric, Banger, and Tess. After an urging from Thomas, Joe joined the group too. If we could help heal the broken trusts in the Felidae, I'd consider the torments of the past year worth it. Even the shootings. Where we went from here, though, I figured none of us knew.

The music continued for hours, thanks to the number of musicians in our group. Banger even produced a keyboard from the music room and played boogie-woogie through Elton John, ending with Chopin as the night wound down. Thomas moved off his position on the wall and came to me. He'd spent the past half hour watching me work the crowd from the shadows. Friends would stop by and chat him up, but every time I looked his way, Thomas's gaze had been on me.

He wrapped an arm around my shoulders and said, "Time for you to head up, don't you think?"

"As if you'd settle for no," I said coyly. Thomas didn't have to worry about me putting up a fight. He left his perch as soon as I yawned.

"Maybe I'm also tired." He pulled me close and ran his hands up and down my arms, warming them. "What happened to the blanket I gave you?"

"Is there anything you miss?" Nights on top of a mountain chilled quickly. I couldn't wait to use the jetted tub. "Deana was shivering. Our management couple left before I thought to ask where the extras are kept, and I didn't want to miss this." I waved my arm in the direction of our guests. "Not that you'd let me."

Thomas pulled me into him and murmured, "After the third time almost losing you, I hate letting you out of my sight."

True to that, my man had observed me like an artist—or a scientist, I guess—since I'd woken up from surgery. I had to remember my recovery was as much for Thomas as it was for me.

I waggled my eyebrows. "Maybe we should work on your PTSD, like we did with me and the garage."

He bent and murmured in my ear. "No excuses needed to fuck you. Ever."

I tilted my head back and grinned, trying to keep the guests from knowing my fiancé's growly ways had started my engine purring. Like they couldn't tell. Everyone I hugged good night to wore the same, knowing smile on their face.

Not for the first time, the mechanics of hosting our wedding frustrated me. All my important people came to witness our vows, but I couldn't spend quality time with anyone individually. We didn't have enough days. I wished we could convince Joe—he offered to officiate in a show of support—to marry Thomas and me right there and be done with it. Then we could turn our wedding into a big vacation.

At the same time, I knew Thomas ticked down the minutes until he could declare naked weekend for just us. He bought the lodge for getaways, but I hoped we could host big events like this often as well. A vision of our future settled over me—family and friends celebrating life's moments out here for years to come. I longed to stay up into the wee hours talking, singing, goofing around.

"I can hear you thinking," Thomas complained as we stepped inside the great room. "Tomorrow's a big day, then you're not getting out of bed the day after."

I caught up to him and bumped his hip. "I'm not complaining about naked weekend, it's just—"

"Let me finish…" We started up the stairs to our suite. "The Matthews—you remember the property managers, right?" Considering the sea of fresh faces swimming in my brain was rather small, I nodded. "Well, the Matthews have a schedule of activities planned for our guests the day after tomorrow. Dining and shopping in Asheville, caves, waterfall tours… you name it."

I sighed at the mention of waterfalls.

"Another time, darlin'. My point is… whoever is still here the day after that is invited to hang with us here." Thomas stopped in the middle of the steps and kissed my temple. "You have more than tonight to enjoy your clan."

This man. He knew me so well. He lifted my heart from promises alone. All my emotions swirled together and hummed beneath my skin. I glowed by the time we entered our room.

51

The Best is Yet to Come

Thomas

She stood in our bedroom beside the french doors to the balcony, studying our guests mingling below. My elfin queen observing her clan from her royal perch.

My sexy wife.

Kick had disappeared after lunch. The bright smile she wore hadn't fooled me. With a quick kiss, she feigned interest in checking on the children gaming in the media room. Her tell was the crease between her brows. *Fatigue.*

She healed faster than even I expected, but we'd packed a lot into the past week. I kept everyone occupied for thirty minutes, giving her a break from hosting. Then I sought her out to make sure everything was fine. I also hated being away from her for more than a few minutes since the shooting. I'd work on it when we returned to Oakville.

I selfishly stood in the hallway's shadow to our suite and dwelled on the vision Kick made as she stared at the distant mountains. Despite my attempts to trick her into telling me about her dress, the sole hint she'd given me about it mentioned vintage Halston as the inspiration. The clue didn't do justice to the dress or her in it. When I laid eyes on Kick in the garden where we married, she paused with her sons on each arm and smiled. The world and everyone in it boiled down to the simper she privately shared with me.

She captured the epitome of my fantasies of her since the day we'd met. Rachel's friend had nailed the dress design. As the boys escorted Kick down the pebbled path, I memorized each square inch of the layers of silk caressing her curves. The end product—my fairy queen—had been all for me.

As if the dress wasn't enough, Kick's soft curves had returned to my prurient delight, thanks to her forced rest and recovery. Material flowed around her with each step like it was intended to optimize her shape. She took my breath away. While Kick stayed lost in her thoughts, I reveled in the memory.

The halter neckline plunged enough for a peek at her spectacular cleavage. Delicate crystals and garden-inspired embroidery caressed her décolletage, complemented her ivory skin. At lunch, she'd told me the delicate pinkish-peach color of the fabric was called "blush." I called it perfect. I'd never seen a color favor her more. A few pleats falling from an empire waist lightly shadowed those lip-biting curves, teasing my eyes with the subtlest movement.

I took in her elegant back. Like a magnet, I felt compelled to touch, to run my fingertips over the angles of her perfect posture. The halter tied in a bow at her neck, daring me to walk up and pull the ends. The bodice disappeared around her sides, returning in another deep V at her sacrum. Here's where the material turned fantastical. From behind, it fell over her perfect ass, simulating a waterfall as she walked.

Drop earrings mingled with curls falling from her sexy updo. Pink and amber stones in the earrings matched the ones at her neckline. The best detail for me came in the form of a Celtic-inspired tiara, her curls artfully woven around it, instead of a veil.

Maybe I'm amazed.

I thought of the song we loved so much we asked Rachel to sing it for us during the ceremony. I was amazed that Kick loved me. Amazed and overwhelmed.

Two things about this view stood out. One, Kick hadn't covered up the scar on her back with makeup or material. Two, the deep back allowed a butterfly wing of her tattoo to peek out. Since the dress was almost finished when Kick was shot, not much could've been done about the scar, but the tattoo had to have been deliberate. She had hid it for years, fearful of judgment from people like her mother. That wing waving across her hip told those people to go fuck themselves. Hell, the material was sheer enough to also catch the essence of the rest of the artwork.

A choked laugh escaped as Kick tipped her head. I thought she might be crying until I caught the ends of a smile at the slight turn to her profile. Her body and spirit continued to call to me, so I stalked over to her—my magnet. My compass.

In an instant, touching her became a matter of life and death. My hands slid inside the dress, around her waist, then up, caressing each breast, savoring the softness and the weight of them. "Hello wife."

Kick's smiling cheek touched my own as she turned in to me. Her body pressed into mine and hummed, like I knew it would.

"You didn't flinch." I moved an errant curl with my nose and kissed her neck. Her exotic floral-mixed-with-lavender scent filled my nose with each press of my lips.

"I wanted you to come to me."

I settled my arms across her stomach, kissing her neck above the bow. "Are you tired? Has today been too much?"

She shook her head. "I took a moment to think." Settling back against me, Kick exhaled. "When… after the sun came out during our pictures… I required a few minutes."

For the past week, while all eyes were on Liam and Kick, something had needled me deep inside. I couldn't put my finger on it until my insecurity bubbled to the surface right before the ceremony. I pulled away and took a guess. "Shane?"

"Yup. But not what you think."

What I thought? Down in my soul, I'd been afraid she secretly wished I could be Shane. Like women I'd been with before, I feared she'd settled for me. She'd told me how awful the NFL spotlight had been, but it was nothing compared to the screwball life I lived. Or so I thought. "Tell me."

"When the clouds parted—during the shot of us with the rhododendrons in the background—the sky was his blue. The color of his eyes." She continued to stare off as she spoke. "Sounds silly, but Shane used to show up when the sky was that color. I'd feel his presence and know I could make it through another day."

"Did he show up during the photo shoot?"

"No. That's the thing. But it's okay."

"You sure?" I started. "You don't... wish this was about him instead of me?"

"No." Kick's chin quivered as she pivoted around fully and embraced me.

She tipped her head back and studied me. Her eyes bore straight through to my secrets. She'd already proved that. "I choose you today and every day. Don't doubt that."

I still tended to wake in the middle of the night—sweaty and at a loss for breath—thinking I'd lost her. "It's ridiculous. Sorry." I kissed Kick's forehead, letting my lips linger as I breathed her in. "You know I don't mind that you think about him, right?"

"You're never ridiculous... except when you give me your middle school smirk. And yes, I know how you feel. It's another reason I love you." She pulled our hands together and brought them to her heart. "I thought about something Rachel said when she saw the inscription on your ring."

"It's inscribed?" I shifted my hands to pull the ring off, but she squeezed tight and said, "Check it later, cowboy. Anyway, we fell into an exchange on whether someone can have two soul mates. I made the case I was fundamentally transformed when Shane died, even at a soul level."

I nodded, contemplating her argument, remembering Alicia's death. "I can see that."

"The sky color startled me. It reminded me of beach skies. Soon I was contrasting the original plan to retire at the beach with this mountain-top retreat you bought us."

I lifted an eyebrow, a little lost, and she shrugged. "I mean, both settings bring me peace. They fit me equally."

I scratched my head. "Would you rather have a beach house?" Shit, what an idiot, surprising her like I knew her deepest desires. That's not how marriages worked. From what I could tell. What did I know anymore?

"Not at all. Will you stop?" She went up on her toes and whispered, "You're supposed to be the confident one in our relationship, Professor."

I rolled my eyes. "Ha." Hardly.

"Emotions are hard to explain. I'm sorry. What I mean is… I feel like my soul's had two lives. You could call the first a beach one. Now it's a mountain one. I'm as thrilled with this as I was with the first."

Like a lightning strike, it hit me. I nuzzled her neck again, peppering her shoulder with kisses, and remembered what she'd said when she woke up in the hospital. I whispered, "You went there, didn't you?"

"Pardon?"

"To the other side. With Shane. We know someone who can do that at will."

"You're kidding?" She started. "Who?"

I lifted an eyebrow. "Alaric. To him, it's like moving into another room. He claims he can stand on the threshold, making it possible to be in both at the same time. In the hospital, you said you were looking for me. Did you see Shane when you were unconscious?"

I knew I'd hit the right nerve when Kick bit her lip. "Shane didn't show. I did go to the beach house we'd started building though. It was finished and furnished. Everything about it was wrong, like what life would have been had he lived. Except my body was a mess. The kids… it was very wrong." A tear came to her eye, and I squeezed her tight. "I wanted to escape it and called for you."

A lump formed in my throat. "I held your hand and demanded you come back to me, as soon as the staff let me."

A pair of eagles circled in the sky, saving us from our thoughts as we watched them hunt prey in a distant meadow. We became lost in their precise teamwork, as if we were spectators at a sporting event. The way they worked together reminded me of Kick asking me to fight her battles with her and not for her. I'd repeated the promise as part of my wedding vows. The events of the past six months had shown me how to do just that for her, made me a better man for it.

My hands lowered to her belly, covering the softness below her navel. "Mmm. Your curves are back." Earlier in the year, as Kick lost weight, her body tightened. She didn't know what to make of the changes then. I loved each manifestation of the process because it was hers. But this…

She shifted her gaze to watch the path my hands traced along her skin. "I hate to admit it, but it's from meditating more than resting. I guess my body and I made peace."

"Are you saying…?"

"You were right about my body obeying what I wanted," she reluctantly said as the corner of her mouth lifted.

I tapped my ear in jest. "Come again? Think I'm hearing things."

Giggling now—the sound went straight through my heart… and down to my cock—Kick repeated, "You were right, Professor Thomas Butler Theodore Harrison. I discovered I liked my body the way it was."

I squeezed her middle. "Wow. I must be a genius."

"You're something."

She leaned back into me and sighed, letting me support her full weight. She laughed again when my cock stiffened. "My admission turns you on?"

"My sexy-as-hell wife turns me on." I pressed into her. "I've had this situation since I saw you standing here. What if I eased up this skirt and played with you right now, make you come? With our guests below us?" My hand pushed up the hidden side of the dress, seeking my desire.

Kick reached for my chin, her thumb stroking the cleft before she licked it. I closed my eyes and let the sensation fill me.

"You… want to fuuuck." She drew out the *u*, and I almost canceled our reception on the spot. We hadn't gone full-tilt since the night in the garage. Even then, her wounds stayed at the front of my mind. "You better give me that big, juicy T-bone later… *husband*."

I growled at the possession of the word, enjoying each syllable. "What about an appetizer now?" I slipped my finger under the silk panel of her little bikini pants. "Christ, these are already wet."

"Thom… as…" Kick purred my name, reminding me of the day we met.

I lost my senses and gave in to desire. My fingers took over, playing with her pussy, easing around her folds, working her bud. Her hips encouraged my actions until the hum under my skin began. I felt Kick's too. Fuck, we were so close.

Then a group of people laughed from below, breaking our spell.

"No appetizer for you, baby. Should've kept my wits." I slowly removed my fingers and let my head fall into the doorframe. "We have to work on this aura business." I pulled my hand to my mouth and licked my fingers, savoring her sweetness.

Her eyes sparked with desire as she watched me. "It is hella hard to hold it in now."

There was an understatement. In order to help her heal faster, every evening we'd been putting all our effort into joining auras, starting with meditation and ending with mind-blowing orgasms. We had inadvertently caused a new problem. The energy now tickled under my skin constantly, like it begged to be released.

"Glowing in front of the guests is not a good look?"

She scrunched her nose. "It's the idea of answering those questions. Hell, I can't explain it. Add in the Felidae knowing why it happens and the word *embarrassing* also comes to mind. Unless you want to hide up here the rest of the day. Lock the door and draw the drapes. Our guests might understand."

Laughter from the veranda floated up again, breaking our bubble for good.

I sighed in resolution. "Sorry, wifey. The next time you call my name, I want you yelling it. Besides, the caterers cleared away our meal and the fire pit's almost ready to make the gluten-free s'mores you requested instead of cake. I, for one, plan to eat a marshmallow off your nose."

Kick brushed her fingertips down the front of my waistcoat. I'd removed the jacket when we ate. "What the hell is it about you in a vested suit?" She inhaled slowly, like she savored me as I had done to her. "Just does it for me. Watching you work the crowd in your dark linen…" She touched my bare forearms. "Cyndi calls this arm porn."

Kick bit her lip, I guess to keep from laughing at the face I made. "I adore your friend, but she can be weird." Who the hell cared about forearms? As long as they worked.

I sniffed the air, confirming my suspicions the fire pit was ready, then grabbed her hand and maneuvered us through the doors to the balcony. "We need to get back. Besides, you also owe me a foxtrot. Oh, and no one else gets to dance with you in this dress." I adjusted my trousers. "I can't handle it."

Her laughter tickled my ears and other areas. "What about my boys, my brother, and Uncle Billy?"

"Alright, they get a pass. One dance each."

Kick squeezed my arm and shook her head.

I pulled a remote from my pocket and pressed a button. The opening bars to Tony Bennett's "The Best is Yet to Come" floated up from the outdoor speakers. Several people turned and began clapping as we descended the steps. Pulling her hand to my mouth, I kissed Kick's knuckles and winked. "Come on, Mrs. Harrison. I have a feeling the party's just begun."

*****

Turn the page to read the cut scenes from the original edition of *Kick Home*.

52

Bonus Cut Scenes

These scenes takes place after the Poker night, when Thomas, Banger, and Dylan interrupt an interchange between Big Jonn and Kick. They have a small fight in the book, but there may have been some unresolved issues the following morning. (Also, the location has changed from Kick's house to the farmhouse, but I can call artistic license on that one. ☺)

The Big Fight

Thomas

THE TOASTY WARMTH AND CLEAN-SCENTED AIR OF MY KITCHEN welcomed me after a hard workout with Eddie. The space was devoid of signs of lunch. Considering Kick's strict schedule had played a key role in bringing her health back in balance so quickly, I was concerned she might not have been feeling well.

The silence in the house was another clue something was off.

Was she sleeping or had she left? An emergency, perhaps? I pulled my phone from my pocket—no missed texts.

The downstairs was empty, along with the second floor, leaving my third-floor office. Since we'd blended our lives, Kick had informally taken the first-floor office, while I worked in the third-floor one—my inner sanctum, as she called it. I heard the faint tune of a song from the eighties as I approached the stair. Another quiet sound of sobs made a chill race down my spine.

Oh no.

I sprinted up the steps. I'd meant to tell her about the damn videos, but the time never seemed right to bring it up.

I spotted Kick at my desk. A stone-cold mask shifted into place when she noticed me. My head dropped in shame. I squeezed my eyes shut, pinching the bridge of my nose as I listened to her click through files, knowing exactly what they were—security footage that I'd kept of her from the fall. I should have thrown them out, but I couldn't bring myself to do it.

Her face turned back to my monitor. In a quiet, detached voice, she stated, "Some over-my-head router issue is happening with my laptop. It wouldn't let me log in, so I came up here. I suppose… it's my fault, really." She double-clicked the mouse. "This file had my name on it. Nosey me wondered if you were working on a surprise." She looked up. Her cool smile refused to reach her eyes, breaking my heart.

"No part of me thought you'd been spying."

The air was acrid from anxiety—mine—and anger—hers. I ran a frantic hand through my hair.

"Swear to Christ, darlin'… meant to tell you about these, but hadn't figured out how to bring it up."

"You spied. On me." Kick's voice stayed deadly calm. I would've given anything for her furious temper right then. "This is all kinds of fucked up."

All my senses woke, but that was my reality now when it came to her. The air in the room seemed to solidify as I struggled to inhale. I shook my head. After all the impossibilities we'd already shared, this couldn't be the uncrossable line. I started cautiously, pleading, "From the first night we met, I had to make sure you were safe. Somehow, I needed it. No matter what happened between us, I knew I always would."

"You needed footage of me falling apart? This feels like something Big Jonn would do."

She was looking at footage from the afternoon of our fight in Mick & Hugh's, when I tossed Young Jonn out of the store, then Kick threw me out a few minutes later. My spine stiffened and my fists clenched. Did she really believe her words, or were they from shock? How dare she put that man and me in the same category. "I've never disrespected you. Graham, on the other hand…"

"Disrespect? Nice," she scoffed, waving her hand in dismissal of me. "Big Jonn's arrogant, but also harmless. Okay, you two almost came to loggerheads last night. But he cleared up the gossip articles."

"You can't seriously believe him." She was damn lucky Graham backed off as easily as he had. "The man doesn't care about you or your boundaries. He behaved because of Jake and Mateo."

"Do you care about them?" She swept her hand in front of the screen. "This looks like disrespecting my boundaries. I've never seen shots from this angle. How are they possible? You crossed a big line here."

I opened my mouth to add to my defense, but she cut me off. "Especially with this one." Kick clicked on the video I'd heard on the walk up. A tear slid from her hazel eyes. "This… I can't abide."

It was footage of her and Macushla on the patio dancing. She forwarded to the part where she collapsed into a sob on her bench.

She stared at the screen, sounding detached as she watched. "I had no idea there were mics on the cameras. My files don't have sound."

My fingers slammed through my hair again, making it stand on end. That whole day would forever stay imprinted in my mind. From finding Young Jonn Graham threatening Kick to her throwing me out of the store and possibly out of her life to seeing this and running a search on her. I'd finally understood her and lost her at the same time. But the video… it haunted me.

"This…this is so…" Kick's jaw had set, but her eyes held her vulnerability, revealing a heart broken.

I'd done that. Again. "I split in half that night."

"You weren't the only one," I mumbled. Damn her for not seeing it, seeing me. I'd been ready to walk away, then I saw this and had to stay.

She leveled a pissed-off glare at me. She had me to rights. The bright afternoon light warming the room mocked the darkness settling in my heart. Deep down, I believed we could work past this, though it would hurt like hell.

"Did you notice that's the last video in the folder?" I asked through gritted teeth. "That night shattered me as much as it did you—"

"I seriously doubt that."

I raised my hands in surrender. "Fine. It shook me to my core, though. I knew then—"

"Knew what?"

"That I'd do anything to keep you safe. That I was falling for you."

Kick jumped up and paced the room. Finally, her fury showed, giving me hope. Kick's temper meant she still cared. Lord help anyone she went cold rock on. "You were falling for me, so you could, what? Stalk me? Do you think having feelings makes this okay?"

"Yes, but no, too. I told Banger to take me out of the surveillance loop the next morning. I had to trust Banger's protection would be enough for the both of us."

She spun on her heel with fury filling her eyes. "Jaysus Thomas! Do you know how this makes me feel? Like I've been handled. Or manipulated. I sure as hell never expected it from you."

Her last comment whipped my head back like I'd been slapped. My temper flared in response. "Of course you were handled, dammit. No one targets a barista for shits and giggles. My instincts were on alert from the first night with the graffiti. Don't be naïve."

"Argh!" Kick slammed her hands on the desktop before jumping up. I cut off any more protests. I'd had enough. "Banger has an entire security team on you. Do you think only Siobhan monitors your feed?"

Kick jammed her hand on her hip. "Are there cameras I don't know about? Inside my house, maybe? Did you watch me in my bedroom?"

Breath shot through my nose like a bull about to charge. "Tell me you're fucking kidding right now."

I took a step toward her and made myself stop. I was too angry. "Your temper's doing the talking, not you. You know me better than that. Banger walked you through each camera's location. He told me so."

Kick stopped moving and became like a statue with her arms folded tightly across her chest. I couldn't tell if I'd gotten through. I moved a few steps again. She did know me. She knew I'd never purposefully violate her. Didn't she? She dropped her arms and took off, charging for the stairs. A sharp spark shot between us when I reached for her arm, to keep her near, to keep her talking. Suddenly, I was terrified she'd leave the house and never return. Kick shouted at the sting, pulling her hand into her abdomen. "Don't follow me!"

I bent down to pet a shaking Macushla as her mama stormed down the steps. "She'll be fine, girl. Won't she?" The dog answered by licking my hand hesitantly. I didn't know if it was to reassure or console me.

The Make-Up

Kick

The back door slammed shut after I stomped over the threshold into the chilly March afternoon, without a jacket and shoes. Cold usually made my joints hurt, so I tried to avoid it at all costs. Furious to my marrow, the chill had no effect on me at the moment. Or I just didn't care.

I pounded my way through the backyard, down the path to the clearing. Roots and slick debris on the ground nearly stopped my progress. The pond seemed to call to me, and pride kept me moving that way.

I'd heard gunshots earlier and figured Banger was on the range. Part of me hoped he was still hanging around, so I could give him a piece of my mind. Another part of me wanted him to be long gone. I wasn't about to get into a battle over semantics with him or Thomas. They were dead wrong for spying on my most intimate moment—the night I broke apart only to have Shane knit me back together.

I halted at the water's edge. Thomas had hurt me, but I'd also hurt him. Did embarrassment over knowing Banger's people and Thomas watched my breakdown fire my temper? Or did guilt?

Thomas had been right about the footage in the garden being the last file. I hadn't noticed anything from inside my house, even though I'd accused him of it. I also didn't tell him about the impossible encounter with Shane. Is that what set me off? He'd come close to a secret I didn't understand myself. I sure as hell couldn't explain it to Thomas. And how silly did that sound, considering everything I knew about the Felidae?

I growled in frustration at a couple of Canada geese doing laps around the pond. Thomas was right.

I'd given an entire security team permission to see those files. If Banger's people could see those moments, why wouldn't I let the man I love in on it? That was easy to answer. Thomas took an advantage I hadn't given him. My cluelessness about the extent of my troubles back then didn't matter.

Anger at the situation spread up my spine again. The truth stared me straight in the face. Like picking at a scab on a wound, I had to admit my family needed help to stay safe. Even with the security improvements, I kept trying to fix everything on my own. The bottom line was I could be vulnerable to the people set on hurting us or to those protecting us. But vulnerability was unavoidable either way.

I squatted down and wrapped my maxi skirt tight to my ankles, then vigorously rubbed my calves.

The chill finally penetrated my adrenaline-fueled state, sparking some sense in me. Pain set in with an unmatched quickness. Mud seeping through my socks, squished between my toes. I dropped my head to my knees in frustration. I'd been an idiot. I hadn't listened to Thomas's defense or trusted his motives. He deserved the benefit of the doubt, not the presumed evil intention.

I had reacted… like my mother would. Fuck. Forty-seven years old and I still defaulted to behavior that I'd learned under her tutelage. Being like Bobby was the worst kind of insult and completely true in this instance. I'd treated Thomas as an enemy instead of an ally, thanks to my embarrassment over the night itself.

I remembered all times Bobby had been her most lethal. The meanness came out when she felt she had an advantage. She was deadly when she'd viewed herself as weak. I had to kill that part of me immediately or Thomas and I wouldn't last.

Tears streamed down my cheeks. I brushed a few away, then let the rest slide unimpeded, as they cleansed the shame.

The first sensations to hit me when I opened the mudroom door were the smell of brewed coffee, then the heat. Pain sliced through my nose on the inhale, thanks to the contrast in temperatures between outside and in. Briskly rubbing my hands together and holding them over my face, I exhaled, hoping to thaw out quicker. The socks came off next, dropping them straight into the garbage can. My nerves turned into sharp knives as my body warmed.

Still amped with adrenaline, I didn't dare touch the coffee. I heard the light tapping of computer keys from the first-floor office and was pulled toward Thomas. The need to make this right was foremost. My body would have to come up to temperature without any help.

Heading straight for the doorway without thinking of cleaning up, I found Thomas at the desk with my laptop. His furrowed brow stirred my shame again. I'd put that concerned and hurt expression on his handsome face.

"Your log-in problem is fixed." He didn't bother to look at me as he clipped his words.

"Thanks, but——"

Thomas looked up at me. What I saw cut off my next thought.

His silver eyes had darkened to a cold charcoal, like he was gearing up for war. My chest lifted in self-defense, but I owed it to him to make the first move.

I inhaled and finished my thought. "I screwed up. I was surprised and hurt that you took liberties before they'd been given. I was so mad, I wanted to spit… or kick you. However, you were right too. I never considered how many eyes are on my security footage every day. In the end, you've always been on my side, my champion. I shouldn't have treated you as if you're one of those who have harassed me. I don't like being vulnerable, and I took it out on you."

Thomas looked shocked at my change in direction. Didn't that convict me more? I bit my lip, wondering what he'd do now.

Trying his best to stifle a smirk, Thomas swiveled the desk chair toward me, spread his knees wide and held his hands out. "If you're that mad, just go for the balls."

"What?" Scrunching my nose at his lunacy, I tittered at the comment. "No way. No one gets to hurt them. Not even me."

"You still want them, then?" He challenged me with a lifted eyebrow. I matched his brow lift, adding a curt nod. I had more to say though. "I'm upset over the timing. Call me naïve, I don't care, but I didn't know Banger had given you access to my files. One of you should've said something."

Thomas rolled his shoulders and raked his fingers through his shaggy hair. "I'd do it all over again."

I threw my hands in the air in frustration. How could he not see my perspective?

"You weren't supposed to happen." Thomas spat out, his hand slapping his thigh. "You've upended me from the beginning."

I folded my arms across my chest. "Are we having a pissing contest about whose life changed more? Hello? Felidae, anyone?"

His expression moved from defensiveness to doubt to surrender as he stared at me. "You know you're my heartbeat and the air I breathe?" I knew and trusted in the depth of his feelings for me, but I'd never considered how quickly they might have developed before he said anything.

I rolled my eyes, instantly regretting the move when Thomas

winced. "Sue me for the cheesy words, but they fit." He continued, "You've got to admit your life's been in danger since the day we met. When I was overseas, it drove me crazy being so far away, not knowing if you were safe. You'd already made these… in-roads into my locked-up heart. It exposed me to vulnerability again. I didn't know what to do about it. So, yeah, I had Banger loop me into the feed reports. The alternative was a constant stream of phone calls, making sure he did everything possible to protect you."

Thomas let out a shaky breath. "It wasn't about stalking you, darlin'. My soul needed easing. Don't you get it? Your safety has never been optional for me." His head dropped. Since he'd never displayed

shame over his emotions, I interpreted his posture as conflict.

"Yes. I get it." I moved to the desk, leaning my hip on the end.

He lifted his gaze. "You do?" His eyes lighted with surprise and a dash of hope. The desperation and defensive set to his jaw vanished.

My heart eased as a grin raised the corner of my mouth. "Did I let you off the hook too easily?"

Thomas reached for my hips and shifted me between his legs. "Christ no. For a while, I thought I'd done the unforgivable."

"People do a lot of fucked up stuff when they're in love." I leaned on my hands and tilted my head to the side. "I can't fathom you doing anything I couldn't forgive, though. Never. Sometimes, I will need a moment to clear my thoughts."

He ran his hands up my back and down my thighs. "Christ, you're freezing. Didn't you grab a coat?"

Thomas's hand traveled down my leg, lifting my foot. His eyes widened in surprise at the dirt and scrapes on my soles. "Or shoes?"

"Case in point to what I just said?" I sat on top of the desk, closed the laptop, and slid it out of the way.

Thomas rucked up my skirt to where it was clean, or at least good enough to wipe my feet. A wisp of air from the floor register caught in the open space and fluttered the rest of the material up.

"Mmm." His eyes hooded as his hands reached farther up.

The differences in our body heat caused more stabbing pain in my legs as the circulation returned.

Placing a foot against his chest, I pushed Thomas back in the chair. The air blew my hem higher, but I didn't care. "Listen, pal, there are some things I need to be certain you understand." One of those cursed jolts that happened whenever we were angry shot through me at our touch. It ran up my leg and beyond.

"Shit!" My foot lifted for a brief second of its own accord, until I set it hesitantly back in his lap. "What the hell?"

"I've never minded the sting." A devilish grin spread across Thomas's face as he examined my muddy legs. The only recognition he'd felt the charge too came from a flex in his jaw. "Not where you're concerned." A molten gaze lifted to mine as his hand moved to his balls. He didn't adjust himself, though.

He grabbed my ankle and rubbed it against him, letting me know where the jolt landed.

"Stop lusting and listen. Please." I leaned in, snapping my fingers in front of him. I'd forgotten I wasn't wearing a bra. Well, it was a Sunday. The scoop-necked tee impeded my efforts to make a point.

That lust-filled glare moved from my chest up to my face. Love softened both the blue in his eyes and the cold steel in his voice. "I'm listening. Say everything you need to."

My foot stayed on his tight abs while the other leg rested on the seat along his thigh. I clasped my hands in my lap. "I was a bitch. I admit to needing physical protection, even if I didn't understand it before. But…" I pressed harder into him. "I'm also no longer the wilting flower who cowed in the shadow of a big, strong man. I fight my battles now. Hell, I've fought the wicked witch my whole life. Honestly, the boogeyman doesn't frighten as much as he pisses me off."

"You think you cowed behind Shane?" Interesting. That was what Thomas picked up from my speech.

"Yes. Him and Dad. I felt safe in their shadows." A shiver ran through me. "Don't know if I'd be as far along in my recovery if I hadn't been forced to face life out in the open though."

Thomas shook his head. "I seriously doubt it." He pulled his chair up to the desk and scooted my ass closer to him. His eyes followed his hands as they rhythmically rubbed up and back. "They gave you what you needed. I'm trying to do the same. Or do you question that?"

"Not at all. Only… you need to hear this, Cowboy. I… I'm done being patronized. And I won't be owned." My foot moved south, rubbing his hardening cock through his jeans.

"Patronizing? Darlin', I respect no one more than you. I hang on to your opinions. I have since we first met." His eyes darkened. "As for owning…" He lurched forward, reaching all the way up my skirt. With the tips of his fingers and a little help from me, Thomas slid my underwear off and threw it on the floor somewhere, leaving me exposed in the good way. "Damn right. I claim ownership of you." He laid his head between my legs, spent a moment nuzzling. Those dark irises glazed over as they lifted back to mine. "What I've been trying to tell you is… you own me too."

The tip of Thomas's straight Roman nose tickled as it softly stroked along one thigh, then the other. Caressing, as he breathed me in. Watching him, as those criminally long, black lashes touched his cheek, he took my breath away. Yeah, I understood why he had those videos. And I probably would've done the same, if I were in his shoes.

The truth of the thought struck deep and quick in my heart. Thomas did own it and my body, not because of some outdated social order, but because I needed him too. Own me? Hell, I wanted him to inhabit me.

My muscles twitch with the need to give him more, to give him everything. But he wrapped his hands around me, holding me in place. His nose slid into my exposed folds, and he gently blew on my clit. A better jolt shot through me—the kind that hummed and set my aura free.

Thomas groaned as he licked along my seam. The sensation mixed with his love set my body aflame.

"Damnitall, you own me. All of me." He placed each of my ankles on his shoulders, forcing me to lean on my elbows. "So beautiful." Then Thomas grabbed my hips and pulled me toward his mouth. "I accept your apology, Baby. Now watch me give you mine."

*****

The End!

THANK YOU FOR READING KICK AND THOMAS'S STORY. I HOPE YOU LOVE these characters as much as I do. What's next, you ask? Sign up for my newsletter by scanning the QR code. You'll find the sign-up there, along with all my social media links.

MY WEBSITE ALSO HAS THE SALES INFORMATION ON CYNDI Sendaydiego's book, *Love You Better*. That's right, Kick's bestie has a standalone book in the same world. She gets a second chance with an ex you haven't met yet. Blake is a successful, handsome restaurateur and single dad. So, why does he scare the pants off her... literally?

- If scanning QR codes isn't your thing, you can also get on the newsletter list by going to www.kallynjones.com. Letters are sent monthly except in the run-up to a book release. You can unsubscribe at any time.
- **You can make a difference in an author's career by leaving a review.** Seriously. Writing a short review helps readers like you find their next favorite book. If composing a review makes you uncomfortable, a rating is a wonderful gift too.
- Like with the first two books, *Kick Home* has a playlist on Spotify, called *Kick Home Tunes*. A link is also on my website.

Author's Note

Thank you so much for taking this journey into Kick and Thomas's world. Early scenes between these two popped into my head nine years ago. Back then, I was sure the cannabis part of the story wouldn't be speculative when published. Alas, it helped me imagine what the scenario might look like in my state when it finally happens (including how the opposition to legalization might play out). This is a reminder, however, that cannabis products are still illegal in real-world North Carolina at the time of publishing.

The secret society of humans with anti-aging genetic variances? Well… ;-)

Acknowledgments

- To my beloved Jones crew: Unending gratitude for your support with this new venture. Thank you for your advice with story ideas. Thank you for cooking for yourselves most nights, now that you're 'big boys.'
- To my editors, D.A. and Lisa: Thank you for fixing all the words. Your enthusiasm for Kick and Thomas's story means so much.
- Hugs go out to Mom, Linda, Joye, Shannon, Jenn M., Bethany, Jeanne, Laura, Annie, Renae, and Jamie. Your evangelism for my work is humbling. Your friendship and support are essential to my spirit.
- To my budding ARC team: I'm indebted to you for helping spread the word about my little series.
- To my first readers: Undying gratitude to you for taking a chance on an unknown author with little "social proof" and a big idea. There are endless books to choose from, and I'm honored you picked mine. You have brought smiles and encouragement to my first year in this publishing venture. Hugs to all of you. XO KJ

About the Author

Kallyn Jones returned to her roots as an author after a successful career as a brand specialist. She brings the same passion for diving into unique stories as she writes about her sexy, down-to-earth characters and their offbeat families. She delights in finding heroes and heroines in unusual places and believes hard-fought happily ever afters are the sweetest.

Kallyn lives in her adopted hometown of Raleigh, North Carolina, with her own hero, their three sons, and their dog. In her spare time, she enjoys trail walks, digital painting, and testing out new, "healthy" recipes. She's proud to say her fellas usually like her experimental dishes. *Usually*.

Follow Kallyn Here:

Website: www.kallynjones.com
Facebook: KallynJonesAuthor
Instagram: KallynJonesWriteNow
Goodreads: Kallyn Jones
BookBub: Kallyn Jones